DIANE ALLEN

*Daughter of
the Dales*

PAN BOOKS

First published 2018 by Macmillan

This edition published in paperback 2018 by Pan Books
an imprint of Pan Macmillan
20 New Wharf Road, London N1 9RR
Associated companies throughout the world
www.panmacmillan.com

ISBN 978-1-4472-9517-4

1 3 5 7 9 8 6 4 2

A CIP catalogue record for this book is available from the British Library.

Typeset by Palimpsest Book Production Limited, Falkirk, Stirlingshire
Printed and bound by CPI Group (UK) Ltd, Croydon, CR0 4YY

Daughter of the Dales

Diane Allen was born in Leeds, but raised at her family's farm deep in the Yorkshire Dales. After working as a glass engraver, raising a family and looking after an ill father, she found her true niche in life, joining a large-print publishing firm in 1990. She now concentrates on her writing full time, and has recently been made Honorary Vice President of the Romantic Novelists' Association. Diane and her husband Ronnie live in Long Preston, in the Yorkshire Dales, and have two children and four beautiful grandchildren.

By Diane Allen

For the Sake of Her Family
For a Mother's Sins
For a Father's Pride
Like Father, Like Son
The Mistress of Windfell Manor
The Windfell Family Secrets
Daughter of the Dales

In memory of Maurice Allen,
a true Dales man

1

Skipton, Yorkshire, 1913

'Get on, Bess.' Sixteen-year-old Luke Fox snapped the reins across the back of the exhausted and sweating horse, which he had been told to take care of by Jethro, as he had handed the horse to him. All Luke could think was that he had to undertake the task of telling his mother that his grandmama was near death, as he swept his hair back out of his eyes. He was dreading having to tell her the news, but knew that it was a son's duty to do so.

The early summer's warm sun beat down upon him and sweat was pouring off both him and the horse as they reached their destination, Skipton High Street. He was breathless, exhausted and thankful that he had got there safely, as he fumbled with the reins while he tied the knackered steed to a safe hold along the setts of the High Street. The horse and trap had flown like the wind from his grandmother's home at Langcliffe to Skipton, a distance of twelve miles, to where both his parents were at work in the family business, Atkinson's department store. In a bid to tell his urgent news, he had driven the trap too hard and knew it, he thought, as he looked back at the sweating horse.

As he pushed through the shining glass-and-brass revolving doors, he was thrust into the highly perfumed shop floor of the sprawling and busy Atkinson empire. A young shop girl sniggered when Luke nearly stumbled, and then quickly corrected herself as she seemed to realize who the unsteady shopper was.

'Where are my mother and father?' Luke asked anxiously, correcting his apparel quickly and blushing at the shame-faced girl.

'Up the stairs, sir. Your mother is taking a fitting and your father is in his photography studio.' The shop girl pointed through the many rows of scarves and accessories that filled the ground floor of the most prestigious shop in the Dales.

Luke made his way past all the shoppers in their finery, who were intent on browsing the luxuries that Atkinson's provided, sniffing at the perfumes and inspecting the latest in fur goods. With his head down, he reached the bottom of the stairs, flushed and anxious to tell his news to his parents.

'Luke, what are you doing here?' James Fox stood at the top of the stairs and looked down at his son, as he pondered how Luke had got there and why he was on his own.

'It's Grandmama, she's dying! I had to come – Jethro couldn't find Ethan to come and tell you, and he couldn't come himself because he had a horse foaling.' Luke had decided to be the bearer of the news instead of Jethro's son, the stable boy, Ethan, who had disappeared as usual, probably to wander and wonder at the surrounding countryside, a regular occupation of his. Luke's voice rang out up the stairs to his father, making the shop girls stop in their tracks and the shoppers shake their heads in acknowledgement of the bad news that Charlotte Atkinson, the owner of Atkinson's, was on her deathbed.

'Quiet, boy. Now tell me: how bad is she?' James came down and stood at the bottom of the stairs, before placing his hand on his son's shoulder to calm him down.

'The doctor says she'll not be with us much longer, and that Mother has to come home. He says Grandmama's had a stroke. Grandpapa found her this morning – she can't move!' Luke looked pleadingly into his father's eyes, secretly regretting now that he had been so hasty to become the bearer of such bad news and realizing just what his message meant to the family. He hung his head and wiped his nose with the back of his hand. He wouldn't cry; young men did not cry and show their emotions, although his grandmama was the mainstay of the family and he loved her dearly.

'Good man for coming to tell your mother.' James patted his son's shoulders. 'I'll go and tell her. Go and see to your horse. Take it to the livery stable at the Red Lion and ask for a fresh one to take you home, or ask for someone to take you both.' He looked around the shop floor, where the staff were trying to go about their jobs, while being aware of the family tragedy unfolding.

3

'I'll take Mama home. I can do it, Father, I want to do it. I'll get a team and leave my horse, then you can ride it home. I'll be outside, waiting for Mama.' Luke looked up at his father; he knew his horse was tired, but he wanted to finish what he'd started. To change it would mean wasting time, and his mother would never notice, if he didn't tell her. He wanted to be the one who took care of his mama, getting her to the bedside of her dying mother as soon as he could. Changing horse would cost precious minutes.

'Very well, I haven't time to argue. But see to it that you do change the horses. Your mother will be with you shortly.'

James watched as his son made his way out into the blazing early summer's heat. He quickly made his way up the three flights of stairs to the fitting room with the news that would change everyone's world.

He glanced around the fitting room at the young bride, who was flushed with excitement as Isabelle – the owner of Atkinson's and his wife, and Luke's mother – swiftly made adjustments to the beautiful bridal gown, while Isabelle's assistant held a measuring tape. The bride stood admiring her own reflection in the full-length mirrors that surrounded the walls of the room, as tucks and pleats were added.

'I'm sorry to interrupt, but I'm afraid I have some grave news. Isabelle, my love – our Luke is here! He's come to take you home. Your mother's been taken ill.' James took the box of pins out of his wife's hand and placed his hand round her waist. 'Your father woke up to find her barely able to move this morning. The doctor says she's had a severe stroke.' James looked at his wife and watched as she struggled to take in the news. He glanced apologetically at the crestfallen bride-to-be.

Isabelle caught her breath and James could see tears welling in her eyes. She glanced quickly at her assistant. 'I'm sorry, I must go. My poor mama, I must go to her.' She looked again at the young bride for whom she had been taking a fitting, and then thrust the box of pins into the hands of Madge Burton, her new seamstress.

'Luke is outside – he's waiting with a horse and trap. I did tell him to change his horse for a fresh one from the Red Lion, as he insists he will take you home, so I hope he's done as I bade him. Take your parasol; the sun is so strong today. Don't worry about anything here. I'll see to closing the store and will be with you as soon as I can. And, Isabelle, be strong; be there for your father, as he will need you before this day is over.'

Isabelle could feel her body trembling as her husband helped her down the stairs and half-heard the bride-to-be complaining that she had been promised Miss Isabelle for her fitting, and that being left with her understudy was most unsatisfactory. Stupid woman, she thought. Had she not heard: her mother was dying! Her dear, darling mother, who had been there for Isabelle every day of her life; the least she could do was be there for her now.

The shop floors were hushed as Isabelle was escorted quickly past the concerned shop girls, the bad news spreading rapidly as they watched with empathy their employer join her son.

'Give my love to your mother, Isabelle, she's very dear to me.' The aged Bert Bannister caught Isabelle's arm just as she stepped out into the blazing sunshine. He was bent nearly double with arthritis and his steps were laboured, but he insisted on working a few hours a week, 'just to keep my hand in'.

'I will, Bert. I only hope I'm not too late, as she sounds seriously ill.' Isabelle smiled wanly at the concerned man. He had been her mother's prop, from the time when she first set up her chain of department stores. If it hadn't been for Bert, Charlotte Atkinson would never have dreamed of owning a string of shops. He had insisted that he would work for her until he dropped, but now it looked as if it was going to be the other way round.

James kissed his wife tenderly on her cheek. 'Give her my love – I'll be thinking of you all. I'll be home as soon as I can.' He watched as Isabelle stepped down the stairs of the busy store, unfurling her parasol to shade her from the ferocious heat of the early summer's day, walking quickly to the trap and horse with Luke, their son, at the reins. Once she had climbed in, he turned and went back into the store to give support to Madge and the disgruntled bride-to-be.

'I thought you were never going to come. I seem to have been standing here for an age, and the horse here is getting hotter and hotter.' Luke looked at his mother as she climbed up beside him in the lightest trap, which Jethro had advised him to take, for speed. 'Even though I've changed the horse, it's not liking the heat and standing out here,' he added quickly.

Isabelle looked at her son and then at the horse, which she instantly recognized as Bess, Jethro's most relied-upon trotter. 'Luke, do you think I don't know my animals? This is Bess, from Windfell. You've not changed the horses, as your father asked. I love my mother dearly, Luke, but I don't want Bess to drop down dead on the way home. Now what are we going to do? My mother wouldn't appreciate the waste of a good horse, for the sake of seeing her on what could be her deathbed. You should have taken your father's advice, or perhaps borrowed a horse and carriage from the Red Lion, for we do have an account with them.'

'I wanted to take you home and look after you,' replied Luke, scowling.

'I know, but there's no need to kill the horse for the sake of it. We could have been with my mother sooner, if you had listened to your father. I suppose the doctor and my father are with her, but I should be there as soon as I can.' She continued looking at her son. He was so stubborn, but she understood why he needed to prove himself to her; he was only showing his love for her. 'Now, if you are not about to change her, just let her trot home at a comfortable pace, and then Jethro or Ethan will cool her down when we reach home.'

Isabelle sat back and said nothing more, as Luke trotted Bess and the trap down the High Street of Skipton, with a surly look upon his face. Local business people and shoppers tipped their hats in recognition of one of the wealthiest shop owners in Skipton and beyond, as they made their way down the heavily used road, passing the church and heading out to the Dales beyond. Once outside Skipton, Isabelle let her feelings begin to show. The more she thought about her mother dying in her bed, the more she wanted to urge Luke and Bess on, but she was right – it was no good flogging the poor beast. Luke had obviously done that in order to reach her, by the look of the sweating animal. She should have made him change it, she thought, as she regretted not being firmer with her son. She bit her lip and fought back the tears and gazed around her over the white drystone walls at the blooming meadows. They were filled with buttercups, clover and daisies, a sea of yellow in the bright summer's sun. How could anyone die on a day like this? she thought, as she looked up into the clear blue sky. It wasn't right that her mother might be taken from her on a day like today.

'Are you alright, Mother? We will get there in time.' Luke dared not glance at his worried mother as they entered the fast-expanding railway village of Hellifield, with the echo of Bess's hooves filling their ears as they passed under the railway line that meandered south into Lancashire. They were getting nearer to home; another few miles and they would be through Long Preston, and then it would be Settle, and home.

'I know, you are doing well.' Isabelle smiled at her youngest. He really should not have been sent for her. He was so like she was and, at sixteen, he'd never known any-one close to him die. He really knew nothing of life yet.

'Is Jane alright – is she comforting your grandfather?' She thought of her seventeen-year-old daughter and hoped she was bearing up. Jane worshipped her grandmother. In fact Isabelle sometimes believed Jane thought more fondly of her grandmother than of her, which was not surprising, given the similarities in their personalities, which were more than noticeable when they were together.

'Aye, our Jane was organizing tea and sympathy as I left. She was there for Grandfather this morning. You'd have been proud of her. As soon as Ethan knocked on the door of Ingfield, to tell us Grandmother was ill, Jane organized us all. She can be so bossy, can our Jane,' said Luke.

'She'll only mean well. She likes to take control.' Isabelle smiled at her son; there was a healthy rivalry between her children, with both being a little jealous of the other. She sighed as they reached the outskirts of Settle. How she wished she was standing on the steps of Windfell, instead of passing her current home of Ingfield House.

'Nearly there, Mother.' Luke took the corner sharply as he passed the River Ribble and the Christies' cotton mill, worrying slightly that the horse was starting to become flecked with sweat along its shoulders.

Isabelle looked up at the open scars of the limestone quarry half a mile down from Windfell and knew she was truly home. Her heart beat fast and she felt sick; would she arrive in time to find her mother still alive?

Turning into the drive, they saw Ethan waiting for their arrival. His father, Jethro, stood in the shadow of the stables. Ethan grabbed Bess's harness and then held his hand out for Isabelle to dismount from the trap.

'Thank you, Ethan. I'm afraid Bess needs your assistance more than I do,' Isabelle said apologetically.

'Don't worry, ma'am, you get into the manor and see how it is with your mother.' Ethan smiled at the worried-looking woman and then led the horse and trap to where his father stood, while Luke climbed down.

'Sorry, I was a bit hasty and asked a little too much of her,' said Luke, as he took his cap off his head and rubbed the sweat on his brow with it.

'Not to worry, we'll look after her now. You look after your mother, and pray for your grandmother.'

Jethro looked at the knackered horse and swore under his breath, as he unfastened the harness and led her into the stables. He knew it was partly the hot day that was to blame for Bess's exhaustion, but the lad had no feeling when it came to animals. He should have insisted that Ethan go. After all, Ethan had only been fishing in the nearby Ribble, but Jethro hadn't said so, as his son could be caught for poaching. But Ethan knew how to get the best out of a horse without breaking it, and he would have had sense to change horses at Skipton, with the day being so close and muggy.

'Ethan, draw me some water – let's cool Bess down. You pour and sponge her down with it over her withers, and then I'll scrape it off, and we'll repeat that until she's cooled down. The main thing is to make sure that she doesn't go into cramp.'

Ethan ran to the water trough outside the stables and

watched as Isabelle and Luke entered the manor. Coming back with loaded buckets, he stood next to his father. 'If I'd have brought the horse back like that, you'd have brayed me.'

'That I would, lad. But Master Luke insisted that he went for his mother, and they've enough on their plates today. There's a storm coming, in more ways than one. I can smell it on the air, and look at how those beech leaves are twisting and turning in a near-breathless sky – a sure sign that a storm is on its way. My father taught me that, when I was knee-high. Bess will soon cool when the storm comes, and hopefully she will be alright; unlike the mistress.'

Ethan glanced at his father. He knew better than to disbelieve him, but right now the day was as hot as the new oven in Windfell Manor. It was common knowledge that his father was part gypsy, and he was invariably right when it came to reading nature's signs.

Isabelle plucked up her courage as she turned the brass door handle of Windfell's front door, not knowing what to expect as she stepped into the hallway.

'Thank heavens you are here, Miss Isabelle, your mother is failing fast,' said Mazy, the housekeeper. 'Dr Burrows was praying that you'd be here in time to say goodbye before she departs this earth. Thank heavens it is Dr Burrows who has attended. Your mother has always trusted him despite his age – he should be retired by now.' Mazy was nearly in tears as she took Isabelle's parasol, and tried to smile reassuringly at Luke as he

11

followed his mother up the grand, winding staircase. She shook her head before disappearing below stairs, where all the rest of the staff at Windfell awaited the impending bad news.

Isabelle opened her mother's bedroom door, with Luke close behind her. She looked around the room and at her mother lying listless in her bed, rasping for breath. Archie – her father, and the man Charlotte had loved all her life – sat by her side holding her hand, his face tired and full of pain as he felt each shallow breath that his beloved wife took.

Dr Burrows patted Isabelle's hand and shook his head as she went and sat down at the bottom of the bed, next to her stepbrother Danny, who smiled at her and put his arm round her as she started to cry.

'I'm glad you are here, Izzy. Mother would be happy that we are all here together,' he whispered.

Isabelle smiled and wiped back the tears that trickled down her cheeks. She loved her mother so much – how could she carry on without her?

'No, tears, our lass, she wouldn't want you to be sad.' Archie looked across at his daughter. 'She's had a good life; she'd be the first to say that.' He bent over and kissed her mother Charlotte on her brow and ran his hand around her pale face. 'She hasn't felt right this last week or two; she knew her health were failing and she hoped that she wasn't going to be bedridden.' Archie looked over at his dying wife. 'I'm right, aren't I, lass – that wouldn't be for you?'

'If I could do more, I would, but her heart is weak. She

will not make nightfall.' The ageing Dr Burrows looked at the heartbroken family around him and thought about his own mortality. He'd seen many a body in and out of the world, but the death of Charlotte Atkinson hurt him as if she were his own. She'd always been a fighter, and now the fight in her was worn out and he couldn't help but think he was heading the same way.

Isabelle touched his hand. 'Thank you, Doctor, we know you have done all you can; there's nothing more that can be done by anybody.'

Charlotte breathed in deeply, causing all the family to look at her. The beautiful grey-haired woman whimpered, held her breath for a second and then, with quiet serenity, breathed a long sigh and silently passed from one world to the next, as if she had just been given permission from Isabelle and from the Lord above.

Dr Burrows rushed to her side and checked for signs of life, as Archie broke down in tears, his head in his hands. He'd lost the love of his life, his darling Lottie.

'Don't cry, Grandad. You said yourself that Grandma wouldn't want us to.' Jane placed her arms around her grandfather, whom she loved dearly. 'You've still got all of us.'

'I have, child. But your grandmother was my very life.' Archie wiped his eyes and looked at the doctor, who shook his head, as no signs of life could be found.

Isabelle broke down and cried, while Danny hugged her. 'I've just lost my best friend as well as my mother,' she sobbed.

'Yes, me too. She may not have been my natural

mother, but she never treated me as anything other than as if I was. Harriet and all my family will miss her – we owe everything to her.' Danny thought back to when his father, Archie, had married Charlotte, his first love, after both had been left bereft following the deaths of their original partners, and both finding that they were very much dependent on one another.

'Are Harriet and the children at Crummock?' Isabelle blew her nose on her lace handkerchief and looked at her stepbrother.

'Yes, our Ben has the German measles, and Georgina sounds as if she's getting it too, she's so twisty and in a mood. Rosie stayed behind to help her mother, else she would be here with me.' Danny felt he had to explain why his side of the family were not with him, at the deathbed of the woman they owed everything to.

'It's alright, lad. Charlotte knew everybody loved her, and that's all that matters.' Archie looked up and across at his son.

Dr Burrows closed his bag and felt that his time with the family had come to an end, and they needed their privacy.

'I'm sure you want to be on your own now. I'll be back tomorrow with a death certificate, in order for you to bury Charlotte.' He shook his head. 'She was one hell of a woman, if you don't mind me saying so. She's going to be missed.' He stood up and shook Archie's hand and patted his old friend on the back. He looked around at the woman who, as a baby, he had brought into the world. 'Big shoes to fill, Isabelle, but she will have taught you well, if I know Charlotte.'

Danny stood up and opened the bedroom door for the doctor to leave, as Isabelle rose and hugged the old man, who felt like part of the family.

'Thank you for being here for her. It is what she would have wanted.' She hugged him tightly.

'You be strong. Your family – especially Archie – will need you.' Dr Burrows put on his top hat and left the grieving family to say goodbye to their loved one.

Thomson, the butler, met Dr Burrows at the bottom of the stairs. Guessing that his mistress had died if the doctor was leaving, he didn't say a word, but simply opened the front door for the sad-looking old man.

'Your mistress is no longer with us. If you can tell the staff, it will give a little ease to the family,' Dr Burrows said as he stood in the doorway. 'She's gone and taken the sunshine with her, by the look of this worsening day. It looks like thunder rolling across those back fells. I'd better get myself home.'

Both butler and doctor looked up to the darkening fells over Malham and listened as a distant rumble of thunder made itself heard.

'She always was too bright to last long, just like the day.' Dr Burrows tapped his hat and stepped out with his cane, then walked down the drive of Windfell Manor, with the storm winds starting to blow their way through the beech trees.

*

'I'm sorry to say that Mistress Charlotte has died. I've just seen the doctor out of the manor,' said Thomson to the staff as they gathered, looking sombre, around the table in the kitchen.

Lily, Charlotte's maid, sobbed. 'She was such a lovely woman. She never lost her temper, and I remember when she first came here – both me and her were not used to the finer things in life, so we learned our roles together.'

'Aye, and she gave me a chance, when I was nothing more than a filthy-mouthed nothing who couldn't stop swearing. I didn't deserve the chance she gave me,' sobbed Mazy. 'I'll have to go and tell Jethro. Ruby, when you've done sobbing, put some tea on for the family; they'll need a drink, if nothing else. Master Archie hasn't eaten all day.' Mazy made for the back door and ran across the yard to the stables, gazing up at the rain-filled skies.

Jethro and Ethan saw her coming and met her in the stable doorway.

'She's gone, hasn't she? I saw the doctor leaving.' Jethro looked as black as the clouds that were scuttling overhead.

'Aye, she's gone, bless her soul. We are all in tears in the house.' Mazy put her arm around her husband, for she knew how much Charlotte had meant to him.

All of them raised their heads as a huge crack of thunder broke directly over the house.

'That's Charlotte and God arranging the furniture in heaven,' joked Mazy as she looked upwards, with tears in her eyes.

'Then he'll have to bloody well behave himself, because

little does he know it yet, but Charlotte will have her own way and will be running the show by nightfall.' Jethro sniffed hard and fought back the tears.

'Aye, that she will. At least Master Archie will get a bit of peace now, for she did lead him a dance some days, but he must be broken-hearted.' Mazy hugged their son Ethan and rubbed his dark head of curls.

'He's not the only one – a finer woman I've never known. She was true to her word, was Miss Charlotte, and never let you down. The world's a sadder place without her. Come, Ethan, let's away and check this horse.' Jethro nearly choked on his words.

Mazy watched as her husband and son strode back into the shadows of the stables. The thunder rumbled above her. 'God bless you, Charlotte Atkinson. You've left more than one broken-hearted man down here, if you did but know it. My Jethro worshipped the ground you walked on.'

2

The curtains at each house along the winding small streets of Austwick were pulled in acknowledgement of the passing of Charlotte Atkinson. Villagers lined the cortège route and bowed their heads, removing their caps and bowlers as the family passed them in the carriage on the route to the church – a route that Charlotte had taken many a time, in good times and bad.

'Look at the people!' Isabelle gasped to Danny. 'There are so many attending, they are even standing outside the church gates. I hope it doesn't rain, for their sakes.'

'It doesn't surprise me. Our mother knew everyone, and everyone knew her. What did you expect, our Isabelle? After all, she was one of the most powerful women in the district.' Danny looked out of the carriage as it pulled up at the church's gates.

'It isn't about the power, lad; it's that she was loved and always tried to do right by people. She could have made or broken half of the families in this district, but she showed each one the respect they deserved. If you and Isabelle both do the same as you go through life, then you'll earn just as much respect as your mother.' Archie stood up and waited for the coachman to open the carriage door, then looked out at the ancient market cross on the small green next to the church. The cross he had chased Charlotte around, when they were children. Where had the days gone?

The vicar stood at the church entrance and shook hands with the family, before nodding to the undertaker to follow him into the building. He was nervous as he looked around the packed church, which was full of dignitaries, family and those who had come to pay their respects to the once-humble farm lass from Crummock. He had never taken a burial service like this and expected not to have to do so again; not for a while anyway, he thought, as he looked over at the fragile Archie Atkinson as he started the service.

The vicar held a good service, knowing Charlotte and her roots in Austwick and the Craven community well. He remembered all her close family members, and spoke of her life without belying the heartache that had made her the strong woman she was. He gave his final blessing as the family gathered around the grave, and watched as those who wished to said their final farewells to the woman they loved and respected.

'I'm glad that's over.' Harriet linked her arm into her husband Danny's, and looked round at their daughter

Rosie. 'Are you going to the funeral tea with your father or are you coming home with me?'

'Would you mind if I go to Windfell with Father? I'd like to attend, if I may.' Sixteen-year-old Rosie looked at her father, hoping that he would back up her request.

'Of course you can come with me, Rosie – and you should come as well, Harriet, despite Ben and Georgina having German measles. You know you have no excuse not to, really,' said Danny quickly. 'The housemaid is quite prepared to see to their needs while you are there. I heard her say so this morning,' he growled at his wife.

'Well, you heard wrong. Ben's over the worst of it, but Georgina has such a fever that I fear for her. Measles is known for making a child's heart weak, and I've known some children have fits because their temperature is so high! Do you think I'd risk my children with a common maid, when your mother is dead and there's nothing further that can be done for her?' Harriet's face was full of fear, remembering the hurt and pain she had suffered over the death of two of her previous children, the twins Daniel and Arthur. She had always blamed herself for putting her work at Atkinson's before their needs. 'Have we not been through enough, losing two children? I will always blame myself for not always being there when they suffered. I should never have listened to your mother and Isabelle, when they assured me that the nanny would look after them while I worked at the store.'

'Harriet, there was nothing we could do to save the two offspring we lost. It was the diphtheria to blame; the disease moved quickly and, even if you had been there with them, there was nothing you could have done. The doctor told you that, and he said you were beyond reproach. You cannot keep blaming yourself for their deaths, nor keep fearing the worst every time our children have a sniffle. Nor blame Isabelle, or my mother. No one knew that day how quickly the disease was going to strike, and how bad the weather was going to turn,' Danny whispered quietly.

Rosie stood back from her parents. She was slightly tired of hearing her parents row, something they now seemed to do on a regular basis.

'I've not got a problem with Isabelle; it is she who has a problem with me. Did you notice that she hardly spoke a word to me in the church? She just doesn't understand that my children come first,' said Harriet.

'That's because she couldn't speak – out of respect for the dead. Perhaps you should be the one to show a bit more respect. After all, my mother did a lot for us and our family, despite what you think. Don't forget that Crummock was hers, and we will have to wait and see how the land lies after the funeral.'

Danny looked worried. What if Charlotte had left Crummock to Isabelle? Harriet would not be happy with that. To her, Isabelle had it all and enjoyed a life of ease. Isabelle being made the landlord of Crummock would be the last straw.

'I'll curse if your mother has left Isabelle Crummock. She's had everything on a plate since the moment she was born. Her mother set her up in business, and even then she was too busy chasing after worthless men, leaving me to do all the work.' Harriet looked as black as thunder as she pulled on her leather gloves.

'You left the business because you wanted to bring up our family. You've only yourself to blame. Mother bent over backwards for you when Rosie was born, following the deaths of our first two. She was always there for you, and fully understood your decision to stay at home and be with Rosie and the rest of the family, as they came along. So stop blaming everybody else for your lifestyle. Besides, you want for nothing; we've a good living – it's a bit rough in winter, but we've all we could wish for.' Danny was tired of hearing the constant moaning of his wife. She had been broken-hearted at the deaths of her two eldest, but so had he. Harriet tended to forget that and withdraw into herself, blaming everyone and anyone who challenged her view on life.

'My children are everything to me, which is more than can be said for Isabelle. Just look at Luke – he doesn't seem to have an ounce of sense in him; and as for Jane, well, she's been brought up by your mother and has every one of her traits, the bossy little madam.'

'Aye, she's a fair lass, is Jane. My mother taught her well.' Danny grinned and looked across at his niece, who was standing next to her mother Isabelle, joining in intently a conversation about some subject that she had an opinion on.

'It's a shame you don't have as much interest in your own lass, Rosie, and a bit more time for the two at home.' Harriet looked across at her husband. She was fed up with her lot in life, and sick of hearing Charlotte's and

Isabelle's names on everyone's lips. She was the one who had helped to start the Atkinson empire; or had they all forgotten? She too had put in many hours designing and sewing, initially in the first little shop at Settle, but then the business had expanded and her family had become her main focus. It was then that she had decided that running a business was not for her, and that her heart lay with her family and home.

'Get yourself home, Harriet. Henry from Sowermire next door to us is about to leave, so get a lift with him back up to Crummock, before you say anything else that you might regret.' Danny scowled at his wife. She had a caustic tongue in her head, when she was that way inclined. Better that she went home before she caused any bother. He watched as she made her way through the mourners, catching Henry at the church gate as he climbed into his trap. At least she had the sense not to argue with Danny there, but he knew he would be in for an onslaught on his return home.

'Well, that's your mother seen to, Rosie. Let's away and keep your grandfather company – he looks a bit lost without your grandmother on his arm.' Danny turned round to his daughter. He loved her dearly, despite what her mother had said. Rosie appreciated the farm and the world around her, and never said a bad word about anyone. At sixteen, a year younger than her cousin Jane, she was just the opposite: a young woman with a love of nature and a gentleness for the people around her. How could Harriet say that he had no time for her? They were as close as a daughter and father could be.

'So, Mother's decided to go home then? She's been worrying all day about our Ben and Georgina. Although Ben seemed well enough this morning; he gave me a load of cheek when I went into his bedroom. He even threw one of his pillows at me as I left.' Rosie smiled at her father – he was everything to her. He was so different from her mother, who always seemed to be fighting the world. He smiled and had time for her, and she loved to be with him, cherishing every moment.

'Aye, well, you know: mothers and sons, there's a special bond.' Danny linked his arm into his daughter's.

'A bit like fathers and daughters?' Rosie smiled as she walked over to her grandfather. She enjoyed having her father to herself.

'Just like that, my dear.' Danny squeezed his daughter's hand tightly before speaking to his father. 'We should be on our way, Father, as the day's doing well to hold the rain back.' He looked up at the grey sky and at his father standing at the grave's edge, looking down upon the coffin of the one he loved.

'Aye, if you say so, lad. Folk have said that they'll see me back at Windfell, so I suppose I'll have to leave her here. You know we have barely ever been apart since the day we married. It is going to be hard to live without her.' Archie leaned on his stick and wiped a tear from his eye, before walking stiffly away from the grave.

'Here, take my arm, Grandpapa.' Rosie left her father's arm and linked her arm through her grandfather's as she smiled with affection at him.

'You are the image of your grandmother – who you

were named after, lass. You've just the same looks and ways. You remind me of her every time I look at you. Your father's mother was sweetness itself and I loved her just as much as my Lottie, but somehow Lottie's light shone brighter, and I was attracted to her like a moth caught around a flame. So she was waiting on me when your grandmother died, and that's how it is. I've loved and I've lost two good women in my life. The world can be hard sometimes.' Archie stopped for a minute and caught his breath, thinking back to his first wife, Rosie.

'But you've still got all of us, Gramps. You've Aunt Isabelle and Uncle James and all my cousins – we will all look after you.' Rosie waited patiently as the elderly man climbed into the carriage to take him home.

'Aye, but you forget, they are not my flesh and blood, not like your father. He's my true son.' Archie paused for a minute. 'Danny, I need to speak to you in the morning, in the study on your own – there's something I need to ask.' Archie looked across at his son as the carriage rocked into action.

'Ask me now, Father.' Danny looked worried, wondering what his father wanted with him. 'Nobody can hear us.'

'No, I'll bide my time because I need to speak to Isabelle first; it's only right.' Archie looked out of the window at the overgrown hedges full of cranesbill and meadowsweet passing by. 'Hey up! It's raining; well, my old lass, tha' did get blessed from heaven afore they filled you in, after all.' Archie sat back and smiled at his granddaughter and thought of the coffin that held Charlotte being rained upon, and of the love she had given him. It was a pity his son hadn't quite the same affection from his own wife. Happen he shouldn't have talked Danny into getting wed to Harriet all those years ago and maybe, if they hadn't lost the children, things would have been different. He sighed and leaned on his stick. Nay, but hindsight was a marvellous thing; if you knew what life was to throw at you, you'd never do anything, he thought. Time would tell if they sank or swam; and the news he was to tell Danny the next morning would have a huge bearing on his son's future, but it was something he had to do before he, too, departed God's good earth.

3

Isabelle looked at her husband lying back in the unmade bed, half-asleep but half-awake as he listened to her ranting. She'd tossed and turned all night, thinking about the repercussions of her mother's death. When she'd asked what was to become of Windfell, Archie had completely ignored her.

'What if Mother has not left me Windfell? It's my home. I hope she realized how much I love the place. You do know that my true father bought it? That's why it should belong to me.'

James yawned and rubbed his head, giving up on getting any peace as he pulled the covers back and sat in his nightshirt on the side of the bed. 'I thought your father was broke and beyond help, until your mother stepped in and saved the day.' He relieved himself in the chamberpot and immediately regretted his response.

'Oh, shut up. You know nothing when it comes to my family.' Isabelle looked at her husband. 'I'm beginning to realize that the family history I was told was perhaps a little bit in favour of my mother, especially if Windfell is not to be mine.'

'All I know is that Archie has always been here for all of us, and your mother loved him,' said James. 'Besides, he didn't say anything. Wait until you've spoken to the solicitor this afternoon. Old Walker will tell you everything.' James pulled his nightshirt off and looked at his brooding wife. 'Do you know how dark you look when you are in such a mood? Be thankful for what you have got, Isabelle, else it looks like you are a money-grabbing bitch. We've got Ingfield, thanks to your aunt, whom nobody had a good word for. It's a grand house, with plenty of bedrooms and all you need in a home. What do you need Windfell Manor for?'

Isabelle stared at her husband and didn't reply as she walked out of the bedroom, slamming the door behind her and leaving James in no doubt that the day ahead was going to be a hard one. She walked along the long adjoining corridor, with its stained-glass window bearing the coat of arms of the Ingfield family upon it, and hesitated at the top of the stairs. Ingfield House, it was true, was a lovely home and she had been lucky to inherit it from her Aunt Dora, although that had only been by default, as Dora had died without making a will, leaving Isabelle – the closest and only traceable heir – to inherit all that was now around her.

She sighed; the shop in Skipton, a property and business in the Queens Arcade in Leeds and a rented shop in Bradford's Foster Square she already knew were hers, as they were in her joint name with her mother. But the place she loved was Windfell, and her heart was yearning to own it. She felt her lip tremble and her eyes started to fill with tears. She broke down as she turned back towards her bedroom, sobbing uncontrollably as she met James on the landing.

'Hey now, enough of this. Your mother was a good woman. She loved you; she will have done right by you. Have patience and wait until you hear what the solicitor has to say.' James knew Isabelle had set her heart on the family home, and he knew how much it was hurting her to realize that possibly it was not going to be hers for the foreseeable future.

'I don't ask for much. But I just wanted Windfell. It's right that Danny and Archie have Crummock, but I had my heart set on Windfell!' She hid her face in James's jacket, crying relentlessly as she remembered the days she had shared with her mother in her old home. How she missed both. Her mother was gone forever, and it had just hit her that she would never hear her voice and feel her kisses again. But she knew she would remember Charlotte every day if she lived at Windfell and spent her life alongside the spirit of her mother, which filled every nook and corner of the manor.

Danny sat across from his father and watched him as he finished his late, leisurely breakfast.

'Are you alright this morning, Father? You looked tired last night, that is why I left you early.' He watched as Archie drew breath between his two rashers of bacon –

the same breakfast he'd eaten for as long as Danny could remember.

'Aye, I'm alright; you have to be, haven't you, lad? Moping about is not going to bring her back, no matter how much I miss her. Lottie was an exceptional woman, and I only hope Isabelle will take a leaf or two out of her book.' Archie sipped his tea and looked across at his son. 'Isabelle can be spiteful sometimes. She's expecting to inherit everything, and I don't like that.' He stirred his tea and noticed the puzzlement on his son's face. 'Lottie has left Windfell to Isabelle, but only after my day – or until I feel I want to leave it. She'll find out this afternoon; Charles Walker will tell her.' Archie grinned. He loved Isabelle, but she had a lot of her true father in her, and he had ignored her prying at the funeral into what was to become of Windfell.

Danny sat back and looked at his father, who was a devil for keeping things to himself when he thought it was for the best.

'Anyway there's something I want you to ask Harriet, and I've something else to tell you – something I think you should know.' Archie's face clouded over.

'Go on then, Father, tell me your worst.' Danny waited.

'Nay, we'll go into the study. Give the servants the chance to clear my breakfast away.' Archie looked at his one place setting on the large mahogany dining table, remembering that there used to be up to six places set most mornings, not that long ago. He rose from his chair and walked across to the study, Danny following behind him. 'Shut the door, lad. I don't want anyone to listen in.'

Danny sat down in the chair that Charlotte had loved so much, noticing the tapestry down by the side of the chair that had never been finished by her, and never would be now.

'What's wrong, Father? You're not ill, are you?' Danny looked at his father and noticed how worried he looked.

'Nay, I'm fine. But I can't see the point in rolling around this big house, and I hate them bloody stairs because of my bad knees – and Isabelle will not want me here, if I offer for her to move in with me. Besides, I couldn't keep my thoughts to myself when it comes to how they spoil Luke. Jane is another matter, but they've ruined that lad.' Archie paused. 'Would you and Harriet be able to put up with me at Crummock? It's more where I belong; and Crummock, I know, will be yours after my day.' Archie looked across at his son. He knew he was asking a lot, for Harriet would not welcome the news gladly.

'Aye, heavens, Father. You don't have to ask. I presume it'll be your farm after today, and you know you can stay with us. It'll save you trailing the road up to us, because it's what you will do, if you live here alone or with Isabelle.' Danny sighed and tried to smile in reassurance at his father, wondering how he was going to break the news to Harriet.

'But what about Harriet – she'll not want me under her feet?' Archie knew what his son was thinking, realizing full well that Harriet would complain.

'I'll not have her say a bad word about it. We've two

spare bedrooms, and we owe you and Charlotte for everything we have, so she will have to lump it,' Danny blustered.

'Right, if you are alright with that, then that's what I'll do, and then Isabelle can have her Windfell. It's where she belongs; this was Lottie's dream, not mine. I'd rather be sitting at Crummock's kitchen table than at that big dumb thing in the dining room all by myself.'

'Is there something else that's bothering you? ' Danny glanced at the worried-looking man across from him and waited. It seemed it was a morning of confessions.

'Aye, this is why I wanted you to close the door.' Archie hesitated. 'I went to Ragged Hall the other day, as somebody told me Bill Brown wasn't too well. So I went to see him, seeing as we've traded things together over the years. And that was when I saw his grandson. I nearly dropped down dead – he was the spit of you.' Archie stopped in his tracks and looked across at his son. 'The baby that Amy Brown was carrying all those years back was yours, lad, and he's back: grown up and living with his grandfather.'

Danny stared at his father, not knowing what to say.

'He even carries your name – Daniel. His grandfather said nowt, and I didn't either, but I'm sure old Bill knows he's yours. It's up to you to introduce yourself, if that's what you want. I think the lad deserves to know who his true father is, and perhaps you could make up for all the lost years. But I thought it fair that I let you know my thoughts.' Archie looked across at his son; he didn't know what to advise: whether to leave the lad alone, or suggest that Danny go to Ragged Hall and make himself known. The decision had to be Danny's.

Danny rubbed his hand through his hair. 'I've never told Harriet about Amy Brown and me – let alone about the baby that I suspected was mine. We aren't seeing eye-to-eye at the moment, as it is, as she's never satisfied with her lot. Finding out I fathered a baby before we were married would be the final nail in the coffin.'

'Aye, I've heard her moaning at you. She'll not really want me living with you, but she might have to bite her tongue a bit, if she thinks I'm listening in. Wait until I'm there with you and then make up your mind. Daniel's not going anywhere. Part of the reason he's with his grand-father is that he and Amy's husband don't get on, so Bill told me. Her husband probably realizes that he's got a cuckoo in his nest.' Archie rubbed his hand over his knees because they were aching, and thought about the young man who had greeted him and taken him by surprise as he entered the yard of Ragged Hall.

'Is he good-looking, Father? How tall is he? Does he really look like me?' Danny leaned forward; he knew full well that, now he was aware of his son's existence, he was going to have to meet him.

'Aye, if you can remember yourself in the mirror from twenty years back, then he's you. A bit thinner perhaps and doesn't look right happy, but by the sounds of it he hasn't had the best home life. He's the oldest of five, and it'll have been a struggle for your Amy, bringing them all up at Slaidburn.' Archie noticed the look of concern on his son's face.

'And Amy – did Bill mention how she is doing?' Danny remembered the wild young lass with dancing eyes who had captured his heart that long, hot summer. He should have married her, not Harriet, but the family had to come first back then.

'He never mentioned her. Sorry, lad.' Archie looked at the disappointment in his son's eyes. 'Best you think what to do about the lad, and leave Amy alone. Remember, you've responsibilities of your own; you've enough on your plate.'

'I know, but I've never forgotten her.' Danny hung his head.

'No – nor I your mother. But they are both in the past. Anyway, I've told you my news. Think about it, but don't go hurting your own family; they should come first. And today let's go and face the music with Isabelle; she'll be in a slightly better mood if she thinks she can move into Windfell and get rid of me from under its roof.' Archie smiled as he watched his son struggle with the news. He wondered if he shouldn't have told him about Daniel, but if his own son had been living across the other side of the dale, unbeknown to him, he'd have wanted to know. Whatever Danny did, it was up to him now.

Isabelle looked at Archie and wiped her nose and eyes as the family group stood outside the solicitor's, after hearing the will being read. She looked at her family group. 'Well, I didn't know what to think when you ignored me yesterday, Father. As it stands, dear Mama has done right by all of us. I presume you will be staying at Windfell,

Father?' Isabelle looked for support from James as he stood next to Danny.

'Nay, lass, you can have Windfell now. It's of no use to me. I've decided to move out. I've asked Danny if I can move in with him and Harriet, then you can have your home back all to yourself. I need nowt with that big posh house. I hate climbing those bloody stairs. With hindsight, I should never have sold my father's home of Butterfield Gap.' Archie looked at Isabelle and watched as her eyes flashed, thinking of Windfell becoming her new home and the consequences of Archie moving into Crummock.

'You are going to live at Crummock? Does Harriet know? She'll not be very happy. She's never happy about anything nowadays.' Isabelle shot a glance at Danny. She was at the end of her tether with her sister-in-law and her surly ways.

'Danny's asking her later in the day. She'll be right with it. After all Crummock will be theirs, after my day, and your mother gave her a sweetener when she left her those few shares in the firm. It'll make Harriet think herself valued at long last.' Archie looked sternly at Isabelle. 'You be right with her, Isabelle – you and Harriet used to be so close. You just made different decisions, but Harriet deserves a bit of the profit from the shops.' Archie had noticed Isabelle's face cloud over when old Walker had disclosed a 10 per cent share in the chain of shops to go to Harriet.

'I am right with her. It's Harriet that's got bitter and twisted over these last few years. I can't help being me.

She shouldn't hide herself away so much up at Crummock. I'd welcome her back any day to help run things, if she would only ask.' Isabelle was tired of trying to be all things to all people. She'd put every waking hour into her mother's chain of shops, as well as having her two precious children, and hadn't time for listening to the gripes and moans of Harriet.

'Aye, well, she's different from you. She prefers to be a wife and mother rather than a hard-headed businesswoman like you and your mother. Harriet lost two bairns, remember that. A mother never gets over losing a child.' Archie looked at James and Danny, who were also like chalk and cheese but never spoke a bad word between them. If only the women of the family were like them. He watched as the two men shared a joke and laughed out loud as they turned to join in the conversation between Isabelle and Archie.

'So, sir, you are to live with Danny?' James looked with concern at Archie. 'You don't have to leave Windfell because of us; we are quite happy where we are at.' He admired his down-to-earth father-in-law and felt that perhaps Archie was being hasty in his decision to live with his son.

'Nay, lad, Windfell's too big for one person. You will fill it well. Jane and Luke will enjoy living there and, besides, it's where Isabelle belongs. I can help our Danny up at Crummock, and I'm sure Harriet will get used to me being about. I don't take a lot of looking after.' Danny smiled at James. He was not a hard northerner, but was softly spoken and gentle, perhaps too gentle for the hard-headed Isabelle.

'As long as you are sure? You can return and live with us if you wish; there will always be a welcome, I'm sure.' James shot a glance at Isabelle and noticed the dark look she gave him.

'Nay, lad. Windfell can be all yours, once I've moved out. It'll make life easier for all.' Archie patted James on the back. 'Now, I'm off for a gill in the King Billy – something I haven't done for years. You lot get yourselves home and explain to your families what's to happen next. I can do no more.' Archie looked at his pocket watch. It was three o'clock; he'd have a gill and then get a carriage back home, just in time for his supper. He needed the peace, some time away from all the squabbling. He could just imagine the chatter and racket at both houses, once they were on their own and able to discuss their futures. Both siblings caused nothing but worry and were never satisfied with their lot. He'd just been happy with a full belly and a roof over his head, and hadn't expected anything from his parents, when he was their age. Where did it all go wrong?

4

Isabelle stood in the hallway of the manor, looked around her and sighed. She was home. She'd always known Windfell would be hers one day, and although she was sad she had lost her mother, she was overjoyed that at last she could move her family there. The clock that Archie had brought from Butterfield Gap chimed, as if to remind her that Windfell was not quite hers yet – not until Archie signed it over to her, as he had agreed earlier in the week. 'Well, you can be thrown out; you never did fit in with the rest of the house,' she said to the chiming clock, as she stood with her hands on her hips. She remembered her mother putting up with it, after it was placed in the hallway on the death of Archie's father. Nevertheless, it was going to be good to be back in her beloved bedroom, and to be able to walk down the sweeping stairs knowing that now she was the new mistress of Windfell.

She turned as the front door opened, realizing that the summer's day had slipped into a warm sultry evening

and that James and her daughter Jane – the new apprentice – had just returned from their first day working
together in the shop at Skipton. *Her shop*; the words
seemed strange as she mulled them over in her head. The
shop that she now owned, along with the one in Leeds
and the one rented in Bradford.

'Well, I can see what you've been doing all day, while
Jane and I have been working hard to earn you more
money.' James hung up his bowler hat on the hatstand
by the door and grinned at his wife. 'Playing lady of the
manor, by the looks of it.'

'I have not, I've just been remembering how many
good times we had here, and looking at what Father is
taking with him and what needs doing before we move
in next week.' Isabelle linked her arm into James's and
smiled at Jane, who was yawning and looked tired, next
to her father. 'Tired after your first day at work?'

'I'm exhausted. Am I expected to do that every day of
the week? Bert Bannister never shut up about my grandmother, and said I had to learn from the bottom of the
firm upwards, just like she had. Can't I be in the office,
Mother, or even learn to dressmake, if I have to?'

'It won't do you any harm to know the warehouse,
and to deal with the orders coming in and out – Bert's
quite right. You've got to know how the firm works, and
get to know everyone we deal with. After all, one day it
will all be yours, just as my mother has left it to me.'

'But, Mother, I could help Father develop his photographs and help tidy his studio. Anything but be with old

Bert Bannister; he's so slow and everything has to be done so precisely,' said Jane.

'You respect your elders, madam,' said James. 'And it is "Mr Bannister" to you. No matter what position he has or age he is. Manners will get you a long way in this life.'

Jane scowled at her father. What did he know? She was sure he had never been her age. 'I'm going out to look at the foal in the paddock. I could hear her whinnying at the sound of us arriving. She must be lonely, she's been used to having someone looking after her all the time.'

'If you find Luke out there, tell him we are going home shortly. I think he said he was going down to the river,' shouted Isabelle after her daughter, as Jane scurried out across the hallway. Turning to James, she pulled him close to her. 'We are going to be so happy here – I love Wind-fell.' She kissed him on the lips and smiled, knowing that she had everything a woman could wish for.

'Perhaps we have too much. I have a strange feeling, when things are going this well, that something is bound to go wrong.' James smiled at his wife and held her tightly as she sighed with contentment.

'Don't be such a pessimist. Nothing – and no one – can touch us now. God bless my dear mama. I do realize that I owe her everything.' Isabelle pulled James closer to her.

'You'd do well to remember that, and dear Archie. He's about to give up his home for you.' James hoped Isabelle's feeling of self-importance would pass quickly. He was uneasy that everything in her life had come easily to her and that sometimes she took things for granted.

*

'She's a bonny thing, isn't she?' Ethan leaned over the drystone wall and chewed a grass stalk as he leaned back and admired the foal and the young woman standing before him.

'She is, she's got spirit.' Jane watched the young chestnut foal race up and down the paddock, its short stubby mane and tail blowing in the wind as it played in excitement at being able to enjoy the freedom of the warm summer's day. 'I wish I was her, wild and free. Not be-holden to anyone.' She flashed her eyes at Ethan and smiled at the dark-haired lad, whom she knew her cousin, Rosie, had feelings for.

'You moving in here then, next week? My father says he's going to miss your grandfather and hopes we will all be keeping our positions.' Ethan moved closer to the lass he'd partly grown up with. He was now starting to real-ize just how beautiful the ugly duckling she had once been had become, and that he had to acknowledge Jane as the next heir to Windfell, along with her brother.

'Yes. Mother says we are moving in next Monday, once Grandfather has moved out. I can't see her chan-ging any of the staff, so your father needn't worry.' Jane turned to look at Ethan, who stood just inches from her face. 'Why, would you miss me, Ethan Haygarth? Would it break your heart not to see me each day?' She smiled.

'Aye, I'd miss looking at you every day. We've always been good friends.' Ethan reached for her hand and pulled it towards him. He'd been building up the courage to kiss the girl, who was now nearly a fully grown woman. The flash of eyes and the warm smile had confirmed Jane's true feelings, and now was the time to make his move.

'What do you think you are doing? I don't want to hold your hand. Remember your place, and be thankful that you'll be keeping it, as stable boy,' Jane spat.

Ethan pulled her towards him and held her tightly as he kissed her hard on the lips. She might be the grand-daughter of his late mistress, but she'd been flirting with him for months, of that he was sure. He held her against him as she wriggled and protested, finally giving in as she kicked him on the shins.

'How dare you!' Jane slapped Ethan hard across the cheeks as he let go of his grip. 'You dirty gypsy, don't you dare put your hands on me again,' she screamed. 'I'll tell my parents, and you and your family can start packing your bags.'

'No, no, Miss Jane – I thought that was what you wanted. You looked so jealous when Rosie and I were talking together the other day. And just then you smiled and encouraged me. You shouldn't have led me on, with your false feelings.' Ethan stood back from the angered young woman.

'I most certainly did not, and I wasn't jealous of farm girl Rosie – you are decidedly wrong. You and she are welcome to one another.' Jane stomped away from her long-faced would-be suitor, stopping only to shout back at him, 'Your days are numbered, Ethan Haygarth,' while she made her way down to the river at the bottom of the parkland, in order to find her brother, Luke.

Jane walked hastily through the flowering grassland, the stalks catching in her laced boots and long skirts as she looked back and saw Ethan following her. This made her break into a run as she tried to escape from him, although secretly she wanted him to catch her. She shouted down towards the river bank in a bid for Luke to hear her, realizing what Ethan could do to her if he caught her, and wanting Luke to be aware of her presence, as back-up.

'Luke! Luke, where are you?' She held onto an ash tree's trunk as she picked her way over its roots and the slippery white limestone of the river's edge. She lifted up her skirts as her feet crunched over the shingle while she made her way to what she knew to be Luke's favourite fishing pool, just below the mighty roar of one of the many waterfalls along the River Ribble. She was aware that she was moving slower than her pursuer, impeded by her long skirts. 'Luke!' she yelled out, as a hand moved over her mouth and Ethan whispered in her ear to be quiet.

Above the waterfall, Luke suddenly heard his name being yelled, and peered over the moss-covered falls to see Ethan and his sister talking and what appeared to be arguing. He waved with his spare hand as he balanced on a particularly slippery boulder, with his rod in the other hand. He edged nearer the falls and waved his rod at the couple, who seemed to be urging him towards them. Picking his way in bare feet, he balanced on the edge of the falls, trying to find an easy way down, as he looked into the gushing waters and the deep pool below him.

'Luke!' Jane yelled out as Ethan suddenly stopped arguing, after realizing the danger Luke was in. Gone were all his thoughts about trying to amend the misinterpretations of earlier, which were what had led him to follow Jane down to the river's edge. Now he had to make sure no harm came to Luke, who was oblivious to the depth of the pool below him.

'Can he swim?' Ethan asked a frantic Jane, as he untied his boots. They both watched Luke balance his rod and wave at both of them again, not concentrating on his actions and deafened by the roar of the river in flood.

Jane shook her head. She screamed as Luke picked his way on the slime-covered stones, only to lose his footing, his rod flying up into the air as he bounced off the moss-covered rocks through the gushing white falls into the deep, dark pool below.

'Stay there, I'll jump in and get him.' Ethan pulled off his waistcoat and pocket watch and quickly jumped into the pool, leaving Jane at the side, frantically yelling Luke's name and peering into the frothy waters of the river. The cold water caught his breath as he dived below the falls, filling his lungs with icy shards while searching deep down for the white shirt of Luke. Ethan gasped for breath as he surfaced and then dived again, after noticing Luke's body trapped between two boulders at the side of the falls.

Jane watched, counting every second that both were under the water, fearing the worst for her brother.

Ethan appeared spluttering, pulling Luke behind him as he splashed awkwardly out of the side of the pool. 'Go and get your father – he's alive, but he's hit his head and is bleeding badly.' Struggling with Luke, Ethan pulled the boy's body out of the water and laid it on the sand and shingle at the pool's edge. 'Go, Jane, go and get help.'

She froze for a second or two as tears ran down her face while she gazed on the lifeless body of her brother. Blood ran down his forehead, staining his white shirt and trickling into the water's edge.

'For God's sake, go!' Ethan yelled as he pummelled Luke's chest to clear his lungs of water.

Jane fled just as Luke was drawing breath. He coughed and spluttered as Ethan talked gently to him and sat him up, before pulling off his own shirt in order to tear a shred off to bandage Luke's bleeding head. Ethan watched and said a silent prayer as Luke whispered his name. Thank God he'd not drowned; he would have been to blame, that was for sure, and he was certain he would have lost both his own and his family's positions, if Jane had opened her mouth.

'You're alright, mate, you fell down the bloody falls. We are going to have to learn you to swim this summer.' Ethan leaned back and watched Luke gain his breath, looking up at the green foliage of the whispering trees above, as they swayed quietly in the gentle summer breeze. He waited for what felt like an age before Jane appeared, with her father and Ethan's behind her.

'Oh my God, Luke – are you alright?' James Fox bent down and picked his son up in his arms, gasping at the sight of so much blood on the white-shirt bandage and at Ethan catching his breath. 'What were you thinking of? How many times have I told you to steer clear of this deep pool?' He helped a sobbing Luke up from the river bank and then passed him to the stronger arms of Jethro. 'Thank God you were there, Ethan – he'd have drowned for sure if you hadn't have jumped into the river after him.'

'I did nothing, sir; really you should not be thanking me.' Ethan hung his head and felt ashamed at the fact that he was standing bare-chested in front of both his master and Jane, waiting for the chastisement that was certainly going to come. He'd dared to touch the new master's daughter and had nearly caused his son's death. He'd be lucky not to get a thrashing.

'Nonsense! Jane told me how you did not hesitate for a second to save Luke. We will always be in your debt.' James held his hand out and shook Ethan's firmly, before turning and running quickly to catch up with Jethro, who was halfway across the field and making his way to the manor, holding Luke up under his arms.

Ethan looked at Jane, who was standing at the river's edge staring at him. 'You didn't say anything to your father?'

'What was there to say? You saved my brother.' She made her way up from the river bank and stood at the edge of the field, waiting for Ethan as he put his boots and socks back on. 'Besides, I lied. I have been flirting with you on the quiet, and I deserved all that I got. Which I must say was very fine, Ethan,' she giggled. 'However, I was only trying to make my milksop cousin Rosie jealous. She's the one who really likes you, but you are too blind to see it. You are a typical man! I've no intentions of courting anyone yet; indeed, I don't think I ever will.'

Ethan hopped on one leg as he pulled his boot onto his left foot.

'Rosie doesn't like me in that way, does she? I thought she was just showing interest in the horses.' He walked quickly to catch Jane up as she ran her hand through the long grasses.

'You are so gullible, Ethan Haygarth. And I'm sorry I slapped you and called you a gypsy.' Jane grinned. 'But yes, Rosie has confessed to me that she thinks you are handsome.'

'It's no skin off my nose. I deserved it, and I'm quite proud I'm part gypsy.' Ethan smirked, thinking about Rosie. So he *had* taken her eye. That was quite something he could be proud of, and Rosie was the nicer of the two girls.

'Well, let's remain friends, and don't you say a word to Rosie about me telling you that she likes you.' Jane stood and waited for his reply as she watched her mother and father lift Luke into the waiting carriage to take him home to Ingfield.

'Won't say a word, I promise. And thanks for not telling on me.' Ethan blushed and looked down at his feet, knowing that he had pushed his luck.

'Jane, come quickly, we need the doctor to look at your brother,' shouted Isabelle as she climbed into the carriage.

'Coming, Mother,' Jane yelled as she rushed across the pebbled drive to join her parents and brother.

Ethan watched as the carriage made its way out of the gates, before joining his father in the stable.

'That was a near do.' Jethro stood by his son and looked at him. 'It could have ended in tragedy. As it is, I think Luke's just knocked the front of his head badly. Better to spoil his beauty than his brains – not that he's got many.'

'Aye, he's going to have to learn to swim. I'll teach him this summer.' Ethan lifted the horse harness that he'd been cleaning earlier, before he'd got distracted by the sight of Jane admiring the foal. He put it back on its peg on the stable wall.

'Now, lad, I'm giving you a bit of advice. There's them – the posh 'uns – and there's us. You can look, but you don't touch. We are not in their class and never will be, and an ill wind will always blow if you dare to do any other. You let his father teach him to swim, if Luke wants to do so. And as for Miss Jane, you leave her be, lad. She's not right for you.' Jethro spat his mouthful of tobacco out and looked at his son.

Ethan dared only glance at his father. Was there nothing he didn't see or know? He'd never noticed him there when he'd tried to kiss Jane.

'Aye, alright, Father.'

Jethro watched as his son sloped off to the barn to fill the horse hay-racks. He leaned against the stable doorway and looked across at the manor house. It didn't seem five minutes since he had had the same feelings for Charlotte, who was at that time the new mistress of Windfell. But he'd known better than to show them. Instead, he'd always been there to support her. Commoners and posh folk should never mix, especially when young Jane had pointed out that they were only gypsies. Her grandmother would never have been so cutting and demeaning. There was a new breed shortly to inhabit Windfell, of that he was sure, and Ethan would be better off away from them. The lad had ideas above his station in life, ideas that were going to get him into trouble.

Back at Ingfield House, Isabelle and James stood over Luke's bed, watching their son sleep.

'Thank God he's alright. The doctor says the wound on his head looks worse than it is. There was so much blood.' James reached for the hand of his fretting wife. 'He'll be fine in the morning.'

'I thought we were going to lose him – he looked so white. I can understand now how Harriet felt when she came home to the news of the twins being dead. Our sons and daughters are the most precious things we will ever have. No wonder she cannot forgive Mama and myself for dragging her in to work that day. Thankfully, in our case Ethan was there to pull him out of the water, otherwise we too would be without our son.' Isabelle ran her hand over Luke's brow and smiled as he turned in his sleep. 'What Ethan was doing down in the river, I don't quite know. Perhaps tickling one of our finest trout, knowing him. Like father, like son. I've seen Jethro down there many a time when I was growing up. Mother and Archie used to turn a blind eye to it. However, I don't see why we should.' She walked to the gas light and turned the flame down, before urging James out of the room.

'The odd fish or two won't hurt, Isabelle. It matters not

that it is not Ethan's right to fish in that part of the river. We need to keep our staff on our side, and if that's what it takes to keep Ethan and Jethro happy, and encourages them to get my horse and carriage ready for me first thing in the morning, then I'm satisfied. Besides, he saved your son's life,' James whispered as he closed the bedroom door silently behind him.

'It starts with one fish, and then we'll find him liming the river for all the fish. I think we should watch that lad. Mazy should never have married into a family like that. She was worth more than becoming a gypsy's wife.' Isabelle strutted along the landing, her skirts rustling as she reached the top of the stairs, and stopped sharply.

'I think you are wrong. Jethro and Ethan have always been good with your family.' James knew that disagreeing with his wife meant harsh words to follow, for she always spoke her mind.

'James, leave the running of Windfell to me. I am the new mistress and I aim to make everyone know that. I appreciate your participation, but the household is my concern. Your help with business is more than enough worry for you, along with your photography studios. After all, you have studios in Leeds and Bradford in our stores – you seem to be always busy with them, the amount of time you spend there.' Jane waited for his reply.

'Yes, my dear. Of course you know best. But I am here, if you ever need—' James was stopped in his tracks.

'I am my mother's daughter. She taught me everything I know. Just like I'm teaching Jane. I was brought up to be strong, and that is what I'll be; and while I know you are more than capable of running the household, it is my job.' She descended the stairs without looking back at her husband.

'Yes, dear,' whispered James. He was married to a stubborn woman.

5

Things had not been easy between Danny and Harriet since he had announced his father's intention of coming to live with them at Crummock. And today was no exception.

'You never once thought of consulting me, did you? You just said, "Of course it will be fine with the wife," because my wants don't even come into it.' Harriet felt stressed. Ben was back on form and had decided to do one of his disappearing tricks, making up for the weeks that he had been confined to his bed with German measles. Plus baby Georgina was still not 100 per cent, crying at the least little upset. On top of that, it was clipping time, and the sheep were in the normally tidy farmyard waiting to be sheared and have their thick woollen coats removed for the hot summer months ahead. The noise of their bleating was driving her mad, and the mess that would have to be swept up after they had been shorn would be unbelievable.

'What would you have me do? Say, "No, Father. We

don't want you"? How ungrateful would that have sounded, after he'd just said that Crummock would be ours, after his day had passed?' said Danny. 'Will you stop your moaning; he'll be no bother, and in fact he will be a blessing. He'll be able to give me advice whenever I want it, and you know how much Ben and Rosie love him. I wish he was as fit as he used to be, because I could really have done with his help this morning, looking at this lot to clip and place our mark on.'

'Well, I'm glad for you, but to me he's just another mouth to feed. I've enough on lately, and it'll mean I'll have to get him a room ready.' Harriet could nearly cry; she'd had enough. Four weeks of sickly children, and the death of Charlotte, had made her spirits low. It was as if nothing was going right, and looking around the yard at more than a hundred and fifty sheep, and all the neighbours who had come to help in the yearly event of clipping, was just about the last straw. She appreciated that everyone was here to help, but they would all want to be fed, and she would be expected to wrap the woollen fleeces up into a ball, ready for the wool merchant from Long Preston to collect later in the year. All of this, with Ben missing, Georgina bawling and Rosie unable to wait a minute longer for her grandfather to arrive, just made Harriet feel like breaking down.

'Get Rosie to make my father's bed up and tidy his room – she's old enough. Ben will turn up when he's hungry; he will be down at the wash-dubs with his mates. It's a good day for having a dip in that pool down there.' Danny looked up at the blue skies and regretted straight away that he'd said Ben might have gone swimming. Harriet would imagine all sorts of calamities.

'A dip in the wash-dubs – he'll be to bury! He's only just got over the measles.' Harriet stood on the steps that led down into the yard and rubbed her face with her hands. She just didn't know where to start.

'Come on, old lass, this isn't like you. You usually take everything in your stride. My father will be no problem and, if he is, we can always send him back to Isabelle to look after, although he is my responsibility really.' Danny put his arm around Harriet and felt her sobbing. He kissed her gently on the neck as she trembled.

'I'm sorry, it's just that I'm not feeling myself at the moment. The children have been a worry, and although I know we owe everything to your father, I don't know if it will work with him living here. Anyway,' Harriet pushed him back, 'take your hands off me. We'll have none of this, Danny Atkinson – you are showing me up. Look at Henry from Sowermire wondering what's up; you'd swear he'd never seen a husband give his wife a hug before.' Harriet pushed him away and wiped back the tear that had trickled down her cheek.

'He probably hasn't, and he definitely won't have hugged his wife for a while. I doubt his arms would reach around her, she's such a size.' Danny tried to brighten Harriet's mood.

'Shush – he'll hear you. Patsy might be big, but she's a good woman; she'll feed you well, when you go there clipping. Which is more than can be said of me, if I don't stir my shanks and get that rhubarb pie in the oven and

54

find a cheese from out of the pantry.' She lifted up her skirts and made for the kitchen doorway. But Danny's shout stopped her in her tracks.

'You've one less worry – here comes our Ben with my father. They are just coming round the end of the wood.' Danny leaned against the garden wall and wiped the sweat off his brow with the back of his cap, as his father opened the farmyard gate with Ben by his side. 'Where do you think you've been trailing? Did you not think to tell your mother where you were off to?' he asked Ben, who was busy chatting to his grandfather.

'I found him on the green lane going over to Wharfe; he was only making his way to play with the Knowles lad. It's a good day for trailing and adventures, isn't it, Ben?' Archie rubbed his small grandson's head of curly brown hair, before whispering that he had to say sorry to his mother for upsetting her.

'Sorry, Mother. I just hadn't seen John for so long, and I didn't think you'd miss me.' Ben bowed his head, knowing he was in a spot of bother as Harriet pulled him into the house by his shoulder.

'Let him stop out with us, lass, we'll keep an eye on him. He can help pick up the loose bits of wool and put them in a sack; it'll keep him out of mischief.' Archie looked at his son, wondering if he had done right.

'Leave her, Father, she'll give Ben a chastising and then he'll be out with us. It'll be like water off a duck's back at the moment, for he tends to do his own thing and have a mind of his own, does our Ben,' sighed Danny.

'Aye, I had one of them, and look what he grew into!

A bloody big stubborn bugger, who still tends to do just what he wants.' Archie laughed and patted his son on the shoulders. 'Right, let's get these sheep clipped.' He reached into the bag on his back and pulled out a shining pair of sharp steel sheep-shears. 'The sooner we get started, the sooner we get done. Is that not right, lads?' he shouted to the four neighbouring farmers, who were already handling sheep, turning each animal onto its buttocks and then holding the struggling sheep fast between their legs. The sharp shears started cutting the fleece away from the sheep's stomach, and then up around the back and next to the head, carefully keeping the fleece whole and not nicking the sheep. Once bare of their fleece, the sheep were then marked with a red waterproof mixture, with the letter A, to denote that the sheep belonged to the Atkinsons, before they were let back out of the farmyard to the holding pasture where their spring-born bleating lambs were waiting. The marking would help if a sheep got lost on the open fell and would reveal who its owner was.

'You needn't think you are clipping, Father. Not on those doddery knees. First sheep that struggled, you'd be knocked over.' Danny looked at his father, whose disappointed face said it all. 'Why don't you roll the fleeces up? Harriet was going to help, but she's got enough on, with the baby still under the weather.'

'But it'll be the first time I've missed clipping my sheep for the last fifty years. I can do the odd old one.'

Archie looked at the yard full of grey-faced Rough Fells and Swaledales, all breathing hard and bleating in the warm summer's sun. The flies they were attracting buzzed around them, and as Archie watched them he realized his son was speaking the truth and he would have to face up to the fact that he'd be more bother than he was worth.

'I suppose you are right. It's a bloody sad day when your father is doing a woman's job. But I don't want to be a burden to anyone.' Archie pushed his way through the flock of sheep and made for the first shearer with a fleece ready for wrapping. He shook out the lanolin-filled fleece, folding all the odd pieces of it into the middle, and just leaving the tail-end to be used for tying the fleece up. He rolled the fleece tight like a rolled-up blanket and then pulled the tail-end tightly around the fleece. Then he tucked it into itself, before throwing the fleece into the huge hessian sack that the wool merchant had left to be filled on the back of the cart in the corner of the farm-yard. He then quickly moved on to the next.

Danny watched his father. He was an awkward old devil. Why didn't he just take it easy and sit and watch them all? Clipping was a young man's job, and he wished Archie had stopped down at Windfell, just for today. He picked up his shears and joined the group of men; as his father had said, the sooner they all started the better. It was going to be a long day.

Archie leaned back and stretched. He ached from bending down and rolling fleeces. He sat back on the edge of the garden steps and watched those who, to him, looked like young men, as Harriet poured a drink of tea into enamel mugs and made sure each man was amply fed with warm bacon and hard fried-egg sandwiches, followed by rhubarb pie and cream. She was a good woman really; the death of her two children had made her hard, though, and had spoilt her onetime gentle ways. He had always thought she was right for Danny, a good farmer's wife as well as being a good mother, despite what Harriet thought of herself. It was a pity they weren't getting on so well at present. No doubt he hadn't helped by wanting to move in; and telling Danny that he had a son at Ragged Hall would only have made him think about what he might have had. Perhaps he shouldn't have said anything.

'Thanks, Harriet, that looks grand. You make a good pie, just like my mother did, and that's a true compliment.' Archie smiled up at her as she stood beside him with the enamel jug of tea, after pouring him a cup.

'Thank you, Father, and thank you for rolling the fleeces for me. It's been a good help.' Harriet pulled her skirts around her and sat next to her father-in-law. She did love him, she just hadn't wanted him to live with them. Things were fraught enough, without another body to look after.

'Our Danny thinks I'm not fit for clipping, so it's the least I can do. It seems he's right anyway, because I feel knackered. I'm not as fit as I used to be, and these lads clip fast. A lot faster than I ever did.' Archie put his head back after a long sip of his tea and looked into the vivid cloud-free blue sky, watching the swallows and swifts as they screeched above his head.

'It'll come to us all, so don't worry. Rosie and I have

made your room up. You are welcome to join us any time now. Danny and the children can't wait for you to arrive.' Harriet looked at Archie and saw how tired and aged he seemed since the death of Charlotte.

'I'll try not to be any bother, lass. I'll keep out of your way and will help when I can. I know I'm just another responsibility, but I'll take young Ben fishing and sing to Georgina when she's twisty. Not that it will stop her gurning,' laughed Archie.

'You'll not be any bother, Father. Now go and have a lie-down, I'll finish rolling the fleeces. Georgina is asleep, Rosie is baking a cake and, as you can see, Ben is helping his father mark the sheep.' Harriet put her arm round Archie. He looked shattered, and her heart softened to the old man.

Together, they looked across at Danny and Ben and smiled.

'Look at Ben: the next owner of Crummock, lass. He's a right farmer.' Archie smiled before standing straight. The truth was that the day was telling on him. 'I might just go and have forty winks. Am I in the end bedroom?' He looked up at the long, ancient farmhouse and yawned.

'Aye, I thought you'd be quietest there.' Harriet watched as her father-in-law stiffly climbed the few steps into the garden and walked up the path. He was old and in need of care; no wonder he wanted to come home to Crummock. She'd have to learn to bite her tongue. She owed a lot to Archie Atkinson, and the least he could expect was a bit of comfort in his dotage. He never took sides and had always been kind to her, she should remember that.

Archie lay on his bed and looked up at the cracked whitewashed ceiling of his new bedroom. It was a step down from the beautifully plastered ceilings of Windfell Manor and their ornate cornicing. He listened to the men in the yard talking and laughing to one another, and smelt the fruitcake that Rosie was baking in the fireside oven of the kitchen. This was what he had missed – the simple things in life – not having to announce to the world his intentions for the day, what he wished to eat and where to eat it. He closed his eyes; life had gone full circle and he was back in the world that he'd been born into, albeit without his Lottie. But she would always be waiting for him in his dreams and thoughts.

6

Isabelle stood back and looked around the drawing room of Ingfield House, watching the parlour maid as she scurried around with the dust covers that were being thrown over the furniture they were going to leave in their abandoned home.

'That's right – I'm taking that vase. Be careful, I don't want it breaking,' shouted Isabelle at the hauliers who were moving the possessions that were to join her in the family's new life at Windfell Manor.

'Do we really need to take all these belongings to Windfell? Where are you going to place them? Windfell is full to the rafters already.' James sat down in one of the covered chairs and watched as his wife gave orders to the scurrying young men. They dared not answer back to his domineering wife.

'Really, James, we need to make our mark on Windfell – make it ours. My mother and Archie have always kept the house smart, but some of their furniture and decor are a bit dated. I aim to stamp my own mark on Windfell and make it our home. I'm so glad that we don't have to sell Ingfield. I hope that one day the house, and most of the contents, will make a good wedding present for our Jane, if and when she is to wed.' Isabelle glanced at her husband as she stood and looked around at the emptying room.

'Jane to wed – I hope not! Or at least not for a few years yet, she's only seventeen and it would be a brave man that tackles her. Do you know I caught her reading one of the ridiculous pamphlets those visiting suffragettes to Skipton were handing out the other day? She's definitely got a mind of her own.' James sighed as he watched his wife remonstrating about how her belongings should be handled, instead of listening to him. 'She even had the cheek the other day to quote their saying, "Deeds, not Words", to me when I said I had not spoken to your father about offering help when he moved out.'

'Perhaps she had a point, my dear. After all, all you have done is sit there and moan, and we are trying to get us moved into Windfell before the evening,' Isabelle said curtly. Her thoughts were both on the move and on where she should really be: making her mark as the new owner of Atkinson's. And she hadn't time for her husband's relaxed ways; he might just as well have gone to Skipton and supported Jane, by coping with some of the backlog of orders that had occurred because of her mother's passing.

'I object to you saying that. I did help Archie with his belongings this morning – not that he took a lot with him. He seems to have turned his back on his old life, now that your mother has gone. I only hope he and Harriet see eye-to-eye, as we both know Archie does things his own way and doesn't think of the consequences.' James rose from his seat and looked out of the window of Ingfield's drawing room onto the busy street in Settle. 'I'm going to miss seeing the people going past our window. At Windfell, all I'll be able to do is see that row of beech trees and listen to the gossip of the staff.'

'Well, there will be enough of that, especially at the moment. I don't think I'll be very popular with Jethro and Mazy, as I've told them Ethan's services will be no longer needed. There's just no need for two in the stables, especially now that Archie is going to live at Crummock.' Isabelle joined her husband at the window and looked out onto the bustling street, full of people going about their business.

'You didn't tell me! Do you not think that decision was a bit hard, after he saved our Luke's life? ' James was shocked.

'I didn't tell you because I knew how you'd react. I know he saved Luke, but I've seen the way he looks at Jane; and he's always creeping about the place, poaching the odd fish and catching the occasional rabbit. Believe me, I'm not often wrong: if he stays at Windfell, Ethan will bring trouble. He doesn't seem to know his place in society – unlike his parents.' Isabelle straightened a cover and turned her back on her husband. She knew her decision would not be popular with him, and she had already felt the coolness of Mazy's reaction to it.

'Have you made any other decisions behind my back?' James waited.

'No, not yet, although we are going to have two lady's maids at Windfell, and I think I might have to let Lily go. After all, she's not getting any younger, and my Dorothy looks after my needs so well.'

'But Lily was your mother's favourite!' James looked horrified.

'Exactly – my mother's favourite – and, as such, she always had my mother's ear. She never treats me as the grown woman I am, and never will.' Isabelle remembered the time when Lily had told tales on her and her former lover, John Sidgwick, something for which she had never forgiven her. 'Everyone else can stay. I don't want to be seen as uncaring.' She had known how James would react and had been hesitant to reveal her thoughts.

'I know that you must be prudent, but Lily was dear to your mother's heart. And you have to deal with Mazy and Jethro every day. I don't think you will be helping your reputation. As the doctor told you, your mother's shoes are hard to fill.' James watched as his wife struggled to realize that she would not be liked for her actions.

'Perhaps if I find Lily somewhere to live, it might look like I do care. It was a trick my mother used to employ, whenever she felt her staff had to leave. Although all the Lock Cottages are occupied, I could perhaps speak to my godfather and see if he has any cottages empty. The ones on Jubilee Terrace at Langcliffe would be ideal. I'm sure he will be able to help. As for Ethan, I'm afraid I stand by my decision.' Isabelle walked over to the doorway and watched as the carriers closed the tailgate of their cart after they finished loading the Fox possessions. 'Can you lock the doors and make sure all is secure?' She turned and looked at her scowling husband.

'Why, where are you going?' James walked over to her side.

'I'm going to Grisedale's on Victoria Street. I'd like a new bedroom suite for Jane's bedroom, and I saw just what I wanted in their window.' Isabelle tidied her plaited hair and placed her elaborately decorated hat on her head, glancing in the hallway mirror as she picked up her parasol from the umbrella stand.

'But, Isabelle, there are four perfectly good bedroom suites upstairs that you could take to Windfell, not to mention the ones already there.' James shook his head.

'She needs a new one, something modern that reflects the age we live in. A new broom sweeps clean, James – you should know that.'

He watched as his wife walked down the path of Ingfield House. He knew Isabelle would have whatever she wanted, despite what he had to say about it. He respected her for being a strong woman, but sometimes she was so stubborn. Stubborn to the point of stupidity, especially when she would not back down after realizing her mistakes. He sighed and gazed around Ingfield House, before closing the heavy oak door and locking it securely behind him.

He ran his hand down the mock-Roman pillars on either side of the porch as he stepped down the pristine white, donkey-stoned steps. He would miss living in

Settle, and would have to get accustomed to the quiet evenings at Windfell. He looked around him at the grand house they were putting into storage. Life would never be the same, now that Isabelle was the new mistress of Windfell. He was just thankful that he worked in Skipton and was his own master in his photography studio at Atkinson's. That was a part of his world that Isabelle knew better than to interfere in. He should be grateful for small mercies.

Archie sat next to Jethro as they made their way gently, with the horse and cart filled with the possessions that Archie had decided he wanted for his new life up at Crummock. The horse ambled amicably along the rutted track out of Austwick, and Archie looked across at the scars of white limestone called Norber, feeling content with his lot.

'We'll miss you at Windfell, sir,' said Jethro quietly, as he gently encouraged the horse while they climbed the hill towards the turn-off to Sowermire Farm and then on towards Crummock itself.

'Aye, well, I'll still be about, and you'll be alright with Isabelle and her family. She's her mother's daughter – she'll take care of you all.' Archie leaned back and looked at the rolling hills and fields that stretched out in front of him.

'Nay, sir, I hope I'm not talking out of term, but Mistress Isabelle is not totally like her mother; she's causing a bit of a stir at our house at the moment.' Jethro had thought about biting his tongue to Archie, but then he had reconsidered, knowing that Archie would not be happy that Ethan had been told to look for work elsewhere.

'What do you mean, lad? What's she been up to?' Archie leaned forward and looked at the worry that lined the tanned face of Jethro, a man he respected for his horsemanship and his country ways.

'Perhaps I shouldn't tell you, but she's told our Ethan he's to look for new employment. That he's not needed.' Jethro paused and waited as a silence came between them. He watched as Archie shook his head and licked his lips as he took in the news.

'Nay, she'd no need to do that, there's plenty of work for both of you. Especially as that lad of hers is worth nowt. But you didn't hear me say that.' Archie shook his head again and looked at Jethro. 'She's obviously not thinking straight. But I'll not see your lad out of work. If she won't see sense, I could perhaps have an answer to your problem.' He thought for a moment, before asking Jethro, 'What would you say if Ethan came and worked for me up at Crummock? I can't make our lass keep him on at Windfell, but he could still work for me.'

'I'd appreciate that, sir. Crummock would be the right spot for Ethan. I'd not deny that he's as wild as a mountain hare, but he's a good lad really.' Jethro breathed out in relief. If Archie Atkinson employed Ethan, he'd have a good master and he was better away from that Miss Jane, whom Ethan had shown more than a passing interest in.

'Right, well, leave it with me, I'll speak to both of

mine and make it right with them, and you tell your Mazy, and then it will be sorted.' Archie gazed in front of him, trying to understand why Isabelle had given Ethan his marching orders. After all she was more beholden to him than to anyone else in her service, after he had saved Luke from drowning.

Spirits were low in the kitchen at Windfell, after the realization that they were to lose both Lily and Ethan.

'You know, I thought better of Miss Isabelle.' Ruby sat back and hugged her cup of tea while she looked around at the crestfallen staff.

'That's the trouble – we all still think of her as "Miss Isabelle", but she isn't the young woman we all knew; she's a grown woman with children of her own. And now Mr Atkinson's gone to live at Crummock, and with Mrs Atkinson at rest, she's our mistress.' Lily's eyes filled with tears. 'She can do what she likes with any of us. Besides, she's laid off all the staff at Ingfield except for Dorothy Baines, so you should think yourselves lucky.'

'But what will you do, Lily? Where are you going to go? Windfell's been your life.' Nancy stopped for a minute from peeling potatoes and looked at the sniffling lady's maid.

'Well, I'm not going into one of the Lock Cottages or into one of Lorenzo Christie's cottages. I've got my pride, I've got savings – I'll find my own little cottage. So she needn't worry her head about where she's going to put me, just to ease her conscience. I'll have a look down in Settle this afternoon; find myself something small, just right for one. And then, when I'm settled in, I'll take in a bit of mending, to earn a little money. I'll not go without, don't you worry.' Lily breathed in and looked around at the long faces that surrounded her. 'Aye, I'm not dead yet – just moving out.' She tried to muster a smile.

'What with you and our Ethan, I don't know what she's thinking about. It isn't as if she's skint.' Mazy leaned against the kitchen sink and looked around her. 'She's even talking about putting that new fancy electric all through the house – imagine the mess! We've only just got over the new boiler and the bathroom being put in.'

'It was good news that Mister Atkinson is going to take Ethan up to Crummock, but you'll miss him, Mazy.' Ruby rose from her chair and put her teacup and saucer next to her, before patting Mazy's shoulder lovingly.

'Aye, both Jethro and I are grateful to the master. He's a good soul. We can grin and bear what life throws at us, but you always wish for something better for your children. Ethan says he'll come back down home on a Sunday and he's not that far away, so we will just have to grin and bear it.' Mazy glanced up at the stairs leading to the main hall, hearing the sound of feet approaching, and placed her finger to her lips to stop everyone from gossiping as Dorothy Baines entered the kitchen.

'Is Mistress Isabelle alright this morning?' Ruby looked at the newest pretty maid to arrive at Windfell, trying to divert the conversation and stop the silence that fell when Dorothy was present.

'Yes, thank you, Mrs Pratt.' Dorothy looked around at the group, which she knew was hostile to her new position at Windfell and which she'd never be part of. 'Look, I'm sorry the mistress has decided to replace Lily with me, and I realize that I will always be the odd one out because you have all been here so long. But what would you all have done, if you were in my shoes? I could hardly have said no to keeping my position. I'm just like the rest of you – I need the money to survive.' She slumped down onto the pine chair at the head of the table and put her head in her hands.

Ruby walked over and ran her hand over the young girl's shoulders as she talked to her. 'We know, lass, but we have all been together so long; and if you kick one of us, we all limp. We know it isn't your fault. We'll just have to adjust to the changes that are coming and make the best of things. God bless Mistress Charlotte – she was one of the best. We can only hope Mistress Isabelle is going to follow in her footsteps. And don't worry, lass, you'll get used to us and our ways and will soon forget these first few weeks.'

Dorothy raised her head and smiled across at Lily. 'Sorry, Lily, I'm so sorry that she has sacked you.'

'Don't be sorry. I was Mistress Charlotte's maid, and not really Isabelle's. My work is done here and it's time to move on. All things come to an end. I wish you all the best, Dorothy, and hope you will be as happy here as I have been.' Lily put her arms around the young girl and smiled at her companions. She was going to miss the kitchen of Windfell and its occupants.

7

'So, I've not only acquired your father, but I've also got his stable lad to feed.' Harriet looked at her husband's reflection in the dressing-table mirror as she brushed her hair with fervour, while she took in the news of Ethan coming to work at Crummock. 'I just knew this would happen – you can never say no to your father.' She swivelled round on her stool and watched as Danny pulled his shirt over his head. He sat on the side of the bed, bare-chested and as handsome as the day she met him.

'Oh, Harriet, Ethan will not be any bother. In fact if he takes after his father, he'll be a blessing. And as for feeding him, he will like enough feed himself. He's a dab hand at catching rabbits and tickling trout, and as long as he supplies the house occasionally, I don't mind turning a blind eye. Unlike our Isabelle, who, as far as I can see, has cut off her nose to spite her face by not keeping Ethan in her employment. The rest of the staff will not be happy with her actions.' Danny looked at his wife, whom he still loved. He just wished that for once she'd see the good side in things instead of being so negative.

'Well, it's typical of your Isabelle: someone helps her and then she does them an injustice. Is Luke making a good recovery? It could have been so much worse, if Ethan had not rescued him. Isabelle should be grateful to that lad. Thinking about it, perhaps he is better off with us. At least he will be appreciated.' Harriet yawned and walked over to the edge of the bed.

'You can ask yourself how Luke is. Isabelle sent word with Father that she would like us to join her for Sunday dinner next weekend. She probably wants to show off her new home to us.' Danny laughed and leaned over and played with the ends of Harriet's long brown hair, hoping that for once she'd be in the mood to please him.

'Oh, do we have to go? I really can't abide the way she talks down to me nowadays. She changed completely when your mother put her in charge of all the stores. As for poor James, I don't know how he puts up with her bossing him about; he's just like her toy poodle.' Harriet sighed. She really didn't want to go to Windfell and feel like the poor relation.

'We will all go. We didn't when it was Mama's funeral; and besides, you now hold shares in the stores, so it would do you good to keep your hand in and make sure all's well with the businesses. You've no excuses; all the children are well now, and it's time you and Isabelle made up. As for James, he enjoys being her poodle. He makes his own way in life, lost in his photography and being

72

given orders to obey.' Danny lay back and pulled gently on Harriet's arm, urging her to join him.

'I'm tired, Danny, leave me be. I've been up since five. Unlike Isabelle, I haven't lots of people looking after my needs.' Harriet pulled the sheets back and climbed into bed, turning away from her husband and the passion he was requesting.

'You are always tired. I sometimes think it's just an excuse and that you don't love me any more.' Danny lay down next to her and kissed Harriet's neck gently, trying to get some of the attention and love that he craved.

'I love you more than life itself, Danny Atkinson, so don't you dare say that. I am genuinely tired; there's always something to do, and the youngest two take so much watching. Rosie does as much as she can, but daydreams looking out of the window all day, wanting to be off over fell and dale, or to be with you. Now her grandfather is here, she's even worse, because he's forever telling her tales of when he was a lad. He fills her head with rubbish.' Harriet turned over and kissed Danny on the lips.

'Aye, they are alike them two, thick as thieves.' Danny ran his fingers through Harriet's hair and held her tightly. 'Our children will soon be grown and away, and then we will have time for ourselves and we will look back and wonder where all the years have gone. Just like my father and Charlotte.' Cradling Harriet tightly, he looked up at the ceiling and thought about the lad that he knew to be his at Ragged Hall. How could he ever admit to having a child with anyone other than Harriet? It would break her heart. The lad would just have to stay where he was for now. And he would have to bide his time and hope that over the next few years, as their own children grew, he would get the opportunity to make good his mistake. His heart was owned by the woman at his side, and always would be. He bent down and kissed Harriet's brow, before both of them pulled the covers up to their chins. 'I love you, Harriet Atkinson,' Danny said quietly.

'And I you, Danny Atkinson,' Harriet whispered, half-asleep.

'Goodnight, my love. All will be well in the end.' Danny turned and blew out the bedside candle and gazed into the darkness of the night, hoping that his words rang true and that all would be well in their world. Time would tell, no doubt.

Bill Brown sat across from his young grandson and decided to say what had been on his mind for some time.

'I'm buggered, lad. This old ticker of mine can't go on for much longer.' He looked at his well-built grandson, the lad he knew was the love-child of his daughter Amy and the farmer Danny Atkinson. 'Now, after my day Ragged Hall is yours, do you hear? Don't let that bastard over at Slaidburn take it off you. It should have been your mother's, but I'm leaving it to you.' Bill caught his breath and dropped his head as he thought of the love-less marriage that his daughter was in.

'Nay, Grandfather, it should be my mother's, not mine. Besides, you are not going anywhere yet, so don't talk of suchlike.' Daniel's eyes filled with tears, for his grandfather had been his saviour, rescuing him from a life no better than a servant with his so-called family.

'You know why I'm leaving it to you, lad. Your mother's told you that you were conceived out of wedlock and to a different father from the rest of her brood. You are Danny Atkinson's son – his bloody father was only in our farmyard a week or two back. I thought then that I should have said something to him, to set you up right, after my day. Like a fool, I didn't, but there's nowt stopping you from making yourself known to them at Windfell Manor after my day. They are a good family. Archie and I went to school together – if you could call the few days we did attend, between helping our fathers out on the farm, schooling. Archie looked at you when I was talking to him, and I know he recognized you as one of his own. With that mop on your head, you stick out like a sore thumb – a right Atkinson. No wonder your stepfather at Slaidburn hated you.'

Daniel hung his head. 'Why didn't Mr Atkinson come and say something to me? Am I something to be ashamed of – a dirty secret, best left alone?'

'Nay, lad, Archie is not like that, nor is his lad, Danny. It's the first time he had seen you. As far as they were aware, you were a Bland. After all, your mother wed and disappeared from Danny's life. Danny went on to wed and have a family of his own, and both your mother and he had to make the best of it.'

'My mother has always told me that the Atkinsons are well-to-do. That they are wealthy, and that part of that wealth should one day be mine. But I'm not bothered about the money. I just want to be acknowledged as Danny Atkinson's son.' Daniel lowered his head, remembering his childhood at Slaidburn with the Bland family. A childhood filled with misery, when he was treated like a dog – not a human being with feelings – by his stepfather and step-brothers. His mother was the only one who showed him affection. She talked about better days before she was married, with a twinkle in her eye and a lightness in her voice.

'Aye, well, like I say, get yourself known to them, after my day. They'll do right by you, once they ken who you are.' Bill breathed in deeply and closed his eyes.

'I will, Grandfather. With your blessing, I will.' Daniel sat back in his chair and looked around the kitchen of Ragged Hall. A farm of his own and a family to call his own – that was all he had ever wished for. And now it lay within his grasp.

Rosie lay on her back next to Ethan. It was a dazzling warm day. The air was alive with the buzz of insects and the hot sun shone down on them both, making them feel lazy. It was a day to relax and enjoy.

'Your father will wonder where I've got to. I don't want to upset the apple cart in my first week of work-ing at Crummock.' Ethan rolled over onto his side and looked at the innocent young woman alongside him. The sun shone on her fine blonde hair, making it look like angel's breath. He watched as she closed her eyes to shel-ter them from the sun's rays. Her long, fine lashes threw shadows on her blushing red cheeks as she lay enjoying the summer heat.

'Don't worry, Ethan, he and my grandfather have gone to the market in Settle. They won't be back until before supper, and they'll not even know you've gone,' she whispered, as she stretched out over the bed of wild thyme that omitted its heady herbal perfume around them.

'But your ma! Won't she be missing you?' Ethan lay back down and looked into the sun.

'She'll not miss me, nor you. I often wander, once I've done my chores. As long as I turn up for my supper, she'll not think anything of it.' Rosie opened her eyes and turned onto her side to look at the young dark-skinned, curly-haired lad. Feeling full of mischief, she picked a sprig of purple-flowering thyme and tickled him under the nose with it, teasing him as he lay back with his arms under his head.

'Stop it, you tease.' Ethan wiped under his nose and laughed. 'Where do you wander to? You shouldn't really, not on your own.' He looked concerned.

'Depends how I feel. Sometimes I just walk down into Wharfe.' She pointed down at the hamlet that lay tucked under the limestone outcrops below them. 'Sometimes I walk over to Clapham and wander through the grand garden that the Farrer family owns. And sometimes I walk over the fells, nearly into Horton. Wherever I go, I prefer to be out on my own. You can smell the breeze and feel the sun on your face while listening to the sky-larks singing, without having to be bothered to talk to anybody.' Rosie tucked her skirts under her knees and sat clasping her hands around her legs. 'I need to be outside, not helping my mother wash or bake in the kitchen. Sometimes I wish I had been born a boy. I'd have been able to help my father more then, and be outside all the time.'

'Well, I'm glad you weren't born a lad.' Ethan looked at the lass with her long blonde hair, which was whipping over her face in the slight breeze of the fellside, and felt a flutter within him that he'd not experienced before. 'Could I come with you on your walks?' Unlike Jane, Rosie had the same love of the natural world around her as he felt. She respected nature and the people in her life, and he in turn respected her for that.

Rosie blushed as she realized what Ethan had said. She enjoyed his company too, his easy ways with animals and his knowledge of plants and flowers. She looked across at him. He was handsome in his corduroy breeches, striped shirt and tight-fitting waistcoat. His curly dark hair matched his almost black eyes, which looked at her, waiting with anticipation for her answer.

'I'd like that – I'd like that a lot.' Rosie grinned. 'Father and Grandfather are always away at the market on a Tuesday, so let's make Tuesday afternoon our time together and not tell anyone.'

'That would suit me; we get on so well and I enjoy your company.' Ethan smiled, showing his perfectly white teeth to Rosie.

'Good, that's a deal. Let's meet at the end of the wood, and then no one will see us. I don't think my mother would be happy with me mixing with the new stable lad,' Rosie whispered.

'You mean it would be the gypsy part of me that she wouldn't want you to mix with. But she should know that my mother and father are both respectable, and that my father doesn't wander the lanes and roads like his own father did.' Ethan bowed his head.

'Have you ever met your grandfather?' Rosie asked quietly.

'Nay, never. My father said he left my grandmother expecting him, and only came back once in a while when he was a lad. He must be a good age now. He's probably dead in a ditch somewhere – best spot for him. Although I'm curious to see how his sort live. I've always fancied going to Appleby Fair, but my father won't hear of it; he says he wants nowt with them ways. But whether he likes it or not, he takes after his father, for nobody can handle a horse like my father, or judge a person just by looking at them – he sometimes knows what I'm thinking better than I do myself.' Ethan looked out over the Dales and pulled at a stalk of fell grass, putting the stalk in his mouth to chew on, as he thought about his lost family and the yearly horse fair at Appleby, which all Romany gypsies attended in order to meet up with their families.

'I've noticed the caravans and horses on the roadsides lately. It's Appleby Fair very soon, isn't it?' Rosie put her arm through Ethan's and smiled.

'Aye, second week in June. They hold it on Gallows Hill, just outside Appleby. I'd love to go and just look around. I'm not bothered about my grandfather, he's not worth looking for. Who could walk out on a woman who was having your baby? He should have done right by her and settled down to a life in Settle. But I would like to see something I've heard about all my life and perhaps, just for once, feel as if I fit in.' Ethan hung his head and twiddled the piece of grass between his fingers.

'You should go. As you say, see what goes on there. Your curiosity will be satisfied then.' Rosie looked at the young man who had been the main topic of conversation in Crummock's kitchen. Her grandfather and father did not understand how her Aunt Isabelle could not keep Ethan in employment, after he had saved her son from drowning. 'I could come with you.'

Ethan lifted his head. 'You couldn't come with me – your parents would not allow it. Besides, how do we get there? It isn't as if it's in the next field. It is at least forty miles away.' He shook his head and pulled a tuft of the herb-filled grass from the earth, then threw it for the wind to blow and do with it what it would. He watched it float away, just like his dreams.

'Leave it with me. You *will* go to Appleby Fair. It's important to you.' Rosie pushed herself up from the warm, fragrant land and twirled round in the breeze as she looked down upon her crestfallen companion. 'Come on, let's walk over to Beggar's Stile and then get home for supper; the day is too good to waste.' She smiled as Ethan pushed himself up and joined her.

'Don't promise something you can't fulfil, and stop teasing me, Rosie Atkinson. Else you are no better than your cousin Jane.' Ethan grabbed her hand, stopping her from dancing in the warm summer sun.

'I never promise something I can't fulfil, and don't insult me by likening me to my cousin. She thinks only of herself and plays with your heart. That is why, if truth were told, you will have been banished to us, at Crummock. We can't have our precious Jane mixing with the lower classes, now can we? Stop that sullen look and catch me if you can. And stop feeling sorry for yourself – we will go to your Appleby Fair.' Rosie pulled away from Ethan and started to run over the short dry grass of the fell land. 'And we will go together.'

'Rosie, we are all waiting for you.' Harriet yelled up the stairs, losing her patience with her teenage daughter.

Rosie appeared slowly at the top of the stairs and looked sheepishly at her mother. 'I don't feel well, Mother, I think I ate too many gooseberries when I was picking them for pies yesterday.' She pulled a face and hoped that the white talcum powder she had covered her face with was convincing enough, from a distance, to back up her story.

'Well, I'm not going without you. I'll only worry the whole time I'm there. Besides, I really don't want to go anyway, as your Aunt Isabelle will only gloat about her new abode.' Harriet reached up and undid the ribbon of her hat and was about to take it off, when Danny stopped her.

'It's only a belly ache, Harriet. Rosie is sixteen, not six, and she's got a tongue in her head. If she gets worse, she can always send for you. Besides, Ethan will be visiting his parents later today, and he can bring word to Windfell if Rosie worsens.' Danny let his hand drop from hers, as Harriet stopped untying the ribbons for a moment. 'She's not a baby, my dear, and don't make her the excuse for not visiting Windfell. It's not every day we get invited for our lunch, so let's make the most of it.'

Harriet sighed and told Rosie, 'Go on, get yourself to bed. As your father says, let Ethan know if you get any worse. It's lucky he said that he'd polish the harnesses and saddles this morning, as otherwise he'd be long gone.' She looked up the stairs and watched as her daughter made good her escape from her gaze.

'She will be fine, my love. Now come, my father and the children are waiting in the carriage and it's a beautiful day, so we can dawdle and enjoy the scenery.' Danny put his arm around his wife and guided her to the kitchen doorway. He was determined that Harriet and Isabelle would talk to one another over lunch, and he knew his sister must feel the same way or she would not have invited them – despite Harriet assuming they were invited just to hear Isabelle gloating.

Harriet looked back. 'I just hope that Rosie will be alright; she never says she's ill, as a rule.'

'She will be fine. As she says, she's been greedy eating those green gooseberries she was top-and-tailing yesterday, that's all.' Danny helped his wife up into the carriage. For once, she had listened to sense and had agreed that Rosie was old enough to look after herself. Perhaps her feelings of inadequacy in motherhood were finally ebbing. He certainly hoped so.

Rosie and Ethan watched out of Crummock's kitchen window as the family's carriage disappeared over the hill, down the rough track towards Austwick.

'When they are past the thorn bushes on the hilltop, we can outride them and take the shortcut down by the wash-dubs, through Wharfe and Helwith Bridge. We will just catch the ten-thirty train at Settle.' Rosie wiped her falsely ashen face with a tea towel and urged Ethan out of the house.

'You are sure you want to do this? Your parents will be so angry with both of us, if they ever find out.' Ethan hesitated. Ever since Rosie had suggested that she pay for the train fair to Appleby he had worried, but at the same time he couldn't help but feel a bit excited at the prospect of his first ride on a train, and a visit to Appleby Fair with a girl on his arm.

'Of course I want to do this. I wouldn't be spending my savings on train tickets if I didn't. Besides, my parents are not going to find out. I heard my father say they were to dawdle and, once they are at Windfell, they won't return until suppertime.' Rosie watched as Ethan mounted the horse that he'd saddled for them both, and which waited outside the back door of Crummock.

Ethan held his hand out for Rosie to join him and sat forward in the saddle to make room for her. 'I know travelling this way isn't very ladylike, but neither of us is heavy and the horse will cope with two of us on it. Using one horse saves money at the Lion's livery stable, and they won't suspect anything if I just take one horse to be stabled.' He hauled on Rosie's hand as she pulled up her skirts and sat down tightly behind him. She wrapped her arms around him. Ethan smiled, enjoying the feel of having her body so close to his. 'Right, hold tight, if we are to catch the train, we've not a minute to waste. You are sure you are alright?'

'I'm fine, Ethan. Don't worry about ladylike manners – you forget that I'm not as precious as my cousin. Now go, just in case my parents take the same road as us and not the road via Settle, as I heard my mother request.'

Ethan flicked the reins of the horse and dug his heels in to urge the animal forward. Together they trotted briskly out of the farmyard and down the bridlepath to Wharfe. Rosie sat close to Ethan and felt the sun on her face as she hugged him tightly. She looked at his dark hair as it shone like jet in the morning's sun and breathed in the smell of him. It was a comforting scent of warm hay, with a hint of the carbolic soap that he had obviously washed in that morning. She wasn't worried that he'd seen her ankles and most of her left leg as she mounted the horse. Her mother would be mortified, but how was she to know?

The horse walked carefully across the stream next to the clapper bridge at the wash-dubs and then carried on trotting down the bridlepath to Wharfe. The limestone walls on either side of them made them nearly invisible on the centuries-old path, until they came to the small hamlet of Wharfe. Luckily it was quiet, with most of the inhabitants at church, praying for the Lord to keep their souls. Once out on the road to Helwith Bridge, Rosie thought she was riding with the devil himself, as Ethan urged his horse into a gallop. She held him even tighter and could feel her long blonde hair whipping her face as they passed the limestone boulders and farms spread along either side of the road. The horse galloped faster and faster, making her cling on for her life as they raced down the road. On reaching the entrance to Windfell, both of them looked up the driveway, hoping that nobody would notice the fleeing pair as they galloped the two miles into Settle. Ethan felt guilty at not seeing his parents on the Sabbath, and Rosie felt guilty at deceiving her parents. Still, it was worth it, just to be near the lad she had feelings for. And the day had only just begun.

Once at the outskirts of Settle, Rosie dismounted, out of view of the prim eyes of the ladies of the district, and walked through the town. She waited on the corner of New Street, and watched as Ethan took the horse into the livery stable of the Golden Lion. She looked across at the clock in the post office's window. It showed twenty past ten; ten minutes to go before the train left for Appleby and then carried on to Carlisle. She felt her stomach churn as she saw Ethan running out of the Golden Lion and, at the same time, her parents' carriage passing the town hall a hundred yards behind him. Hiding around the corner of New Street, she waited for Ethan to join her and hoped that he had not been recognized.

'Bloody hell, that was a close one! Your father's just stabling his horse and carriage while the rest of your family has a look around Settle. I was so close I heard him instruct the stable lad as he drew into the yard,' Ethan panted.

'Come on, we've no time to waste – the train will be pulling into the station, if it's not already there. I can see steam rising. The engine will be filling up with water, before going down the line.' Rosie grabbed Ethan's hand and ran the two hundred yards to the station, then gasped as they saw the train waiting on the far platform. 'We need tickets!' They pushed past people dressed in their Sunday best, and opened the crimson-coloured doors of the ticket office to purchase their tickets.

'Two tickets for Appleby, please.' Rosie caught her breath as she looked across at the ticket officer, with his LMS hat upon his head.

'Return, first-, second- or third-class?' the bespectacled man asked.

'Return and second-class, please.' Rosie wished that he'd hurry up.

'Two-and-six, please, next train is at two.' He waited as Rosie counted out her money, before passing the tickets under his grilled window.

'We're not waiting for the two o'clock train – we aim to catch this one.' Ethan pulled on Rosie's arm as they both turned on their heels and dashed out through the crowds, who were wishing family and loved ones farewell from the safety of the platform. They flew up and over the metal bridge traversing the railway line, both of them gasping for breath as they reached the other platform, breathing in the smoke and fumes of the waiting train.

'All aboard!' The stationmaster started closing the carriage doors as the engine built up steam, ready to leave the platform.

Ethan pushed Rosie into the second-class carriage, with its door still ajar. They were just in time, as the door slammed shut behind them and the stationmaster blew his whistle for the train to depart. Both collapsed giggling into their seats, while the other passengers shook their heads in disbelief at such bad behaviour from the young.

'We made it! We are on our way to Appleby.' Ethan's eyes were filled with anticipation as they looked out of the open window as the train pulled away from the station.

'Yes, we've done it.' Rosie smiled and then sighed, looking at the solitary penny she had left in her posy bag, as they left Settle and the station behind. 'I should have said third-class, then I would have had more money to spend at the fair. But we were in such a rush.'

'We'll make our own amusement, Rosie. Besides, I've sixpence, so we'll not go hungry, and at least you had the sense to get return tickets, so we can get home.' Ethan was excited. Unlike Rosie, he had never ridden on a train before and was watching the houses and scenery fly by. 'Look, there goes Windfell.'

Both craned their necks out of the carriage's window and took in a fleeting glimpse of Windfell Manor. A further pang of guilt clouded their faces as they thought of the lies they had told, to enable their day together.

'We will be back before them, won't we?' Rosie looked across for reassurance from Ethan.

'Yes, didn't you say we can have a few hours at Appleby and will be back in Settle for five o'clock? We won't be that long at the fair.' He looked across at a worried Rosie.

'I guess we will be fine. We won't be missed, I'm sure.' She sat down and looked out at the scenery rushing past her. 'Please don't let us be late,' she whispered to herself. Her parents would never forgive her. As for Ethan, he'd never work for anyone ever again.

8

Jane picked up the morning newspaper and read the headlines with horror.

'Have you seen this, Mother, and you, Father? The poor woman, how could the King's horse run her over like that?'

'I don't think the jockey did it deliberately, my dear. The stupid woman ran directly in front of him, and he couldn't stop.' Isabelle looked across at James for support.

'Poor Emily Davison. She was only trying to make a point by pinning a banner for "Votes for Women" on the horse. Perhaps the King and Parliament will listen to us women, after a death at the Epsom Derby.' Jane lifted her hand up to the violet, green and white pendant that she wore as a sign of solidarity with the fight for the newly named Suffragette movement and its causes. 'Surely they've got to, now that women are going on hunger strike and nearly dying. They must realize how strongly the modern-day woman feels about having equal rights to men.' She sat staring defiantly at her father, knowing that he thought her ideals were rubbish.

'I do wish you would stop your fascination with these troublemakers, Jane. This is a man's world, and women should know their place.' James looked at his young daughter, who had a mind of her own, and sighed.

'Where's that, then? Tied to the kitchen sink, doing sewing and needlework and looking pretty on a man's arm? Grandmama never did any of that, nor did you, Mama. Both of you were your own women – and you still are. Yet we don't get a say in the running of the country. Surely that's not fair?' She folded the newspaper and looked at her father, who was about to explode.

'Enough, Jane, we have visitors about to join us. In fact I can hear their carriage coming up the drive this minute. Now no more talk of suffragettes, women's rights or anything else that crosses your mind. And try to be right with Rosie. I know you are not alike, but you can at least show her a little respect. After all, she is your cousin.' Isabelle rose from her chair and made her way to the hallway, giving James a dark look as she went, in the hope that he would say something along the same lines to Jane while she went to meet their guests.

'Your mother's right: you know nothing about such-like. You should just concentrate on your role in the firm. That's enough for you to think about at present,' James said gruffly.

'Grandmama would understand. She always knew what was right.' Jane crossed her arms in a sulk.

'Well, she isn't here. So just for once, smile and be pleasant.' James rose to his feet and went to join Isabelle, who was busy making their guests welcome, leaving Jane to continue feeling upset about the death of Emily Davison.

'Harriet, how lovely that you can be with us today. And just look at young Ben and Georgina – how quickly they grow!' Isabelle welcomed Danny and his family to Windfell with open arms. She was genuinely glad that Harriet had accepted her invitation to lunch. 'No Rosie? Jane will be disappointed. She was hoping that Rosie would be with you.'

'I'm afraid Rosie was feeling a little unwell this morning, so she could not join us.' Harriet smiled at Isabelle, feeling that her welcome was slightly over the top.

'She ate too many gooseberries yesterday, giving herself a belly ache, that's all.' Danny sat down in a chair and looked at Harriet and hoped she wasn't going to fret about Rosie being left at home.

Jane had moved to sit next to the window. She sniggered but quickly hid her reaction, as her Aunt Harriet gave her a warning glance.

'That is unfortunate! But easily done, and I do hope Rosie soon recovers. Luke, would you and Jane like to show Ben the foal? She is growing so quickly, and you will all be bored while we adults chat before lunch.' Isabelle watched as Georgina, the baby of the family, crawled around the room, leaving fingerprints on the highly polished furniture. 'I'll ask Lily to take charge of Georgina while we enjoy one another's company. If that

91

is alright with you, Harriet. Lily's got a good way with children, and it is a pity she has no family of her own and will be leaving our service soon.'

'I'd prefer that Georgina stayed with me; she does not know who Lily is and doesn't like strangers.' Harriet looked worried and glanced across at Danny for support.

Archie had said nothing up until this point. He looked around at his grandchildren and thought that he'd rather enjoy their company than sit in the newly decorated parlour of Windfell. 'I'll take Georgina out with me, and we will all go and see this young foal. It'll give you four a chance to catch up in peace and say what you want, out of my earshot.' Archie picked up young Georgina, noticing the worried look between Danny and Harriet as he held her tightly in his arms. He laughed as she tried to pinch his pocket watch out of his pocket. 'Come on, li'l 'un, let's go and look around outside while the grownups talk. Jane, you open the doors; and you two lads behave yourselves, otherwise you'll have me to answer to.' Archie made his way out of the parlour like the Pied Piper of Hamelin, with his grandchildren around his feet. It had been the excuse that he had needed. He still hurt when he thought of Charlotte sitting in the chair that Isabelle had now claimed as her own.

'Would you like a sherry, Harriet and Danny? Or perhaps a cup of tea?' James looked across at the couple, who rarely visited them, and noticed Harriet's worried gaze once the children had left her side. He wanted to make them both feel at home.

'A cup of tea would be grand, James.' Danny stood up

and looked out of the parlour window, turning round as James rang the bell for Thomson to come running, on command. 'So, you've settled in, I see. I like the new wallpaper, Isabelle, it must have cost a pretty penny.' He looked round at the newly decorated parlour and grinned at James, who was shaking his head in despair.

'I always did want this room to be decorated with this wallpaper, but Mama would never hear of it. The pattern is called "Strawberry Thief" and is by William Morris. It is so pretty and suits this room so well. What do you think, Harriet? You always had a good eye for style.' Isabelle smiled and sat down next to her sister-in-law.

'Yes, it is very you, and it suits the parlour well. Who else would think of bringing nature into a living space, for us all to enjoy.' Harriet looked around at the patterned wallpaper, depicting birds feasting on strawberries, and remembered the wedding dress that Isabelle had designed for her, after meeting the artist William Morris. They had been so close then, enjoying one another's company and sharing their secrets together.

'It's a bit too posh for the walls at Crummock. So don't be getting any ideas, our lass.' Danny looked around him.

'It cost an arm and a leg. I told Isabelle we could do without it, but she would insist. She likes to get her own way, don't you, my dear?' James stood behind his wife and ran his hand along her shoulders.

'Crummock's walls are practical, and are fine just whitewashed each year, so you needn't fret, Danny.' Harriet looked up as Thomson entered with tea for four, and the conversation stopped until he left.

'Harriet, how are you keeping? I sometimes worry about you, for we seem to have drifted apart and I can't ignore that any longer. We were once so close.' Isabelle reached out for her sister-in-law's hand and squeezed it tightly, after sipping her tea. 'You will have heard that we nearly lost our Luke, when he fell into the river? It was then that I realized how hard and uncaring I had been over the loss of your twins. I hope you can forgive me? It's just that until you have children of your own, you don't realize how precious they are to you. You must have been heartbroken, as I know you both were, but I was too wrapped up in the business and was blinkered to your loss.'

Isabelle's eyes filled with tears as she looked at Harriet, whose head was bowed as she remembered the pain Isabelle had caused when she had flippantly remarked that infant death was something nearly every family endured. It was true and it was part of the times they lived in, but to lose two boys cruelly in one afternoon, without their mother by their side, was a pain of Harriet's that Isabelle would have to live with all her life, and something she hoped she would never have to experience herself. Now, all these years later, she realized how callous she had been, and she wanted to sweep any misunderstandings to one side.

Harriet shook as she remembered the day twenty years ago when she could not get home to her children in time, after working in the shop at Skipton in the run-up to Christmas. 'I still feel so guilty. I put my work first and placed the children in the care of their nanny. I thought it was just a cold they both had. If I'd been there with them, and had noticed their suffering and seen them fighting for breath before I set off for the shop, they might still be with us, if I had called the doctor out in time.' She pulled her handkerchief out of her sleeve and sobbed into it.

'Diphtheria took a lot of lives that year, and it moves so fast – it was not your fault, my dear Harriet. You must not constantly blame yourself. It is I who was to blame, if anyone, by insisting that we finished off the orders before we went home. I know I seemed very uncaring. I beg your forgiveness, dear sister-in-law. And I regret I have not had it in my heart to say these words earlier. Mama often chastised me for not being more caring, and told me that one day I would realize how you felt. Well, I do now, after Luke's brush with death.' Isabelle hugged Harriet to her, as Danny and James looked on, thankful that at last the two women had spoken about exactly how they felt.

'I thought you hated me for staying at home and looking after my children. I know the business was everything for Mama and you, but my children are my world, along with Danny.' Harriet sobbed anew, looking into Isabelle's tear-filled eyes.

'I know, and Mama knew that too. I don't hate you; we've just grown apart, which is truly a shame. From this day forward, let us get back to being friends. After all, Mama wished that to happen, and she left you part of the shares in Atkinson's. Both she and I have never forgotten that without you we would never have been so successful.' Isabelle looked up at her husband and urged James to back up her words.

'All these tears. What are we to do, Danny?' James looked over at a worried-looking Danny. 'Put the past behind you, both of you, and let's all look forward to a better future. I think that is what Danny and I hope for, as we love you both dearly.'

'Aye, that we do. I'm getting a bit fed up of walking on eggshells. Especially now we've got my father living with us, for he's a liability in his own right. He forgets that I've been farming Crummock for nearly twenty-four years without his help every day. And I don't know why Archie has decided he wants Ethan to work for us, as I've hardly any work for him. Although he will come in handy, come hay-time,' said Danny.

'I enjoy having your father living with us,' Harriet sniffed. 'He's good with the children. Ben loves him, and Rosie won't have a bad word said about him. And as for bringing Ethan with him, well, he's no trouble. I hardly ever see him.'

'I'm sorry Archie has burdened you with Ethan. That's the trouble with him: you don't ever see Ethan, and he was never to be found when there was work to be done here. My mother was too easy on him, because she had always held his father in great esteem. And Ethan helps himself to trout out of the river and the odd rabbit or two. I just don't know why Father took him up to Crummock.' Isabelle looked over at James.

'Probably because he cares about Ethan and feels liable for his welfare, my dear. Especially as he saved our Luke's life,' James added quickly.

'Well, if I were you, Danny, I'd keep an eye on him. But

let us forget about Ethan for the moment because the family is more important. My dear Harriet, let us put our differences aside and get back to being the friends we were, all those years ago. We don't have dear Mama as our buffer any more, and I would so like us to be there for one another.' Isabelle looked at Harriet with pleading eyes, meaning every word she said. She needed her sister-in-law, and especially her knowledge of the business. Jane would take years of training, but Harriet knew everything about the trade and would be an asset to the firm, if she could get her interested in it again. 'Come and have afternoon tea in Atkinson's next week with the children and see our new designs – they are stunning this year.'

'I'd like that. Rosie would, too.' Harriet smiled and cast her mind back to the fitting and cutting room, which she had enjoyed working in, until the fateful day when her life had stopped.

'Is Wednesday alright with you? James can take the children's photographs while you visit me. Can't you, James?' Isabelle smiled.

'Certainly, my dear. Dress them up in their Sunday finery and I'll do my very best.' James grinned across at Harriet, knowing full well that his wife was sweet-talking Harriet back into the firm.

'Splendid! Now, let's see where Father has gone to with those children. You will be wanting your lunch and to get back to Rosie, if she is not feeling well.'

'Yes, I would appreciate getting back a little earlier than we anticipated, just to make sure she's alright.' Harriet was relieved that Isabelle understood.

'I understand. I'll ask Thomson to hurry Cook along.' Isabelle linked her arm through Harriet's as they walked into the hallway. 'Danny, do you want that old grandfather clock? It really does not fit in this hallway; it was another thing that my mother put up with, but didn't like.'

'It's belonged to my father's family for years – you can't just throw it out. We'll have it up at Crummock, won't we, Harriet?' Danny looked shocked at Isabelle's lack of love for a family heirloom.

'Yes, it will fit well at the bottom of the stairs. Archie will no doubt like to have it back with him.' Harriet smiled.

'Then I'll get Jethro to bring it up to you on the flat cart next week. Now, where are those children?'

The train pulled into Appleby station after making its way through the tunnels and cuttings that spread along the length of the remote railway track. The engine heaved a sigh of relief as it came to rest after the steepest climb on the line, known as 'the long drag'.

'That was a journey! How beautiful did Dentdale and Garsdale look as we passed through them? The houses looked so small, way down in the bottom of the valleys.' Rosie smiled and tried to keep up with Ethan as he made his way through the station gates, following the crowd down into the town of Appleby.

'Mallerstang looks so rugged, even on a beautiful day like this. Just think what it would have been like when they were building the railway line. It's a wonder they didn't freeze to death when they were laying the track down.' Ethan stopped in his tracks and watched in wonder the number of horses and travelling people that lined the streets of Appleby. Flat-bedded wagons and round green-topped caravans painted with bright-green, red and gold decoration crowded through the narrow streets, drawn by horses of every description. Black-and-white pintos, brown-and-white skewbalds, chestnuts and roans were all were being led and ridden by their owners, who were not bashful when it came to showing off their horsemanship. Amongst the horses, droves of sheep and cattle were also being driven in the direction of Gallows Hill, the main field for Appleby Fair.

'White heather for your girl, Mister?' A beautiful, sultry young gypsy girl came and enticed Ethan with a basket full of heather and wooden clothes pegs. 'It'll bring you both luck.'

Ethan shook his head and looked at Rosie, knowing that between them they had very little money.

'Some pegs for your ma, then?' She tugged on his sleeve.

'Sorry, no money.' Ethan hung his head.

'Good luck to ya anyway.' The young girl moved on to her next victim, and both Ethan and Rosie watched her as she wove her way through the crowds. Her long colourful skirt swayed and her bracelets jangled as she cleared a passage away from them, watched by the visitors to Appleby.

'Sorry, Rosie. I would have bought you some heather, but we both need whatever money we've got.'

'It doesn't matter, Ethan – we can pick our own

heather. I've never seen anywhere so busy. There's so many people, and they are all selling something or riding horses. You can't walk safely along the street because of the horses racing up and down.'

'It's called "flashing", and they are riding them to the places I've heard my father talking about, called Flashing Lane and Long Marton Road. It's where all the gypsy men show off their horses by riding them up and down the lane to put them through their paces, and to show their best points before selling them. We can go there, if you want; or down into the village to watch the horses being washed down at a place called "the Sands", which is just under the main bridge that spans the River Eden.' Ethan waited as Rosie made up her mind.

'Can we go and see the horse being washed? I don't want to go near the racing horses. It looks dangerous, and there are so many people. I don't want to offend you, Ethan, but some look like they can't be trusted.' Rosie had never seen such a raggle-taggle collection of people, and she was beginning to regret agreeing to spend the day at Appleby Horse Fair.

'They are only travelling folk, Rosie. They love their horses and country ways. You'd look a bit worse for wear, if you didn't know where you were going to rest your head from one night to the next and were out in all weathers. Besides, somewhere in these people will be my relations, so they can't be that different from me.' Ethan looked at the fear on Rosie's face. 'Here, put your arm through mine, I'll look after you.'

She looked up at Ethan and saw the excitement in

his eyes. He was loving the smell and the mix of what he thought to be his own people, but at the same time he wanted to protect her. She smiled and put her arm through his, and felt safe as they pushed their way past the crowds to stand on the top of the bridge that crossed the mighty River Eden. There they looked down, watching the gypsy men washing their horses in the deep waters. The two of them gasped as they watched the horses swim in the deepest parts of the river with their riders on their backs, and cringed as the riders made the horses climb the banks out of the river with a deft whipping.

'I think it's cruel.' Rosie held Ethan's arm tight.

'It's good horsemanship, that's all.' He watched as a beautiful black-and-white stallion snorted and tossed its head, in defiance of its owner.

'No, I don't like these ways.' Rosie looked around at the crowds and decided that Appleby Fair was not for her. She saw linnets that were being sold in cages so small they could hardly stretch their wings, and women offering to tell fortunes to people who only wanted to hear good things. 'These aren't our people, Ethan, we belong back home.'

'We'll be home soon enough. Give us another hour and we'll catch the train. I'd like to go up onto the main field and just have a look around the horses for sale, and wander through the caravans. I don't know what my grandfather looks like, or if he is even alive, but I'd like to see his lifestyle and his ways, while we have time.' He pulled on Rosie's arm and they made their way back through the crowds towards Gallows Hill.

'Alright, I know it's important to you. I know you would really like to find your grandfather, if you were truthful. Just an hour, though, and then we must return.' Rosie tried to smile, worrying that Ethan was getting carried away with the atmosphere of the fair.

'I promise we will only be another an hour, and then we will catch the train.' Ethan flashed his winning smile at the girl on his arm and set off in earnest pursuit of his grandfather. They wandered around the covered wagons and flat carts, with the families that lived in them huddled around camp fires, telling stories and exchanging the year's news together. Dogs barked and sniffed around their feet, with a lurcher showing its teeth at Rosie, as Ethan dragged her away from harm.

'Please let's go home. We'll not find your grandfather here.' She looked at the tanned, weather-worn faces and at the women in their colourful skirts, and wanted the safety of her home. These were not her ways, although they were country folk like her.

'Alright, we'll be away. But I'm going to return because somebody somewhere will know my grandfather.' Ethan looked disappointed, but knew Rosie was right: if they didn't go back now, they would miss their train home. He looked back at the campsites they were leaving behind and vowed to visit them again on his own, for this was a life he could enjoy.

Rosie sat quietly, lost in her own thoughts as she watched the scenery pass by her outside the train carriage. Her hair and clothes smelt of the camp fires they had wandered amongst, in their pursuit of an elusive grandfather whom both of them knew they would never find. Her skirt and boots were covered with mud from the churned-up field at Gallows Hill. She knew she looked a mess, and she only hoped she could change and wash before her parents returned home. With every clatter of the railway line beneath her she wished she was home, safe and sound. She cast her mind back over the day, at the horses being put through their paces, and the beggars selling whatever produce they could; the smell of rabbit stew drifting on the wind, and the brightness of the painted wagons that were home to the wandering gypsies. It was a completely different way of life from hers and a different language. She had not understood a word that some of them had spoken, and had felt as if she was an outsider in her own world.

Ethan sat across from her, half-asleep, content that he'd visited the legendary Appleby Fair and unconcerned that his presence might be missed at home – unlike Rosie. With every mile they were nearer home she felt sick at the thought of having to explain her disappearance, if her parents had already returned to Crummock. She'd not thought of the consequences of her trip; but now, with hindsight, her mother was going to be frantic, whereas Ethan had no one to answer to. He'd not lied to his parents, he just hadn't gone to visit them, and he'd not spent every penny that he had. The sixpence he said he had in his pocket had remained there all day and they were both going home hungry, filthy and tired. Rosie wondered if Ethan had any money on him at all, for they had drunk from a spring that fed the River Eden, rather than Ethan spending his elusive sixpence. How she wished she had not been so easily led. It was her fault; after all, it had been her idea and she had no one else to blame.

'She's not in her room. Where is she, Danny?' Harriet came rushing down the stairs, frantic with worry.

'She'll not be far.' Danny tried to calm his wife. 'I'll go and look outside and ask Ethan if he's seen her.' He reached for the kitchen door, while Archie looked out of the kitchen window and spotted a horse and riders galloping like the wind, up the lane to Crummock.

'Don't bother going to look for either Ethan or Rosie. Come and look here. God only knows where they've been, but they are in a hell of a hurry to get back home.' Archie sat down in the chair next to the unlit fire and looked up at his son's scowling face.

'I'll bloody kill him! What does he think he's doing, taking one of the horses and putting our Rosie up behind him? You should never have brought him here, Father. Isabelle said he was more bother than he was worth.' Danny made it to the back door and opened it wide.

'Now just think on. Rosie was the one who said she was too ill to join us today. They've obviously planned their day out together. Besides, they might not have been far.' Archie tried to talk some sense into his son. It was no good that he was just blaming Ethan.

'The fire's not been stoked since the minute we left this house, nothing has been touched – she's been out with him all day. By God, they are both going to tell me what they've been up to,' Danny swore as he closed the door behind him.

Sensing the tension within the house, baby Georgina started wailing, and Harriet sent Ben to his room as her eyes filled up with tears at the thought that her daughter had lied to her.

'She's at that age, Harriet. She's not your little lass any more, she's nearly a grown woman,' Archie said, as he crumpled newspaper into the dead hearth and added a few dry kindling sticks, before lighting the fire with a match. 'She'll have been alright, don't you worry. Ethan is not the devil that Isabelle makes him out to be. There will be an explanation.' Archie watched as the kindling sticks took hold, and then gently added pieces of coal until a good blaze roared.

'She's still our little girl, she's only sixteen. Danny will kill Ethan.' Harriet consoled Georgina with a biscuit from the tin above the fire, and sat her down on the pegged rug next to her grandfather.

'Nay, he won't. Not if he remembers that he was young himself.' Archie smiled down at his youngest grandchild. 'They are no bother when they are your age, but they are nowt but worry when they grow up, eh, li'l 'un?' He listened as he heard his son raising his voice at the pair, who had just entered the farmyard on the hard-driven horse. He knew that perhaps he was to blame, after introducing Ethan to Crummock; lately he had noticed the smile on Rosie's face whenever he was mentioned. It was worth it, just for that. Besides, Ethan was a good lad; a bit wild maybe, but he hadn't a bad bone in his body. The back door was flung open and Rosie walked in, tears streaming down her face and her clothes splattered with mud.

'They've been on the bloody train, up to Appleby. Just look at her, coming back looking and smelling like a bloody gyppo!' Danny pushed Rosie into the kitchen. 'That bloody lad – he trailed her up there, to be with his own. They'll be running away together before you know it.' He was fuming.

Rosie pulled her arm away from her father and looked at her mother and grandfather. 'It's my fault, not Ethan's. He didn't make me go. I suggested it – it was my idea. He really wanted to see if we could find his grandfather. I'm sorry I lied, but I knew you'd not let us go, even if we asked,' she cried.

'Too bloody right, lass. Now get yourself up the stairs, and don't let me see your face until the morning. Just be glad you are not going to get the braying I'm going to give Ethan, before I send him on his way,' Danny growled.

'No, Father, please don't send him away. It wasn't his fault; please, it was mine. I'd rather you took your belt to me,' sobbed Rosie.

'Just get yourself to bed, Rosie.' Harriet watched as her daughter, still sobbing, made her way down the passage and up the stairs to bed. 'You can't belt Ethan. And, like you said, you'll need him in the next month or two for hay-time. Have a word with his father – he'll sort Ethan out. Rosie's come to no harm, and it's as clear as the nose on your face that she's sweet on him, otherwise she wouldn't have lied to us.' Harriet glanced quickly at Archie as she put the kettle on the now-blazing fire.

'It's all your bloody fault, Father. I should have said no to Ethan coming here.' Danny spat into the fire.

'Nay, lad, you can't blame me for his curiosity about where he comes from. Everybody wants to know that. Rosie was only being kind.' Archie looked up at his son and then poked the fire, knowing he shouldn't say another word on the subject.

'Aye, well, she's back now, I suppose that's all that matters,' said Danny. 'But I will have a word with his father; happen he can square Ethan up a bit.'

Harriet went quietly to the pantry and cut a slice of bread and cheese, then took it up to her heartbroken daughter without Danny noticing. 'Don't cry, Rosie, your father's not going to do anything to Ethan. He's never hit anybody yet, and he knows he needs him this summertime.' She ran her fingers through her daughter's long hair as she sobbed in her arms. 'You know, you may think a lot of Ethan, but he's just the first boy in your life, and there will be a lot more yet. And he isn't worth lying for.' Harriet kissed her daughter on her brow and hugged her tightly. 'He didn't do anything to you, did he, Rosie?'

'What do you mean, Mother?' Rosie looked up at Isabelle.

'You didn't lift your skirts for him, did you, dear?' Harriet hated asking, but it was one of the first things that had entered her head when Rosie came into the kitchen.

'Only to climb onto the horse. He did see my ankles, Mama.' Rosie blushed.

'That's alright, dear, we'll let him get away with that. Remember, though, that Ethan's nearly a man – a man with urges. Don't get too close to him. Now you eat your bread and cheese and tidy yourself up. Your father will

107

have calmed down by the morning and will soon forgive you both.' She stood up and looked down at her distraught daughter.

'I'm sorry, Mama,' Rosie sniffed.

'Just don't let your heart rule your head, Rosie. You are almost a woman, and you can't act like a child any more. Perhaps more time with your cousin Jane would help. She's quite the young lady, and you could do worse than follow her lead.'

'Please, Mama, I think I'd rather be belted by my father than spend time with Jane.'

'We will be visiting Skipton and the store next week. You are having your photograph taken by Uncle James. You can see Jane then, while I spend time with your Aunt Isabelle. Thank heavens she can't see you in this state. Now, get yourself washed and to bed, for tomorrow is another day.' Harriet closed the bedroom door behind her, listening to the sobs of her daughter. Archie was right: she was growing up, but she was still a little girl really, and always would be, in her mother's eyes.

Jethro pulled the ropes tight, securing the old grandfather clock from Windfell's hallway tightly onto the cart.

'You'll not be too hard on him, Jethro? Ethan's only young and curious.' Mazy looked at her husband, who had been in a mood since Danny Atkinson had told him of their son's trip to Appleby with his daughter.

'I'll tell you what, woman: he's got to learn his place in the world, instead of looking at what he can't have. Bloody running away with Miss Rosie in search of his grandfather.

I'll give him something to remember his grandfather by. This isn't the first time he's messed about with the lasses of the big house. I saw him trying to kiss Miss Jane, and told him to leave well alone. What's wrong with the lad?'

'Nowt's wrong with him – he's just young.' Mazy watched as Jethro climbed up onto the cart and whipped the horses into action, making the bell on the grand-father clock chime with the jolting vehicle. It was rare that Jethro lost his temper, but he'd had time to brood on his son's wild ways and that was always a bad thing.

'I'm glad you could find time to bring the clock from Windfell, Jethro,' said Archie as he watched the strong man lifting the oak-cased clock down from the cart, before hauling it on his shoulder into the farmhouse at Crum-mock. Jethro returned to the cart for the clock face's case, then helped Archie carry the weight that pulled on the clock's chains to make it work.

'Aye, well, I need to square up that lad of mine while I'm here. I'm sorry he's caused you and your family bother. He should have known better than to do that. You don't bite the hand that feeds you.' Jethro stood in front of Archie and wiped his brow with his neckerchief.

'Nay, it was our Rosie just as much to blame. She'd paid for the tickets and put the idea in his head; they are a lot alike, those two.' Archie looked at the brooding man and knew that Ethan was going to get the rough side of Jethro's tongue.

'Nay, they are not alike, if you don't mind me saying, sir. Your Rosie is a lady, and my lad needs to know his place.' Jethro spat out a mouthful of saliva and grabbed the horses' reins. 'Is he in the stable, our lad?'

'No, he's in the calf shed, mucking it out. Danny kept him near home today, knowing you were coming. Don't be too hard on him, Jethro. Nobody was hurt, and they both came home none the worse for their day out.' Archie was trying to calm him down, but knew Ethan was going to be in for a belting, even though he was old enough to take on his father.

'He'll not be doing the same again, sir. And thank you for keeping Ethan on here. I wouldn't have blamed either you or Master Danny if you had sent him packing. It's what he deserves.' Jethro grabbed the reins of his horses, unable to talk to his former master any more without showing his true feelings. He led the horses around the back of the farmhouse to the stables, stopping for a moment as he watched his lad busy with a pitchfork, mucking out the calf shed into a wheelbarrow.

Ethan looked up from his work, after hearing the horses and cart come into the yard. 'Father, I knew you would come. Before you do anything, I'm sorry if I've upset you.'

'Too bloody right, lad. And aye, well, you know why I'm here.' Jethro dropped his horses' reins and strode over to his son, undoing his thick leather belt from around his waist and wrapping the buckle end around his fist.

Ethan cringed and cowered back into the calf shed. He knew all too well what his father's temper was like, when pushed. He stood with his back against the wall.

'I'm too old for that now, Father, you can't belt me any more. I didn't do any harm. Rosie and I just had a day away together, that's all.'

'Rosie, is it? It's "Miss Atkinson" to you, lad.' Jethro raised his left hand and slapped Ethan across the face and then, with the belt buckle round his right hand, belted Ethan again and again over his back, as his son begged for him to stop. 'You'll show the Atkinson family some respect. You owe your very existence to them. Know your place, lad, and leave their young women alone.' The belt cracked repeatedly on Ethan's back, cutting through his shirt and raising blood across his back.

Jethro stood over his son, who lay sprawled in the manure of the calf shed, shaking with fear at his father's wrath, not daring to fight back.

'Miss Rosie is not for you, lad, and the sooner you realize that the better. And as for finding that grandfather of yours, get the idea out of your head because I hope he's dancing with the devil. He did nowt for my mother and nowt for me.'

'Jethro! Stop at once. There was no need to go that far,' shouted Danny across the farmyard, after hearing Ethan's screams from within the house. 'He only needed a word, not flaying to within an inch of his life.'

'Nay, words are wasted on him; he's been told once before. This time he knew what was coming.' Jethro picked up his cap from where it had fallen after his attack on his son. 'He'll not be giving you any more bother. Will you, lad?' Jethro scowled at his son and didn't show an ounce of pity.

Ethan looked up at Danny Atkinson, with his blood-ied back against the whitewashed walls of the calf shed and tears in his eyes, and mumbled, 'No, sir, I know my place.' But within him still flashed defiance. He dared to look at Jethro, who was grovelling next to his master, instead of being proud of his son. No wonder his father was still just a groom; he had no ambition and didn't dare to dream. Ethan vowed that would be the last beat-ing he would ever take from his father, or any man.

'Get yourself home, Jethro. Ethan, go up to your room above the stables and take care of yourself for the rest of the day. Mrs Atkinson will bring you a bite to eat.' Danny watched as Jethro mounted the steps to the cart and moved the horses out of the yard. It was a side to Jethro he had never seen before and didn't want to see again. The lad hadn't deserved such a belting. As his father had pointed out, neither of the youngsters were the worse for their trip away together. So why be so harsh?

Ethan pulled himself up and made his way slowly to the stables, climbing up the ladder to the warm, safe hay-loft where his mattress lay in one corner. Lying down on it, he ran his finger over the welts that he could reach and looked at the blood on his fingers. He'd not let his father do that again. In fact he'd make a point of never seeing his father again, if he could help it. Nobody would tell him what to do from now on, unless it was worth his while. As for Rosie, well, she was still his girl. Belting or no belting.

*

'Ethan? Are you there, Ethan?' Rosie whispered into the darkness.

'Aye, I'm up here.' He crawled to the edge of the loft and looked down at Rosie in the dim light of the candle. She was in her nightshift, and her golden hair hung loose around her angelic face.

'I've brought some of my mother's best salve for your cuts. But they don't know I'm here. I've sneaked out while they are all asleep.' Rosie climbed up the wooden ladder in her bare feet, placing the candle and the pot of salve next to Ethan.

'They'll hang us, if they find us both together,' Ethan whispered as she sat down beside him.

'They'll not find out, if you are quiet. Now, take off your shirt and let me put this on your cuts.' Rosie unscrewed the lid of the pot and looked at the face of Ethan, who she knew had taken a beating for her. She ran her fingers gently over the welts and heard him gasp with pain as the salve seeped into his wounds. 'I'm sorry, Ethan, this is all my fault. It was me who bought the tickets, and me who thought it was a good idea.' She sat back into the darkness of the hay-loft as she watched him replace his tattered shirt.

'I'd do it all again, just for you to visit me like you are tonight.' Ethan leaned over to Rosie and pulled her towards him. 'My father was wrong: we are not that dissimilar. Kiss me, Rosie. Let them not part us, no matter what our differences.'

Rosie looked across at the lad she knew she had feelings for. She knew she shouldn't have, but she closed her eyes and waited for the kiss she had been dreaming of.

113

She held Ethan tightly and kissed his lips, before drawing back from his arms as she caught her breath.

'I'll have to go,' she whispered. 'They might miss me.' She liked the feel of Ethan's warm, firm hands on her body, and knew that if she stayed any longer it would be asking for trouble. She picked up the candle and climbed down the ladder, looking up at the face she knew she loved, before disappearing into the night.

Ethan watched the small flame blend into the darkness. Now that was a dream worth chasing, and one that merited the thrashing of his life.

9

Isabelle sat back in her office chair and gazed out of the window. Papers and invoices were strewn over her desk, along with cloth samples and designs. She was snowed under with work, but still she could not concentrate on the tasks in hand. Something was wrong with James, but she didn't quite know what. Ever since they had moved to Windfell, he had been more distant towards her. Perhaps he missed the busy streets of Settle, as he did seem to be going out walking on his own more of late.

She picked up the latest pattern books from Viyella and looked at them, barely giving the latest fashion of hobble skirts a second look before throwing the books back on the desk; she just couldn't settle. She decided to take a walk through the store, which usually made her feel more relaxed and ready to take on her duties. She'd go and see how Bert was getting on with Jane, down in the warehouse, after visiting each department.

'Morning, Mrs Fox.' The waitress quickly curtsied

and then went about her business as she served the demanding visitors in the upstairs tea-room.

'Morning, Grace.' Isabelle prided herself that she knew every one of her staff and always made a point of remembering their names. Heads turned as she walked around her welcoming tea-room. She spoke to the people she knew, and watched as they ate delicately cut sandwiches or fancies and cream cakes while chatting to their friends and neighbours. Atkinson's was the place to be seen, and the clientele reflected this, with only the best-dressed people and the highly reputable eating there.

'Isabelle, my dear, how lovely to see you. I trust you are keeping well?' Lady Crofts caught her by the wrist.

'Yes, thank you, extremely well. And you?' Isabelle smiled at the round-figured elderly woman, who was known by everyone and was a terrible gossip.

'Yes, I'm fine, dear. Just enjoying some of your delicious cakes with my friends. We were all hoping to catch a glimpse of that husband of yours – he's a dashing fellow and such a charmer.' Lady Crofts smiled and looked round at the group of ladies, who hung on her every word.

'I'm afraid he is in Leeds today, at our shop in the Queens Arcade, along with my new seamstress. They won't be back until much later.' Isabelle smiled and looked around at the wealthily dressed group, most of whom were clad in her designs.

'That's such a pity, my dear, but still we have enjoyed spending a moment with you. And we just needed an excuse to visit your store and catch up with any news over a nice cup of tea.' Lady Crofts picked up her teacup and took a long sip, before turning her back on Isabelle, putting an end to their conversation.

Isabelle walked away and made for the doorway before looking back at the group, who were intent on gossiping. She noticed that they were all looking at her as she left the busy tea-room, and she smiled. If they were talking about her, then at least they were leaving someone else alone. And what they didn't know they made up, she thought, as she made her way down to the warehouse.

'Now, you are in bother, lass – your mother's come to check up on you.' Bert Bannister looked across at his new ward, Jane, who was busy unpacking the latest consignment of Devon Violets perfume and moaning about how much she hated the smell.

'How's Jane doing, Bert?' Isabelle leaned over the packing table and looked at the old man and her daughter, who seemed bored.

'She's alright; could perhaps do with working upstairs for a while, in the perfume department, seeing as she loves the scent she is unpacking at the moment.' Bert grinned at Jane. If her mother had not been there, she would have pulled a face at her instructor, knowing that she could get away with it, as Bert was more a family friend than an employee.

'I just don't know why anyone would wish to smell so sickly. It's so sweet.' Jane blew the packing straw off yet another bottle and straightened the green ribbon around its neck.

'Violets were your grandmother's favourite flowers,

117

along with primroses. She always had to have a bunch on her desk, once spring was upon us.' Bert looked across at Jane and smiled.

'You miss her, don't you, Bert? We all do. In fact, since her death I can't seem to turn my hand to anything with vigour,' Isabelle confessed.

'It's only to be expected; she held everyone together and was always there for them. A good woman, that's what she was.' Bert shook his head as he thought about days past.

'I've some good news anyway, Bert. Harriet and her family are visiting us on Wednesday. James is to take a family photograph, and then I hope to try and persuade Harriet that the firm still needs her.' Isabelle looked around her and watched as a carter dropped off his load for Bert and his small team to unload and unpack. Bert just had to look at the two warehouse men for them to know what was expected of them.

'It will be good to see Miss Harriet back with us. It's what your mother would have wanted. How old is her youngest now? I lose track of time.' He looked across at Isabelle, remembering when the two sisters-in-law used to work together.

'She's one next week. That's why I thought a photograph of the children was apt.' Isabelle smiled.

'Aye, that'll mean a lot to Miss Harriet. Especially since the two twins died. It broke her heart and she's never been the same since, despite going on to have more family. You never get over the loss of a child. My old lass and me have lost two – one at birth and one who was just not born right. They were always sickly, but we still remember them.' Bert looked across at young Jane and smiled. 'Is Mr Fox at Leeds today with Madge Burton? They were saying upstairs that she's quite a good seamstress.'

'Yes, James has a full day of bookings, and Madge is meeting the manager at the shop in Queens Arcade. I thought it was time she made herself known to him. They went on the seven o'clock train together this morning.' Isabelle twiddled with the string that sat on the packing bench and thought about James and his visit to Leeds with Madge. He hadn't wanted to go with her, and had made such a fuss when he left her that morning.

'She's a bonny woman, is Madge; she could do with finding herself a good single man.' Bert's face clouded over.

'You don't always have to be dependent on a man,' young Jane spouted up. 'Women should be independent. I don't think I will ever marry.'

Both looked across at the young lass with a mind of her own.

'Jane, will you stop reading the rubbish that the stupid women of the Women's Social and Political Union keep feeding you? Of course you will marry; it is what is expected of you, when the right man comes along.' Isabelle sighed.

'The times are changing, Mistress Isabelle, even I know that. Better to be single than unhappily married.' Bert looked at his mistress, who was oblivious to all the gossip within the store, which he had tried to ignore.

'Well, I never thought I'd hear that, Bert Bannister:

you telling me, at your age, to move with the times. It must be working with our Jane; you must have heard too many of her radical ideas.' Isabelle stood back and looked at the pair who were trying to tell her the way of the world.

'Aye, well, sometimes we can't see what's going on under our own noses, and I'm as guilty as the next man of that.' Bert walked over to the consignment of goods that had just arrived and thought better of saying anything about his concerns. After all, it was only idle gossip that he'd heard and there was always plenty of that in Atkinson's department store.

10

James Fox sat across from the new love in his life and did not feel one bit guilty for his thoughts about the sweet-faced young woman who had captured his heart.

'I can't believe we are travelling to Leeds together, James, and that your wife knows and doesn't suspect a thing.' Madge giggled and looked at her employer, and the man she had made it her business to fall in love with.

'Ssshh! Keep your voice down. Nearly everyone knows me on this train, as I make this journey regularly. Anyway you've to meet the manager at Queens Arcade, and I have a full morning of photography. The afternoon, however, will be ours to spend as we please, and I can think of lots of ways to pass an hour or two.' James winked at the young blonde-haired woman with cupid-bow lips and come-to-bed eyes, and couldn't believe that someone her age would possibly look at a middle-aged man with greying hair. A slight pang of guilt caught him by surprise when he thought of Isabelle, hard at work in the main store at Skipton; but he shook it off as Madge smiled at him in such a seductive way that all thoughts of guilt were banished. If only Isabelle would look at him that way and have time for him, instead of being hardheaded and caught up in her work. It was always the children, Atkinson's or Windfell; there was no time in Isabelle's life for him. Or at least that was how it felt.

This afternoon he would enjoy his time with Madge, who showed him quite openly the love he craved. He'd booked a room at the new Queens Hotel at the station, which wasn't out of the ordinary, as he had stayed there in the recent past when he was needed for more than one day in the studio at Leeds. He was going to make the most of his day with the alluring Madge, and no one need be any the wiser. He smiled as his new flame looked out of the window at the passing countryside. The afternoon could not come soon enough – a bottle of champagne and a nice double bed were already calling him away from his work.

Nearly a week had passed since James and Madge had shared an afternoon of illicit passion together, and Madge was beginning to wonder about the true reason for Isabelle's invitation for Harriet and her family to visit Atkinson's.

'What's Harriet like? Is she like your wife?' Madge looked out of the window of the photographic studio down onto the busy High Street of Skipton, while quizzing James about the impending visit of his sister-in-law and her family.

'Oh Lord, no! She's anything but. Harriet is very

maternal – her family is everything to her. She's not material in the least.' He looked across at the woman he was besotted with, as he made ready for the Atkinson family photograph. 'Why do you ask?'

'I just wondered. Everyone seems to be talking about Harriet with a wistful fondness and, as I've never met her, I am curious. And, if I'm truthful, a little worried, as everyone says she is an expert seamstress. Your wife won't be replacing me with her, will she?' Madge turned to face James and looked at him with a worried expression.

'Madge, my dear, whatever gave you that idea? Isabelle would not replace you – I'd not let her.' James walked over to her and ran his hand down her back and kissed her on the cheek. 'My wife is just hoping that now her mother has died, Harriet will come back to the fold, as it were. She needs Harriet's support when it comes to running the firm, until Jane shows more interest.' James let go of Madge and looked out of the window. 'There's Harriet, over on the other side of the street, with baby Georgina in her arms and her daughter Rosie and son Ben. They are making their way here, so you'd better make yourself scarce.' James held her at arm's length and quickly glanced around the studio to make sure everything was in place for the photo he was about to take. 'Go on, get back to your dressmaking before you are missed.' He patted Madge fondly on her bottom.

'It's just that I know some of the workers in Atkinson's don't like me. I hear them whispering about me, and have done ever since I arrived here.' Madge turned into James's arms and looked up into his face.

'You imagine it, my dear. Besides, they are always gossiping about somebody on the shop floor. It's the nature of shop girls; too busy living somebody else's lives, when they should be living their own.' James pushed her away. 'Go on, get gone.'

'But—' Madge stopped quickly as the door opened.

'There you are! Mrs Middleton is waiting in the fitting room. Had you forgotten your eleven o'clock appointment? And what are you doing here?' Isabelle looked angrily at Madge. She'd had to pacify Mrs Middleton with a free cup of tea, as she and Jane had scoured the building for Madge.

'It's my fault, dear. I asked Madge to give me hand putting up the backdrop for Harriet's photograph. That will be all, Madge, you had better go quickly and see to Mrs Middleton.' James dismissed her without blinking and smiled tenderly at his wife.

'Yes, sir.' Madge curtsied and quickly gave him a loving smile behind Isabelle's back.

'Really, James, you have Jane to help you with little jobs like that. Don't drag Madge away from her duties again. She is already a bad timekeeper and doesn't need any further encouragement to get behind with her work,' Isabelle said haughtily, glancing around the studio.

'Harriet is on her way. I've just seen her and the family cross the road. It will be good to see them here. There was a time when I didn't think she would ever step into Atkinson's again.' James quickly changed the subject and walked to line up the camera with the backdrop, ready for the family shot.

'I'm glad we have made up and that I decided to show Harriet some sympathy. Madge has such an air of superiority about her, as if she has no respect for me. Even though she is excellent with a needle, I often think I'd prefer to work with Harriet, if I could persuade her to return to the fold. After all, she is part owner, and Mother would have approved. I only hope she has forgotten now the words that we both said in anger. I personally regret every word I said.' Isabelle stood with her hands on her hips and watched as James played with the lens, getting the focus right.

'Don't even consider it, Isabelle! All the times I have heard you cursing Harriet and her family for letting you down. Besides, Harriet wouldn't leave her youngest. Georgina's not quite one yet.' James turned and looked sternly at his wife. Madge had read the situation correctly and Isabelle was plotting her downfall.

'We'll see. I'm going to try and tempt Harriet back, despite what you say. Perhaps with a little sweetener at first. Now, if you'll excuse me, I'll go downstairs and greet them.' Isabelle looked at her husband, whose face was set sternly.

'I'll be late home tonight. I thought I might go and look at the new motorcycles that Pratt's are displaying. I've had my eye on one for a while, and now I think I may treat myself,' James shouted after her.

'What on earth do you want one of those for? They are noisy, dirty things; they will never catch on.' Isabelle stood in the doorway and sighed. 'I suppose you will suit yourself, despite what I have to say about it.' She lingered there and then decided not to wait for a reply, as she heard her guests coming up the stairs. James would do as he chose, and at the moment seemed to be his own master. She was getting tired and a little worried about him and his changing ways.

Rosie stood alongside her mother. She'd been told to put on her best clothes and had protested while Harriet put a ribbon in her hair. She hated the ribbon, it made her look like a child. The big pink satin bow hung down at the side of her head and irritated her, as she stood in front of the camera with her mother and siblings. She tried to smile, as her Uncle James made silly comments so that they all laughed, but it didn't help that Jane was standing at the back of the room looking every inch the young lady, while in her own eyes Rosie looked stupid. But she tried her best. The sooner it was over, the sooner she could go home, so she forced a smile as the shot was taken.

'There, that wasn't too bad now, was it, children?' Harriet looked round at her family and ushered them off the make-believe set of a grand house, and smiled as Isabelle took baby Georgina from her arms. 'Rosie, are you going to go with Jane? I think she wants to show you around the firm. I'm going to have tea with Aunt Isabelle and will take Ben and Georgina with me; you can both join us when you've seen enough.'

Jane looked almost as excited about taking Rosie under her wing as Rosie herself did. In truth, neither girl particularly liked the other, but both knew they had to be polite in their parents' company.

'Yes, Mama.' Rosie walked over to Jane, who scowled

at her as she opened the door, leaving the adults talking and Ben seeing how the camera worked with his Uncle James.

'Don't you think you are a bit too old for wearing ribbons?' Jane looked at her cousin and smirked. 'I haven't worn ribbons since I left school.'

Rosie reached her hand up to her hair and pulled the offending satin bow out of her blonde locks. 'Mama made me wear it. I hate the thing.' She shoved the ribbon into her pocket and walked down the stairs onto the shop floor, trying to walk as elegantly as her cousin. 'Is Luke not here today?' Rosie enquired.

'All Luke thinks about at the moment is the Officers' Training Corps that he's volunteered for. He's always down at Giggleswick School, even in his holidays. And if he's not there, he's over at the outdoor range they've got at Attermire Scar. He's even got his own rifle. Mother hates seeing him cleaning it; she's frightened he will fire the thing, even though he's told her that he is allowed only blank cartridges.' Jane stopped at the bottom of the stairs and waited for her cousin. 'Luke's not fit to look after himself, let alone be in possession of a gun, if you ask me.'

'I think I can hear them firing when I'm at the top of Moughton Scar – at least, that's what Ethan says it is. You can hear the guns distantly above the skylarks singing, they disturb the peace up there,' Rosie said innocently.

'You walk up Moughton Scar with Ethan! He's only a stable boy, you know, you shouldn't even talk to him.' Jane looked with disdain as she weaved in and out of the customers, making her way to the warehouse and delivery bay.

'Grandfather says we all come from the same maker, and no one's better than anyone else. Besides, Ethan and I are good friends, he likes the same things as I do.' Rosie blushed.

'He's a dirty gypsy. One you should keep your eye on. I certainly would not want him near me.' Jane opened the warehouse doors for Rosie to pass by her and, as she did so, Rosie looked her snobbish cousin up and down.

Jane might be better dressed than her, in a pin-tucked, high-collared white blouse adorned by a silver brooch and a tight beige skirt, with her hair piled high upon her head, but she was not a nice person. In fact she could be downright vicious. From now on, Rosie would not mention Ethan's name to her ever again.

'Miss Rosie, I meant to talk to you at your grandmother's funeral, but I never got the chance.' Bert Bannister looked across from his bench and smiled at the young woman he'd known all her life. 'I heard that you and your family were coming to visit, so a good thing may have come out of your grandmother's passing. It will be good to see your mother taking an interest in the firm again.'

'Thank you, Mr Bannister. We are only here for a few hours, but it is nice to be able to look around at where my mother once worked alongside Aunt Isabelle.' Rosie smiled at the old man whom her grandmother had revered.

'She did more than work here, lass. She was the one who built it, along with Miss Isabelle. They worked well together back then; it was a shame bad things got in the way of their happiness.' Bert breathed in deeply and thought of all the years and bad feelings that had built up since the opening of Atkinson's department store.

'It was Grandmama's store – she was the one with the money. Atkinson's is nothing to do with Rosie or her side of the family,' Jane said curtly.

'Nay, that's where you are wrong, lass. Archie, your grandfather, pulled his weight alongside his Lottie. They worked together, and he was her prop. She might have had the brass, but Archie was the rudder that steered your grandmother's ship, keeping her straight. Rosie has as much right to be here than any one of us – she's a true Atkinson.' Bert grinned and patted Rosie on the shoulder. 'Here, I've something for you: a bottle of your grandmother's favourite perfume, "Devon Violets". We couldn't put it out on the shelf because the label is torn, and Jane here doesn't like it, so I kept it to one side, thinking I'd give it to my old woman. But it's more right for you, as violets were what your grandfather always picked his Lottie in the spring.' Bert smiled and looked at the delight on Rosie's face as she glanced at the little green bottle with a violet ribbon attached.

'It stinks, I don't know how anyone can wear it,' growled Jane as she watched Rosie place the precious bottle in her pocket.

'It can't smell that badly – it's one of our leading sellers, Miss Jane. Perhaps it is a matter of differing tastes.' Bert grinned. 'Now, I'd better get on with my work, but do mention me to your mother, Rosie, and tell her that I'm glad to see her back within these walls.'

'I will, Mr Bannister, and thank you for the perfume.' Rosie smiled.

'No problem, lass. I know it's gone to a good home, someone who will appreciate it.' He threw a knowing look at Jane as he made his way down to the bottom of the warehouse.

'I think old Bert is losing it a bit; all he talks about is the good old days. He never talks about the here and now, and it is always about Grandmama and when he first worked for her. I swear he doesn't like me, although he seems to like you well enough, giving you some of Mother's products to take home with you.' Jane looked at Rosie, who was handling her precious gift.

'I can give it back to you, if Bert shouldn't have given me it. I don't want to get him into trouble.' Rosie touched the bottle and hoped that she could keep it.

'No, Mama won't mind. It's only cheap stuff and, as I say, it stinks, despite what Bert says. I wouldn't be seen dead wearing it.' Jane put her nose in the air and walked through the shop floor, strutting like a prize peacock, ignoring the shop girls and smiling a sickly grin at the customers she knew. 'We only attract the best customers at Atkinson's; they deserve the best, and that is what I will definitely give them, once the store is mine.'

Rosie listened and watched as her cousin showed her all the way round the store. She was amazed at all that was on offer and at the number of customers the goods attracted, but what also amazed her was Jane's arrogance.

She only worked in the warehouse with Bert and was still learning the job, with fewer responsibilities than she herself had back at Crummock Farm. Jane's mother might own most of the firm, but Rosie's mother owned a part of it, too – a fact that Jane was definitely overlooking. Rosie breathed out with relief when they finally climbed the stairs to join their parents in the tea-room. She'd had enough of the precious Jane and her forthright views, and was ready for home.

'So, I can't entice you back for a day or two each week? Just to take fittings and help Madge Burton, while I look over the accounts and do the other things that I now find myself doing.' Isabelle lifted her teacup to her lips, curling her little finger elegantly as she sipped.

'I'm sorry, but no, those days have gone. I've got the children and the farm and, now that Archie is living with us, he takes looking after as well. He's not as good on his legs as he used to be.' Harriet shook her head. She had been tempted as she looked through the design books and at work in progress in the busy cutting room. It had reminded her of the love she had once felt for her work. But she knew her place was at Crummock, helping Danny with the farm and bringing up her children.

'You could bring baby Georgina with you, and you need only work when Ben is at school. Surely Rosie is old enough to take on some more responsibilities, like my Jane? After all, she's not far off seventeen.' Isabelle smiled at her sister-in-law. She'd noticed the glint in Harriet's eye as she looked around the cutting and fitting room; there was still a love of fashion running through her veins. A love that she aimed to rekindle.

'Rosie has enough on. Besides, she helps her father more than me, as she loves the farm more than house-work.' Harriet smiled at her daughter and caught a smirk on Jane's face; a smirk that she would have liked to wipe off it, if Jane's mother had not been there.

'Well, think about it. You don't have to decide here and now. I'm just glad we are back on better terms with one another, and that I had the chance to tell you how much I have missed you.' Isabelle looked across at Rosie. 'You know, your mother is a wonderful seamstress – a hundred times better than the one I've got at present. I do wish that you'd try to persuade her, my dear.'

Rosie glanced at her mother and then smiled at her aunt. She knew why her mother didn't want to return to work at Atkinson's. It was true, Harriet did live for her children and the farm, but Rosie also knew that deep down Harriet did not want to become involved in family politics again. That was what had torn the family apart previously, and it was likely to continue to put strain on the situation for some time, if Jane was ever put in charge of the firm.

'It's up to Mother, Aunt Isabelle, but I will try and persuade her, if you wish,' said Rosie. She glanced at her dark-faced uncle, who definitely did not look amused at her aunt's suggestion.

'Thank you, my dear. I hope Jane looked after you this afternoon? She's such a well-mannered young lady that I'm sure she did. I think I've taught her well.' Isabelle glanced at her daughter.

'She was the perfect host, Aunt Isabelle, thank you,' said Rosie. Although she didn't enjoy it, she could play the game as well as anyone else.

11

'Well, how did you go on today with Isabelle?' Danny looked across the table at Harriet.

'Alright. I think she wants me to come back and join her again.' Harriet looked at her father-in-law as he grunted.

'Missing her mother's work already, is she? She never was one for hard work.' Archie looked up from his supper plate and thought of the hours that his darling Lottie had given to Atkinson's. The hours that his stepdaughter was now beginning to appreciate.

'I might be wrong, but I don't think she likes her new seamstress, although even I found her a bit demanding. She's only young, but she has this air of complete confidence about her.' Harriet had not been impressed by her first meeting with Madge. It had only been brief, but she could see why Madge perhaps did not fit into the ethics of Atkinson's.

'It's called being young, my dear. Can't you remember

134

when you and Isabelle had your first shop in Settle? You would have taken on the world, back then. Besides, our Isabelle can be a funny one, and you of all people should know that.' Danny sat back in his chair and smiled at Harriet. 'Would you like to go back and do a few hours? It would probably do you good. Rosie can do a bit more around the house, and we could always get somebody else in for a few days. I can tell that you've missed it – you look full of life this evening.' Danny was pleased that Harriet had enjoyed her day with his stepsister. It had been a long time in coming, but the wounds were gradually healing.

'I don't know, I'll think about it. Georgina is still so young. Perhaps in another few years; then it gives Rosie more time to enjoy her life before settling down in her own marriage and home.' Harriet drank her tea and smiled.

'Where is Rosie anyway? I know Ben and Georgina are in bed, but Rosie is usually around the table with us.' Danny breathed in and watched as his father finished his supper.

'She asked if she could take some bread and cheese and a piece of bannock for her supper. She's been cooped up with Jane all day today, and you know she hates not being outside, so she said she was going for a wander before it gets dark. She'll not have gone far, she'll be back before nightfall.' Harriet stood up and collected the dirty plates.

'I'd want to be out and all, if I'd been with Jane all day,' said Archie. 'I used to think she took after my

Lottie, but lately she's got an edge to her. One I don't like. I think I might have to bring her up sharply soon. She should be a kinder soul. Not everyone is as privileged as her, she should remember that,' he commented as he made his way from the kitchen table to his usual resting place next to the kitchen fire. He sat down in his trusted Windsor chair and reached for his pipe from above the fireplace. 'She does right, does Rosie. She needs a bit of fresh mountain air to clear her head of all the sarcastic remarks she will have had to have put up with today. I don't blame her.' He lit his pipe with a spill and leaned back and looked at his son. 'She's like you, is your Rosie. Happy with the land, and doesn't want owt else.'

'She's growing up, Father. Soon lads will be coming a-calling.' Danny joined his father, sitting across from him next to the fire.

'Time enough for that yet, lad. Let her enjoy trailing the fells first. Then she can find herself a fella.' Archie puffed on his pipe, content with his lot. He loved Rosie; she was a grand lass and he hoped she would stay young and innocent for as long as possible, God willing.

'I thought you were never coming!' Ethan propped himself up on one elbow and looked across at Rosie as she ran across the clapper bridge to the grassy bank where he lay.

'I couldn't make it too obvious. Besides, I'd the dogs to feed and the eggs to collect, as I'd missed doing that this morning, with going to Skipton.' Rosie sat down beside him and kissed him quickly on the cheek. 'Don't complain anyway, I've brought us both our suppers. Mother said I'd to help myself to cheese and bread and a bannock, so I made sure there was enough for both of us.' She untied the napkin that held their supper and laid the contents out amongst the grass and flowers that grew on the banks of the river at the wash-dubs.

'That looks bloody good. Here, let me supply the pudding.' Ethan leaned over to the side of the dry limestone wall that stood behind him and pulled some small wild bilberries from the stumpy, wiry bush that grew below it. 'And this is for my girl, to match her eyes.' He leaned over again and picked a sky-blue scabious, then placed it behind Rosie's ear, kissing her as he did so and touching her cheeks lovingly with his hand.

'We shouldn't, Ethan, we vowed we would just be good friends.' Rosie blushed and looked coyly at him.

'I can't help it – you know I can't. I feel different when I'm with you. I couldn't stop thinking about you all day. This evening couldn't come quick enough.' Ethan kissed her again and held her in his arms.

'Me, too. I hated my time with Jane. She is such a clever devil, but, in all honesty, knows nothing.' Rosie lay back in Ethan's arms. His breath was slow and sure next to her and she let her fingers trace the opening of his shirt, which revealed the dark hairs of his chest.

'Don't! Now you are teasing and I don't think I can control myself.' Ethan sighed. 'You know, I do think a lot of you. But you also know that what we are doing is wrong – your father and grandfather would kill me, as would my father. Well, you saw last time what my own father would do to me.'

'Well, they are not about to find out. I'm not going to say anything, and who else is there to witness our meetings? I think I love you, Ethan, I really do.' Rosie rolled onto her side and looked into his eyes as she opened his shirt more and ran her hands over his chest as she kissed him.

'Rosie, my Rosie, we shouldn't, you know we shouldn't.' He breathed in deeply and kissed her hard on the mouth, before rolling her onto her back and lying upon her. 'I'll be gentle, I promise. This is our secret,' he whispered as he pulled her skirts up and undid his buttons. He'd been waiting for this moment all summer and could resist no longer.

'You do love me, don't you, Ethan?' Rosie whispered, her heart pounding as he could hold back no longer. But Ethan didn't reply, he just kissed her and carried on undoing his trousers, before entering her and taking over her body with every thrust that he made. She winced with both the pain and the thrill of having sex with her wild lover. 'You do love me. Don't you?' she whispered again. But Ethan still didn't reply, as he put his finger to her mouth and smiled down at her. She'd given herself willingly to him and now he was making sure he enjoyed his innocent farm girl.

The bread and cheese had gone stale in the dying summer's sun, untouched and unwanted, as they lay back in one another's arms and thought about what they had just done.

Rosie pulled her skirts down and didn't know if she wanted to cry or laugh. She'd taken part in something that, up until now, she had only seen animals do, but she knew what the consequences might be. She lay back and worried. It had been her fault, as she had teased Ethan; she should have known what she was leading him towards, and that a decent woman would have waited until they were married.

'What if I'm . . .?' She turned and looked at Ethan.

'You won't be, I pulled out in time. You'll be fine – stop worrying. That's the last thing we both need. I'm not that daft.' Ethan sat up and looked across the trickling stream as a dragonfly darted and skimmed over the waters in the dying light. In truth, he didn't know for certain, but he hoped nothing would come of the dalliance. 'The sun's going down, you'd better be off, or else you'll have to answer to your father.' He got up onto his feet and offered Rosie his hand. She took it and pulled herself up next to him. 'Stop worrying, you'll be fine.' He kissed her on her cheek.

'I'm sure I will, but I can't help worrying. I shouldn't have egged you on; it was my fault.' Rosie smoothed her skirts and threw the wasted bread and cheese into the river, before picking up the napkin.

'It was both our faults,' Ethan said, as he kissed her once more. 'Now, get yourself home. I'll walk up by the Wharfe track, just in case someone comes looking for you. You go up the home track, it's not as far.' He held her at arm's length and noticed she was near crying. 'Don't cry, you'll be fine.'

'I know, but if I'm not . . . you'll stand by me?' Rosie whispered.

'Of course. But it hasn't come to that yet. Now, go.' Ethan watched as Rosie balanced over the clapper bridge and made her way home along the lane. He stood and looked over to the rocky outcrop of Norber and watched the sun slowly sink, filling the sky with oranges and pinks as it disappeared from sight.

What had he done? He didn't even know if he did love her, in truth. Rosie was just a young girl, and he had known she would be an easy first conquest. Tomorrow he would tell her not to visit him in the loft. After all, the Irishmen were coming to help with hay-time and he didn't want them knowing their secret. It would give them both time to come to their senses.

12

'Doesn't Luke look smart? Just look at him in his uniform, like a true soldier.' Isabelle gazed proudly at her young son, dressed in his latest cadet's uniform, with his Lee Enfield rifle strapped over his shoulder. He stood in front of both of his parents in his khaki breeches and tunic, peaked cap, knee-length puttees and brown leather boots, loaded down with belts and ammunition pouches. The brass badges on his shoulders and cap, stamped with 'Giggleswick OTC School', shone in the sun.

'I'm lucky to have got this rifle.' Luke grinned. 'My mate Palmer still has to use his old Martini–Henri carbine, which is really heavy to carry when you have the full kit on, and it only fires blanks.' He touched and stroked his rifle lovingly and smiled at his father as he did so.

'Just mind what you are doing with the thing. I never have liked guns. I still can't believe that Giggleswick School has been given a sub-target machine. I don't think they should really be offering military training. I really don't believe in this wave of militarism that is sweeping through the school.' James looked up from his paper and scowled at his young son. 'Besides, that uniform has cost all of thirty shillings, and that is on top of the subscription of seven-and-six, and the use of that damn rifle at two-and-six per term. You'd think we were made of money. And for what – for our son to learn to kill someone or perhaps be killed, if a war comes?'

'James, we are not at war, nor likely to be. This makes our Luke happy and he's good at it. Captain Pierce said Luke was one of this year's leading cadets. He's already put his name down to go to Hagley Park next year, to train with cadets from Eton and Harrow and elsewhere in the country. You should be proud of him.' Isabelle smiled at Luke, who looked a little crestfallen. 'Luke, sing your father the song that I heard you and the other cadets singing about Giggleswick forming a military band – you know, the one that is sung along to the tune of "The British Grenadiers".'

'Do I have to, Mother? Father is obviously not impressed.' Luke stood uncomfortably and ran his finger around his high-collared tunic.

'Yes, go on, and then he will understand the pride that you boys have in being an officer-in-training at Giggleswick.'

James sighed as his son stood awkwardly in front of him and started to sing:

'Our numbers have increased this term; our
    Recruitment Sergeant's grand.
To make us quite complete, we lack but a stirring
    military band;
And if our CO speaks the truth, next term
    there'll surely be
An ear-splitting Rat-a-plan, Toot, Toot, Toot,
    from the Giggleswick OTC.'

Luke breathed in deeply as he finished and looked across at his father, waiting for any praise that might come his way.

'Perhaps you would be better joining that band, instead of being so handy with that gun of yours. But, as per usual, your mother will decide, and I will not be listened to.' James rose from his seat and walked away from his wife and son, who was intent on going down the military path even though there was unrest in the world. Neither of them knew what they were doing; to Luke, it was just a game, and in Isabelle's eyes he was doing something she could be proud of.

'Don't listen to your father, he's just in one of his moods. You concentrate on doing as well as you can in all your subjects, and with the OTC. I can see you making an officer, if what Captain Pierce says is correct.' Isabelle smiled at her son.

'Yes, Mother, I enjoy my role in the cadets. I feel that I'm doing something special for my country. And Father is right that we are training in case war ever comes, but

I'm not even seventeen yet, so I'd be too young to go anyway.'

'Don't talk of such things. War will never happen, despite the war in the Balkans, and Germany building up its naval fleet. Prime Minister Asquith is anti-war, and he'll not let Britain get drawn into anything. You enjoy the training. I'll settle your father down, and he'll come round to the idea.' Isabelle watched as her son left the room. Perhaps James was right, and perhaps Luke should not be training as a soldier; but as Archie had said, it was giving her boy discipline and a purpose in life, and Luke was good at it.

James walked out of Windfell, slamming the door behind him as he put on his jerkin and new motorcycle goggles. He needed to get away from his family, and his new acquisition was calling him – as well as his mistress – as he strode across the pebbled driveway to where it stood.

'Going for a ride out, sir?' Jethro looked at his master, dressed in his new attire, and watched as he lovingly rubbed his hands along the handlebars of his motorcycle.

'I am, Jethro. I thought I'd have a ride down the road and happen up to Ingleton. I'm still getting used to what my machine can do. Isn't it beautiful?' James stood back and looked at the Scott motorcycle that he had acquired through the new motorcycle company based in Saltaire. 'She's a twin-stroke, you know? I've got her to go as fast as thirty miles an hour – it feels like you are flying.' James smiled at Jethro, who was shaking his head.

'You'd not get me on the back of one of them. Give

me a horse any day. They are a lot less noisy, for a start, and probably more reliable. And I haven't got a clue what a twin-stroke is, so you're wasting your breath telling me that.' Jethro thought nowt of the new machine that was his master's pride and joy. 'What do you want to go that fast for, anyway?' He watched as James put his leg over the motorcycle and beamed as he pulled his goggles down, before kick-starting it into action.

'Until you've done it, Jethro, you don't know what it feels like. Otherwise, you'd want to do it,' James shouted above the roar of the engine, urging it into action as Jethro looked on.

Jethro shook his head again as the smell of fumes filled the yard, and he listened as James and the motor-cycle made their way out of the drive of Windfell Manor and down the road towards Settle. Give him a horse any day, not a noisy heap of metal. These young folk, with their new ideas, had no respect of the old ways. He shook his head again and made for his beloved horses; at least they showed him respect.

James sat back on the bike's seat. He could feel the purr of the engine beneath his legs. He felt he was com-pletely in control of the machine. It made him feel like the man he had longed to be for some time, especially now that he had Madge hanging on his every word and giving him her complete attention, unlike Isabelle. His life was beginning to be more bearable.

He smiled to himself as he let out the bike's throttle to climb the steep hill – called Buckhaw Brow – outside the village of Giggleswick and then cut off along the rutted road to the small hamlet of Feizor. He couldn't wait to hear what Madge had to say, once she saw him on his motorcycle. He knew her reaction would be different from that of Isabelle, who had moaned about what it had cost and the fact that she had no intention of ever being seen on the thing. He made his way across the small ford that ran through the hamlet of Feizor and hoped that the motorcycle wouldn't splutter and fail as he came out the other side and drove it over the limestone roadway to the cottage where Madge lived.

'Oh, my Lord! you've gone and got one of those contraptions,' Madge squealed as she opened the door, wondering what the noise was outside her quiet home. 'You've come to see me on it. Everyone will be talking!' She giggled and screamed as she looked at her lover, whilst he took his goggles off and brushed back his greying hair. She gasped as she gazed at the bike in amazement, and then kissed James on the cheek. 'I've got to have a go on it, you've got to give me a ride!' she shouted as she walked around the bike, looking at every inch of it.

'I don't know, Madge. I'm only just learning to handle it myself. Besides, it's not very ladylike. You'd have to pull your skirts up and sit in tight next to me. What if someone sees you?' James looked shocked.

'I don't care, I've got to have a go.' Madge hoisted her skirts up and sat sharply on the small leather seat, holding James close to her on the back of the bike.

'Mind your legs – the exhaust is hot, it will burn them. Tuck your skirts in tight, I don't want them catching in the chain. I don't think we should do this, Madge.'

James breathed in deeply – he didn't want her to think he was not man enough to be seen with her behind him – and decided to kick-start his bike with her still on it. The closeness of her body to his made him forget his fears and he shouted above the roar of the engine, 'Hold on tight and remember, mind your skirts.'

They made their way unsteadily down the rough road from Feizor and then onto the better road that led back down Buckhaw Brow into Giggleswick and Settle. Madge laughed and screamed at every corner, as James tried to counterbalance the weight behind him, stopping at the top of the brow of the hill and looking down upon the slate roofs of the houses of Settle in the valley below.

'Go on – what have we stopped for? Take me down, I dare you!' Madge laughed and urged him on as she pulled her long, knotted scarf around her neck and checked her hair. 'Are you frightened that we might be seen? Or is it that the bike's too big for you?' She giggled, squeezing him tight.

'No, it's just that I shouldn't be on it with you. The bike's new to me. And I worry what people will think of you, if they see us together.' James put both of his feet on the ground and steadied the two of them.

'There's no one about. Look, you can see the road is clear almost until Settle. People are eventually going to know about us anyway, if your promise to leave Isabelle for me is true,' she cried. 'Go on, keep driving, then turn around and take me back home. I'll have had my thrills for the day by then.' Madge kissed him on the ear and hugged him close. 'Please,' she whispered. 'You know I love you.'

James breathed in deeply. Despite his better judgement, he fired the engine up and started down the hill. Madge screamed with delight and her scarf flew like a pennant behind her. The road dipped and the wind lessened, making the scarf fly low and limp, until it dragged downwards near the back-wheel sprocket and chain. She paid it no heed as the bike built up speed and she screamed with excitement. But all too quickly her screams of joy turned to screams of panic, as the scarf became entwined in the motorcycle's chain and back wheel, pulling at Madge's neck and making her unable to breathe. The scarf became more and more entwined as the motorbike picked up speed and dragged her from behind James. She tried to yell and scream and she clawed at James to save her, as she and the bike flew across the road, unseating James and leaving Madge, still and unbreathing, on the stony road of Buckhaw Brow. Battered and bleeding and with a broken neck, her body was lifeless. The scarf was still entwined in the gears of the motorbike, while its wheels continued to turn.

James lifted his head. His leg hurt and he could see that blood was beginning to pour and seep into his moleskin trousers, leaving a dark-red pool on the white of the stony road. 'Madge, Madge!' he yelled as he dragged himself across to her, every inch of road being more painful than the first. His face and arms became peppered with grit and stones as he pulled himself over to where Madge lay, and he realized that he must have broken his leg, as he pulled at the body of his love. He looked at the twisted scarf and the once-beautiful face of the carefree woman who had been so full of life until a few minutes before. Now she was covered with blood, bashed and torn as the bike pulled her underneath it.

'What have I done? I knew you shouldn't have got on it – you knew I was worried about your skirts. Why didn't you think to secure your scarf?' He sobbed and then winced in pain. The two loves of his life lay broken and exposed on the wild fellside, with the sun glistening on Madge's blonde hair and on the gleaming metal bike frame. James lay back and looked up at the sky. His head felt faint and his stomach was nauseous. God, what had he done? How was he ever going to live with himself? And how would he explain Madge's death to Isabelle? She'd never understand, and he knew she would never, ever forgive him.

13

'Dr Burrows has gone. He's happy with your progress.'
Isabelle pulled the morning room's door to and sat down
next to James. She glanced at him, sitting upright in his
invalid chair, and breathed in deeply. She couldn't bear
the sight of him at the moment; he'd bought shame on her
family and, most of all, to her. They were the talk of the
community.

James looked at Isabelle. She had hardly spoken to
him since the afternoon the Bradley brothers had carried
him into Windfell, after finding him unconscious and
Madge dead and broken on the road at Buckhaw Brow.

'Isabelle, I'm sorry. How many times have I to tell you
that I'm sorry?' James held out his hand for her to hold.

'Sorry – you're sorry. Sorry that you were found out,
and that Madge Burton is dead because of your unfaith-
fulness. That's all you are sorry about. I should throw
you out, along with that awful machine, but I've to think
of our family. So just be grateful that you still have a roof

over your head and that I'm even talking to you.' She glared at him.

'Madge meant nothing to me. I keep telling you: she just saw me riding my motorcycle on the road to Ingleton and begged for a ride. How could I refuse her? You know what she was like. I just wish both of us had not been so foolish.' James looked out of the window, unable to keep eye contact with her. He knew she knew that he was lying.

'So that's why all the locals are talking about you calling at Madge's door at all hours of the day and night. And I suppose there is a valid reason for all the staff at Atkinson's to be smirking and talking about your little tête-à-têtes with Madge behind my back. I must have been blind and stupid!' Isabelle pulled her handkerchief from her pocket and dabbed her eyes. 'This isn't the first time a man thinks that I'm too stupid to realize what's going on under my nose. But this time it's not going to get the better of me.'

'I don't think you are stupid. Honestly, there was nothing going on. People gossip, you know that. They put two and two together and make six. I just wish poor Madge was still alive to back me up. I'd do anything for her to be here, standing now in front of us both.' James sighed and tried to get comfortable in his invalid chair as he gingerly moved his splintered leg.

'I bet you do. I suppose you'd rather it was me they were burying on Tuesday, and not Madge. That would have been more convenient for you.' Isabelle breathed in deeply, waiting for the next round of attack.

'The funeral's set for Tuesday then. I must try and go.' James looked down at his broken leg.

'You will not even think of it. You've brought enough disgrace to this house, without showing up at her funeral. I personally hope she's rotting in hell, the little hussy. I gave her a good job, paid her well and gave her responsibilities. But no, Madge was not happy with that; she wanted my husband and, like a fool, he fell for her charms. To think that I even let you go to Leeds together. I bet, if I checked, there would be a room for that date at the Queens booked in your name. I'll go to the funeral. I'll hold my head up high and suffer the indignant looks that people will give me. We owe her parents that much at least.'

Isabelle turned round in her seat and opened the roll-top desk that her mother had sat at when she was alive; she couldn't help but think of how her mother must have felt when she discovered that Joseph Dawson, her husband and Isabelle's father, had another woman in his life. It had been the making of Charlotte Atkinson in the long run. She herself would just have to ensure that James had not endangered her family and all their futures.

'Aye, Isabelle, I've heard your news.' Danny looked across at his sister and felt for her.

Archie looked up from lighting his pipe and also looked at Isabelle. 'I'd never have thought James was capable of that. I always thought he'd eyes for nobody but you. Folk are awful gossips, and sometimes they get it wrong. It's a sad do that the lass died, like, but happen best that she's out of the picture, as it is.' Archie noticed how crestfallen Isabelle appeared. Usually she was as hard as nails, but today she looked vulnerable.

'Father, I meant that we'd heard about Madge dying and that James broke his leg. Not the other rubbish that folk are gossiping and saying.' Danny quickly corrected his father and gave a pleading look for help to Harriet, as she placed a cup of tea down beside her sister-in-law.

'You don't have to pussyfoot around me. I know the stories and I can tell you now that they are probably true, although at the moment James denies it all. But I can tell when he's lying, and he has not been acting himself these last few months, so I knew something was wrong, but didn't know what.' Isabelle pulled off her crocheted gloves and took a sip of her tea. 'I just hope the children don't hear. People can be so cruel, and I have made a few enemies of late. It's not easy following in Mother's footsteps.'

'Oh, Isabelle, I'm so sorry. You must be hurting. I would really like to say what I think to James and give him a piece of my mind. I knew I didn't like that Madge as soon as I saw her at Atkinson's. There was just something about her, as if she had one-up over everybody else. I shouldn't talk ill of the dead, but that is how I felt, as if she was superior to us.' Harriet put her hand on Isabelle's arm and squeezed it lovingly.

'I've been blind, but life goes on. We will have to try and make the best of it. I think, looking back, that Bert Bannister tried to tell me a few weeks ago, but I didn't take the hint. I wish he'd come straight out with it. At least then Madge would still be alive.' Isabelle dropped her head and stared into her teacup.

'Bert always did know everything. That's why your mother thought a lot of him. He always looked out for my Lottie. He's a good man, but getting a bit long in the tooth, like us all.' Archie stared out of the kitchen window and looked wistfully across the valley below to his first home of Eldroth.

'Are you off to the funeral? And what are you going to do at Atkinson's? James won't be able to open the studio up for a while, and you'll need a new seamstress.' Danny sat back in his chair and looked at his sister. He was certain she hadn't come to Crummock on a social visit. She was here for a reason, and it would probably involve Atkinson's.

'I'm closing the studio for a few months, until James gets back on his feet. As for a new seamstress, I don't know what to do. I'm at a loss and my order books are full.' Isabelle paused and then looked up at Harriet. 'I don't suppose I could ask for your help, Harriet? Just for a few weeks, until I find a replacement? I'd arrange transport there and back for you, and pay you a wage. I'd even employ a first-class nanny to look after Georgina. It would be such a help and I'd be so grateful.'

Harriet looked across at Isabelle. She knew that what Isabelle was saying was genuine, but she hesitated in answering.

'I really am in a mess and I need those that I trust and love around me. Just as you helped once before, when you gave me the strength to pick myself up and move on when I was hurt by that awful man, John Sidgwick. Help me again, Harriet, please.'

'I don't know. Georgina is still young and there's the house and the farm. We've only just finished hay-time, and it will be winter before we know it. I'd like to, but I already have enough on my plate.' Harriet saw all eyes watching her make her decision.

'Rosie will look after the house; it's time she was more of a lady than a tomboy,' said Danny. 'And if you get a nanny, Georgina and Ben will be fine. Just start with two days a week and take it from there. See how it pans out. You've talked of nothing else since your visit to Skipton.' He looked across at Harriet. He knew that she secretly yearned to be back working again, despite her life as a mother and housewife at Crummock. She could also give Isabelle a run for her money – something he knew Harriet had been wanting to do since their disagreement all those years ago.

'I'll see – give me some time to think about it. I don't want to be hurried into something I might regret.' Harriet breathed in deeply and looked at Isabelle. 'You'd get me a nanny and transport, and I could come and go as I please?'

'Yes, I said so, and I'd be so grateful. It would be like old times, except that we are both much wiser.' Isabelle smiled and knew that she'd got what she'd come for.

'Aye, old times. Remember the bad as well as the good, and then hopefully neither of you will fall out again.' Archie spat his mouthful of tobacco into the fire, making it hiss.

'We'll not fall out, we've both learned a lot since those days.' Harriet smiled wistfully, remembering the better days with her sister-in-law. 'I'll come and help. Only a few days, mind, and we will see how it goes.'

'Thank you, I just need somebody to be there for me. And I knew I could count on you.' Isabelle rose from the table and hugged Harriet and then looked around her. 'Crummock looks lovely. Mind, it always did at this time of year.'

'Aye, you've got to learn to take the sunshine with the rain, otherwise you'll not survive long up here, or in life. Get home to your man now, you've done your business; and make sure you look after him first. Happen then he won't wander off again,' said Archie.

'Father, be quiet.' Danny stood up and tried to stop his father from saying any more.

'It's alright, Danny. Father always says what he thinks, we both know that. And perhaps I don't always put James first, but he doesn't with me, either, so on that score I think we are even.' Isabelle made her way to the doorway. 'Harriet, I'll let you meet all the nannies that I think are suitable, and Jethro will pick you up for the station in the mornings.' Isabelle smiled as she made her way out into the late summer's day. 'I'm so grateful, believe me,' she said as she made for her carriage.

'She's just like her bloody father. Crafty and cunning, but you can never say no to her. That James will have to pay for his hour or two of pleasure, if I know Isabelle. He'll rue the day he went behind her back – although I think he'll be doing that already.' Archie looked at

156

Danny and Harriet. 'Make sure she's right with you this time, lass; take no rubbish from her.'

'I won't, Father. This time I know she needs me more than I need her.' Harriet smiled.

Isabelle stood at Madge's graveside. It had begun to rain and she looked up towards the falling raindrops pattering onto the spreading leaves of the sycamore trees that surrounded the churchyard. The weather matched her mood. She could have cried, too, shedding tears of hurt as she watched the coffin being lowered into the ground. How could her husband have deceived her so, with her own seamstress, whom she had trusted? Looking back, she should have known something was wrong: all the times James had returned home late, and the occasions when she had found them both together, looking coy and secretive. She should have known. Instead she had been oblivious to the people sniggering behind her back. All of them had known more than she did about what was going on under her own nose.

She looked up at Madge's parents, who were heartbroken and at a loss to make sense of their daughter's death and the scandal that had enveloped them. Their daughter found lying dead, next to James Fox on his new contraption of a motorcycle. The whole district was talking about it. Isabelle breathed in deeply; she wouldn't give her condolences to the family, she would just walk away and leave them in their grief. Besides, if Madge wasn't dead, she would have wished her so; nobody took anything off her, especially not her husband. She looked around her at the whispering mourners and made herself scarce, leaving them to gossip for as long as they liked. No doubt the rumours would give birth to more rumours, and this would just be the start, for the gossips. She must protect the good name of Atkinson's above all else. James would have to learn who was really in charge of his life.

14

'Are you there, Ethan?' Rosie whispered quietly as she climbed the ladder up to Ethan's sleeping quarters above the stable. The smell of newly harvested hay filled her nostrils. It was a reminder that summer was nearly over and that soon it would be autumn. She heard Ethan move as she peered into the darkness and rubbed her eyes to adjust to the light of the hay-loft.

'Aye, I'm here. What are you doing, creeping up here at this time of night? I thought I told you to keep away until the two Paddies had gone home.' Ethan turned on his side and looked towards where Rosie's voice came from.

'I had to come and see you. It couldn't wait any longer,' she whispered as she hoisted herself up on the wooden floorboards and made out the form of Ethan, who reached his hand out to light the stub of a candle in its candlestick.

'What couldn't wait?' Even by the light of the candle, Ethan looked concerned and his voice whispered shakily.

'I . . . I'm worried Ethan. I think I might be having

your baby.' Rosie felt her eyes filling with tears and she started to sob. She'd practised saying the words over and over again in her head as she tossed and turned in her bed, wondering what to do and how to tell Ethan of her predicament.

'Stop it! Stop blubbing and keep your voice down. Else those Irishmen will hear and tell your father, and you don't want him to know. Besides, you can't be – we've only done it once and I was careful. That is, unless you've been with someone else.' Ethan looked at Rosie in the flickering yellow candlelight and saw how upset she was. He knew she wouldn't have been with anyone else, but didn't want to admit it.

'How could you say that? I'd never lift my skirts to someone else. Didn't I tell you that I loved you? But I've hardly seen anything of you these last few weeks; it's as if you have kept out of my way.' Rosie sobbed. She'd thought Ethan would tell her that he loved her and that everything would be alright. Instead he was lying there, accusing her of being unfaithful, and his dark eyes looked straight through her.

'I've been busy helping your father with the hay, and I thought it couldn't be mine. Anyway, you might be wrong. It's only a few weeks since we were down at the wash-dubs. How do you know already?'

'Do I have to say? I don't like talking about suchlike. But you should know – you are not daft. We both know what goes on.' Rosie caught her breath and trembled as she tried to control her sobs.

'Give it another week. You may be wrong. And it'll

give me time to think. We can't do owt yet. But I know one thing: we are both going to get the hidings of our lives, if you are having a baby.' Ethan ran his fingers through his hair and looked at Rosie in the candlelight. He wished he'd behaved himself that warm afternoon; he'd no intention of being cornered by the farmer's daughter, not yet. There was too much of the world to see before he did that.

'I won't be wrong. I'm never late, if you know what I mean,' mumbled Rosie as she wrung her hands, not daring to look into Ethan's face. She sobbed and wished Ethan would show more concern.

'Well, there's always a first time, and this might be it. It's no good worrying yet. Now get yourself back home, before you are missed and before those two over the yard hear you. We'll sort things out, no matter what. I'm not going anywhere and you aren't, so we will just have to take the consequences.' Ethan smiled and finally hugged Rosie.

'You do love me, though, don't you, Ethan? You will stand by me?' she said as she turned to make her way back down the ladder.

'Aye, I'm upset that you even feel you need to ask me that. You should know what my answer is to both. Now get yourself to bed and stop worrying, it'll be alright.' Ethan kissed her on the cheek and watched as she climbed down the ladder and made her way quietly out of the stable, leaving him to blow out the candle and look into the dark of the night. It was a darkness that was nearly suffocating him with the news that he was about to be a father.

'Have any of you seen Ethan? I've had to take the two Irishmen down into Settle myself, as there was no sight nor sound of him first thing this morning.' Danny threw his cap down onto his chair and stood looking at Harriet and his father.

'He'll be bloody wandering off somewhere, making the most of the day.' Archie looked up at his scowling son.

'He'd better not be – not while I'm paying him. He can just get his backside home, wherever he is,' said Danny.

'I haven't seen him at all this morning. Give Rosie a shout – she might have finished, she's upstairs making the beds.' Harriet raised her head from concentrating on kneading the bread, and wiped her hair with the back of her hand as she looked at her annoyed husband.

'If anyone knows where he is, Rosie will. They are, I think, still as thick as thieves, regardless of his father giving Ethan a hiding earlier on in the year. Although, saying that, I haven't seen him loitering about her of late. I suppose we should be thankful for that, and at least she's not with him this time.' Danny walked down the passageway and stood at the bottom of the stairs and yelled up to Rosie in the bedrooms above. 'Rosie, have you seen Ethan today? He's not about, and he was supposed to do a job for me this morning.'

Rosie stopped shaking the bolster into its slip as she

heard her father shouting at her. Her stomach churned as she heard him say that Ethan was missing. Ethan might wander, but only after he had finished his jobs, and he would never have missed doing something that was expected of him. She knew instantly something was wrong. She breathed in deeply; she didn't want her father to see the worry on her face as she walked to the top of the stairs.

'No, I've not seen him, Father. I've been helping Mother all morning.' She leaned over the banister and looked at the anger on her father's face.

'That bloody lad, he's more bother than he's worth,' Danny muttered as he made his way back into the kitchen.

Rosie's legs shook as she made her way back to her parents' bedroom and the task in hand. She felt sick as she sat on the edge of the bed and looked out of the window at the world outside. Where was Ethan? Was it just a coincidence that he was not to be found this morning, after she had spoken to him the previous day, or had he left knowing that she was carrying his child? He was leaving her, just like his grandfather had left his grandmother all those years ago. She didn't know what to do, as she sat and shed a tear, thinking of the plight she might be in. Her father would surely not take kindly to the fact that she was pregnant, let alone that it was with the farm boy and that he had abandoned her, alone with her guilt. And then she thought of her mother's plans being spoilt by her stupidity. Harriet had never stopped talking about reviving her seamstress skills, back in Atkinson's fold, since Isabelle had visited; and Rosie had seen her mother filled with new life as she counted the days until she re-joined the family firm.

She sighed; her minute of weakness on the grassy bank that sultry evening was going to be her undoing. If Ethan had left her, she would have to face the consequences on her own, but until she was sure, she would say nothing to anybody. She breathed in deeply and controlled her sobs; her mother must not find her like this. She'd check Ethan's home above the stable and then decide what to do. However, if he had gone, she'd keep her predicament to herself for as long as possible, for it would be for the best.

'The ungrateful sod!' Danny swore at the supper table and banged his cutlery down. 'Buggering off without a "by your leave". By, I should have listened to Isabelle.' He scowled across at his father. 'It was you who brought Ethan here, and now he's buggered off to God knows where. I'll go down to Windfell tomorrow and see if he's trailed himself home.'

'He'll happen turn up. You know what he's like.' Archie seemed unperturbed by Ethan's absence and carried on eating his supper.

'Nay, he'll not; he's taken all his belongings with him, even the old straw mattress, and it is as if he was never with us. Are you sure he said nothing to you, our Rosie? You are looking a bit sheepish. You two have always been close.' Danny shot a questioning glance at his rather quiet daughter, who looked white and upset.

'No, he said nothing to me. I'm as shocked as you

are.' Rosie held back the tears as her father questioned her.

'At least we've got hay-time over and done with. Plus, he couldn't have slept above the stable this winter. I'd have had to find room for him here, or where the Irishmen have slept in the storeroom. I didn't fancy having him sleeping under our roof. He's such a wild one.' Harriet rose from the table and looked at Rosie. 'You'll miss him no doubt – you look upset. He's best gone, for perhaps you were both getting too close.' She looked at her crestfallen daughter and then smiled. 'I'll have to make you a dress for the dances this coming winter, once I'm back at work. One to attract some lad from out of the village, seeing as you will be seventeen soon.'

'Aye, one with brass. Not a black-haired gyppo, like Ethan. Make your father proud.' Danny grinned at his daughter, teasing her.

'I'm sorry, I have remembered that I need to feed Jip. I forgot earlier on.' Rosie got up from the table; she had to hold back the tears until she got outside, for nobody must know her plight. She pushed her chair back and made her way quickly to the door.

'Look what you've done now! Can't you see she's brokenhearted over Ethan not saying goodbye to her?' Harriet shook her head over Danny's lack of empathy.

'It's good riddance to bad rubbish.' Danny said. 'He's best gone, if she was that fond of him.'

'He'll not be far. He'll land back when he's ready.' Archie moved next to the fire. 'He's making the most of the last days of summer, if you ask me. And, as you say, he'd have said his farewells to Rosie, if nobody else, and you can tell she knew nowt.'

'Aye, well, we will see. If he does turn up, I may not want him back, the trailing little bugger.' Danny wished his father had never brought Ethan to Crummock in the first place.

Rosie sat up high on the hillock called the Knot and looked down on the farmhouse. Swallows and house martins were diving and swooping, catching the last flies and midges of the summer's evening as the sun began to sink lower and lower in the sky. They too were going to take flight to warmer shores for the onset of winter. She hugged her knees close to her and rocked to console herself. Please let Ethan return, she thought to herself. Don't let him be the gypsy that everyone has branded him to be. She loved him and thought he loved her. At least it had felt like that. How could she have been so wrong? Her heart would always be his, of that she was sure. As for their secret, well, that was what it would be kept as, for the next few months at least, until his return.

15

Danny rode up the path to Windfell, straight to the stables, and dismounted at once when he saw Jethro came out to meet him.

'Mister Danny, it's good to see you.' Jethro took the horse's reins and patted its neck. 'Mistress Isabelle is at Skipton, if you were looking for her, but Mister James is at home.'

'It's you I've come to see really, Jethro.' Danny looked at the well-built man and searched his face for any inkling that he knew why he was here. 'It's Ethan; he's left us, and I wondered if perhaps he'd come home.'

'Nay, he's not here, we hardly see him nowadays. He breaks my Mazy's heart many a day, never showing his face. He used to come regular, but he seems to be a law unto himself since he went to live at Crummock. I'll make sure I send him straight back to you, if I see anything of him. He's got wandering feet, has our Ethan, never knows when he's well off. The silly bugger.' Jethro sighed and looked at Danny. 'He's not done owt he shouldn't, has he?'

'Not that I know of, Jethro. But he has taken everything with him and it looks like he's left for good.' Danny looked as the old man's face as it clouded over with worry.

'I'll have to tell our Mazy. She'll be sick with anxiety. It's a good job he's our only one, because he hasn't half given us some trouble over the years. I'm sorry that he's not been decent enough to hand his notice in, and that he's caused you this bother, Mister Danny.' Jethro pulled on the horse's reins as it raised its head, impatient to be off again or stabled with something to eat.

'Well, I just hope he turns up. If he were my son, I'd be worried. Even though Ethan is big enough to look after himself, I'm sure you'd still like to know where he is.' Danny patted the stableman's back and looked at the worry on his face. 'Can you stable my horse for an hour, Jethro? I'll just have a catch-up with James, keep him company for a while.'

'That I can, sir. Mister James will be glad of the company. I think his days are long, since the accident.' Jethro led the horse to the stables. He hadn't wanted to show how much the news of Ethan's disappearance had upset him. But deep down he knew that his son would not have left the safety of a good job for no reason, so something had gone wrong.

'Danny, it's good to see you. You've dared to visit the black sheep of the family then? I thought everyone had 'washed their hands of me.' James patted his brother-in-law on the back while trying to balance on his crutches.

'Aye, well, I can't say I'm suited with your escapade, but I've only heard part of the story, no doubt. It's up to you to tell me the rest, if you want to.' Danny made himself comfortable in the morning room of Windfell and looked out at the immaculate lawns, remembering the days when he strolled around them with Harriet on his arm.

'I don't know what to say, Danny. I've been a fool, and my head was turned by Madge's beauty and attention. And now look where it has got us: her six foot under, and my marriage in tatters. I'm only telling you this because at this moment I need a friend, and a fellow man to talk to. Isabelle is making my life hell, which she has every right to do. Even though I tell her we were just good friends, she has guessed the truth about Madge and me.' James sat down cautiously in a chair next to his brother-in-law and put his head in his hands.

'Well, mate, you've only yourself to blame – what else can I say?' Danny felt for his distraught brother-in-law; he'd guessed that Isabelle would be making James's life hell. He knew she could never live with infidelity in her marriage. 'Our Isabelle has a hell of a tongue on her, and I'm glad I'm not in your shoes. But look on the bright side: at least she hasn't thrown you out.'

'Don't think she hasn't threatened it. But she couldn't live with the scandal, of that I'm sure. The servants are very cold towards me, and as for our Jane, she either goes to work with her mother or hides in her room reading her precious *Votes for Women* newspaper, which is filling her head with nonsense. Thank God Luke is at school at Giggleswick. Even if I do worry about him, now that he's joined the OTC. He'd be first in line if ever there was a war. But I'm wasting my time with my opinions at the moment.'

'You are in a bad way, my old mate. But like I said, you do only have yourself to blame. Although I'd be a hypocrite if I didn't say most of us have been swayed by a bonny face from time to time. It's just that we don't get caught.' Danny sat back in his chair and looked sympathetically at his usually laid-back brother-in-law.

'Why do you say that? You've never been unfaithful to Harriet. I know you've had your ups and downs, but you always seem to love one another, regardless of how tough it gets.' James peered at Danny, interested that he was confessing to having an eye for a good-looking woman.

'No, I've never been tempted since I was wed, but I nearly didn't get married because of a lass who was very similar to your Madge. She took my eye and my heart, if truth be told. She was everything that Harriet wasn't. There was no talk of marriage and family; she just lived for the day.' Danny sat back in his chair and recollected the time he had spent with Amy Brown.

'That's different – you weren't married. You can't be blamed. Did Harriet ever suspect?' James looked at Danny and saw the wistful look come over him of a man once in love.

'I don't think so. But occasionally she says that I should never have married her, that she doesn't make me happy. She was worst just after after our two boys died, because she blamed herself – and the world – for the loss of them.' Danny hesitated. 'She's come round a lot lately, and I think she will improve even more when she goes back to working with Isabelle. They can plan our downfall together, it will be like old times.' Danny laughed.

'Aye, she's back with Isabelle next week, isn't she? I heard Isabelle arranging a nanny for Georgina, I think. Will Harriet be alright with that?' James leaned forward and looked hard at Danny.

'She seems to be taking it in her stride. Isabelle sent details of some girls who had responded to her advert, and Harriet chose from them. As it is, there was a young woman from down in Austwick that she knew and trusted who had applied, so she was happy with her. We will have to see how she does next Tuesday, and how our Rosie copes with a few more tasks to do around the house. She's got a long face on her at the moment and I don't know why. Perhaps she's not going to have the time she used to have to wander and be with me. And I think Ethan disappearing hasn't helped.'

'Ethan's gone? Jethro hasn't said anything.' James leaned forward, trying to make his broken leg comfortable.

'Aye, packed up and gone. God knows why. His father swears he knows nothing about it. At least we'd finished hay-time. I could have done with Ethan's help for another month, just until I'd sorted out the lambs for sale. Rosie will have to help me with them next week. It'll take her mind off housework, because my father's not up to much these days, and my other farm man is beginning to show his age.'

'Well, I've not seen hide nor hair of the lad around here, and Mazy hasn't mentioned him. I'll let you know if he shows up.' James yawned.

'I'd be grateful for that. Now, I'll be away. And you behave yourself! Don't get yourself any more fancy contraptions and even faster women. Look what they've done to you. I'd have thought our Isabelle was more than you could handle anyway, you silly fool.' Danny looked at James, who was a broken man: responsible for the death of his lover and probably broken-hearted, if he did but tell the truth. Still, it could be worse, for they both could have died.

'Don't worry. I've learned my lesson and I won't be able to forget it, not in this house. It's good to see you. I'm thankful for your company, I've been feeling like a leper of late.' James closed his eyes. He'd not been sleeping. Instead he'd been remembering the broken body of Madge, as the night and the darkness fell around him.

'Take care; things will get better with time.' Danny closed the door to the morning room and let himself out of Windfell. His thoughts returned to his fling with the lovely Amy. He couldn't blame poor James, for sometimes the temptation was just too much. At least James wasn't the father to a child he had never seen; a child Danny was sure would come back and haunt him eventually.

16

'Now, can you think of anything that I've not told you?' Harriet looked at her new employee and at baby Georgina, who had taken instantly to her new carer.

'No, Mrs Atkinson, I think you've covered everything. Besides, as you say, I'm sure Rosie will help me out if I can't find anything.' Mary Harrison smiled. She had been shown around Crummock and told the needs of the two youngest Atkinson children more times than she'd had hot dinners. But she understood their mother's concerns and would have felt the same, if they were her own children.

'The main thing is that Georgina does not get out of her routine, otherwise she becomes so bad-tempered that she doesn't know what to do with herself. And don't let Ben twist you around his little finger. His bedtime is seven, although I hope to be back by then. He's usually home about four o'clock after school; he walks up home with the lad from Sowermire, so he only has the last half-mile to walk home on his own. If he's any later than that you'd better go and look for him, as he's known for dawdling.' Harriet looked around her. She was looking forward to her new life starting in the morning, but at the same time she was dreading leaving her family behind. 'Otherwise, I think you know where everything is. Rosie will see to the meals and cleaning. Not that she wants to, for she's a love of the outside more than home-making, and she's with her father now. She'd much rather be handling sheep than dusting and polishing.' Harriet sighed.

'I'll help her, Mrs Atkinson, don't worry. I can turn my hand to most things – us country lasses have to.' Mary smiled; she was being generously paid by the well-to-do Fox family and knew when she was on to a good thing, despite the recent scandal and the awful death linked to James Fox. 'And I'll make sure Mr Atkinson senior is looked after, although he seems to be quite sprightly for his age.'

'Mr Atkinson will look after himself. As long as he's fed, he'll potter around the house and farm. He's learning to take it easy after all these years, giving my husband guidance on occasion. Although sometimes my husband does not appreciate his advice or help, as he is a bit set in his ways. He forgets that it is now 1913, and things have progressed from when he was a lad. Well, I think that is it. I look forward to seeing you in the morning. The breakfast table will be laid. You can eat with my family or on your own, whichever you prefer. Rosie knows what everyone has to eat, so don't worry about that.'

Harriet held her arms out for Georgina, who was playing with Mary's pendant around her neck. Georgina complained about being removed from her new play-thing as her mother prised her away.

'You can play with it again tomorrow.' Mary smiled at Georgina. 'Now, you behave for your mother.' She passed the crying Georgina to Harriet and then pacified her by reaching for a spoon from the table to play with. 'You are easy to suit.' She smiled as Georgina waved the spoon in the air and then grinned as Mary kissed her on the cheek to say farewell. 'Don't worry, Mrs Atkinson. Georgina and Ben will be well looked after, and I'll see that Rosie gets my support too.' She picked up her gloves and put them on, before being shown the door.

Harriet walked back into the kitchen and put Georgina down on the pegged rug. She watched as the baby pulled herself up to her full height and ventured on wobbly steps over to the doorway. 'I only hope I'm doing the right thing,' she whispered to herself. 'I do love my children, but I need my own time, or is that terribly self-ish of me? Besides, Isabelle needs me, especially after James and his public fling.' Time would tell, no doubt, she thought as she set about her work.

'Rosie, hold this gate open for me, to let this old ewe through. She can't be sent to market, she won't make the drive down the valley.' Danny yelled at his daughter as he walked amongst his flock, sorting out which sheep he needed to sell before winter and which ones he wanted to keep.

'That's what you want to be selling.' Archie lifted his

stick and pointed at the old grey-faced ewe as she bleated her way out onto the open fellside.

'She's on her last legs, Father. It's better that she dies where she knows, rather than being slaughtered at the knacker's yard, because that's all she's worth.' Danny pulled another of his flock to one side and felt how fit it was, as he replied to his father.

'It would save you digging a hole for her in another week or two and you'd get a bit of something for her. Those down in t'mill towns of Lancashire don't know she's not fit to eat. Because that's where she'd end up, on their dinner tables.' Archie shook his head. His lad was too soft, he'd never make a millionaire.

'Grandfather, I really do not like to eat lamb and mutton, as it is, without you reminding me where a lot of these are going. I'm helping to send them to their deaths.' Rosie quickly shut the fell gate, letting another sheep get a reprieve from the butcher's knife.

'That's what farming's about, lass. I don't see you complaining on a Sunday lunchtime when you are tucking into your mother's best roast beef. That's just the same. We butchered that beef, and you saw that calf growing up, but you were still licking your lips after your meal.' Archie grinned.

'No, but it's different with sheep. Some of these I've fed with a bottle of milk when they were first born. Like that big tup lamb over there, with the black-striped face and horns, just coming through. I couldn't eat him,' shouted Rosie to her grandfather over the bleating.

'Well, I can tell you now, he's one to go,' Danny

shouted. 'He's become a bloody nuisance; you've fed him so well he expects something from you every time you go near him. He's getting to be dangerous now because he's such a size. Plus, he nearly stabbed me the other day with them horns, tore a bit out of my trousers with his bullying tactics.' Danny looked at his daughter. He hadn't wanted to tell her, but there was no other way – the tup lamb was beginning to make a pest of himself and was one that had to go to market.

'No, you can't sell my Billy, I won't let you.' Rosie climbed the fence of the enclosure and made her way through the rest of the sheep to her favourite lamb of the last spring. 'Look at him, Father, he's such a grand, big ram. He'll breed well next year, you've got to keep him.' She folded her arms round the ram's neck and hugged him, burying her face in his fleece, smelling the lanolin in his coat.

'He's a bloody nuisance; he's off to market, so leave him be, and you mind what you are doing.' Danny looked at Archie as he sorted another sheep from being sold, and his father opened the gate to give it its freedom.

Rosie clung to the tup's neck, but he wasn't having any of it. If there were no tasty sheep nuts or a mouthful of hay, he didn't want to know. He lifted his head in defiance of her grip. He was too strong for Rosie to control. Then he turned round and butted her in the stomach, before stamping his foot in defiance, as he looked at her with contempt.

Rosie fell over amongst the sheep and her skirts became covered with sheep droppings. She was near to tears. Her ribs and stomach hurt as she swore at her favoured lamb.

'I told you – he's turned into a right bastard. Are you alright?' Danny looked at his daughter as she sat up. 'Another month and he'll be even more of a nuisance. He's come and butted me a time or two, it's time he was off.'

'Aye, let him go, lass, he'll fetch a good price at market. As you say, he's a good one for breeding from; he'll not go for meat.' Archie looked across at Danny and gave Rosie his hand as she climbed back over the fence to regain her place opening the gate. 'Tha's a bit fragrant. You'd better find time to fill the tin bath before supper, or your mother will have something to say.'

Rosie looked down at her long dress. It was stained with sheep droppings and urine, from where she had fallen on the cobbles of the pen. 'Bloody ungrateful thing. And he's hurt my ribs.'

'Now then, lass, no need to swear. Its nobbut a bit of muck, it'll wash off. I think it's your pride that's been hurt, more than yourself. You looked to climb that fence alright.' Archie grinned. 'Go and get washed, I can manage the ones we have left.'

'No, I'll stay. This is my job and I'm not letting him get the better of me.' Rosie leaned over the gate and looked at the wild-eyed tup lamb that had been so ungrateful for her affections. 'I don't care if he is butchered now, the stupid animal.'

Rosie stepped into the warmth of the water in the tin bath, which she had filled from the nearby boiler. The waters were soothing. Her ribs and stomach ached with a dull, nagging pain where the tup had butted her, and she lay back in the quietness of the scullery. Her mother had scowled at her and told her to get changed and washed while she put Georgina to bed. Rosie washed herself with the flannel. She knew that the rest of the house was awaiting the stew that had been cooking in the oven next to the fire that afternoon, so she couldn't be long. Mutton stew, it was all they ever seemed to eat, along with home cured bacon and rabbits that were caught on the land. But that was part of being self-sufficient and Rosie knew that, even though she had protested about the marketing of her favourite spring lamb.

She leaned back in the bath and sighed. She felt tired and sickly of a morning. She rubbed her hands over her stomach and thought about the baby she was nearly certain she was carrying, and the fact that Ethan had deserted her in her hour of need. How could he? She was on her own and frightened, trying hard to block out any thoughts about having to tell both her parents the news that she thought she was with child by Ethan. A tear trickled down her cheek and she breathed in deeply, trying to control herself. She knew all too well that her mother could walk into the scullery at any moment and she would have to explain her misery. She quickly washed herself down with the carbolic soap and then pulled herself out of the bath, realizing just how hard she had fallen when the tup had butted her. She ached all over and winced as she dried herself, pulling on her garments, before emptying the water down the main drain of the scullery and hanging the tin bath back on the wall and then rejoining her family in the kitchen.

'You smell a bit fresher, but you look a bit pale. Are you alright, lass?' Her grandfather reached out for Rosie's hand as she walked past him. 'That tup didn't half give you a belt. It's best that he's off – you've spoilt him too much.'

'I'm fine, Grandfather. Just a bit bruised, but I feel better for a hot bath.' Rosie looked at the half-laid table and decided to help her mother out by finishing the job and getting the bread from the pantry. She didn't like the attention her grandfather was giving her, so she deliberately made herself busy.

'You'll have to get used to this, after this evening; it'll be your job three nights a week. That'll put an end to your trailing.' Danny looked at his daughter, who had been quiet of late, and he suspected that she was sulking about her mother's new role in life.

'I'm looking forward to it. Mother has shown me all that I should be doing, and I know what food I've to make you all for the next few meals. It isn't as if I've never turned my hand to being in the kitchen before. I just prefer to be outside.' Rosie smiled at her father as she went to stir the stew. A pain in the bottom of her stomach made her stop for a minute, and she caught her breath in front of her grandfather. He looked concerned.

'Are you alright, lass?' Archie put his hand on her arm.

'Yes, yes, I'm fine. It's just my ribs, where Billy butted me. They are sore.' Rosie was lying. She knew something was amiss, and it was not just the bruising from her tussle with the tup lamb. 'Can you tell Mama that I'm going to take my supper up to bed with me – it's been a long day and the fall has shaken me up slightly?' Rosie ladled a portion of stew into a bowl and picked up a slice of bread and a spoon from the table.

'Your mother would like you to stay with us tonight, for she's feeling guilty about leaving us all, as it is.' Danny looked up at his daughter, who was acting a little out of character.

'I'm sorry. I'll see her in the morning before she goes, but now I'm going to have to go to my bed. My ribs hurt.' Rosie quickly made for the bottom of the stairs, hoping that she did not meet her mother on the way down from putting Georgina to bed, as the pain in her stomach worsened.

'She doesn't look well, Danny.' Archie looked across at his son, who was looking out of the window, watching Ben teasing the dog.

'She's alright. She never complained when she was helping us finish with the last of the sheep. She's sulking, Father; she doesn't want to take responsibility for the home. Don't let her pull the wool over your eyes. Remember her play-acting when her and Ethan buggered off to Appleby Fair. Well, she's doing it again.' Danny sat back and breathed in deeply. 'There's nowt up with her, she's just got to realize that she's got to grow up – and grow up quickly.'

'Well, I hope you are right, lad.' Archie looked into the fire. It wasn't his place to say any more, but he was worried about Rosie.

*

Rosie lay in her bed. She'd been feeling under the weather before the tup lamb had butted her, but now she was worse, much worse. She'd managed to eat her supper by sharing it with the farmhouse cat, and had put on a brave face when her mother had come to check on her, withholding just how ill she was, but now all she wanted to do was cry. The pain had been so intense and she could feel that the bedclothes beneath her were soiled with blood. If there had been a baby, there wasn't now; it was dead, and her nightdress and bedding were stained with its remains.

She hugged her pillow to her and didn't dare look underneath the sheet at the extent of the blood she had lost, and whether there was anything that resembled a baby. She daren't tell anyone, although she longed to confide in her mother. She wished her mother could be there to comfort her in her arms. Instead, in the morning before anyone else awoke, she'd put her sheets and nightclothes in the boiler to wash and would hope that nobody suspected her plight. At least then neither she nor Ethan would be chastised, and nobody would know any different or suspect that she had been with child. It was the best thing she could do, and perhaps her accident had been a blessing.

She looked up at the ceiling and sobbed. She no longer had a baby to worry about, but there was still no sign of Ethan. He had shown his true colours and she was without anyone. How stupid she had been to fall in love with the stable boy, a gypsy. Her love for him must never be known by anyone and now, with the baby gone, it would be her secret.

17

'What are you doing?' It was only just breaking light when Harriet opened the scullery door to find Rosie swilling her bed linen in the brown earthenware sink and stoking up the boiler.

'Mother, I didn't hear you!' Rosie blushed and looked across at her mother; she'd hoped to get the sheets swilled and into the boiler to soak in the mixture of water and soda crystals before her mother had arisen. 'I didn't want Mary to see my accident. I wanted to wash my sheets before she arrived. I feel so ashamed that I have marked my sheets with my monthly.' Rosie bowed her head and bit her lip. She could have cried quite openly as she looked at her mother.

'Oh, Rosie, is that why you were feeling so ill last night? I lay awake and worried about you into the early hours, but now I know it was that, I feel better. It's a woman's curse, for sure, and something that we have all to bear. Mary would have understood; and besides, there is no reason for her to come into your room. You need not have rushed to wash them. Are you feeling better this morning?' Harriet put her arm around Rosie and kissed her on the brow.

Rosie held her tightly. She wanted to confess all, but didn't say a word about her ordeal. She put her head on her mother's shoulder and smelled the perfume that Harriet wore, the perfume she only wore on special occasions. Today it had been put on for her first day back at Atkinson's. 'I love you, Mother.' She held back a tear.

'Hey, what's all this about? I'll be back later this evening – all is sorted for you. There's a pie in the pantry for you to put in the oven; you only need to peel the potatoes, and all the cleaning has been done. I bottomed everything last week and Mary, I'm sure, will fit in fine. She'll look after Georgina and Ben, once he's back from school.' Harriet held her daughter tightly. If Isabelle hadn't been in such a fix, she wouldn't even be thinking of going back to work at Atkinson's. But now that the chance had occurred, she had to admit she was looking forward to it. She hadn't banked on Rosie being this upset; it was Rosie who had acted strangely, from the moment she had agreed to step into Madge's shoes, albeit just temporarily.

'I know, Mother. I can manage all that. I'll just miss you.' Rosie stood back and wiped her tears. 'You've never been away from home before for so long.'

'It's not forever, my love. And you've got Grandfather and your father at home. Just let me help your Aunty Isabelle for a while; she needs her family at the moment, what with your Uncle James having no more sense than that scrubbing brush of yours.' Harriet looked across at the white sheets in the sink and the red smears that were still on them. 'Finish doing your washing and then come in and have a cup of tea with me, before Jethro picks me up and Mary shows her face. Just you and me, like we used to be. I used to nurse you for hours in front of the kitchen fire, unable to believe that I'd been given such a beautiful baby girl, after the death of my two sons. I didn't think I deserved you. You are more precious to me than life itself and, if you don't want me to go today, then I will tell Jethro to return without me.' Harriet held Rosie tightly.

'No, Mother, go. I know it will be good for you, and we will all manage.' Rosie stood back and wiped her eyes. 'I bet Ben won't argue with Mary; he wouldn't dare. And Georgina already loves her – anyone can see that. We will be fine.'

'I know you will, or at least I hope so. I'm finding it hard to leave you all, as it takes lot to entrust my family to another person's care. Now, let me get that kettle on and let me stir your father. Mary won't want to see him in his nightshirt, like he sometimes wanders down in. I don't know who would be more shocked: your father or her!' Harriet sighed as she left Rosie to her washing. Her little girl was growing up into a fine woman, although she was learning the hard way, as all young women did.

'Back full circle, Mistress Harriet.' Jethro pulled up the gig just outside the gates of Settle railway station and helped Harriet alight.

'Indeed, Jethro. I didn't think I'd be doing this ever

185

again. Strange how life works out. I just wish it was in better circumstances and that Madge was still alive to be doing her job, despite the rumours.' Harriet looked at the man who was part of the backbone of the workings of Windfell and wondered just how much gossip had reached his ears.

'Aye, well, I never listen to gossip – no good ever comes of it. I know that, because there's been plenty spread over the years about my family.' Jethro held his horse's bridle and looked concerned.

'Speaking of family, have you heard anything of your son, Ethan? I still don't know why he left us. He'd not been reprimanded or done anything wrong, to my knowledge.' Harriet knew that Jethro must be worried, as indeed she was. After all, Ethan was only a few months older than Rosie, and she would have been worried sick if Rosie had upped and left without a 'by your leave'.

'No, not heard a thing. He'll turn up, though; he never could be nailed down, always liked to trail somewhere. Mind you, Mazy is worried. I keep telling her he'll be back in his own time. I'm just sorry that he's caused you some worries up at Crummock. He should have been grateful that Master Archie gave him that job in the first place.'

'Don't you worry, Jethro. And keep me informed if Ethan does return home. I must go now. The train's due, and I can see steam rising down the track.' Harriet picked up her skirts and her bag and made her way to the platform's edge to join the other passengers who were awaiting the seven-thirty to Leeds. She looked around her.

They were mainly business people, mostly men dressed in their suits, waiting anxiously for the train to draw onto the platform and take them to their positions of importance. Women – especially those of her age and station – were expected to stay at home and take care of their families, leaving the man to be the breadwinner. Harriet felt very self-conscious while she waited her turn to board the train as it pulled into the station.

Once seated in a carriage with her fellow passengers, she looked out of the window and waited for the station-master and porter to clear the platform and blow the whistle. She watched as the steam from the engine blew down next to her window and wisps of white fluff drifted into the early-morning sky. She looked around her. A man in a bowler hat sat across from her, engrossed in his morning's newspaper, while an older gentleman sat with his briefcase on his knee, guarding it with his life.

Harriet rearranged her long grey skirt and breathed in deeply. Closing her eyes, she thought back to her home. Hopefully Mary would nearly have finished getting Ben ready for school, and Georgina would be sitting up at the table in her highchair, eating her chopped-up egg with a toasted bread soldier, if she had not thrown it onto the floor by now. It was a game that she liked to play and one that tested her mother's patience. Harriet knew Rosie would be coping, but she had looked pale this morning; the poor girl was still getting used to her more adult body. Would they all manage without her? What if Georgina took ill? Perhaps she should get off the train and put an end to the stupid idea of helping out at Atkinson's again.

It was too late. The whistle blew and the train jolted into action. The wheels turned slowly at first, and then picked up speed as the carriages swayed backwards and forwards over the tracks, chattering as they went over the points. She was on her way to join Isabelle, for her first day back in work for nearly nineteen years. She only hoped she had not lost her touch, and that Isabelle would hold her tongue if she made any mistakes. That day would tell, and she need not return in the morning if things went badly. But most of all Harriet hoped that her children would not miss her too much and that they would be safe until her return.

'Harriet, I'm so glad you didn't change your mind. I know it must be strange to have to leave your children behind and, honestly, I can't find the words to say how grateful I am.' Isabelle rushed over to Harriet's side as she opened the door and made her way into the cutting and sample room in Atkinson's. She kissed her lovingly on the cheek and held out her hand for Harriet to join her in a morning coffee before they both started work. 'Please do sit down, I had Nancy make enough for us both. Have you eaten? I can always order you some breakfast. Cook is already preparing for our luncheon rush in the restaurant. He wouldn't mind.' Isabelle smiled as Harriet took off her coat and sat down beside her.

'No, I'm fine, thank you, just a little nervous and worried about leaving my family.' Harriet fidgeted in her chair as Isabelle poured her a coffee from the silver pot that had just been delivered to her. Strict instructions had been given to all staff to make Harriet feel most welcome.

'They'll be fine, I'm sure. You made a good choice with Mary, she seemed very sensible and reliable. And of course Rosie is growing up so fast now. I keep forgetting that she's nearly seventeen. She and Jane are so dissimilar, don't you think?' Isabelle sat back and sipped her coffee, watching Harriet worrying.

'Yes, you are quite right. Jane and Rosie have nothing in common, both of them are quite different.' Harriet looked nervous and suddenly came out with what she was thinking. 'I don't know if I should be here. What if somebody takes ill? What if Ben doesn't return from school?' She was beginning to fret.

'Look, it's not like when we were first starting out. We are not under as much pressure as we were the last time you worked here. Atkinson's has grown beyond all recognition. Plus the transport is better, you'd get home quicker; and Archie will keep an eye on everybody for you. God, I never thought I'd say this, but it's a good job we have him. He's a blessing in disguise and he loves his grandchildren – he'll look after everyone. Now let me show you the workbook. It will take your mind off home and get you into the swing of things. The first fittings are in an hour. Mrs Tattersall is wanting a blouse-coat making in crêpe de Chine. She's going to watch her son rowing on the river at Cambridge, and someone has told her that is what all the fashionable ladies are wearing over their hobble skirts.'

Isabelle looked at Harriet. 'It's just a simple, long

open coat, Harriet. I've got a pattern out for you to look at, and the rolls of crêpe de Chine are over there. Try and persuade her to go for a natural colour. She's a tendency to choose such garish colours, and it doesn't look good on a woman her age – she should know better.'

'I think I know Mrs Tattersall. Her family farms down near Gisburn, they have horses.' Harriet looked up from her cup.

'Yes, that's her. The youngest son won a scholarship to Cambridge, and she's so proud of him. That's why we have to make her feel, and look, special. Remember that feeling you used to get, when we knew the women in front of us could not be dressed any finer, not even if they had gone to the finest dress shops in Paris?' Isabelle smiled at her sister-in-law.

'Yes, I remember. I enjoyed those days, we worked well together.' Harriet stopped sipping her coffee. 'I've missed them, really.'

'I know, and it was all my fault that you didn't return after that terrible day. But Atkinson's was everything to me then, and I didn't know or realize the deep uncon-ditional love between a mother and her child. I should have listened to you when you said the boys were ill, and sent you back home, regardless of the amount of work we had.' Isabelle put her arms around her sister-in-law.

'You weren't to know what was going to happen. Even I didn't realize they were so ill. Let's not talk about it again – it's in the past. Now, show me the pattern books. What colour do you suggest for Mrs Tattersall? She's got auburn hair. Perhaps a green, quite plain, but well cut, to show her still-decent figure?' Harriet breathed in; she had to move on, for things had changed. Her mother-in-law was no longer in charge, and she and Isabelle had to bury past differences. Today was a fresh start for both of them.

18

Jane sat in her chair, looking out at the rain coming down outside her bedroom window. If the evening had been fine, she would have gone for a short stroll, to get away from the atmosphere that had filled the house since her father's more-than-public accident. But as it was, she had nowhere to hide from the poisonous talk of her parents. They tried to act as if everything was alright, never exchanging words while she was around them, but she knew differently. Her father was now sleeping in the spare room and her mother was acting strangely, as if nothing was wrong, and yet everything was wrong. Raised voices could frequently be heard, especially after her father had reached for his glass of port of an evening. She longed to yell at them, 'I'm no longer a child', but daren't. To make matters worse, the staff at Atkinson's tittered and laughed behind her back and she'd come close to losing her temper, when overhearing their comments on several occasions.

And the staff at Windfell didn't seem to be as jovial as usual and hardly bothered with her. They didn't know exactly what to say to her. It was if she had no feelings, and nobody cared. She couldn't even discuss it with Luke, as now that the new term had started he was back boarding at Giggleswick School, conveniently out of the way, but looked after while her mother and father went about their business. The only refuge was her room, and there Jane lost herself in a good book or reading the latest suffragette news in her *Votes for Women*, which was delivered weekly to Windfell. Her mother abhorred her reading it, and hated even more the friendships that she had built through it, especially with the bobbin girls at Dewhurst's. Isabelle especially abhorred Nellie Taylor, whom she thought to be common and mouthy, and she often reprimanded Jane for becoming friends with a mill girl. But Nellie was different: she stood up for women's rights, often talking about demanding equal pay with the menfolk at the mills, and the need for women to have a vote and a say on how the country was run. And even Jane realized that women were not equal with men, and was not happy to accept her lot in life. After all, she was Charlotte Atkinson's granddaughter, and her grandmother had always striven to be as good as – or even better than – any businessman in the area. She always had to work that little bit harder than most men, but was unable to have a say in the local elections. Surely that wasn't right; everyone should be equal, regardless of their gender.

Jane picked up her latest edition of *Votes for Women*

and read the dedication, to remind herself of the cause she believed in:

To the brave women who today are fighting for freedom: to the noble women who all down the ages kept the flag flying and looked forward to this day without seeing it: to all women all over the world of whatever race or creed or calling, whether they be with us or against us in this fight, we dedicate this paper.

She put the paper to one side. It wasn't just her mother and father falling out that she felt upset about. It was the fact that her mother had put her Aunt Harriet in Madge's place. Why hadn't she asked Jane herself to come and learn alongside her? She knew how to sew and could follow a pattern. Instead, she was treating Harriet as if she was someone special. To make matters worse, the whole of Atkinson's was singing Harriet's praises, saying how nice it was to see the pair working back together. If Bert Bannister had said it once to Jane, he'd said it a hundred times, and she was a little tired of hearing about the glorious Harriet and her skills. Bloody Harriet! All Jane needed now was for the simple Rosie to follow her mother into work at Atkinson's, and that would never do. Rosie didn't even dress well.

Jane looked at herself in her bedroom mirror. Her long auburn hair and pale skin made her stand out from the crowd, but how she hated her hair colour; she had always been teased as a child for the redness of it. Even now, even though people commented on her good looks, she still hated it. Everything was wrong in her life, and nobody cared.

'Jane, Harriet has run out of this red-coloured Sylko. Can you go down to Dewhurst's and pick up six reels, please?' Isabelle entered the warehouse at Atkinson's and gave Jane her latest instructions, showing her a near-empty bobbin reel with a hint of the colour she needed.

'Why me, Mother? Can't one of the warehouse lads go for you? It isn't really my job, fetching and carrying.' Jane looked at her mother and pulled a sulky face. She wasn't a gofer – she would be the heiress one day of Atkinson's.

'You are to go because you were the first one I set eyes on who was doing nothing. Besides, I thought you'd appreciate the walk. But don't think I'll not be timing you. There will be no dilly-dallying with those mill girls, especially that Nellie Taylor. She's nothing but trouble. Now get gone. Tell them to put it on my account – and look lively, as Harriet is waiting for it.' Isabelle looked at her surly daughter. She knew Jane wasn't happy and realized that things were not that pleasant at home for her, but 'there were worse things happening at sea', as her mother used to say to her, when she thought she was having a bad time. She watched as Jane grabbed her shawl and made her way out of the warehouse doors.

'I don't know, Bert, she's nothing but a worry at the moment. I can't do right for doing wrong. What with her and her father, no wonder I'm showing signs of ageing.'

Isabelle sighed and looked at the old man across the warehouse table.

'Tha's nobbut a spring chicken yet, ma'am. Wait until you get to my age. It'll not be long before I'm pushing up the daisies. Or so it would be, if I didn't have this place to keep me going. Isn't it grand having Miss Harriet back with us? It's just like old times. How are you both getting on?' Bert leaned on the table and looked across at Isabelle. His body ached, but he wasn't going to let her know of his pain.

'It's lovely, Bert. I don't have to explain anything to Harriet, as she knows exactly what to do, and the customers love her. She's no problem. It's Miss Clever-clogs I'm worried about; she seems so angry about everything. What with her and her father, I'm beside myself.' Isabelle pushed a loose strand of her greying hair behind her ear.

'It'll settle down in a bit. Give it time, and folk will find something else to talk about other than your husband. As for Miss Jane, well, she hears and sees everything down here. Perhaps you could find her a job on the shop floor, or upstairs with you. I think she's feeling a bit lost and neglected.' Bert had watched the young lass becoming more and more discontented over the weeks, and knew Jane was eager to learn elsewhere in the shop.

'I'll see, Bert, but she should have the patience to learn from the bottom up. Perhaps in another week or two, once her father is back, she could help him, because he will need some assistance for a while.' Isabelle turned to go.

'She's like her grandmother, that 'un. She will never

be satisfied – a bit like yourself at the same age. But she'll enjoy being with her father. And besides, I've learned her all I can, so let her be with him.' Bert leaned over and winked. 'She'll keep an eye on him and all.'

'Thank you, Bert, I hear what you are saying.' Isabelle looked haughty as she walked out of the warehouse. Sometimes Bert did not know his place. Unfortunately, he was nearly always right in what he said.

'Six reels of this cotton, please, and book it to Atkinson's.' Jane handed the cotton bobbin over to the young lad in the warehouse of Dewhurst's and waited. The large, five-storeyed mill was made out of local stone and stood down Broughton Road, on the edge of the Leeds-to-Liverpool canal. The towering red-brick chimney dominated the Skipton skyline. The mill kept more than two hundred people in work, and prior to that had been the place of employment of more than four hundred people – all of them families that relied on King Cotton and the cotton-weaving Belle Vue Mill. But now, along with its original name being almost forgotten, and Dewhurst's making it into a mill spinning cotton silk known as Sylko, its weaving rooms were not as busy. But still the clatter of the spinning machines filled the air, along with the dust from the fibres.

'Jane! Jane, I thought it was you. I was just making my way up to the top office.' Nellie Taylor grinned at her comrade-in-arms, who also defied the non-believers in the Suffragette movement.

'Hello, Nellie. I'm just collecting some Sylko for my

mother. I wondered if you'd be about.' Jane looked at her working-class friend. They made an odd partnership, and sometimes Jane was ashamed of the way Nellie dressed, in her work clogs, grey stockings and drab dresses. But when she listened to Nellie talking, she realized there was more to her than just an ordinary mill lass. Nellie was a firebrand for the Suffragette movement.

'I can't talk long, for old Dewhurst is on my back. He says he's fed up of me whipping up the work lasses with my dangerous talk. It's only dangerous if you are an ignorant man. But then again, he is.' Nellie grinned, her face lit up with wickedness as she beamed from under her mob cap.

'Yes, and my mother's timing me, so I can't be long, either.' Jane shook her head.

'The more money they have, the tighter the bastards get! No disrespect to your mother, Jane. But you know what I mean. Here, are you joining us on our march next Saturday? We aim to walk through Skipton, demanding our rights from the government. I think there's about ten of us so far.' Nellie looked at her posh friend and waited for an answer.

'I don't know. My mother wouldn't want me to be involved. I don't know if I could get away.' Jane saw the warehouse boy coming back with her reels of cotton and was thankful for an excuse to leave. She supported the movement, but it would only give her mother more worry if she joined the protest.

'Go on, lass, we won't get into any trouble. The local bobbies know us all too well – you know what it's like

around here. You can't fart unless somebody hears you.'
Nellie laughed out loud.

'I'll see. I can't promise.' Jane took the bobbins from
the warehouse boy and started to walk away from her
friend.

'Twelve-thirty, top of the High Street next to the
churchyard. Wear your sash, you can help me carry
the banner,' shouted Nellie after her, before walking in the
opposite direction. 'I'll see you there. We need you to
help organize.'

Jane walked down the cobbled mill yard and made
her way over Belmont Bridge, stopping on the top to
look at the barges on the canal make their way underneath and unload their cargo along the quayside. She
watched as an elderly man kept lowering a bucket full of
holes down into the dirty waters of the canal. His body
was nearly bent double with age, and she watched as he
dragged the bucket along the bottom of the canal until
the weight told him it was full of what he was dredging
for: black gold, coal from the barges that had supplied
Dewhurst's powerful engines and had fallen into the
canal. She saw him sort the rubbish from the coal, throwing it back into the canal. He put the lumps of coal into
the old wooden cart that she'd seen him trundling
around Skipton with, to hawk his stolen gains to those
who'd buy it.

What a way to make a living, she thought, as she
started her walk back home. But then again, there were
many who earned a living from nothing – she knew that.
Then there were the likes of her mother's customers,

some of whom had more money than sense. Jane realized that she was privileged, but she also knew it was as a result of her grandmother's hard work. How she missed her grandmama, who'd always been there for her; she'd have sorted out the mess at home and would have been there for Jane to talk to. Instead, she had been shoved down into the warehouse and told to collect the bobbins that she now held in her hand, like a common errand girl. Her mother thought nothing of her; all she thought of was her precious business. That's why her father's head had been turned – Isabelle had no time for him, just as she hadn't for her.

Damn it, she would go on Saturday's march just to defy her mother, if nothing else.

19

'Hey up! I didn't think you were going to show.' Nellie Taylor stood with her folded banner at the top of Skipton High Street, grinning, as Jane joined the small group. 'We've not got a very good show today. There's only five of us. Nevertheless, we might be small in number, but we are determined in our beliefs. Let's show Skipton that we mean business, that women can no longer be treated like second-class human beings.' She lifted her banner and looked at all her comrades-in-arms, waiting hopefully for any more followers of the cause. 'What's up with you, Lady Jane? You look as if you are in a mood. All not well in your world?' Nellie didn't believe anything could be wrong in a world filled with the amount of money the Atkinsons and Foxes had.

'It's Mama. She tried to stop me joining you, she just doesn't understand. I hate her at the moment. All she thinks about is the business, nothing else.' Jane scowled and pulled her sash of green, cream and violet straight, as she made ready for the march down the High Street.

'It's people like your mother who are keeping the women of this town chained to their homes and husbands. She pampers to their needs as ignorant kept women – prizes for their men, dressed in their hobble skirts and smelling of perfume. They don't have time to think for themselves. That's why she's so against you being with us.' Nellie was in full voice. 'I've been thinking; we should do what Kitty Marion's done: break a few windows, make folk sit up and take note. Her and Clara Giveen even set fire to the grandstand at Hurst Park to show how strongly they feel. It's no good us feebly walking down the High Street and doing nothing. Nobody's going to give us a second glance,' Nellie yelled.

'I don't know, Nellie. Sergeant Monks is watching us, I saw him when I walked out of the store. He's got his eye on us.' Jane looked worried.

'Nah, he'll be more bothered about his pork pie from the butcher's; he just thinks we are a lot of silly girls and women. Right, come on, ladies: best foot forward. Let's show the good people of Skipton what we want.' Nellie thrust the banner to two girls behind her and linked arms with Jane, stepping out in her black lace-up boots and long full skirt, ready to take on the world.

'Votes for women. Votes for women!'

Nellie yelled as she pushed her way down the bustling High Street, ignoring the jeers from men and the disgusted looks from women of higher society. Jane was pulled along beside her.

'What do we want? We want justice, we want equality,' she yelled, and her followers took up the chant.

The small group made itself known, but it wasn't enough in Nellie's eyes. She wanted everybody's head to be turned and to acknowledge that the Suffragette movement was now amongst them. As they passed Atkinson's beautiful display windows, Nellie stopped. She noticed a loose stone among the market setts and bent down to pick it up.

'This'll make your mother take note. She'll know just how serious you are with this.' Nellie stopped and looked at Jane as she held back her arm, stone in hand ready to be flung.

'What are you doing? Stop it, you'll get us arrested,' Jane yelled, as Nellie lobbed the stone straight through the largest window of Atkinson's. The crash of glass made everyone stop in their tracks. They all stared at a mannequin as its head came off and rolled down the street. The glass shattered everywhere, and women screamed. Such a disturbance had never been seen before on Skipton High Street.

Sergeant Monks blew his whistle loud and clear, calling for backup from the station on Swadford Street. He made a beeline for Nellie and Jane.

'That bloody showed them, they'll know we mean business now, girl! Now, let's bugger off. How fast can you run?' Nellie grinned at the group behind her and took to her heels, leaving Jane wondering why she had become involved in such a fracas and having to turn and run herself, along with the other demonstrating women.

'Votes for women,' Nellie shouted once more, as she ran down to the turn-off for Broughton Road.

'Votes for women, my arse!' a constable shouted after her, knowing Nellie and where she lived. He'd soon catch up with her.

Jane was frantic. She bobbed and tried to hide in the crowd that had now gathered around the scene of Nellie's crime. She daren't go into her mother's firm, but instead watched as her mother came out of the doorway to look at the damage done. Jane quickly took off her sash, which she been wearing had so proudly, and thrust it into her pocket, out of the sight of the gossiping crowds.

'Now, Miss Fox, I think you may have been party to the crime just committed. You should be more careful who your friends are, or at least hide that auburn hair of yours, if you don't want to be caught.' Sergeant Monks put a gentle hand on her shoulder. 'Now let's do this quietly, without making a further scene. I'm sure both you and your mother would appreciate it that way. You just go to the station with Constable Stavely here, and I'll go and talk to your mother.' Sergeant Monks looked at the young lass he'd know all her life and shook his head. 'Take her away, Mike. I'll follow up shortly with her mother. She'll not give you any bother, will you, Miss Fox?'

'No, I didn't know Nellie was going to do that. I couldn't stop her. Mother will kill me for being involved.' Jane hung her head as the constable took her arm and walked her through the crowd. She watched as they muttered her name and shook their heads. 'It's the Fox lass.

Her mother will have something to say about this,' she heard one of her mother's customers exclaim.

'All I did was walk with Nellie, I didn't do anything,' Jane protested. 'You don't have to take me to the station. I'll not do it again.' She pulled on the constable's arm.

'Now, Miss, Sergeant Monks says I've to take you there, so just you be quiet and give me no bother.' Constable Stavely held her arm in a vicelike grip and walked Jane up Swadford Street and into the station.

'Got one of these mad women, Bill. Or should I say "girl". A bloody suffragette – she's just broken Atkinson's window, along with her mate. She'll soon be joining us as well.' Constable Stavely leaned over the station's desk and laughed with his fellow officer as they looked Jane up and down. 'Sarge says she'll give us no bother, for he knows the family.'

Jane was near tears. She'd never been in trouble before. She was secretly in fear of the police and, together with the thought of her mother's anger once she came to save her, felt scared stiff.

'Put her in one of the cells – that'll calm her down. Bloody stupid women!' Constable Stavely's colleague passed him the keys to one of the two cells in the station and looked Jane up and down again. 'I'll wait to see what Sarge says, before I take her details and book her.'

'Come on then, you.' Constable Stavely pulled on Jane's arm and led her to the cells at the back of the station, showing her into a small, stark room, with just a wooden bench with a cover on it acting as a bed, and a bucket for a toilet. He then left, closing the door behind him and turning the key in the lock.

Jane looked around her. She'd never been in such a place, and she couldn't even see out of the small window, it was so high above her. The key turning in the lock might have incarcerated her in her cell, but it also unlocked the flood of tears that had been welling up inside her since her capture. She sat on the edge of the hard bed and sobbed. Oh God, what would her mother say? She loved her Atkinson's store. Indeed, Jane did, just as much. She'd known how hard her grandmother had worked for the string of shops to become a success. It was her inheritance and it meant everything to her. How could Nellie Taylor have been so stupid, and how could she herself have let her be?

'You are telling me that my Jane was responsible for this!' Isabelle looked at Sergeant Monks in disbelief. 'She told me she was going to the library, and that she would have no part in the stupid protest we had argued over this morning. The stupid girl!' Isabelle watched as Bert Bannister swept the broken glass up from the High Street and made safe the window.

'Aye, well, she wasn't the ringleader and it wasn't her that threw the stone, you'll be glad to hear. But she did cause an affray, so one of my constables has taken her to the station. That will cool her down, along with the knowledge that you'll have plenty to say, no doubt.' Sergeant Monks looked at Isabelle. She didn't deserve any further scandal in her life. That was why he'd tried to whisk Jane away as quietly as he could.

'Oh, yes, Officer, I'll have plenty to say alright. I bet it was that terrible little Nellie Taylor who was the ring-leader. She drip-feeds her suffragette propaganda into our Jane's ear whenever she can. And I was stupid enough to send Jane to Dewhurst's for some cotton last week.' Isabelle could have cursed. 'Will you be pressing charges? I suppose you'll have to.'

'Aye, you are right – it was Nellie who threw the stone. As for Jane, I'll see how she's behaved, once we get back to the station. She's not as headstrong as her partner-in-crime, so I'm hoping that a few hours in the cells will give her something to think about. I could do without the paperwork, and the last thing I want is a lot of screaming women in my station. Once I've brought Nellie Taylor in, I'll more than likely have that.' Sergeant Monks looked at Isabelle. 'A strict talking-to from both of us should be sufficient. Let Jane stew until you've closed up the shop; it'll not do her any harm.'

'Thank you, Officer, I'd be grateful if that is what we could do between us.' Isabelle hesitated. 'It isn't that I don't believe in the suffragette cause. After all, my mother was a firebrand in her own right, and I believe any woman is equal to any man and should therefore have the same rights. But causing chaos and violence is not the right way to go about it. I will emphasize that most carefully to Jane when I pick her up this evening. I also think that matters at home have perhaps not encouraged her to see things in a better light. I will make it my responsibility that she doesn't give you any more trouble, Sergeant Monks.'

'Aye, things have not been good for you. Perhaps it is Jane's way of letting of a little steam, while protesting for her ideals. Don't worry, Mrs Fox, I do understand. Now, if you don't mind, I'll go and arrest the true culprit. Will you be wanting your day in court with her, ma'am?' Sergeant Monks waited as Isabelle turned to look at him in the doorway.

'I think not, Sergeant Monks. It would play right into Nellie Taylor's hands because it would be a day of hearing her own voice in a packed courtroom, telling everyone the virtues of the Suffragette movement. My mother and myself – and hopefully, one day, my headstrong daughter – have been standing up to men for generations. The world will change, and women will be equal one day, but not through violence. I will be at your station around six, Sergeant Monks. Do with Nellie Taylor what you want, but keep her away from my daughter.'

Isabelle lifted her skirts and stepped back through the revolving doors of Atkinson's. As she did so she sighed; her silly daughter; she applauded Jane's beliefs, but not to the extent of getting arrested. She would talk to her tonight and get to the bottom of what had been upsetting her of late. Although, deep down, she knew that it was because of her father's actions; their home life was not good just now, and it was time to forgive and forget and try to make life return to normal at Windfell. She and James must stop shouting at one another and think of their family, before it was too late and irrefutable damage was done.

20

'This is all your fault. She's upset and rebelling because of the shame you have brought upon the family.' Isabelle was taking her frustration with Jane out on James, as she paced backwards and forwards in the parlour of Windfell Manor.

'It's more than that. She must be missing her grandmother, and I know that she must be upset with us arguing constantly,' said James. 'I am upset about it myself. Isn't it time we put an end to it? What's done is done. I can't amend the past, and I admit that I have been a fool.' He looked at his wife. He'd found it hard to believe that his daughter had as good as been arrested for being involved in smashing her own mother's window. Yes, it was for a cause that was worthy, in Jane's eyes, but it was not like her to be so demonstrative. She'd say what she thought, yes, but she wouldn't normally have caused criminal damage.

'I was going to suggest that, once you return to work,

Jane could be your assistant, as she's not enjoying working in the warehouse. And you will need someone to help you, once you return, in the next week or two. That might give her more purpose in life, and she always has been closer to you than to me. You know what daughters are like with their fathers – in their eyes, fathers can do no wrong. Even if he is the biggest cad in the district.' Isabelle's eyes flashed at James. She would never forgive him for doing her wrong, no matter how hard he tried.

'There you go again – you cannot let it lie. But yes, I'd welcome Jane into the studio to help me. She knows the basics already, and it would save me having to train someone else. I hope to be back next week, once I regain a little more strength in my leg. It would get Jane into a position that makes her feel more important. I don't think she has appreciated having to learn the workings of the firm from the bottom up. I also think she may be a little jealous of Harriet helping you out. Perhaps Jane thought she would be given a better position in the firm, given that she is our daughter, despite not showing one bit of interest in using a needle.' James hoisted himself up and looked out of the window. 'Autumn is here, the beech leaves have turned already. It'll soon be winter and then we will have problems getting ourselves into work, let alone Harriet getting there from up at Crummock.'

'We've always managed, and if Harriet can't make her way from Crummock, then I will have to do without her. I'm going to have to find somebody anyway, I think. We have so many orders and, to be honest, at the moment Harriet is a godsend, but all she talks about is her children and the farm. It's a bit never-ending, and I switch off after a while.' Isabelle walked over to James and stood beside him.

He turned to look at her. 'I'm sorry, Isabelle, I didn't mean to cause you all this worry. I've been stupid. I love you, and our family. It was a few moments of self-indulgence that ended in disaster. A disaster that none of us will ever forget. But maybe it can make our marriage stronger, if we can overcome it.' He leaned on his walking stick and looked at Isabelle. How could he have been such a fool and have allowed his head to be turned by Madge, when the woman he truly loved had always been by his side?

'I can never forget what you have put us through, James. It will never be the same, but we must make the best of it. For all our sakes.' Isabelle's eyes filled with tears; she had missed her soulmate, the man she had always loved. But now, hopefully, he was hers once more. Perhaps some good had come out of Jane's rash actions. She only hoped so.

'That's good to see.' Jane entered the room quietly just as her father kissed her mother tenderly on the brow. 'At least you are not shouting at one another.' She walked past her parents, her eyes still red from crying, after the lecture and strong talking-to that both parents had given her, following the terrible few hours she had endured, locked up in the police cell. She'd been made to feel so unsure of herself, and as if the world was conspiring against her. She had, however, realized just how fervent her friend Nellie Taylor was in defence of the suffragettes, and had listened to Nellie shouting from the next cell, as she too was caught and detained. Poor Nellie, would she still be there?

Even though her mother had told the police to do what they wished with Nellie, Isabelle did not want to press charges. Jane knew the reason behind this was to protect herself and the family, as she would have been called as a witness, and it would be another scandal that her family was involved in. What a fool she had been to get so involved. Nellie, on the other hand, would stand her corner and probably do something more serious next time, following the call of the Pankhurst sisters and their like. That was not for her; she had learned her lesson.

'We were just talking about you, my dear. Your father and I have decided that perhaps it would be a good idea, on his return to work shortly, for you to help him in his studio, instead of being downstairs with Bert.' Isabelle went and stood behind her daughter and put her hand on her shoulder. She hated to see Jane so upset. 'Then perhaps, when he is not so busy, you could come and learn some sewing skills with Aunt Harriet and myself, if you wish.' She glanced over to James for reassurance.

'Yes, we'd work well together. You've always liked arranging the props and you'd get to deal with the customers, and that is what Atkinson's is all about.' James smiled at his daughter and made his way back to his chair.

'That's just it: you always think about what's good for Atkinson's. You never ask me what I'd like, or what I think!' Jane hung her head and started sobbing again.

'Jane, you are always first in our thoughts, along with Luke. We always do what is best for you both. Atkinson's is yours as much as it is mine. I thought you loved the place; you've been a part of it since you could barely walk, and Grandmama used to take you around the shop with so much pride, knowing that some day you would step into her shoes and mine.' Isabelle bent down and took her daughter's hands. 'You miss your grandmama, don't you? We all do. And I threw myself into my work, wanting to prove myself, and forgot that you need attention, too. I'm sorry, my love. These have been terrible times for us all. I still miss my mama; she was such a strong woman to follow, and I know I'll never have the respect she had.' Isabelle held Jane tightly to her.

Jane sobbed even louder.

James looked at mother and daughter. 'We will listen more to you, Jane. We forget that you are nearly a grown woman, and you should have more say in your life. But perhaps not to the extent of hurling stones at businesses down Skipton High Street. No matter how good the cause! Now dry your eyes and stop sobbing. Your mother and I have decided to make amends and, as she says, I would dearly like to have you as my assistant, if you wish. At least then you won't have to put up with the gossip and the looks that the shop floor and warehouse staff will be giving you.' James patted his daughter; he hated to see her upset. 'Have a day or two off and let the dust settle, so to speak, then start back at work with me. We can be two outcasts together, if you are worried about the gossip. I'm sure your mother will agree.'

'I'm not bothered what folk say, as I did nothing wrong. It was Nellie. But yes, Father, I would like to do that. If that's alright with you, Mother? I do feel so ashamed that I let Nellie do it, and I'm sorry. It is because everyone's been so wrapped up in themselves, and I have no one except old Bert Bannister to talk to. I miss Grandmama so much.' Jane raised her head and looked into her mother's dark eyes. 'I love you, Mama, and I'm so sorry for all the worry I've given you.'

'Don't worry, my dear. I was just as headstrong at your age. You always hurt the ones you love, because they are the ones who love you the most and you know you can get away with it. We all have to vent our wrath occasionally.' Isabelle looked up at her husband; he would never know just how much he had hurt her. It was true, she'd hurt those she loved around her too, with words of anger and her actions, most of which she regretted, with hindsight. The trouble was that time was a slow healer, and it would take a long time to amend the last six month's happenings. Jane wasn't the only one who felt unloved.

'What's the matter, Isabelle? Are you still worrying about the smashed window? It's been replaced, and folk will soon forget about it.' Harriet looked up from her sewing and waited for a reply from her sister-in-law, who had been in a mood with her all day. 'It wasn't as if Jane was responsible; it was her friend.'

'It isn't just that, Harriet. My life's in such a mess. I just feel like crying. I didn't think James would ever hurt me the way he has done. I'm trying to put on a strong face and hold the family together, but it is so hard. I've even let him back into my bed at night, but to be honest, I don't want him near me, because all I think of is her and what they got up to.' Isabelle stopped pinning the clothes on her mannequin and sat down next to her sister-in-law. 'The business takes all my time, and my children feel neglected. And in all honesty, I didn't realize just how much my mother did for our families. Since her death everything's gone wrong, and even Archie never comes near me.' Isabelle wiped away a tear that was falling.

'Well, you don't have to worry about Archie; he's just content up at Crummock. You know he was never one for finery, and he'd be the first one to come to your aid if he thought you needed him. He doesn't visit much because he knows you are all busy. Besides, he's better with sheep than folk, as he tends to say what he thinks nowadays and doesn't realize the consequences.' Harriet smiled. 'As for the rest, things are bound to get better. It's just been a bad year so far, so let's hope 1914 will put an end to our run of bad luck.'

'I still can't believe that James cheated on me. I look at him and sometimes I want to slap his face. And what's more, if Madge wasn't already dead, I think I'd want to murder her, for all the hurt she has caused. To think it was going on under my very nose; they were probably touching each other in here.' Isabelle looked around her and started to sob.

'It's not worth tears, Isabelle. She's gone and James is back with you. Just make sure he doesn't wander again.

Stop dwelling on it, and welcome him back into your bed – it's what we women have to do.' Harriet breathed in deeply and looked across at Isabelle, who lifted her head and looked at her.

'But you know nothing about how it feels, to be hurt by someone you love. Danny will never have looked at another woman since he married you. You've no idea of the pain Madge has caused,' she sobbed.

Harriet hesitated. 'No, Danny's always been faithful since we married. But there was a time, just before we were to marry, that I found out he was not being faithful to me, and I never will forget the pain it caused me.' Harriet stopped sewing and breathed in deeply. 'Like you, I didn't know what to do. I loved him so much and didn't want to lose him. I couldn't compete with Amy Brown – she was the talk of the Dales and the sweetheart of all the farm lads, with her easy ways. So I closed my eyes and ears and carried on with the charade of our courtship, in the hope that Danny would see sense some day.'

'You knew about Amy Brown?' Isabelle lifted her head and wiped her face. 'And you still married him.'

'Oh, so you knew, too? I should have guessed, for he always confided in you.' Harriet looked at Isabelle. 'Yes, I knew she was giving him something that I wouldn't until we were married, but I still married him. Unlike Amy, I had my morals. And I knew that was why she was adored by half the male population.'

'I told Danny what Amy was like, Harriet. I told him he was a fool. I didn't say anything to you because I knew you loved him. It was just that Amy let him have his own way.' Isabelle looked across at Harriet, with her head held high.

'I know, you were torn between us. Don't worry, Isabelle, I understand. What I'm trying to tell you, though, is that Madge must not come between you and James. She's done what Amy Brown did to us – given James an easy distraction, and that's all she was. Like Amy, Madge was someone who made him feel he was special when she lifted her skirts. When really it was both of us who loved them more.' Harriet went and put her arms around Isabelle. 'At least you haven't the worry of knowing that a child was born from James's fling. I sometimes wonder if Amy's firstborn could be Danny's, and I hear that he's come back to live at Ragged Hall, which makes me worry even more.'

'Oh, Harriet, I'm sure he won't be Danny's. She married someone from over Slaidburn. He's just come to look after his grandfather while he's unwell.' Isabelle breathed in deeply and blew her nose.

'We'll see, because one day he will turn up like a bad penny, of that I'm sure, and I will know instantly if I'm right or not. Anyway, let's get back to Jane. Bring her to me when she's not busy helping her father and I'll show her how to cut out a pattern. Then we will take it from there. It is what she should be doing: following in your footsteps. Although looking through the store today, I couldn't help but notice how many people are purchasing our finished garments from our suppliers. The fact that people are able to make their own clothing now, too, means that I think our role in life may soon be forgotten, and only needed for very special occasions.' Harriet went back to her sewing and put her head down.

'I'm glad Mother left you shares in Atkinson's, for you are still a part of the family and always will be, Harriet. And don't you worry: Danny loves you and always will. And as for James, well, I've no option but to forgive him, for the sake of our family.'

21

'Well, bugger me, you'll never guess who's just casually sloped back into the yard, with his mattress over his back and two dead rabbits in his hands, as if nothing's happened.' Danny came into the kitchen and looked at his father as he gazed out of the window.

'It can only be Ethan. I told you he'd be back. What did you say to him?' Archie turned around with a grin on his face. 'Welcomed him back with open arms, did you?'

'I bloody well didn't. I asked him where he'd been and said that he'd no right to trail off like he did. I also said that he'd caused no end of worry, both for us here and for his parents.' Danny pulled up his chair and warmed his hands next to the fire. 'There's a touch of frost out there this morning.'

'That's why he's back – summer's come to an end. He's not daft, he knows where he'll be warm and fed. You'll have him now until spring and then he might need another wander. That is if tha wants him.' Archie looked at his son.

'To be honest, I've missed the little bugger. Happen I didn't appreciate him when he was here. He kept the yard tidy and the horse harness was always polished, and the horses loved him. He's a good hand with the two Clydesdales and we will start ploughing that bottom field to plant turnips before long. I should really send him packing, but he's asked if he can talk to me this evening. He looked serious, so he knows I'll not mince my words.'

'This 'un will be glad. Have you heard your father, Rosie? Ethan's turned up, as bold as brass.' Archie grinned at Rosie, with her arms full of washing as she entered the kitchen. 'Tha's had a face as long as a wet weekend in Blackpool since he's been away.'

'What do I care about him? Ethan can trail where he wants. I hope you are not taking him back on, Father.' Rosie stood with her sheets nearly falling out of her arms, secretly feeling her heart flutter as she heard the news. At the same time she was short with her words, for he'd left her in her hour of need and she couldn't forgive him.

'He wants to see me tonight. I told him to go about his work until then. I'll have a think about it. Ethan is a law unto himself, but not a bad worker when he puts his back into it.' Danny looked at his daughter, who seemed flushed. His father was right: since Ethan had been gone, Rosie had been miserable. Happen there was something he was missing here.

'Well, regardless of what Grandpapa thinks, I'm not

bothered if he stays or goes.' Rosie turned on her heels and went quickly to the wash-house with her load.

'Methinks the lady doth protest too much,' Archie muttered.

'I didn't realize you knew Shakespeare, Father.' Danny looked at the old man. 'I do think tha's hit the nail on the head – something that's been happening since that day they both buggered off to Appleby together, now that I think about it.' Danny rubbed his brow.

'Well, we'll have to see what he's got to say tonight – he's been up to something.' Archie looked at his son. Danny had forgotten what it was like to be young, but Archie hadn't.

Rosie quickly pushed the washing into the dolly-tub and started to stir the clothes with the posser. She'd wash the sheets, rinse them and hang them on the line next to the duckpond as soon as she could, regardless of the chill wind that was blowing. She had to see Ethan, before he spoke to her father. She thought of him while she pummelled the clothes. Where had he been, these past few weeks? What had he been up to, and why had he returned now? Happen he did care for her after all.

She swept her hair back from her face and leaned into the dolly-tub. The steam from the hot water hit her face as she lifted the sheets into the earthenware sink to be rinsed. The cold water was icy this morning, and she didn't dally long before she threaded them through the mangle to get rid of the excess water. She swore under her breath as her sleeves and skirt got wet, leaving her arms and stomach cold to the touch. Then she carried the heavy washing basket out of the wash-house, across the yard to the green where the duckpond and clothes line were, sheltered by a small plantation of trees that ran alongside the track down to Austwick. Even there the wind was biting, and Rosie wished that she had grabbed her shawl before setting about her task. Her hands were numb and red as she finally pegged the last of the sheets out and turned to look at them blowing in the breeze. Drops of water fell from them, as if they were white clouds full of rain, as she turned to shoo the goose that was Crummock's guard dog from around her feet. She hated the honking bird; it was never quiet and had a habit of pecking you if you let it get near.

'I see old Napoleon hasn't lost his squawk.' She turned and looked towards the garden gate and saw Ethan leaning over it. 'He doesn't know who his friend is and who his enemy is.' He grinned; the grin that Rosie loved, the one that had made her his, on that fateful day of passion.

'If it were up to me, I'd shoot the thing. Along with a few other things that are worth nowt around here.' Rosie picked up her washing basket and walked over to him. She walked with a swagger, hoping to catch Ethan's eye even more.

'Now, Rosie Atkinson, you are not aiming your words at me, are you? There's me come back specially to be with you, and I could be looking down two barrels, for all you care.' Ethan opened the gate and leaned against it next to her. 'How are you? How are things . . . you

222

know?' He nodded to Rosie's stomach and looked worriedly at her.

'You needn't worry. In fact you need not have come back. I lost the baby, if indeed there was one there at all – I'm still not sure. Nobody knows, I managed to keep it to myself. I lost it through the night and cleaned myself up before anyone suspected anything.' Rosie stumbled over her words. She'd needed him that morning; she'd needed Ethan's arms to be put around her and tell her it was alright and that he loved her, but he hadn't been there. She'd been alone with her loss and hadn't even known where he was.

'Rosie, I'm so sorry, I didn't know. Are you alright? Did you not go to see the doctor? You should have told your mother.' Ethan put his arm around her as she trembled, both with the cold and with the trauma of remembering the terrible night when she had lost her unformed baby.

'What, and have to tell everybody that you were the father and that you had left me? What would that have achieved? We'd both have been cast out by our families. Remember what your father did when we went to Appleby; he'd have been even worse, once he'd found out the baby was yours.' Rosie buried her head in Ethan's shoulder and cried. His tweed jacket and strong arms comforted her as he held her close. She could smell the mountain air on his clothes and realized just how much she had missed him, and how much she loved her wild rambler.

'I've only been living in the shooting hut below Moughton Scar. I had to have time to myself to think things through. To see what I thought about the future for both of us – for all of us.' Ethan put a finger under Rosie's chin and lifted her face up for her to look at him. 'I didn't leave you, Rosie, I just needed time to think. I do love you.'

'But you left and didn't say anything, so what was I to think?' Rosie wiped her eyes clear of tears.

'Aye, but I'm back now, and I was going to tell your father all and ask for his permission for me to marry you. Regardless of who I am. Now, with things like they are, perhaps asking his permission to court you would be a better idea. It'll not be as rushed, and then there's no more sneaking about. Neither of us have enjoyed lying and being secretive.'

'My father would never agree, nor will my mother, especially with you disappearing like you did.' Rosie looked up at him, thinking it was a hopeless request.

'Nay, I don't think they will. But your grandfather knows we are made for one another. I can tell from the way he looks at us when we are just talking together. It's better to marry for love than for money. After all, isn't that what he did?' Ethan held Rosie tight. 'I can but try and, if they are truly against us, then we will continue like we have done, until they realize that we are meant for one another.'

'Alright, but they will both say I'm too young and that I should set my sights higher. I know they will.' Rosie held Ethan tightly; he was everything to her, she had known that when he'd left her on her own in her grief.

'Tonight, then, I'll ask them after supper.' Ethan bent

down and kissed her. 'And yes, I do love you, Rosie Atkinson, and now I can truly say it, as we are under no pressure. I would have married you, if you were still carrying our baby. I would not have deserted you, no matter what.'

'Now then, lad, I suppose you've come to plead for your job back and tell us why you went wandering without leave.' Danny looked at Ethan. For once he looked respectable: his shirt was clean, his corduroy trousers were stainless and his long dark hair was brushed and in place.

'Aye, I'd be grateful if I could keep my job, especially after I tell you why I left. I hope that perhaps you'll respect the dilemma I find myself in.' Ethan looked at Danny and Archie, as they both sat at the polished dining-room table, in a room that was not often used by the farming family. It was one Ethan had never been in before. It was obvious to him that this was just as an important meeting to them as it was to him, and he felt uneasy as he glanced around the room at the oil paintings on the walls and the polished silver upon the dressers. There he stood, a stable boy asking for no less than the hand of the lass that all this would belong to one day, so perhaps he did have ideas above his station.

'Well, go on then, lad, let's be hearing you.' Archie looked at the nervous lad; he'd known Ethan since he was born and, no matter what else was said of him, he knew Ethan never did things without a cause.

'I had to leave. I needed time to think and to see if what I was feeling was right.' Ethan paused and looked at both burly farmers. 'I've been living in the shooting hut below Moughton these last few weeks, because I had to get away from here. I couldn't let my feelings get the better of me until I knew what to do. Rosie has felt the same.'

'Rosie – what has this got do with Rosie?' Danny sat up in his chair and gazed at the swarthy lad, who stood looking uncomfortably at them.

'Let the lad finish, Danny.' Archie pulled on his son's sleeve.

'I, er . . . we, both think a great deal of one another. We can't help it, we are just alike. But I know my father would give me another braying, and I know that I'm way below Rosie's station in life and I shouldn't even be thinking of her in that way. That's why I needed time to think. But I'm hoping that you'll both understand and that you'll give me permission to court her properly.' Ethan blurted it all out. What he'd rehearsed so carefully was nothing like what had come out of his mouth, but at least they knew how he felt.

Danny sat back in his chair. 'I bloody knew it! I've been as blind as a bat, until I saw Rosie's face when I told her that he was back.' He turned and stared at his father. After all, Archie was to blame for making this happen, by bringing Ethan up to Crummock and turning his young daughter's head. 'She pretended not to care, but she cared alright.'

'Hold your noise, lad. It's not the end of the world. Rosie's nearly seventeen, and Ethan here is not a bad soul. At least you know all about him, and he is right: they are alike. Two wild 'uns together. And he's doing the proper thing, instead of sneaking about – give him some credit.' Archie winked at Ethan as he stood, almost trembling.

'But he has nowt, not a bloody penny. I wanted better for Rosie.' Danny sat back and looked at Ethan. 'Oh God, Harriet will not be happy.'

'You are forgetting, lad. I was in the same shoes as Ethan and couldn't afford the clothes on my back, when I fell in love with my Lottie. Then your mother came along and we were happy, but Lottie was always at the back of my mind and I knew she would one day be mine, no matter how poor I was. There's no price on true love, lad, you should know that. Let the lad court her, see how they feel about one another in six months' time. It might come to something or it might disappear like the morning's dew.' Archie smiled at Ethan; he liked the boy's determination and knew he was right for Rosie.

'Bloody hell, Father. Think of what you are saying. He's a stable lad; at least your father had land. I should say no and send you on your way.' Danny looked at the lad who stood in front of him and thought of how unhappy Rosie had been the last few weeks, which he'd put down to her mother giving her extra work, but now he realized differently. 'Rosie is everything to me and I want to see her happy. I can't stand the sullen face we have had the last few weeks. If I say yes, it's on the understanding that you don't get up to anything untoward; no wandering hands – you respect her like a lady and you treat her right. Else it won't just be your father that gives you a braying. As my father says, six months and we will see how you still feel about one another. You can join us on a Sunday for dinner and can have the use of the parlour for an hour.' Danny stared at the young lad who had captured his daughter's heart. 'I'll ask Mrs Atkinson to make the room above the storehouse available for you; it'll be a bit warmer than the stable. We were going to have to find you somewhere before the onset of winter, and I've been thinking of that for a while. There's already a bed in there, although you might have mice as company.' Danny looked at the lad, who was now trying to hide his happiness and couldn't believe his luck. 'You treat her right, otherwise God help you.'

'I will, Mr Atkinson, I will. Thank you.' Ethan beamed.

'Now go on, get your arse out of here. I expect hard work out of you and no loitering about, looking at our Rosie. God knows what her mother will say!' Danny shook his head. Harriet wouldn't understand. She had wanted Rosie to be a lady all her life, but Rosie had always had other ideas, he'd known that. She loved the land.

Rosie lay in her bed. She could hear her mother and father talking through the wall that divided them, and knew she was the subject of discussion. She'd gone to her room early that night, avoiding any contact with Ethan and the conversation that would follow between her parents. But now she found herself unable to sleep. She imagined the disgust of her mother, at her setting her sights as low as the gypsy stable boy. She recalled all the times Harriet had sighed and said she wished Rosie was more like her cousin Jane. Jane would never do that, Jane would always be a lady and would marry into higher society, so long as everyone forgot her mad moment of fighting for the suffragette cause.

No matter. Ethan had broken their silence, and no doubt she'd be confronted by an irate mother in the morning. It was a pity it wasn't Harriet's day helping out at Skipton, for she would have to endure her mother lecturing her all day as she helped her. Whatever happened, her mother must never find out that they had already been intimate with one another, and the terrible consequences it had caused. That would always be her own and Ethan's secret; no one else must ever know. Rosie pulled her bedclothes up to her chin and tried to sleep, tugging her pillow around her ears. Tomorrow would be hell, but Ethan was worth every minute, she thought, as she gazed into the darkness of the night.

'I swear this place would go to the dogs if I wasn't here. I'm gone just a few days a week, and then this happens behind my back. And your father seems to have no more sense than he was born with – saying yes to Ethan! For heaven's sake, Rosie, you are only sixteen and, of all the lads in the dale, it's Ethan that takes your eye. Could you not have set your heart on the lad from Woodend or Sowermire? At least their fathers own some land.' Harriet looked across the table at her young daughter.

'But they are not the same, Mother. Ethan and I get on so well; we both have the same love of the countryside, and we are happy in one another's company.' Rosie lowered her head. She'd had earache from her mother all morning – lecture after lecture on how to behave, and on setting her sights higher than a common gypsy.

'Well, I suppose I'll have to make the best of it. Your father says Ethan's not a bad lad, and your grandfather seems to be relishing the thought of you two walking out together. Even told me he was looking forward to a wedding, instead of a funeral. I personally hope it doesn't come to that – wedding indeed! You'd better both behave yourselves, for we are not having the embarrassment of a hurried wedding in the family, so don't be lifting your skirts, my girl, else I'll wipe my hands of you.' The bread she was making got the pummelling of its life as Harriet vented her frustration on the dough.

'No, Mother, we would never do that.' Rosie blushed and passed her mother the greased bread tins, hoping to be out of her earshot soon.

'You can go and sweep out the feed-room and make up Ethan a bed in it. Take them old sheets that the Irishmen have been using, seeing as your father has said Ethan can sleep in there. I'm just glad he's not let him into the main house. I'd never have slept for listening for him and you sneaking about the place. Because that's what he'd do, I just know it.'

Harriet looked across at her daughter. She'd wanted better for her, but Rosie's happiness was the main thing and she was in better spirits this morning.

'Take that old piece of gingham that's in the bedding box at the end of my bed – it'll make him some curtains. And I don't want to see him with next to nothing on in a morning, when I'm off about my work. There's two old chairs that Archie brought with him and a table in the outhouse; take him those as well. We'd better give him a better standard of living, if he's to walk out with you.' Harriet watched as Rosie grinned at her. 'You can grin, my lass, but you behave with him! Just until we know what he's about. And time will tell us that – if you're still on his arm this coming spring.'

Rosie stood back and looked at Ethan's new living quarters. The room smelled of the barley, wheat and corn maize used to feed the hens and pigs, stacked in one corner. But it was warm and dry and quite homely now. The spare bed, which had been there for any travellers and drovers, was now made up with clean sheets, and Rosie had hung the red gingham curtains around the windows and whitewashed walls, as her mother had suggested. In the corner she had placed the old kitchen table and two chairs from Windfell, which had once been in her grandfather's kitchen at Butterfield Gap. They had found a home, just like Ethan, she thought, as she placed a jam jar of late-flowering Michaelmas daisies on the table to brighten the room up.

Ethan was gradually being made welcome at Crummock Farm. Perhaps it was a blessing that she had lost her baby; this way everyone would know that both of them were serious about one another. It didn't matter that Ethan was a stable boy. Anyway he wasn't any more; he could say he was the farm man now, and he'd hopefully have an even better position in the future.

Rosie smiled as she closed the paint-worn door behind

her and climbed down the stone steps that led into the farmyard. Ethan had made it this far and, with her love, he'd get even further with her beside him, of that she was sure. Sunday could not come soon enough, and in six months' time hopefully they would be able to marry.

22

'Seen any tarts on bikes, lately, Fox?' Geoffrey Brunskill, the school bully and prefect, hit Luke hard around the head as he walked down the dormitory, checking that all was in order for night. 'Oh no, sorry – your father just kills them, I'd forgotten.'

Luke hung his head and then pulled his covers back to climb into bed, watching as Brunskill left the room. How he hated him. Since his father's accident Brunskill and his little gang of followers had made his life hell.

'Take no notice, Luke, he's a bastard.' Bill Palmer looked across at his best friend, who he knew was upset about events at home and the fact that he'd been sniggered about for weeks. 'Nobody else even gives a damn about what they heard. Besides, he's only having a go at you tonight because you've received your rifle badge so quickly. It took him ages, and he still hasn't received his red star and fully qualified as an NCO. I bet you get there before him – he's too thick to become an officer. I'd like to know what his parents are like. He's only from Bradford, and they can't be that posh.'

'I'm just a little tired of him constantly having a dig. One day I'm going to get him and make him pay. But at the moment it's not worth it.' Luke got into his bed, before giving another glance at the uniform that was now hanging up, adorned with the newly awarded rifle badge on the left arm. He was proud of himself, so Brunskill could say what he wanted.

'Lights out, no talking. Especially you, Fox, I can hear you and that rat-like Palmer.' Brunskill hit the side of his leg with the newly acquired silver-topped swagger stick that all the cadets had been given, for parade purposes. But in Brunskill's case it was an extra bullying tool, one he did not hesitate to use.

Luke and Bill went quiet, waiting until the gas lights had been turned off and the bully had left them in darkness.

'It's feels strange with half the dorm missing and in the sanatorium,' Bill whispered.

'Yes, have you had German measles, like me? Mother said I'd had them when I was just over five, but I can't remember,' Luke whispered back.

'Yes, I've had them, and you can't catch them again.' Bill looked at the empty beds in the darkness, devoid of their inhabitants, who had either been sent back home or were being looked after by matron elsewhere, in isolation from the rest of the pupils.

'I can see our visit to camp being postponed; they won't be sending a load of spotty, ill lads anywhere. God forbid if half the War Office developed German measles because of Giggleswick School,' Luke whispered back. 'Still, it's drill parade in the morning and instruction lecture after tea. We'll probably find out more tomorrow.'

'Now that will annoy Brunskill, as he'll be hoping for his red star and his proficiency certificate to say he's assured of a commission, if we do go to camp. His brother got both at Bordon Camp last year, and he needs to keep up with him. God help us, if we don't go.' Bill sighed.

'We can't do anything about it. I'm tired, Bill – sorry, I'm off to sleep now.' Luke pulled his covers up around his face and thought about the camp he had so wanted to attend. There he would have mixed and made friends with other cadets from around the country, and they would all have the same patriotic feelings that he had. Then his thoughts wandered to home and his mother and father, and the stony silence there had been on his last weekend visit. He hoped things had improved, but now his sister had written to him telling him of her escapades, the fool. Between school and home, there wasn't much to like, but the cadets made him feel special, especially now that he had reached a first-class honour. The military was the life for him and he'd give it all that he'd got.

'Now then, men, I'm afraid I have some bad news for you. As you know, we were due to go to camp next week, but in view of the outbreak of German measles, I'm afraid it has had to be cancelled.' The Commanding

Officer stood in front of the cadets, after putting them through their paces on the square outside the historic school rooms. 'Now I know that you were particularly looking forward to this event, so for those of you who are well enough, I suggest that we have a few days up at Attermire Scar on the practice ranges. The miniature range under the cloisters has poor light, though it serves some purpose, but I propose that we march through Settle and then camp out on the fellside in readiness for using the ranges.' The CO watched and listened as a mumble of discontent ran through the cadets on parade. 'There's always next year, and as you know we will be going to Hagley Park in Staffordshire, so set your sights on that event in late June.'

'I bloody well knew it.' Luke walked back into the school with Bill next to him.

'Well, at least we get a few days off at camp on the side of Attermire, that's better than nothing. I wasn't looking forward to more than a week in this weather anyway, it's gone so cold of late.' Bill patted his mate on the back.

'You'll never make a soldier, you are too soft,' said Luke.

'I don't intend to. Politics is more my thing. I'll make the bullets that you will fire on my behalf – that way it's a lot safer. Isn't that what all politicians do?' Bill laughed.

'Too bloody right; it's them lot that cause half the wars in the first place, but you won't catch them on the battlefield.' Luke sat down at his desk and grinned at his mate.

'No, they've more sense. I'll leave it to the likes of you, if there's ever a war. It's best I sit behind a nice warm desk and let the others do the fighting.' Bill looked at the blackboard, and at the teacher coming in.

'Coward,' Luke whispered.

'Too true, but at least I'll still be around to tell the tale.'

Luke looked around him, stopping to catch his breath as the steep track rose in front of him out of Settle, leading on towards Malham. He turned round to see down to the market town of Settle, and a little further afield he could see the majestic copper dome of Giggleswick School chapel. It rose above all else, stating its importance before the students and school below it. Further to his right, he could just make out the rooftop of his home at Windfell. He looked at it for a brief second, before putting his best foot forward as the CO yelled at them all to keep marching. He missed home, but had decided a while ago that the army was to be his life.

They had marched through the centre of Settle, past the ancient Shambles and up through the market towards the narrow cobbled street of upper Settle, turning all the locals' heads as they swung their arms and walked in time together. Over their shoulders were their trusted rifles and on their backs were their backpacks, filled with what they would need for their two nights on the wild fellside. Luke was quietly looking forward to staying out in the wilds. He knew that he did not excel in his studies, so he devoted his time to becoming a soldier and to one day serving the King. It was what he most desired. And two days of scouting and shooting practice were right up his street; anything to get away from the musty-smelling oak-clad rooms of the ancient school, which his mother had thought he would be happy in.

The troop marched onwards to the winding Stockdale Road, high above the market town of Settle on the remote landscape leading over to Malham. There in front of them stood the high limestone crags of Attermire Scar, and the rifle butts were just visible at the bottom of the crag known as Warrendale Knotts, nearly half a mile from the road. Luke remembered when he had been at the site with his father on Whit Monday, when he taken part in the full-day shoot known as the 'Tradesman's shoot'. The shops in Settle and the surrounding district donated prizes for the best shot. His father had donated and awarded a clock to one of the local boys from the TA and had patted Luke on the back, then turned to him saying, 'Next year it could be you, son.' At the time Luke had doubted it, but now he had progressed with his skills and was certain that the prize would be his in the coming year.

'Right, men, we are staying in the field over the road. Sort yourselves into two groups. Group one needs to erect the tents, while group two will dig holes for the latrines and find some kindling and wood to build a fire. And look lively.' The CO bellowed as Luke and Bill Palmer decided which group to be in, and finally opted to be the ones digging the latrines and gathering firewood.

'Shit attracts shit,' Brunskill laughed as he pushed his way past Luke and Bill, carrying the tent poles into place.

'Piss off, Brunskill,' Luke shouted to the well-known bully. 'Shove your pole up your arse!'

Brunskill glowered at him, and then grabbed Luke by the shirt neck, quickly letting him go as the CO looked his way. 'Go and dig your hole and bury yourself in it,' he whispered as he strode off with his followers on his heels.

'Don't annoy him, Luke. He's not worth it. And we might have to sleep in the same tent as him.' Bill picked up his shovel and made for the wall side, ready to dig.

'I hate him. I'll make him think twice about picking on us, one day. He's nothing but a coward anyway.' Luke walked off, with Bill following. He would get even with Brunskill. He might be older and larger than him, but one day he'd regret being such a bully towards him.

Unfortunately Bill had been right, and the first night of camping neither Luke nor Bill hardly slept, conscious the whole time that a few feet away from them lay Brunskill and his mob of friends. They'd kept themselves out of the way of them all evening, as they had been made to tramp up and down the scar with laden backpacks to improve their fitness. But when night-time had come, they had had to put up with the jeers and mockery of Brunskill as they settled down to sleep. Now Luke was trying to keep awake, frightened that Brunskill would do something to him or Bill while they were asleep. He rubbed his eyes and listened to the snores coming from everyone else, and felt his head getting heavy as the night slowly crept into morning. Then sleep eventually got the better of him.

'Wakey-wakey, sleepy Foxy.'

Luke woke up feeling the warm, foul-smelling liquid being poured over his head and the sound of a voice coming from the person he hated.

'I couldn't be arsed to go out to the latrine, so I've given you a morning wash instead.' Brunskill kicked him slightly and then buttoned up his trousers as he put his dick away.

Luke lay in his bed as he realized that Brunskill had urinated over his head. The smell of pee made him want to be sick. 'You bastard!' He got out from under his soaked grey blanket and was about to confront the laughing Brunskill when the CO entered the tent, on hearing all the commotion.

'All of you, out across to the range in ten minutes. A spot of breakfast is to be served in the wooden hut next to the wall and then practice will begin. Fox, get up and get dressed, and tidy yourself up, man.' He turned and left the group and walked out of the tent.

'Yes, you stink, Fox, anyone would think you'd pissed the bed.' Brunskill swaggered as he led his followers out of the tent, leaving just Bill hunched up in a corner, looking shame-faced at his best friend.

'Sorry, Luke, I couldn't stop them.' Bill watched as Luke emptied his billy can of water over his head, trying to get rid of Brunskill's smell from his hair and his skin.

'It's alright, Bill, I know. But I'll not let this lie, believe me.' Luke made himself tidy and put his uniform on while his best friend watched. He vowed to get his revenge and show up Brunskill for the bully he was.

Bill and Luke ate their breakfast in silence. Luke watched as Brunskill sniggered across at him, making his friends laugh as he held his nose and commented about the smell around the table.

As soon as breakfast was over, the troop went out to the range, which was tucked away under the limestone scar. Raised areas of shooting platforms were distanced at various yards from the targets – one hundred and fifty yards being the easiest and the hardest being set at the lane edge, a distance of eight hundred and eighty yards. Only the most proficient shot could manage to hit the target from there. The six-foot target on a rotating iron axle was only a speck in the distance.

The group started off at the shortest distance and everyone hit the target. Captain Pierce, who had joined the group that morning, was keeping score.

'This is bloody easy – I wish we could get a move on,' Luke complained, as everyone lined up to take shots at the first three distances.

'It might be easy for you, but I missed the target altogether last time. There is no way I'm going to manage the last two distances.' Bill looked around him. He was beginning to wonder why he had bothered entering the Officers' Training Corps, for he was not military-minded, but his father had told him it would make him more of a man, so he'd agreed to give it a go.

'You don't concentrate enough. Hold your gun steady and gently squeeze the trigger. Like the CO says, you've got to treat your gun like the most precious thing in your life.' Luke and Bill walked towards the platform set at seven hundred and fifty yards from the target. In their footsteps came Brunskill, who overheard their conversation.

'Perhaps he's not like you. He's got more precious things in his life. Unlike you, who's not even loved by your family – boarded out, when your family only live two miles away from the school. Let's face it, nobody wants you,' sneered Brunskill.

'They are busy, they work hard, so shut your mouth, you.' Luke stared at Brunskill. How he hated him.

'Aye, we know exactly how busy your father was, especially on that bike of his.' Brunskill sniggered as he walked off and lined up to position himself at the next platform.

'Don't let him get to you.' Bill pulled on Luke's sleeve, holding him back from tackling Brunskill. 'He's not worth it.'

'I'm going to show that bastard he's not perfect. I'm sick of him picking on me and my family.' Luke lined up along with Bill and took his next round of cartridges from the CO before loading his gun, his face set, determined to outshoot Brunskill, if nothing else.

'Right, men, whoever hits this target will go on to try the platform furthest away. This will really test you all,' shouted the CO, as the cadets looked at the distance and knew what was being asked of them.

One by one, each cadet stepped up to the platform, taking his time to line up his scope and fire. All the cadets missed, bar Brunskill, who boasted about his victory. Bill stepped up and did as Luke had told him to, but to no avail, for he was no marksman and he knew it. Then Luke stood behind the wooden platform, resting his gun solidly and holding it firmly within his hand. He squeezed the trigger. He stood back and grinned as the bullet sped to the centre of the target, and Captain Pierce waved the white flag to say the target had been successfully hit.

'Well done, Luke. That means there's just you and Brunskill to try the next platform.' Bill patted his mate on the back and looked at the anger on Brunskill's face as they made their way across the wild grassland to the platform next to the wall. Brunskill's mob was cheering him on and he was full of himself as he opted to shoot first, when given the choice.

The cadets went quiet as he posed himself, taking time lining up the small speck in the distance. Bang! The shot was fired and all eyes turned to Captain Pierce as he rotated the target, and it looked as if it had been hit. But his arm rose and waved a red flag to show that the target had not been damaged, and a gasp of disappointment was heard from Brunskill and his followers.

'Good luck, Luke,' Bill whispered, as the rest of the cadets watched him.

'Aye, good luck, mate,' one of the group shouted as Luke took his position.

He licked his lips and twisted his cap round. Looking through his sights, he lined up the target as best as he could, aimed and fired! It seemed an age before the target was turned round and examined by Captain Pierce, and Luke couldn't believe it when a white flag was raised and a cheer went up from all the cadets. They patted him and congratulated him, swarming round him like bees around a honey pot.

'Right through the bloody centre, Fox, a pure bullseye.' Captain Pierce came running up with the paper target showing the impact of his shot. 'Good man.'

Luke grinned and was speechless. He turned and looked at a downcast Brunskill, whose friends seemed to have deserted him. Luke held his hand out to him and watched as Brunskill couldn't quite take in his act of comradeship.

'Hard luck, Brunskill, better luck next time.' Luke shook the hand of the lad who had been a bully to him for so long. He'd no need to prove his worth to him any more. He'd been shown to be the better shot, and now everyone knew it.

Brunskill was silent as he shook Luke's hand. He knew he had to look like a gentleman, but he also knew that his days of being top dog among the cadets were over. No one was even giving him the time of day as he went and sat down behind the drystone wall and lit a cigarette. Bloody Luke Fox – his sort always won.

23

'Really, Harriet, I'd have thought that you would have set your sights a little higher than Ethan, for Rosie.' Isabelle looked across at her sister-in-law in amazement at the news she'd just been told.

'I did – I said anybody but Ethan. There's so many more suitable than him, but it is as Danny says: they are both happy with one another, and that counts for a lot. Besides, they are both young; we are hoping that it will come to nothing and that their so-called love for one another will dwindle. I don't think Ethan has even told his parents. He won't dare, as Jethro would have something to say about it, so he can't be that serious. I just hope he doesn't break Rosie's heart in the process.' Harriet looked up from her sewing and noticed Isabelle scowling.

'Well, I certainly expect better of my Jane, even though she is trying me to within an inch of my patience at the moment. There's plenty of young eligible men in the dale and she's older than your Rosie, so she needs to get a move on. I keep encouraging her to attend socials and the local dances, but with no luck. I think we will have to have a Christmas Ball this year at Windfell, just like Mama used to have, and then perhaps I can invite someone who's suitable along for her. Besides, it will do the family good and will disperse any rumours about James and me having a failed marriage.' Isabelle stood back and admired the dress that she had been finishing off for a customer and smiled. 'If Jane wore something like this, she would have no end of admirers.' She pulled out the long skirts of the deep-red velvet ballgown and sat back in satisfaction at her work. 'Mrs Capstick is a very lucky lady. I hope her husband appreciates her keeping up appearances.'

'I'm sure he does, I've never seen a more devoted couple.' Harriet smiled. 'Should Jane not be with us by now? I was going to watch her as she cut out the pattern for the blouse that Amelia Hall ordered. I thought it was a good one to start with.'

'She's just doing an errand for James; he needed some ink to be collected from the printer's. He barely had to ask her and could hardly believe her eagerness, for she usually turns her nose up at errands, but she went straight away. I think she knows that he is still in quite a bit of pain with his leg, although he dare not complain when he's in my company. He knows that he will not get any sympathy from me. After all, he's only got himself to blame.' Isabelle sighed. It would take longer than a few months for her to forgive James for all the hurt he'd caused, and she was not about to show any weakness on her side of the marriage.

'I was hoping you would have advertised for a new seamstress by now. Winter is fast approaching and I don't want to be travelling from up at Crummock to Skipton each day. Besides, I probably won't be able to, for the road soon gets blocked with snow, you know that.' Harriet looked at Isabelle.

'How can I forget, Harriet? Don't you worry – I placed an advertisement in the local paper just last week, as I knew that although you are enjoying your time with us, it would not be practical for you to work here over the winter. Let's say that I have learned from my shameful past mistakes. Hopefully, by spring, Jane will have learned well enough to follow in your footsteps anyway. Then, if you wish, you can join us as and when you please, as it is a joy to be working with you again, dear sister.' Isabelle walked over to her sister-in-law and hugged her tightly. 'Are you doing anything special for Rosie's birthday next week? It's not every day a girl is seventeen.'

'No, she says she doesn't want any fuss, she just wants a quiet day. No doubt Ethan will come into it somewhere along the line. He seems to have replaced us in her affections. I just wish she wasn't so young, for there will be time for men in her life, and he's the first one she's known.' Harriet looked up at Isabelle and then decided to keep her thoughts to herself. Isabelle was being very understanding, but she was no doubt hiding her true thoughts about her niece's love affair. She remembered the caustic remarks about Ethan the last time he had come up in conversation. Still, she was glad that Isabelle had placed an advertisement for her position, for during the winter she was better up at the farm, which was where she belonged the most and where she would be needed, if snow came.

'Ethan, these are absolutely beautiful. I can't believe you have made them yourself.' Rosie smiled as she admired the miniature set of drawers that Ethan had lovingly made for her birthday present. They both sat outside on the stone steps that led up to his new lodgings in the feed-room. They sat as close to one another as they dared, given that Rosie's father kept walking across the yard as he went about his work, before the family tea that had been arranged for Rosie's birthday.

'I thought they could be put towards our home, when we get wed. They'll look good on top of the mantelpiece. That is, if we can ever afford a home.' Ethan kissed Rosie quickly on the cheek, hoping not to get caught in the act. 'I love you – you do know that. I was just frightened when you said you were with child. I'd have stood by you.'

'I know, and I was frightened too. It was perhaps a good thing I lost it. It makes days like this more special.' Rosie opened the small drawers that could hold various bits and bobs, and looked at the handles that Ethan had fashioned out of offcuts of brass from around the farm and from old brass curtain rings. 'I've been thinking that if we do wed and need a home, I could perhaps persuade Grandfather to let us live in his Great-aunt Lucy's cottage in Austwick. It's been empty for years and needs a lot of repair, but it would be lovely for just us two.'

'I don't think your mother will agree. She doesn't seem to think that I'm good enough for you, but I aim to prove her wrong. There's not much I can't turn my hand to, and your father keeps saying what a good job I'm doing, now I've decided what's important to me in life. I don't want to be just the lad that mucks out the stable and cleans the harness – I can do better than that. Where's the cottage at? Should we go and have a look at it, when we can get away together?' Ethan had decided it was time to show his commitment to Rosie and to prove to her parents that he was a worker, now that he had something to aim for. He didn't want to be excluded from the family as the outcast that he currently felt he was.

'It's down on the back green, just set back a bit off the main road. The garden's overgrown, but the roof is alright and so are the doors and windows. Should we go and have a look at it on Sunday? We are both allowed time together then.' Rosie looked excitedly at him.

'Aye, we can do that. I like Austwick and it would be just right, as you say. Plus, your grandfather is always right with me. I've a lot to thank him for, as it was him who brought me here.' Ethan smiled and wanted to hug Rosie again, but quickly put thoughts of that to one side as her mother came to the garden gate opposite them.

'Rosie, come on in now – tea is on the table and, as it's your birthday, I've made a trifle, so you'd better get yourself in before your grandfather eats the lot of it.'

Harriet looked across at the two love-birds sitting on the step. She remembered how she used to look at her Danny that way, and her heart melted a little towards Ethan. 'Are you coming and all? After all, there's no show without Punch, and it'll make our Rosie happy.' Harriet folded her arms and waited, watching the disbelief on both of their faces. 'Aye, get yourselves in. I might not be suited with this courtship, but I'll not have you miserable on your birthday.'

'Thank you, Mother. It is kind of you to ask Ethan in. Look what he's made for me.' Rosie passed the miniature set of drawers to her mother to inspect, as Ethan took his cap off and walked quietly past her.

'Not a bad job, lad. They are right bonny. I wouldn't mind some of them myself.' Harriet passed the miniatures back to Rosie. 'You're not as daft as you look.'

'Thank you, Mrs Atkinson. I'll make you some, if you want.' Ethan grinned.

'Aye, you can – in your own time, though. You've enough on this next week or two, gathering the fell with Mr Atkinson and bringing the sheep down for winter. He's decided to give you a few more responsibilities.' Harriet passed Rosie the set of drawers back and smiled. 'Now get yourselves in for some tea; there's salmon sandwiches and a present waiting for you, Rosie, because no doubt you'll be expecting something.' Harriet watched the two of them enter Crummock. Her eldest was no longer a little girl; she was a woman, and she'd have to realize that.

Ethan felt uncomfortable sitting at the table in the

dining room of Crummock Farm. He looked around him at the fine china that embellished the oak plate-rack and didn't quite know what to do with his hands and arms, as Harriet sat down opposite to him, giving him a knowing glance.

'Pass Ethan a sandwich, Rosie. Do you like salmon or would you have preferred something else?' Harriet looked at him as he gingerly took a sandwich from the gilt-edged plate, then watched as everybody else helped themselves and started to eat.

'Aye, tuck in, lad – fill your boots. Make best of it while there's stuff on the table.' Archie grinned; he'd been in the same position, the first time he'd sat in the exact same spot and not been wanted by old Father Booth, as he'd eyed his daughter.

'Yes, I like salmon, but what I've caught from the beck is nowt like this.' Ethan looked at the red-coloured fish, which showed barely any resemblance to what he usually caught.

'This is tinned salmon – a real delicacy. We only have it on special occasions, birthdays and Christmas. I thought it would be a treat on Rosie's birthday.' Harriet looked across at Ethan, who didn't appear that impressed.

'Mam, why is Ethan eating with us? He's usually out in the stable,' Ben spouted up as he looked at Ethan, while hiding his bread crusts under his plate edge.

'Because he is – that's all you need to know for now.' Harriet smiled at her young son. 'Now eat your crusts up, they'll make your hair curl.'

'I don't want curly hair. I know why he's here. I saw

251

him kissing our Rosie in the cowshed last week. They didn't see me because I kept quiet; they are always kissing. Blaaa . . .' He put his tongue out and pulled a face.

'You shut up, our Ben, you don't know anything. You are nothing but a peeping Tom.' Rosie kicked her brother under the table and glared at him.

'Now you make Ethan welcome at our table. Him and your sister are courting, and we will have none of your cheek, Ben Atkinson.' Danny looked across at his son and stirred his tea. 'Else you can go and join Georgina in a sleep upstairs in your bedroom.' He looked across at the two lovers and saw Rosie's cheeks blush. 'I'm off down to Windfell tomorrow, Ethan, do you want to come with me? We can see your mother and father, and then we can tell them how things are between you and Rosie. They've a right to know and, if I tell your father that we are somewhat happy with the situation, he should treat you right.'

Ethan bowed his head. 'I expect my father will bray me again. I shouldn't even be looking at Rosie, let alone walking out with her, in his eyes. But I'll come, and then both my mother and father will know what I'm about. If you'd back me up, Mr Atkinson, I'd appreciate that.' He lifted his head up and looked at Rosie and smiled.

'Right, we'll go first thing. I need to call in at the blacksmith's in Settle, so it will give you a bit of time to be alone with them. But I'll tell your father to behave himself while I'm gone. I'm not having you the worse for wear, just for the sake of setting your eye on our lass.' Danny looked across at his father and hoped that he'd want to come with them both. But Archie said nothing,

252

as he was too busy watching Harriet dishing up the sherry trifle that had been made earlier and passing it to everyone, before she reached for the two parcels that were on the sideboard.

'This is from me and your father.' She passed the larger of the two brown paper parcels to her daughter. 'The smaller one is from your Aunt Isabelle and Uncle James.' She watched as Rosie's eyes lit up with excitement as she pulled on the string bow of the large parcel, unfolding the paper carefully.

'Oh, it's beautiful, Mother, but when will I wear it? It's too grand for everyday use.' Rosie pulled away the paper and pushed her chair back, standing to hold the beautiful dress that had been concealed within the package.

'Now, that is a picture. Aye, lad.' Archie grinned as Ethan looked at Rosie holding her present of a blue taffeta ballgown up next to her.

'Yes, sir.' Ethan looked at the girl he loved and felt unsure of himself for the first time. Perhaps his father was right: he shouldn't be aiming for a girl like Rosie. She was far too high above him, and he should know his place.

'Well, you are old enough to go to one or two of the local dances now, and Aunt Isabelle is going to hold a Christmas Ball this year, so you'll be needing it for that, I'm sure. We can't have you letting the side down.' Harriet looked across at Ethan and noticed his face starting to cloud over. 'Open your other present – that was Aunt Isabelle's doing.'

Rosie's face was beaming as she placed her new dress down behind her chair and quickly tugged on the string of the other parcel, pulling back the paper to reveal a blue-and-silver beaded evening bag. 'Oh, I've never seen anything like it.' She ran the beaded fringe that hung from the bag through her fingers and looked around the tea table at everybody.

'And here, lass, I'm no good at buying presents, but I thought you could make use of this.' Archie passed Rosie the money he had put in his pocket specially for her.

'I couldn't take that, Grandpapa, it's a pound – that's more money than I've managed to save up all year.' Rosie went round the table and hugged him and tried to give it back, but Archie shook his head and thrust it back in her hand. 'Tha'll need it someday, lass, I'm sure it will come in handy. Besides, I'd rather see you happy while I'm still here to see it, than when I'm six foot under and no good to anyone.'

'That's a long way off yet, Grandpapa.' Rosie kissed Archie on the cheek and looked at Ethan, who looked as black as thunder and had not touched the trifle in front of him.

'I'm sorry, but I've things to do. The calf pen wants mucking out, and I need to go and clean the horse harness.' Ethan got up from the table, taking everybody by surprise.

'But you've not had your trifle, and I thought we could go for a walk after tea,' Rosie exclaimed.

'No, I've too much to do. I thank you all for asking me, and I'm glad that you've had a good birthday, Rosie. Now please excuse me, I'll be away.' Ethan pushed his chair back while the family watched him walk off. Rosie was nearly in tears. As he left, he looked at the miniature set of drawers that it had taken him hours to carve and make. They were rubbish; he could never compete with her family and he was a fool even to have thought it. If Rosie started attending all the social events in the district, her head would soon be turned. Perhaps that was what her mother was hoping, when she had given her that fancy dress and the posh evening bag. He was a fool to think she would ever be his, and he was sure his father would say the same to him in the morning, if he went.

'Ethan! Ethan, wait!' Rosie got up from her chair, dropping her precious gifts to the floor, and rushed to be with him as she heard him close the kitchen door.

'He takes after his father, does that 'un.' Archie looked across at Harriet. 'Doesn't like to think he's been shown up or outdone.'

'I wish we'd never invited him in. And yes, I'm not ashamed to admit that if Rosie goes to the dances and balls coming up, in that dress, I hope she'll meet somebody a lot better suited to her than Ethan Haygarth.' Harriet looked at the untouched trifle and sighed.

'Be careful what you wish for, and don't try to alter the path of true love, for you'll only get hurt.' Archie looked across at Danny. 'What does thou say, lad?'

'I'm not saying owt. But he seems nowt but trouble, does that lad,' Danny said.

'Ethan, what's wrong? Why have you come out here? You know full well that you've done all there is to do for today.' Rosie strode across the farmyard. Her skirts billowed in the wind that had suddenly sprung up, making the last of the autumn leaves cascade around her, and her hair lash her face.

Ethan turned and looked at her. 'I'm not good enough for you, Rosie. Go and find somebody else – somebody with more brass, somebody with land and that's been brought up the same way as you. I've come from nowt, and my father's right: I shouldn't even be setting eyes on you, let alone touching you.'

'Why are you saying this now? What's changed from an hour ago, when we were going to look at the cottage in the village and were making plans for our life together?' Rosie stood in front of him and held back the tears.

'I've realized how little I have to give you, that's what's changed. I've nothing, and never will have, and you deserve better. I could never buy you fancy clothes and bags, and go with you to society balls and dances. They would all look at me and whisper behind my back, "He's the gyppo that the Atkinsons let court their daughter." I can hear it now. You deserve better.'

'Well, let them talk, I don't care. I want only you, and I'm not bothered about fancy clothes and snobby social balls. We'll go to the local dance down in the village hall – everyone goes to that, and nobody stands on ceremony there. As long as I have you, I don't care.' Rosie put her arms around him and hugged him close to her. 'I love you, Ethan Haygarth, and only you, so stop being so bloody proud, and go and see your father tomorrow.

He'll have to take it in his stride, if my father tells him that he must.'

Rosie looked up at Ethan, whose black hair was blowing in the wind and whose eyes were dark and as wild as the weather.

'We don't need anything or anybody, if we have one another.' Rosie took his face in her hands and kissed him. 'My wild rover: that's what you are and always will be, and that's why I love you.'

'So, you've finally decided to show your face. Do you know how much worry you've put your mother through? I suppose you've been trailing around looking for your grandfather again. When I told you to bloody well forget about him.' Jethro scowled at his son and spat out a mouthful of saliva as he watched Ethan drive up to the stables and stop next to him, with Danny beside him on the buckboard.

'Now then, Jethro. Ethan landed back the other day and I've told him to come and make his peace with you and his mother, but I need a word before you set into him. That's why I'm here, stopping off on my way to see the blacksmith at Settle.' Danny looked at Ethan. He had been quiet all the way to Windfell. He knew Ethan was not looking forward to confronting his father. 'Let him go into Windfell and see his mother first, while I have a word with you. I'm sure she will be glad to see him.'

Ethan climbed down from the flat wagon and watched as Danny walked into the stable, his hand on his father's shoulder, talking quietly; he hoped that was the way it would stay, as he tied up the team of horses to the metal ring outside the stable, before making his way around the back of Windfell Manor. He stopped just outside the kitchen door as he plucked up courage to face his mother, Mazy, thinking of the fuss she would make of him, now that he had returned, and of the shock she would show at his confession of love for Rosie.

'Hey up, young Ethan! Now you are a stranger, but I know someone who will be glad to see you.' Ruby the cook turned to see who was entering her kitchen as she stirred the year's last batch of blackberry jelly on the stove. 'Mazy! Mazy, look what the cat's dragged in,' she yelled through to the pantry, where Ethan's mother was checking the supplies, ready for winter.

'What are you yelling at, Ruby? I'm only here, not a mile away?' Mazy stepped into the kitchen and stopped in her tracks as she saw her son standing in the doorway. 'Ethan, you are home! Thank God for that. Where have you been? I've missed you so much.' She rushed to his side and hugged him as he put his arms around his mother.

'I'm sorry, Mother, I should have come earlier, but I . . .' Ethan put his head down, not wanting to say that he hadn't forgiven – and couldn't – his father for the braying he'd been given, and that he'd missed her so much.

'Shh . . . I know, your father shouldn't have lost his temper with you. He should have known better.' Mazy held Ethan's face in her hands and kissed him on the cheek. 'You are home now and that's all that matters.' She sniffed and wiped her nose and pushed away the tears that were falling. 'I just didn't know where you were, and if I'd ever see you again, when Mr Atkinson said you'd gone missing. And you know what your father is like; he wouldn't let me come up and see you when you were at Crummock. He said that it was your duty to come and see us.' Mazy breathed in deeply.

'I'll leave you two together. The kettle's nearly boiling, and you know where the teacups are.' Ruby pulled the pan full of boiling jelly off the heat and watched as mother and son sat down together, wanting to make up for lost time in private, as she made her way out of the kitchen.

'I'm sorry, I seem to be good at causing upset and worry. And I'll be making more this morning, when Mr Atkinson finishes telling my father what I'm about.' Ethan dropped his head and looked down at his hands.

'What's up, Ethan? You're not in trouble, are you? Is that why you disappeared?' Mazy reached for her son's hands and held them tightly as she looked at him with love and concern.

'It depends what you call trouble, and if Father is going to lose his temper again.' Ethan sighed. 'I'm hoping that you will both give me your blessing to court Rosie – that's why her father is here with me. He's outside with Father, telling him that they have concerns, but they are happy for us to walk out together on certain days, rather than sneak behind their backs. We can't help it, Mother. I love her and she loves me – we can't stop it. That's why I went away, to see if I could stop thinking about Rosie, but I couldn't and she feels just the same about me.' Ethan looked at his mother and at the shock on her face.

'Oh, Ethan, she's way above us. It's Miss Rosie you are talking about, Master Archie's granddaughter. She's not for the likes of us.' Mazy looked at her son and sat back in her chair, taking in the news. 'Your father will be saying just the same. He'll be going mad, you know he will, despite what Master Danny says. And you say the Atkinsons are alright about it? I just can't believe that. You are a grand, lovely lad, but you can't keep Rosie in the lifestyle she's used to – we have nothing.' Mazy sat back and looked at her son, taking in his news and remembering all the times the Atkinson and Fox children had been part of Ethan's life and realizing that perhaps the inevitable had happened. He'd always thought a lot of Rosie and was better off loving Rosie than Jane, who was way out of his reach, and Mrs Fox would not even be happy if he so much as looked at her.

'I'm sorry, but we do love one another,' said Ethan, without hearing the kitchen door open and his father step in.

'Love! What do you know about love, lad?' Jethro stepped in and stood in front of his son. 'You only bloody hurt folk – not showing your face to us for weeks on end. Making your mother cry of a night and making her wonder whether you were dead or alive. And all for some slip of a lass that you should not be looking at, let alone thinking you are in love with. I thought you'd have learned your lesson after I gave you that braying, but no, you've brought more bother to our door.' Jethro stood in front of his son, while Mazy pulled on his arm to try and hold him back from hitting their son.

'Leave him be, Jethro, don't you hurt our lad,' she shouted.

'I'll not bloody hurt him. Danny Atkinson has warned me off him. But he does deserve his arse being kicked, with him thinking himself something that he isn't and setting his cap at Rosie Atkinson. He should know his bloody place,' Jethro snarled.

'Just like you had to? Don't you realize I know that you worshipped the ground Charlotte Atkinson walked on? I used to watch you helping her with her horses and doing anything you could for her. She could have asked for the moon and you would have tried to get it for her. It's no good lecturing our Ethan; he's only doing what his father wanted to do, and courting the lass from Crummock.' Mazy stopped short; she hadn't meant to say what she had, but over the years of her marriage to Jethro it had become clear to her that he secretly loved his employer. But now it was out, she realized that's why he had vented his wrath on their son so much, for Ethan had done what Jethro had never dared to.

'You are talking daft, woman. I never thought anything about her. I married you, didn't I?' Jethro looked blackly at his son and wife as they stood together, ready to take him on. 'Do what you bloody like. You always have hidden behind your mother's skirts, and if Danny bloody Atkinson has no more sense than to let you see his lass, then I'll have to be bloody quiet. It'll all end in nowt anyway, but don't think you can come trailing home again, because I'll not make you welcome.' Jethro turned and walked towards the door. 'Behave your bloody self and don't bring us any shame.' He grabbed the door handle and slammed the door behind him, leaving both Mazy and Ethan looking at one another.

'Don't fret, he'll come round. You know what he's like.' Mazy reached for the teacups and kettle.

'I thought he'd bray me again.' Ethan breathed in deeply.

'Nay, he won't do that, not if Mr Atkinson says that he is alright with you courting Rosie. Now, we never mention what I said to your father – it's not to be talked about ever again, and I only said it because I knew if he'd have been in your shoes now, he'd have done the same. You enjoy your time with Miss Rosie and leave your father to me.' Mazy poured the tea and smiled at her beloved son.

Ethan looked at his mother, trying to understand his father's secret love for his employer, and the love that his mother must feel for Jethro. She'd been second best all her married life, and had only just now let his father know that she was aware of this. That was no marriage; he and Rosie would be more secure than that – of that he was going to make sure.

'We could make this look lovely. Just look at the garden, Ethan, we could fill it with vegetables. And it looks like there are two bedrooms. Room enough for a family, if we are ever so lucky again.' Rosie blushed and felt a pang of sadness for the trauma and worry that she had been through, while thinking of the future and hoping for better times ahead with Ethan by her side.

Ethan looked around him at the overgrown garden and the ivy-clad walls of the unoccupied cottage. 'Aye, I reckon we could make something of it. But I daren't dream too much about it. Your grandfather might have plans for it and he may not even agree to us living here.' He looked at the excitement on Rosie's face as she peered through the peeling, paint-cracked windows into the kitchen and small living room.

'Grandpapa would only be too happy to let us live here – it's always been empty. He used to say that he would live in it sometime, but now he's happy to be back with us up at Crummock.' Rosie stood back next to Ethan and put her arm through his. 'I'll wait a bit longer and then I'll ask him, once we have proved that we do love one another and that we are serious.' She squeezed Ethan's arm tightly and smiled. 'Our own little house – just us two, where no one can tell us what to do. Won't that be fine?'

'It will, Rosie. In fact I could make a start on the garden in my spare time. I can clear the weeds over this winter, cut back these brambles and give the garden gate a lick of paint. Then everyone will know we are serious about each other. It'll not do the cottage any harm anyway, as it looks so uncared for.' Ethan looked around him. He would give the garden his time, as and when he could. 'I hope that when the time comes your grandfather will agree, because it is, as you say, the perfect home for us. A home that we will cherish between us. We'll do this, Rosie. Despite whatever obstacles they put in our way, we will show them.'

Ethan held Rosie tightly and looked around him. It was a lot of responsibility, but Rosie was worth it. That spring he had been a young lad without any cares. Now he had grown into a man, and he aimed always to be there for his Rosie.

24

'Jane, you might as well make yourself useful today, while Harriet and I interview the new seamstress. You can go into Settle and give Lambert's my instructions for the invitations that I need printing for our Christmas Ball. There's no need for you to come into work, Aunt Harriet won't have time for you and nor will I.' Isabelle looked across at her daughter as she spread marmalade on her second slice of toast. 'Have you any need of Jane today, James?'

James was engrossed in his morning newspaper and didn't realize that he was being talked to, as he read about the latest divisions between the Triple Entente of Britain, Russia and France and the Triple Alliance of Germany, Austria–Hungary and Italy. The division between the two military camps was beginning to make him more aware and anxious that all was not well in the world. Especially with the Irish Home Rule movement insisting on Irish self-government. The world was not a safe place.

'James, are you listening or am I talking to a brick wall, as usual?' Isabelle put her knife down sharply.

'Sorry, my dear, I was just reading about the worries of the world. It will only take a small spark to throw the world into chaos.' He sighed and folded his newspaper. 'Now, what did you ask?'

'Do you need Jane today or can she have the day at home?' Isabelle looked disdainfully at her husband. All he did was worry about world affairs, and consequently she had lost count of the times he had condemned her compliments about Luke excelling in the cadets at school, as he feared that war would soon be rearing its ugly head.

'No, no, I don't think so. I've quite an easy day today. But she can join me in the Leeds branch tomorrow, and then she can keep an eye on me. I'm sure you'll be happier if she does.' James looked sharply at Isabelle, knowing full well that she still didn't trust him.

'You never told me that you were interviewing today. Could I not take the interviews with you, instead of Aunt Harriet – surely it would be more fitting?'

Jane looked at her mother. She still wasn't being included fully in the running of Atkinson's and resented the fact.

'You will get your chance in time, Jane, but at this moment leave it to Harriet and me. She has the experience, and it is her position they will be filling. She does tell me, however, that you are showing promise in your sewing and cutting skills. She was quite impressed when I spoke to her about you.' Isabelle sipped at her tea. 'Now, are you willing to walk into Settle and take my instructions to the printer's? It would be a good help, and the weather is quite pleasant for the first day in November.'

'I suppose I could. I'm obviously not needed in the store.' Jane looked across at her father. 'Am I really to come with you to Leeds tomorrow? Will I have time to look around the arcades and perhaps do some shopping?'

'If your mother agrees, I don't see why not. You haven't been for a while, and it won't hurt the staff there to meet you and realize that you are the future face of Atkinson's.' James smiled at the excitement his daughter was showing. 'And I suppose you will be wanting some spending money – so I'd say "yes" to delivering your mother's invitation instructions. Although I can't say I'm looking forward to a ball. Opening our house to half the dale does not fill me with pleasure.'

'I don't know what to do regarding the invitation to Harriet and Danny and their family. Harriet told me the other day that Rosie is walking out with Ethan – Mazy and Jethro's son. Now I don't want to sound a snob, but I do hope they don't bring him along as part of their family. Imagine, the stable boy coming as a guest into our home on such a grand occasion. What would people say?' Isabelle breathed in deeply and shook her head in disbelief.

'Rosie is walking out with Ethan?' Jane squealed.

'Has she no pride? I wouldn't be seen dead walking out with him, he's so common.'

'Keep your voice down, Jane, Mazy will be able to hear you.' Isabelle quietened her daughter quickly.

'He's not a bad lad. I'd have thought Rosie might have set her sights higher. It will suit your stepfather, Isabelle. I can't see your problem. Just ask them all as a family and then, if Ethan comes with them, he does; and if not, you have no problem.' James smiled to himself. Jane was so much like her mother.

'I just hope he doesn't. It could be quite embarrassing. Now, come with me, Jane, and I'll give you the instructions for the printer, before your father and I catch the train into work. Make sure you ask to have them printed for the middle of the month. I want us to be the first in the district to announce our intentions. I want to get one ahead of the Fosters at Anley Hall. Mary Foster is always bragging about how grand her Christmas Ball is, so let's better her this year.' Isabelle got up from the table, leaving James thinking how mother and daughter both had attitude; if they thought themselves far better than the rest of society, they were heading for a fall.

'My mother would like two hundred invitations to be delivered no later than the fifteenth of this month to us at Windfell.' Jane stood next to the counter, looking at the printer with his blue ink-stained hands.

'Two hundred, you say, with envelopes?' The printer looked up over his glasses at Jane and waited for a reply.

'Yes, and my mother asked if you could place a design

around the invitation, something tasteful, like bells or holly?' Jane looked around the small printing-press room, whose walls were covered with posters and wooden printing blocks, with all different typefaces and designs upon them.

'Perhaps you would like to have a look at some ideas, while I see what this young man behind you is in need of? I'm sure he won't take long to serve.' The printer looked over Jane's shoulder at the young blond-haired man who stood waiting his turn, then reached for some Christmas prints for the decoration on the ball invitations.

'Yes, I suppose I could.' Jane turned to look at the customer behind her as she moved to one side to choose the decoration. She stopped for a second as she glanced up at the young man. He reminded her of someone, but she couldn't quite think who. She smiled at him as he stepped up to the counter while she made her way to the side of the office.

She listened in to the conversation between him and the printer as she looked slowly through the selection.

'So that's fifty funeral cards to be picked up by yourself tomorrow. We can deliver them for you, but that will of course be extra,' the printer said quietly.

'Nay, I'll deliver them myself. My grandfather would have liked that and it's only right that I do so,' the young man said.

'Right you are, sir, they will be ready for you by midday tomorrow. May I give you my condolences from all at Lambert's? We will be thinking of you and your loss.' The printer passed the details over to his young apprentice and watched as his customer left the shop.

'I think we will have this one, Mr Lambert, it looks very seasonal and I think it will be tasteful enough for Mama.' Jane pointed at a print of a holly swag with a silver bell in the centre. 'It's very eye-catching and should look good on our invitations.'

'That's a good choice, Miss Fox, it is very popular.' Mr Lambert folded the corner of the print down to remind him of her choice and put it to one side. 'Anything else, Miss?'

'Erm, no. Well, yes, there is! Can I ask who the young man is that you've just served? I thought I recognized him, but his name escapes me.' Jane peered at the old man while he answered her.

'That'll be old Bill Brown's grandson, Daniel. He's just lost his grandfather and was ordering his funeral cards. Your grandfather will know them – they farm over at Ragged Hall. No doubt he'll be delivering an invitation to your grandfather, as all the farmers in the district knew and respected the old gent.'

'Oh, I didn't think I knew him. I just thought his face looked familiar. I must be thinking of someone else. However, you are correct in thinking that my grandfather will have dealt with his grandfather, if they farm.' Jane picked up her posy bag and looked at the printer.

'Aye, he might not know Daniel Bland, for he's just come to live with the old man, from what I hear. He's been keeping him company in his hour of need. It's a sad day for him.' Mr Lambert shook his head as he turned away from Jane.

'Indeed, Mr Lambert. I should have given my condolences to him as well. I do hope he calls in at Windfell so that I may do so.' She looked sympathetically at the printer. 'Good day, Mr Lambert.'

'Aye, good day, lass. I'll see to your invitations for you.' The printer watched as Jane made her way out of the shop.

She walked up through busy Duke Street, her head held high as she acknowledged fellow shoppers and neighbours. But her mind was on the good-looking man who had stood behind her at the printer's. What a pity he would probably be taking the funeral card to Crummock and not to Windfell, for she would have liked to have seen more of him and introduce herself. He had seemed strangely familiar, but at the same time she had never seen him before in her life. She smiled to herself as she thought of the mop of blond hair and the blue eyes; he was a good-looking man, that was for sure.

'So, you enjoyed your day with your father?' Isabelle looked at her daughter as Jane flicked through the pages of *The Lady*, seemingly uninterested in the contents, just as she was in the *Weldon's Ladies' Journal* that had been discarded to one side, as she decided that she couldn't be bothered to read either magazine on this quiet Sunday morning.

'Yes, it is so different from here. Leeds is so full of life, and the shops . . . well, our little shopkeepers in Settle just can't be compared to the bustling arcades in Leeds. The ladies are more fashionable and the gentleman are that well groomed, I swear even I must have stood out like a country bumpkin.' Jane sighed.

'I'm sure you didn't. As you know, you and I keep well abreast of fashion. It's just that the ladies who attend our Leeds shop are wealthy, as with most of the shops in the arcade. Step a few streets back and you would see another side of Leeds – the poverty and the slums that townspeople still live in. So you must think yourself fortunate, Jane. You have been born into a privileged lifestyle. Did your father have a good day?' Isabelle wanted to quiz her daughter. It had been James's first day back in Leeds since the fateful crash, and she had done nothing but wonder how the Leeds store had reacted to his return.

'Yes, he was busy all day. He had a queue of people wanting their picture taken, so we were both kept on our toes. We barely had time for lunch, let alone anything else. I was hoping I would have had time to browse in a few shops, but all I managed to get was this magazine at the station. And this is full of what the perfect wife and mother should be, and it doesn't keep my interest.' Jane flung *The Lady* to one side. 'Did you find a replacement for Aunt Harriet – one you both agreed on – without my input?'

'Yes, we did, thank you. She's called Margery Sutcliffe and lives in Skipton, so she's ideal. Her seamstress skills are excellent, and she comes highly recommended by her previous employer. I think you and she will get on well.

272

She's a bit plain in looks, but perhaps that is not a bad thing. She dresses well, and that's more important.' Isabelle pulled on her gloves and looked at her daughter, who didn't look happy, knowing that she had not been trusted to interview the new seamstress. 'Come to church with me and your father. You know you should attend, no matter how much you despise going. The walk there will do you good, and will stop you from brooding.'

'I'm not brooding. I just dislike Sundays. Perhaps Luke will come and brighten up the day, although all he thinks about is how to shoot his gun and how smart he looks in that uniform of his. Stupid idiot!' Jane sighed again. 'But church is one step worse, so I'll find something to do. I'll write a letter or two in the morning room and tell my friends about the ball at Christmas, then they've time to plan their dresses.'

'Suit yourself, my lady. But going to church shows your standing in the local community, and it doesn't hurt to be seen there. We will be back for lunch, so we won't be long.' Isabelle walked over to the doorway and left her daughter in the morning room, reaching for pen and paper from the desk next to the window. Jane was in a mood and was best left alone.

Jane watched her mother and father walk down the drive and past the beech trees that were blowing in the northerly wind. Her mother was holding onto her hat, despite the hat pin keeping it in place, and Jane shook her head, wondering why they hadn't taken the trap instead of walking the half-mile to Langcliffe.

She reached for her pen and looked at the blank pages of paper in front of her. She didn't feel like writing, but as usual on a Sunday that was all there was to do – that and a gentle walk, as her mother had reminded her. She breathed in deeply, sat back in her chair and looked outside: a walk or letter writing? Both were equally boring, she thought, as she picked up the pen again and dipped it in the inkpot. She stopped when she heard the sound of horses' hooves as they disturbed the pebbles on the drive outside the window. She looked out, but could see nobody, so presumed it was Jethro or someone visiting him, or one of the staff, as she couldn't hear the doorbell being rung and answered. She picked up her pen once again and started to write.

She stopped quickly, almost knocking her inkpot over, as there was a knock on the morning-room door.

'Enter,' Jane shouted, as she looked at the words written half-heartedly on the nearly blank piece of paper.

'Begging your pardon, Miss, but there is a gentleman here. He came to the back door, wanting to see your grandfather. I've told him that he no longer lives here, but once he explained what his business was, I thought that perhaps you would like to save him the bother of travelling all the way to Crummock. Our Ethan will be calling on us this afternoon, and he could take the card back with him.' Mazy looked at Jane and waited, with the visitor standing patiently behind her.

'The card?' Jane looked up.

'Yes, Miss. Mr Bland here is delivering his grandfather's funeral card.'

Jane got up from her desk and looked past Mazy, ignoring her question.

'Mr Bland, how good it is to make your acquaintance. Please do accept my deepest condolences, on behalf of myself and all my family, on the loss of your grandfather. I'm afraid it is as Mazy says: my grandfather is now living at Crummock with his son. But, as Mazy is suggesting, we can make sure the invitation reaches him safely later in the day.' Jane looked up at the blond-haired young man she now knew to be Daniel Bland, and was even more taken with his striking features.

'I thank you, Miss Atkinson. That would take a few miles off my journey, so I am most willing to accept you and your maid's suggestion.' Daniel smiled at both of the women, who were staring at him in a most bemusing way. 'Who do I give the invite to?' He looked at both and waited for an answer.

'I'll take it, Mr Bland. My son will take it back to Crummock with him this evening – he works for Mr Atkinson.'

'Thank you.' Daniel gave the invitation to Mazy and turned to go.

'Mr Bland, would you like to join me in a drink of coffee? I must confess, I was about to put pen to paper, but cannot be bothered with writing this morning. My parents are at church and I could do with some company. I'm sure some warm refreshment would be just the thing for you.' Jane looked at Daniel and then at Mazy, noticing that she too couldn't keep her eyes off the visitor.

'I would not say no to that. Especially as I can see that

you have a grand roaring fire.' Daniel smiled at his host and walked past Mazy, who stared at him as he made his way into the morning room.

'Coffee for two, please, Mazy, and perhaps some of Cook's rock-cakes?' Jane quickly dismissed the gawping housekeeper and joined her visitor in a chair next to the fire. She looked him up and down, noting how tall he was, at least six foot; and although he was dressed like any other local farmer, in a shirt and waistcoat with corduroy breeches and jacket, he carried them with a swagger. His high cheekbones and blue eyes, framed by his blond hair, made him a most handsome man – and one that Jane found quite fascinating.

'I feel I'd better introduce myself, Mr Bland. I'm not, as you called me, Miss Atkinson, but Jane Fox. Mr Archie Atkinson, your late grandfather's friend, is my mother's stepfather and she took the Atkinson name when her own father died, until she married my father, James Fox. So we are in no way related, although my grandfather – as we have always called him – is loved by me and my brother and is just as good as a true grandfather, of that I'm sure.'

'Families can be a terrible mix-up. I know that myself, but I'll not bore you with mine just now. It is far too complicated.' Daniel looked across at Jane and thought how good-looking she was, with her long auburn hair; it was nearly how he remembered his mother, Amy, when she was young – before years of living with his so-called father and four brothers had taken their toll on her. She too had been beautiful, until all life's dreams had been beaten and wrung out of her by her husband and his family. He'd hated leaving her over at Slaidburn so he could look after his grandfather, but knew he could not stand living at home another minute. He knew that his mother was better off without him there, as a reminder of her free-living past. It was a thorn in the side of her husband, who frequently reminded both Daniel and Amy of the differences between Daniel and his other sons. He was different; he was not his father's child and all the world knew it, it was that obvious.

'It is as you say. I doubt anything would shock me, when it comes to families, but we have said enough about our family, I'm sure.' Jane smiled. 'When is your grandfather's funeral, and will you be leaving us and going back to Slaidburn when he has been buried?'

'It is on Friday, at Rathmell, at two p.m. And no, I won't be going back to Slaidburn. My grandfather left his farm, Ragged Hall, to me, so I aim to stay there, build the farm into what it used to be before my grandfather took ill.' Daniel looked into the fire as Mazy entered with a tray laden with coffee and rock-cakes. She bobbed a curtsy as she left the young couple helping themselves.

'Mazy's son will deliver your card – you've no need to worry on that score. I'm sure my grandfather will attend, and also his son, who shares your Christian name, although we call him "Uncle Danny". We never use his "Sunday name" of Daniel, as he calls it.' Jane smiled at her guest as she poured him his coffee and passed him a rock-cake. 'He has the same-coloured hair as you, too – strange, that!' Jane paused and then bit into her rock-cake and watched Daniel's every move, as she realized that it was her Uncle Danny that her guest reminded her of.

'Aye, well, we are all Dales folk around here. All inter-related, one way or another, and folk often look alike.' Daniel bit into his bun and looked at his hostess. 'Were you not in the printer's when I ordered the cards? You were looking at some fancy designs.'

'Yes, I was. That's how I recognized you, when Mazy introduced you. My mother had asked me to go to Lambert's to get some Christmas Ball invitations printed. I was looking at what I thought she would like printed on them, while you were placing your order.' Jane breathed in, wondering if she dared say the next line. 'You must come as my guest. I know it will be a little soon after the death of your grandfather, but I'm sure he would approve. And I know Grandfather Archie would like to see you there. It's on Christmas Eve, at eight p.m. I'll send you an invitation, to remind you.' She blushed. She had never been that forward before, but Daniel Bland was so good-looking and he was about to get his own farm, so her parents could not complain.

'Aye, I might just do that. My grandfather would want me to. His dying words to me were to get on with life, after his day, and not mope about. You remind me, with an invitation, and I'll be here.' Daniel smiled across at the young woman who had made him welcome; he'd like to see a bit more of her, now that he knew who she was.

'It's a deal then.' Jane laughed.

'That it is, but now I'd better be on my way. Thank you for the drink and the warm-up. I'll get on with the business of handing out my cards and telling everyone my bad news. It's going to be a long day, if everyone I meet invites me in for a drink and to get warm. My grandfather must have been well liked.'

Daniel rose from his chair and looked at the young woman in front of him and at the house she lived in. It was a million miles from the hovel he'd been brought up in, and yet he had been told by his mother that this house was where his true father had lived nearly all his life. His true father, whom he had yet to meet.

25

'Well, that's another bugger gone. There's hardly anybody left that I played and grew up with.' Archie looked at the funeral card that Ethan had just handed him.

'The devil looks after his own. You'll be with us for a good time yet.' Danny patted his father on his back as he stared at the notice of Bill Brown's demise.

'I suppose I will have to show my face at his funeral. Now, are you going to come along with me? It could be awkward for you. You'll get to see the lad, though.' Archie looked at his son and knew this was the moment that perhaps Danny had been waiting for: a glimpse of his former lover and their son, both of whom, he knew, must have been playing on his mind.

'Well, you can't go without me really. I'll come, but I'll keep a low profile and sit at the back of the church, away from the family.' Danny glanced quickly at his father. The old bugger knew him too well; he knew exactly what he was thinking.

'I wonder what's to become of Ragged Hall. Will Bill have left it to his lass, or perhaps her lad will have been given it? He's the one that deserves it – he was there when he was needed.' Archie leaned upon the kitchen table and looked out of the window, deep in thought. 'Ragged Hall's always been in the Brown family. Bill will not have wanted it to go to any of that lot over in Slaidburn. I bet your lad's got it.'

'Father, he may not be my lad. Just because he's blond, it means nowt,' Danny snapped.

'Tha'll see for yourself. He's yours alright, and he's back where he belongs. A cuckoo never falls far from its nest. He'll be back at Ragged Hall, I'll bet you my last penny.' Archie grinned.

'Now, we can't have you looking like that. Here, let me straighten your tie. And keep your trilby on if you can, at the graveside, as your hair needs cutting.' Harriet fussed over Danny, making sure he looked respectable for the funeral that both he and his father were attending. She turned to Archie and straightened the white handkerchief in his pocket. 'Now, don't worry if you are late back for milking. Rosie and Ethan have it in hand. We all know how these funerals drag on, especially with you farmers. You'll be discussing the price of sheep and what the weather is doing, while poor old Bill's grave is filled in and he's already forgotten about.'

'Nay, lass, we will try and be back in good time. Now Bill's gone, his family doesn't have anything in common with us.' Archie smiled at Harriet and then glanced quickly at Danny. 'Right, lad, let's be away. It's only a little chapel at Rathmell and I need a seat, as my old legs won't be able to hold me up through the full service.'

'Bye, Harriet. We should be back before milking, so don't worry. As you say, the time we get back will depend on this old gasbag and who he gets talking to.' Danny leaned forward and kissed Harriet on the cheek. He rarely did this and Harriet knew exactly why he had done it today, as she watched father and son leave the warmth of her kitchen.

She sat down and glanced out of the kitchen window, looking out over the Dales and watching Danny and Archie going down the road from Crummock on their way to Bill Brown's funeral. She breathed in deeply, trying to control her thoughts as she watched the horse and buggy carrying father and son disappear over the hill on their way down into Austwick, and then on to the sleepy hamlet of Rathmell. Today Danny would see her rival, for the first time in nearly twenty-five years. Yet she could not suppress the jealousy and hatred she felt for the woman who had nearly stolen her man from her, albeit briefly, all those years ago. She held back the tears that were threatening to fall and looked out to the fells in the distance. 'God help you, Amy Brown, if you look at my man the way I know you did all those years ago. He's mine now. We have a family and a home, and I would fight you with every breath of my body this time, if you tempt my man again,' she whispered to herself. Then she let her tears fall, as she remembered the hurt she had once felt – a hurt that had nearly destroyed them.

*

'I knew there'd be a lot of people here. Bill was highly thought of.' Archie sat next to Danny in the pew that was one back from the last row, in the small chapel in the centre of Rathmell. 'He was well respected, had damn good sheep in his day,' whispered Archie, as they stood when the vicar could be heard entering the chapel, followed by the coffin and the mourners.

'I am the resurrection and the life. Whoever believes . . .' The vicar walked slowly in front of the grieving family and stood before the coffin, which the pall-bearers rested next to the altar in the small chapel.

Danny caught his breath and looked at the grey-haired, weeping woman who stood behind it. That couldn't be Amy – not his Amy. Then four dark-haired men joined her in the front pew, after following the path of the coffin. Danny looked at the onetime love of his life and couldn't believe his eyes. Where was Amy's thick auburn hair and the spring in her step, and the smile he had loved so much? He knew it was her father's funeral, but he'd expected Amy to look just as beautiful as he'd remembered her to be. Instead, she was an old woman. Her once-vibrant hair had turned grey and was pinned up in a bun under her black mourning hat, and her face was tanned and covered with lines, showing the hard life she had endured since her marriage.

Amy's sons and husband sat next to her, like black crows, hanging on every word the vicar spoke and guarding her from prying eyes. Their dark hair was slicked back, covering the white collars of their shirts and blending with the blackness of their suits, making the pew look like one of death and grieving. Seated on his own on the other side of the chapel was a lone figure, quite the opposite of those in the adjacent pew. There sat a man with blond hair, his black suit showing it off as if a halo shone around his head, as he listened intently to the vicar reading the life story of Bill Brown.

'Let us rise to sing psalm number twenty-three, "The Lord is my shepherd",' the vicar called out and the congregation all stood.

'I told you – he's your lad alright. Just look at him,' whispered Archie to Danny. 'He's not one of them, anyway.' He nodded in the direction of the pew containing Amy and the rest of her family.

'Quiet, Father, folk will hear you.' Danny looked ahead of him and sang. He looked at the lad who was singing all alone. His father was right: there was no doubting the fact that he was a cuckoo in the nest and that he had come home, whether Danny himself liked it or not. It was obvious to one and all who his father was.

'You are home soon, did you not go to the funeral tea?' Harriet stood back and looked at both of her men as they came back into the kitchen.

'No, we didn't even go to the graveside. My father was struggling with walking and it looked like rain, so we just did the service.' Danny threw his trilby on the table and pulled the black tie from around his neck, placing it on the back of the kitchen chair. 'Come here, you bundle of rubbish.' He reached down for baby Georgina and held her on his knee, as Harriet placed the kettle on the hob.

'We didn't want to impose on the family. And besides, I don't ken the lad that Bill's daughter married, but he looks a moody bugger. Plus she's changed out of all recognition, and she didn't bother looking to the side we were on. So we didn't stop.' Archie pulled up the other chair next to his son and smiled at his youngest grandchild as she played with the teaspoons on the table.

'Oh, so there was no gossip or anything? That's not like you two.' Harriet poured out two cups of tea and took Georgina onto her lap, to hold her tightly next to her.

'No. I don't suppose we'll have much to do with Ragged Hall again, now Bill's gone.' Archie sipped deeply from his cup and sat back in his chair. 'It will no doubt be put up for sale, unless one of his grandchildren farms it.'

'Well, perhaps that would be for the best. Their home will be Slaidburn, after all.' Harriet smiled and sat back, content with the news she had been given. There was no need to worry about Amy Brown; obviously time had favoured herself, for keeping her looks, otherwise Danny would not have returned so quickly. He was still hers, and always would be.

26

'Close your eyes. No peeking.' Ethan held Rosie's hand and guided her across the back green to the garden of her Great-aunt Lucy's cottage. 'You are cheating – keep your eyes closed. Here, stop there and I'll tie my neckerchief around you and then I know you can't see.' Ethan stopped Rosie in her tracks and undid the red-and-white spotted neckerchief from around his neck. He tied it securely round her eyes, making sure she couldn't squint through it. 'There, that's better. Now I know you definitely can't see.'

'But why do I have to close my eyes? What is there so special to see?' Rosie held out her hands, grasping Ethan's as he guided her over the green and through the garden gate of the small, dilapidated cottage. She held tightly on to Ethan as he guided her up the path to the back door and then turned her round, before untying her blindfold.

'There, what do you think? I've cleared all the brambles and dug the flowerbeds ready for spring, and I've taken the ivy off the walls of the cottage. At least you can see into the rooms more easily now.' Ethan stood back and watched Rosie's face light up.

'Oh, Ethan, you've even made a birdtable?' She rushed over to where a birdtable stood in the middle of the paved garden area, and looked at the workmanship that had gone into it and how tidy the garden looked. 'It looks lovely, Ethan.'

'Snowdrops are already beginning to show. I told them to keep their heads down for a while longer yet, as we are only just into December. And there's a Christmas rose over here by the back door – it will flower shortly. Your Great-aunt Lucy must have known her plants.' Ethan grinned. 'It's a grand garden and there's enough room for a veg plot round the side, so we'd never go hungry.'

'Now we've just got to convince everybody that we are serious; that it's not just "puppy love", as my mother keeps calling it.' Rosie walked over to the cleared windows and peered in. 'I could see us two living here. It would be ideal, and we'd be away from my family and yours, in our own little home. Although you'd still have to work for my father or find something else.'

Rosie turned and looked at the lad who had stolen her heart. She was going to have to speak to her grandfather. He understood her and had always stood by her, no matter what her parents had said.

'I'll ask my grandfather for the key, just to have a look around at the moment. And then I'll ask if he'd give his blessing for this to be our first home, if we are still together in the spring. Which, of course, we will be. I know he wouldn't approve of us going behind his back.' She smiled and held Ethan close to her as he kissed her and ran his fingers through her long hair.

'I love you, Rosie Atkinson. I always will. Spring is only like a day away to me. This cottage will be ours – I'll wish it so. Just like I wished for you.' Ethan held her tightly and kissed her passionately as they stood outside the back door of the old cottage, hoping their dreams would come true and that one day they'd wed and live there.

'I wish that too, Ethan. I don't want anyone else, just you.' Rosie held him tightly. She knew that if her parents had their way, they would prefer anyone other than Ethan, for he just wasn't good enough for her in their eyes. But they didn't know him like she did.

'I don't know, Rosie, your father won't be that suited.' Archie looked with concern at his granddaughter. 'I know the cottage is empty and could do with a bit of attention, but I don't think your father would be happy if I was encouraging your affections for Ethan.'

'But, Grandfather, we only want to have a look around. We wouldn't get up to anything while we were there. Please . . .' Rosie at her grandfather looked like an appealing puppy as she tried to get her own way.

'Oh, alright, I suppose a quick look round is not going to get you into any harm. Now you take care and behave yourselves, else I'll be out on my arse if your mother finds out I'm encouraging you both. I'll give you the key and I expect it back later today. You just look round, and you say nowt to your parents. Otherwise I'll not be welcome living here no more, and I'll need the cottage.' Archie scratched his head and went over to the drawer in his desk. 'My Aunt Lucy will be looking down and laughing at me. She always used to have a soft spot for me and Charlotte, and now I'm in the same situation with you and Ethan. I know true love when I see it, even if you are both too young.' He looked at Rosie. 'Now you do nowt you'd be ashamed to tell me of and you return this key to me tonight, and then I'll say nowt to nobody.'

'I promise, Grandfather, and thank you. I knew you'd understand.' Rosie took the key and kissed Archie on the cheek. She hesitated before leaving him to walk down into Austwick with Ethan. 'I do love him, Grandfather.'

'I know, lass, just be careful. I'd hate to see you hurt.' Archie sat on the end of his bed and sighed as he watched Rosie nearly skipping out of the doorway. She was only young – too young to be wanting a home and family of her own, especially with raggle-taggle Ethan, even if they were made for one another. Anyway, it might all come to nothing. Time would tell.

'It's perfect Rosie. I know it's only got two bedrooms, but that's all we'd need for a start.' Ethan looked around him.

'For a start, Ethan Haygarth! How many children were you thinking of us having? I might not want any.' Rosie looked out of the window at the limestone scars of the fell called Moughton and smiled to herself. Then she remembered the night when she had lain alone with her worries and her pain, bringing a pang of uncertainty back to her.

'I'm sorry, Rosie, I should think more of what I say.

But I'd love a big family. And after a good paint with whitewash, and new homes found for the various spiders that seem to be everywhere, I think we could not wish for anything better for a brood of our own.' Ethan put his arms around her waist and kissed her neck as she looked out of the window. 'We could be really happy here.'

'I know, Ethan, but I'm scared,' Rosie whispered.

'Don't be scared. I'll always be by your side, I promise,' he whispered as he held her tight.

'I can't help it, not after . . .'

'Shhh. If I'd known what had happened, I'd never have gone away. I'm sorry for the hurt, Rosie.' Ethan kissed her again. 'We will always be together, I promise. Now let's get the key back to your grandfather, so he isn't worrying.' He smiled. He'd found a spare key hanging up in the back kitchen, and now he felt for it in his pocket. He would keep his find a secret. Over the winter he would secretly put every hour he could into the cottage, because come spring Rosie would be his, and he aimed to have a home ready for them both.

'I hope you can all make it?' Isabelle passed to Harriet the newly printed invitation to her Christmas Ball.

'Oh, Isabelle, it'll be like old times. Your mother gave such grand balls in her time. I was in awe of them and inspired by the grandeur. It was the special part of Christmas – an excuse to dress in your finest clothes. I felt like a queen, when I had Danny on my arm and we were dancing in the hall.' Harriet looked lovingly at the invitation and smiled, remembering the good times when she was younger.

'I'm surprised he didn't cripple you – he's always had two left feet, our Danny. Knowing him, he'd stand on your feet more than lead you in a dance.' Isabelle looked at her sister-in-law and wondered how to word the invitation for Rosie, but not for Ethan, without offending her.

Harriet interrupted her thoughts. 'Is Rosie included? She can wear the new dress I made her. It matches the evening bag that you gave her. I hope you will include her in the invitation. I need her to see what she is missing, and to stop making a fool with herself with that Ethan. He's not good enough for her. I don't know why Danny and Archie make a fuss of him.' Harriet looked at her sister-in-law and recognized a look of relief, as she talked yet again about her unhappiness with her daughter's courtship.

'Rosie is invited, but I would prefer it if Ethan didn't attend. It just wouldn't be right, with Mazy being our housekeeper and Jethro being the groom. He would be so out of his depth and it would be embarrassing for us all.' Isabelle breathed in deeply and waited for Harriet's comments.

'I just wish Rosie was not so infatuated with him. Do you and Jane know a few eligible young men who might catch her eye and encourage Rosie not to lose her way with Ethan? Anybody would be better than him.' Harriet put down her sewing, as she admitted her despair over the love affair that was unfolding between Ethan and Rosie.

'Leave it to me. We both know a few young men who

might take her fancy. There's the Knowles lad at Feizor, and the Robinson lad at Horton. He's just been left some land by his grandfather – he would be a good catch. And let's face it, your Rosie is a good-looking girl. Dress her up and I'm sure, by the end of the night, we will find somebody more suitable.' Isabelle smiled. 'Now about work: when do you want to call it your last day? Do you agree with my choice of Margery Sutcliffe? I think she was the most adept of the bunch and, between you and me, she is too old and set in her ways to turn James's head. I've learned by my mistakes, Harriet, I really have.' Isabelle looked thoughtful as she thought back to the flighty Madge, and then of the woman she had just employed. 'Plus, Margery will be a steadying influence on Jane to learn the skill of dressmaking, and it looks like she will not take any nonsense when it comes to her work.'

'She's a bit stern, but she does have very good skills. So, yes, you have made the best choice. If she is to start next week, as you have agreed, I'll finish working here the following week. We seem to have caught up with the orders now. Another week here will give Margery time to settle in, and time for me to spend with Jane, although she is showing great promise in her skills. I don't think you will have any worries with Jane. She seems to have settled down and realizes now, after her silliness with her so-called suffragette friend, just how much she thinks of this wonderful shop. Especially as she knows that one day it will be hers. I wish Rosie had as much sense. I'm sure she is going to ruin her life, if she doesn't see sense soon. The more I moan at her, the more she digs in her heels and swears undying love for her Ethan.'

'Oh, Harriet, it will work out alright; she'll see the error of her ways eventually. I'll ask Jane to make a fuss of Rosie at the ball and to introduce her, as I say, to some of the eligible young men in the district. Hopefully she will return home with her eyes open and realize that Ethan is not for her. Now, once winter is over, and if you are not too busy on the farm, you must come back and keep your hand in at Atkinson's. After all, you are a part shareholder and you should have your say in the running of the stores. We could have tea together, if there is nothing to discuss, and it is just good that we are close again. Mother would be so happy that we are no longer at loggerheads with one another.' Isabelle smiled at her sister-in-law; she had missed Harriet over the years and was glad of her being there now for support.

'I will. It is just the travelling to Skipton this winter that will keep me away. The nanny has been perfect with Georgina, and Rosie is good with her, too. And as for Ben, well, he's growing up quickly, so I would like to come back in spring, once the worst of the weather has gone. I've enjoyed my time here with you, albeit brief and under terrible circumstances.' Harriet bowed her head, thinking of all the hurt James had caused with his fling. But at the same time she was glad that the misfortune had brought down the barrier between her and Isabelle.

'Well, what he did to me still hurts me and the family, but hopefully it will make us stronger. He chose his moment, though, didn't he? Just after my mother dying – a time when

I was at my most vulnerable. It will take me a long time to forgive him. And I think a lot of Jane's behaviour lately is a result of his stupidity and his actions. Thank heavens Luke is away from it all at Giggleswick.' Isabelle sighed. 'Still, some good has come out of the bad, and just look at us two: thick as thieves once more, and for that I'm thankful.'

'Yes, me too. We were both young and foolish, and you think only of yourself at that age. We should not forget that when chastising our own children. Even though we want the best for them.' Harriet looked around her and remembered the time when Atkinson's was just starting out, and all the excitement there had been in the air. Her mother-in-law had been dressed to the nines, and she and Isabelle had taken orders and fittings for dresses and clothes that no one in the district could compete with. Now things were changing. Some working-class households – the ones that could afford it – owned their own sewing machines and bought ready-made patterns in different sizes, to make their own clothes more easily. Coupled with the new ready-to-wear range that Atkinson's now had in store, tailor-made clothes would soon be solely for the few, with alterations perhaps being the most that Atkinson's seamstresses could offer. Times were changing, and the economy was more austere. She couldn't help but think that the best times for Atkinson's had perhaps been and gone now. Anyway, time would tell and she could do nothing about the ways of the world, even if she wanted to.

27

Windfell Manor was thronged with staff getting the hall ready for Christmas and the coming ball. The kitchen was especially busy, as they prepared for the many meals that would be expected of them.

'I'm rushed off my feet. I don't know how the mistress thinks we can cope,' said Ruby. 'She's not offered any extra staff, or told me yet how many guests we have at this ball. I haven't even got Lily any more; she used to help, if she thought we were busy. But you won't find Dorothy getting her hands dirty down in the kitchen. Oh no, she's far too much up her own arse to come down here too often. Too busy making sure everyone's wardrobe is correct – as if that takes much doing in this house!'

Turkey feathers filled the air as Ruby and Nancy plucked the four birds that Jethro had brought in from Settle market.

'You'd think Jethro would have plucked these birds

for us, but no, he's too busy faffing about with his horses and moaning about his lad. I don't know why he's so bothered about Ethan. I say, "Good lad." There's nowt wrong with aiming high, and Rosie is a grand lass – unlike our snooty Miss Jane.'

'I can understand Jethro not being happy about it. Ethan should know his place. Although I'd never say so to Mazy – her lad can do no wrong, in her eyes. We should never mix with them above us; it only ends in tears. Think of that flighty bit that turned Master James's head.' Nancy picked up the meat cleaver and aimed it at the feet of the turkey she had just plucked and came down hard with it onto the chopping block, before moving on to cutting off the crinkled pink-and-blue wattle. 'I don't mind plucking the birds, but I hate cleaning them.' She went over to the kitchen sink and put her hand down the turkey's neck to remove the crop, which was filled with the remains of the turkey's last corn supper. 'It's the smell.' Nancy retched as the odour hit her nostrils.

'You have never had a strong stomach.' Ruby turned round quickly and shook her head at Nancy. 'Thank heavens Christmas is only once a year, and at least I can prepare quite a bit in advance. But I'm sure it was never this chaotic in Miss Charlotte's time, and she'd have been down here making sure we were alright. Mistress Isabelle just says what she wants and doesn't think of the consequences – she's always been like that. Always wanted her own way and never thought how it affected anybody else. Miss Jane is just like her; she'll have to learn by her mistakes or it'll be the worse for her.' Ruby examined her plucked turkey. 'I'll have to singe this fine down off. I'm tearing the skin, trying to pluck it off.' She walked over to the mantelpiece and got a spill from the container above the fire and lit it. Holding the turkey up in one hand, she ran the lit spill over the fluffy down on the turkey's neck and chest, watching it brown and curl up and disappear, while filling the kitchen with the smell of burnt feathers and acrid smoke. 'I can't hold this bird much longer, it'll have to do.' Ruby looked at her handiwork and then put the heavy turkey down on the kitchen table. 'Open the back door and then clean me this one, Nancy. At least we've done half of them. It's coming up to lunchtime, I need to put the cock-a-leekie soup on the stove.'

Nancy opened the back door wide, letting fresh, cold air into the kitchen, before returning to cleaning the turkey. 'I don't want any dinner.' Her stomach churned as she looked at her next victim and thought of the chicken in the soup that she usually enjoyed, but not today.

'You don't know what's good for you, lass. You've got to eat,' grinned Ruby, as Nancy retched again and gave her a look that said everything.

'I know I do, but the thought of any fowl in anything makes me want to be sick. You could have made mushroom soup – or anything other than what I can envisage running around a farmyard.' Nancy breathed in and took courage as she picked up her carving knife to operate on the dead bird.

*

'Now, doesn't that look beautiful?' Mazy stood back and admired the decorated pine Christmas tree that stood proudly in the hallway of Windfell.

'It certainly does. I do love Christmas.' Dorothy Baines stood next to her with an armful of mending and cast-offs from the Fox family.

The tree looked magnificent; glass baubles shone and tinsel glittered in the light of the chandelier that had recently been hung in the entrance hall. The tip of the tree was finished off with a sparkling golden star reaching halfway up the staircase from the base on the marbled hallway's floor.

'The mistress has really gone to town on things this year. I thought it would be a quiet Christmas, after she lost her mother this spring and after the scandal that hit the family, but it seems it has not affected her Christmas plans.' Mazy looked at Dorothy, knowing that she was her mistress's ears when it came to the staff.

'I think that is exactly why she has planned such a big event. To show that there is new life in Windfell, and to make her and Mr Fox look strong. You can't mourn forever – life goes on.' Dorothy balanced her pile of clothes over her arm and watched as Eve wrapped a long garland made of holly and fir around the iron handrail of the stairs. She smiled slightly as she watched Eve stop and nearly swear as the holly pricked her, in defiance of being twined around the banisters.

'You've got an armful of mending, I'd better not keep you.' Mazy had tried to make friends with Dorothy, but she found her hard work and even though she knew it was not Dorothy's fault that she had replaced Lily as lady's maid, she couldn't forgive her for filling her shoes so readily.

'Oh, most of this is to be thrown out. It mainly belongs to Mister James. The mistress says he should have a new dinner suit for the party, and Miss Jane goes through clothes like nobody's business. In fact let me give them to you, and then you can give them to the rag-and-bone man when he comes again.' Dorothy held each item up, passing nearly all of them to Mazy as she did so, before going into the morning room to sit and mend the few items she had kept.

Mazy looked at the armful of garments that Dorothy could have taken to the outhouse herself, to await the weekly rag-and-bone man's visit. She was so lazy, thought Mazy. But she knew Dorothy didn't want to show her face in the kitchen, realizing that she would probably be given a job to do. Mazy picked through the garments one by one: the pretty silks that had once adorned Jane, the frills and fancies of the best quality. On the bottom of the pile was a perfectly good dinner suit, which Isabelle had decided was not good enough for her unfaithful husband, with a bow tie still attached. Perhaps she was getting rid of it because he had worn it with his lover, Mazy thought, as she held it up and looked at it carefully. Whatever the reason, the suit was too good to give to the rag-and-bone man. Neither of her two would ever wear anything like it, but she could sell it to the second-hand shop in Settle and boost her pay a little. Snooty-drawers Dorothy need never know it had not gone to its rightful place, she thought, as she moved to put the contents of her arms in a secret location in the stable, to be taken home later. The money was better in her purse than in the kitchen funds, where it would have gone if the rag-and-bone man had bought them, she thought, as she walked back smiling into the kitchen.

'Been to see your Jethro, have you? Did you tell him it's nearly lunchtime, if he fancies joining us in this kitchen that's in disarray?' Ruby looked up from stirring her soup.

'He's not here today; he's gone to the blacksmith's to shoe two of the horses.' Mazy glanced at the red-faced cook, who looked as if she was going to burst with heat and stress from running the busy kitchen.

'There you go – nobody tells me anything. I've made enough soup for an army and there's only going to be the four of us having it, because madam here says she doesn't want anything, and Thomson has gone into Settle to pick up Master James's new shoes. I suppose he will have gone in with Jethro, when I think about it. Those upstairs will have to have cock-a-leekie for their starter tonight, and they'll just have to lump it.' Ruby placed the bread board down on the table in front of Mazy and looked at her face. 'Aye, and you needn't pull that face – that's what we are having, despite the smell of turkey guts. If your Jethro had cleaned them, then my kitchen wouldn't smell like it does.'

'He's busy as well, you know. You are not the only one who's rushed off their feet. He's been told to collect people all over the dale, for this ball at the weekend, and he's busy with Christmas jobs just like the rest of us.' Mazy was holding her own with the angry cook.

'Busy poaching pheasants off the Maudsley estate, I suspect. I don't suppose he's got a spare brace, has he? I could do with one, if he's some spare. Only if he has the time, of course,' blustered Ruby.

'Here, I'll make your life easier and take Dorothy her dinner. She won't be able to sit in here with this smell, you know what she's like. Yes, I'll tell Jethro you need a brace of pheasants – he's got some hanging already, if you need them with a bit of taste. They should just be right for Christmas Day.'

Mazy reached for a tray and placed a cruet set, spoon, bowl of soup and plate with buttered bread on it. 'That should do Her Ladyship Dorothy. Not that she'll show her face anyway, because she knows you are busy in here and she's in the morning room, mending clothes as usual. I'll give Eve a shout – she's busy in the hall seeing to the decorations – before I'm on my way to serve madam.' Mazy lifted up the tray and left Ruby and Nancy shaking their heads in disbelief at how one of their group could get away with doing nowt.

'Is your Ethan coming to the ball? He should, you know, if he's courting young Rosie.' Ruby sat down next to Mazy, on her return, and sipped her soup, waiting for her to reply.

'Oh no. It's not his place to be with the family. Mistress Isabelle won't want him there. After all, he'll be bringing the Atkinson family along in their carriage, and it wouldn't be right.' Mazy shook her head. She was proud that Ethan was courting Rosie, but knew his father did not agree with his son's love for her and thought Ethan should know his place.

'I don't see why he shouldn't. Miss Jane will have asked plenty of her friends. It's not like it is a formal occasion, it's only Christmas celebrations, and everyone should be welcome,' said Eve as she enjoyed her soup, oblivious to the smell, which had dissipated into the cold air.

'Nay, his father would not approve. Besides, what would he wear? You know how they all dress up on occasions like this. He'd only be embarrassed by looking out of place.' Mazy thought about the dinner suit she had hidden; it might be a bit on the large side, but she was adept with a needle and could alter it to fit her Ethan. Perhaps Eve was right: he should attend; he should be with Rosie and be proud to be seen there.

'Well, if I were him, I'd be there. Poor Miss Rosie is going to be lonely without him. And Miss Jane will not help, as she always seems to be slightly jealous of Rosie. Although I don't know why; she has everything she needs in her life and always will have, while poor Rosie has always had to be more grounded and is more like us.' Nancy leaned back next to the sink and watched the others eating their lunch. 'I bet he scrubs up well, your Ethan; under that long, wild hair there's a good-looking man hiding.'

'Nancy, hold your tongue – he's half your age.' Ruby looked at her second-in-command and shook her head.

'I don't know how you can even think about him like that. He's Mazy's son, and perhaps she's right: them and us shouldn't mix. Only thing is: Miss Rosie is not one of them, she is more like us. So there's no wonder Ethan has taken her eye. Still, it's a shame he'll miss dancing to the Beresford Band. Especially when they are coming all the way over nearly every dale in the area. I just hope the weather is good for them and that there's no snow. I might have a dance myself, down here in my kitchen, if I can interest that miserable Thomson.' Ruby sat back and laughed. 'Tell your lad to come and dance with me in the kitchen; he can't sit out in the stable feeling sorry for himself all night. Nancy will make him smile, by the sound of it.'

'I'll see. Perhaps he should attend. He is Rosie's beau.' Mazy looked around her at the faces she knew supported her.

'Aye, tog him up smart and sneak him in, just for Miss Rosie. It'll make her night.' Nancy turned round to start plucking her next turkey, making feathers fill the kitchen again.

'I'll see. He might be asked yet anyway, and then there is no need to sneak him anywhere.' Mazy stood up and cleared her dish.

'Nay, he won't, not with Mistress Isabelle, but you can dream.' Ruby pushed her chair back. 'Here, Nancy, I'm plucking, you are cleaning. Wash these dishes up, while I finish plucking your bird. I know just how much you can't wait to get your hands into that bird, and I wouldn't deprive you of the pleasure.'

303

Nancy got hold of the half-plucked turkey and watched Ruby nearly swear as she did so. Bloody birds, she thought, they were nowt but work, and these are just the first of many to be eaten over Christmas.

It was the Sunday before Christmas, and Rosie sat with her mother next to the kitchen window, looking out on the frosted landscape while having a quiet family moment. Georgina was lying asleep on her mother's knee and Ben was laid out in front of the open kitchen fire, reading his latest copy of *The Boy's Best*, occasionally letting out a chuckle as he read about the character's latest exploits.

Rosie concentrated on the darning that she had been given and felt content in the warmth of the kitchen. The smells of Christmas filled it, as the plum pudding steamed on the stove top and the scent of pine from the newly erected Christmas tree in the parlour drifted through the whole house.

'It's nice to have you back home all the time, Mother. We've managed, but in all honesty we have missed you when you have been at Skipton.' Rosie looked up at her mother and smiled; it was a rare day when all was quiet at Crummock. The cattle were in for winter, the sheep were down from the fells and the two blazing fires were keeping the long farmhouse warm throughout.

'Yes, I'm best at home in this weather. Come spring, I'll give them a hand again. I think your Aunt Isabelle enjoys me participating a little in the business, and you all seem to cope without me for at least two days of the week. It's good to be back in my kitchen, though, without wondering what exactly is going on at home. Speaking of which, will Ethan be joining us this afternoon, as usual on Sunday? We will have to stir them two sleepy heads, if you need the parlour to yourselves.'

'No, Mother, it doesn't matter today; he's gone down to see his mother and father this afternoon and we've arranged to see one another later, after supper. I can tell him to join us for Christmas dinner, can't I, Mother? I want him to share Christmas with us.' Rosie blushed. She still found it hard to display her love for Ethan openly, knowing that her mother did not approve of her choice.

Harriet shifted slightly in her chair as Georgina weighed on her arm. 'He can come to Christmas Day dinner, but he does not join you at the Windfell ball. Your Aunt Isabelle has requested that, as a family, we come alone and said that Ethan will not be welcome. You can see her point of view; there will be dignitaries and people of all standing there, and she will not want a simple stable lad there on your arm.' Harriet looked across at Rosie and waited for the temper that was about to erupt from her daughter. She saw her face turn from smiling happiness to a dark scowl. She was a creature with plenty to say.

'How can she? If I'm going, Ethan is going. What's she going to do when I marry him? Because that's what I'm going to do. Tell her, Mother, or I will.' Rosie threw the darning down and stood up, scowling in front of her mother and watching as baby Georgina awoke as she vented her wrath. 'She's nothing but a snob, and so is Jane. Well, she can keep her Christmas Ball – I'm not going.'

Rosie stormed out of the kitchen and up to her bedroom and lay sobbing on her bed, staring at the unworn ballgown that she had been admiring since her mother had given it to her, as she waited for her first ball at Windfell with the love of her life on her arm. If Ethan wasn't welcome, then she wasn't, either, and wild horses would not drag her there.

28

'I'm so glad you've seen sense, Rosie. Just look how beautiful you are – you deserve to go to the ball. Ethan will understand; he would only feel uncomfortable, because – let's face it – he will have tethered the horses of most of the guests and he's bound to feel inadequate around them.' Harriet stood back and admired her daughter, who was all dressed up for the Christmas Eve Ball at Windfell. 'Isn't she beautiful?' Harriet turned and looked at Danny and Archie, wanting them to give Rosie the same assurance.

'Aye, a right bonny lass. You'll put everybody else to shame.' Archie looked up at his granddaughter and smiled; she was the spitting image of her grandmother and, being so, was especially dear to him. 'Never mind, lass, Ethan's not going anywhere. He'll be happier sitting in the kitchen with his mother, and you could always go down and visit him there. They'll probably be better company than half of the buggers upstairs.'

'Father, think on what you say! It's a big night for Isabelle – she needs to prove her standing in society, and show that she and James have recovered from his wanderings.' Danny looked at his father as he pulled a face and tugged on his collar and bow tie. He hated these sorts of event, and the fact that he had to toe the line and be polite to people he didn't normally have time for.

'It's nowt but a bloody sham. Folk are still going to remember James for being the first to have a motorbike in this area and killing his lover on it. Despite how big the show is tonight. And as for her ladyship not inviting Ethan, she's wrong. If he makes our Rosie happy, he should come with her.'

'Just keep your thoughts to yourself, Father. Remember the children's carer is in the next room.' Harriet looked sternly at her father-in-law as she pulled on her gloves and put the fireguard up to safeguard the kitchen fire, after filling a small metal-lined wooden box with warm ashes to keep them warm in the carriage.

'It's alright, Grandfather. Ethan wasn't too worried and, who knows, I might just enjoy myself with whoever may be there.' Rosie smiled at her grandfather. He always fought her corner for her, no matter how annoying it was to her parents.

'Right, if we are to get there in time, let's go. Ethan is outside with the carriage and team, and at least it's a fine frosty night. The weather is in our favour, albeit a little chilly. Have you all got everything?' Danny looked at the two women in his life and thought how fine they both looked. 'Mrs Atkinson, would you care to take my arm?'

'Why yes, sir, it would be a pleasure.' Harriet smiled and linked her arm through her husband's.

'That means you are with me, lass. Never mind – I'm the one with the brass. You remember that.' Archie winked at Rosie as she took his arm.

'I'd love you if you hadn't a penny to your name, Grandpapa. Money isn't everything.' Rosie kissed his cheek and took his arm as they walked out into the crisp winter's evening and towards Ethan waiting with the team.

'Good evening, so glad you could join us.'

Isabelle smiled at each guest as they entered Windfell, with James by her side in a show of unity. The hallway and ballroom were filled with well-to-do locals and dignitaries and their wives, and were awash with the bright colours and glitter of precious jewels.

'I don't think even Mama had as many guests as this. I don't even know everyone who is here. I think some are friends of Jane's, and of course there are some masters from Giggleswick School. It was only right that Luke asked them. It will do his standing at the school good. I do wish he had worn his dinner suit, though, instead of his cadet's uniform,' whispered Isabelle to James as he stood next to her, shaking hands with each guest and guiding them towards the drinks and food, which were being served by all the staff of Windfell.

'Just how many people have you invited? And tell me, do you recognize the tall blond lad who's with Jane? She keeps batting her eyelashes at him and I haven't a clue who he is. He's not in a dinner suit, so he can't be one of yours.' James smiled yet again at the incoming guests and glanced across at his daughter and her companion.

'I haven't got a clue who he is, but he is quite good-looking, although not well dressed. I'm just glad that she's entertaining him, instead of sitting like a wallflower or telling everybody the virtues of the Suffragette movement.' Isabelle smiled yet again and then looked out onto the driveway as the carriage from Crummock drove up. 'Here's the rest of the family. I hope Archie doesn't speak out of turn, and I do hope Harriet has told Rosie that Ethan is not welcome.

'Harriet, Danny and Papa, how lovely that you have joined us. And just look at you, Rosie, aren't you beautiful – quite the young lady. You'll be fighting the young men away from you.' Isabelle kissed Harriet on the cheek and smiled at her family.

'You've put on a good show, Isabelle; we could hear the band playing as we came past Stainforth. I hope you've invited your neighbours.' Archie kissed his step-daughter.

'Yes, the neighbours have been invited. The Maudsleys are mingling somewhere, so you can catch up with them, Father, and I'm sure you will know more people than I do. Rosie, Jane is over there in the corner, if you wish to join her. Although she seems to be giving all her attention to a certain young man, who I must admit seems familiar, though I'm sure I don't know him.' She smiled at Rosie, who struggled to reply to her and wasn't looking at where Jane was. Isabelle looked at Harriet, realizing that her request that Ethan did not attend had not been popular with her niece. 'I'm so glad you could all come. It's quite like old times.' She smiled as Harriet passed Thomson her wrap and put her arm through Danny's.

'Indeed it is. Let's hope this is the beginning of a wonderful Christmas, full of magic.' Harriet put her arm around Rosie and pulled her close to her. She noticed Rosie glance at the lad who was talking to Jane, with his back towards them, and saw that he was not well dressed, so Ethan would not have looked too out of place. She guessed Rosie was thinking the same thing.

'Go and enjoy yourselves. Just shout when you want a drink and Thomson will serve you. There's cold platters laid out in the dining room and, as Archie says, there's the Beresford Band playing in the ballroom. They would have been a bit too racy in Charlotte's day, but we've moved with the times.' James patted Danny on the shoulder and watched as the family walked into the throng and were made welcome by the other guests.

'Please excuse me, dear; most of the guests have arrived now and I want to have a talk to the officer who is standing next to Luke and his friend. Just to get an idea of how he thinks our country stands in these turbulent times.' James smiled at Isabelle. He'd done his duty, standing like a stuffed dummy, meeting and greeting while some of the so-called ladies looked at him and then giggled as they walked away, and their husbands chastised them even for looking at him. It would be a long time before his transgression with Madge Burton was forgotten, of that he was sure. Nobody forgot anything in the Dales, especially when it came to a scandal.

'Certainly, dear, I'm about to mix myself and make everyone welcome to our home. Isn't it wonderful to have the manor filled again with so many people – we must do it again next year.' Isabelle picked up her champagne flute and made a beeline for Jane, as she needed to know who the mystery guest was that was keeping her daughter so enthralled.

'The world is in chaos, sir. Every country has its eye on another one, and before long the alliances between countries will be tested beyond belief.'

Captain Pierce looked sternly at James as he stood alongside Luke and his best friend, Bill.

'The decline of the Ottoman Empire when the Balkan League captured the Ottoman lands in south-eastern Europe has been a major factor in the unrest. Those Russkies thought it would be a very useful tool to access the Adriatic Sea; and as for Germany, it is busy building a railway between Berlin and Baghdad through Istanbul, so it can't afford to fall out with anybody yet. I'm just thankful that the London Conference this year resolved the conflict in Serbia and formed an independent Albania. That was one less conflict. But it's only a matter of time – the world is a powder keg, sir. That's why we need stout fellows like your son here to fight for his King and country.'

'That's what I am afraid of. It's alright playing at soldiers in the grounds of Giggleswick School, but I would not want to see my son go to war. I'm glad that he is the age he is; at least he is too young for action yet.' James looked across at Luke, whose face showed that he thought otherwise.

'A war, if it came, wouldn't last long. No country can afford it, and most countries are in an economic mess. But as for playing soldiers, I beg to differ, sir. I train my cadets better than any of the officer classes of the Duke of Wellington Brigade. They are officers and gentlemen by the time they leave Giggleswick and my care. My training and values will be with your son all his life and he is one of our leading cadets, especially on the firing range. Something you are proud of, I'm sure?' Captain Pierce slapped Luke on the back and looked at James for his response.

'I am indeed proud of him, but I'd have been even prouder if he took my stance on life and didn't believe in war, for it only brings death and despair. There are other means to ensure peace.' James looked at the captain and then at his son.

'Father, please!' Luke sighed.

'You are not one of those conscientious objectors, are you, sir? With no backbone, and someone who would rather see other people die in their place than fight for their country?' Captain Pierce stuttered.

'No, but I'm not one for needless war and the slaughter of innocents, especially when one of them may be my son. Now, please excuse me. I'm afraid my wife is urging me to mingle and I've wasted enough of your time.' James looked at the man whose whole life revolved around fighting and war, and who had influenced his son far too much for his liking. He needed to make his excuses and speak to Isabelle regarding taking Luke away from the school, which acted as an army recruitment centre, before it was too late and the war that was threatening broke out.

'Now, Jane, who is this? Are you not going to introduce us?' Isabelle touched the arm of the young man who had captivated her daughter. 'I don't believe you made yourself known to me as you entered Windfell.' She caught her breath as he turned to smile at her.

'Mother, may I introduce Daniel Bland. He is the grandson of Ragged Hall's Mr Brown. I met him when he came to inform Grandfather of Mr Brown's death. I hope you didn't mind me inviting him this evening.' Jane beamed at the handsome young man who stood next to her.

'Delighted to meet you, Mrs Fox. My grandfather spoke often of your family and was insistent that I made myself known to you and your brother.' Daniel looked at Isabelle and recognized a change in her manner as she studied his features.

'Please accept my condolences on the loss of your grandfather. He will be missed by the local community. I know my stepfather and stepbrother knew him very well. Tell me, Mr Bland, are you his only grandchild? I have quite lost track of your mother and what family she has, since she moved over to Slaidburn.' Isabelle fished cautiously for what she already knew was the answer. It was clear to her who this young man was – and who his father was, for the likeness was uncanny.

'I'm the oldest and I have left four brothers back in Slaidburn. However, I'm afraid I have fallen out of favour with them, as my grandfather left me Ragged Hall upon his death. My father is not happy that he did not see fit to will it to my mother, for some reason. There is nothing stranger than families, but I was always there for my grandfather, and he was there for me. I seem to be the odd one out in the family, but blessed when it comes to luck.' Daniel smiled, knowing full well what Isabelle was thinking.

'So, will you be staying in the area? I'm sure it would have pleased your grandfather to know that his farm is in good hands and will be remaining in the family.' Isabelle looked at Jane, who kept glancing at her companion. She was smitten by him, even though he was improperly dressed for the occasion and of little standing in the community.

'Yes, it needs a lot of work and a great deal of time spending on it. But I'm willing to give it both, so you won't be seeing the back of me quite yet.' Daniel grinned. Isabelle knew who he was, and his grandfather had told him that the stepsister and brother were very close. She knew that he was Danny Atkinson's son – something his mother had told him when he was old enough to understand.

'Well, I wish you well, Mr Bland. Jane, I know you are enjoying Mr Bland's company, but don't neglect our other guests.' Isabelle gave a tight smile as she stepped away from the young couple.

'Please, Mrs Fox, my name is Daniel. In future, please call me Daniel – I'm sure you know why.' He caught her arm.

'Oh yes, I know why. I only hope you are not here to cause trouble or hurt any of my family,' whispered Isabelle out of earshot of Jane, thankful that the band was extremely loud.

'No, I simply want to meet my father, and this is one way to do it. My mother loved him, and still does, but I'll keep that to myself. There's been enough hurt in my life, without causing it in somebody else's. I'll take care.'

Daniel looked earnest as he watched Isabelle make her way to her husband and then on towards her step-brother, and then lead Danny away from his wife and family. He didn't want to hurt anyone, not in the way he had been hurt in his life; he just wanted to fit in. The more he had talked to Jane, the more he knew he was where he belonged, and that this was his true family. The family his mother had wanted to be part of, but had never had the chance.

29

'I can't be down here long, Ethan, they will miss me.' Mazy stood back in the bustling kitchen of Windfell and looked at her son. 'Heavens, you look different. Nancy's done a right good job of cutting your hair and shortening the trousers – I couldn't have managed without her. I feel real tearful, just looking at you: my son dressed up like a gentleman. A handsome one at that.' Mazy bit her lip and stood back to look at her son, dressed in the evening suit that had been discarded for the rag-and-bone man. He looked handsome, clean-shaven, his black hair slick and neat; a match for any man on the dance floor.

'Aye, I don't think Rosie will look at another bloke once she sees me. I may have no money, but even I'm surprised at how well I scrub up.' Ethan looked down at his black trousers and at the work shoes that were just hidden under the length of them. 'Pity he wasn't throwing out some shoes as well, but you can't have everything.'

'Yes, your feet are too small for anybody's cast-offs

– I did try. Well, you had better get yourself up our stairs and make a quiet entrance; don't be too flash. If Miss Rosie's meeting you by the Christmas tree, I'll stand there with you and serve drinks, to support you both. Mistress Isabelle won't dare make a scene, once you are both up and dancing, as she won't want her night spoiled. So she'll just have to accept you.' Mazy looked at her precious son. He was good enough for anybody, in her eyes, and she would walk through hell to protect him.

'Thank you, Mother. You know how I feel about Rosie, I had to be with her tonight.' Ethan kissed his mother and held her tightly.

'Aye, well, your father will have something to say to us both in the morning no doubt. But it'll be worth it, just for the pair of you to turn a few heads and to let them know nothing's going to stand between you.' Mazy wiped her eyes with her hanky and led the way up the servants' stairs, weaving through the crowds to where the Christmas tree stood.

'She's not here yet. I can see her father talking to Mrs Fox, but I can't see Rosie, nor her mother.' Ethan gazed around the room at all the well-to-do guests and tried to hide behind his mother, as she picked up a tray of full champagne glasses from the dresser and offered them to passing revellers.

'She'll be here, don't fret. She keeps her promises, does Rosie – not like that Jane, who seems to be occupied with a young man. Although her mother and Mr Atkinson don't seem that happy with her, by the look of the glances they are giving her and the young man.

318

Happen you won't be the scandal of the evening after all.' Mazy smiled as her tray started to empty to all the partygoers.

'Ethan! Ethan, I'm here.' Rosie tugged on his jacket and pulled him towards her into the relative quiet of the drawing-room doorway.

'I couldn't see you. How do I look – swanky, eh? Not so much a stable boy now.' Ethan grinned. He held his hands and arms out and looked himself up and down. 'Do you think you can afford to be seen with me, Miss Atkinson?'

'Oh, Ethan, I wouldn't be bothered if you were still in your old work clothes, as long as we are together. But yes, I'm right proud to be on the arm of such a good-looking man. Let's see what they do about us now.' Rosie grinned.

'Could I interest you in a dance, madam? I do believe the band is playing a waltz and, as that is the only dance I can do, we had better make a move and show them how it is done.' Ethan winked; he was going to enjoy himself, just like everybody else.

'Do you think we should? My mother will have a fit when she sees you. She's been trying to introduce me to eligible young men all evening. The only one she hasn't bothered with is the one Jane is talking to, and although Mother says she doesn't know him, she keeps looking at him strangely.' Rosie took Ethan's arm as he led her onto the dance floor, feeling excitement and a little fear as she realized that people were looking at what, in their eyes, was a handsome young couple making the most of Christmas at Windfell.

'That's our Rosie. Who's she with? Oh my Lord, it's Ethan. Just look at him, he's in a suit. You can hardly tell it's the same boy that drove us down here tonight. Oh, I could die with embarrassment!' Harriet turned to Archie and then looked around her, at the faces watching the couple as they glided around the room. 'Where's Danny? Has he seen? What will Isabelle say about this? Oh, heavens! She'll never talk to me again.'

'Stop getting yourself flustered. Just look at them, they are the bonniest couple here tonight, and they know it. You should be proud of them, especially Rosie – she loves that lad, you know. And you can't say you haven't been there yourself, because you have. My lad had money, and you didn't have much, so how do you think we felt when you became part of the family? It didn't worry us, and it shouldn't worry you now. Just look at them, they are as pretty as a picture.' Archie leaned on his stick as he sat at the edge of the ballroom and watched Rosie and Ethan holding one another tightly as they waltzed around the room. Rosie's face was full of love, and Ethan looked so proud as he concentrated on his footwork. 'Bonniest couple in Yorkshire, that's what they are.' He sat back and shook his head as Harriet pushed her way through the crowds in search of Danny and Isabelle, to reassure her sister-in-law that she had known nothing of Ethan and Rosie's plans.

'I know – I've seen him, he's here!' Flustered, Harriet broke into the conversation that Danny and Isabelle

320

were having. She didn't notice the look of worry on both their faces when she spoke to them, and was nearly in tears as she saw the anger on Isabelle's face.

Isabelle looked shocked at Harriet's words.

'Oh, Harriet, I'm sorry. I had no idea he was going to attend. I didn't know Jane had invited him, otherwise I would never have allowed Daniel Bland to come. I'm sorry, it must be deeply upsetting for you. Danny knew nothing about him until just recently, I can assure you. But how long have you known? Please don't upset yourself; it is only us who knows who he really is, after all.' Isabelle looked at Harriet, distraught, and then pleadingly at Danny, who now had to face his wife and then make himself known to his illegitimate son.

'Harriet, I'm sorry you've had to find out this way. You do know that I loved only you, and that Amy was just an easy distraction – there was never anything between us.' Danny tried to put his arms around his wife, who looked puzzled by their responses.

'What are you both on about? Who is Daniel Bland, and why are you mentioning Amy Brown? At least I presume it is Amy Brown, considering that I told you, Isabelle, that I knew Danny had been unfaithful to me all those years ago. Don't look so shocked, Danny, you made it so obvious at the time, and I've always known I was second best.' Harriet looked at brother and sister and knew something untoward was in the making, with this so-called Daniel Bland. 'I was referring to the fact that Ethan is dressed up to the nines and is parading our daughter around the dance floor, for all the world to see.

So whatever it is that I'm not supposed to know and will be so shocked by, tell me now.' She breathed in and looked at them both. It must be bad, as neither of them had blinked regarding the news of Ethan and Rosie's escapade.

'I think I have a son! That's who Daniel Bland is. And he's caught the eye of Jane; she's been with him all night. That's what Isabelle was telling me when you came over to us. I'd no idea – I'm so sorry Harriet, I must have hurt you all those years back, and now for you to have all this thrown in your face. He's not thought of his actions.' Danny reached for Harriet's hand, but she pulled it away from him.

'He's not the only one who hasn't thought about his rash actions, is he? Where are they? Does he know you are his father?' Harriet gazed around the dance floor. Her eyes flitted from person to person, and the noise of the band and the sight of her Rosie and Ethan making fools of themselves to one and all made her feel quite faint.

'They are over there by the window. I am sorry to say that when you look at him, I don't think there is any doubt about his parentage.' Isabelle put her arm around her sister-in-law, feeling her body shake and seeing tears well up in her eyes.

'And does he know that Danny is his father?' Harriet spotted Jane and Daniel standing together, lost in conversation. 'He is more like you, Danny, than any of our children are, so I'd say there is no doubt whatsoever.' Harriet pulled her handkerchief out of her pocket and held it against her mouth, stifling a cry.

322

'I think so. From the way he talked, I believe his mother has told him who he is and that he is named after his true father.' Isabelle breathed in deeply. This was not the night she had planned. Yet again family scandals were being played out under the roof of Windfell Manor.

'I'm sorry, Harriet, I'm so sorry. I was young and I was foolish, and when Amy got married to the fella from Slaidburn, I thought that would be the last I'd see or hear of her.' Danny tried to put his arm around his wife, but she pulled away.

'You mean you hoped that your sins would not be found out! Well, he's standing there and looking every inch like you. And there I was, worried about Ethan showing us up with Rosie. At least they are not sneaking about with their love; they are proud to declare it to the world.' Harriet looked across at Daniel and then at Danny. 'No wonder you didn't stay long at Bill Brown's funeral. You and Archie realized then. You both had nothing much to say about how it went, because you had seen Daniel and noticed the resemblance and knew instantly that he was your son.'

'Oh, Harriet, if only you had said that you knew about Amy. I've been carrying the guilt for years.' Danny looked at his wife. All around him people were enjoying the festive season, but his world was falling apart.

'Guilt – you know nothing about guilt. Remember that I was to blame for the death of our two boys. It was my fault I put my work before them both. I lost my first-born, while Amy kept her son and your heart.' Harriet looked across at Jane laughing and flirting with Daniel.

'You make it right by him; go and tell him that you are his father, and then he has no hold over us.'

'I can't. How do I do that?' Danny looked at the hurt in his wife's eyes. Their marriage had been tempestuous, but now he knew why, for Harriet had always known about his love for Amy and had kept it her secret. A secret that had eaten away at her, every year she had been married to him. Every time life's trials went against them, she had questioned his love for her and it had gnawed away inside her.

Isabelle put her hand on Danny's arm. 'I'll distract Jane. It is best if Daniel gets to know that his secret is out. Take him into the drawing room and speak to him, find out what he is about. Although it sounded to me as if he just aims to farm Ragged Hall and is not here to cause trouble.' Isabelle looked at her brother and sister-in-law. Her perfect evening had been spoilt, but that was of little consequence compared to what Harriet and Danny were going through. She stepped through the crowds, passing Ethan and Rosie lost in one another's arms on the dance floor. Both stopped in their tracks as they watched Danny and Harriet following Isabelle over to where Jane and her admirer stood.

'Looks like Jane is in more trouble than we are.' Ethan smiled as Rosie watched her parents looking distressed, while following her aunt.

'No, something is wrong – my mother's nearly in tears.' Rosie let go of Ethan's arms and walked to her parents' side.

'Go back to Ethan, Rosie.' Danny glanced round at

his daughter as Harriet stepped in front of Isabelle, intent on getting to Jane and Daniel first.

'No, let her stay, she should hear this. In fact everyone should hear this; it is yet another dirty secret that has made itself known tonight,' yelled Harriet, making everyone around her fall quiet as she strode up to Daniel and Jane. 'Yes, yet another scandal – more for you all to talk about.'

Everyone looked at Harriet acting so strangely.

'My daughter is courting a stable lad, and now my husband has another son in our midst. Is that not right, Daniel? For is my husband and the father of my children not your father, too?' Harriet stood in front of Daniel Bland and the startled Jane, as tears flowed down her cheeks.

Daniel put his head down and looked at the faces of the revellers. The band had stopped playing and all eyes were on him and Jane, and the Atkinson family.

'I believe so. That is what my mother has always told me, since I was young.' Daniel looked at his father. 'Although I had no intention of making my parentage so public. I didn't come here to make trouble, just to see the family that my mother had talked about for as long as I can remember.'

'Harriet, lass, come here to me, don't get yourself so upset.' Archie made his way through the crowd and put his arm around the hysterical woman, whose heart had been broken once more. 'Come on – come over here with me, away from these folk. Rosie, you and Ethan go and tell Jethro to take us back to Crummock. I don't think your mother will want to stay and see Christmas in with these good folk.'

'Yes, Grandfather.' Rosie looked as bewildered as everyone else, as she and Ethan ran to fetch Jethro to take her mother home. The man who was with Jane was her own half-brother? Where had he come from? Who was his mother? Rosie glanced back as she watched Archie and her mother walk steadily out of the hallway, her mother in tears; and then the crowds of guests turned their attention to her father, standing with his namesake. There was no doubt in anybody's minds that Danny Atkinson had another son, and Rosie a half-brother.

'I'm sorry, good people, please don't let this outburst spoil your evening.' James stood on the band's platform and tried to draw attention away from Danny and his new-found son, as they made their way into the drawing room of Windfell. 'Families, eh, who would have them?' He was trying to make light of the situation. 'Come on, we've still got a few hours until Christmas Day. Enjoy the band and food, and forget your worries, because compared to ours they will be nothing.'

James grinned and instructed the band to start playing again, as he looked across at his wife and daughter. He was not the first in the family to fall from grace and he certainly wouldn't be the last, he was sure of that. Right now, he hoped that Danny was doing right by his new son, but also that he would return to Crummock and tell Harriet just how much she meant to him and that he had always loved her. He knew that, like his own fling with Madge, it must have ensued from the thrill of the moment, but unfortunately a son had been born from Danny's forbidden passion.

'Thank you, James. Isn't it all a mess?' Isabelle linked her arm into James's and looked at Jane, standing alone and aghast, until Rosie reappeared without Ethan on her arm, making her way to where her father and her newly announced brother had been standing with Jane. Luke was moving through the crowd to join them, not wanting to be disassociated from the breaking scandal. 'You try to protect your children from hurt and then you, as a parent, do more damage than you could possibly dream of,' said Isabelle regretfully.

'What do you expect? It's been the year from hell. It is only fitting that we end it on a high note – or should that be a low note? Did you know about Danny's affair and that he had a son?' James looked at his wife and noticed how shaken she seemed.

'Yes, I've always know about his love for Amy Brown. He nearly didn't marry Harriet because of her. Poor Harriet, she doesn't deserve all this worry.' Isabelle stopped short as Jane, Luke and Rosie came to join them both.

'Rosie, are you alright? Would you like to stay with us at Windfell tonight? I know it's Christmas Eve, but perhaps your mother and father might appreciate you staying here. Ethan would be more than welcome to stay with his mother and father tonight – I'm sure Mazy would like that. You can see him first thing in the morning and then go back with him to Crummock in the evening.' Isabelle's eyes had been opened; it didn't matter

327

about your standing in the world; it was love for one another that mattered.

'I don't know, I'll see. Ethan has taken my mother home, along with my grandfather. It seemed only right that he took her home. I should have gone with her, but Grandpapa said I had to stay here and wait for my father. Ethan's father will take us back to Crummock, when my father is ready.' Rosie looked at her cousin Jane and Luke, and for once they looked sympathetically at her.

'Well, this must have been a shock for you, too. A brother you knew nothing about, being made so public. Your poor mother was distraught. Now, if you do stay, I'm sure you will be able to find a few presents under the tree with your name on. Won't she, Jane?' Isabelle gave her daughter a knowing look, to acknowledge that what was to have been hers might have to be reallocated.

'Yes, of course, and you can help me out by listening to the boring conversations about the cadet school at Giggleswick with this one.' Jane glanced at her brother and put her arm around her cousin. 'I didn't know who he was, Rosie, else I wouldn't have invited him. I didn't mean any harm.'

'I know. It's just been a shock to my poor mama.' Rosie glanced over at the closed drawing-room doors.

'Don't worry, Rosie. Your father still loves you just as much. Your mother will calm down, and life will carry on as normal.' Isabelle kissed her niece's brow as she tried to ease the worry that the night had caused.

'It's very strange to find out that I've got a big brother I knew nothing about.' Rosie smiled.

'Well, at least you haven't been fluttering your eyelashes at him like I have all night. I had no idea who he really was.' Jane looked at her mother.

'That's typical of you. No more sense than the day you were born on,' Luke teased his sister. 'Desperate – that's what you were!'

'Why, you cheeky devil!' Jane scalped her brother with her hand. 'Come on, let's go outside and get a bit of fresh air. It will stop all these folk from looking at us as if we are exhibits in a showground.' She looked at her mother and father.

'Christmas sky tonight, let's see if Saint Nick is on his way.' James laughed, for the magic of Christmas could not be forgotten.

'I hope he's put his hand in his pocket this year. Nuts and sweets are alright, but I wouldn't mind a surprise or two.' Luke grinned.

'You'll get what you are given,' said Isabelle. 'Now go on, get some fresh air while we make sure all's calmed down among our guests.' Isabelle watched as the three of them walked arm-in-arm out of the ballroom and hallway into the winter's evening.

'They are growing up, James. They are no longer children.' She sighed.

'I know, and I fear for their futures. We can but be here for them. We can't tell what 1914 will bring, but if it's anything like this last one, we are all going to have to be strong.' James kissed Isabelle, before stepping out with her on his arm to mingle with their guests. War was coming, of that he was sure. But for tonight he would try and forget, and would be there for his family.

'Just look at those stars.' Jane looked up to the star-studded sky. 'Listen, you can hear the church bells in Settle.'

All three children looked up at the sky over Windfell.

'I hope my mother and father will be alright, and that the appearance of Daniel Bland does not cause even more upset in the family.'

'I know. Let's make a wish all together, a Christmas wish to the stars – as Father said, it's bound to come true.' Jane put her arm around Rosie.

'I know what I'm going to wish for. My red star, so that I can become an officer,' said Luke as he closed his eyes and made his wish.

'Shush . . . you shouldn't tell us,' Rosie said, as she closed her eyes and wished for herself and Ethan to be allowed to wed, and for peace at home.

'Well, I'm not telling you mine, but it is hopefully going to come true, if I have my way.' Jane closed her eyes and thought of Daniel Bland, despite the scandal he had brought with him.

All three stood on the gate leading to Windfell Manor, lost in their thoughts, until Danny's voice was heard calling down the drive.

'Rosie! Rosie, come here and meet Daniel.'

Rosie breathed in deeply. She looked at her cousins and didn't say a word as she walked back up the drive to her father and the tall blond-haired young man she now knew to be her brother.

'Rosie, this is Daniel. Although he has a different mother from you, he is my son and your brother, and I want you to make him welcome in our home.' Danny put his arm around his precious daughter and looked at Daniel.

'Hello, Rosie. I've always wanted a sister, and now I have one.' Daniel smiled at her.

Rosie looked up at his open face. He was the image of her father – a father she loved so dearly. She wanted to vent her wrath on him for being unfaithful to her mother, and then she remembered her own love and passion for Ethan. She could have been like Daniel's mother: alone and pregnant and desperate to find a father for her child, if she had not lost her baby. She thought of the fear and the scandal there could have been. She bowed her head and then lifted it to look at her new brother.

'Welcome to our family, Daniel. A big brother for Christmas – now that's different. Better than any present I could have wished for. Happy Christmas, Brother.' She linked her arm through Daniel's and her father's, and looked towards where Ethan stood waiting with the horses to take them home. Ethan was the main love of her life, the one whose love made her strong. Unlike her father, she would marry her wild rover, regardless of the scandal. She knew that her Christmas wish would come true.

30

'Harriet, I love only you, and have done since the day we met. My fling with Amy Brown was just that. We both were young and stupid. I knew you were the only one for me, but she was just too much of a temptation.' Danny lay next to his wife as she sobbed, with the bedclothes pulled up around her.

'But you have a son, and you have brought him home! How am I supposed to feel and deal with that?' Harriet turned and faced her husband with tear-filled eyes.

'I'd hope you would deal with it like you always do with our children. I know he's not yours, but he is mine. My son, who I've just found. And by the sound of it, he has had a very bad deal in life up until now.' Danny sighed as he held his wife close to him.

'Do you think I care about his upbringing? I hated Amy Brown and everything she stood for – she was wild and uncaring, while my mother always groomed me to behave like a lady, to find a good man and settle down. But just as I had done so, Amy came along and stole you from me, albeit just for a brief time. She deserved all she got. At least your firstborn is alive, while mine are dead in the grave and I will never see them again.'

'Oh, Harriet, we can't do anything about the past. I loved our sons, too, but we must look to the future. We have both gained a son tonight – if you let Daniel into your heart. He's not come to make any bother. His grandfather's left him Ragged Hall. He'll not ask anything of us, except recognition of him as my son.'

Harriet looked up at the husband she loved. It was true that she could not alter the past, and she had always known about Danny's affair with Amy, so a child from the dalliance should not come as a shock. 'It was the way I found out – I made such a fool of myself. I was more worried about Rosie and Ethan dancing together, and then Isabelle looked at me like I was mad, not realizing I knew nothing of Daniel Bland's presence.'

'Surprisingly, Isabelle handled it well, and so did James. However, I wish Daniel's arrival into the family could have been a little less public.' Danny smiled. 'On the way back home, he and Rosie talked as if they had known one another all their lives.' He ran his fingers through Harriet's long hair and kissed her brow. 'Forgive me, and make our black sheep welcome into our fold.'

Harriet nodded her head, before turning over in bed and keeping her thoughts to herself. Daniel was Danny's son, and she would grow to love him. In the morning another two places would be laid at the Christmas dinner table: one for Ethan and one for Daniel. Her family was complete once again. They would celebrate Christmas with the living, and would look to the future.

Archie lay in his bed with the bright moon shining down through his bedroom window, the ghostly ribbons of light illuminating the room and making him unable to sleep. It was his first Christmas without his beloved Charlotte next to him. He thought of her laughter, and of her love of Christmas and her family. What would she have made of Daniel's appearance? he wondered. He pulled the blankets up over him, trying to keep warm against the hard frost that was being laid down in the outside world.

'God bless, and happy Christmas, Charlotte, my love,' he whispered as he closed his eyes and dreamed of Christmases past, and of the love that he and Charlotte had shared. 'One in, one out,' he muttered as he drifted off to sleep, thinking of Daniel sitting at the Christmas table. What the future held, they would have to wait and see, but whatever it was, he knew he'd never love another like his Lottie.

'Noel: Christmas Eve 1913'
by Robert Seymour Bridges

A frosty Christmas Eve
when the stars where shining
Fared I forth alone
where westward falls the hill,
And from many a village
in the water'd valley
Distant music reach'd me
peals of bells aringing:
The constellated sounds
ran sprinkling on earth's floor
As the dark vault above
with stars was spangled o'er.
Then sped my thoughts to keep
that first Christmas of all
When the shepherds watching
by their folds ere the dawn
Heard music in the fields
and marvelling could not tell
Whether it were angels
or the bright stars singing.

Now blessed be the tow'rs
that crown England so fair
That stand up strong in prayer
unto God for our souls
Blessed be their founders
(said I) an' our country folk

335

Who are ringing for Christ
in the belfries to-night
With arms lifted to clutch
the rattling ropes that race
Into the dark above
and the mad romping din.

But to me heard afar
it was starry music
Angels' song, comforting
as the comfort of Christ
When he spake tenderly
to his sorrowful flock:
The old words came to me
by the riches of time
Mellow'd and transfigured
as I stood on the hill
Heark'ning in the aspect
of th' eternal silence.

For the Sake of Her Family

DIANE ALLEN

It's 1912 in the Yorkshire Dales, and Alice Bentham and her brother Will have lost their mother to cancer. Money is scarce and pride doesn't pay the doctor or put food on the table.

Alice gets work at Whernside Manor, looking after Lord Frankland's fragile sister Miss Nancy. Meanwhile Will and his best friend Jack begin working for the Lord of the Manor at the marble mill. But their purpose there is not an entirely honest one.

For a while everything runs smoothly, but corruption, attempted murder and misplaced love are just waiting in the wings. Nothing is as it seems and before they know it, Alice and Will's lives are entwined with those of the Franklands' – and nothing will ever be the same again.

OUT NOW

For a Mother's Sins

DIANE ALLEN

It is 1870 and railway workers and their families have flocked to the wild and inhospitable moorland known as Batty Green. Here they are building a viaduct on the Midland Railway Company's ambitious new Leeds to Carlisle line.

Among them are three very different women – tough widow Molly Mason, honest and God-fearing Rose Pratt, and Helen Parker, downtrodden by her husband and seeking a better life.

When tragedy strikes, the lives of the three women are bound together, and each is forced to confront the secrets and calamities that threaten to tear their families apart.

OUT NOW

For a Father's Pride

DIANE ALLEN

In 1871, young Daisy Fraser is living in the Yorkshire Dales with her beloved family. Her sister Kitty is set to marry the handsome and wealthy Clifford Middleton. But on the eve of the wedding, Clifford commits a terrible act that shatters Daisy's happy life. She carries her secret for the next nine months, but is left devastated when she gives birth and the baby is pronounced dead. Soon she is cast out by her family and has no choice but to make her own way in the world.

When further tragedy strikes, Daisy sets out for the bustling streets of Leeds. There she encounters poverty and hardship, but also friendship. What she really longs for is a love of her own. Yet Daisy doesn't realize that the key to her happiness may not be as far away as she thinks . . .

OUT NOW

Like Father, Like Son

DIANE ALLEN

From birth, Polly Harper seems destined for tragedy. Raised by her loving grandparents on Paradise Farm, she is unknowingly tangled in a web of secrecy regarding her parentage.

When she falls in love with Tobias, the wealthy son of a local landowner of disrepute, her anxious grandparents send her to work in a dairy. There she becomes instantly drawn to the handsome Matt Dinsdale, propelling her further into the depths of forbidden romance and dark family secrets.

But when tragedy strikes, Polly is forced to confront her past and decide the fate of her future. Will she lose everything, or will she finally realize that her roots and love lie in Paradise?

OUT NOW

The Mistress of Windfell Manor

DIANE ALLEN

Charlotte Booth loves her father and the home they share, which is set high up in the limestone escarpments of Crummockdale. But when a new businessman in the form of Joseph Dawson enters their lives, both Charlotte and her father decide he's the man for her and, within six months, Charlotte marries the dashing mill owner from Accrington.

Then a young mill worker is found dead in the swollen River Ribble. With Joseph's business nearly bankrupt, it becomes apparent that all is not as it seems and Joseph is not the man he pretends to be. Heavily pregnant, penniless and heartbroken, Charlotte is forced to face the reality that life may never be the same again . . .

OUT NOW

The Windfell Family Secrets

DIANE ALLEN

Twenty-one years have passed since Charlotte Booth fought to keep her home at Windfell Manor, following her traumatic first marriage. Now, happily married to her childhood sweetheart, she seeks only the best for their children, Isabelle and Danny. But history has a habit of repeating itself when Danny's head is turned by a local girl of ill repute.

Meanwhile, the beautiful and secretive Isabelle shares all the undesirable traits of her biological father. And when she announces that she is to marry John Sidgwick, the owner of High Mill in Skipton, her mother quickly warns her against him. An ex-drinking mate of her late father who faces bankruptcy, Charlotte fears his interest in Isabelle is far from honourable. What she doesn't realize is how far he's willing to go to protect his future . . .

OUT NOW

Information Systems Development: Methodologies, Techniques, and Tools

Third Edition

Information Systems Development: Methodologies, Techniques, and Tools

Third Edition

David Avison

ESSEC Business School, Cergy-Pontoise, France

Guy Fitzgerald

Brunel University, Uxbridge, UK

McGRAW-HILL PUBLISHING COMPANY

LONDON · BOSTON · BURR RIDGE, IL · DUBUQUE, IA · MADISON, WI · NEW YORK · SAN FRANCISCO
ST LOUIS · BANGKOK · BOGOTÁ · CARACAS · KUALA LUMPUR · LISBON · MADRID · MEXICO CITY
MILAN · MONTREAL · NEW DELHI · SANTIAGO · SEOUL · SINGAPORE · SYDNEY · TAIPEI · TORONTO

Information Systems Development: Methodologies, Techniques, and Tools
David Avison and Guy Fitzgerald
Published by McGraw-Hill Education

Shoppenhangers Road
Maidenhead
Berkshire
SL6 2QL
Telephone: 44 (0) 1628 502 500
Fax: 44 (0) 1628 770 224
Website: www.mcgraw-hill.co.uk

British Library Cataloguing in Publication Data
A catalogue record for this book is available from the British Library

Library of Congress Cataloging in Publication Data
The Library of Congress data for this book has been applied for from the
Library of Congress

Acquisitions Editor:	Conor Graham
Senior Development Editor:	Caroline Howell
Editorial Assistant:	Paul von Kesmark
Senior Marketing Manager:	Jackie Harbor
Senior Production Manager:	Max Elvey
New Media Developer:	Douglas Greenwood
Produced for McGraw-Hill by:	Steven Gardiner Ltd
Cover design by:	The Senate
Text design by:	Claire Brodmann Book Designs
Printed and bound in Spain by:	Mateu Cromo, Madrid

ISBN 0–07–709626–6

Dedicated to

Léone, Marie-Anne, and Thomas
and
Lin, Anna, and Jane
with love

Brief Table of Contents

Contents

· · · · · · · · · · · · ·

Preface to the Third Edition

First published 15 years ago, and extensively updated for the Second Edition in 1995, David Avison and Guy Fitzgerald's *Information Systems Development: Methodologies, Techniques, and Tools* is the key text on this subject and is used by lecturers and students worldwide. Through long experience of teaching with the text and feedback from colleagues and students, the authors have continued to build from this solid foundation to produce a new Third Edition. This new edition has been greatly enhanced and updated to reflect the latest developments in the field, and to meet the needs of a new generation of students.

Current users of the text, apart from valuing the content and material, particularly appreciated its unique structure in providing separate chapters on the *themes*, *techniques*, *tools*, and *methodologies* of information systems, enabling them to use the book in a variety of flexible ways. In the new edition this strength of structure has been retained, although due to the increased size and breadth of coverage, the seven original chapters now become seven parts. Each part is now made up of a number of chapters, either new or based on the original sections. This provides consistency for lecturers, while making the book much more manageable and accessible for all.

So much has happened in the world of information systems since the Second Edition that there are now new themes and issues, such as:

- the information systems development context;
- project management;
- method engineering;
- web-based development;
- enterprise resource planning;
- flexibility in information systems;
- legacy systems;
- outsourcing.

Additional techniques, include:

- Unified Modelling Language (UML);
- risk analysis;
- cognitive mapping;
- stakeholder analysis;
- lateral thinking;

- critical success factors (CSFs);
- SWOT analysis;
- scenario planning;
- case-based reasoning.

New methodologies, include:

- RUP (Rational Unified Process), an object-oriented methodology;
- DSDM (Dynamic System Development Method), an RAD methodology;
- CMM, a capability maturity model framework;
- Welti ERP development, an Enterprise Resource Planning methodology;
- XP, an extreme programming methodology;
- WISDM, a web-development methodology;
- CommonKADS, a knowledge management development approach;
- PRINCE, a project management methodology;
- Renaissance, a methodology for dealing with legacy systems;
- SODA, a cognitive mapping-based framework.

And this is in addition to all the existing methodologies from the Second Edition. Some of these are less well used than they were, but because they typically exemplify principles, or techniques and tools that are still important in the field of information systems development, they have been retained.

The tools and toolsets to support systems development have also been substantially updated and now include:

- Groupware;
- Dreamweaver;
- Oracle;
- Select Enterprise.

Finally, all the existing material, including the critical sections on methodology issues and frameworks, have been reviewed and updated as appropriate.

Because of this broad and effective content base together with its excellent structure, the text provides a sound basis for courses in information systems at all levels, from introductory through to specialist, and is relevant for courses with both an information technology and management perspective. It is of course particularly relevant for specialist courses in information systems development at both undergraduate and postgraduate level.

It is both a theoretical and practical text with, for the first time, web-based support material available for both lecturers and students. The Online Learning Centre can be found at:

http://www.mcgraw-hill.co.uk/textbooks/avison-fitzgerald

The authors

David Avison is Professor of Information Systems at ESSEC Business School, near Paris, France after being Professor at the School of Management at Southampton University for nine years. He is also Visiting Professor at University Technology, Sydney, Australia and Brunel University in England. He is Joint Editor (with Guy Fitzgerald) of Blackwell Science's *Information Systems Journal*, now in its 13th volume. He has authored over 20 books as well as a large number of papers in learned journals, edited texts, and conference papers. He is Chair of the International Federation of Information Processing (IFIP) 8.2 Group on the impact of IS/IT on organizations and was past President of the UK Academy for Information Systems. He will be Program Chair of ICIS 2005 in Las Vegas and has chaired several other international conferences.

Guy Fitzgerald is Professor of Information Systems at Brunel University. Before this he was the Cable and Wireless Professor of Business Information Systems at Birkbeck College, University of London, and he has also worked at Templeton College, Oxford and Warwick University. Most recently he has been a Visiting Scholar at Georgia State University in Atlanta, USA. He has worked in the computer industry for many years with companies such as British Telecom, Mitsubishi and CACI Inc, International. His research interests are concerned with information systems and information management and he has published widely in these areas. He has undertaken an in-depth study of IT outsourcing in the UK (with Leslie Willcocks) and his most recent work addresses the flexibility of information systems.

Acknowledgements

The authors would like to thank the following academics who have helped in the development of the third edition: Carl Adams, University of Portsmouth; Dr Aziz Ait-Braham, South Bank University; Christine Cuthbertson, Templeton College; Martin Hancox, Manchester Metropolitan University; Chris Kimble, University of York; Nicolas Prat, ESSEC Business School; Jeremy Rose, Manchester Metropolitan University; Hanifa Shah, Staffordshire University; Richard Trounce, University of Central England; Duane Truex, Florida International University; Richard Vidgen, University of Bath; Trevor Wood-Harper, University of Salford. We would also like to thank the anonymous reviewers whose comments and criticisms helped us to improve the book significantly. Finally we would especially like to thank Alfred Waller, who has supported, guided, and cajoled us on all three editions of this book plus all the current team at McGraw-Hill.

Preface

· · · · · · · · · · · ·

First published almost ten years ago, *Information Systems Development* is used by lecturers and students worldwide. Through long experience of teaching with the text and feedback from colleagues and students, the authors have continued to build on the solid foundations of the original text. The new third edition of *Information Systems Development* has been updated and enhanced to reflect the latest developments in IS technology, and to meet the needs of a new generation in IS studies.

The book contains comprehensive coverage of diverse topics including Oracle applications, UML notation, RUP, RAD, and DSDM. There is a new section on SAP and other ERP systems. E-commerce and web applications such as Dreamweaver are examined, as well as additional information on package development and component based design. The authors further illustrate how these various technologies integrate with social and economic factors to provide a thorough examination of *Information Systems Development*.

Due to this broad content base, *Information Systems Development* is suitable for a wide range of degree programs without impacting the unique requirements of either computer science, or business and management courses. Both theoretical models and real-world examples provide an engaging and practical text, and there is considerable web-based support material available for both lecturers and students.

The Online Learning Centre can be found at:

http://www.mcgraw-hill.co.uk/textbooks/avison-fitzgerald

Key features:

- Expanded material on Use-case modelling, RAD and DSDM, SAP, JSD, ISAC, and KADS.

- Increased coverage of Euromethod, Yourdon, Knowledge Management, CMM, and stages of growth.

- Enhanced management aspects (e.g. project management, TQM, quality issues)

- Contingency approaches Ethical issues in IS development

David Avison is Professor of Information Systems in the Department of SID at the ESSEC Business School in Cergy-Pontoise, France. He has published and edited over 20 leading texts on Information Systems. Guy Fitzgerald is Professor of Information Systems at the School of Information Systems and Computing at Brunel University. He has published numerous books for both business and academic audiences, many in conjunction with Professor Avison.

PART

1

INTRODUCTION

In Part 1 we introduce the context and main topics of this book. The domain of information systems is an exciting world. In Chapter 1 we discuss the context in which the developments that are the subject of this book take place. For example, the following issues are discussed: the increased rate of technological change, increased globalization of systems, growing importance of the knowledge-based economy, Web and Internet technologies, role of stakeholders and drivers for change. We stress the organizational and human aspects at least as much as the technology. We provide early definitions of the major themes of the book. In Chapter 2 we define information systems and give examples of the different types of information system in organizations. Reasons are given for the need to use a methodology to develop information systems and suggestions made regarding the requirements of such a methodology.

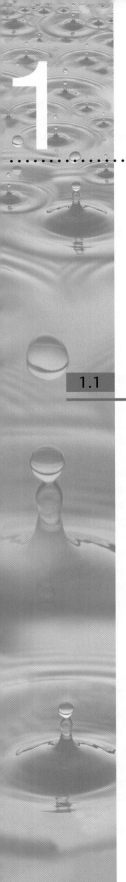

1 CONTEXT

INFORMATION SYSTEMS

This text is about information **systems** and specifically about ways of developing information systems. In this chapter we introduce the nature of information systems and illustrate this with examples. We develop this further and introduce other related concepts in Chapter 2. The main thrust of Chapter 1, however, is the context in which information systems are developed. We tend to stress the human and organization aspects to counteract the stress placed on the technology, which is a feature of many texts on this topic.

An **information system** in an organization provides processes and information useful to its members and clients. These should help it operate more effectively. The information might concern its customers, suppliers, products, equipment, procedures, operations, and so on. Information systems in a bank might concern the payment of its employees, the operation of its customer accounts, or the efficient running of its branches.

All organizations have information systems. The organization might be a commercial business, a government organization, or a community organization, for example, a bank, trade union, church, hospital, university, library, charity, or co-operative. This book concerns itself with **formalized information systems**. By formalized, we do not mean 'mathematical'. We use the term to distinguish information systems discussed here from less formalized information systems such as the 'grapevine', which consists of rumour, gossip, ideas, and preferences. These informal information systems may also be valid information systems and tend to be intuitive or qualitative in nature. Business discussions at the golf club or over lunch are also valid for disseminating information. However, organizations also need to develop formalized systems that will provide information on a regular basis and in a predefined manner, and these are the concern of this book.

We are mainly concerned with **computer-based information systems**, for the computer can process data (the basic facts) speedily and accurately, and provide information when and where required, which is complete and at the correct level of detail, so that it is useful for some purpose. By comparison, manual systems may be slower (information must be timely to be of value) and unable to deal with large volumes (of customers, suppliers, or transactions). Further, manual systems may be less accurate because checking procedures can be tedious, and not failure-proof (inaccurate 'information' can lead to poor decision making). In some circumstances, however, manual systems can be perfectly adequate or indeed superior to computerized information systems, such as in a small business, or where particular flexibility or human judgement is required.

In modern information systems, the basic data to be processed can include pictures, graphics, video, sound, and text as well as traditional alphanumeric data, such as a customer record. The computer system might be used to store data or convert the data to useful information by producing reports, pictures, graphics, or handling management enquiries. This does not mean that a computerized information system is 'purely' a computer system – there may well be manual (or clerical) aspects, such as inputting the data or some cross-checking – it simply means that part of the system is likely to be computerized. Nor does it mean that the computer technology itself is the most important aspect of the information system (in the same way that a word processor is certainly not the most important aspect of the system whereby an author produces a novel). Thus, in the main, technology itself is not the major emphasis of this book, and nor should it be. It mainly is about information systems (IS) not information technology (IT).

The information systems of an organization will be required to help it analyse the business, along with its environment, and formulate and check that it achieves its goals. These goals might be related to profitability, long-term survival, service provision, expansion, greater market share, and employee and customer satisfaction. The information system may help the organization to achieve improved efficiency of its operations and effectiveness through better managerial decisions. Information systems are sometimes regarded as providing competitive advantage. Another way of looking at this would be to say that, without good information systems, a business would be at a considerable competitive disadvantage. They are therefore an important organizational resource.

1.2   EXAMPLE INFORMATION SYSTEMS

Although many information systems are unique to particular types of organization – such as a system for placing and paying out bets in a betting office, a system to register voters for a local authority, a ticket reservation system for an airline, or a system for recording lottery choices – many information systems are common to a wide range of organizations. These include payroll, invoicing, project planning, decision-support, and so on. Even systems designed for a particular type of organization can be of a more general type. Therefore, reservation systems, for example, can be found in travel agents, cinemas, theatres, and libraries as well as in airlines. The generic nature of such systems is not always recognized in systems development as many systems have been developed as a one-off for a particular company or industry sector. Application packages, such as word processing or project management, are an exception and they have been developed for generic use in different types of organization.

For the moment we need to think about some examples of information systems before considering how they might be developed. We will outline two example information systems:

- A payroll system is an information system. This was one of the first applications to be computerized. Why? Because producing the payroll manually became very time-consuming and labour-intensive as the number of employees grew in an organization. If the payroll was late or contained errors there would be trouble, possibly even strikes. Organizations needed to get this right so they turned to computerization. It is difficult to imagine that such processes could be undertaken manually. Today, all but the smallest organization (or maybe those wishing to avoid taxation!) utilize a computerized payroll package to pay wages and salaries. The raw data of a payroll system might include the number of hours worked, rates of pay, deductions, such as tax, pensions, union subscriptions, national insurance, and savings schemes. The information system typically produces payslips, which contain information about gross wage, net wage, and details of the deductions made, reports for management, historical records, and the provision of information for the tax office, other government departments, banks, etc. The management information reports produced might help management make decisions relating to increasing or decreasing staff levels, incentive schemes, and appraising the performance of employees. Payroll systems are not simple, there exists a wealth of legislation that the system has to cope and comply with, for example, relating to company cars, pensions, employee savings schemes, and share options, above and beyond the basic production of the payroll. A payroll system must also be flexible and maintainable, for almost every few days there are changes, some required by staff (e.g. they get married), some by the company (e.g. they change salaries and rates of pay), or by the government (e.g. they change tax rates). So, payroll is a classic computerized information system; it is used (it may be internal or outsourced) in virtually all organizations; it is clearly of great importance (everybody wants to be accurately paid); but it does not cause many problems or issues (except occasionally after a Budget). It is what is termed a mature application. It is not very exciting, it uses traditional technology, yet over time it has evolved to become a sophisticated system that works well and efficiently. It does not provide any competitive advantage to an organization, it is just a necessary system for an organization to have to enable it to be in business. In terms of development, it was originally developed in-house but today is typically provided and procured as an application package. There are many such mature systems in organizations, e.g. invoicing systems, billing systems, order processing systems, inventory systems and personnel systems. They may not all work as effectively and efficiently as payroll, but they are in application terms mature and traditional.

- Our next example system is very different. It is an electronic auction house (such as eBay). It is relatively new (eBay started in 1995) and exciting, and uses the World Wide Web as its user interface. Yet, essentially, it is just an information system. It matches buyers with sellers utilizing an auction concept. This concept is not new, there have been auctions for hundreds of years, but the electronic auction enables buyers and sellers to be geographically distributed across the world, whereas the traditional auction required the buyers and sellers (well, strictly, just the potential buyers), and the product being auctioned, to be together in a particular place at a particular time. The electronic auction breaks the tradition in terms of both time and space. The electronic auction house (known as an intermediary) provides all the necessary support services to enable someone to put an item up for auction and for potential buyers to find the item, examine information about it, and bid for it. The auction house then 'conducts' the auction based on bids received over a period of time, defined by the seller. Actually, the information system usually just records the bids as they are received and makes them available online, so everyone can see the current state of play. If a potential buyer has had their bid beaten by someone else they can see this and bid again. At the end of the auction period, the item goes to the highest bidder, provided the reserve price is met, and the system puts the successful bidder and the seller in touch. They can then arrange payment and delivery. The auction house usually provides payment, insurance, delivery, security, and other services to its clients if required and in general provides an environment that enables people to participate easily and securely in an auction from the comfort of their home or workplace, or indeed anywhere. They also provide information on the seller, and whether he or she can be trusted, gathered from the responses of people who have dealt with him/her previously.

Figure 1.1 shows an example from an auction on eBay.co.uk. Someone has put a Hofner President guitar up for auction, and the seller has provided details of the guitar plus some pictures. It has attracted eight bids and the current high bid is £412. The auction has about 21 hours to run, so it may yet attract further bids. The seller appears to have a good history on eBay and has received many positive responses from people he has previously traded with (not shown).

The electronic auction is an information system, comprising people, rules, procedures, technology, software, communications and allied services, such as delivery companies and third-party insurance companies. Such auctions have proved very popular for selling almost anything. eBay began by providing a marketplace for toys and stamps, but quickly embraced the sale of almost anything, goods as well as services, including cars, jewellery, musical instruments, cameras, computers, furniture, sporting goods, boats, and event tickets. It is now the leading online auction place in the world with a turnover (value of goods sold) of over $5 billion per annum. It claims that, on any given day, 'there are millions of items listed for auction across thousands of categories'. It also claims to have 42.4 million registered users, although this probably includes people who registered for the site but 'are just looking' and maybe only looked once. Nevertheless, there is clearly a large community of people who like auctions and appear to be having fun, and such electronic auction houses have created a new kind of marketplace that has attracted significant numbers of people and trade. eBay is even thought to be making a profit, through its commission on sales. eBay now also provides a live auction facility enabling people to conduct an auction in the more traditional way but with online real-time bidding from home.

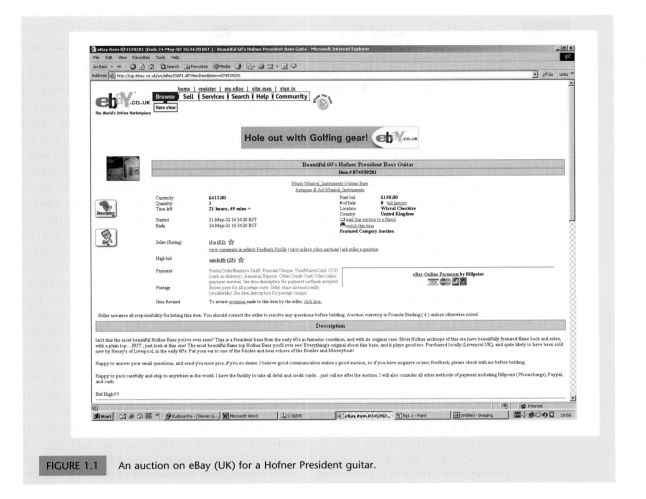

FIGURE 1.1 An auction on eBay (UK) for a Hofner President guitar.

We have provided two examples of information systems, at somewhat different ends of the spectrum which we hope will help form the background when we address different ways of developing such information systems. Another important factor is the environment and context in which such information systems are developed.

1.3 ENVIRONMENT AND CONTEXT

Information systems do not exist in a vacuum. Clearly, they are developed and operate within an environmental context that has a significant effect on them. This environment is increasingly complex and dynamic. Businesses today are said to be facing increased competition, global challenges, and market shifts, together with continuing, rapid, technological developments. We will look briefly at some of these factors driving the environment and context in which information systems exist and are developed.

1.4 GLOBAL ECONOMY

No longer do companies face competition only from other local companies. Competition can come from anywhere in the world, and frequently does. There has been a reduction in barriers to trade and competition. This is a result of an opening up of a number of countries to a more market orientation, for example China and Russia, and specific legislation within, for example, the European Union and as a result of the North American Free Trade Agreement. Continuing deregulation, removal of trading restrictions, and the breaking up of monopolies are a feature of many economies throughout the world and are helping to drive a more global economy. Other barriers are also being removed. For example, the adoption of the Euro is the latest in a series of initiatives to make international trade easier in the European Union and beyond. Another factor is improved physical transport capabilities, for example, developments in motorways, airlines, railways, and packaging. To give one example, UK supermarkets now display perishable and exotic produce that has originated in Africa, South America, or indeed from almost anywhere around the world. Together with improved packaging and storage techniques, such produce can now be shipped in timescales that mean they are almost as good in the UK as in the town next to their area of origin. Local seasons for fruit and vegetables have almost disappeared, strawberries are now available at almost any time of the year, although usually at a premium price. Information systems support such transactions.

A further impact of the global economy is that, although markets may be more open and accessible, costs can still differ significantly from country to country, particularly labour costs. So, economies with higher labour costs have to compete directly with those that have lower labour costs. No longer can companies rely on such competition being prevented by tariff barriers or dissipated by large transportation costs. The UK success story of Dyson, an innovative company which designed and developed a revolutionary new cyclonic vacuum cleaner product, recently announced that manufacturing would cease in the UK and be transferred to a country with cheaper labour costs. The global economy therefore took its toll on what was perceived as an important contribution to UK manufacturing, but Dyson felt that in order to survive it had to react in this way.

1.5 DIGITAL ECONOMY

Another element in the dynamic context of business is the digital economy, resulting from the convergence of computing and telecommunications technologies. This has had a significant effect on businesses and society in general and is epitomized by the impact of the Internet and the World Wide Web. Organizations have found that their operations, products, services, information, markets, competition, and economic environment are all potentially affected. Companies are seeking to create more digital content in their products and services and deliver them over digital networks. This has been characterized by the term 'from place to space'. So, for example, banks are attempting to shift their communication and service delivery channels with their customers from personal interactions at branches to call centres and finally to the Internet. The product is mainly digital information and transactions can be undertaken without a high street presence, although this is still seen as some customers are wedded to visiting their branch. However, the impact of this change is enormous for the banking sector. We are currently seeing competition (in the UK) with the existing banks offering a range of Internet-based products and services, but we are also seeing the advent of new entrants who have found they can enter this new digital banking world relatively easily. Egg, for example, is a bank established by the Prudential, traditionally an insurance company. This indicates that the world is under significant change. Further, if banking products and services are essentially digital and can be delivered via the Internet, then they can potentially be delivered in the UK by a non-UK provider, for example a European or American bank, or indeed in America by a British bank. We have not yet seen much evidence of this because of legislation and regulation barriers, but it is surely only a matter of time. The global and digital economies are not universally welcomed and there are some who see this as exploitation, particularly of poorer people. The term 'digital divide' is sometimes used to express this view.

1.6   ELECTRONIC COMMERCE

The digital economy includes electronic commerce or e-commerce which is simply the conducting of commercial transactions electronically, typically via the Internet, between geographically separated parties. It may involve some or all parts of the transaction process relating to pre-sale, execution, settlement and after-sale activities. Clearly, e-commerce has been the subject of much debate over recent years, and it has been suggested that it has revolutionized business for the following reasons:

- eases access to global markets (known as reach);
- extends business hours to 24 hours, 7 days a week;
- reduces the costs of transacting business;
- reduces the costs of marketing;
- facilitates customized one-to-one communication with customers;
- shortens the transaction cycle;
- provides a more perfect market; that is, it is easy for customers to find and compare prices (sometimes termed electronic market places).

Whether this is yet a true revolution is debatable, and whether all these benefits necessarily or automatically accrue is open to question. For example, the cost of marketing is thought by some to be higher because of the broader, more diverse markets that need be covered. Further, it is argued that the need for, and thus the cost of, establishing good brands and brand images might be greater than for traditional commerce. Except for a few notable exceptions, the revenue generated from purely e-commerce activities has been disappointing and, in terms of the global picture, accounts for only about 1% of world trade. There is also a view that e-commerce is really very little different from traditional commerce. The business processes are essentially the same, it is just the way that they are implemented that is different. In a few years nobody will bother to make a distinction in the way that transactions are carried out. Nevertheless, e-commerce is certainly very important and here to stay and it is likely to continue to be influential even if all the early hype is not quite justified.

1.7 NON-COMMERCIAL IMPACTS

Although e-commerce has taken most of the headlines recently, there are non-commercial impacts of the digital economy that may prove equally important. Throughout the world, and especially in the UK, there is a large public sector that is responsible for many activities, including transportation, education, taxation, regulation, employment, customs and excise, the law, and the environment, together with 388 English local government authorities. Together, these government departments and associated agencies are responsible for a large section of the economy and a large number of employees.

The UK government has recognized the importance of actively promoting the public sector and government agencies on the World Wide Web (or web). They regard this as a key opportunity to provide higher quality services directly to citizens at lower cost and more efficiently, 24 hours a day. It is thought that government departments should be able to achieve significant improvements in the provision of information to the public, especially allied with the push to more 'open government' and increasing freedom of information. This vision is not just confined to the provision of information. In time, citizens will be able to conduct their business with the government online. According to a report from the UK National Audit Office, it 'requires a fundamental transformation of many central departments' and agencies' business processes' (National Audit Office, 1999). To this end the UK government committed itself to having a quarter of transactions between citizens and government capable of being conducted 'electronically' by 2002 and further that all public services that can be conducted electronically should be online and available for citizens and companies by 2005. In order to help ensure that these targets are met, the UK government has set up the office of the e-Envoy, which is the key central agency responsible for e-government. It is a policy-oriented organization, which has run a number of campaigns to encourage central and local agencies to develop their electronic services. In 2001 it launched the government portal site (www.ukonline.gov.uk) to co-ordinate access to over 900 government sites. Although the results, so far, have been described as 'mixed' (National Audit Office, 2002), there is no doubt that the e-government initiative is a potentially important element of the digital economy, alongside the usual, more commercial elements.

1.8 CHANGE

The environmental context of this book is also described as increasingly dynamic and turbulent (Wielemaker et al., 2000) with change being endemic and the norm, rather than the exception (Prahalad and Hamel, 1994). Successful organizations are often thought to be those that are capable of dealing with such change and the opportunities it presents. Ciborra (1996) suggests that 'within a firm ... what seems to matter is the flexibility and adaptive capability in the face of environmental discontinuities'. Modern organizations seek to be responsive, adaptive, and flexible in their operations and strategy.

However, even those organizations that embrace the challenge of change have found that it is not easy to achieve, not least because their information systems (IS) and information technology (IT) are anything but flexible and adaptive. As we have suggested, technology has enabled many new and innovative information systems. Ironically, some managers have found that in practice IT can be a barrier to change as well as an enabler of change. The problems of 'legacy systems' (Section 6.1) (i.e. information systems that have been running for many years) are well known. It is sometimes difficult to be innovative in organizations because the existing systems are so ingrained, represent such large investments, and are difficult to change. Further, business cannot be suspended for a period while these significant changes are implemented. In addition, organizations have found that the cycle of business change is often shorter than the cycle for IT/IS change, which produces bottlenecks. As early as 1990, *The Economist* magazine suggested that 'businessmen have discovered a ... disconcerting problem: markets change, but computer systems do not', and the challenge for businesses is to break these rules of the past, and structure IS to meet the variety of changing information requirements that businesses are now facing.

So, the environment and context is dynamic. Wielemaker et al. (2000) argue that 'business is moving at 150 miles an hour' and 'the business models are morphing at an incredible speed ... a year in this business is really like five, six, seven years in traditional business'. Further, decisions are made much faster, often accepting higher risks because less data are available to make the decision. The knock-on effect of this on information systems and information systems development is profound. More is demanded from them, they have to be developed quickly, they have to be easily updatable, and they must utilize resources effectively. The pressures are enormous and the effects on the people involved are significant. We look at this human dimension next.

1.9 HUMAN DIMENSION

In this book we stress the human and organizational aspects of information systems development at least as much as the technological aspects. Today, the pressures are such that the human elements are the key to success. Indeed, in many of the information systems failures that have occurred, the conclusion has been placed squarely on human and organizational factors rather than technical ones (see, for example, reports into the failure and later success of the London Ambulance Service: Fitzgerald, 2000). A lack of planning may lead to unexpected costs and project abandonment. Poor training may result in people not co-operating with or supporting the information system. The same result may be caused by the system not making use of the users' business knowledge. Failure may also be due to poor methods, techniques, and tools. We consider the need for an information systems development methodology in Section 2.2 and also distinguish between techniques and tools.

Here we look at the people who will probably be involved in the in-house development of a computer information system. We identify a number of groups or **stakeholders** (see also Section 16.1). First, we identify those on the system development side:

- *Programmers* code and develop a system in a computer programming language.

- *Systems analysts* specify the requirements for a system and the outline designs and solutions that will meet the requirements. Typically, they are the interface or liaison between the business users/analysts and the programmers.

- *Business analysts* understand the complexities of the business and its needs and liaise with the systems analysts. They are typically from the business side of the organization but adopt this role in the context of a particular development project for a specific period.

- *Project managers* manage the project with particular emphasis on schedules and resources.

- *Senior IT management* are responsible for IT and managing it overall within the organization.

- *Chief information officer (CIO)* is responsible for IT, IS, and information strategy and aligning them to the needs of the business as a whole. Although usually a member of the IT department, it is essential that the CIO is part of the organization's top management team and understands the implications of the global and digital economy (Ross and Feeny, 2000). Sometimes, this position is known as the chief knowledge officer, recognizing the importance of knowledge as well as information (see Section 2.1).

The above groups may not exist as distinct groups in all organizations. The boundaries between them have undoubtedly become blurred over the years. In some circumstances one person may undertake a number of roles, or a group may flexibly undertake all roles as needed. The situation is even more confused by the tendency of the IT industry to have a wide and varied range of overlapping job titles for these roles. Further, many organizations no longer have rigid separations between the IT systems development side and the business. Often multi-skilled development teams, capable in both business and IT, are formed for a particular development project, often managed and led by the business units themselves.

Next, we identify those in the business or organization for whom the system is required. This group is often generically known as 'users', but this is misleading as they are not homogeneous and there is a range of different types of user. Indeed, 'users' can also be 'developers'. We break this category down as follows:

- *End users* use the system in an operational sense. They may be intermediaries between the system and the business users.

- *Business users* are people in the particular business function that have a need for the system. They might or might not physically interact with the system itself. They are interested in its functions and output, as support for achieving their business objectives.

■ *Business management* have responsibility for the business function that the system addresses and may have been responsible for commissioning the system and financing it from their budget. They are responsible for the strategic use of IT in their business unit.

■ *Business strategy management* are responsible for the overall strategy of the organization and the way that information systems can both support and enable the strategy.

Again, we are describing roles for people here. They may be combined or separated. Sometimes, different categories of user are identified, for example, *regular user* and *occasional* or *casual user*. This categorization is important for determining what type of user interface may be required in a system, or what type of training is needed. Clearly, these will be different for regular users and occasional users. A regular user may not require a lot of help and explanation and just the minimum of interactions, whereas an occasional user will require detailed help and guidance when using the system.

An example is provided by an airline reservation system. If occasional users decide to book a flight on the Internet, they are carefully guided through the process and have to enter exact details, such as the dates, the originating and destination airport, the class, and so on. Regular and experienced users, such as travel agents, often have a different interface, which enables them to enter shorthand details using airline codes. Once learned, this is much quicker than the occasional user interface, and indeed if the travel agents were forced to interact in the latter way, they would become very frustrated. Travel agents also often have the ability to do wider searches, for ranges of dates, multiple destinations, fare types, etc. Sometimes, information systems must be able to cater for a range of different users including both regular and occasional.

Our next category is external users. These are stakeholders outside the boundaries of the company in which the system exists:

■ *Customers* or *potential customers* use the system to buy products and services, or search for information relating to products. They are generally not employees of the company and thus have a different relationship to the earlier categories of user. Too often, customers are ignored when systems are being designed and developed, even though they are obviously important stakeholders with specific requirements. We look at this issue in Section 7.5.

■ *Information users* are people external to the organization who may use the system but are not customers, in that they do not buy anything. Users of a government website may just be looking for information on building regulations, for example. This category of user is also often ignored when the system is designed.

■ *Trusted external users* have a particular relationship with the organization and may be given special privileges in the system. Suppliers are examples of such users. There are likely to be specific design requirements and security implications for this category of user.

■ *Shareholders, other owners or sponsors* are people who have invested in the organization and have a financial interest. They may be only peripherally concerned with the information systems in the organization but they will want to ensure that they are contributing to the financial development and success of the organization.

- *Society* includes those people who may be affected by the system without necessarily being traditional customers or users in any way. This is a broad category and relates to people, or society as a whole, who may be potentially affected by the system in some way. People may be put out of work by a system or it may disseminate inaccurate or private information. It might be that a system refuses credit to someone based on old or inaccurate information, or it may be that the credit rating system discriminates against particular groups of people in some way. Society is an important stakeholder in systems development and societal impacts also need to be considered.

In general, we believe that it is desirable that all stakeholders of a system are involved in the development process. They all have some kind of stake in the success of the information system.

In the information systems development process, some users might be part of a group, such as the information systems strategy group, the steering committee, and the development team. We will examine this in more detail when looking at organizational aspects. Although we have said that it is desirable that all users are involved in the development process, systems development has in the past been dominated by professional users, in particular computer programmers and computer systems analysts. Some of the approaches to information systems development discussed in this book attempt to redress the balance. Certainly, it helps if these professional users see their task as supporting the other users of the system.

1.10   ORGANIZATIONAL ASPECTS

Although methodologies, techniques, and tools are all a necessary part of the infrastructure to develop information systems, so are management aspects. Information systems development as a whole and each individual information systems project need to be managed. Organizations differ, but a common arrangement is to have an information systems strategy group, a steering committee, and a systems development team.

The aim of the **information systems strategy group** is to develop a plan for information systems development in the organization and ensure that the plan is carried out and tuned as circumstances change. It is a high-level group, usually meeting each month, representing top management, heads of the various divisions, and head of the information systems function. We discuss information systems strategy in Section 4.2.

The **steering committee** will oversee each project within the overall plan, ensuring that the wishes of the information systems strategy group are met, and setting its own standards for the project including performance requirements, approving the personnel working on the project, and approving the final system. Project management and control (see Section 4.7), such a major element affecting the success or failure of the information systems project, will largely rest on the steering committee. The head of the information systems function will frequently be a member of both groups. The steering committee may also specify the information systems development approach to be used in a particular project, although this may be a standard for all information systems development in the organization. The steering committee is very likely to include the head of the department affected by the information system being developed and may also include the finance director, personnel manager, and, possibly, outside consultants, as well as the systems development project team leader.

The **systems development team** will concern itself with the day-to-day development of the information system and includes the analysts, programmers, and users working on the project. The composition of the team will differ as the system progresses through the stages of the systems development life cycle (see Chapter 3), although there will normally be one **project team leader** ensuring continuity throughout.

1.11   SUMMARY

- An information system in an organization provides processes and information useful to its members and clients. These should help the organization operate more effectively. The information might concern its customers, suppliers, products, equipment, procedures, operations, and so on.

- Information systems are developed and operate within an environmental context, which has a significant effect on them. This environment is increasingly complex and dynamic. We have discussed the global economy, the digital economy, e-commerce, and change as part of this context.

- Stakeholders closely involved in driving an IS development project include programmers, systems analysts, business analysts, project managers, senior IT management, and the chief information officer.

- User stakeholders include end-users, business users, business management, and business strategy management.

- Other stakeholders include customers, information users, trusted external users, shareholders, and society as a whole.

QUESTIONS

1 We have discussed some issues that we consider as providing environmental 'context' to information systems development. Discuss other issues that form part of this context.

2 Discuss the role of the various stakeholders in an IS development project.

3 Read about an IS failure or success. What part of the story can be attributed to technological, human, and organization aspects? Was 'context' important to success or failure?

1.12 FURTHER READING

Braa, K., Sorensen, C., and Dahlbom, B. (eds) (2000) *Planet Internet*, Studentliteratur, Lund, Sweden. This book contains a number of useful papers on many of the topics discussed in this chapter, though keeping up to date with information on the Web and in the media is essential.

2 INFORMATION SYSTEMS DEVELOPMENT

KEY CONCEPTS

In Chapter 1 we discussed what information systems are and provided some context in which they are developed. In this chapter we discuss the need for an information systems development methodology and the requirements of such a methodology. This leads on to Chapter 3 where we discuss the information systems development life cycle, which has had an enormous influence as a general approach to develop information systems.

However, we start by providing some definitions of the main concepts discussed in the book. Of course, we will provide more 'meat' to these early definitions as we explore them in later chapters. We provide these early definitions to help the reader understand what follows rather than provide 'ideal-type' definitions which everyone can accept.

One problem in this area is that many of the terms used in this section are used differently and inconsistently elsewhere. We will attempt to be consistent in our usage or explain where usage differs. This is a fairly new discipline, and differences of opinion are to be expected, but it does not make our task easy.

Data represent unstructured facts about events, objects, or people. When three 'strings' of data '250792', '78700199', and '19873' are associated, they could be used to give the information that a person whose identity number is 19873 possesses a driving licence (number 78700199), even though that person is under the minimum legal age for driving motor vehicles. The string of data 250792 is interpreted as the date of birth, 25 July 1992, showing that the holder is only 10 years old in January 2002. The essential difference between data and information, therefore, is that data are not interpreted, whereas **information** has a meaning and use to a particular recipient in a particular context and can be used for decision making. Information comes from selecting data, summarizing it, and presenting it in such a way that it is useful to the recipient. Too often, this process is not well refined and vast amounts of data are output. This is often referred to as 'information overload', although, strictly speaking, it is not information but data, because it is not useful.

Some writers equate knowledge with information. Buckingham et al. (1987) define information as 'explicit knowledge'. In other words, information expresses what is meant clearly, with nothing left implied. Knowledge may also be seen as accumulated information. Most importantly, people with knowledge know the meaning and implications of the information presented and how to use it effectively. They should therefore be competent in completing their tasks. So, **knowledge** contains the ability to use information effectively for particular purposes.

The distinction between data, information, and knowledge is context-dependent. Let us look at another example where a line manager analyses the departmental figures and presents the results to the planning department. For the line manager, the results are an interpretation of events and are therefore information rather than data. They have meaning for the line manager. For the central planners, these figures are the raw input for their own analyses, not yet interpreted, and are therefore data rather than information. Therefore, information is such because it is relevant and understandable to some person or group. But the central planners need to have the knowledge to use this information effectively. This may be explicit, that is, communicable to others or tacit, that is, only implicitly understood.

Having given a preliminary definition of information, we need to discuss what is meant by a **system**. This is more difficult because it is a term that is used widely in many different fields of activity. Therefore, the ecological system is a view of the world that includes the relationship between flora and fauna which we call the balance of nature, and the educational system could be viewed as our understanding of the relationship between teachers, students, books, and colleges whose purpose is to pass on knowledge to all members of the community. Systems are related to each other. Telephone bills are produced by a billing system, forwarded by a postal system, and paid using a banking system. The banking system will have a customer service system, a cheque processing system, and a payroll system, among others. Smaller systems within larger systems are called subsystems. An information system will also have subsystems within it. An airline information system may have subsystems to report on the status of passengers, report on flights, and to analyse costs and profits. All these examples of systems include a collection of parts or subsystems that work together.

The 'system' part of 'information system' represents a way of seeing the set of interacting components, such as:

- people (for example, systems analysts, business users, line managers);
- objects (for example, computer hardware devices, a user interface, telecommunications networks, the World Wide Web);
- procedures (for example, business processes, an information systems development methodology, business rules).

All this must take place within a boundary that separates those components relevant to the system (for example, to do with purchasing a product or service online) and those concerned with the environment around the system (for example, other information systems, customers, suppliers, governments, laws, and so on).

Systems also have a purpose. For example, many information systems are designed to provide relevant information to users to help their decision making. Information needs to be presented at the right time, at the appropriate level of detail, and of sufficient accuracy to be of use to its recipient. This will help to ensure that the corporate information resource is utilized fully.

Buckingham et al. (1987) define an **information system** as:

> A system which assembles, stores, processes and delivers information relevant to an organisation (or to society), in such a way that the information is accessible and useful to those who wish to use it, including managers, staff, clients and citizens. An information system is a human activity (social) system which may or may not involve the use of computer systems.

This definition is useful in that it emphasizes the human and organizational aspects of information systems. It suggests that the information system is useful, in other words, has a purpose, usually improving the effectiveness in the way that the organization does things – information systems do not exist for their own sake. The definition also makes clear that not all information systems use information technology, though this book is mainly about information systems that are computer-based – they use information technology for at least some of the work.

This book is about **information systems development**, that is, the way in which information systems are conceived, analysed, designed, and implemented. In Chapter 3 we suggest a generic approach to information systems development called the information systems development life cycle. At first, it might sound like a prescriptive, mechanistic process. In reality, however, it is very often far from that. Indeed, there are different ways of developing information systems: there are many methodologies, techniques, and tools to help support the development process.

2.2　NEED FOR A METHODOLOGY

The early applications of computers – say, until the 1960s – were largely implemented without the aid of an explicit information systems development methodology. In these early days, the emphasis of computer applications was toward programming, and the skills of programmers were particularly appreciated. The systems developers were therefore technically trained but were not necessarily good communicators. This often meant that the needs of users in the application area were not well established, with the consequence that the information systems design was sometimes inappropriate for the application.

Few programmers would follow any formal methodology. Frequently they would use rule-of-thumb and rely on experience. Estimating the date on which the system would be operational was difficult, and applications were frequently behind schedule. Programmers were usually overworked, and frequently spent a very large proportion of their time correcting and enhancing the applications that were operational.

Typically, a member of the user department would come to the programmers asking for a new report or a modification of one that was already supplied. This might occur because the present system did not work as specified or because of changes in the organization and its environment. Often, implementing these changes had undesirable and unexpected effects on other parts of the system, which also had to be corrected. This vicious circle would continue, causing frustration to both programmers and users. This was not a methodology, it was only an attempt to survive the day.

As computers were used more and more and management was demanding more appropriate systems for their expensive outlay, this state of affairs could not go on. There were three main changes:

- There was a growing appreciation of that part of the development of the system that concerns analysis and design and therefore of the role of the systems analyst as well as that of the programmer.

- There was a realization that, as organizations were growing in size and complexity, it was desirable to move away from one-off solutions to a particular problem and toward a more integrated information system.

- There was an appreciation of the desirability of an accepted methodology for the development of information systems.

2.3   INFORMATION SYSTEMS DEVELOPMENT METHODOLOGY

It was to answer the problems discussed in the previous section that methodologies were devised and adopted by many organizations. We have already discussed the term methodology. An **information systems development methodology** can be defined as:

> A collection of procedures, techniques, tools, and documentation aids which will help the systems developers in their efforts to implement a new information system. A methodology will consist of phases, themselves consisting of subphases, which will guide the systems developers in their choice of the techniques that might be appropriate at each stage of the project and also help them plan, manage, control, and evaluate information systems projects.

But a methodology is more than merely a collection of these things. It is usually based on some 'philosophical' view, otherwise it is merely a method, like a recipe. Methodologies may differ in the techniques recommended or the contents of each phase, but sometimes their differences are more fundamental. Some methodologies emphasize the human aspects of developing an information system, others aim to be scientific in approach, others pragmatic, and others attempt to automate as much of the work of developing a project as possible. These differences may be best illustrated by their different assumptions, stemming from their 'philosophy' which, when greatly simplified, might be that, for example:

- a system that makes most use of computers is a good solution;
- a system that produces the most appropriate documentation is a good solution;
- a system that is the cheapest to run is a good solution;
- a system that is implemented earliest is a good solution;
- a system that is the most adaptable is a good solution;

- a system that makes the best use of the techniques and tools available is a good solution;
- a system that is liked by the stakeholders is a good solution.

Techniques and tools feature in each methodology. Particular techniques and tools may feature in a number of methodologies. A **technique** is a way of doing a particular activity in the information systems development process, and any particular methodology may recommend techniques to carry out many of these activities.

Each technique may involve the use of one or more **tools** that represent some of the artefacts used in information systems development. A non-computer-oriented example may help. Two techniques used in the making of meringues are (1) separating the whites of eggs from the yolks and (2) beating the whites. The methodology may recommend the use of tools in these processes, for example, an egg separator and a whisk. In this text, tools are usually automated, that is, computer tools, normally software to help the development of an information system. These tools might enable some development tasks to be done automatically or semi-automatically. Indeed, some tools have been designed specifically to support activities in a particular methodology. Others are more general purpose and are used in different methodologies.

This book is about methodologies, the differences between them, why these differences exist, and which methodology might be appropriate in given circumstances. As we shall see, methodologies differ greatly, often addressing different objectives. These objectives could be:

1. *To record accurately the requirements for an information system.* The methodology should help users specify their requirements or systems developers investigate and analyse user requirements, otherwise the resultant information system will not meet the needs of the users.

2. *To provide a systematic method of development so that progress can be effectively monitored.* Controlling large-scale projects is not easy, and a project that does not meet its deadlines can have serious cost and other implications for the organization. The provision of checkpoints and well-defined stages in a methodology should ensure that project-planning techniques could be applied effectively.

3. *To provide an information system within an appropriate time limit and at an acceptable cost.* Unless the time spent using some of the techniques included in methodologies is limited, it is possible to devote an enormous amount of time attempting to achieve perfection.

4. *To produce a system which is well documented and easy to maintain.* The need for future modifications to the information system is inevitable as a result of changes taking place in the organization and its environment. These modifications should be made with the least effect on the rest of the system. This requires good documentation.

5. *To provide an indication of any changes that need to be made as early as possible in the development process.* As an information system progresses from analysis through design to implementation, the costs associated with making changes increases. Therefore, the earlier changes are effected, the better.

6 *To provide a system that is liked by those people affected by that system.* The people affected by the information system, that is, the stakeholders, may include clients, managers, auditors and users. If a system is liked by the stakeholders, it is more likely that the system will be used and be successful.

An information systems development methodology, in attempting to make effective use of information technology, may also attempt to make effective use of the techniques and tools available. Information systems development methodologies are also about balancing technical aspects with behavioural (people-oriented) aspects. As we shall see in the book, there are many views as to where this balance lies and how the balance is achieved in methodologies. At one extreme are the methodologies aiming at full automation of information systems development as well as the information system itself. However, even in these systems people need to interact with the system. At the other extreme, perhaps, are attempts at full user participation in the information systems development project and user-led design. Even here, user solutions may make full use of the technology, and there are a growing number of tools designed to aid users develop their own information systems. The balance between technological aspects and people aspects is one that we will return to as it is a continual theme in information systems development.

Having stated that this book is about information systems development methodologies, not all organizations use a standard methodology. They might have developed their own or adapted one to be more appropriate for their own circumstances. Many organizations may only use some aspects of a standard methodology. Other organizations use no methodology at all. The ways that organizations use (or do not use) information systems development methodologies will be another theme of the book.

2.4 SUMMARY

- Data represent unstructured facts about events, objects, or people.

- Information has a meaning and use to a particular recipient in a particular context and can be used for decision making.

- Knowledge is accumulated information and contains the ability to use information effectively for particular purposes.

- An information system is a system that assembles, stores, processes, and delivers information relevant to an organization (or to society), in such a way that the information is accessible and useful to those who wish to use it, including managers, staff, clients, and citizens. An information system is a human activity (social) system that may or may not involve the use of computer systems.

- An information systems development methodology is a collection of procedures, techniques, tools, and documentation aids which will help the systems developers in their efforts to implement a new information system. A methodology will consist of phases, themselves consisting of subphases, which will guide the systems developers in their choice of the techniques that might be appropriate at each stage of the project and also help them plan, manage, control, and evaluate information systems projects.

QUESTIONS

1 Discuss the definitions of data, information, knowledge, information system, methodology, technique, and tools, and look for alternatives in the literature. Do you think our definitions are adequate? Do they miss out on any important aspect?

2 Why do you think there is a need for a methodology to develop information systems? Why do you think that many organizations do not use them?

3 Of the six objectives for an information systems development methodology discussed above, what for you counts as most important, and why?

2.5   FURTHER READING

Kendall, K. and Kendall, J. (2002) *Systems Analysis and Design*, 5th edn, Prentice Hall, Englewood Cliffs, New Jersey. This is one of a large number of American texts that cover the basic field of systems analysis attractively and thoroughly. Most texts of this type tend, however, to emphasize technological aspects.

THE LIFE CYCLE APPROACH

In Part 2 we introduce the information systems development life cycle, which is a general approach to developing systems. It has been the basis of many systems development projects since the 1970s. The phases in the approach are described along with the strengths of the approach. We use this approach as an exemplar and introduce methodologies, techniques, and tools by means of this approach. However, we also discuss its weaknesses, or at least problems relating to the way it has been used in practice, as they lead on to the alternative approaches to developing information systems, which are introduced in Part 3 of the book. Many of the alternative themes discussed there have in their roots attempts to address some of these weaknesses.

3 INFORMATION SYSTEMS DEVELOPMENT LIFE CYCLE

3.1 INFORMATION SYSTEMS DEVELOPMENT LIFE CYCLE (SDLC)

The SDLC has had an enormous influence as a general approach to develop information systems. Although there are many variants, it has the following basic structure:

- feasibility study;
- system investigation;
- systems analysis;
- systems design;
- implementation;
- review and maintenance.

These stages together are frequently referred to as 'conventional systems analysis', 'traditional systems analysis', 'information systems development life cycle', or, more frequently in the USA, the **waterfall model**. The term 'life cycle' indicates the staged nature of the process. Further, by the time the review stage comes, the information system must be found to be inadequate and it may not be long before the process starts again with a feasibility study to develop another information system to replace it. In the next few sections we describe each stage in turn.

1 Feasibility study

Among other reasons, a computer system might be contemplated to replace an old system because increasing workloads have overloaded the present system, suitable staff are expensive and difficult to recruit, advancing technology leads to new possibilities, there is a change in the type of work, or there are frequent errors. The next stage is to look in more detail at the present system and then to determine the requirements of the new one.

The feasibility study looks at the present system, the requirements that it was intended to meet, problems in meeting these requirements, new requirements that have come to light since it was first implemented, and briefly investigates alternative solutions. These must be within the terms of reference given to the analyst relating to the boundaries of the system and constraints, particularly those associated with resources. The alternatives suggested might include leaving things alone and improved manual as well as computer solutions.

For each of these, a description is given in terms of the technical, human, organizational, and economic costs and benefits of developing and operating the system. So, any proposed system must be feasible:

- *legally*, that is, it does not infringe any national or, if relevant, international company law;
- *organizationally and socially*, that is, it is acceptable for the organization and its staff, particularly if it involves major changes to the way in which the organization presently carries out its processing;
- *technically*, that is, it can be supported by the technology available and there is sufficient expertise to build it;
- *economically*, that is, it is financially affordable and the expense justifiable.

Of the possible alternatives, a 'recommended solution' is proposed with an outline functional specification. This information is given to management as a formal report and often through an oral presentation by the systems analysts to management who will then decide whether to accept the recommendations of the analysts. This is one of the decision points in the SDLC – whether to proceed or not.

2   Systems investigation

If management has given its approval to proceed, the next stage is a detailed fact-finding phase. This purports to be a thorough investigation of the application area. The information obtained will be much more detailed than that recorded in the feasibility report. It will look at:

- the functional requirements of the existing system (if there is one) and whether these requirements are being achieved;
- the requirements of the new system as there may be new situations or opportunities that suggest altered requirements;
- any constraints imposed;
- the range of data types and volumes that have to be processed;
- exception conditions;
- problems of the present working methods.

These facts are gained by interviewing personnel (both management and operational staff), through the use of questionnaires, by direct observation of the application area of interest, by sampling, and by looking at records and other written material related to the application area:

- *observation* can give a useful insight into the problems, work conditions, bottlenecks, and methods of work;

- *interviewing*, which may be conducted with individuals and groups of users, is usually the most helpful technique for establishing and verifying information, and provides an opportunity to meet the users and to start to overcome possible resistance to change;

- *questionnaires* are usually used where similar types of information need to be obtained from a large number of respondents or from remote locations;

- *searching records and documentation* may highlight problems, but the analyst has to be aware that the documentation may be out of date;

- *sampling* may be used but often requires specialist help from people with statistical and other skills.

A great deal of skill is required to use any of these effectively, and results need to be cross-checked by using a number of these approaches. It may be possible to find out about similar systems implemented elsewhere as the experience of others could be invaluable.

3   Systems analysis

Armed with the facts, the systems analyst proceeds to the systems analysis phase and analyses the present system by asking such questions as:

- Why do the problems exist?
- Why were certain methods of work adopted?
- Are there alternative methods?
- What are the likely growth rates of data?

In other words, it is an attempt to understand all aspects of the present system and why it developed as it did, and eventually indicate how things might be improved by any new system. So, systems analysis provides pointers to the new design. In particular, the analysts will emphasize the need to ascertain what are the requirements for the new system.

4   Systems design

Although usually modelled on the design suggested at the feasibility study stage, the new facts may lead to the analyst adopting a rather different design to that proposed at that time. Much will depend on the willingness to be thorough in the investigation phase and questioning in the analysis phase. Typically, however, the new design might be similar to the previous system, but avoiding the problems that occurred with the old system and without including any new ones. Sometimes, the new system is somewhat more radical.

This stage involves the design of both the computer and manual parts of the system. The design documentation set will contain details of:

■ input data and how the data is to be captured (entered in the system);

■ outputs of the system;

■ processes, many carried out by computer programs, involved in converting the inputs to the outputs;

■ structure of the computer and manual files that might be referenced in the system;

■ security and back-up provisions to be made;

■ systems testing and implementation plans.

5 Implementation

Following the systems design phase are the various procedures that lead to the implementation of the new system. If the design includes computer programs, these have to be written and tested. New hardware and software systems need to be purchased and installed if they are not available in the organization at present. It is important that all aspects of the system are proven before **cutover** to the new system, otherwise failure will cause a lack of confidence in this and, possibly, future computer applications. The design and coding of the programs might be carried out by computer programmers. Alternatively, application packages might be purchased to form part of the final system. In this approach, the analysis and programming functions are separate tasks carried out by different people.

A major aspect of this phase is that of **quality control**. The manual procedures, along with the hardware and software, need to be tested to the satisfaction of users as well as analysts. The users need to be comfortable with the new methods. The departmental staff can practise using the system and any difficulties experienced should be ironed out. The **education and training** of user staff is therefore an important element of this phase. Without thorough training, users will be unfamiliar with the new system and unlikely to cope with the new approach (unless it is very similar to the old system).

Documentation, such as the operations and user manuals, will be produced and approved and the live (real, rather than test) data will be collected and validated so that the master files can be set up. **Security** procedures need to be tested, so that there is no unauthorized access and recovery is possible in case of failure. Once all this has been carried out, the system can be operated and the old one discontinued. If cutover to the new system is done 'overnight', then there could be problems associated with the new system. It is usually too risky an approach to cutover. Frequently, therefore, there is a period of parallel running, where old and new systems are run together, until there is complete confidence in the new system. Alternatively, parts of the new system can be implemented in turn, forming a phased implementation. If one part of the system is implemented 'to test the water' before the rest of the system is implemented, this is referred to as a pilot run. Acceptance testing comes to an end when the users feel assured that the new system is running satisfactory and it is at this point that the new system becomes fully operational (or 'live').

6   **Review and maintenance**

The final stage in the system development process occurs once the system is operational. There are bound to be some changes necessary and some staff will be set aside for maintenance, which aims to ensure the continued efficient running of the system. Some of the changes will be due to changes in the organization or its environment, some to technological advances, and some to 'extras' added to the system at an agreed period following operational running. Inevitably, however, some maintenance work is associated with the correction of errors found since the system became operational.

At some stage there will also be a review of the system to ensure that it does conform to the requirements set out at the feasibility study stage, and the costs have not exceeded those predicted. The evaluation process might lead to an improvement in the way other systems are developed through the process of **organizational learning**.

As commented earlier, because there is frequently a divergence between the operational system and the requirements laid out in the feasibility study, there is sometimes a decision made to look again at the application and enhance it or even develop another new system to replace it. This could also occur for another reason. Changes in the application area could be such that the operational system is no longer appropriate and should be replaced. The SDLC then finishes and starts at the point where there is a recognition that needs are not being met efficiently and effectively and the feasibility of a replacement system is then considered and the life cycle begins again.

In the following sections we discuss the key concepts of methodologies, techniques, and tools in the particular context of the SDLC.

3.2   METHODOLOGY

There were many variants of the SDLC. The earliest in the UK was that proposed by the National Computing Centre (NCC) in the late 1960s. At the time, the NCC was sponsored by the UK government to provide a lead in computing for both government and private organizations. One of its functions, therefore, was to suggest good standards for developing computer applications. It had a great impact on the data processing community, particularly in the UK, and represented a typical methodology of the 1970s based on the SDLC. This methodology has been improved and altered since, so that a number of approaches used today can be regarded as a modern variant of this approach, the most obvious being SSADM (Section 20.1).

The use of a methodology improves the practice of information systems development. The attributes that we would expect of a methodology include:

  A series of **phases** starting from the feasibility study through to review and maintenance. The phases are expected to be carried out as a sequential process. Each of these phases has subphases. The activities to be carried out in each of the subphases are usually spelt out clearly in the methodology documentation, usually found in manuals. The outputs (or 'deliverables') of each subphase are also detailed. Deliverables may include documents, plans, or computer programs.

2 A series of **techniques**, which include ways to evaluate the costs and benefits of different solutions and methods to formulate the detailed design necessary to develop computer applications, are also detailed. We illustrate some of these techniques in Section 3.3.

3 A series of **tools** to help the systems analysts in their work. By tools, we mean, in this book, software packages that aid some aspect of the approach. We discuss some of these tools in Section 3.4.

4 A **training** scheme so that all analysts and others new to their roles and responsibilities could adopt the standards suggested. Typically, there may be a training course offered that might take up to six weeks. A qualification might be offered.

5 A **philosophy**, perhaps implied rather than stated, which might be that 'computer systems are usually good solutions to organizational problems and processing'. We suggest this because the assumption is that the inevitable consequence of using most methodologies is a new computer application to perform the required functions.

Of course, the NCC methodology itself became dated and was replaced by other methodologies, many of which were also based on the life cycle but incorporated the latest methods, techniques, and tools. Many more modern methodologies such as SSADM, Merise, and Yourdon Systems Methodology, which are described later in the book, are life cycle approaches.

For example, SSADM (Section 20.1) has the following stages:

- Stage 0 – feasibility;
- Stage 1 – investigation of current environment;
- Stage 2 – business systems options;
- Stage 3 – definition of requirements;
- Stage 4 – technical system options;
- Stage 5 – logical design;
- Stage 6 – physical design.

Although the terminology used for each stage seems different, we can see the progress through the life cycle from feasibility study, via investigation and requirements analysis, through to design. In fact, SSADM does not offer much specific advice regarding implementation, as this is seen as being particular to the application environment and the assumption is made that little general advice can be given. Each of these seven stages of SSADM are further detailed into several steps (the methodology documentation consists of several manuals).

Although we have argued that most methodologies follow a life cycle of sorts, some circumvent stages in the wish to develop applications quickly, such as James Martin's Rapid Application Development (Section 22.1), for example; whereas others do not assume such a logical step-by-step approach (Multiview, for example – Section 25.1). Yet others concentrate on only part of the life cycle, like soft systems methodology (Section 24.1). Finally, some methodologies concentrate on particular views about the emphasis that should be placed when developing applications, such as ETHICS (Section 23.1), which emphasizes people aspects and participation.

3.3 TECHNIQUES

Most methodologies recommend a number of documentation aids to ensure that the investigation is thorough. The early methodologies might have included:

- various flowcharts, which might, for example, help the analyst trace the flow of documents through a department;
- an organization chart, showing the reporting structure of people in a company or department;
- manual document specifications, giving details of documents used in the manual system;
- grid charts, showing how different components of the system, such as people and machines, interact with each other;
- discussion records on which the notes taken at interviews could be recorded;
- file and record specifications describing, in the former case, all the data items in a record, including their names and descriptions, size, format, and possible range of values.

Many of the documentation techniques outlined above have been replaced. The most well-used techniques are probably now data flow diagramming (Section 12.1), which is important in specifying the process aspects of the system, and entity-relationship diagramming (Section 11.1), which detail the data aspects. Data flow diagrams that describe the logic of the system or the physical implementation of the new design show:

- data flows into the system from the environment;
- data flows out of the system into the environment;
- processes that change the data within the system;
- data storage within the system;
- the boundary and scope of the system.

Entity-relationship diagrams, on the other hand, represent the data aspects. An entity is a data type, such as a student, lecturer, course, and classroom. These diagrams show how these entities relate to each other and they also show the detail about each entity, similar to that provided in a record specification form.

As we will see in Part 4, there are many techniques used in information systems development. Some are associated with particular methodologies, like rich pictures (Section 10.1) in Soft Systems Methodology, others are more generic, such as dataflow diagrams and entity-relationship diagrams, which are recommended in many methodologies.

3.4 TOOLS

When we talk of tools, we are referring to software packages that aid aspects of information systems development. Most tools require significant computing power and good graphics capabilities. Most tools available now were not available in the early days, although there were project management tools (we discuss Project 2000 in Section 17.4) and report-generating packages, such as RPGII. Users of RPGII would complete a series of forms specifying how the required report should be structured and what files contained the data necessary to be on the report. This has been incorporated as one aspect of modern toolsets (Chapter 18). Oracle, for example, will have an application generator as part of its toolset. Other tools support the production of documents, such as dataflow diagrams and entity-relationship diagrams. They include Visio, discussed in Section 17.3, but again this feature is included in many toolsets. As you will see in Part 5, there are many different types of tool available, which ease much of the systems development process.

Probably the greatest benefit of using tools is that analysts and designers are not reluctant to change documents, because the change process is simple. Frequent manual redrawing is not satisfactory, because of the effort involved and the potential of introducing errors when redrawing. Without such drawing tools many a small change required by a user would not be incorporated into the documentation of the system.

3.5 POTENTIAL STRENGTHS OF THE SDLC

The SDLC has a number of features to commend it. Methodologies incorporating this view of applications development have been well tried and tested. The use of documentation standards in such methodologies helps to ensure that the specifications are complete, and that they are communicated to systems development staff, the users in the department, and the computer operations staff. It also ensures that these people are trained to use the system. The education of users on subjects such as the general use of computers is also recommended, and helps to dispel fears about the effects of computers. Following such a methodology also prevents, to some extent at least, missed cutover dates (the date when the system is due to become operational) and unexpectedly high costs and lower than expected benefits. At the end of each phase the technologists and the users have an opportunity to review progress. By dividing the development of a system into phases, each subdivided into more manageable tasks, along with the improved training and the techniques of communication offered, we have the opportunity for control of the applications development process.

3.6 POTENTIAL WEAKNESSES OF THE SDLC

The criticisms of the systems development approach to applications development, or, to be more precise, of the way in which it was used include:

- failure to meet the needs of management;
- instability;
- inflexibility;
- user dissatisfaction;

- problems with documentation;
- lack of control;
- incomplete systems;
- application backlog;
- maintenance workload;
- problems with the 'ideal' approach;
- emphasis on 'hard' thinking.

We will discuss each of these in turn.

1   Failure to meet the needs of management

As can be seen in Figure 3.1, although systems developed by this approach often success-fully deal with such operational processing as the various accounting routines, the needs of middle management and top management can be ignored. Management information needs, such as that required when making decisions about where to locate a new factory, which products to stop selling, what sales or production targets to aim for and how sales can be increased, are neglected. Although some information may filter up to provide summary or exception reports, the computer is being used largely only for routine and repetitive tasks. Instead of meeting corporate objectives, computers are being used to help solve low-level operational tasks. In general, the danger is that such systems are rather limited in their scope and rather unambitious.

2   Models of processes are unstable

The conventional SDLC approach attempts to improve the way that the processes in businesses are carried out. However, businesses do change, and processes need to change frequently to adapt to new circumstances in the business environment. Because these

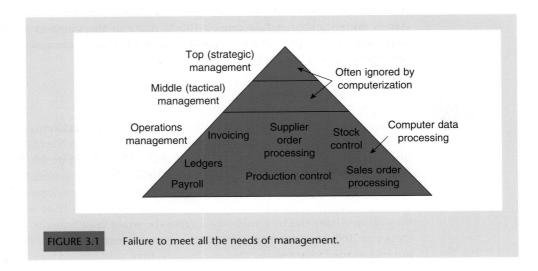

FIGURE 3.1   Failure to meet all the needs of management.

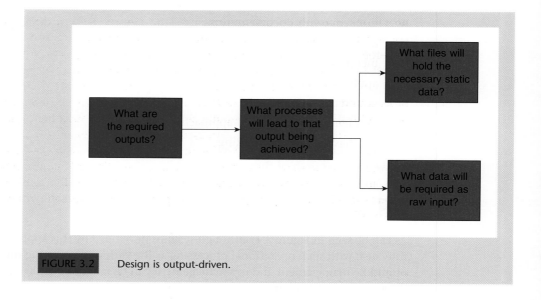

FIGURE 3.2   Design is output-driven.

computer systems model processes, they have to be modified or rewritten frequently. It could be said therefore that computer systems, which are to some extent 'models' of processes, are unstable because the real world processes themselves are unstable.

3   **Output-driven design leads to inflexibility**

The outputs that the system is meant to produce are usually decided very early in the systems development process. Design is 'output driven' (see Figure 3.2) in that, once the output is agreed, the inputs required, the file contents, and the processes involved to convert the inputs to the outputs, can all be designed. However, changes to required outputs are frequent and, because the system has been designed from the outputs backwards, changes in requirements usually necessitate a very large change to the system design and therefore cause either a delay in the implementation schedule or are left undone, leading to an unsatisfactory and inappropriate system.

4   **User dissatisfaction**

This is often a feature of many computer systems. Sometimes systems are rejected as soon as they are implemented. It may well be only at this time that the users see the repercussions of their 'decisions'. These decisions have been assumed by the analysts to be firm ones and, as computer systems can prove inflexible, it is normally very difficult to incorporate changes in requirements once the systems development is under way. Many companies expect users to 'sign off' their requirements at an early stage when they do not have the information to agree the exact requirements of the system. The users sign documentation completed by computer-oriented people. The documents may not be designed for the users. On the contrary, they are designed for the systems analysts, operations staff, and programming staff who are involved in developing the system. Users cannot be expected to be familiar with the technology and its full potential, and therefore find it difficult to contribute to the debate to produce better systems. The period between 'sign-off' and implementation tends to be one where the users are very uncertain about the outcome and they are not involved in the development process and therefore may lose their commitment to the system. They might have become disillusioned with computer systems and, as a consequence, fail to co-operate with the systems development staff. Systems people, as they see the situation, talk about user staff as being awkward or unable to make a decision. Users may first see the system only on implementation and find it inappropriate. This alienation between technologists and users has even been known to lead to users developing their own informal systems which are used alongside the computer system, ultimately causing the latter to be superfluous.

5   Problems with documentation

We have suggested that one of the benefits of the methodology is the standardization and documentation that methodologies use. Yet this is not ideal. The orientation of the documentation is frequently toward the computer person and not the user, and this represents a potential source of problems. The main purpose of documentation is that of communication, and a technically-oriented document is not ideal.

6   Lack of control

Despite the methodological approach enabling estimates of the time, people, and other resources needed, these estimates can be unreliable because of the complexity of some phases and the inexperience of the estimators. Computer people have been seen as unreliable and some disenchantment has ensued in relation to computer applications.

7   Incomplete systems

Computers are particularly good at processing a large amount of data speedily. They excel where the processing is the same for all items: where the processing is structured, stable, and routine. This often means that the unusual (exceptional conditions) are frequently ignored in the computer system. They are too expensive to cater for. If they are diagnosed in the system investigation stage, then clerical staff are often assigned to deal with these exceptions. Frequently they are not diagnosed, the exceptions being ignored or forgotten, and the system is falsely believed to be complete. These exceptions cause problems early on in the operational life of the system. These problems mark a particular technical failure, but they also indicate a systems failure, a failure to analyse and design the system properly.

8   Application backlog

A further problem is the application backlog. There may well be a number of systems waiting to be developed. The users may have to wait some years before the development process can get under way for any proposed system. The process to develop an information system will itself take many months and frequently years from feasibility study to implementation. Users may also postpone requests for systems because they know it is not worth doing because of the backlog. This phenomenon is referred to as the invisible backlog.

9   Maintenance workload

The temptation, then, is toward 'quick and dirty' solutions. The deadline for cutover may seem sacrosanct. It might be politically expedient to patch over poor design rather than spend time on good design. This is one of the factors that has led to the great problem of keeping operational systems going. With many firms, the effort given to maintenance can be as high as 60–80 per cent of the total workload. With so many resources being devoted to maintenance, which often take priority, it is understandable that there is a long queue of applications in the pipeline. The users are discouraged by such delay in developing and implementing 'their' applications because of the necessity to maintain the legacy systems (see Section 6.1).

10   Problems with the 'ideal' approach

The SDLC model assumes a step-by-step, top-down process. This is somewhat naive. It is inevitably necessary to carry out a series of iterations when, for example, new requirements are discovered or subphases might prove unnecessary. In other words, information systems development is an iterative process, whatever textbooks say. The political dimension where, for example, people have their own 'agenda' transcends the rationale of any methodology. Users and analysts will need to interpret the methodology, and its techniques and tools, to be relevant to a particular problem situation. It also assumes a tailor-made rather than packaged solution, usually for a medium- or large-scale application using mainframe computers. With the widespread use of PC systems, such an approach may be inappropriate and unwieldy.

11   Emphasis on 'hard' thinking

The SDLC approach may make a number of simplistic assumptions. It assumes that there are 'facts' that only need to be investigated and identified; it assumes that there can be a 'best solution' identified that will 'solve the problem'; it assumes that this 'ideal solution' can be easily engineered by following a step-by-step methodology; and it assumes that the techniques offered will analyse and design all that needs to be done. But we are not engineering a simple mechanical object. The world of information systems is concerned with organizations and people as much as technology. The situations encountered are often ambiguous, issue-laden, messy, and problematical, and an alternative approach might well be more appropriate in these difficult but common situations.

The above criticisms of the SDLC should be regarded as 'potential' criticisms, as many organizations using the approach do not fall into all or even most of the potential traps. However, this book concerns itself with improving information systems development by adapting the SDLC or using alternative approaches to developing information systems.

In Part 3, we will look at themes regarding views about information systems development. They can be seen as ways in which people in the field have reacted to the potential problems of the SDLC. This has resulted in many views about what a methodology should emphasize: people aspects, planning aspects, automation ... there are many such views. To some extent these can be seen as representing different philosophies, for example, a people-oriented approach might be seen as being based on the philosophy that people have a right to design their organizational environment. But these themes also reflect greater possibilities, for example, software tools that can both make the process easier and faster, and also make some approaches possible, which aim toward automation of the development process. Similarly, the craft of systems analysis has been improved greatly through the use of alternative techniques.

3.7 CONCLUSION

Before we consider approaches to systems analysis, which represent advances on the traditional SDLC approach, the reader should stop and consider that many systems developed today are still done using no real methodology at all. This is particularly true in organizations using PCs, perhaps developing websites as their first experience of computing. The SDLC has many advantages over trial and error.

The SDLC is being used successfully. In many respects, there is nothing intrinsically wrong with the SDLC. Much depends on the way in which it is used. There must be sufficient resources assigned to the process; it needs to be well managed and controlled so that any deviation from the plan is noticed and dealt with; it should be seen not as a rigid process but as a flexible and iterative one; the feasibility study needs to be seen as a way of exploring alternatives rather than as a way of advancing a limited point of view; and systems development should not be seen as a purely technological process but one involving all users and developers, indeed the organization as a whole. However, many of the alternative approaches address some of the potential weaknesses suggested above. This may mean improving one or more of the phases, including the use of an alternative technique or a new software tool.

We also do not wish to assert that any of the alternative methodologies represents a panacea. Major concerns in computing remain, for example:

- meeting project deadlines;
- system maintenance;
- staff recruitment and retention;

- user dissatisfaction;
- changing requirements.

Notwithstanding these continuing pessimistic trends, there are many successful information systems, some developed using the basic SDLC approach. In Part 3 we will look at the various themes in information systems development methodologies that are seen as developments or alternatives to the basic approach discussed in this chapter. These alternative approaches usually address one or more of the potential criticisms of the SDLC approach discussed in the previous section.

3.8 SUMMARY

- The SDLC has had an enormous influence as a general approach to develop information systems. Although there are many variants, it has the following basic structure: feasibility study; system investigation; systems analysis; systems design; implementation; review and maintenance.
- An information systems development methodology is likely to include: a series of phases with subphases, each having expected outputs (or 'deliverables'); a series of techniques; a series of tools; a training scheme and some underlying philosophy.
- Although the SDLC has many strengths and is still used today, it also has many potential weaknesses, which has led to alternative methodologies, techniques, and tools being available.

QUESTIONS

1 Distinguish between techniques, tools, and methodologies in the context of the SDLC.

2 Discuss the strengths and the limitations of the traditional systems development life cycle.

3 Would you adopt the SDLC for developing a small application on a PC? Would you modify it in any way? Give reasons for your answer.

3.8 FURTHER READING

Avison, D.E. and Shah, H.U. (1995) *The Information Systems Development Cycle: A First Course in Information Systems*, McGraw-Hill, Maidenhead, UK. Avison and Shah describe an up-to-date approach modelled on the SDLC. It can be regarded as a prequel to this present book.

The structure of the book is based on separate descriptions of information systems development themes, techniques, tools, and methodologies. In Part 3 we explore some of the themes that have evolved in relation to information systems development. A theme represents a particular foundation, school of thought, or focus that has influenced information systems. Some of these themes are particular responses to one or more of the perceived limitations of the traditional systems development life cycle (SDLC) approach discussed in Chapter 3. However, none of them are panaceas and no one approach solves all the problems.

Themes may relate to, or are part of the philosophical background of, particular techniques, tools, or methodologies. Therefore, the theme of participation relates to, and has been influential on, the ETHICS methodology. As techniques, tools, and methodologies are described separately, the reader should be aware that these relationships exist and that some of them are quite complex. So, as an illustration of one such set of linkages we have produced a 'road map' (see Diagram 1). This shows, from the

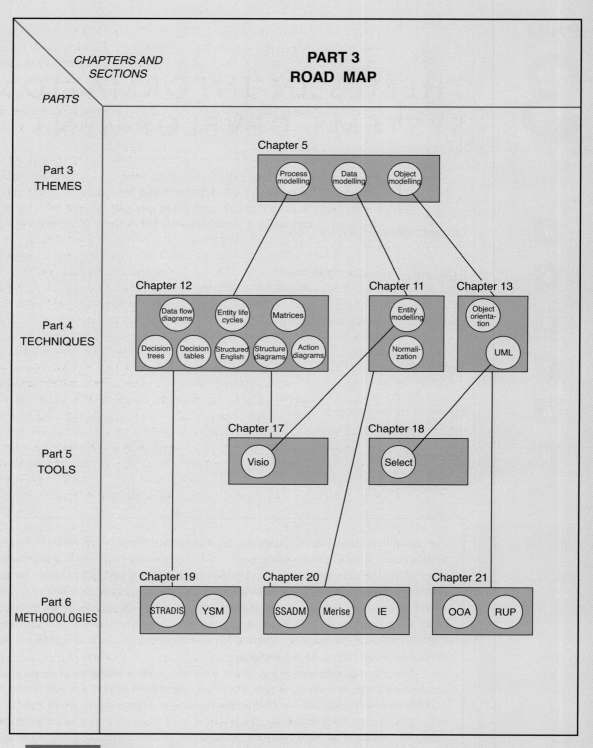

CHAPTERS AND
SECTIONS

PARTS

**PART 3
ROAD MAP**

Part 3
THEMES

Chapter 5

Process modelling   Data modelling   Object modelling

Chapter 12

Data flow diagrams   Entity life cycles   Matrices

Decision trees   Decision tables   Structured English   Structure diagrams   Action diagrams

Part 4
TECHNIQUES

Chapter 11

Entity modelling

Normali-zation

Chapter 13

Object orienta-tion

UML

Chapter 17

Visio

Part 5
TOOLS

Chapter 18

Select

Part 6
METHODOLOGIES

Chapter 19

STRADIS   YSM

Chapter 20

SSADM   Merise   IE

Chapter 21

OOA   RUP

DIAGRAM 1   Modelling theme 'road map' (shows relationship between themes and techniques, tools, and methodologies for the modelling theme).

perspective of the theme of 'modelling', the linkages to techniques, tools, and methodologies. So, if a reader wants to explore and follow through from the theme of modelling to the related techniques, tools, and methods, he or she should look at the highlighted sections. This is simply one example of the way techniques, tools, or methodologies interconnect, and the reader will need to explore his or her own road maps for the others. Potential links are cross-referenced in the text to help in this task.

In Part IV we attempt to group various themes into categories or groups, for convenience. However, there exist a range of alternative groupings. One reason for this is that a theme has a number of characteristics or features that might justify it being grouped in some other theme. This is inevitable and it should be realized that these groupings are not definitive. But, hopefully, they make some sense and prove helpful.

Chapter 4 group together themes that address information systems for the organization as a whole: their inter-connection, strategic use, re-engineering, and planning. We first look at the systems approach, which presents a holistic view of organizations and therefore addresses the piecemeal aspect of the traditional SDLC, which we criticized in Chapter 3, because the systems approach looks at the problem situation as a whole. Strategic information systems, which address the needs of top management, could be said to be a 'head-on' attack at the emphasis placed on computer applications at the operational level of the firm in the traditional approach. Strategic aspects are obviously crucial to the success of the information systems effort. Business process re-engineering is again a re-examination of the present systems, including the information systems of the organization. Such re-examination leads to redesign within the context of both the other processes and the needs of the organization as a whole. We look at planning approaches which emphasize the way future information systems development can be organized and integrated so that strategic as well as the tactical and operational needs are included. The stages of growth model shows how information systems and information technology might typically develop as a whole in organizations over time. We then look at the issues of flexibility and risk. Another major theme is managing the project in the hope that projects are delivered 'at cost and on time' and we look at this in the last section of Chapter 4.

In Chapter 5 we look at modelling and approaches that emphasize the modelling aspects, either on the process side or on the data side. Modelling represents an important aspect of many methodologies. We look at structured approaches, which centre on the techniques and tools for modelling processes. The next theme, data modelling, concentrates on understanding and classifying data and the relationships between data in an organization and is therefore related to the development of databases. Object orientation is an alternative view, and in this approach we model objects of all kinds in the organization: data, processes, people, and software can all be modelled as objects. This is therefore a unifying approach within the overall theme of modelling.

Another major area is that of engineering and construction and this is discussed in Chapter 6. The first theme in this category concerns legacy systems, that is, what to do with the systems already existing in the organization. We then turn to evolutionary development, that is, the gradual development of applications over time. Prototyping enables users to see and comment on the application before it is implemented. It uses system development software tools in a bid to improve requirements analysis, that is, ensure 'what the users want is what they get'. Prototyping is also claimed to lead to more rapid application development and we discuss this as a separate issue. We then look at the particular issues of engineering methodologies from components of other approaches. Finally in this chapter we look at developing web applications.

Chapter 7 will emphasize the role of people in developing and using an information system. The importance of the people using the information systems and other interested parties, frequently called stakeholders, is addressed in the theme of participation. This participation can be strengthened so that there is joint application development, or so strong that it is the end-user who is developing the system. We then look at expertise and knowledge and include a section on expert systems and another on knowledge management. In expert systems one of the important areas is capturing the knowledge of people who are considered experts in the particular application domain so that users can build on this expertise. Finally, we look at customer orientation. This suggests that the stakeholders of most importance are the customers (not so much technologists or even users). This is most strong, perhaps, in web applications.

Of course, one alternative approach is to buy the software as an application package, or as a full-scale enterprise resource planning system, and these are discussed in Chapter 8. We also look at outsourcing, which might lead to system development as well as information systems being completely done externally.

We then consider software engineering in Chapter 9. This concentrates on quality software, which is, of course, an important part of any computerized information system. Attempts have been made to automate all aspects of the systems development process and there are now a number of software tools, which support automated development. This is discussed in detail in Part 5. We then look at building applications through the use of components. Database management is then discussed, as it is a concern of much applications development work.

Most of the themes discussed in Part 3 have their counterparts in Part 6: actual methodologies that are used in organizations. Even if they are not directly linked, most of the methodologies used today will have been greatly influenced by aspects of these themes.

4 ORGANIZATIONAL THEMES

4.1 SYSTEMS THEORY

In Chapter 2 we attempted to define the nature of **systems**. We saw how systems relate to each other and that they themselves consisted of subsystems. This gives rise to the definition of a system as a set of interrelated elements (Ackoff, 1971). A system will have a set of inputs going into it, a set of outputs going out of it, and a set of processes that convert the inputs to the outputs.

We define a **boundary** of a system when we describe it. This may not correspond to any physical or cultural division. A payroll system might include all the activities involved in the payment of staff in a business. These activities fall within the boundary of that system. Those systems outside it, with which it relates, are referred to as the **environment**. Systems thinking concerns itself with interactions between the system and its environment, not so much with how the system works, which can be seen as a 'black box'. The staff recruitment system and production systems within the firm will be part of the environment of the payroll system, as will the government's system to increase employment.

One of the bases of systems theory concerns Aristotle's dictum that the whole is greater than the sum of the parts. This would suggest that we must try to develop information systems for the widest possible context: an organization as a whole rather than for functions in isolation. If we fail to follow this principle then a small part of the organization may be operating to the detriment of the organization as a whole. If we do break up a complex problem into smaller manageable units, we need to keep the whole in mind. Otherwise, this may be reductionist, the process of decomposition distorting our understanding of the overall system. Users of many of the approaches discussed, in particular the structured approach, part of process modelling (described in Section 5.2), may succumb to this danger unless they use the approach with care. Decomposing complex structures is the accepted approach in a scientific discipline, but information systems concern people and organizations as well as technology, and the interactions are such that in these human activity systems it is important to see the whole picture. The human components in particular may react differently when examined singly as when they play a role in the whole system.

Organizational systems are not predictable as they concern human beings. The outputs of computer programs may be predictable and capable of mathematical formalism. Human activity systems are less predictable because human beings may not follow instructions in the way a piece of software does, nor interpret instructions in the same way as other people do or in the way that they themselves might have done on previous occasions.

Another aspect of systems theory is that organizations are **open systems**. They are not closed and self-contained, and therefore the relationship between the organization and its environment is important. They will exchange information with the environment, both influencing the environment and being influenced by it. The system, which we call the organization, will be affected by, for example, policies of the government, competitors, suppliers, and customers, and unless these are taken into account, predictions regarding the organization will be incorrect. As organizations are complex systems, this would suggest that we require a wide range of expertise and experience to understand their nature and how they react with the outside world. Multidisciplinary teams might be needed to attempt to understand organizations and analyse and develop information systems.

Human activity systems should have a **purpose** and the interrelated elements interact to achieve this purpose. What then is the purpose of an information system? Depending on the application area, an information system may be constructed to help managers decide on where to build a new factory. It may provide information about customers so that decisions can be made about their credit rating. It might be to maximize the use of aircraft seats in an airline ticket reservation system. With this information provided, it is possible to control the environment rather than passively react to it.

Information systems usually have human and computer elements and both aspects of the system are interrelated. However, the computer aspects are closed and predictable, the human aspects are open and non-deterministic. Although not simple, the technological aspects are less complex than the human aspects in an information system, because the former are predictable in nature. However, many information systems methodologies only stress the technological aspects. This may lead to a solution that is not ideal, because the methodologies underestimate the importance and complexity of the human element.

Systems theory has had widespread influence in information systems work. It would suggest, for example, that whatever methodology is adopted, the systems analyst ought to look at the organization as a whole and also be aware of externalities beyond the obvious boundaries of the system. These include customers, competitors, governments, and so on. Systems theory would also suggest that a multidisciplinary team of analysts, not all computer-oriented, is much more likely to understand the organization and suggest better solutions to problems. After all, specialisms are artificial and arbitrary divisions. Such an approach should prevent the automatic assumption that computer solutions are always appropriate, as well as preventing a study of problem situations from only one narrow point of view. With this approach comes the acknowledgement that there may be a variety of possible solutions, none of them obviously 'best' perhaps, but each having some advantages. These solutions may involve structural, procedural, attitudinal, and environmental change.

Checkland (1981), developed further in Checkland and Scholes (1990), has attempted to turn the tenets of systems theory into a practical methodology, which is called Soft Systems Methodology (SSM) (see Section 24.1). Checkland argues that systems analysts apply their craft to problems that are not well defined and soft thinking attempts to understand the fuzzy world of complex organizations. By contrast, 'hard' approaches, such as the structured and data analysis methods, emphasize the certain and the precise in a particular domain and tend to look at the domain from one point of view, a major contrast compared to soft systems thinking.

Checkland's description of human activity systems also acknowledges the importance of people in organizations. It is relatively easy to model data and processes, but to understand organizations it is essential to include people in the model. This is difficult because of their unpredictable nature. The claims of the proponents of this approach are that a better understanding of these complex problem situations is more likely to result when compared to using hard approaches alone.

We will now look at one final contrast in hard and soft systems viewpoints. Analysts following hard approaches think in terms of systems as though they exist as such and can be engineered. The soft systems viewpoint is that systems do not exist but represent a way of viewing, and therefore understanding, complex real-world activities. However, the implication of this is that different analysts will see the real world in different ways, depending on their background, experience, and so on. The discussion between different analysts can therefore provide understanding of the real world as well as expose its complexity. It may lead to a completely different systems view of the organization being studied.

There are other approaches that have used systems ideas in their design. Beer's Viable Systems Model, for example (see Espejo and Harnden, 1989), provides a tool to study organizations holistically, analysing their structure and their information systems from many viewpoints. Multiview (Section 25.1) incorporates these ideas as well as 'hard' systems ideas in its approach.

4.2 INFORMATION SYSTEMS STRATEGY

The first business activities that were computerized tended to be the basic transaction processing systems such as payroll, sales order processing, stock control, and invoicing. The approach used was simple and did not involve changing the nature of the business activities performed. In the early days, change usually only concerned the means by which existing activities were undertaken. The same activities were computerized to make them more **efficient**. Payroll, for example, previously required large numbers of manual payroll clerks to perform the activity. When computerized, it did not need all these clerks. Early computerization therefore aimed to promote efficiency and in particular to reduce labour costs. This kind of computerization is termed efficiency projects, defined by Fitzgerald (1998) as:

> Projects that seek to reduce the cost of performing a particular process or task by utilising information technology. They do not seek to radically change the nature

of the objectives that those tasks and processes were originally devised to fulfill, they simply seek to achieve the same objectives at lower cost, i.e. to perform existing tasks more efficiently.

Silk (1990) argues that cost displacement savings are relatively easy to quantify and that a clear financial case for investment can be demonstrated, using any of the available financial analysis techniques, such as Internal Rate of Return (IRR), Net Present Value (NPV), Return on Investment (ROI), or Payback Period. Such savings are quantifiable; for example, the cost savings of payroll clerks were the salary savings, and cost justification was easy to make.

This does not mean that **cost/benefit analysis** (or any other technique) is an effective evaluation method; indeed, it has been argued that the predicted benefits were rarely achieved. Sometimes the benefits or savings were exaggerated and the costs of the required computer staff underestimated or ignored. So, replacing relatively cheap payroll clerks with a computer system and relatively expensive systems analysts, programmers, operators, etc. did not always produce the large predicted benefits. Nevertheless, the mechanical evaluation process itself was relatively straightforward. IBM, for example, developed a method known as SESAME that used a cost/benefit technique to assess a computer project in comparison with a non-computerized system (Lincoln and Shorrock, 1992).

However, in more recent times, the opportunity for further information systems investments based on efficiency and labour displacement criteria have been limited. First, the number of opportunities are reduced, as more and more projects are implemented, and, second, the returns are declining, as the most clear-cut efficiency improving opportunities have already been addressed. In most large organizations almost all the activities are now computerized or supported by computers in some way. So, overall, the propensity for reducing traditional labour costs via information systems is declining.

The cost justification for revamping systems that have already been computerized, i.e. recomputerizing, is more difficult because the labour displacement opportunities are no longer available – those savings have already been made in the original computerization. However, more recently, there have been a number of justifications based on cost savings relating to reductions in the managerial workforce, particularly middle management levels associated in particular with enterprise resource planning systems (Section 8.2). It is this area that will probably provide the basis for most labour-saving cost displacement information systems projects in the future.

Labour costs have formed the largest and easiest costs to displace using information technology (IT), but other costs have also been amenable to displacement, at least to some degree. Paper and postage costs have been displaced, at least to some extent, by Electronic Data Interchange (EDI), electronic mail, and electronic commerce. Property costs have been displaced, or reduced, where organizations have used IT to enable the move of back-office functions away from town centres to cheaper areas (or even to home working). Inventory costs have been displaced by information systems-enabled Just In Time (JIT) systems. Such cost displacement savings can be relatively easily quantified in these systems which seek to perform essentially the same functions as before, but to perform them at less cost.

A major problem with the cost/benefit justification (based on labour displacement cost savings or other efficiencies) of new computer systems or IT investments in organizations is that it is very difficult to justify systems that do not deliver savings but may deliver benefits such as increased market share, new opportunities, or, in general better management information. These kinds of investment are very unlikely to pass the usual efficiency-based evaluation or justification process that is used in most organizations.

Over the years computing and technology investment has moved from just being about cost savings and efficiencies to more strategic or effectiveness systems. This in particular regards the use of information systems and IT as a direct tool for obtaining competitive advantage. Information systems can be used to improve the business in the marketplace and in this way to help:

- redefine the boundaries of particular industries;
- develop new products or services;
- change the relationships between suppliers and customers;
- establish barriers to deter new entrants to marketplaces.

The basic objectives of this type of information system is to identify better ways of doing things, leading to increased revenues, greater functionality, better products and services, improved presentation or image, and improvement of the organization's competitive positioning. This is usually referred to as using information systems to gain **competitive advantage**. This is IT for **effectiveness** rather than efficiency. The basic objectives of effectiveness projects are not simply to reduce the costs of performing existing tasks but to identify ways of doing different things that better achieve the required results, leading to increased revenues and better service. Effectiveness projects are not addressing efficiency criteria but seek to improve organizational effectiveness. The distinction between efficiency and effectiveness hinges on the notion of objectives. It is perfectly possible to perform some set of tasks very well and efficiently, i.e. in the cheapest possible way, but this does not mean that performing that particular set of tasks is the best way of achieving the objectives associated with those tasks. Efficiency is broadly concerned with how we do things, whereas effectiveness is concerned with what we do.

Although making justifications based on effectiveness criteria is not impossible, it is much more difficult than making a financial case on the basis of efficiency/savings obtained. One of the reasons for this increased difficulty is because there is an extra stage of proof to go through.

For effectiveness projects it is not just necessary to identify the benefits, for example, better service, but also that the recipient of those benefits will recognize and value the improvement and change their behaviour in some positive way as a result, e.g. by existing customers buying more services, by not transferring their allegiances elsewhere, or for the improved service to attract new customers. Customers or potential customers must first be aware of the change and second perceive it as an improvement over the service they currently use (which may be no service at all or a competitor's service). So, the **benefit realization** process comprises at least two stages, first the provision or implementation of the project to provide benefit and second the effect of that benefit on the wider environment and any resultant behaviour change.

Figure 4.1 illustrates this notion; for efficiency projects the identified efficiency concept is implemented and the benefit accrues, usually as reduced costs, (or not) and

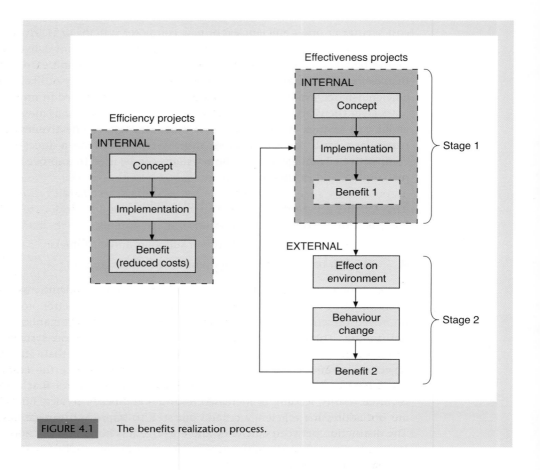

FIGURE 4.1   The benefits realization process.

that is the end of the process. It is internally controllable by the organization and usually does not depend on any interaction with the outside environment. Effectiveness projects have a similar first stage process which may result in some Stage 1 benefits. However, it is not necessary for any cost benefits to accrue at this stage. The second stage of the process is the effect of the implementation of Stage 1 on the environment and any resultant change in behaviour leading to Stage 2 benefits. Stage 2 benefits may be, for example, improved sales resulting in improved revenues.

The fact that there are two stages to the process unfortunately provides greater opportunities for the potential benefits to get lost or become dissipated and makes the evaluation of such effectiveness projects so difficult. In the case of cost displacement the organization is more in control of the realization of benefits whereas in the improved services case (i.e. effectiveness justifications) the organization is in control of achieving the first stage but not the second stage which is the impact on others, for example suppliers, customers, and potential customers. This second stage has been the area where miscalculations are frequently made; for example, it is often assumed that the move from Stage 1 to Stage 2 is a logical and deterministic process: that an improved service will lead to more people buying that service, or that better information will lead to better decision making.

In some information systems development methodologies, a phase or stage relating to realizing projected benefits has been included to ensure that any measure implemented in the information system leads to the hoped-for change in behaviour. This is long term and difficult to prove and it has often been the case that organizations have abandoned any attempt at justification and instead rely on management perception of the benefits, sometimes referred to as strategic insight, intuition, or blind faith.

The use of information systems for effectiveness or competitive advantage has been shown to have the possibility of generating very significant rewards for the organization in terms of income generation rather than cost savings. There are some 'classic' examples which purport to show how some organizations 'have seized the opportunity to use information systems to gain competitive advantage' (see Eardley et al. 1996). In particular, American Hospital Supply Corporation's then 'revolutionary' 1978 order-entry system directly linked customers into their systems, which made ordering by the customer very easy. Customers have access to the order-distribution system so that, for example, customers could perform various functions, such as inventory control, for themselves using the system. This helped reduce costs for both the company and their customers, and enabled American Hospital Supply to develop and manage pricing incentives to the customer across all product lines.

There are a variety of other examples where information systems have been used to establish competitive advantage, such as DEC XCON, Xerox's customer support system, Merrill Lynch's cash management account system, American Airlines Sabre reservation system (followed by Apollo), and the 'electronic' newspaper, *USA Today*. More recently there have been notable examples such as Dell Computers and Amazon who have made strategic investments in IT in attempts to change the nature of business in their particular industries, with Dell achieving significant success and Amazon less so, at least in terms of financial returns. In the UK there are also some well-known examples, such as Thompson's Tour Operator Reservation System, Sainsbury's laser scanning point of sale system, and First Direct bank.

It is from these kinds of early pioneering strategic examples that the concept of using information systems to gain competitive advantage has evolved.

Porter (1980) offers an industry analysis framework of competitive strategy to help identify the competitive forces that any company needs to consider. These five forces are illustrated diagrammatically in Figure 4.2 and Porter suggests that significant strategic advantage can be gained by diminishing supplier or customer power, holding off new entrants into the industry, lowering the possibility of substitution for its products, or gaining a competitive edge within the existing industry. This framework can be helpful in focusing the role of information systems to improve competitive positioning. Earl (1989), for example, identifies four ways in which Porter's model helps:

- it deals with the industry and competitive dynamics;
- it highlights that competition is not simply concerned with the action of rivals;
- it facilitates discussion and is based on sound principles of industrial economics;
- it focuses on the few dominant forces necessary.

Figure 4.3 shows an extension to Porter's work by Earl to illustrate the strategic role that IT can play on each of Porter's dimensions. American Hospital Supply, for example, illustrates the use of IT to address the customer competitive force. IT was used to help

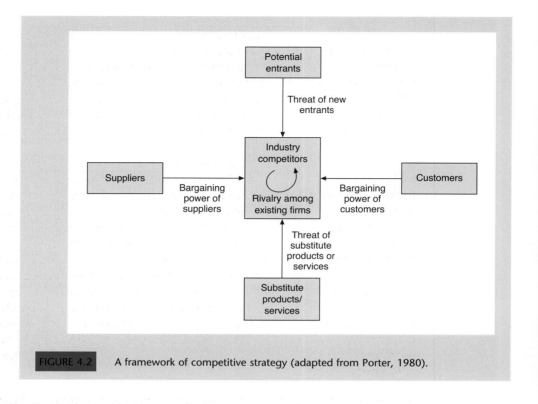

FIGURE 4.2   A framework of competitive strategy (adapted from Porter, 1980).

Competitive force	Potential of IT	Mechanism
New entrants	Barriers to entry	1. Erect 2. Demolish
Suppliers	Reduce bargaining power	1. Erode 2. Share
Customers	Lock in	1. Switching costs 2. Customer information
Substitute products/services	Innovation	1. New products 2. Add value
Rivalry	Change the relationship	1. Compete 2. Collaborate/alliances

FIGURE 4.3   The strategic role of IT (adapted from Earl, 1989).

lock in the customers using both mechanisms. Another aspect of this case is the role of a dedicated champion to push the ideas in the organization, to overcome all the inevitable objections, to sustain the momentum over a fairly long period, and to inspire people with the vision. This person is unlikely to come from the information systems domain, although he or she may be a 'hybrid manager', that is, a person having knowledge and experience in both the IT and user domains. The role of people in successful information systems development is stressed further in the theme on participation, discussed in Section 7.1.

Although many organizations now recognize the need to address effectiveness as well as efficiency in their use of IT and the resulting need for an IT strategy, the approach to developing such a strategy is by no means clear or universally agreed upon. Indeed, there has been a degree of scepticism that cast doubts on some of the more simplistic approaches to IT for competitive advantage. It has been argued that some of the successes are due to the fact that the product or service offered was good rather than having anything to do with the information system. Other criticisms relate to sustainability, i.e. even if the IT investment has generated a strategic benefit how long will it last? Can competitors copy the IT system easily and reproduce the benefits in their own organizations. Obviously not being able to sustain the advantage is problematic, and in such cases maybe all that has been achieved is an increase in the cost of doing business in that particular industry. It is clear that investing in IT to gain competitive advantage is not a simple panacea and some organizations have adopted rather simplistic approaches as follows:

■ *Technology-driven model* – the reaction of some organizations has been implicitly to make the assumption that investment in IT will automatically result in business success and the achievement of competitive advantage. It is the embodiment of the view that if the technology exists it should be employed. It might be seen in the unthinking purchase of the latest IT product. This strategy is usually driven by technologists. A result of this approach is information technology that may not be appropriate for the needs of the organization and a lack of control over IT budgets. As no business benefits are stated, there is no way of measuring whether any such benefits accrue. This strategy is obviously irrational although understandable in some ways due to the rapid pace of technological change exceeding the ability of many managers to keep up. Technology adopted in this way may cause disruption in the organization and incompatibilities between information systems, rather than making for greater efficiency and effectiveness. For example, the introduction of the personal computer in many organizations was unplanned and could be described as technology-driven, and although this led to many individual benefits there were often other longer term problems of compatibility, support, and integration. Strassmann (1990) concludes that there is little evidence that technology-based systems of information management have produced benefits that could be claimed to justify their costs. Even if the claimed (and unproved) individual gains are summed, they do not lead to an overall improved performance of the organization. It would thus appear that an approach based purely on the technology-driven model is unlikely to prove adequate.

■ *Competitor-driven model* – an alternative model or approach that some organizations have adopted is to react to their competitors by copying them. There is evidence

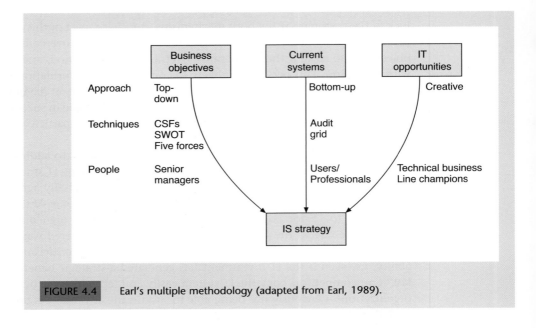

FIGURE 4.4 Earl's multiple methodology (adapted from Earl, 1989).

that this happens in some sectors rather more than others. In the UK banking sector, for example, there seems to be a 'knee-jerk' reaction to copy each other in terms of technology and services. In manufacturing, there appears to be an assumption that anything Japanese was by definition the best approach to follow. The competitor-driven model is an approach based upon the fear that an organization's competitors will use information technology to gain significant advantage over them. Therefore, they must be 'tracked' and copied at each stage of their development. The fear is that companies that do not follow the same path in information technology will ultimately be squeezed out. The competitor model says that we will not allow this to happen by matching our competitors at every point. The problems with this approach are threefold. First, that by simply following competitors, the organization will never innovate to its own particular strengths and advantages. Second, it may miss opportunities for being a leader itself. Third, it may still lose out by not itself being the first in the field, particularly in situations where being first in the field enables barriers to entry to be constructed.

A more thoughtful approach to the formulation of IT strategy and the alignment of IS development with business needs has been defined by Earl on the basis that no one-dimensional approach is likely to be successful. He suggests an approach that combines a variety of different elements and techniques, including both top-down and bottom-up analysis. The individual elements are not necessarily new but they are combined into what is argued to be a comprehensive and effective approach. Figure 4.4 illustrates this 'multiple methodology'.

The first element of the model is a top-down analysis of the business and its goals and objectives leading to an identification of the potential role that IT might play in achieving these objectives. This is a top-down business-led activity in which IT people would play a supporting role rather than the other way round. It is best achieved by the

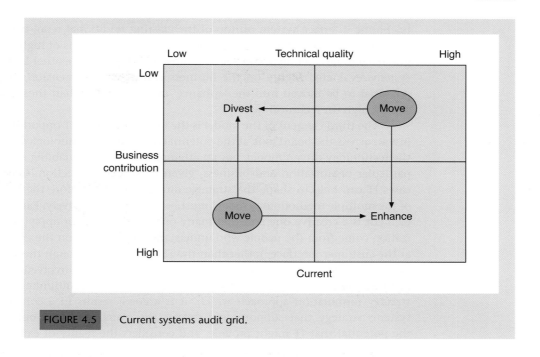

FIGURE 4.5   Current systems audit grid.

use of established techniques such as Critical Success Factors (CSFs) (see Section 15.2), SWOT analysis (see Section 15.5), and Porter's 'five forces' model (see above) to help assess competitive positioning, industry factors, competitor strengths, etc. with a view to using IT to address strengths and counter weaknesses.

The second element of Earl's model is a bottom-up analysis of the organization's current systems. This is a critical element of the model because, as in so many approaches to strategy formulation, the current systems are ignored and a 'green field' situation is assumed. This is usually quite unrealistic and leads to failure because the existing legacy systems in an organization have been ignored. The analysis consists of evaluating the strengths and weaknesses of the existing IT provision and existing systems on the basis of, first, business contribution and value to users and, second, technical quality.

Figure 4.5 shows a typical systems audit grid that might be helpful in this analysis. One point of the analysis is to try to run down and exit from systems that perform poorly on both dimensions. It is frequently found that there are many such systems, particularly in organizations where IT has evolved in the organization in a somewhat *ad hoc* manner. These systems are often expensive to run and maintain, and contribute little to the organization in the direction that is required by the strategy. They should be phased out in order to free up valuable resources. On the other hand, those that are high on both dimensions should be enhanced and evolved. Earl makes the point that many strategic systems, or systems that have helped to provide competitive benefit, have in fact been based on enhancements and redirection of existing systems rather than the construction of totally new ones. Where this can be achieved it obviously provides a head start and potentially a reduction in the cost and lead times for developing strategic systems. An example is the telephone banking system of First Direct in the UK which built a strategic telephone interface system on top of the existing traditional retail banking systems of Midland Bank (now HSBC). Those systems with combinations of highs and lows on the grid need to be carefully evaluated and moved into one of the other boxes. Probably the systems evaluated highly on the business contribution dimension would have more potential to be moved into the 'enhance' category rather than those systems that are simply high on technical quality.

The third element of the model is the identification of IT opportunities. This is not just an across-the-board look at the potential of the latest technological innovation, as in the technology-driven model, but an attempt to assess the enabling effects of IT on the particular organization and business, given its strategic direction. Of course, in some cases IT can help to shape the strategic direction and therefore the left and right legs of the multiple methodology model must be developed iteratively. Earl suggests that this element is a creative one and that many of the best ideas for applying IT in an organization come from the people who understand the business on the ground, particularly at the customer interface, rather than the IT specialists, although the specialists can act as catalysts in this process. So, a range of people need to be involved in this part of the process. The three elements of the model thus provide a multidimensional, integrated strategy formulation approach which, it is argued, results in a coherent information systems strategy that supports and reflects the overall business objectives, addresses the potential that IT might provide, and considers the reality of existing IS provision.

The emphasis on strategic information systems and a top management view has led to a number of implications for methodologies. Many, such as Information Engineering (Section 20.3) have strategic planning as an important early phase in the development at information system. In the next two sections we look at business process re-engineering and then at information systems planning.

4.3   BUSINESS PROCESS RE-ENGINEERING (BPR)

One approach to information systems development, which takes into account strategic aspects, is business process re-engineering. It has presented organizations with the opportunity to rethink outdated procedures, rules, and assumptions underlying their business activities. This opportunity is usually enabled partly by the application of technology to outdated processes.

Although it can be argued that BPR is evident in some of the notions of Scientific Management, it is usually suggested that the more modern origins of BPR are the descriptions of Hammer (1990) and Davenport and Short (1990) and its rapid adoption by consultancies around the same time. This was followed by its popularization with books, such as Davenport (1993) and Hammer and Champy (1993), who define BPR as:

> The fundamental rethinking and radical redesign of business processes to achieve dramatic improvements in critical, contemporary measures of performance, such as cost, quality, service, and speed.

Re-engineering determines what an organization should do, how it should do it, and what its concerns should be, as opposed to what they currently are. It is a radical approach and entails 'business reinvention – not business improvement, business enhancement, or business modification'. This early view of BPR is thus very different to incremental change (such as might be apparent when 'computerising' clerical systems or 're-computerising' computer systems), it is about fundamental change. Emphasis is placed on the business processes (and therefore information systems that reflect them and enable the change), but it also encompasses managerial behaviour, work patterns, and organizational structure. BPR is thus a total approach, involving top management, total organizational restructuring, and a change in the way people think. According to Hammer and Champy, organizations re-engineer for four main reasons:

- they face severe commercial pressures and have no choice;
- competitive forces present problems unless the organization takes radical steps to realign business processes with strategic positioning;
- management in the organization regard re-engineering as an opportunity to take a lead over the competition;
- publicity about BPR has prompted organizations to follow the lead established by others.

The essential first steps in planning a BPR programme are: to develop business vision and process objectives; to identify processes to be redesigned; to understand and measure the existing processes and to identify information systems levers that help push the changes; and finally to design and build prototypes.

The model of BPR created by Hammer and Champy describes the characteristics of re-engineered processes as follows. Several jobs are combined, performed by a 'case worker' responsible for a process. 'Case team' members are empowered to find innovative ways to improve service, quality, and reduce costs and cycle times. Due to process integration, fewer controls and checks are necessary, and defects are minimized by an entire process being followed through by those ultimately responsible for the finished product. Workers make decisions according to the requirements of the whole process. The steps in a process are performed in the order decided upon by those doing the work, rather than on the basis of fragmented and sequential tasks, and this enables the parallel processing of entire operations.

The outcomes of such BPR programmes often include:

- flatter organizational structures;
- greater focus on customers;
- improved teamwork, leading to a more widespread understanding of the roles of others.

As originally conceived in the early 1990s, BPR often necessitated the recruitment of re-engineering teams consisting of, for example, strategists in information systems, business analysts with computer skills, organizational development specialists, and organization and methods experts. Customer service teams were used to maintain and develop a focus on future business, and team 'facilitators' to coach team members, resolve conflicts, and rectify operational problems.

According to Davenport and Short (1990), information systems and BPR have a recursive relationship. On the one hand, IT usage was to be determined on the basis of how well it supported redesigned business processes. On the other, BPR was often enabled by information technology and information systems. The combination of information systems and BPR presented the key opportunity to change the way in which business was conducted radically. A successful BPR programme was fundamental enough to lead to sustainable competitive advantage for organizations brave enough to seize such opportunities.

However, the original enthusiasm for BPR has subsequently been tempered by a number of factors. The very radical approach, which often resulted in large numbers of redundancies, typified by the 'don't automate, obliterate' (Hammer, 1990) view of BPR has proved alienating. Grover (2001) has characterized this as the 'slash and burn mentality' of BPR, arguing that:

> Unfortunately, many corporations responded to reengineering by performing major work force reductions under the aegis of reengineering. Such efforts were not strategically driven, and led to firms losing vital components of the work force that reduced their ability to be creative and productive ... Optimizing process at the cost of people has been a major problem of reengineering.

But perhaps the most significant factor is the reported failure rates of BPR initiatives. Wysocki and DeMitchiell (1997) suggest that failure rates as high as 70 per cent are common. Even Hammer and Champy (1993) quote failure rates of 50–70 per cent, but in their view this is because companies and managers are not radical enough. They highlight senior managers' lack of ambition for radical change, and their unwillingness to embrace the BPR concept fully. Furthermore, they argue that managers fail to comprehend the degree of change required, not only in business processes, but also in managerial behaviour and organizational structure. Moad (1993) identifies lack of resources and senior management support as well as the time that it takes to achieve returns, which result in pressure to abandon the BPR programme.

These factors have resulted in something of a backlash against BPR. Critics have suggested that there is little new theory underpinning the ideas and that it has been usurped by consultancies for their own ends (Earl and Khan, 1994, Peppard and Preece, 1995; Grover and Malhotra, 1997).

BPR, according to Melao and Pidd (2000), is itself now undergoing re-engineering. They suggest that more recent literature (e.g. Davenport and Stoddard, 1994, and Burke and Peppard, 1995) has begun to 'soften' the radical approach to change, associated with the early versions of BPR and they identify nine issues, or continuums, for thinking about BPR (see Figure 4.6).

In Figure 4.6, the first column indicates the issue or element of the continuum, the second column represents the traditional or classic view of BPR, and the third column is the newer, broader, and softer, concept of BPR which they argue is now becoming the more common approach. So, for example, the first identified element is 'novel vs established', where novel is the original BPR which was argued to require a 'conceptually new business model' whereas established is the newer view, which argues that it does not have to be novel but can be 'the linking together of existing approaches in a novel way'. The second element of the framework of analysis is 'radical vs incremental'. Here it is argued that in the new view of BPR, the improvements or benefits need not be completely radical but can be incremental. Third is 'clean slate vs existing' with the classic BPR typically requiring organizations to start from scratch, whereas the new

Issues	Classic	New
Novel vs Established	Conceptually new model	Linking existing models
Radical vs Incremental	Radical	Incremental
Clean slate vs Existing	Starting from scratch	Existing
Broad vs Narrow	Cross-functional	Not necessarily
IT-led vs IT-enabled	IT-led	IT-enabled
Mechanistic vs Holistic	Mechanistic	Holistic
Dramatic vs Modest	Dramatic	More modest
Top-down vs Bottom-up	Top-down	Bottom-up
Methodology vs Inspiration	Methodology	Inspiration

FIGURE 4.6   Framework of BPR (Melao and Pidd, 2000).

BPR can build on existing initiatives. The fourth is 'broad vs narrow' which is normally interpreted as to whether the area of concern is cross-functional (broad) or whether it can be narrower, and so on. Grover (2001) adopts a similar view and states that:

> We now use the term 'business process change' to reflect the importance of process instead of radical change. The strong positions of 'radical change,' 'core processes,' 'top-down,' 'break-through performance,' and so on, are giving way to the reality that there is more than one way of conducting change. Incremental and continuous approaches with bottom-up involvement within functions might be appropriate for some companies and not for others. Classical reengineering might be appropriate for others.

Grover also relates this newer approach to BPR with Total Quality Management (TQM) initiatives and suggests that these approaches, which were diverging just a couple of years ago, now seem to be converging. The point is that BPR is changing from its original concept and is being adapted by organizations to fit new circumstances and the concept, which still has merits, is now much more flexible.

4.4   INFORMATION SYSTEMS PLANNING

Information systems planning is an essential aspect of developing successful systems. In this section we focus on strategic planning and alignment of information systems with the overall strategic direction of the organization. Rather than look at individual applications and subsystems in detail, strategic planning needs to involve the top management of the organization (the managing director, finance director, operations director, and so on) in the analysis and determination of the objectives of that organization. Management should assess the possible ways in which these objectives might be achieved utilizing the information resource. The approach therefore requires the involvement of strategic management in planning information systems.

Because of the requirement to develop an overall plan for information systems development in the organization (within organizational planning as a whole), there are obvious links with systems theory (Section 4.1), and because of its emphasis on the role of strategic management, there are also obvious links to information systems strategy (Section 4.2). Further, because of this top management involvement, there are also links with the participative approach (Chapter 7) as well as business process re-engineering (Section 4.3).

Planning approaches are designed to counteract the possibility that information systems will be implemented in a piecemeal fashion, a criticism often made of applications in the past. A narrow function-by-function approach could lead to the various subsystems failing to integrate satisfactorily. Further, it fails to align information systems with the business strategy. Both top management and IS personnel should look at organizational needs in the early stages and develop a strategic plan for information systems development as a whole so that information systems are integrated and compatible. This becomes a framework for more detailed plans. Individual information systems are then developed within the confines of these plans. Plans could be made at three levels:

1. Long-term planning of information systems considers the objectives of the information systems function and provides rough estimates of resources required to meet these needs. It will normally involve producing a 'mission statement' for the information systems group, which should reflect that of the organization as a whole. The information systems plan at this stage will be an overview document, for example, providing only prospective project titles.

2. Medium-term planning concerns itself with the ways in which the long-term plan can be put into effect. It considers the present information requirements of the organization and the information systems that need to be developed or adapted to meet these needs. Information about each potential information system will be spelt out in detail, including the ways in which they address the overall strategic objectives of the organization. The ways in which the information systems are to be integrated will be stated. Priorities for development will also be established and again these will reflect the long-term plan and mission statement. A planning document will usually will be produced which shows the current situation along with an action plan for future development.

3. Short-term planning, perhaps covering the next 12 months, will provide a further level of detail. It concerns the schedule for change, assigning resources to effect the change, and putting into place project control measures to ensure effectiveness. As well as detailing the resources required for each application in terms of personnel, hardware, and budget, it will contain details of each stage in the development process as suggested in the systems development life cycle described in Chapter 3.

As indicated there is a need for information systems to address corporate objectives directly and so planning should ensure that management needs are met by information systems. Sometimes information systems are designed around management needs, a sort of 'top-down' approach, ignoring operational needs which are assumed to be fulfilled elsewhere. Managers may also set standards for information systems, and one of these requirements will be choosing an approach and a methodology for developing information systems.

There are many general information systems planning approaches, often utilizing techniques such as Critical Success Factors (Section 15.2) and SWOT (15.5). Business analysis might be the first stage of the development of an information system and involves the creation of an information systems strategy group to undertake the following tasks:

■ an assessment of the strategic goals of the organization, which could be long-term survival, increasing market share, increasing profits, increasing return on capital, increasing turnover, or improving public image;

■ an assessment of the medium-term objectives to be used as a basis for allocating resources, evaluating managers' performances, monitoring progress toward achieving long-term goals, establishing priorities;

■ an appreciation of the activities in the organization, such as sales, purchasing, research and development, personnel, and finance;

■ an appreciation of the environment of the organization, that is, customers, suppliers, government, trade unions, and financial institutions, whose actions will affect business performance;

■ an appreciation of the organizational culture relating to values, networks, and 'rites and rituals';

■ an appreciation of the managerial structure in terms of the layers of management or matrix structure, types of decision made, the key personnel, and types of information needed to support the key personnel in their decision making;

■ an analysis of the roles of key personnel in the organization.

With this knowledge, it is possible to assess the type of information that an information system might provide. The first stages of Information Engineering (see Section 20.3) also concerns itself with planning aspects.

Addressing a more detailed later stage in the planning process, Lederer and Mendelow (1989) suggest a number of guidelines which should be considered when planning:

■ *develop a formal plan* – set objectives and policies in relation to the achievement of organizational goals and thereby enable the effective and efficient deployment of resources;

■ *link the information systems plan to the corporate plan* – provide an 'optimal project mix' which will be consistent with and link to the corporate plan, ideally over the same time period;

■ *plan for disaster* – ensure that dependencies are identified and damage likelihood identified;

■ *audit new systems* – evaluate present systems to identify mistakes and hence avoid their repetition and to identify areas where a small resource input might have led to a larger benefit;

■ *perform a cost/benefit analysis* – identify intangible and tangible benefits and costs before putting in the required resources;

■ *develop staff* – make use of and develop the skills of staff;

- *be prepared to change* – as relationships, structures, and processes change;
- *ensure information systems development satisfies user needs* – understand the tasks and processes involved to establish the true user requirements;
- *establish credibility through success* – build up user confidence through previous success, thereby promoting co-operation and lowering barriers.

The effective strategic planning of information systems and the close alignment of IS with the overall business strategy is key to organizational success. However, many methodologies, including the traditional life cycle approach, failed to emphasize this or have a strategic planning activity in their development phases. As a result, planning sometimes got ignored and information systems failed to be as effective in organizations as they might otherwise have been.

4.5   STAGES OF GROWTH

The Stages of Growth (SoG) concept has been around in economics, marketing, organizational studies, and many other areas for a long time. The concept in outline is that an entity (a country, an organization, a department, a product, an individual, or whatever) is perceived to go through a number of discernible and distinct phases, over time, before it can reach a particular point of development, or maturity (they are sometimes also called Maturity Models). Usually each of the identified stages has to be gone through in order for maturity to be achieved, although sometimes there can be shortcuts in particular circumstances. Sometimes the SoG are simply an observation based on empirical studies, i.e. it appears that these are the stages of development or growth which in general the entity goes through, but it is also frequently used to prescribe the stages that the entity *should* go through, and this can be much more contentious.

In relation to information systems and information management, there are a number of SoG models. Most of these relate to the stages that organizations go through in their use, management, and experience of IT. Probably the first was Gibson and Nolan's (1974) model, which identified four stages of growth in the use of IT before maturity was reached (see Figure 4.7).

The stages closely reflect the relative amount spent on IT in an organization, as a proportion of their size, but this also happens to reflect the development and learning path in their utilization of IT. This development and expenditure was argued to follow an 'S-shaped curve' that could be divided into four stages: initiation, contagion, control, and integration. There are four elements that have to be tracked to identify where an organization is in terms of this model:

- *Scope of the applications portfolio* – typically an organization would start its IT development by implementing mainly financial and accounting applications. This would then be increased until most major functions would be supported by IT systems, through to the development of information systems to support management and decision making in mature organizations.
- *Focus of the IT organization* – initially this would be centralized and IT-focused and move to decentralized and data resource-focused in maturity.

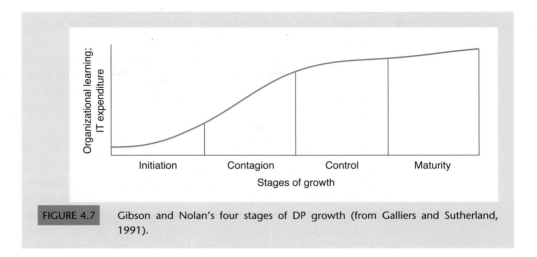

| FIGURE 4.7 | Gibson and Nolan's four stages of DP growth (from Galliers and Sutherland, 1991). |

- *Focus of IT planning and control* – initially this would be an internal focus through to a more external focus in maturity.

- *Level of user awareness* – this concerns the source of the IT initiatives in the organization. Initially users would be reactive to what was on offer from the IT department, then user awareness would move to users becoming the drivers of IT initiatives, through to a partnership in maturity.

Subsequently, Nolan added another two stages, data administration and integration, thereby creating a 6-stage model (Nolan, 1979). Nolan's SoG model was used to identify not only where organizations were in terms of the four stages but more importantly how they should develop in order to achieve maturity. The model became very influential and a prescription for the development of the IT function in organizations in terms of structure, activities, management, etc. It was widely used by consultants and consultancy companies to drive what organizations needed to do to be mature in their use of IT.

However, the model has been criticized in a number of ways. First, it was not empirically proven, i.e. it did not originate from a quantitative study of IT organizations. It was based on what the authors had observed in organizations in their consulting roles but could not be proved. Second, not everyone agreed that this view of maturity was in fact desirable. For example, it seemed to imply ever-increasing expenditure on IT. Third, it was based on a particular view of technology at the time and a view of the IT department. This was related to 'the exploitation of a single broad strand of technology for business data processing' (Feeny et al., 1996). However, Gibson and Nolan did recognize that there would be other 'S-shaped curves' relevant to new technologies as they emerged.

Other SoG models have emerged. For example, Hirschheim et al. (1988) have evolved the Nolan model but focus on IT delivery, management, and leadership. They identify three stages:

- *Delivery* – the focus of IT is internal, reactive, and is concerned with delivering applications on time and within budget to build credibility.

■ *Reorientation* – the focus moves to the exploitation of IT to support the business (what is called using IT to generate strategic advantage).

■ *Reorganization* – the focus is now on relationships with the business, and ideally a partnership or coalition with the business. The application portfolio is balanced, depending on strategy and need, and the structure is probably federal with IT both in the centre and in the business units, according to what makes the most sense.

These are distinct SoG and need to be progressed through. So, for example, when IT cannot deliver (i.e. deadlines are missed, the costs run out of control, and the applications are not delivering the required functionality), there is a kind of pre-stage or Stage 0. Here, there is no possibility of IT having a relationship with the business. There is no credibility with senior business managers. Therefore, the 'delivery' stage concentrates on addressing this issue, getting to the position where the basic provision of applications can be trusted and relied upon. Once this is achieved consistently, then the IT department can be taken seriously and move to 'reorientation'. Here critical, strategic, applications can be considered and developed. IT is aligned with the business, the IT function is now typically led by a business person who can drive the new business focus. Once these applications are achieved and successful, then the IT needs to be 'reorganized' for an overall perspective and a sustainable steady state. IT is now critical to the business and may be represented at Board level as a partner with the business. IT is integrated into the business units where appropriate, and certain functions are kept central, e.g. standards, procurement, IT careers, etc.

So, a number of different SoG models exist, and continue to be developed. Galliers and Sutherland (1991) have revisited and revised some of the earlier models and come up with the following stages:

■ *ad hoc*racy;

■ starting the foundations;

■ centralized dictatorship;

■ democratic dialectic and co-operation;

■ entrepreneurial opportunity;

■ integrated harmonious relationships.

Stages of growth models have also been applied to specific areas of IS; for example, IS planning and strategy, the development of end-user computing (EUC) (see Section 7.2) and information centres (IC) (also see Section 7.2). More recently SoG models have been developed to assess electronic business in organizations and the implementation and exploitation of ERP systems (see Section 8.2) (Holland and Light, 2001).

The related area of innovation and diffusion of technology has also been conceptualized in terms of stages; for example, Brancheau and Wetherbe (1990) used innovation and diffusion concepts in connection with the adoption of spreadsheet software, and Cooper and Zmud (1990) in connection with the adoption and infusion of Materials Requirement Planning. The Capability Maturity Model (CMM) of software is also essentially an SoG model and is described in Section 25.3.

4.6 FLEXIBILITY

The term 'flexibility' is used in a variety of different contexts. It is variously used to describe the inherent properties of a system, the nature of a change or implementation process, and a property of business, information, or other strategies. The term is also used in distinct senses, such as describing systems that can respond effectively to planned or unanticipated changes either where the response leads to changes in the nature of the system (flexibility is 'designed in') or where the response involves the organization changing or transforming itself (a characteristic of an 'organic' rather than a 'bureaucratic' organization). It has always been an important theme in information systems development, because computer applications have proved very poor at responding to changes in the environment that they are supposed to represent.

The flexibility of a system is typically described in terms of dimensions, such as speed of response and the range of activities that the system can perform. Implicitly, both dimensions are judged relative to some norm; for example, a *flexible* manufacturing system can do more things than 'typical' manufacturing systems. In general terms, flexible management systems may include devolved responsibility for decision making, the appropriate size of teams, a culture that can cope with broadly defined roles and *informated* team members (Zuboff, 1988).

Technical systems requisites for flexibility may include initial design, where flexibility is designed into the system, and appropriately trained operators. There may, however, be trade-offs between flexibility and other system characteristics. These trade-offs may be with political realities within an organization, system complexity, effectiveness in relation to particular objectives, the need for standardization and other factors. There may be a trade-off between organizations' needs to have uniform data standards and the need for local discretion in the face of unpredictable demands.

Flexibility is nearly always seen as a 'good thing'. It appears to have three broad advantages. First, it improves the quality of internal processes in ways that may offer a variety of performance improvements. Advantages accruing might include higher staff morale. Second, it may give firms a competitive edge, for example, through the speed of response to an unexpected increase in sales orders, which other firms could not meet. Third, it is part of the 'survival kit' of an organization. It may be that a measure of flexibility is necessary in a turbulent world: 'be flexible or cease operating'. As a number of writers have noted, the acquisition of flexibility is not without costs, and these need to be compared with the likely benefits. In terms of information systems, real costs may include hardware, software, training, reorganization, and ongoing costs.

Flexibility is a useful attribute for any organization operating in an uncertain environment. Different aspects of flexibility are apparent in related concepts such as adaptability, resilience, robustness, agility, versatility, manoeuvrability, and responsiveness. Resilience suggests an emphasis on the ability to cope with uncertainty and to withstand shocks, without fundamentally changing products or processes. However, the concept of flexibility is most closely related to, but distinguishable from, robustness.

Rosenhead (1989) has defined robustness as the extent to which future options are available. The implication is that leaving future options open is a desirable thing. He contrasts robust decision making with conventional decision making. It may be that outcomes are too far in the future to know what the aims and objectives of the decision maker may then be. Under such circumstances, it can be argued that a good decision is one that retains, as reachable, as many outcomes as possible. Concepts like adaptability, agility, and versatility suggest an ability to respond more positively when faced with a changed environment. Described in these terms, flexibility is an attribute that can enable an organization to react to developments. But flexibility and associated concepts can also describe an ability to prepare for and manage an uncertain future in a more proactive way. Therefore, flexibility can involve actions before or after events and involve either defensive or offensive measures. From this perspective, Evans (1991) identifies four archetypal manoeuvres which provide strategic flexibility:

- *pre-emptive manoeuvres* – creating options, inflicting surprise, or seizing initiatives;
- *protective manoeuvres* – insuring against losses, hedging, or creating buffers against adverse conditions;
- *corrective manoeuvres* – the ability to recover from adverse situations and learn from mistakes;
- *exploitive manoeuvres* – capitalizing on opportunities and consolidating advantages.

There are a number of circumstances in which an organization might wish to design any information system robustly or flexibly; for example, where:

- *The designers do not know what the information system is to do*. If the user/analyst team is unable to define precisely, or even imprecisely, what it is the system is likely to be called upon to do, then a flexible system, which can easily be adapted to a variety of purposes, seems potentially desirable.
- *The organization may not know how user requirements will develop after the information system has been introduced*. Traditionally, system builders believe their responsibility for the system ends with its initial implementation. However, they should be committed to developing the system beyond this time, and a flexible system, with the potential for development in various ways, is desirable because the introduction of an information system may itself be the catalyst for organizational change or development of requirements.
- *The designers may not be certain that the chosen development methodology will deliver precisely what is required*. Even if there is a precise specification of requirements, and a guarantee that these requirements will never change, there may be some doubt as to whether such a system can be delivered first time. To prevent missing the target specifications, or commencing a lengthy and costly redevelopment exercise, a flexible system, which can be altered fairly easily, is desirable.

Thus, there appear to be two essential features that make flexibility desirable: ill-defined and shifting system requirements, and mismatches between system performance and requirements. In both cases the ability to change system performance would be helpful.

Successful business strategies are often characterized by initial flexibility, vagueness, and sometimes deliberate ambiguity. In recent years, partially to cope with this, information system developers have moved away from rigid methodologies typified by the systems development life cycle (SDLC) approach, though not always successfully. For instance, Multiview (Section 25.1) emphasizes flexibility in information systems development.

Strategy needs to be most flexible when the organization operates in an unstable or turbulent environment. However, there is evidence that information technology (IT) increases environmental turbulence (indeed, it could be argued that this may be a primary motive for investment). This may, in turn, cause strategy to be couched in more nebulous terms. There is evidence both that successful firms have flexible strategies and that this stems, to some extent, from senior management preference for qualitative language which would preclude explicit statements of objectives. Flexibility is necessary in a fast-changing environment but may not be so in a stable one. The conditions under which flexibility is valued will be contingent on factors such as the rate of change of the environment and the values held by senior executives.

The need for flexibility arises partly from the nature of the strategy-making process which contains both objective and subjective elements. Such decision making has to fulfil a set of conflicting objectives, including the need to measure and combine objective and subjective aspects, to forecast future uncertain events, and reconcile different interest groups. Problems arise due to the evolutionary nature of systems. If evolutionary systems are difficult to evaluate then it seems likely that evaluation in terms of changing strategy will be even more problematic.

It may be that flexibility has a further role: as a critical success factor (Section 15.2) in its own right. The vision of senior management, not just their support, may enhance or determine success rates. Since competitive advantage comes from uniqueness, methodologies are likely to be a constraint on the identification and exploitation of such attributes.

Although some of the maintenance effort is spent on correcting systems poorly specified in the first place, enhancement maintenance, that is, adapting the systems to accommodate changes in the specification, has always taken the lion's share of total maintenance. According to Ward (1985), 98 per cent is devoted to enhancement maintenance. Software engineering techniques (Section 9.1) improve the quality of the software, but not the systems analysis. It is obvious, therefore, that time spent identifying possible changes in the investigation phase of the information systems development life cycle would be time well spent.

There are different ways to consider future requirements. They can be considered as new requirements that will arise in the future. This is the conventional way of viewing them. This is not very helpful as it implies high unpredictability, almost suggesting that it would be a waste of time to try to account for them at the design stage. More helpful, perhaps, is to consider them as existing requirements that will come to light in the future. This might suggest that if every effort was made, every technique followed, and every avenue explored, that it may be possible to identify them before the design is set. In any case, new requirements that will arise in the future can also be considered as 'current requirements', because an information system should be designed so that change can be facilitated. In other words, systems should have inbuilt flexibility. Either way, the identification of future requirements and their incorporation in the new information system will reduce the maintenance burden following implementation. This suggests two things. First, that it is possible to identify future requirements at an earlier stage and, second, that systems should be designed so that it is easy to make changes to cater for requirements that are identified after implementation.

Information systems should be capable of incorporating a range of possible or most probable futures. This emphasis should diminish the maintenance problem by making change easier to incorporate. However, this may have the effect of shifting costs from maintenance to development. With these costs often coming from different budgets and development costs being, to some extent, avoidable while maintenance costs are not, the effects of making projects appear more expensive needs to be carefully handled.

The difficulty of identifying future requirements discussed above and the inherent inflexibility of most information systems may lead to information systems failure or obsolescence. Later in Part 4, we discuss some techniques that might be used to help identify future requirements. In particular, we consider future analysis, risk analysis, and lateral thinking. All the techniques are concerned with reducing uncertainty.

4.7   PROJECT MANAGEMENT

One of the goals of an information systems development methodology is to manage information systems development projects efficiently and effectively. So, to some extent, project control is a theme that pervades methodologies themselves and the entire book. After all, methodologies were introduced largely to manage an information systems development project and to try to make the mantra 'within cost and on time' more likely, therefore reducing the risk of failure. To this we should add: 'with the required functionality and quality'.

In Chapter 14 we look at techniques, such as Gantt charts, work breakdown structures, networks (critical path or PERT analysis), CoCoMo, and function point analysis, which all attempt to help control project development. In Section 17.4, we show the features of Microsoft Project 2000, which is a software tool for project control. A project control package can help to ensure that projects are scheduled at the earliest possible date, with the least drain on resources. Many of the methodologies discussed in Part 6, in particular, those designed for large projects (e.g. SSADM, Merise and RUP) emphasize project management and control aspects. Further, PRINCE (Section 24.5) is specifically designed as a methodology supporting the management of projects. When they are used together, SSADM defines the technical work to be done and PRINCE defines the project management aspects. In this section, we look at the issues concerned with project management and control in general.

The aim of project management is to deliver the project on schedule, within budget, complete, and of the highest quality. Poor project management is a major reason for the failure of many information systems projects. Indications of poor project management might be a lack of identification and control of the activities in a project, poor estimation of the human, time, cost, and other resources required for successful completion, resistance to change, and a lack of focus on the deliverables in detail and how success can be measured.

Much of what we consider 'normal' in a methodology – for example, defining the scope, agreeing times and deadlines, allocating human resources, regular progress reporting, ensuring quality control – are within the scope of project management. They are important issues, whether the project concerns a large tailor-made system or a smaller one centred on an application package, whether the system is developed by technologists or users, indeed whatever the project. Further, project management is also closely linked with IS planning (Section 4.4).

Estimation of the resources required is difficult unless the analysis of the work involved is completed in detail. By breaking up the large project into smaller tasks and then again into activities, the process is easier. Estimation of times and costs for each activity can be based on experience of similar activities on other occasions, an average of estimates from experienced people, and by using techniques, such as CoCoMo and function point analysis (see Section 14.1).

This work breakdown structure can go down through a number of levels. PRINCE facilitates the process of breaking up the work into a series of lower levels. The analyst can better estimate the resources required for each activity because it is smaller, more tangible, and probably within the analyst's experience. The analyst also needs to work out whether some tasks need to be done on completion of other tasks or whether some tasks can be done in parallel. With all this information, and with the possible help of project management tools, it is feasible to start estimating the time and resources required for the project. Information about holidays, other interruptions such as possible sickness leave, and some slack, needs to be incorporated to make the estimate more realistic. Even so, it will not be 100 per cent accurate, so the analyst may suggest a range in the estimate, from most optimistic, through most likely, through to most pessimistic.

Project management implies the existence of some sort of project manager or management team. This role requires good leadership skills, communication skills, administrative skills, and technical competence, as well as a position that is senior enough to command respect. In most organizations, there is a person allocated to this role for each project and this project leader reports to the steering committee and senior management. A member of the senior management on the steering committee may be nominated project manager and act as 'champion' of the project.

As seen by the list of requirements, the project leader role can be very demanding. Part of this role concerns people: getting people working together on the project, and getting people committed to the change, building confidence, and avoiding resistance. Change is never easy for people, so managing the change is a key aspect of the project leader's task. Much will depend on the experience that individuals have had with change in the past, which collectively is part of the organization's 'culture'.

We saw in our discussion of the SDLC in Chapter 3 that methodologies tend to break up projects into phases, subphases and tasks. Project management is partly about estimating the resources required for each (and hence compounded for the whole project) and ensuring that this forecast is achieved to the required quality as the project develops. A lot of the estimating will be done in the feasibility stage, and these estimates will form one basis for management deciding to go ahead with the project.

Identifying critical success factors and ensuring that they are thought about in every stage of the information systems project is also an important part of project management. Sometimes this aspect is distinguished through a **benefits realization programme**. People in the project team may be set aside to ensure that benefits are being realized and there may also be quality managers assigned as well, to ensure that deliverables are achieved at the right quality level. These roles add to those of the project manager, team leader, representatives from the user community, managers, directors, and others.

Of course, the project leader is concerned about ensuring all 'deliverables' are indeed delivered at the agreed levels of quality. However, the project leader should also ensure that the resources allocated to the project are realistic enough to achieve these goals. These resources include people (who have the required experience and skills for the role or training required), infrastructure (in terms of office space, hardware and software tools, training programmes) as well as an appropriate methodology.

We have mentioned the issue of quality without specifying what is meant by this potentially ambiguous term. **Quality** means that the product conforms to the requirements defined for it. An information system should have defined quality expectancies for performance (e.g. for speed of processing, the time to process 10,000 transactions), efficiency (defined levels of storage and other resources it will use), and reliability (e.g. mean time between failure of the system). Some aspects of quality may be more difficult to measure, for example, ease of use, though even here there may be some level of customer satisfaction defined through Likert scale tests (say, an average minimum of 4 on a scale of 1=bad and 5=good). 'Quality' needs to be on the agenda throughout the development of a project – a 'total quality approach'. There are quality standards, such as those of the International Standards Organisation (ISO), that should be adhered to, though reaching these standards is not sufficient (nor is following a methodology, including PRINCE, a guarantee that the standard has been met).

An important aspect of project management is that of progress monitoring: the ability to reveal a separation of actual progress compared to the estimate. This will be revealed using the tools discussed in Part 5 (e.g. Project 2000). In that event, managers will be able either to make corrective actions, such as increase resources to make the estimate more likely, or to reschedule the project. If the decision is to 'accept the inevitable', at least management have been forewarned. It is obviously better than to discover there will be a delay only at the time the system was due to be operational. Further, through reporting, this is communicated to all concerned, leading to trust and understanding rather than alienation.

However, it is obviously better to have a realistic project plan and keep to that plan. In that regard, an assessment of the risks associated with the plan represents an important aspect. Risks (Section 15.7) need to be identified, their likelihood and impact estimated, measures to counteract the risk identified, and measures to be put in place if the event occurs agreed. The latter may include risk transference procedures, such as taking out insurance or imposing penalty clauses on suppliers.

But this suggests a somewhat mechanical view of project management. Good project management has a lot to do with people management as well. It requires members of the team implementing the change to be well motivated. It also requires good management of those affected by the change. Inadequate attention to change management is one of the main reasons for project failure. Clients and users should not be disappointed, and so managing expectations so that they are realistic is important. New information systems are likely to affect the people and culture of the organization and can be gradual/incremental or sudden/transformational. The project manager needs to identify the type of change and the forces working for and against the change, listed under people, resources, time, external factors, and corporate culture. From that information it is possible to formulate an appropriate strategy corresponding to that analysis, indeed many of the arguments discussed earlier in this chapter on strategy relate also to project management. Conflicts are bound to occur, although paying heed to the above will reduce their number, and good negotiating skills could prove crucial. All this would suggest that strong top management support, good leadership and communication skills, as well as good project management processes are key to the effective management of projects.

4.8   SUMMARY

- Systems theory has had widespread influence in information systems work. It suggests a holistic approach to viewing organizations rather than a scientific approach.

- Strategic information systems attempt to identify better ways of doing things, leading to increased revenues, greater functionality, better products and services, improved presentation or image, improvement to the organization's competitive positioning, etc. to gain competitive advantage. They emphasize effectiveness rather than efficiency.

- Business process re-engineering is the fundamental rethinking and radical redesign of business processes to achieve dramatic improvements in critical, contemporary measures of performance, such as cost, quality, service, and speed. In its more recent guise, it has itself been re-engineered and it is less radical.

- Information systems planning involves top management assessing the possible ways in which their objectives might be achieved utilizing the information resource and therefore in planning information systems.

- The stages of growth model shows how information systems in an organization tend to go through a number of discernible and distinct phases, over time, before they reach a particular point of development, or maturity. One model suggests that information systems develop from initiation, to contagion, control, and finally to maturity.

- Flexibility in information systems is seen as an important positive attribute. It is typically described in terms of dimensions, such as speed of response and the range of activities that the system can perform.

- Project management is a theme that is important in most methodologies. It is about managing information systems development projects efficiently and effectively, delivering the project on time, within budget, complete, and of the highest quality.

QUESTIONS

1 In what ways are the themes of this chapter 'organizational'? What links these themes and what separates them?

2 What is 'strategic' about strategic information systems?

3 Discuss why business process re-engineering has been softened or toned down. Do you think this movement has reduced its potential?

4 For an organization of your choice, identify the 'stages of growth' that it passed through, and discuss whether these are similar to any SoG model discussed in the text.

5 Discuss the difficulties related to making information systems flexible so that implementing future change is easier.

4.9 FURTHER READING

Cadle, J. and Yeates, D. (2001) *Project Management for Information Systems*, Prentice Hall, Harlow, UK.

Checkland, P. and Scholes, J. (1990) *Soft Systems Methodology in Action*. John Wiley & Sons, Chichester, UK.

Currie, W.L. and Galliers, R. (1999) *Rethinking Management Information Systems*, Oxford University Press, Oxford.

Earl, M.J. (ed.) (1996) *Information Management: The Organisational Dimension*, Oxford University Press, Oxford.

Galliers, R.D. and Sutherland, A.R. (1991) Information systems management and strategy formulation: The 'stages of growth model' revisited, *Journal of Information Systems*, Vol. 1, No. 2.

Hammer, M. and Champy, J. (1993) *Re-engineering the Corporation: A Manifesto for Business Revolution*, Harper Business, New York.

Melao, N. and Pidd, M. (2000) A conceptual framework for understanding business processes and business process modelling, *Information Systems Journal*, Vol. 10, No. 2, pp. 105–129.

5 MODELLING THEMES

5.1 MODELLING

In Chapter 4 we looked at approaches to information systems development that seek to address the needs of the organization as a whole. We now look at another overriding theme in modern information systems development: modelling.

A model is an abstraction, a representation of part of the real world. An abstraction is often viewed as the process of stripping an idea or a system of its concrete or physical features. Abstraction can be viewed as a simplified representation of the lower level. A benefit of abstraction is the easier development of complex applications. It provides a way of viewing what the model indicates are the important aspects of a system at various levels, so that high levels have the 'essence' of the system and low levels have the detail that does not compromise that 'essence'. The process of abstraction loses information and so a model should only lose that information which is not part of the 'essence' of the system.

It has been suggested that in information systems there are some 'natural' or 'inherent' levels, and these are the conceptual level, the logical level, and the physical level. The conceptual level is a high level overview description of the universe of discourse (UoD), i.e. the domain of interest; this might, for example, be the overall information system, the business system, or society. The logical level is a description of the information system without any reference to the technology that could be used to implement it. Its scope is the information system itself, or part of it, and it is not concerned with modelling the UoD. The physical level is a description of the information system including the technology of a particular implementation.

The elements of the real world that the model chooses to represent are crucial. In the context of this book, it may concern a representation of one or more aspects of the current or proposed information system. Section 5.2 looks at process models in which the key element represented in the model is process. Section 5.3 looks at data models in which the key element represented in the model is data. Processes and data have traditionally been modelled separately but the object-oriented approach has modelled these elements encapsulated together (see Section 5.4) along with other elements such as people.

5.2 PROCESS MODELLING

Structured methodologies use many techniques of process modelling. They have as their unifying elements an emphasis on the processes and the basic technique of functional **decomposition**; that is, the breaking down of a complex problem into more and more detail, in a disciplined way. At the lowest level the units are simple and manageable enough so that they could be reflected in a few lines of computer program code. An example of functional decomposition, which represents a simplification of a payroll system, is seen in Figure 5.1. As well as enabling understanding of complex processes, it also enables people to view the processes at different levels. For example, systems analysts and users may wish to view the system at a high level of abstraction and programmers at a lower level.

Structured systems analysis and design has been associated with a number of consultancy houses and authors. These include Gane and Sarson (1979), DeMarco (1979) and Yourdon (1989). In Section 19.1, we look specifically at the Gane and Sarson methodology (STRADIS). This is a good example of the original structured approach. In Section 19.2 we look at a later development of the approach, Yourdon Systems Methodology (YSM). Other methodologies, for example, SSADM (Section 20.1) and Merise (Section 20.2), have been greatly influenced by this school.

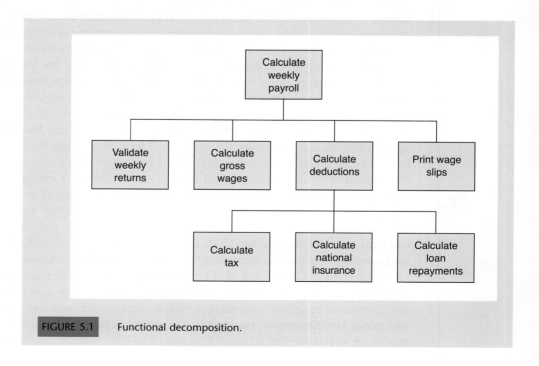

FIGURE 5.1 Functional decomposition.

Some of the techniques associated with structured systems analysis and design, specifically functional decomposition, decision trees, decision tables, data flow diagrams, data structure diagrams, and structured English are looked at in Chapter 12. Many of these models are supported by tools and toolsets (Chapters 17 and 18). Many of the representations are graphical and this encourages user involvement to some extent. Although the emphasis of the structured school is on processes, there is also a consideration of the structure of the data in some of the techniques and tools.

Process modelling describes the logical (real-world) analysis of the processes and not just their physical (implementation) level designs. In other words, there is usually a clear distinction between any application logic (what a system is trying to achieve) and the computer representation of that logic (how the computer system achieves it). In process-oriented approaches the documentation is produced as part of the analysis and design process as 'deliverables' and these models can be cross-checked to ensure consistency in analysis and design and hence enable quality control.

There is also a separation of data structures as seen by the user in the processing and its physical representation (a file or part of a database). This separation of logical and physical designs is an important element of a number of methodologies discussed in Part 6. It gives a level of **data independence**: in other words, the processes can change without necessarily changing the computer files. Similarly, the files can change without necessarily altering the user views of the data.

Two process modelling techniques are data flow diagramming (Section 12.1) and structured English (Section 12.4). Data flow diagrams are a particularly useful aid in communicating the analyst's understanding of the system and are a feature of many commercial methodologies. Users, both end-users and user management, of the area or department concerned can see if the data flow diagram accurately represents the system and, once there is agreement that it reflects their requirements, it can be converted to a design. Structured English is like a 'readable' computer program. It is not a programming language though it can be readily converted to a program, because it is a strict and logical form of English and the constructs reflect structured programming.

There are other variations on the 'English-like' languages used in these methodologies. Although 'English-like', they are not natural languages, which tend to be ambiguous and long-winded. Structured English and its variants, such as pseudo-code and tight English, are designed to express process logic simply, clearly, and unambiguously. This is particularly important to ensure that the system developed represents a system that is actually required.

5.3   DATA MODELLING

Whereas structured analysis and design emphasizes processes, data analysis concentrates on understanding and documenting data which, it is argued, represents the 'fundamental building blocks of systems'. These approaches focus on the modelling of data. High-level data analysis is orientated toward modelling the 'real world' or that part of the real world of concern (e.g. organization, department, or whatever), and is implementation independent. This means that the data model, and therefore the data analysis process that derives it, is suitable whether the physical model is a database, file, or even a card index. There is therefore a separation of logical from physical data; that is, data independence. It also means that, even if applications change, the data already collected may still be relevant to the new or revised systems and therefore need not be collected and validated again.

Early database experience did not always bring about the expected flexibility of computer applications, usually because the database was not a good reflection of the organization it was supposed to represent. Modelling the organization on a computer database is not simple. It is argued that data analysis helps to achieve a data model that is independent of any database, accurate, unambiguous, and complete enough for most applications and users. Its success comes in the systematic way by which it identifies the data in organizations and, more particularly, the relationships between these data elements (i.e. the 'data structure').

Data analysis techniques attempt to identify the data elements and analyse the structure and meaning of data in the organization. This is achieved by interviewing people in the organization, studying documents, observation, and so on, and then formalizing the results through a process known as entity modelling (see Section 11.1).

Data analysis does not necessarily precede the implementation of a database or computer system; it can be an end in itself, to help in understanding aspects of a complex organization. Good models will be a fair representation of the 'real world' and can be used as a basis for discussion and understanding of the organization.

There are a number of alternative approaches to data analysis, one of the most well known is entity modelling. The basic information is obtained in a variety of ways, including the interviewing of users and management in the organization, to identify the key entities (important data groupings). Typical entities might be customer, supplier, parts (see Figure 5.2), and finished goods. Next the relationships between these entities are identified and then the entities and their relationships are expressed as a graphical model.

Data analysis is a feature of a number of methodologies. It is sometimes argued that data is more stable than processes (i.e. that processes are more susceptible to change than data). Therefore, data constitute a better, more stable, basis for the design of an information system than something that is likely to change, such as the processes. This argument

PART NUMBER	COST	NAME	SUPPLIER
344	£10.00	Widgets	Smith
346	£12.00	Widgets	Jones
540	£10.00	Widget tops	Smith

FIGURE 5.2   Part relation.

suggests that in a university, for example, the data concerning students is more stable than the functions or processes that the university may perform on a student. So, there will always be students, they will have names, addresses, registration numbers, degrees they take, and so on. However, the processes, such as the detail of the registration process, may change. This argument has been questioned and some argue that data and processes are in fact equally stable (or unstable) but nevertheless data modelling is important in many methodologies. Most, including object-oriented methodologies, focus equally on the modelling of both data and processes. Additional strengths of data modelling are as follows:

- it is a model which is readily understandable by both developers and users because of its graphical form;
- it is independent of any physical implementation (i.e. it is at a logical level);
- it does not show bias toward particular users or departmental views. The data model can reflect a variety of different views of the data.

Of course, any model can only be *a* model and not *the* model of that part of the real world being investigated. It cannot reflect reality completely and accurately for all purposes. The data model cannot be a completely objective representation of an organization, it is clearly the subjective view of those involved in its creation. Having said this, however, the data model derived from data analysis usually proves in practice to be suitable for the purpose (i.e. to represent the necessary data and to build an information system).

5.4   OBJECT MODELLING

The object-orientated (OO) approach to systems development is increasingly important in the development of information systems. For some it is the means by which many of the existing problems of development, which have proved so tenacious and hard to overcome in the past, will be solved. The concepts of object-orientated modelling and object-oriented systems development are introduced in this section as a modelling theme and further developed in Chapter 13 in relation to object-oriented techniques, including UML, and then again in Chapter 21 in relation to two object-orientated methodologies.

Booch (1991) suggests that the concept of object orientation emerged simultaneously in a number of different fields in the 1970s including computer architecture and operating systems, databases, cognitive science, and artificial intelligence. However, for others its development is associated with the early programming languages, in particular, Simula and Smalltalk; in fact, according to Bahrami (1999), the term object in this context was first used in Simula. Given that the concepts of object orientation have been around since the early 1970s, it is surprising, perhaps, that they have only relatively recently become so influential. This can be said of a number of 'new' themes discussed in Part 3. It may be that it takes up to 20 years for such conceptual and theoretical advances to make their impact in practice. The basic object-orientated concepts are quite different to traditional ones in systems analysis and design and this helps to explain why OO has taken some time to be widely adopted and why some systems developers have found it difficult to come to grips with in practice.

Coad and Yourdon (1991) suggest that the object-oriented concepts are based on those we first learned as children; that is, objects and attributes, wholes and parts, classes and members. We learn by identifying particular objects, such as a tree, and then identifying their component parts (i.e. their attributes), for example, branches and leaves, and then to distinguish between different classes of objects, for example, those of trees and rocks. This implies that the concepts should be simple and indeed the language Smalltalk was originally developed for children to use.

Object-oriented development is different from other models, such as process and data modelling described in the previous sections. Clearly it still involves the modelling of data and processes (or functionality), as these are the fundamentals of a system, but it does it in a completely different way. It does not treat data and processes separately but combines or encapsulates them into an object.

An object represents something in the real world, so an example might be an object representing a car, in a car rental application. It has data, such as the manufacturer, model, colour, number of seats, mileage, etc. It also has processes or actions (methods as they are termed in the object-oriented world), such as go forward, go backward, go up a gear, go down a gear, brake, accelerate, etc. But we are not particularly interested in these processes in the car rental system so we do not model them (i.e. we only model what is relevant for our application environment). In the context of a car rental application, we might be more interested in processes such as servicing a car, booking a car to a client, client returning car, checking a car for damage, etc. Some of these might be processes the car object can perform, others might be processes other objects perform on the car object. The processes that the car object can perform might be limited, but we might be interested in the car's capability of transmitting its position, its display mileage function or its self-diagnosis feature. In which case we would model them. Objects are independent of each other and exist independently (i.e. the exact way that it performs its processes and the data are unknown to other objects). This means that the internal workings or implementation of the object can be changed without it causing any problems or affecting other objects, an important benefit. So, a system is made up of a series of discrete objects that interact together by the passing of messages from one object to another, which trigger the processes of the object. So, a booking object might check the mileage of a particular car before reserving it to check if it is due for a service.

Object-oriented modelling is concerned with representing objects, including their data and processes, and the interaction of objects, in a system. We also model hierarchies of objects (called classes), so we might have a high-level car vehicle object that breaks down into various objects of cars of particular manufacturers. These concepts are described in more detail in Section 13.1.

There are a number of benefits of the object-oriented approach:

■ Object-oriented concepts unify many aspects of the information systems development process. For example, the analysis of the application area can be undertaken using object analysis and object modelling, the design of the new system can use object orientation as the design approach, the human–computer interfaces can be designed using object-oriented methods, applications can be developed using object programming languages, object-oriented tools, and 'data' (using a broad definition of the term to include text, audio, pictures, video, and so on) once collected can use object-oriented multimedia databases. There is no need to transform the objects into other representations. The object-oriented theme is relevant and consistent throughout. This contrasts with other methodologies which somehow have to blend and reconcile the results of different approaches, such as that of the data and process views discussed in the previous two sections. For example, attempting to reconcile entity-relationship diagrams and data flow diagrams is not trivial because they represent different objects in different ways. The object-oriented approach represents data, processes, people, and so on, all as objects.

- It facilitates the realistic reuse of software code and therefore makes application development quicker and more robust. In theory the organization will develop a library of object classes that deal with all the basic activities that the organization undertakes. Software development therefore becomes the selection and connection of existing classes into relevant applications, and because those classes are well tried and tested as independent classes, when they are connected together they provide immediate industrial-strength applications that run correctly in a shorter period of time. Only completely new classes will need to be developed or purchased. Proponents of object orientation believe that eventually there will exist international libraries of object classes that developers will be able to browse to find the classes they require and then simply buy them. The classes in these libraries will be guaranteed to perform as specified, and so new applications are easily developed and existing (object-oriented) applications can be modified and extended in functionality just as easily. Software development is not only quicker and cheaper but the resulting applications are robust and error-free. This still remains somewhat of a theoretical benefit as we have not yet seen very much evidence of libraries of object classes developed for reuse.

- It integrates methods of systems development with the systems context. Mathiassen et al. (2000) suggest that this is an increasingly important benefit because modern systems are not just about replacing labour-intensive operations as was the case in the past. In most organizations such labour displacement systems have all been developed, we are now at a stage of developing the second or third version of them, or developing systems with other objectives, such as supporting individuals in problem solving or communication. For such systems the method must focus on the context as well as the system. For example, in a system that dispatches ambulances to emergencies it is important that the system models the context and methods of interaction of the ambulances, the other emergency vehicles and services, the ambulance drivers and their way of working, the patients and their potential injuries and problems, and the hospitals that may receive the patients. If this context is ignored then the system may well fail, as indeed happened in the London Ambulance Service (Fitzgerald, 2000). Of course, traditional systems development has always attempted to deal with context (e.g. Checkland, 1981) but the benefit object orientation is said to provide is that it specifically addresses the modelling and understanding of context using the same methods and principles as for modelling the system itself.

Coad and Yourdon (1991) suggest a number of other motivations and benefits for object-oriented analysis (OOA), including:

1   the ability to tackle more challenging problem situations because of the understanding that the approach brings to the problem situation;

2   the improvement of analyst–user relationships, because the approach can be understood by both equally and because it is not computer-oriented;

3   the improvement in the consistency of results, because it models all aspects of the problem in the same way;

4   the ability to represent factors for change in the model so leading to a more resilient model.

These are ambitious claims, and in a later section these claims can be evaluated in the context of OOA and the RUP methodologies (see Chapter 21) and more detail on the concepts and techniques of object-oriented analysis and design are provided in Chapter 13.

5.5   SUMMARY

- A model is an abstraction, a representation of part of the real world.
- In a three-level view, the conceptual level is a high-level overview description of the universe of discourse (UoD), i.e. the domain of interest. The logical level is a description of the information system without any reference to the technology that could be used to implement it. The physical level is a description of the information system including the technology of a particular implementation.
- Process modelling describes the logical (real-world) analysis of the processes and not just their physical (implementation) level designs. The basic technique of process modelling is functional decomposition; that is, the breaking down of a complex problem into more and more detail, in a disciplined way.
- Data analysis concentrates on understanding and documenting the data elements and their relationships.
- The object-oriented (OO) approach models objects, which represent something in the real world including people, data and processes, and the interaction of objects.

QUESTIONS

1 What are the differences between modelling an airplane and modelling an information system?

2 Why are process and data modelling separate? What else should be modelled in an information system?

3 Why do you think object modelling has been gaining more users at the expense of process and data models?

5.6 FURTHER READING

Avison, D.E. and Shah, H.U. (1995) *The Information Systems Development Cycle: A First Course in Information Systems*, McGraw-Hill, Maidenhead, UK.

Mathiassen, L., Munk-Madsen, A., Nielsen, P.A., and Sage, J. (2000) *Object Oriented Analysis and Design*, Marko Publishing, Aalborg, Denmark.

Teorey, T.J. (1998) *Database Modelling and Design: The Fundamental Principles*, Morgan Kaufman, San Francisco.

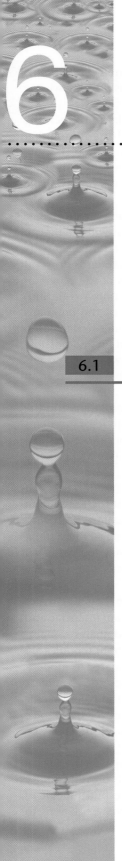

6 ENGINEERING AND CONSTRUCTION

....

LEGACY SYSTEMS

In this book we concern ourselves in the main with developing new computer applications. However, established organizations will also be concerned with running systems that have been in operation for some time. These are its legacy systems, and some may even have been originally developed as early as the 1960s and 1970s. Because of this, some legacy systems are likely to be high-volume transactions data processing applications running on mainframe computers – commercial systems frequently written in the Cobol programming language using structured files rather than database systems. With high maintenance costs, use of obsolete hardware and software, poor documentation, and lack of people support with the knowledge required to maintain them, it is not surprising that legacy systems have become an enduring and problematic theme!

Legacy systems may well perform critical processes, a reason for their early development, and be valuable assets of the organization. However, during their lifetime they could have undergone many changes in the review and maintenance phase of the SDLC. These changes are likely to have made them more complex. Sometimes, documentation might have been neglected and is therefore not up to date. For all these reasons legacy systems will probably have become more and more expensive and difficult to maintain.

Sometimes new systems will be developed to replace legacy systems that no longer achieve their objectives, use outdated technology, or are very costly to maintain. At the other extreme are those systems that have been performing effectively with minimal maintenance necessary, sometimes for many years. However, for most organizations, many legacy systems are a major problem: both expensive to maintain and to replace.

A critical point in many legacy systems comes when a change in the environment requires a major change in the system, such as the ability to handle increasing data volumes or differing functionality (or in the recent past ensure that they will run successfully in the year 2000). The organization needs to decide whether to invest in maintenance or replacement. This is not only a question of cost. As Warren (1999) points out, if you abandon a legacy system 'you face the risk of losing vital business knowledge which is embedded in many old systems'.

If the choice is maintenance, then the organization may consider implementing new features that make the system more efficient and effective, as well as ensuring that the system incorporates new functional requirements and existing problems are corrected. If the choice is replacement, then the project is likely to be very expensive unless there is an appropriate application package (Section 8.1) that was not available previously or components available that can be conveniently reused.

One alternative to continued maintenance or replacement is to **reverse engineer** and then **forward engineer** the application. Software tools exist that will attempt to analyse the application programs, in terms of the rules and procedures that they embody (reverse engineering), and modify them so that they conform to new standards (forward engineering). The new standards could relate to a more recent version of the programming language or an alternative one, a restructuring of the programming code into modules that can be easier to change in the future, a restructuring of the programs (sets of modules), or a restructuring of the data source, perhaps from files to databases. Such analysis and redesign should make the application easier to maintain and possibly enable it to integrate with other applications. This is potentially a lower cost and less risky solution to a legacy problem when compared to developing a new system from scratch.

Oracle (Section 18.3) has modules designed to reverse engineer programs and the Renaissance methodology (Section 24.5) presents one approach to adapt legacy systems so that they do conform to an organization's new vision for information systems. An alternative approach is Application System Asset Management (ASAM) (see McKeen and Smith, 1996).

The implementation of an enterprise resource planning system (Section 8.2) can also address effectively the problem of legacy systems. Some modules of the ERP system may be implemented that replace legacy systems; indeed, many organizations dealt with the Year 2000 problem by replacing their legacy systems with a new ERP system. However, ERP implementation does not necessarily involve decommissioning of all legacy systems. Others might remain but be adapted so that they interface with the new ERP system.

Another way to deal with legacy systems is to manage them better. Greater resources might be given to the maintenance of such systems so that financial and other rewards make maintenance work attractive for programmers and analysts; maintenance is seen as a requirement for personnel to gain promotion; program modules are revised in turn to ensure the code is efficient; and documentation is updated to modern standards. Some organizations give their systems an annual 'service' or 'complete overhaul', rather like a piece of machinery, others have sidestepped the issue by outsourcing the maintenance of their legacy systems (Section 8.3). Whatever the choice between the above approaches, neglect is not the answer as organizations could be seriously affected by the failure of their key established applications.

Of course, today's new applications, even ERP systems, will become the legacy systems of tomorrow. Hence it is important to build into today's applications flexibility so that future change is easier to implement. This is easy to argue for, but difficult to implement, and much of the concern of good practice suggested in this book aims to ensure that the 'legacy' of today's systems are not the problems of many legacy systems implemented in the past.

6.2 EVOLUTIONARY DEVELOPMENT

Evolutionary systems development is a staged or incremental approach that periodically delivers a system that is increasingly complete (i.e. it evolves) over time. Evolutionary development is sometimes termed incremental development. The first (or even subsequent) implementation is not seen as the main objective but is just part of the continuing evolution and improvement of the system until an optimal solution to the original problem or requirements is achieved. Frequently, as the system matures only minor iterations occur until a major step change is required as a result of technological obsolescence, change of business mission, or a fundamental redesign of the required processes, in which case the system is completely thrown out and a new one begun.

When this happens the orderly, evolutionary changes are replaced by large, abrupt changes, creating shock waves throughout the organization and the process begins again. Of course, the idea that a system ever reaches an equilibrium state, where it requires relatively little maintenance and change, is not often seen because in practice the business needs and user requirements are usually evolving and changing, necessitating continual evolution.

Evolutionary systems are thus not in their final form at their first iteration or delivery. Each delivery achieves something useful and usable but is not necessarily complete. The design process stretches over the entire life of the system providing a better approximation to the ideal required product at each iteration. Figure 6.1 illustrates the concept.

It can be seen that there are a series of development efforts. The first iteration begins at a particular point in time and contains a full set of stages or phases from the identification of requirements through analysis, design, and implementation. Although not specifically mentioned here, it is frequently assumed that a prototyping approach will be used and prototyping is closely associated with evolutionary development (see Section 6.3); however, this is not strictly necessary for it to be evolutionary. The system developed in the first iteration will probably be only a subset of the total requirements, or just a first stab at them. In the bottom half of the diagram it can be seen that only a relatively small part of the total potential needs and requirements have actually been achieved at the end of the first iteration. After this, a period of learning about the system, and gaining experience of using the system, may occur. (In fact, iterations can have a time gap between them, butt up to each other, or even overlap.)

With the experience and knowledge gained, a second iteration of the system is initiated with revised and refined requirements. This second iteration essentially takes the existing system from Iteration 1 and evolves it and integrates it with the new requirements discovered in Iteration 2. This is typically a demanding task but probably involves less effort than building the original system of Iteration 1. Thus, in theory at least, the amount of effort declines at each successive iteration.

At the end of Iteration 2 a significantly greater proportion of needs should now be fulfilled. However, it is important to ensure that the environment has not changed

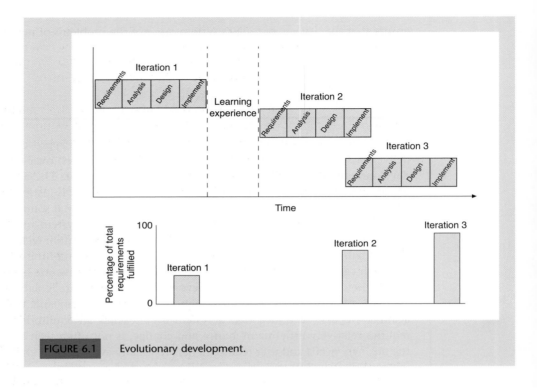

FIGURE 6.1 Evolutionary development.

before starting Iteration 3. For example, the system might need to reflect the introduction of some new government regulations. As well as these mandatory changes, additional improvements are also implemented resulting in a large proportion of the total requirements now being fulfilled, indeed close to 100 per cent. This might mean that the equilibrium mentioned above has been achieved; however, it is more likely that further iterations occur from time to time, as a result of further changes in the business needs and environment.

Orman (1998/9) makes the point that evolutionary development is characterized not just by its ongoing and iterative nature, but by the evolutionary nature of the system's original creation as well. Therefore, the original design, and indeed designs of subsequent iterations, should be geared to evolution. This can be achieved in a number of ways:

- *The design does not have to be perfect.* It can be just a first attempt, good enough, rather than an ideal or perfect solution. The first design often focuses on the core of the system.
- *It can allow or accommodate future change, or at least not impede such change.* This might be achieved in a number of ways, for example by building in some flexibility or redundancy, or by parameterizing as much as possible.
- *It does not have to be comprehensive.* It need only address part of the required system to begin with rather than everything that might possibly be required.

Therefore, improvements and enhancements to the system can be added later in subsequent iterations, as the system is used and experience is gained. A further benefit of this approach is that it can be quick, or at least getting to the first implementation can be relatively quick. It may not be a complete nor ideal solution but at least it is something, and it has probably been delivered more quickly than a full, traditionally developed system. Rapid application development (Section 6.4) uses many of the concepts of evolutionary development to achieve speed of delivery.

Another major benefit of evolutionary development (and something that distinguishes it from other development models) is that changing requirements over time are expected and catered for as part of the incremental development. As a change is required it is just built into the next iteration of the development. Change is seen as the norm and not a surprise or a reflection of failure in some way. What might normally be thought of as maintenance of a system, with its negative connotations, is regarded as positive (McCracken and Jackson, 1982).

Evolutionary development is regarded as highly appropriate for situations where requirements are difficult to discover in advance (or indeed where they are impossible to discover), or where the system is particularly complex. According to Orman (1998/9), it may be 'the only feasible strategy for highly unstructured or unstable systems where the traditional requirements and analysis techniques frequently fail'. He also argues that most 'strategic management applications and decision support systems fall into this category as their requirements are generally vague, and the objectives are fluid, even in the minds of end users'.

Evolutionary development differs from the SDLC (Chapter 3) in that it is not a linear development. The SDLC is designed for 'straight line development' (Pressman, 2000); that is, it assumes that a complete solution will be delivered at the end of a linear sequence. At each stage of the SDLC, as complete and comprehensive a job as possible is undertaken. For example, in the early stages, a complete and detailed set of requirements is specified in great detail. These then are typically 'frozen'; that is, they cannot be changed during the development phase. These requirements then drive the design and implementation of the complete and finished system.

This is clearly not the case in evolutionary development. With evolutionary development, just a first set of outline requirements, perhaps only for a subset of the system, would typically be identified at first, the detail of which would be assumed to be changing and changeable. These would then be used to design the core of the system that would deliver something useful but that would undoubtedly need to be changed in some way and evolve with later iterations.

Attempts have been made to combine the rigour and the management control of the SDLC with the benefits of the evolutionary approach, which has been criticized as being difficult to manage and control. Most notably, Boehm (1988) has proposed the spiral model (see Figure 6.2), which adopts the concept of a series of incremental developments or releases. As can be seen, development spirals outward from the centre in a clockwise direction with each cycle of the spiral resulting in successive refinement of the system.

In each cycle of the spiral there are four main activities, represented by the four quadrants. First, there is planning (bottom left quadrant) and at each cycle round the spiral this is about planning the next part or phase, and different elements will be involved depending on what stage the project has reached. Second, there is an objectives phase (top left), then, third, a risk analysis stage (top right) concerned with the identification and resolution of risks in the system. Risks, such as design flaws, failing to meet

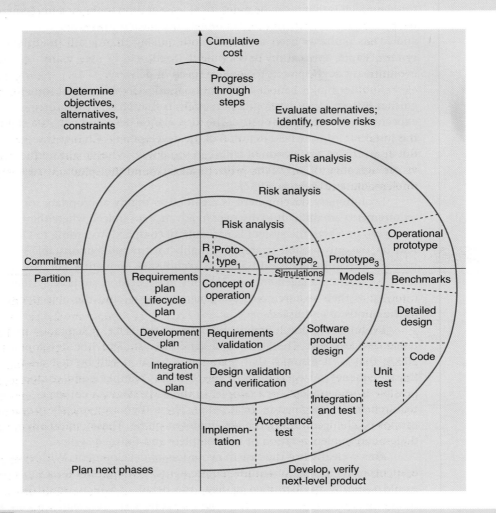

Cumulative
cost

Progress
through
steps

Determine
objectives,
alternatives,
constraints

Evaluate alternatives;
identify, resolve risks

Risk analysis

Risk analysis

Risk analysis

Operational
prototype

Commitment

R Proto-
A type₁

Prototype₂   Prototype₃

Partition

Requirements
plan
Lifecycle
plan

Concept of
operation

Simulations   Models

Benchmarks

Development
plan

Requirements
validation

Software
product
design

Detailed
design

Code

Integration
and test
plan

Design validation
and verification

Unit
test

Integration
and test

Implemen-
tation

Acceptance
test

Plan next phases

Develop, verify
next-level product

FIGURE 6.2   Boehm's spiral model. (Source: Boehm, B. W. (1988) A spiral model for software development and enhancement, IEEE Computer, Vol. 21, No. 5. © 1988 IEEE.)

user needs, escalating costs, losing sight of the perceived system benefits, etc. are detected early in the development process. The spiral model, apart from its evolutionary nature, is particularly focused on addressing risk. This is not generally a strength of other models of development. Indeed, it is sometimes known as the 'risk-driven model'. The fourth stage is development (bottom right). In the early stages this might concern the development of manual or paper models, it might involve the development of a prototype (see below). The prototype might be used to help define and understand the requirements or illustrate a user interface for users to react to, or whatever. These may then evolve into the delivered system, and in later cycles they become more complete systems until finally they are the fully tested and engineered releases of the system. The exact number of cycles is not defined. It depends on the nature and characteristics of the particular project and the difficulties encountered in the cycles.

The vertical axis in the model represents the cumulative cost of the development project, which increases with each cycle. Similarly, the horizontal axis represents the commitment to the project, also increasing with each cycle. Prototyping is an important element of the spiral model but some commentators regard this aspect as its main characteristic, often forgetting the importance of the other quadrants.

Although described in this section concerning evolution, it should be noted that the spiral model is not evolutionary in iterative implementations, as indicated in Figure 6.1. It is evolutionary only in its revisiting of each of the stages. The same stages are visited again and again as the project cycles around the spiral until a complete systems implementation is produced.

6.3 PROTOTYPING

Information systems tend also to be one-offs, but the cost of building a software prototype has been difficult in the past because building a prototype was often almost as expensive and took nearly as long as developing the final system, and therefore was rarely undertaken. This has changed with the availability of software tools which have greatly reduced the costs and speeded up the process of developing a prototype. Hardgrave (1995) suggests that over 70 per cent of systems development efforts involve prototyping of some kind, and Coad and Yourdon (1991) suggest prototyping should be used for all object-oriented projects. This, together with the use of prototyping in RAD (Section 6.6) and its growing use in relation to web development (Section 6.6), suggests that prototyping is here to stay and as popular as ever.

Prototyping addresses some of the problems of traditional systems analysis; in particular, the complaint that users only see their information system at implementation time when it is too late to make changes. If a prototype version of the information system is not developed first, the systems analysts are experimenting on the user. The first version of the type is also the final version and this brings about an obvious risk of failure, including outright user rejection. Therefore, the prototyping approach is a response to the user dissatisfaction found when using the traditional approach to information systems development.

According to Chen (2001), the prototyping method was formally introduced to the information systems community in the early 1980s to combat the weakness of the traditional waterfall model (Chapter 3). The early prototyping process was for developers to design and build a scaled-down functional model of the desired system and then the developers demonstrate the working model to the user. This results in comments and feedback on its suitability and effectiveness. The developer then continues to develop the prototype until the developers and the users agree that the prototype is satisfactory.

At that point, an important distinction is made in the literature, as to whether the prototype is then thrown away, that is, used solely to help establish and elicit the user requirements, or whether the prototype is then evolved or enhanced to form the actual system that is provided to the user for real use. So, there are two types of prototype:

- a throwaway (or expendable) prototype;
- an evolutionary prototype.

This distinction often leads to differences in the design of the prototyping tool. Some are designed to develop prototypes that are expendable only, focusing on quickly building graphical interfaces and some basic processing and functionality. Such tools develop prototypes that are:

- inefficient for operational use;
- incomplete, performing only some of the required tasks;
- inadequate, sometimes being designed for one type of user or one purpose only;
- poorly documented;
- unsuitable, or difficult to integrate with other operational systems;
- incapable of scaling to the required volumes of operational use.

It is suggested that the use of evolutionary prototyping tools leads to slightly quicker applications development, as the developers are building on something that already exists, rather than starting from scratch. However, they need to blend the power of the prototype with the ability to evolve the prototype into an effective, live running system, which can handle large volumes and has the speedy response, high functionality, security, etc. that operational systems require.

With prototyping, user acceptance of a system is regarded as far more likely. By implementing a prototype first, the analyst can show the users something tangible – inputs, intermediary stages, and outputs – before finally committing to the new design. These prototypes are not diagrammatic approximations, which tend to be looked at as abstract things, but actual physical outputs, screens, databases, etc. The formats can be changed quickly, as the users suggest amendments and enhancements, until the users see a reasonable approximation of their requirements. Further, it may only be by using this approach that the users discover exactly what they really want from the system, as well as what is feasible. It is also often possible to try out an example run using data generated by the users themselves or with real data. This helps to ensure that the system and processes can handle the inputs and data thrown at it. Without a prototype this might not happen until very late in the development process, often just prior to implementation. The key benefit of prototyping is finding out such problems as early as possible. The earlier it is discovered the easier and cheaper it is to fix.

In information systems there are different kinds of prototype with different objectives. The most common use of prototypes is to examine areas where the users and analysts are unsure of the requirements and feel they need to tease out and explore the real needs by showing and amending a physical approximation of a system. With this objective, prototyping is argued to be an improvement on the traditional form of requirements gathering. Prototyping may form part of a methodology itself, or it can be used contingently as part of an existing methodology, used when and where appropriate. It is particularly useful where:

- the application area is not well defined;

- the organization is not familiar with the technology (hardware, software, communications, designs, and so on) required for the application;
- the communications between analysts and users are not good;
- the cost of rejection by users would be very high, and it is essential to ensure that the final version has got users' needs right;
- there is a requirement to assess the impact of prospective information systems.

Alternate forms of prototyping in information systems, apart from requirements elicitation objectives, are:

- *functional prototypes* for demonstrating, testing, and evaluating the functionality of a system;
- *process prototypes* for demonstrating, testing, and evaluating the processes, sequences, responses, etc. of a system;
- *design prototypes* for demonstrating and evaluating a variety of alternate designs or solutions;
- *performance prototypes* for testing response times, loads, volumes, etc.;
- *organizational prototypes* for demonstrating and evaluating different organizational designs, cross-functional work, organizational processes, and their integration with information systems (see, e.g. Hume et al., 1999).

Often, prototyping in practice combines two or more of these objectives.

There are a variety of factors that have been suggested as important when considering whether prototyping is appropriate. Those characteristics of a project where it is normally suggested that prototyping would be particularly beneficial are as follows:

- unclear requirements;
- unstable requirements;
- high innovativeness;
- high system impact on the organization (although not safety critical);
- high system impact on users;
- relatively small project size;
- relatively small number of users;
- relatively short project duration;
- where commitment of users to a project is required.

Although these characteristics may be recommended as appropriate in the literature, of course there are always examples where they have been ignored or success has been achieved in spite of them.

Prototyping may be more than just another tool available to the analyst. It could be used as a basis for a methodology of systems development in the organization. This may have:

- *an analysis phase* designed to understand the present system and to suggest the functional requirements of an alternative system;

- *a prototyping phase* to construct a prototype for evaluation by users;
- *a set of evaluation and prototype modification stages*;
- *a phase to design and develop the target system* using the prototype as part of the specification.

Prototyping is also regarded as a way of encouraging user participation (see Section 7.1 and Chapter 16). The hands-on use of prototypes by users provides experience, understanding, and the opportunity for evaluation. Once users and managers realize that things could be changed and that they could exert influence, it can lead to improved participation and commitment to the project.

Some analysts recommend that only the most critical aspects of a new system should be prototyped. Alternatively, the prototype may be built up using the most straightforward aspects and add to the prototype, as users and analysts understand the application area more fully. This is somewhat akin to the evolutionary approach discussed in the previous section.

A prototype is frequently built using special tools such as screen painters and report generators which facilitate the quick design of screens and reports. The user may be able to see what the outputs will look like quickly. Whereas a hand drawing of the screen layout will need to be drawn again for each iteration that leads to a satisfactory solution, the prototype is quickly redrawn (or repainted) using the tools available. As with word processing systems, the savings come in making changes, as only these need to be drawn. Therefore, the ease and speed with which prototypes can be modified are as important as the advantages gained from building the prototype in the first place. Iteration of screens and designs becomes a practical possibility.

Frequently a prototype system can be developed in a few days, and it may not take more than 10 per cent of the time and other resources necessary compared to developing the full operational system. This can be a good investment of time and it can speed up the overall development process. Analysts can usually achieve rapid feedback from the users so that the iterative cycle can quickly work to a version acceptable to the users. It has been suggested that this typically cuts in half the time that requirements determination normally takes, with better results.

Some systems teams use the prototype itself as the artefact that the users sign off (i.e. if they are happy with the prototype and the way it performs then that is good enough). This can be a more effective approach to obtaining a user decision than signing off the traditional manual specification.

Prototyping, although having many benefits, is not without its critics. It is certainly not a panacea to all the problems of traditional development and should be used appropriately. Prototypes have been criticized on a number of fronts (see, e.g. Janson and Smith, 1985) for leading to inadequate, or partial, system designs. Designs resulting from prototyping are not properly engineered, it is argued, they just emerge, leading to poor operational systems. Some situations are just too complex for systems to be designed in this way and that more formal and deliberate design strategies are needed. This is essentially the 'quick and dirty' criticism of prototyping, which is often made. These criticisms are particularly, and probably rightly, made in connection with safety critical applications. Developers who practise prototyping have been highlighted as not having the necessary design skills. Prototyping has also been criticized for the difficulties it presents in connection with testing. Normally, systems are tested against detailed specifications but with prototyping there may not be any specification.

Prototyping is sometimes regarded as difficult to manage and control, and the danger of forever seeming to cycle around minor differences has been experienced in practice (Fitzgerald, 1999). The proliferation of requirements that prototyping leads to is sometimes regarded as a problem, as is getting users to participate. Sometimes users have questioned the long time required to develop an operational system when the time taken to develop the prototype was so short. The managing of expectations in prototyping is very important to overcome this problem. Sometimes prototypes designed to be thrown away become used as operational systems due to the pressures of managers and users who want the system immediately and cannot understand why they cannot use the prototype, especially after they have seen it 'work'. Plato (1995) states that 'prototypes have an amazing tendency to become operational systems … and they wind up becoming half-baked operational contraptions'. Some users are disappointed that the operational system is not as quick as the prototype to run. Tudhope (2000) even suggests, 'some developers go so far as to introduce code for the purpose of producing delays in the speed of operation of early prototypes to avoid unrealistic user judgements of final system response'!

There is also the risk that the system requirements may change in the meantime. Some users may argue that the time, effort, and money used to develop a prototype is 'wasted'. It is sometimes difficult to persuade busy people that this effort does lead to improved information systems.

Many of the criticisms of prototyping are really concerned with its inappropriate use. Clearly, prototyping is not a substitute for thorough analysis and design. Implementation compromises should not be made as they are likely to remain in the final system. This includes the documentation, which might be neglected as analysts argue, 'it is only a prototype'. One of the necessary components of successful prototyping is management and control so as to ensure that compromises are not made and the process of repeated iteration does not go on too long.

The information system may be implemented in stages. At each stage, the missing components are those that give the poorest ratio of benefits over costs. The analysts in this case will have to be aware of robust design and good documentation when the prototype is being developed. The prototype must be able to handle the quantities of live data that are unlikely to be incorporated when giving end-users examples of the prototype's capabilities. Otherwise, prototyping will not improve the quality of systems development. Therefore, although prototyping is frequently regarded as a 'quick and dirty' method, it need not be 'dirty'. If the prototype is well designed, the prototype can feature as part of a successful operational information system. The temptation, however, is for a quick and dirty solution because the tools can produce a quick result and analysts are tempted to move quickly on to the development phase before sufficient analysis has been carried out. The emphasis on controls in prototyping is therefore necessary. Corners should be cut only in situations where the information system will have a very short lifespan (or is set up for once-only use).

Up to this point it has been assumed that prototyping was undertaken and facilitated by professional systems developers building a prototype for users to comment upon and react to, and this is indeed the normal approach. However, sometimes prototyping is undertaken by the users themselves without specialist IS developer help. This is part of the end-user computing concept (see Section 7.2). The prototyping tools must be relatively straightforward and easy to use and the users need to be self-motivated and committed to the project. It also has the benefit of freeing up the IS specialists for other activities or projects and means that the users drive the project forward at their pace and on their terms.

As indicated above prototyping has been used for many years in systems development but recent development approaches also use prototyping (see Section 6.4). Even more recently development of web-based systems have frequently used prototyping. This may seem a little odd at first because many web-based systems do not have the internal users of traditional systems, but, for example, Chen (2001) argues that 'prototyping methods are especially suitable for web-based applications because of the ease of system delivery and updates afforded by web technology'. However, he does go on to say that 'the unique requirements of web applications require the designers to take additional considerations when using these models (i.e. *prototypes*)'.

In Chen's Modified Prototype Method (MPM) for web application development, the basic functionality of a desired system, or a component of it, is formally deployed right away, via a prototype. The maintenance phase begins right after the deployment and it continually evolves. Once a prototype is deployed, its online users' actions are monitored using web server logging facilities. The subsequent analysis of these user actions determines which parts of the application are being used the most and which are being used the least, and the information is used to evolve future development and add efficiency to the application. So, the live system is essentially a prototype and the users, out there, contribute to its development and enhancement by their actions. Another Web development methodology is WISDOM (Section 22.4).

6.4   RAPID APPLICATION DEVELOPMENT (RAD)

Rapid Application Development (RAD) has evolved as an important theme in information systems development over the last few years. The term appears to have first been used by James Martin in 1991; the Martin RAD methodology is described in Section 22.1. As with many themes, RAD was developed as a reaction to the problems of traditional development, in particular the problems of long development lead times. It also addresses the problems associated with changing and evolving requirements during the development process. RAD has a number of general characteristics or features as follows:

1   Incremental development

An important element of the philosophy of RAD is the belief that not all a system's requirements can necessarily be identified and specified in advance. Some requirements will only emerge when the users see and experience the system in use, others may not emerge even then, particularly complex ones. Requirements are also never seen as complete but evolve and change over time with changing circumstances (Section 6.2). Therefore, trying fully to specify a system completely in advance is not only a waste of time but often impossible. So why attempt to do it? RAD starts with a high-level, rather imprecise list of requirements, which are refined and changed during the process, typically using toolsets (Chapter 18). RAD identifies the easy, obvious requirements and, in conjunction with the 80/20 rule (see the Pareto principle below), just uses these as the starting point for a development, recognizing that future iterations and timeboxes (see below) will be able to handle the evolving requirements over time. Hough (1993) suggests using the technique of functional decomposition (see Section 5.2) and each function identified and the requirements listed, but, he says, 'the precise design specifications, technical issues, and other concerns should be deferred until the function is actually to be developed'.

2 Timeboxing

The system to be developed is divided up into a number of components or timeboxes that are developed separately. The most important requirements, and those with the largest potential benefit, are developed first and delivered as quickly as possible in the first timebox. Some argue that no single component should take more than 90 days to develop, while others suggest a maximum of six months. Whichever timebox period is chosen, the point is that it is quick compared with the more traditional systems development timescale.

Systems development is sometimes argued to have three key elements. In traditional development two are typically variable: time and resources (see Figure 6.3). In traditional development when projects are in difficulty, either the delivery time is extended or more resources are allocated or both but the functionality is treated as fixed. In RAD the opposite applies, resources and time are regarded as fixed (allocating more resources is viewed as counterproductive although this does sometimes happen), and so that only leaves functionality as a variable. So, under pressure and when projects are in difficulty, time and resources remain constant but the functionality is reduced.

RAD compartmentalizes the development and delivers quickly and often. This provides the business and the users with a quick, but it is hoped, useful part of the

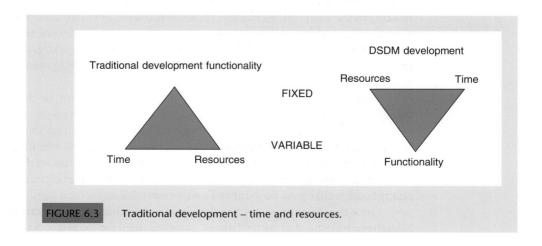

FIGURE 6.3   Traditional development – time and resources.

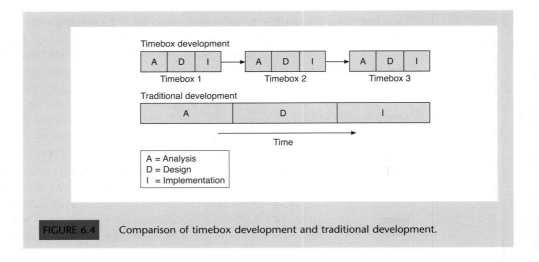

FIGURE 6.4   Comparison of timebox development and traditional development.

system in a refreshingly short timescale. The system at this stage is probably quite limited in relation to the total requirements, but at least something has been delivered. This rapid delivery of the most important requirements also helps to build credibility and enthusiasm from the users and the business. Often for the first time they experience a system that is delivered on time. This is radically different from the conventional delivery mode of most methodologies which is a long development period of often two to three years followed by the implementation of the complete system. The benefits of RAD development is that users trade off unnecessary (or at least initially unnecessary) requirements and wish lists (i.e. features that it would be 'nice to have' in an ideal world) for speed of development. This also has the benefit that, if requirements change over time, the total system has not been completed and each timebox can accommodate the changes that become necessary as requirements change and evolve during the previous timebox. It also has the advantage that the users become experienced with using and working with the system and learn what they really require from the early features that are implemented.

Figure 6.4 illustrates three chunks of development and, although the overall time to achieve the full implementation could be the same as with a traditional development, the likelihood is that the system actually developed at the end of the three timeboxes will be radically different from that developed at the end of one large chunk as a result of the learning and evolving processes which leads to change being made to each specification at the beginning of each timebox.

Some RAD proponents argue that, if the system cannot be divided into 90 day timeboxes, then it should not be undertaken at all. Obviously such an approach requires a radically different development culture from that required for traditional or formalized methodologies. The focus is on speed of delivery, the identification of the absolutely essential requirements, implementation as a learning vehicle, and the expectation that the requirements will change in the next timebox. Clearly such radical changes are unlikely to be achieved using conventional techniques.

Once the duration of the timebox has been decided it is imperative that the system is delivered at the end of it without slippage, as timeboxes are fixed. So how is this achieved? Well, first, by hard work and long hours and, secondly, by the use of the other RAD techniques discussed below. But also if slippage is experienced during development of a timebox then the requirements are reduced still further (i.e. some of the things that the system was going to do will be jettisoned).

3   The Pareto principle

This is essentially the 80/20 rule and is thought to apply to requirements. The belief of RAD proponents is that around 80 per cent of a systems' functionality can be delivered with around 20 per cent of the effort needed to complete 100 per cent of the requirements. This means that it is the last, and probably most complex, 20 per cent of requirements that take most of the effort and time. Thus why do it? – just choose as much of the 80 per cent to deliver as possible in the timebox, or at least the first timebox. The rest, if it proves necessary, can be delivered in subsequent timeboxes.

4   MoSCoW rules

In RAD the requirements of a project are prioritized using what is termed the MoSCoW Rules:

- M = 'the Must Haves'. Without these features the project is not viable (i.e. these are the minimum critical success factors fundamental to the project's success).
- S = 'the Should Haves'. To gain maximum benefit these features will be delivered but the project's success does not rely on them.
- C = 'the Could Haves'. If time and resources allow these features will be delivered but they can easily be left out without impacting on the project.
- W = 'the Won't Haves'. These features will not be delivered. They can be left out and possibly, although not necessarily, be done in a later timebox.

The MoSCoW rules ensure that a critical examination is made of requirements and that no 'wish lists' are made by users. All requirements have to be justified and categorized. Normally in a timebox all the 'must haves' and at least some of the 'should haves' and a few of the 'could haves' would be included. Of course, as has been mentioned, under pressure during the development the 'could haves' may well be dropped and even possibly the 'should haves' as well.

5   JAD workshops

RAD requires high levels of participation (see Sections 7.1 and 16.1) from all stakeholders in a project as a point of principle and achieves this partly through the JAD workshop. JAD (Joint Application Development) is a facilitated meeting designed to overcome the problems of traditional requirements gathering (see Section 16.2), in particular interviewing users. It overcomes the long time that the cycle of interviews take by getting all the relevant people together in a short period to hammer out decisions. Normally, in the context of RAD, a JAD workshop will occur early on in the development process to help establish and agree the initial requirements, the length of the timebox, what should be included and what excluded from the timebox, and most importantly to manage expectations and gain commitment from the stakeholders. Sometimes a subsequent JAD workshop is used to firm up on the details of the initial requirements, etc. In some RAD approaches the whole process is driven by a series of JAD meetings that occur throughout the timebox.

The fourth element is the presence of an executive sponsor. This is the person who wants the system (or whatever the focus of the meeting is), is committed to achieving it, and is prepared to fund it. This person is usually a senior executive who understands and believes in the JAD approach and who can overcome the bureaucracy and politics that tend to get in the way of fast decision making that usually bedevils traditional meetings.

6 Prototyping

Prototyping is an important part of RAD and is used to help establish the user requirements and in some cases the prototype evolves to become the system itself. Prototyping helps speed up the process of eliciting requirements, and speed is obviously important in RAD, but it also fits the RAD view of evolving requirements and users not knowing exactly what they want until they see or experience the system. Obviously the prototype is very helpful in this respect. Prototyping is discussed further in Section 6.3.

7 Sponsor and champion

Having a committed sponsor and a **champion** of the systems is an important requirement for RAD and for its success. We have discussed the sponsor above. A champion is someone, often at a lower level of seniority, who is also committed to the project, who understands and believes in RAD, and is prepared to drive the project forward and overcome some of the bureaucracy and politics.

8 Toolsets

RAD usually adopts, although not necessarily, the use of toolsets (Chapter 18) to help speed up the process and improve productivity. In general it is usually argued that the routine and time-consuming tasks can be automated as well as using available tools for change control, configuration management, and even code reuse. Reuse of code (see also Section 9.3) is another way that RAD speeds the development process. However, it is not just about speed but also quality because existing code or modules have usually already been well tested, not just in development, but in real use. RAD searches for shortcuts and reuses code, may be clones existing code and modifies it, or utilizes commercial packages, etc. where applicable. This may be code within the organization or bought from outside. Sometimes more than just a little piece of code is used; for example, complete applications may be used and the developers use this as the basis of the new system and change the interface to produce the desired results. Many 'new' e-commerce or Internet applications have been developed in this way using the legacy systems and then providing a new 'umbrella' set of applications and user interfaces on top. The idea is to leverage existing code, systems, experience, etc.

Specific RAD productivity tools have been around for some time and are developing fast, and existing tools and languages are being enhanced for RAD, particularly for rapid development of Internet and e-business-based applications.

RAD appears to be becoming relatively widely used in practice in organizations (Russo and Wynekoop, 1995; Eva and Guilford, 1996). Boehm (1999) suggests that there are 'good business reasons' why RAD has become increasingly popular. He argues that 'in general, RAD gives you earlier product payback and more payback time, before the pace of technology makes your product obsolete'. Subramanian et al. (1996) suggest that the shorter elapsed time between design and implementation of RAD often results in the system being much closer to the user/business needs.

Despite the proposed advantages of the RAD approach it has been criticized as being 'quick but dirty', suggesting that some shortcuts are taken for the sake of speed, especially in relation to systems quality and documentation. One of the reasons for the establishment of the DSDM consortium was to counter such criticisms and this consortium believes that RAD can deliver quality systems (see Section 22.2).

Yourdon (2000) suggests that: 'When RAD was first introduced, developers sometimes used it as an excuse to abandon all discipline and resort to extemporaneous hacking.' Unfortunately he feels that this temptation is even greater in the current environment, particularly with the pressures to develop e-business projects rapidly.

The issue of infrastructure or underlying architecture is clearly important but often seems to be ignored or forgotten in accounts of RAD. Hough (1993) believes that the design of an application alone is not sufficient. He states:

> To realize the full potential of an application, it must be based on a sound architecture … It is relatively easy to design a simple house (e.g. one with three bedrooms, a kitchen, etc.); however, only individuals with specific skills can properly design the architecture of a 50-storey building (how the walls are built, how big the foundations must be, etc.). Design implies caring for today's needs, whereas architecture suggests that long-term issues, including expansion, have been taken into consideration. Therefore, of key importance to Rapid Delivery is the ability to continuously add increasing functionality to the evolving application. If the overall application architecture is not sufficiently addressed early on, it will be difficult to integrate application segments over time.

Hough identifies the key architectures as: application, data, process, and technology, but he also suggests that others are important, such as presentation, control, security, and communications architectures.

Not all projects are thought to be suitable for RAD and in our opinion there are some areas in which RAD should not be used (e.g. safety-critical systems). The authors do not want the 'fly by wire' systems of the aircraft they fly to have been developed using RAD or with a fixed timebox! There may also be areas where RAD does not make sense, e.g. if the application does not need to be developed quickly, or if the requirements can be completely 'known' in advance, or if there are only 'must have' requirements, then traditional methods would still seem appropriate. This leaves a lot of areas in-between, and we would not go as far as to advise that no large systems, or business-critical systems, or transaction processing systems, should ever be developed using RAD. Rather we would look to the maturity of the organization in using RAD and say that these areas are potentially more risky, but if the organization (developers, users, and management) are experienced and have a history of success with RAD, then they may well be able to undertake RAD in such areas.

This raises the issue of the culture change necessary for using RAD in organizations. It is clear that some developers brought up in traditional development environments find RAD very difficult to come to terms with as it goes against some of the norms that they believe are central to systems development. Others can take to it quickly but in either case a great deal of education and training in the new approach is usually required. The authors know of one organization where the culture change for existing developers was too great and they had to appoint a new team for RAD development rather than use the existing team. It is also clear that management and users need to be aware of the RAD culture. It typically requires them to have higher levels of commitment and participation throughout the process, and because of the evolutionary nature this commitment often has to be ongoing. Some of the cultural changes involved relate to the following:

- The need for interdisciplinary team working as opposed to individual specializations.

- The empowering of users and developers to make decisions as opposed to the decisions being made on high.

- The acceptance of 'good enough in the context' and fit for purpose as opposed to striving for perfection or the best possible solution.

- The notion that change is expected and not a surprise as opposed to change not being allowed once the requirements have been specified.

- The engendering of a non-blame culture and all pulling together as opposed to a search for scapegoats when things go wrong.

All these make implementing the RAD approach a challenging management of change activity.

6.5 METHOD ENGINEERING (ME)

Method engineering (ME), sometimes referred to as methodology engineering, is the process of designing, constructing, and merging methods and techniques to support information systems development. Method engineering is often associated with the hierarchical and bureaucratic approaches of the 1980s as techniques were combined to form meta-methodologies. Normally it is concerned with the blending of methods and techniques into a methodology or framework. However, its most recent form is enterprise resource planning (ERP) systems (Section 8.2), which are combinations of application types rather than methods and techniques.

In this section, adapted from Avison and Truex (2002), we reflect on the genealogy of method engineering and look to how it must evolve to meet the needs of contemporary IS development. As guides and as method engineering source books, we point the

Type	Focus	Intent	Added-value	Orientation	Examples	Modelling types
Type I	Uniview	Standardize on best practice in systems development	Bring order to chaos, structured, methodological approach	Technical Technologist	STRADIS (process view) D2S2 (data view)	Modelling data or processes
Type II	Making approach more ecumenical (filling in the gaps)	Connect univiews to engineer an overall approach	More generalizable, universal More complete	Technical Technologist	SSADM Merise	Modelling data and processes
Type III	Identifying and linking method fragments	Add technical richness by adding modules or method components	Broaden scope further Ability to interconnect methods into whole 'super (meta)-method'	Technical Technologist	Information Engineering with CASE	Modelling various systems components
Type IV	Contingent frameworks	Provide guidance to use techniques Bring in organizational and social richness	Provides guidance about how and why we use method components Broaden scope further	Social and organizational as well as technical Middle managers and users	Multiview	Modelling the proper match of components
Type V	Enterprise resource planning	BPR – Re-engineer whole organizations (to fit the system?)	Provides more structure to organizational frameworks Adds BPR and workflow	Organizational and technical Top managers	SAP, BAAN, Peoplesoft	Modelling the ideal organization

FIGURE 6.5   Movements in method engineering (modified from Avison and Truex, 2002).

reader to Brinkkemper et al. (1996). We will discuss these challenges and point to potential directions for ME that are more likely to address the basic problems and needs of information systems development. In so doing, we briefly review five phases in the ME movement, with the fifth being ERP systems.

Early ME involved creating a standardized approach to 'engineer' systems development, usually based on process or data modelling (see Chapter 5), bringing order to work that had previously been largely trial-and-error and software-oriented. In general, this contained techniques, phases, and standards put together to form a coherent methodology to be used by systems analysts and programmers. This embodied the best practice available at the time. An example of such an approach on the process side was STRADIS (Section 19.1). We refer to this as Type I method engineering (Figure 6.5).

In Type II method engineering, ME was carried out to improve IS development methodologies so that they captured best practice by including techniques in other methodologies, such as data flow diagrams and entity modelling, or take account of newly proposed ones, such as object-oriented methods. Many were extended to address more phases of the life cycle. This resulted in larger, generalized, perhaps bureaucratic, approaches. These widened the scope of methodologies to be more general-purpose and made them more commercially viable. Information Engineering, Merise, SSADM and Yourdon Systems Method (see Part 6) are examples of these methodologies.

But this general-purpose, universal approach did not address the problems of complexity nor the skills required to develop IS. One response was the development of tools (Part 5). As a reaction to the complexity and inflexibility of methods, systems analysts frequently paid 'lip service' to a methodology, rarely following the phases exactly as described in the manual and sometimes omitting, adding, or modifying phases. Some organizations stopped using methodologies altogether.

Type III method engineering, the next development, links method fragments or components to form a 'meta-methodology'. This aimed to increase the flexibility of approaches and the customization of a 'one-off' methodology for a particular application. One major difficulty is that the analyst is confronted with a 'hodgepodge' of techniques and tools, some of which may be inappropriately linked to others; therefore, most approaches of this type provided a framework and control system to guide the analyst in choosing the appropriate method fragments. Some of these frameworks proposed sets of situational (or contingent) factors that guided the selection of method fragments (Van Slooten, 1996). However, these frameworks tended toward a very technical view of the development of IS, indeed they have been dominated by toolsets (see Chapter 18).

Type IV method engineering recognizes that organizations are social constructs – they are about relationships between people – and artefacts do not determine how people behave. Information systems development is not just about choosing technique fragments. It was therefore broadened to include human and organization factors at least as much as technical ones. These approaches, such as Multiview (Section 25.1), recognize that IS development is constrained by organizational context while providing the means to change that context. It is not just a set of tools and techniques, however, frameworks such as Multiview provide guidance on when and where it might be appropriate to use them. We cannot assume that technical improvements will lead to organizational improvement. Any IS development endeavour can suffer the unintended consequences of action. This suggests that IS approaches applied contingently should also be applied thoughtfully.

Another concern relates to the burden on the systems analyst to choose the 'appropriate' techniques and tools for the situation, even with the guidance of such a framework. In such an informal approach, a further concern is the lack of control and application of standards in information systems development.

Avison and Truex (2002) propose, perhaps controversially, that enterprise resource planning systems (Type V in Figure 6.5) represent a type of ME approach. Enterprise resource planning (ERP) systems, such as SAP, attempt to re-engineer whole organizations and, in effect, model an ideal organization (making the actual organization fit with this ideal). Like most of its precursors to the ME movement, it became fashionable but is now being critically scrutinized.

ERP systems are built upon highly normalized, robust data models and industry-specific reference models, purported to represent 'best-of-class' process and work flow models. As such, they represent a composite of systems views and models ranging from data through process and work flow to object models. Ideally, they seek to integrate all views, such that data and process knowledge may be available to any of the application components wherever appropriate or needed.

There is a certain irony associated with ERP systems when they are seen as forms of method engineering. To some extent they hark back to the Type II ME approaches, which imply a universal view of organizational systems. The tools associated with ME approaches enforced the sequence and the description of design upon the developer. So, too, do ERP systems, by virtue of the various models and components enforcing a kind of discipline upon the organization. A final irony is that if most organizations do not take advantage of the configurability of the system, and they tend not to because of the cost, then most organizations using ERP will look very much alike in terms of business processes and organization. Moreover, legacy systems tend to incorporate aspects of organizational distinctiveness and incorporated organizational memory. Many of these legacy systems have been abandoned with the adoption of an ERP system. However, with the reduction of ERP sales growth following high demand due to the Y2K crisis, methodologists and management alike have begun to consider how to overcome the inherent problems of this universal approach to creating information systems.

Method engineering will always be a theme in IS development as it is a sign of progress in the adaptation of methodologies to changing IS/IT environments and progress in methodology design itself. We return to some of these issues again in Chapter 26.

6.6 WEB-BASED DEVELOPMENT

In a review of three companies working in Internet time, Baskerville and Pries-Heje (2001) identified 10 concepts relevant to IS development for the Internet. We will explore these concepts to gain an insight into the real-world characteristics of web development projects. The first two, time pressure and vague requirements, link all the concepts:

- *Time pressure* – competitive pressures may mean that any advantage is short-lived and will be copied quickly. So, it is important to take advantage of any short-term gain to lead to more long-term advantages.

- *Vague requirements* – requirements are often imprecise or not known at all and have to be created through imagination and innovation. It is not infrequent that it is only on implementation and use that the real requirements are revealed.

- *Prototyping* – the software prototype is the specification of requirements, not the thick paper report. This prototype is frequently rejected so that a more well-founded design can be constructed.

- *Release orientation* – these earlier ideas and others suggest early release and frequent re-release. Rapid application development is even more relevant to Internet projects.

- *Parallel development* – database development can take place at the same time as the graphical design, and requirements analysis and design become hard to separate.

- *Fixed architecture* – complexity needs to be tamed. A three-tier architecture where the business data, business logic, and the user interface are separated out allows for team members to work in parallel with a degree of independence.

- *Coding your way out* – when the going gets tough, the developers need to code their way out of problems. Hacking was not originally a pejorative term, but was used to identify programmers who could write elegant and effective code quickly.

- *Quality is negotiable* – the question often arises as to whether software is developed to achieve high quality, a quick product, or a cheap one. In some senses, quality has always been negotiable. In web-based projects the overriding view of quality tends to be the customer perspective and experience, rather than by a defined and repeatable development process or a software product that survives an internal audit.

■ *Dependence on good people* – Internet projects are completed under time pressure and typically in small teams where all members need to pull their weight. Key staff can make or break a project.

■ *Need for structure* – the old structures of systems development, for example, keeping business analysts separate from software engineers, may be inappropriate to building applications in Internet time.

As Vidgen et al. (2002) show, although the 10 concepts capture the emergent aspects of web IS development well, if the term 'business urgency' is substituted for the concept 'Internet time', then it is clear that the 10 concepts have a more general relevance to understanding the IS development process. In situations characterized by time pressure and definitional uncertainty, the response of IS developers has long been to adopt a flexible strategy to IS development using techniques such as rapid application development and prototyping. However, there are some concrete differences between Internet projects and traditional IS development:

■ *Internet time* – the development time is reduced greatly: two years is unthinkable, six months is often unacceptable, and many significant e-commerce projects are implemented in weeks. This means that the 10 concepts above tend to be the norm rather than the exception.

■ *Strategic implications* – the strategic implications are directly related to business goals, particularly in e-commerce projects where a revenue stream is generated.

■ *Emphasis on graphical user interface* – there is a need for talented graphic designers.

■ *Customer orientation* – the user is a customer rather than an employee. E-commerce applications need customer focus and marketing input.

On the other hand, there are also similarities:

■ *Databases* – sophisticated Internet applications rely on databases and require traditional skills to implement them.

■ *Integration* – Internet applications need to be integrated with enterprise applications. For example, a car ordering system that gives consumers a delivery date needs to communicate with manufacturing requirements planning (MRP) software. Enterprise Application Integration (EAI) is a challenge for Internet applications.

As Internet projects become broader in scope requiring greater integration with front office, back office, and legacy IT systems of all sorts, then Internet projects will become yet more difficult to distinguish from traditional IT projects. Traditional IS projects would also benefit from being giving more attention to strategy, customers, and design aesthetics and therefore the distinctions should, over time, become less pronounced and even disappear altogether as web-based IS development becomes 'business as usual'. Figure 6.6 shows the stereotypical differences between traditional IS and Internet development projects. Their work forms the basis of the web development methodology WISDM (Section 22.4).

Dimension	Traditional IS projects	Internet projects
Strategy	The strategic dimension is abstract	The strategic dimension is tangible and visible and relates closely to business goals
	The strategic dimension is addressed indirectly, through broad notions such as strategic alignment. Often the strategic dimension is not addressed at all	Strategy is addressed directly, particularly for e-commerce projects in which a revenue stream is generated
User	The typical user is an employee	The typical user is a customer who makes payment for goods and services
	Users can be trained and consulted directly. System use might be mandatory	Usage is not mandatory and the customer will not attend training sessions
	User needs can be understood through work studies	User needs can be understood through sales and marketing methods
	Job satisfaction is a key aim	Customer satisfaction is a key aim
Design	The development focus is on the internals of the design: the database, the programs and an architecture (e.g. three-tier)	The development focus is on the website as a visual artefact. The development cycle might start with a mock-up of the user interface
	The user interface is almost an afterthought	Graphic design skills and a feel for web aesthetics are essential

FIGURE 6.6   Traditional and Internet-based applications (from Vidgen et al. 2002).

6.7   SUMMARY

- Legacy systems are systems that have been in operation for some time. They may well perform critical processes, but they are often seen as a problem as they may have high maintenance costs, use obsolete hardware and software, be poorly documented, and lack people support with the knowledge required to maintain them.

- Evolutionary systems development is a staged or incremental approach that periodically delivers a system that is increasingly complete as it evolves over time.

- A prototype is an approximation of the information system to be built. Developers can design and build a scaled-down functional model of the desired system and then demonstrate this to the users to gain feedback.

- Rapid application development (RAD) follows principles and uses techniques including incremental development, timeboxing, MoSCow rules, JAD workshops, prototyping, and toolsets to achieve speedier development.

- Method engineering (ME) is the process of designing, constructing, and merging methods and techniques to support information systems development. It might be a blending of methods and techniques into a framework, methodology, or meta-methodology. Its most recent form is enterprise resource planning (ERP) systems, which are combinations of application types rather than methods and techniques.

■ Web-based information systems development is just another, albeit newer, application type, but it does have some particular emphases including time pressures, design and user interface requirements, security concerns, and customer orientation.

QUESTIONS

1 Provide a balanced argument to an IT manager asking: 'What should we do about our legacy systems, continue to maintain them or replace them?'

2 Compare and contrast the various approaches to information systems development discussed in this chapter to the SDLC discussed in Chapter 3.

3 Are there any problems to counteract the apparent advantages of blending techniques to engineer a best or ideal methodology?

4 Argue a case that there are fundamental differences between web development and any other information systems development.

6.8 FURTHER READING

Brinkkemper, S., Lyytinen, K., and Welke, R.J. (eds) (1996) *Method Engineering: Principles of Method Construction and Tool Support*, Chapman and Hall, London.

Chen, J. (2001) Building web applications, *Information Systems Management*, Winter, Vol. 18, No. 1.

Martin, J. (1991) *Rapid Application Development*, Prentice Hall, Englewood Cliffs, New Jersey.

Orman, L. (1998/9) Evolutionary development of information systems, *Journal of Management Information Systems*, Vol. 5, No. 3.

Vidgen, R., Avison, D.E., Wood, R., and Wood-Harper, A.T. (2002) *Developing Web Information Systems*, Butterworth-Heinemann, London.

Warren, I. (1999) *The Renaissance of Legacy Systems*, Springer-Verlag, London.

7 PEOPLE THEMES

PARTICIPATION

In Part 3 so far we have covered a number of themes within various movements in the information systems development arena. The first emphasized an organizational view and the needs of top management regarding strategic level decision making; the second concerned modelling, in particular, that of data and process modelling and object orientation; and the third emphasized engineering and software themes in the development process. We now turn to another major theme, that of the people concerned in the development of an information system, particularly users and other stakeholders; that is, people having a stake in the information systems project.

In the traditional systems analysis methodology, the importance of user involvement was frequently stressed. However, the computer professional was the person who was making the real decisions and driving the development process. Systems analysts were trained in, and knowledgeable of, the technological and economic aspects of computer applications but far more rarely on the human (or behavioural) aspects which are at least as important. The end-user (the person who is going to use the system) frequently felt resentment, and top management did little more than pay lip service to computing. The systems analyst may be happy with the system when it is implemented. It may conform to what the systems analysts understand are the requirements and does so efficiently. However, this is of little significance if the users, who are the customers, are not satisfied with it.

The strategic view of information systems highlighted the necessity for top management to play a role in information systems development. The approach discussed in this section highlights the role of all users who may control and take the lead in the development process. If the users are involved in the analysis, design, and implementation of information systems relevant to their own work, particularly if this involvement has meant users being involved in the decision-making process, these users are more likely to be fully committed to the information system when operational. This will increase the likelihood of its success. Indeed, in some Scandinavian countries such a requirement may be embodied in law, with technological change needing the approval of trade unions and those who are to work with the new system.

Some information systems may 'work' in that they are technically viable, but fail because of 'people problems'. For example, users may feel that the new system will make their job more demanding, less secure, will change their relationship with others, or will lead to a loss of the independence that they previously enjoyed. As a result of these feelings, users may do their best to ensure that the computer system does not succeed. This **aggression** may show itself in attempts to 'beat the system'; for example, by 'losing' documents or even by more obvious acts of sabotage. Frequently it manifests itself in people blaming the system for causing difficulties that may well be caused by other factors. This is sometimes referred to as **projection**; that is, they project their problems on to the system. Some people may just want to have 'nothing to do with the computer system', a kind of **avoidance** tactic. In this kind of situation, information systems are unlikely to be successful or, at the very least, fail to achieve their potential.

These reactions against a new computer system may stem from a number of factors, largely historical, but the proponents of participation would argue that they will have to be corrected if future computer applications are going to succeed and that it is important that the following views are addressed:

- users may regard the IT department as having too much power and control over other departments through the use of technology;

- users may regard computer people as having too great a status in the organization or not seeming to be governed by the same conditions of work as the rest of the organization;

- users may consider the pay scales of computer staff to be higher than their own and that the poor track record of computer applications should have led to reduced salaries and status, not the opposite.

These are only three of the arguments. Some views are valid, others less so, but the poor communications between computer people and others in the organization, symptomatic of the prevalence of computer jargon, have not helped. Training and education for both users and computer people can help address the cultural clash between them, as can time spent in user and IT departments for all. Somehow these barriers have to be broken down if computer applications are really going to succeed.

One way to help both the process of breaking down barriers and to achieve more successful information systems is to involve all those affected by computer systems in the process of developing them. This includes the top management of the organization as well as operational-level staff. Until recently, top management have avoided much direct contact with computer systems. Managers have probably sanctioned the purchase of computer hardware and software but have not involved themselves with their use. They have preferred to keep themselves at a 'safe' distance from computers. This lack of leadership by example is unlikely to lead to successful implementation of computer systems: managers need to participate in the change and this will motivate their subordinates. With the implementation of executive information systems (information systems designed for the use of top managers) and the like, this attitude is becoming less prevalent.

Attitudes are also changing because managers can see that computer systems will directly help them in their decision making. The widespread use of PCs and the information about the technology available in newspapers and other sources has also diminished the 'mystique' that used to surround computing. Earlier computing concerned itself with the operational level of the firm; modern information systems concern themselves with decision support as well, and managers are demanding sophisticated computer applications and are wishing to play a leading role in their development and implementation.

Communications between computer specialists and others within the organization also need to improve. This should establish a more mutually trusting and co-operative atmosphere. The training and educating of all staff affected by computers is therefore important. In turn, computer people should also be aware of the various operating areas of the business. This should bring down barriers caused by a lack of knowledge and technical jargon and encourage users to become involved in technological change.

Another useful way of encouraging user involvement is to improve the human–computer interface. There are a number of qualities that will help in this matter. These include visibility, simplicity, consistency, and flexibility:

1. *Visibility*. This has two aspects. First, it means that the way that the system works is seen by the users. This aspect is related to participation, because, if users understand the system, they are more likely to be able to control it. Second, visibility means providing information on the current activity through messages to the users so that they know what is happening when the system is being run.

2. *Simplicity*. This means that the presentation of information to the users should be well structured, that the range of options at each point is well presented, and that it is easy to decide on which option to choose.

3. *Consistency*. This means that the human–computer interface follows a similar pattern (sometimes referred to as 'look and feel') throughout the system. Indeed, wherever possible, all systems that are likely to be used by one set of users should follow this pattern.

4. *Flexibility*. This means that the users can adapt the interface to suit their own requirements.

User involvement should mean much more than agreeing to be interviewed by the analyst and working extra hours as the operational date for the new system nears. This is 'pseudo-participation' because users are not playing a very active role. If users participated more, even being responsible for the design, they are far more likely to be satisfied with, and committed to, the system once it is implemented. It is 'their baby' as well as that of the computer people. There is therefore every reason to suppose that the interests of the users and technologists might coincide. Both will look for the success of the new system. With a low level of participation, job satisfaction is likely to decrease, particularly if the new system reduces skilled work. The result may be absenteeism, low efficiency, a higher staff turnover, and failure of the information system.

The advocates of the participative approach recommend a working environment where the users and analysts work as a team rather than as expert and non-expert. Although the technologist might be more expert in computing matters, the user has the expertise in the application area. It can be argued that the latter is the more important when determining the success or failure of the system. An information system can make do with poor technology, but not poor knowledge of the application. Where the users and technologist work hand in hand, there is less likely to be misunderstandings by the analyst which might result in an inappropriate system. The user will also know how the new system operates by the time it is implemented, with the result that there are likely to be fewer teething troubles with the new system.

The role of systems analysts in this scenario may be more of facilitators, implementing the choices of users. This movement can be aided by the use of application packages which the users can try out, and therefore choose what is best for them. Another possibility is the development of a prototype which users can use as a basis from which to agree final design.

Mumford (1983b) distinguishes between three levels of participation:

1 *Consultative participation* is the lowest level of participation and leaves the main design tasks to the systems analysts, but tries to ensure that all staff in the user department are consulted about the change. The systems analysts are encouraged to provide opportunity for increasing job satisfaction when redesigning the system. It may be possible to organize the users into groups to discuss aspects of the new system and make suggestions to the analysts. Most advocates of the traditional approach to system development would probably accept that there is a need for this level of participation in the design process.

2 *Representative participation* requires a higher level of involvement of user department staff. Here, the 'design group' consists of user representatives and systems analysts. No longer is it expected that the technologist dictates to the users the design of their work system. Users have an equal say in any decision. It is to be hoped that the representatives do indeed represent the interests of all the users affected by the design decisions.

3 *Consensus participation* attempts to involve all user department staff throughout the design process, indeed this process is user-driven. It may be more difficult to make quick decisions, but it has the merit of making the design decisions those of the staff as a whole. Sometimes the sets of tasks in a system can be distinguished and those people involved in each set of tasks make their own design decisions.

In Section 23.1 we discuss the ETHICS methodology which has been designed around the principles of user participation.

Of course, participation does have its problems. It might result in polarizing or fragmenting user groups, and there is a possibility of manipulating the process by selecting only those participants who are considered 'right' or by suggesting that users decide 'this ... or there will be unhappy consequences'. Further, participation may cause resentment, either from analysts, who might see this as their own job being taken over by unskilled people, or by users, who feel that their job is accountancy, managing, or whatever, and this is being cramped by demands to participate in the development of computer systems.

One reaction to lip service participation is the growth in *end-user computing*; that is, users developing their own applications (Section 7.2). With the increase in computer literacy, software tools being designed with end-user computing in mind and low-cost hardware, end-user computing is indeed feasible. It is also one reaction to the application backlog as users see the only way that applications development will take place is to

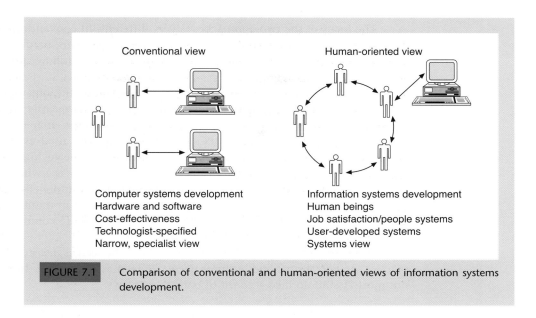

Conventional view

Human-oriented view

Computer systems development
Hardware and software
Cost-effectiveness
Technologist-specified
Narrow, specialist view

Information systems development
Human beings
Job satisfaction/people systems
User-developed systems
Systems view

FIGURE 7.1   Comparison of conventional and human-oriented views of information systems development.

develop the applications themselves. It can be relatively unsophisticated; for example, users using menu-driven office systems, such as word processing, spreadsheet, and database packages running on the PC with Windows, through to users writing their own software using programming languages. Such end-user computing gives users control over their applications. Potential weaknesses relate to the possible inefficiency, neglect of integrity, and security issues, and the lack of an organization-wide perspective of these application 'islands'. Information centres, which are a source of advice to end-users developing their own applications and cheaper hardware and software through bulk-buying opportunities, represent one response to some of the potential disadvantages. However, this is a centralizing move which is resented by some end-user departments. Some user departments might have their own specialist computer people who are members of the department, not that of the computing department or information centre, and their role might be to provide general advice through to acting as facilitators.

Another response to the excessive power of computing people in information systems development is joint requirements planning (JRP) and joint application design (JAD) (see Section 16.2). Representatives from the user groups and computer people conduct workshops to progress the information system through the planning and design stages. The leader of the workshops has a particularly crucial role and should be trained and experienced. Executives are likely to be involved in the JRP workshops along with end-users, but they are unlikely to play a leading role in the design phase. Computer people will also be more prevalent in JAD workshops, and the use of tools and prototypes may help the process. In some organizations JAD workshops may take place in group decision support rooms consisting of linked computer systems with software, database, and other support but these can be dominated by the technology and the role of the human facilitator is again crucial.

Grundén (1986) suggests that participation implies even more fundamental changes in the organization. Figure 7.1, adapted from that paper, gives some of the characteristics of this approach when compared to the traditional approach.

The focus of the two approaches is very different. In conventional systems development, the emphasis is on the technology: computer systems, hardware, and software. The technologist drives the system. Users are given rules to follow and departures from these norms are not tolerated.

The human-oriented view focuses on the people in the organization. This may result in less complex, smaller systems which are not necessarily the most efficient from a technical point of view. Nevertheless, they are more manageable, less reliant on technology and on 'experts'. PCs are more frequently used as the technological base than mainframes. The traditional view emphasizes the technology, whereas the human-oriented view is more interested in the organization as a whole and the user as creator in that environment. Such a view is likely to lead to more effective systems. The implication is that the conventional view is more common in traditional, hierarchical, bureaucratic organizations; the human-oriented view is more common in democratic, growing, and changing organizations.

However, to some extent, both views can now be seen as distortions. In theory and practice, organizational and business needs are seen as paramount. In practice, many if not most IT staff do take account of both these views.

7.2 END-USER COMPUTING

End-User Computing (EUC) evolved as a concept with the development of the PC and the arrival of application packages designed for use by non-specialist IS people, particularly the spreadsheet. Prior to this, computing was seen as a black art performed by professionals using large main-frame computers hidden away in air-conditioned rooms. EUC was also driven by the backlog of applications that users required but could not get built by such professionals (see Section 3.6).

Users began to develop their own applications and some users found that they were successful and even quite liked it. In the early stages, they were usually self-taught enthusiasts. They had the advantage of knowing the requirements of their part of the business very well and they did not need to communicate that to a systems analyst, they just built a system themselves to meet their needs. Typically, this was either a spreadsheet model or even a small database system, and some users advanced to writing programs in languages such as VisualBASIC, and even integrating their applications into the enterprise computer systems.

There are many definitions of End-User Computing, some are brief, such as 'the practice of end-users developing, maintaining, and using their own information systems' (Mirani and King, 1994) through to 'the direct use, development and maintenance of information systems by those whose primary role is to achieve a business purpose rather than the indirect development and management through information systems professionals' (Smith, 1997).

As EUC developed, different kinds of user were identified. We discussed different users in Chapter 1, but in relation to EUC Rockart and Flannery (1983) identify four distinct types:

■   *non-programming end-users* – users have relatively little IT skills and use limited, typically menu-driven environments or a structured set of procedures, and use software provided by others;

- *command-level users* – they perform inquiries and simple calculations and generate reports for themselves, using limited 4GLs (Fourth Generation languages) or database query languages;

- *end-user programmers* – these users can use procedural-type programming languages to develop applications for their own personal information needs;

- *functional support personnel* – these are users who have the skills to develop systems and who also become informal supporters of other end-users to develop applications within their functional areas (i.e. they provide IT support and training for other end-users).

Research has found that EUC provides an effective way of providing some of the information systems in organizations, and it results in a good deal of user satisfaction. EUC also has the benefit of taking pressure off the central IS development function, who were struggling to meet all the demands for new systems being generated in the typical business, and free up the specialist IS personnel to address those activities that EUC could not provide (e.g. the transaction processing systems, the corporate databases).

This development of EUC provided some additional benefits. It enabled the fulfilling of some needs that probably would never have been satisfied through the traditional IT department. Much of the demand for systems and applications by end-users were for things that would possibly never have passed the cost/benefit hurdles imposed by the business or been developed in the necessary time frame to be effective. But because it was the end-users developing them, they could be resourced and undertaken within the user departments. Indeed end-users often felt 'held back' and constrained by the IT department.

So, at one level the situation appeared quite healthy, the users were happy, so was the IT department, and the business was benefiting. However, problems began to emerge and EUC proved unsustainable in some organizations. The users needed more IT support to continue to be effective in their EUC, and the IT department was often reluctant to give such access and support. IT departments did not want these user-developed systems coming into any contact with the live-running operational systems as they tended to ignore security, back-up procedures, and recovery. They ignored IT and corporate standards, and not many user developers appreciated the need for normalized databases or referential integrity.

These end-user-developed systems, therefore, although providing benefits, were proving difficult to maintain. Sometimes they were highly dependent on one person, and there were problems when that person left or was moved, or promoted. When IT tried to take over the maintenance and upgrade of these systems, it proved extremely difficult, as there was typically no documentation and poor design. There was also some concern relating to duplication of effort and data (where the same data are held in different systems, they inevitably get out of synchronization), as local systems were produced in each unit or department. Different hardware and software proliferated throughout the organization as each department bought its own, usually in the retail market, and different contracts were entered into. An unco-ordinated organizational quagmire was emerging. The situation is not dissimilar to the original *ad hoc* development of computing in organizations in the 1960s.

Corporations were justifiably beginning to worry about this situation. They could not really stop EUC because the users would revolt, and it was providing some benefits and plugging a hole that the IT department could not fill, but they could not let EUC run out of control in this way.

One 'solution' was the setting up of **Information Centres** (ICs). An IC was a unit set up by the organization, usually run by the IT department, but somewhat separate, to support and control EUC. So, the provision of a support infrastructure, the IC, was to maximize the benefits and minimize the risks of EUC.

The role of the IC varied but typically it involved some or all the following:

■ defining the domains of responsibility (e.g. what could be developed using EUC and what could not);

■ provision of an EUC infrastructure (e.g. PCs, communications, networks, databases, information streams, etc.);

■ provision of software and tools, including evaluation, support commitments, etc.;

■ support of EUC users, including education, training, help (along with development and design), help desks, etc.;

■ setting of standards for EUC, including back-up, security, privacy, etc.;

■ co-ordination and control of EUC in the organization, to encourage reuse and prevent duplication, encouraging cross-functionality, integration, etc.;

■ procurement, to enable economies of scale to be achieved, etc.;

■ dealing with external partners (e.g. contractors, suppliers, vendors, service providers, etc.).

Successful ICs were regarded by some as being critical to the success of organizational goals as a whole and their perceived importance would seem to be reflected by 78 per cent of organizations having an IC (Guimaraes, 1996). The success of ICs varied, but a number of factors have been identified as contributing to success (see Essex and Magal, 1998):

■ organizational commitment to the IC, including top management support;

■ rank of the IC executive;

■ commitment from end-users;

■ adequate budget;

■ active promotion of IC services;

■ quality of IC staff.

EUC and the IC were responses to developments of the 1980s and 1990s and were important concepts and solutions in large organizations trying to manage their IT, but what role do they now play? Some argue that their time has passed and that, with the increasing sophistication of users and their ability to use and develop systems for the new distributed Internet world, they have proved that they no longer need the old-style IC, and that the client part of the client/server architecture is now 'folded into mainstream applications development' (Tayntor, 1994). For others the whole notion of EUC is no longer relevant when almost everyone in business is a user and developer of some kind.

On the other hand there are those who argue that the IC is as relevant in concept today as it ever was, although perhaps its focus has changed. It is not about supporting end-users in developing their own internal systems. It is now more about supporting them in building customer-facing systems in collaboration with specialist corporate developers and developments and delivering value to the customer. In this new world the IC must transfer from a tactical problem-solving perspective to a more strategic, consultant-like role.

Whatever happens it seems that EUC is here to stay, in some form or other, although perhaps the term EUC itself may change as it looks and feels quite dated. End-users and business people (i.e. those whose prime role is not information systems development), it seems, are going to continue to have a role to play in developing systems, particularly given their increasing IT knowledge and the increasing sophistication and usability of the tools and packages available (see for example Section 17.2 on Dreamweaver). The fate of the IC is probably similar. Support for this new kind of EUC is still going to be required. Therefore, there is a need for the concept of the IC, but whether it is called that in the future is highly unlikely. What it turns out to be remains to be seen. It may, of course, just be called the IT department again!

7.3 EXPERT SYSTEMS

The term 'expert system' derives from the fuller, and more descriptive term, 'knowledge-based expert system', and these terms tend to be used synonymously. Therefore, there are obvious links with knowledge management (Section 7.4). An expert system (ES) is a system that simulates the role of an expert. It is distinguished from other applications because its usefulness is derived from the knowledge and reasoning ability of the expert system and not from number crunching (carrying out large and complex calculations) or the repetitive processing of data, which characterize most scientific and business computing applications, respectively.

Feigenbaum (1982), one of the early pioneers in the area, defines an expert system as: 'an intelligent computer program that uses knowledge and inference procedures to solve problems that are difficult enough to require significant human expertise for their solution'. Somewhat more formally, the British Computer Society's Expert Systems Specialist Group defines an expert system as follows:

> An expert system is regarded as the embodiment within a computer of a knowledge-based component from an expert skill in such a form that the system can offer intelligent advice or take an intelligent decision about a processing function. A desirable additional characteristic, which many would consider fundamental, is the capability of the system, on demand, to justify its own line of reasoning in a manner directly intelligible to the enquirer. The style adopted to attain these characteristics is rule-based programming.

Expert systems are essentially artificial intelligence programs that contain (in some way) some of the knowledge that human specialists have (hence their inclusion in a chapter

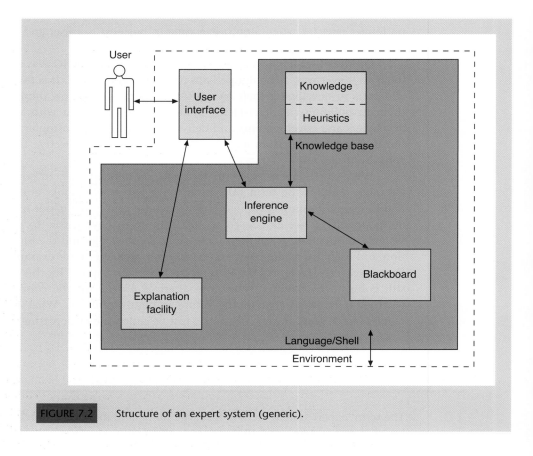

FIGURE 7.2 Structure of an expert system (generic).

on people themes). This does not imply that an expert system builds a psychological model of how the specialist thinks, but rather that it contains a model of the expert's own model of the domain. The domain of the expert system may be a discipline or knowledge area, such as geology or medicine. Alternatively, it may be a particular narrow subset, such as 'risk factors and insurance premiums in California'.

An expert system is basically an intelligent adviser concerning one or more areas or domains of knowledge. This knowledge exists in the minds of human experts, it has been developed and evolved over time by education and experience, and it has to be captured in some way by the expert system, usually in the form of sets of rules and groups of facts. The expert system is then informed about a particular situation of concern to a user, usually achieved by the user answering questions posed by the expert system. Then the expert system comes up with intelligent advice concerning that situation. Ideally, it is able to explain to the user how it arrived at the particular advice.

In practice, expert systems vary considerably, but there are a number of common components in a structure as illustrated in Figure 7.2:

■ *The knowledge base.* This contains two elements. The first is the knowledge necessary for understanding the domain, essentially the facts of the problem area. The second element is the heuristics that indicate how to use the facts to solve specific problems, essentially the rules. For example, a rule might be that 'if *X* is a bird then conclude that X can fly'. This rule is not true in all circumstances because emus are birds but they cannot fly. We might then introduce another rule that states that 'if X is a bird and X is an emu then conclude that X cannot fly' or we might say that 'if X is a bird then conclude with a probability of 0.99 that X can fly'. The facts contained in the knowledgebase are simply assertions, for example, a robin is a bird.

- Although such rules are very common in expert systems, they are not the only way of representing knowledge. Recently, rules have been complemented by frames in some expert systems. A frame is a representation of a group of related knowledge about a particular object. These are useful in situations where there are stereotypical objects. The characteristics of a car give an example. Most cars have stereotypical characteristics, for example, they all have engines, wheels, acceleration speeds, and so on. All these characteristics are gathered together in a frame. Frames are often structured into hierarchies and are good for structuring managerial and business knowledge.

- *An inference engine.* The inference engine controls the process of invoking the rules that pertain to the solution of the problems posed to the system. It is used for reasoning about the information in the knowledgebase and in the 'blackboard' (see below) and for formulating conclusions. It provides directions and organizes and controls the processing of the knowledge and the rules to make inferences based on the problems, that is, the procedures for problem solving. Three elements of the inference engine can be identified. The first is the rule interpreter which effectively executes the rules. The second is the scheduler which controls when things should be performed and in what order. The third is the consistency checker which maintains a consistent form of the process and solution. The inference engine usually keeps track of the execution steps so that the user can backtrack through the interaction as necessary.

- *A language.* This is the language in which the expert system is written. A number of specific expert system programming languages have been developed, probably the best known being Prolog and LISP.

- Probably the most common approach to expert systems development is to use a shell. A shell is an expert system with all the inference capability but without any domain-specific knowledge. It is thus ready for users to input their own rules and knowledge to create their own specific expert systems application. Using a shell obviously saves time as all of the system, except for the specific application knowledge, is already programmed. Many shells were originally full expert systems applications that subsequently were converted to general purpose shells by removing their knowledge component. There are a variety of different types of shell, some are PC-based, while others are for large mainframe computers. They are continuing to evolve, and some are even classed as end-user tools in which domain experts can build their own expert systems. Shells help focus the effort on the domain and knowledge acquisition rather than on the program development. They are not suitable for all types of application and can be limiting and inflexible.

- *An explanation generator or facility.* This is the part of the system that presents the reasoning behind how the system arrived at its conclusions.

- *A blackboard.* This is a temporary workspace that records intermediate hypotheses and decisions that the expert system makes as the problem and the solution evolve. It consists of three elements. The first is the plan and approach to the current problem; the second is the agenda, which records the potential actions awaiting execution, that is, the rules that appear to be relevant; and the third is the solution elements, which are the candidate hypotheses and decisions the system has generated so far. Blackboards do not exist in all expert systems, but they are particularly relevant in systems which work by generating a variety of solutions to the problem posed. They are also important in systems that integrate the knowledge of several different specialists.

- *A user interface.* This varies widely, but is a very important element in the architecture of an expert system. There will be an interface for the user and also one for entering and updating the knowledgebase.

- *The environment.* This is the variety of hardware and software that surrounds the expert system. An expert system may be a stand-alone system or it may be embedded within other systems.

Expert systems emerged as an identifiable element of artificial intelligence (AI) in the late 1960s and early 1970s when it was realized that, in certain subject areas, advances could be better achieved by providing a program with substantial subject-specific knowledge and relatively simple inference capabilities rather than following the previous approach, which was to make deductions based on the general axioms of a subject area.

Expert systems have proved to be of value in certain scientific applications, particularly medical ones, but have been slower to establish themselves in commercial or business areas. Many commentators thought that business applications should be amenable to expert systems as many areas of business rely on the expertise and knowledge of specialists. Areas of finance, such as tax, credit and risk assessment, and portfolio management provide examples. A number of business-based expert systems were developed in the mid-1980s including XCON and XSEL from Digital Equipment Corporation (DEC), ExpertTax by Coopers & Lybrand, Credit Clearinghouse by Dun & Bradstreet and Authorizer's Assistant by American Express. However, although there were some successful business applications of expert systems, they were relatively few, and in general they have not lived up to their expectations. The excitement about the possibilities of expert systems in the business domain has been overshadowed somewhat by the more recent enthusiasm for knowledge management systems (see Section 7.4).

The reasons for the lack of successful business applications of expert systems are varied, but certainly one reason is the rather ill defined and uncertain nature of most business domains. Although experts do exist, their expertise is not of the same nature as that of a chemist or a doctor. In business, there are very few hard and fast rules that everybody will agree on. One expert's views may be totally different from another. This has meant that a consensus on definitions of rules (more where probabilities are included) has proved very difficult to achieve. Most business-based expert systems have restricted themselves to areas where the domain is relatively narrow and where there exists a basic set of rules and standards.

Apart from the problem of finding the right applications, the process of knowledge acquisition or knowledge elicitation has proved problematical. This is essentially the process of obtaining the expertise from human experts, although it may also involve the obtaining of knowledge from books, papers, files, systems, manuals, and so on. There are also a variety of different types of knowledge. This variety can be expressed in many different ways, but we categorize it in two types. Descriptive knowledge consists of the facts and descriptions, including the associations and relationships between them. Procedural knowledge is information about processes, procedures, and constraints involved in applying the information, for example, for decision making.

In designing expert systems, the particular level of knowledge is important. The first level is the domain knowledge. This is information specific to the domain under consideration, for example, 'knowledge of corporation tax'. A second level is also domain-specific, but at a higher level, for example, the national taxation system, in which corporation tax is a part. A final level might be the environment at large within which the taxation system operates, and relevant knowledge here might be cultural or philosophical, or it might relate to the belief and value systems. All these are potentially important to an expert system concerned with corporation tax as a way of explaining and understanding the context, constraints, ethics, history, and so on. However, the difficulties of capturing and representing the knowledge becomes progressively more difficult as the levels get higher. There are many potential levels, but, in practice, expert systems concern themselves mainly with the first level and then the rest as one general level.

The formulation of decision rules is no easy task, as we have seen above, but it is not just because business knowledge is not scientific and that the views of experts may differ considerably. It is also to do with the fact that experts are not always good at structuring or organizing their knowledge and decision-making criteria in any formal way. Experts cannot always explain why they know something or the basis for their decisions. The definition of probabilities is also extremely difficult, as is achieving consensus. Even when experts are in agreement, the knowledge still has to be formulated in ways that enable the expert systems to make use of this knowledge. The representation of knowledge, sometimes known as the construction of a knowledge map, is extremely problematical. It is these problems of knowledge acquisition and representation that are the real bottleneck in the development of expert systems for business applications.

There are also a number of other problems concerning business expert systems; one concerns the difficulties of testing and validating. It is difficult to prove that the expertise has been captured correctly and that the rules and inferences will lead to good and effective results when applied. Some companies have found this such a problem that they have abandoned their expert systems. In the USA, in particular, the fear of litigation for proffering incorrect commercial advice is very high. Yoon et al. (1995) identify a number of other characteristics that were found to be important for successful expert systems. The study was based on a study of 69 projects. The factors considered important included:

- high levels of management support for the project;
- high user participation;
- skilled expert systems developers;
- use of a systems approach to analyse the business problems;
- management of unrealistic expectations;

- use of good domain experts;
- understanding of the impact on end-user jobs.

Students of non-expert systems development will not be surprised at these findings. This raises the question of the relevance of expert systems to methodologies. Expert systems can be used for handling and applying the rules of a systems development methodology in a toolset. Another area relates to the use of methodologies, not just to develop standard information systems, but to develop expert systems. The approach to their development has been very *ad hoc*, and there is no such thing as a standard expert systems development methodology. Indeed, up until recently, there has been little interest in methodological issues in the expert systems community (but see Section 23.2). The prevailing approach to the development of expert systems may be characterized as prototyping or evolutionary. This has evolved from the trial and error approach of the early expert systems where the developers would code up a few rules and then try out the program on the users, find it was inadequate, and change or add some more rules, try it out again, and so on.

More recently, there has been an increasing focus on approaches which first attempt to acquire and structure the knowledge and then build the system. Most expert systems developments have typically been separate from information systems development methodologies, in the sense that different people are involved and the focus tends to be on solving the technical problems rather than on the process of development. For some people, expert systems have particular characteristics that mean that information systems development approaches are not relevant. They argue that the knowledge domain is more complex, and that the knowledge acquisition process and the representation of rules are the key issues in expert systems development. This complexity implies that to develop expert systems might require somebody to interface between the domain experts and the technical expert systems developers. This person is known as a knowledge engineer and typically has good cognitive and interpersonal skills.

Whether developing expert systems is radically different from developing information systems is a matter of debate. It may be that current methodologies may not need too much adapting to handle knowledge acquisition and representation as well as the acquisition and representation of data and processes. Another area of interest relates to whether any of the approaches to expert systems development have anything to offer information systems development methodologies. Some of these issues are further discussed in Section 23.2 where an expert systems development methodology (KADS) is described.

7.4 KNOWLEDGE MANAGEMENT

We discussed the meaning of data, information, and knowledge in Chapter 2, and we explore the latter further in this section. During recent years, knowledge management has been seen to be of vital importance to organizations, as important indeed as information management. Knowledge management concerns getting information to the appropriate people, when required, helping them to share this information and experience, enabling them to use it to improve organizational performance, and putting all that in action for a specific purpose. But knowledge is more than 'information'. As Davenport and Prusak (1998) suggest:

> Knowledge is a fluid mix of framed experience, values, contextual information, expert insight, and grounded intuition that provides an environment and framework for evaluating and incorporating new experiences and information. It originates and is applied in the minds of knowers. In organizations, it often becomes embedded not only in documents or repositories but also in organizational routines, processes, practices, and norms.

If we consider the knowledge repository, for example, it can hold best practices, skills inventories, expert databases, competitive intelligence, sales presentations, and product information. It can also contain features that can be said to be a directory to help those who are searching for knowledge. Competitive advantage might be achieved through this knowledge sharing, encouraging innovation, building on past experience, and creating new capabilities within the organization. Its aim is therefore to build on organizational memory through the process of organizational learning. Its use may be apparent after a conversion process when the knowledge seekers convert the knowledge back into information relevant to their purpose.

Tiwana (2000) suggests that there are 24 key drivers that make knowledge management such an important issue for management and organizations.

1　Knowledge-centric drivers

1. The failure of companies to know what they already know.
2. The emergent need for smart knowledge distribution.
3. Knowledge velocity and sluggishness.
4. The problem of knowledge walkouts and high dependence on tacit knowledge.
5. The need to deal with knowledge-hoarding propensity among employees.
6. A need for systemic unlearning.

These knowledge-centric drivers emphasize the situation that most organizations find themselves in: important knowledge exists within the firm but it is not being used effectively. This is partly because they do not know what knowledge their employees have and the lack of motivation for knowledge sharing.

2　Technology drivers

7. The decline of technology as a viable long-term differentiator.
8. Compression of product and process life cycles.
9. The need for a perfect link between knowledge, business strategy, and information technology.

These technology drivers suggest that competitive advantage no longer can be gained from technology itself – your competitors also have this advantage. Further the speed of change is getting even faster, not just from the point of view of technology, but also product and process life cycles. The key to competitive advantage would seem to lie on using the organization's knowledge better, and ensuring it is available for strategic decision making.

3   **Organizational structure-based drivers**

10   Functional convergence.

11   The emergence of project-centric organizational structures.

12   Challenges brought about by deregulation.

13   The inability of companies to keep pace with competitive changes due to globalization.

14   Convergence of products and services.

The organizational structure-based drivers emphasize the great changes that are taking place within organizations due to both internal and external drivers. When these great changes are taking place, there is a danger that the knowledge of the organization might be lost. It is therefore vital that knowledge management is seen as great a priority as implementing change due to the inevitable organizational changes.

4   **Personnel drivers**

15   Widespread functional convergence.

16   The need to support effective cross-functional collaboration.

17   Team mobility and fluidity.

18   The need to deal with complex corporate expectations.

With personnel changing roles, teams, functions, and so on, there is again a danger that the knowledge, skills, and experience are lost. People think about their new challenges rather than their knowledge of previous work.

5   **Process-focused drivers**

19   The need to avoid repeated and often expensive mistakes.

20   Need to avoid unnecessary reinvention.

21   The need for accurate predictive anticipation.

22   The emerging need for competitive responsiveness.

We often hear of the expression, 'don't reinvent the wheel', yet it occurs regularly in practice as people do not use the knowledge gained by others or it is not available.

6   Economic drivers

23   The potential for creating extraordinary leverage through knowledge; the attractive economics of increasing returns.

24   The quest for a silver bullet for product and service differentiation.

There have been lots of 'silver bullets' claimed over the years, many relating to the use of information technology. These have provided short-term competitive advantage at best. Yet one key to competitive advantage is surely the knowledge that organizations possess. Knowledge management is about exploiting this to full effect.

Too often, organizations forget what they know, and one aspect of knowledge management is identifying its knowledge assets, and then to manage and make use of these assets by diffusion. But it is not just about forgetting knowledge already learnt. It is also about communicating quickly new knowledge just discovered in this period of rapid change. It is through the knowledge of their people that organizations have real competitive advantage, not through their technology.

Knowledge management is difficult: how can we identify and manage something that we do not know exists? In the long term, organizations try to change the culture so that knowledge sharing is the norm. In doing that, it needs to counteract the view that knowledge is power and therefore sharing it loses personal power. Reward schemes can help to make the sharing of knowledge (and also using other people's knowledge) advantageous to the individual. The theme is encouraging people to share and exploit each other's knowledge partly through the support of IT, not the use of IT to replace people. Organizations need to develop a 'culture of knowledge sharing'.

Another way to encourage knowledge sharing and knowledge management is to have an executive level role with the title of chief knowledge officer (CKO). This shows top level commitment to the importance of knowledge. The CKO might replace the chief information officer (CIO) title discussed in Chapter 1, though the roles are very different. The CKO, for example, will not have responsibility for IT, the CIO may well have this responsibility.

An important aspect of knowledge management relates to tacit knowledge, which is knowledge that is difficult to express in words and therefore can be hidden from the rest of the organization. Among other things, a knowledge management system attempts to make this tacit knowledge explicit and public. This might be achieved through attempting to explain the knowledge with others and clarifying the knowledge through questions and answers. Further, this enables additional change. The knowledge changes from being an individual's own, to that of the community. Knowledge management is about sharing knowledge.

From the organization's point of view, knowledge management is about sharing best practice, but externally it wants to make capabilities rare, valuable, and difficult to imitate. Sun Microsystems, a company that sells hardware and software, makes available knowledge about new systems to staff out in the field for training purposes while they are at work. Staff are therefore up to date without the need to go to frequent formal training courses. Ernst & Young, a consultancy company, provides knowledge to its customers about auditing, tax updates, methods, and tools. These customers pay for the particular service, belonging to the knowledge network of Ernst & Young. 3M, a company relying on innovation, uses knowledge management systems to diffuse knowledge on best practices in their research and development and their technical communities. Their Intranet site includes the ability to access library and information services, a corporate learning management system (including access to e-learning), a news management facility, a directory of e-business contacts, and communities of knowledge management and knowledge exchange.

7.5 CUSTOMER ORIENTATION

A common progression stressed in the late 20th century was the emphasis placed on the user rather than the technologist and technology. We have reflected this in a number of sections in the book and in particular in this chapter. However, toward the end of the 20th century and since, much emphasis has been placed 'further down the line' of stakeholders to the customer. Companies say they are 'customer focused'. This has been most prominent in the information systems domain in web applications where the users are likely to be customers, in data mining applications where, for example, the customers' use of the web might be traced and, more generally, in customer relationship management (CRM).

CRM is concerned with attracting valuable customers in the first place and keeping them loyal to the company. Technology is used to improve customer service and provide competitive advantage. The customer, it is hoped, is treated as an individual through this technology and finds experiences with the company very positive. Essentially the philosophy of CRM is contained in the motto 'delivering value to customers will bring value to the organization'.

Although good CRM does not necessarily mean use of the Internet, the latter has played a major part in organizations' emphasis on CRM. Internet search engines and other software have facilitated tracking customers' use of the web, and analysis of this has led to systems providing relevant information to customers. These customer data are potentially good customer knowledge, but fulfilling this potential necessitates good systems analysis and support technology.

Customers are only the final link in the supply chain and CRM also relates to other parts of the supply chain, for example, suppliers in business to business (B2B) electronic commerce.

Outside the web, similar tracking is performed through customers' use of the supermarket loyalty card. Special offers directed to the individual customer can be made based on previous purchase records, all automatically generated using computer systems. Another major application area for CRM concerns call centres where customers have their queries dealt with using on-screen tips to enable the query to be dealt with quickly and efficiently.

There are a number of implications for information systems development. One concerns ascertaining customer requirements during the investigation. A common technique is to carry out electronic surveys of customers. This is likely to achieve general information, but can be somewhat superficial. Typical customers, focus groups, and the like might be interviewed as much as users and managers were in the past. As the customers are not part of the company and therefore not 'captive', this may require even better communication skills than those required for interviewing other employees of the organization. The development team may be somewhat different than conventionally; for example, containing marketing experts and segment managers and experts in design, data mining, and data warehousing, as well as privacy and security officers.

Emphasis is also placed on good design so that it is easy for customers of various kinds to use the systems. Some customers (like users) may be experienced and do not require nor want detailed instructions. Others may be less experienced and require detailed guidance to use the system. Further, instead of one or two user interfaces for the system, there may be a large number depending on the range of types of customer.

For help desk and call centre applications, systems analysts need to prioritize the different types of information being provided, so that particularly important information is provided first, such as information about customer name and address, product guarantee period, and other repairs made for a product, all following the customer's product serial number being input. The customers need to feel that they are getting good customer care and service. Therefore, call centre staff need to be trained to deal with customers as well as use the computer information system. Knowledge management systems may be used here, for example, as a means of tracking down faults. The system may also keep a log of each customer transaction so that the system can 'learn' from each customer experience. Certainly sophisticated systems will analyse each set of transactions. Data mining and data warehouse systems can also be used to analyse the data gathered.

Another concern relates to security aspects, because if customers have access so will hackers. Poor customer-oriented systems from the point of view of security are far more vulnerable than similar internal ones, although all systems are vulnerable to some extent. The company must also be seen as one that is very protective of customers' privacy. Privacy should be seen as a right, not a preference. Again, flexibility might gain greater emphasis, as these systems must keep up with competitors, and changing design, as well as content, is likely to be far more frequent than is the case with internal systems. Yet the designer has to have speed as a priority as well, for Internet users expect very good response rates. This is also an important aspect of customer satisfaction.

Although the gains of CRM are potentially high, customers might become alienated by poor systems analysis and design. The analysts' task will therefore include the ability to persuade management to bear the cost of developing effective CRM systems. Arguments such as competitive advantage, decreased customer attrition, and increased sales can help here. The impact may be great, but effective investment might include changing the business processes, even a business process re-engineering exercise, to emphasize greater attention to customer requirements, and this could be difficult. The integration necessary of the CRM system with the basic systems of the company could also be a major concern.

7.6   SUMMARY

- The movement concerned with involving all those affected by information systems in the process of developing them is usually referred to as participation.

- End-user computing is a participative approach whereby the users, not specialists, develop their own information systems.

- An expert system is an information system that simulates the role of an expert. Its usefulness is derived from its knowledge and reasoning ability.

- Knowledge management is a further development and sophistication of expert systems concerned with getting information to the appropriate people, when required, helping them to share this information and experience, enabling them to use it to improbe organizational performance, and putting all that in action for a specific purpose.

- Customer relationship management (CRM) is concerned with using information technology to attract customers to the organization and keeping them loyal to the company.

QUESTIONS

1 A systems analyst suggests that user participation increases development times, leads to inefficient applications, and makes his or her job less satisfying. Provide a counterargument to this view.

2 Do you agree that knowledge management is simply a further development of expert systems or do you think there are fundamental differences?

3 Do you think the prime stakeholder of an information systems development project is the developer, user, or customer? Argue a case for each.

7.7   FURTHER READING

Dyché, J. (2002) *The CRM Handbook, A Business Guide to Customer Relationship Management*, Addison-Wesley, New Jersey.

Jackson, P. (1999) *Introduction to Expert Systems*, Addison-Wesley, Harlow, UK.

Mahmood, M.A. (2002) *Advanced Topics in End User Computing*, Idea Group Publishing, Hershey, PA, USA.

Mumford, E. (1996) *Systems Design: Ethical Tools for Ethical Change*, Palgrave, Macmillan, Houndmills, Hampshire.

Tiwana, A. (2001) *The Essential Guide to Knowledge Management*, Prentice-Hall, New Jersey.

8 EXTERNAL DEVELOPMENT

APPLICATION PACKAGES

An enduring theme of application development concerns the wish to reduce the effort involved by purchasing a ready-made solution. Usually this means the purchase of an application package. Most packages used carry out applications that any type of business has. Typically, these are word processing, spreadsheet, database, calendar management, e-mail, and so on. There are also packages designed for particular market sectors, for example, hotels, shops, and transport companies. A rather more ambitious type of application package are the enterprise resource planning systems (ERP) which are integrated packages that cover a range of applications for businesses, for example, sales order processing, invoicing, ledger systems, production control, stock control, human resource management, and the rest.

Although the purchase of application packages and ERP systems means that much of the development work is done externally, it does not mean that there is no systems development work in-house, as the packages need to be tailored for the company. In the case of ERP systems, this tailoring can be very substantial and implementation, a long-term exercise. However, the use of outside consultants can ease the burden on in-house staff. An alternative approach is to purchase development, implementation, and the operation of computer applications from outsourcing suppliers.

The purchase of an application package can be a daunting task. Most businesses purchasing office applications will purchase a well-adopted package, such as those from Microsoft. However, it is much more difficult when purchasing other types of package. It is imperative that the company set up a requirements definition for the package. This will involve looking at the problems of the present system and deciding on the requirements for the new system. Very often, the old system may need replacing: the business or its environment is changing, customer service is deteriorating, or poor management decisions may be made because of inappropriate, inaccurate, or untimely information being provided. Statements about desired service levels and workload will

127

be particularized into the provision of reports, enquiry facilities, levels of security, volumes to be processed, and timescales. There may also be constraints, such as a budget maximum, personnel restriction, and a target date for implementation.

In evaluating a particular application package, the following questions should be asked.

1   Does it meet the functional requirements?

This is of course the issue of fundamental importance. If the package does meet the functional requirements then:

■   Is all the input required by the package readily available?

■   Is its capacity large enough for present use or too restricting for the future?

■   Does it process the data fast enough?

If only some of the requirements are fulfilled then some other questions should be asked:

■   What percentage of the requirements are fulfilled without amending the application package?

■   Are the limitations of the package acceptable?

■   How easily can the extra requirements be fulfilled?

2   What resources are required to buy and run the package?

■   What is the basic cost, maintenance cost, and the cost of extra hardware and support required?

■   What labour is required to set up and run the system?

■   Can the package be run on other computers (which may be important later)?

3   How many people are presently using the package?

■   Is it possible to get their reactions to it?

■   Were there many set-up and teething problems?

■   Has it proved reliable?

■   Are they presently happy with the system?

■   Are they happy with the help provided by the supplier?

■   What would they have done differently now?

4   What is the quality of the documentation?

This relates to any hard-copy documentation and the help and other facilities provided in the package itself:

(a) Package/ Criterion	A	B	C		(b) Package/ Criterion	A	B	C		(c) Package/ Criterion	Weight	A	B	C
1	X	X	X		1	6	9	8		1	2	12	18	16
2	X		X		2	6		9		2	10	60		90
3	X		X		3	7		9		3	10	70		90
4	X	X			4	7	10			4	1	7	10	
5		X			5		10			5	2		20	
Total	4	(3)	3		Total	26	(29)	26		Total		149	48	(196)

FIGURE 8.1   Evaluating application packages.

■ Is it geared to computer experts, or are the users of the system likely to understand it?

■ Is it well written? The documentation should be assessed on its appropriateness for the people who are going to use the package.

■ Is it good for reading, learning, teaching, referring to, reminding, and diagnosing problems?

One way of presenting the various solutions is to create a matrix, listing the requirements (and therefore ignoring irrelevant features) on the left-hand side of a table, and then listing the solutions that might be appropriate along the top.

Let us assume that the alternative solutions are three application packages. Where the package meets any criterion, put a cross at the intersection. For evaluating the package, the more crosses the better, and therefore the recommended solution will be the one with the most crosses. This is package A in Figure 8.1(a).

A package may only partly meet any requirement. The technique can therefore be improved by giving a mark out of 10 for each package/criterion. The marks for each package can be added up and the package that scores the most is chosen. This is package B in Figure 8.1(b).

The technique can be further improved by giving a weight to each criterion. Some requirements are more important than others. To emphasize the relative importance of criteria, a weight is allocated to each of them so that if a weight of 4 is assigned, then this criterion is considered to be four times as important as a criterion allocated a weight of 1. Thus, if a package scores 7 out of 10 where the weight is 3, this counts as 21 on the total. Criteria that are considered essential can be given large weights, so that packages that do not meet these requirements will be excluded. In Figure 8.1(c), the allocation of different weights to criteria has led to package C being the recommended solution. The example shows that different recommendations could be made depending on the way the technique is applied.

We will now look in more detail at some of the important considerations that need to be taken into account in evaluating and purchasing application packages and the hardware to run them.

1   A requirements shortfall

In some circumstances even the best hardware and software choice performs only some of the requirements defined. The business is then faced with a further choice in order to deal with this:

- Should it adapt the business to fit in with the requirements of the computer system?

- Should it call in the services of its computing team, consultants, or software house to adapt the package so that it does conform to the needs of the business?

- Should it decide that application packages are inappropriate and decide to develop a completely new in-house solution?

All these are feasible in certain circumstances. Whatever the choice, it is likely that some variation of the Pareto 80:20 rule will apply (see Section 6.4): about 80 per cent of the application requirements will be covered by the package, but about 20 per cent will not be covered. Conversely, it is this 20 per cent of the application requirements that will absorb something like 80 per cent of the costs.

At least the prospective purchaser has had the foresight to detect the mismatch before purchasing the system. Too often the system has been purchased and the manager has discovered to his horror that some vital function is not performed. Further, as the problem was not analysed beforehand, the manager may have chosen an application package that is particularly difficult to adapt.

It may seem surprising that the extra 20 per cent of the requirements are so comparatively expensive. The reason is that the writers of an application package expect to sell many copies. This means that the initial expense of writing it is absorbed by the profit on the number of copies sold. Writing a package may cost one hundred times its selling price. However, as soon as more than one hundred copies are sold, the supplier begins to make a profit. The 'tuning' of the package for an individual user will be expensive. Although software houses design packages to be of use to as many prospective customers as possible, such a generalized package is unlikely to fulfil all the requirements of all of them. In estimating the costs and benefits of an application package, it is essential that the cost of fulfilling all the requirements are included, otherwise the justification for the purchase will be distorted.

2   Intangible costs and benefits

In evaluating systems, it is necessary to include intangible costs and benefits in the calculations. Intangible costs include: the time and effort spent looking at potential packages; and the time and effort involved in training and educating people to use the computer system and overcoming their resistance to the new technology.

Training and education are vital. The morale of staff may improve with the implementation of computer systems. But it might deteriorate if measures are not taken to maintain the confidence of employees. Staff may view computers as a threat because they may lead to a loss of work status, work satisfaction, and employment. These intangible costs are difficult to evaluate. Intangible benefits such as greater speed of data processing, improved levels of security, greater accuracy, and greater reliability are equally difficult to evaluate in money terms, but should be included in the assessment. In Section 18.5 we discuss fully the issues relating to the potential benefits and problems that might accrue from using large software packages supporting applications development known as integrated toolsets.

8.2 ENTERPRISE RESOURCE PLANNING (ERP)

Enterprise resource planning (ERP) systems are much more ambitious application packages. We therefore discuss these in a separate section, although they are in essence a type of application package. The success of an organization may depend largely on integrated systems, and in particular on the effective transfer of information throughout the supply chain. ERP systems form a complex series of software modules used to integrate many business processes. Originally, these included production, inventory management, and logistics modules for manufacturing organizations. Later, they developed from materials requirement planning and manufacturing resource planning systems to encompass the capabilities of money resources planning systems, so that ERP systems supported all the basic financial applications and other organizational functions, such as human resource management. Now they include strategic planning, sales and distribution, marketing, financials, controls, quality management, supply management, materials management, plant maintenance, production planning, workflow, and human resource management; indeed, all the standard business processes and functions of the organization. More recently still, modules have been incorporated that provide the capability for e-commerce. In this way ERP systems impact outside the organization as well as within it, as they allow for communication with suppliers and customers. Indeed, they attempt to provide a complete IT solution for businesses.

Many potential advantages are obvious. The business gains from a fully integrated system that enables visibility and integrity of data throughout the organization. Some of the potential disadvantages are also obvious; in particular, the complexity of integrating many or most of the organization's applications and the consequent cost in terms of money and time to achieve this. There is therefore some risk associated with the implementation of ERP systems.

As we have said, the latest versions incorporate Internet technology to pull suppliers and customers closer together in the supply chain. An example might be a customer buying a new car from a dealer. The customer may be able to find where the car is in the manufacturer's production schedule, and the suppliers of raw materials are able to predict manufacturer requirements based on dealers' forward orders.

Enterprise resource planning systems are supplied by SAP, Oracle, JD Edwards, Baan, and PeopleSoft, among others. The 'sales pitch' is obvious – there is support for every aspect of the business, each system is seen as the 'best of breed', top management can see the implications of one part of the business on others, and 'discipline' can be imposed on the workforce as all activities can be costed and controlled.

The market leader SAP has around 40 per cent of the overall market, over 15,000 installed sites worldwide and over US$6 billion in development. The temptation to join this bandwagon has been difficult to resist. It is even possible to have such software configured for certain sectors, including universities, banks, airlines, and retailers. Along with the software itself, there is a huge business in training and consulting.

However, many organizations have found that it is not that simple. The long implementation time span, the huge investment, the impact of everything changing at the same time, and the sheer direct and indirect costs are just some of the complaints offsetting some of the claims. Further, in order to make the likelihood of success greater, many firms change processes to fit the software (i.e. minimal customization or 'vanilla ERP'), and this causes problems. In practice, implementation of ERP systems have often coincided with downsizing (in all but ERP expertise) as companies try to alleviate costs, and middle management in particular suffers. Nevertheless, many businesses have found that their ERP implementation has proved to be a great success.

ERP are a realization of ME goals in that they provide a consolidated and integrated tool kit of method fragments and tools for modelling and building applications. The ERP vendors and the systems analysts enforce a framework by which the systems are brought online. ERP are not simply technologically centric, because they incorporate business process re-engineering and modelling tools. Nor do they simply assume given process models, because, depending on the management's choice of implementation, they have a very definite focus on organizational considerations.

ERP systems are significant breaks with the past in two ways. First, most organizations find them so complex that they forego significant customization and effectively redesign the organization to fit the software system, frequently through business process re-engineering (Section 4.3). This trend is wholly anathematic to past practice in which the goal of information systems development has been to build systems that fit organizations, like custom-tailored gloves fit the hand. A second significant difference is that the driving force behind the acquisition of these systems tends to be *top corporate management* rather than IT management or even business unit management. Finally, as business process re-engineering assumptions and values are a part of these approaches and systems, the focus has moved away from the integration of existing IS and the improvement or enhancement of current systems, to a philosophy of wholesale replacement and abandonment of existing systems and ways of doing work. Organizational restructuring and significant reductions in headcount throughout the organizational hierarchy generally accompany ERP. Significantly, the organizational re-engineering usually follows the introduction of the ERP system rather than preceding its adoption. Therefore, it represents the instance of the software system calling the organizational tune as compared to a more traditional development setting in which the software is constructed to meld with the organizational demands.

ERP systems are a great deal more than a set of methods and tools; they are also regarded as infrastructures in that they incorporate a type of front-end, back-end, and middle-tier architecture that runs on a host of different networks and hardware platforms. An initial appeal of these systems has been that they provided certain interoperability and sharing of enterprise data while allowing custom configuration of the applications set. This is a point that has proven to be problematic, and we return to this later. However, the sheer complexity and the cost of bringing custom-solution ERP up and running has proved so high that the pendulum has swung in the direction of standard, 'no change', implementation on rapid deployment product versions using special implementation teams. Implementation is relatively quick but does not address organizational issues such as restructuring and training. We are therefore at a stage where there is some dissatisfaction with ERP systems (see also Section 6.5).

OUTSOURCING

Outsourcing of activities to third-party organizations has been a significant business practice for many years. For example, a manufacturing organization may outsource all its catering or cleaning needs to a third-party company who may do it cheaper, but probably the main reason is that the organization just does not want to devote their energies to catering and cleaning. Their efforts are better directed toward their own manufacturing business activities, at which, it is hoped, they are very good, and leave the catering and cleaning to a third-party company that specializes in providing these services to a high standard. In theory the client organization does not have to worry about the service provision, except to specify and set it up originally, pay the monthly charge, and renegotiate (or terminate) at the end of the contract. However, things sometimes go wrong so they probably also need to be able to monitor the quality of the service and negotiate rectification when any shortfalls occur.

These same principles have been used in connection with IT provision over the years. In the early days of computing, organizations sometimes used third-party 'service bureaux' to prepare input for a system (prepare punchcards, etc.), to run applications on the bureau's mainframe, or to provide a range of other computer services. More recently it has been common to 'outsource' some or all telecommunications provision, networking, PC maintenance, help desks, training, etc.

Exactly what is meant by the term outsourcing presents problems, and a survey by Michell (1994) illustrated the wide variety of interpretations that outsourcing vendors themselves have for what constitutes outsourcing. In relation to IT, Fitzgerald and Willcocks (1994) have defined outsourcing as 'the commissioning of a third party (or a number of third parties) to manage a client organization's IT assets, people, and/or activities to required results'. The focus here is on the management of the activity by the outsourcing vendor to a defined specification or service level. This can, and often does, involve a degree of transfer of assets, including staff, to the third-party organization. So defined, outsourcing does not exhaust the ways in which markets can be used. Therefore, a distinction is made between contracts that specify a service, and results which the market is to provide and manage ('outsourcing'). This means that the focus of outsourcing is on the result or outcome of the service being outsourced rather than specifying how it is to be undertaken. So an outsourcing contract might specify that a particular computer service has to be available for 24 hours a day, 7 days a week, with an uptime of 98 per cent over the period; it does not specify how that is to be achieved. That is up to the vendor. This contrasts with using the market to provide resources from outside to be deployed under the client organization's management and control, for example the hiring of contract programmers into an existing development team would not be outsourcing. Feeny et al. (1993) have termed this 'insourcing'.

In the early and mid-1990s outsourcing in IT developed a new impetus, driven by the influence of the strategic management concept of 'core competencies' or 'core business focus'. Prior to this, in the 1970s, vertical integration of activities was in fashion, which suggested that competitive advantage could be gained by organizations seeking to undertake activities up and down their supply chain. So a manufacturing organization might also seek to own or make the constituent parts of their product, make their own packaging, own the distribution channel, do their own marketing, etc. Core competencies was diametrically opposed to this. It believed that it was difficult, if not impossible, for organizations to be up to world-class standards in everything they did. To achieve world-class standards is difficult enough but to be world class in non-core activities as well is virtually impossible, and to attempt this is likely to lead to a dissipation of resources and energies resulting in failure in all activities. So, organizations should strive to be of world-class standard in only their core activities and outsource the non-core activities to third parties or vendors where those activities are their core business and therefore they can do them to world-class standards.

When organizations examined their core activities they often found that IT was not part of that core and therefore it should be outsourced. One of the most influential examples of this was Eastman Kodak in the USA who decided that film was their core business and that IT was not, so they outsourced all their IT (Lacity and Hirschheim, 1993). This was a very influential decision and many other companies followed suit or at least reviewed their core business and considered outsourcing some if not all of their IT. In the UK, British Home Stores (BHS) outsourced all their IT as a result of a 'core focus' strategic analysis (Willcocks and Fitzgerald, 1993). This was also a change of philosophy in relation to IT which had previously suggested that IT was key to competitive advantage, particularly in information-intensive industries, but even banks and other information-intensive industries were not immune to outsourcing. The outsourcing of the whole of a company's IT to a third party is still relatively rare, although these are the deals that hit the trade press headlines; more common is the selective outsourcing of parts of a company's IT. Those areas that make most sense may be outsourced. This is known as 'selective outsourcing'.

There are other reasons for outsourcing IT (see G. Fitzgerald, 1994). One reason is to obtain IT services at less cost. Why might a third party be able to provide a product or service at lower cost? The answer is usually related to economies of scale which is essentially the notion that the greater the output the less will be the costs of production per unit of output. In IT terms there is some evidence that economies of scale are to be found in the running of mainframes, data centres, telecommunications networks, and help desks.

This growth in the outsourcing of IT to third-party companies has resulted in the development of some very large IT outsourcing vendors. Indeed the business is dominated by a few very large companies, such as EDS and IBM, with a larger number of much smaller niche players, specializing in, for example, a particular area such as information systems development or a particular sector such as financial trading systems. The structure of the industry has certainly changed with the development of large-scale outsourcing, and some large client organizations which would previously have had a large internal IT department often now have almost no internal IT and now focus on managing and organizing suppliers rather than doing it themselves.

Of course, not all outsourcing has been successful and there is evidence of some degree of dissatisfaction, particularly in the early days. Organizations have terminated and renegotiated agreements, but over time the vendors have probably improved and there is more knowledge about the best areas to outsource and the processes to be undertaken for success.

The outsourcing of information systems development has been an important subset of IT outsourcing, and the 'core competencies' argument has sometimes been the justification. For example, a motor vehicle manufacturer might say that although we need software systems our competencies and capabilities are not in this area, therefore we will outsource it. Or it might be that, although a company has the competencies in ISD and it might be core to their business, they may not be able to keep up with the demand for new systems. This was the justification made by one of the mobile telephone companies to outsource some of their IS development recently. For others, the continuing problems of systems development and the difficulties of delivering systems on time and within budget, has been the justification for outsourcing. The trend for downsizing has also resulted in the outsourcing of ISD. Some companies no longer have IS staff to undertake in-house development projects. Others have found that their existing IS personnel lack the skills necessary to build systems, especially distributed and client/server development.

Whatever the reason there has been a growing tendency for organizations to outsource some or all of their systems development. However, it is not an easy option. In all outsourcing the specification of the service that is being outsourced has proved difficult and problematic, but this is a particular issue with ISD. Many of the problems encountered in ISD relate to the problems of gathering requirements from users, the changing nature of requirements, and the difficulty of accurately specifying requirements, plus the 'freezing' of requirements while the system is constructed. If it is difficult in-house to achieve it can only be even more difficult if it is outsourced. Nevertheless, it is frequently attempted and is sometimes successful. In outsourcing systems development the specification of what is needed must be very tight and exact. Some have argued that the use of an outside vendor to develop systems is actually helpful in this respect because users better realize that the specification has to be precise and stable, and they are prepared to make compromises and not demand that everything is provided. The fact that they are also paying 'real' money also tends to focus the mind on the objectives and a realistic set of requirements.

Sometimes the whole development is outsourced including the gathering of user requirements, but more commonly it is not the whole process but a subset of it, for example just the programming, or the programming and implementation. However, even if a vendor is just undertaking the building phase the client often 'implicitly expects some help on the design', according to Goldsmith (1994), and this can lead to serious problems. Therefore he argues for expending even more effort than usual on defining requirements when outsourcing ISD. Goldsmith also finds that client companies are much more confident about selecting software packages than they are in their ability to select software development services. A particular problem is that the vendor cannot easily convey a tangible example of what will be provided, 'because the vendor is proposing to develop software that does not exist yet, the buyer cannot see it or try it out. Thus, the vendor essentially is asking the buyer to evaluate a promise rather than a product' Goldsmith (1994). A famous example of the failure of ISD outsourcing is that of the London Ambulance Service's disastrous Computer Aided ambulance Dispatch system which failed a few days after implementation due to lack of proper specification, design, and testing together with a poor choice of vendor (Beynon-Davis, 1995).

As in all outsourcing the issue of the contract, and the contract framework, is very important. The type of contracting framework used may have a significant effect on the price paid, the business value accruing, and on the probability of completion.

The client company outsourcing its systems development has to develop skills in selecting the correct vendor, specifying requirements in detail, and writing and negotiating contracts, rather than thinking about systems development methodologies. Again this represents a significant shift in emphasis and downplays the importance of the way the application is developed. Client companies are no longer so interested in what methodology is used – they leave that to the vendor – they just want the outcome to be successful (see Chapter 26). There are other potential, long-term effects for the client organization. The experience and expertise of developing and running systems in-house is being lost. This skill and expertise is being transferred to the vendor with the result that the organization is increasingly dependent on outside vendors. This can be particularly problematic if IT is strategic to the business, or where it becomes strategic after outsourcing. Some organizations, because they have outsourced their IT fail to keep track of strategy in relation to IT and may miss a trick or become overtaken by competitors who have kept up.

Outsourcing has also been driven in some sectors and organizations, by a requirement to test any new work or project in the market place. This is seen as a way of ensuring best value for money by having in-house provision compared with the best that the market can provide. In the UK for example the public sector was required to do this and choose the lowest cost provider. This resulted in a large number of public sector IT projects being outsourced.

One area which has recently seen an increase in outsourcing is that of web development (see Section 6.6) and web technology provision. In this case, the motivation is usually that the client company does not have the necessary expertise in-house, but it can also be driven by the need to develop quickly or not really knowing whether it is going to be a key area and hedging their bets by outsourcing. There has been a significant growth in what is termed Application Service Provision (ASP) (Currie, 2001).

The practice of outsourcing to a vendor in a geographically different area has become known as 'offshore outsourcing', and it has become increasingly popular in recent times. It has been made possible by advances in telecommunications technology, thus effectively removing traditional geographic boundaries. Electronic transfer of data and instructions, email, videoconferencing, etc. can enable the feasible development of a system in a country many thousands of miles away from the client.

The main reasons for this growth in offshore ISD are identified as follows (Patane and Jurison, 1994):

■ the low cost of labour compared with the USA and Western Europe;

■ the ease of access to, and relatively low costs of, high-speed telecommunication networks;

■ worldwide availability of PCs;

■ relatively low entry costs in terms of capital expenditure;

■ the trend toward free-market economies and free trade;

■ the reduction of cultural barriers, such as different working practices and values;

■ the broadening of education opportunities and in particular the worldwide nature of computing knowledge.

India was one of the first to offer such services, with more than 100 software companies located in the city of Bangalore alone, according to Patane and Jurison (1994). India has the benefit of a well-educated sector of the population in computing and the advantage of being able to communicate in English. Other countries like Singapore, Malaysia, Philippines, Hong Kong, and Taiwan are also in this market, as well as some in Europe, such as Ireland and Hungary.

Significant cost-savings can be obtained by having a system developed (or part-developed) overseas due to the low costs of labour, the wages of programmers can be around 10–20 per cent of those in the West. However, cost is only one of the considerations that must be weighed in any outsourcing decision. Application systems development is regarded as particularly suitable for offshore outsourcing, according to Patane and Jurison (1994), although those tasks requiring significant interaction with users are usually performed by in-house analysts. These are typically the front-end tasks of user requirements, elicitation, and outline design and the back-end tasks such as integrated testing and implementation in the client site. This leaves detailed design, programming, and program testing as the most suitable areas to be outsourced.

Maintenance of offshore developed software can be a problem. Systems which have been originally developed by offshore vendors may also be maintained offshore by the original developers. So there may be a long-term commitment to any offshore outsourcing decision.

8.4   SUMMARY

- An application package is a ready-made information system. Being developed externally, the package may need to be tailored for the company.

- Enterprise resource planning (ERP) systems are application packages, but they are integrated systems, transferring information throughout the supply chain. ERP systems form a complex series of software modules used to integrate many business processes.

- Outsourcing is the commissioning of a third party (or a number of third parties) to manage a client organization's IT assets, people, and/or activities to a defined specification or service level.

QUESTIONS

1 Create a list of criteria that you might use to assess whether an information system is developed in-house, through an application package or through an outsourcing supplier.

2 What are the special features that distinguish ERP from other information systems?

3 Evaluate an application package or packages on the basis of the weighting systems discussed in Section 8.1 and make a case for its purchase or otherwise.

8.5   FURTHER READING

Hirschheim, R. (ed.) (2002) *Information Systems Outsourcing*, Springer-Verlag, Berlin.

Janson, M.A. and Subramanian, A. (1996) Packaged software: Selection and implementation policies, *INFOR*, Vol. 34, No. 2.

Norris, G., Wright, I., Hurley, J.R., Dunleavy, J., and Gibson, A. (1998) *SAP: An Executive's Comprehensive Guide*, John Wiley & Sons, New York.

9 SOFTWARE

SOFTWARE ENGINEERING

Software forms part of any information system, but in this chapter we look at those themes that address in particular the role of software and developing software in an information systems project. Software engineering concerns the use of sound engineering principles, good management practice, applicable tools, and methods for software development. This was thought to be the solution to the software crisis, that is, the ability to maintain programs, fulfil the growing demand for larger and more complex programs and the increased potential of hardware which has not been exploited fully by the software. The principles established in software engineering have now generally been accepted as a genuine advance and an improvement to programming practice, primarily by achieving better designed programs and hence making them easier to maintain and more reliable. This has led to improved software quality.

In the period before the advent of software engineering, the conventional way of developing computer programs was to pick up a pencil or to sit at a computer terminal and code the program without a thorough design phase. This *ad hoc* process was also frequently used for larger programs, but a better method for these large programs was to develop a flowchart and code from this. However, even this method was not very satisfactory.

The time taken to develop a fully tested program will be far greater in the long run if effort is not spent on thorough design. Without this design, it is difficult to incorporate all the necessary features required of the program. However, these omissions will only be brought to light at the program testing stage, and it will be difficult to incorporate the changes required at such a late stage. Problem solving carried out by haphazard, trial and error methods is far less successful than where good analysis and design comes before coding.

One solution to better program design was the use of flowcharting methods, but although program flowcharting does discipline the programmer to design the program,

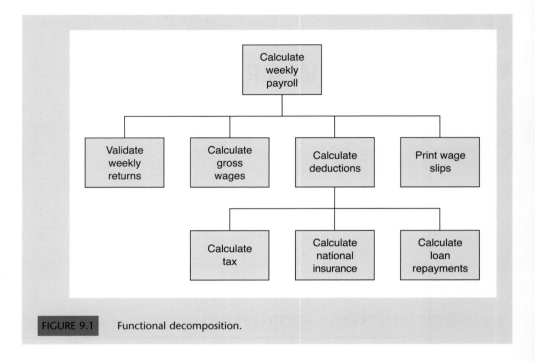

Functional decomposition.

the resultant design can prove inflexible, particularly for large programs. Flowcharting usually leads to programs which have a number of branches. With this method, it is difficult to incorporate even the smallest amendments to the program in a way which does not have repercussions elsewhere. These repercussions are usually very difficult to predict, and programmers find that after making a change to correct a program, some other part of the program begins to fail.

Software engineering offers a more disciplined approach to programming which is likely to increase the time devoted to program design, but will greatly increase productivity through savings in testing and maintenance time. A good design is one achievement of the 'software engineering school' and a second is good documentation, which greatly enhances the program's 'maintainability'. A third is related to both: the regular taking of software metrics (measurements) can help general control of the project (see below).

One of the key elements of software engineering is functional decomposition (Section 5.1). Here a complex process is broken down into increasingly smaller subsets. In Figure 9.1, 'Calculate weekly payroll' at the top level can be broken down into first-level boxes named 'validate weekly returns', 'calculate gross wages', 'calculate deductions', and 'print wage slips'. Each of these boxes is a separate task and can be altered without affecting other boxes (provided output remains unchanged). Each of these can then be further broken down. For example, 'calculate deductions' can be broken down into its constituent parts, 'calculate tax', 'calculate national insurance', and 'calculate loan payments'. Eventually this top-down approach can lead to the level where each **module** can be represented as a few simple English statements or a small amount of programming code, the target base level. This hierarchy is sometimes

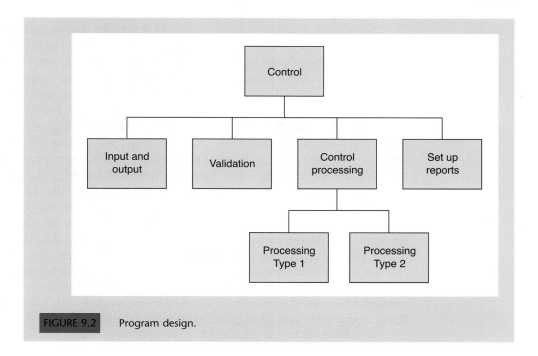

FIGURE 9.2   Program design.

described as a tree with the root at the top and the smallest leaves at the bottom. This is similar to the process referred to as stepwise (or successive) refinement (Wirth, 1971).

Figure 9.1 shows the way a process could be broken down into its constituent parts. Many programs can be broken down into the general structure shown as Figure 9.2. The top-level module controls the overall processing of the program. Separate modules at the lower level control the input and output routines (reading data and updating files), validation routines (checking that the data are correct), the processing routines, and the setting up of reports. Sometimes these structure charts include details of the data (called parameters) which are passed between modules. This information is written on the connecting lines in the diagram.

So far, we have equated software engineering with good practice in programming design. But this is a narrow interpretation. The term is frequently used to cover the areas of requirements definition, testing, maintenance and control of software projects, as well as the design of software.

The requirements definition must be clear and unambiguous so that the software designer knows what the piece of software should do. The designer can then devise the way that these requirements will be achieved. Even the best design will not lead to a successful implementation if the requirements are not clear. The problem with natural language is that it is frequently ambiguous, although there is a series of techniques that can be used to clarify the requirements. We may here be going beyond the boundary of software engineering into information systems development. We take the view that the requirements of the software designer will be made clear by the systems analyst. Certainly where the software is associated with a part of the overall methodology for information systems development, the likelihood of success is increased.

Supporters of software engineering practice claim that the reliability of software designed in this way is improved. These improvements do not only derive directly from better design. There is an indirect benefit. If the software is better designed, it makes adequate testing of that software much easier. By designing the program so that it is split into smaller and separate elements, it is possible to construct a series of tests for each of them. The number of tests for a larger program will be much greater. Perhaps simplistically (but it illustrates the point), a program split into four modules each containing five processing paths will require $5 + 5 + 5 + 5$ (20) tests plus one for the program as a whole once the modules are tested, whereas testing one program will require $5 \times 5 \times 5 \times 5$ (625) tests, because for each of the first five paths there will be five of the second, and so on.

Maintenance is also important because it is an activity that takes up much of the analysts' and programmers' time. Maintenance can involve the update of programs whose requirements have changed, as well as the correction of programs that do not work properly. Maintenance will be made easier by the good documentation and good design, which comes from the software engineering approach. The person making the changes will find that the software will be easier to understand because of the documentation. Further, as the program has been split into separate modules each performing a particular task, it will be easy to locate the relevant module and change it as appropriate. These changes will not affect other modules unexpectedly.

It is essential to use good control techniques to ensure that the implementation schedule for software is reasonable. Otherwise, the users and management will be unhappy about the system even if the requirements definition and software design work is first class, because expectations, which proved to be unrealistic, are dashed. A good methodology for the construction of software will be amenable to project control techniques. Breaking a system down into its parts makes estimating easier and more accurate.

As mentioned above, a major aspect of control is the ability to measure software complexity, size of task, and so on. In this way it will be possible to assess how long the software task should take and how many people should be involved and therefore be able to plan the whole process. Software metrics has become an important element of the software engineering school. Risk analysis, that is estimating the degree of uncertainty surrounding the metrics, has also become increasingly important.

Another aspect of control is ensuring the high quality of software. This implies that software is well tested; that standards, including those about documentation, have been applied; that it proves maintainable; that it is efficient; and that it meets the specification. There are now a number of official British, Australian, and international standards relating to software.

The term software engineering, therefore, is often used to cover much more than simply the design of computer programs. This is the view of many of the writers of texts on software. However, in this text the term is used to refer to the development of quality software. The wider 'environmental' issues are the concern of information systems.

In this text we are interested in producing quality information systems. We regard software engineering as a skill, which improves program design and thereby makes software, an important element of computer information systems, more effective once implemented, and easier to maintain.

A software engineering phase is usually part (though sometimes not explicitly stated) of an information system development methodology, and is explicitly part of structured approaches. Areas such as the following lie outside the scope of software engineering:

■ understanding the problem area;

■ understanding the needs of the user;

■ looking at alternatives;

■ deciding whether a computer system is needed.

If a computer system is recommended, then there will be a software engineering phase. However, the skills of software engineering should be separated from those required for information systems analysis and design. Further, it is important that the requirements of the analyst are expressed to the technologists in a way that the technologist can appreciate, and this provides one impetus in the movement toward the techniques of structured systems analysis and design which parallel, to some extent at least, those in software engineering.

9.2 AUTOMATED TOOLS

We now turn to a number of themes that relate to the overall theme of automation of the information systems development process and a greater emphasis on the software part of the information system. Here we provide some background. Part 5 of this book is devoted to a detailed look at the facilities of modern tools. The hope of automating some aspects or even all of the information systems development process is an abiding one, and has intrigued developers for many years. It has often been recognized that certain aspects of the information systems development process are repetitive or rule-based and therefore susceptible to automation. Early examples include decision table software which could generate accurate code directly from a decision table (Section 12.3), project control packages (Section 17.4) to help organize and control the development process, and toolsets (Chapter 18) to help speed up some common programming tasks. On the analysis side, software has existed for many years to help in the construction of traditional programming flowcharts.

Yet, it has often been noted by users that computer professionals have been very keen to automate everybody else but have shown a certain reticence to 'take their own medicine'. Apart from innate conservatism, there appear to have been a variety of reasons for this: some of the software was not very good or easy to use; it was often found that the benefits were outweighed by the effort and costs involved; and the technology was also a limiting factor.

Recently, some of these factors have changed. The technology is clearly more powerful, cheaper, and widely available. Improved graphics facilities have also had an impact. The quality of the software has improved, and in general there is a growing climate of opinion that automated tools may be beneficial.

There are now a number of tools that support the analysis and design process. These are tools that help the user use the techniques described in Part 4, such as data flow diagrams, entity models, and so on. They are sometimes described as documentation support tools, being designed to take the drudgery out of revising documents, because they make the implementation of changes very easy. In addition, they can contribute to the accuracy and consistency of diagrams. The diagrammer can, for example, cross-check that levels of data flow diagrams are accurate and that terminology is consistent. They can ensure that certain documentation standards are adhered to. Probably the greatest benefit is that analysts and designers are not reluctant to change diagrams, because the change process is simple. Manual redrawing is not satisfactory, not just because of the effort involved but the potential of introducing errors in redrawing. Many a small change required by a user was never incorporated into the system due to the effort required to redraw all the documentation. These kinds of documentation tool have proved both practical and useful so that the change process is not now inhibited.

Tools supporting the use of single techniques have, however, also proved limited in the sense that much of the information required for a data flow diagram, for example, would also be required, in a slightly different form, for the process logic software, and so on. It was realized that it would make more sense to have a central repository of all the information required for the development project irrespective of its graphical representation. In fact, this is the data dictionary, or perhaps as it is more correctly known, because it contains information about processes as well as data, the systems dictionary, systems encyclopaedia, or systems repository (Section 18.1).

Once most of the information concerning a development project is on a data dictionary, it is in theory only a short step to the automation, or at least the automated support, of many of the stages of the development project. Further, one of the goals of a number of methodologies is to provide automated support for all their stages. Some have the automatic generation of code as the end result of the automation of the information systems development process.

More modern software tools include:

- graphical facilities for modelling and design;
- data dictionary;
- automated documentation;
- code generation from systems specification or from the models designed using the tool;
- automatic audit trail of all changes;
- critical path scheduling with resource availability (i.e. project control);
- automatic enforcement of the standards of a chosen software development methodology.

It is important that these facilities are completely integrated (Chapter 18) so that they provide consistency in analysis and design. They are particularly effective in this regard if they are associated with a particular methodology.

Perhaps it is appropriate to provide a few warning bells in relation to tools. They are said to reduce the skill, complexity, time, error, and maintenance associated with the development of information systems. However, many are modest in their facilities. Typically, they help people to draw diagrams, such as entity-relationship diagrams and data flow diagrams, and perform validation checks. Many of the more sophisticated tools are very costly in terms of price, but also in terms of training and support. They may also be appropriate for use with only one methodology, which ties the users to that approach and also may make updates (as the methodology is updated) both essential and expensive.

COMPONENT DEVELOPMENT

In this section we consider component development, discussing **open source software** as the main example. According to Feller and Fitzgerald (2002), the term was coined in 1998 having previously being known as free software. Although the Linux operating system, the Perl programming language, and other complete products are frequently associated with open source software, we are particularly focusing here on the adoption of open source components. Here, people have free access to the code, and this software can be used by anybody as a component of their own aggregate software freely. Collections of routines are publicly available, frequently downloadable from the web, to help build applications. 'Free' is confusing here. It does not necessarily mean that the user does not pay the supplier a fee!

These components include drivers (e.g. for networks and audio applications), system utilities (e.g. emulation, file, graphics, and back-up components), Internet utilities (e.g. file transfer and log analysis), software development software (e.g. build tools and code generators, debuggers), and games, security, and database components, among others. It is notable that most of the systems development components focus on implementation, rather than analysis and design, aspects. There are numerous sources of these components, though IBM, Red Hat, and Cosource are major players.

Feller and Fitzgerald (2002) draw attention to the frequent use of object-oriented languages as being 'not too surprising, as object-orientation supports modular development and component-based reuse'. The modularity of much open source code enables it to be integrated with other code relatively easily. There are also Perl (a programming language) modules available for database interfaces, user interfaces, internationalization, security, compression, and interface modules to commercial software.

Another interesting aspect of open source in the context of this book is the software development process in this environment. Frequently, software is developed by different individuals and groups in parallel. Even though not working on the same project with the same company nor following a standard project management approach, the peer review taking place leads to better debugging and speed of development as well as the more obvious cost advantage of this approach. Peer review is also provided by users who are seen as co-developers. Because of the independent peer review and prompt feedback, open source software can be very robust. This is partly due to the process, but equally due to the spirit in which the process is undertaken: there is a great sense of community felt by open source software developers along with cultural norms (Raymond 2001).

Outside the community itself, developers use open source software to support their development work, users use these products both directly and indirectly (perhaps adapting them for their own particular use), and companies adopt, publicize, and distribute open source software.

However, though we have concentrated on open source as an exemplar, it is certainly not the only basis for component development. For example, Microsoft supports component development but perhaps not in an open source environment. The object management group, which suggests standards for object development, also supports the approach. The use of components avoids 'reinventing the wheel'. Component-based development requires assembly of components (both already available in libraries, from other applications, and new ones), adaptation, and integration. Again this approach may reduce cost, increase speed of development, increase consistency between and within applications, increase reliability, and, in general terms, increase the quality of software.

9.4 DATABASE MANAGEMENT

A large collection of books owned by the local council is not a public library. It only becomes one when, among other things, the books have been catalogued and cross-referenced so that they can be found easily and used for many purposes and by many readers. Similarly, a database is more than a collection of data. It has to be organized and integrated. It is also expected to be used by a number of users in different ways. In some companies the whole organization is modelled on a database, so that, in theory at least, users can find out any information about any aspect of the organization by making enquiries using the database.

In order to make this feasible, there needs to be a large piece of software which will handle the many accesses to the database. This software is the database management system (DBMS). The DBMS will store the data and the data relationships on storage devices. It must also provide an effective means of retrieval of that data when the applications require it, so that this important resource of the business, the data resource, is used effectively. Efficient data retrieval may be accomplished by computer programs written in conventional computer programming languages accessing the database. It can also be accomplished through the use of a query language, such as SQL, or in other ways which are more suitable to people who are not computer experts. In this section we discuss both the potential facilities of a DBMS and the data retrieval methods to access the data on the database using the DBMS.

Figure 9.3 represents a potential architecture for a database system. It has three views of the database: external, conceptual, and internal views.

The external view is the view of the data as 'seen' by application programs and users. It will be a subset of the conceptual model, which is a global or organizational view of the data. There may be a number of different user views, and different users and programs may share views. In the diagram, two users share the same view (External View 2), but their methods of accessing the data are different. This arrangement enables aspects of the database to which a user may not be interested or does not have rights of access to be hidden from that user. This reduces the complexity from the users' points of view. To enable this, there is a series of mappings or transformations between the external views and the conceptual view, which is handled by the DBMS software.

The conceptual view here is different to the conceptual models referred to in Section 10.3. Readers have been warned about the non-standard terminology in information systems! Indeed, the conceptual view expressed in this model is normally that of the

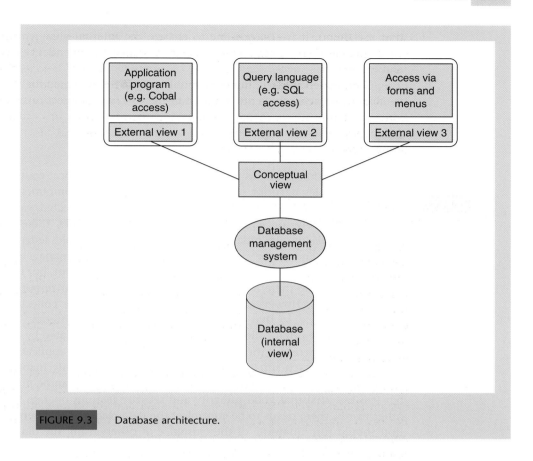

FIGURE 9.3   Database architecture.

entity models described in Section 11.1. In these sections, we describe techniques providing a global data model. The conceptual model discussed in this section is the data model of the organization. It describes the whole database for the organization (or community of users), which could be in terms of entities, attributes, and relationships.

The internal view of the data describes how and where the data are stored. It describes the access paths to the data storage and provides details of the data storage. Again there is a mapping between the conceptual and internal views. The latter will not be of direct interest to the users, but will be of indirect interest in terms of speed of access and the general efficiency of database use. It will be of direct interest to the database administrator (see below) who is normally responsible, among other things, for the efficient organization and effective use of the database.

There is a series of mappings from the conceptual view (the overall data model) to the various external views (the subsets of the data which applications or users have access to) and to the internal view (the way in which the data are organized on computer storage devices). These mappings will be carried out by the database management system software.

The separation of different views of the data enables data independence, which is a crucial element in the database approach. This means that it is possible to change the conceptual view without changing the external views (and the application programs that use them). It is also possible to change the internal view without changing the conceptual and external views. In other words, data independence provides flexibility and efficiency.

Data independence represents only one of the hoped-for advantages of the database approach, which are outlined in the following subsections:

1 Increase data shareability

Large organizations, such as insurance companies, banks, local councils, and manufacturing companies have for some time been putting large amounts of data onto their computer systems. Frequently the same data were being collected, validated, stored, and accessed separately for a number of purposes. For example, there could be a file of customer details for sales order processing and another for sales ledger. This 'data redundancy' is costly and can be avoided by the use of a database management system. In fact some data duplication is reasonable in a database environment, but it should be known, controlled, and be there for a purpose, such as the efficient response to some regular database queries. However, the underlying data should be collected only once, and verified only once, so that there is little chance of inconsistency. With conventional files, the data are often collected at different times and validated by different validation routines, and therefore the output produced by different applications could well be inconsistent. In such situations the data resource is not easily managed and this leads to a number of problems. With reduced redundancy, data can be managed and shared, but it is essential that good integrity and security features operate in such systems. In other words, there needs to be control of the data resource. Furthermore, each application should run 'unaware' of the existence of others using the database. Good shareability implies ready availability of the data to all users. The computer system must therefore be powerful enough so that performance is good even when a large number of users are accessing the database concurrently.

2 Increase data integrity

In a shared environment, it is crucial for the success of the database system to control the creation, deletion, and update of data and to ensure their correctness and 'up-to-dateness'; in general, to ensure the quality of the data. Furthermore, with so many users accessing the database, there must be some control to prevent failed transactions leaving the database in an inconsistent state. However, this should be easier to effect in a database environment, because of the possibilities of central management of the data resource (through the database administrator), than one where each application sets up its own files. Standards need only be agreed and set up once for all users.

3 Increase speed of implementing applications

Applications ought to be implemented in less time, since systems development staff can concentrate largely on the processes involved in the application itself, rather than on the collection, validation, sorting, and storage of data. Much of the data required for a new application may already be held in the database, put there for another application. Accessing the data will also be easier because the data manipulation features of the database management system will handle this.

4   Ease data access by programmers and users

Early database management systems used well-known programming languages, such as Cobol and Fortran, to access the database. Cobol, for example, was extended to include new instructions, which were used when it was necessary to access data on the database. These 'host language' extensions were not difficult for experienced computer programmers to learn and to use. Later came query languages and other methods to access the data, which eased the process of applications development and data access in a database environment. Once the database had been set up, applications development time should be greatly reduced.

5   Increase data independence

We have already introduced this, but it has many aspects. It is the ability to change the format of the data, the medium on which the data is held and the data structures, without having to change the programs which use the data. Conversely, it also means that it is possible to change the logic of the programs without having to change the file definitions, so that programmer productivity is increased. It also means that there can be different user views of the data even though they are stored only once. This separation of the issues concerning processes from the issues concerning data is a key reason for opting for the database solution.

6   Reduce program maintenance

Stored data will need to be changed frequently as the real world that it represents changes. New data types may be added, formats changed, or new access methods introduced. Whereas in a conventional file environment all application programs that use the data will need to be modified for each of these changes, the data independence of a database environment, discussed above, circumvents this. It is necessary only to change the database and the data dictionary (or systems repository), which will contain information about the data in the database (among other things). We discuss these in Section 18.1.

7   Provide a management view

With conventional systems, management does not get the benefits from the expensive computing resource that it has sanctioned. However, managers have become aware of the need for a corporate view of their organization. Such a view requires data from a number of sections, departments, divisions, and sometimes companies in a large organization. This corporate view cannot be obtained if files are established on an application-by-application basis and not integrated as in a database. With decision-support systems using the database, it becomes possible for problems previously considered solvable only by intuition and judgement to be solved with an added ingredient, that of information, which is timely, accurate, and presented at the required level of detail. Some of this information could be provided on a regular basis, while some will be of a 'one-off' nature. Database systems should respond to both requirements.

8   Improve standards

In traditional systems development, applications are implemented by different project teams of systems analysts and programmers, but it is difficult to apply standards and conventions for all applications. Computer people are reputed to dislike following the general norms of the organization, and it is difficult to impose standards where applications are developed piecemeal. With a central database and database management systems, it is possible to impose standards for file creation, access, and update, and to impose good controls, enabling unauthorized access to be restricted and providing adequate back-up and security features.

Much of the success or failure of a DBMS lies in the role of the **database administrator** (DBA), who will be responsible for ensuring that the required levels of privacy, security, and integrity of the database are maintained. The DBA could be said to be the manager of the database and, because the design of the database involves trade-offs, will have to balance conflicting requirements and make decisions on behalf of the whole organization, rather than on behalf of any particular user or according to a particular departmental objective. The role is multi-varied and is usually carried out by a database administration team. In some organizations, the information resource is regarded as one of the key elements of success (which it surely must be) and there is a high-level data administration function that includes the lower level database administration team, responsible for the computer data. In some organizations, the board includes a chief information officer.

There are many database management systems available. These include Oracle and Access, both of which are discussed in Part 5. Some of these run on large computers, others on PCs. Most DBMSs are relational or object-oriented (or a combination of the two). In a relational DBMS, the data model that the user sees is the relational one (i.e. sets of tables). In an object-oriented database management system, the data management and programming language aspects are integrated: all data is represented as objects and the programming language manipulates objects.

Of particular interest to users developing systems in a database environment is the way in which access can be made to the database. We will now turn our attention to this aspect of DBMSs. Data access may be made using soft-copy forms, menus, conventional computer languages, and query languages. Many DBMSs provide alternative ways of access. This can be a useful facility as there are many types of user. Users can be untrained and intermittent in their use of the system. These casual users should be encouraged by its ease of use. Regular users may make frequent, perhaps daily, use of the database and are usually willing to learn a simple syntax. Other users will be professional users who are computer people and will apply their long experience as computer and database users. They may be more concerned about efficiency considerations than ease of use.

As reference to Figure 9.3 makes clear, the external view of the database is that which each user 'sees'. It is derived from the conceptual view. The external view is the subset of the database which is relevant to the particular user, and, although it may be a summarized and a very restricted subset, the user may think that it represents the whole view, because it is the whole view as far as that user is concerned. The presentation and sequence of the data will also suit the context in which they are presented. The format will depend on the particular host language, query language, report writer, or other software used. Indeed, there may well be several external views, perhaps as much as one per application or user that accesses the database. But whatever the description given to the user, the underlying data will be the same.

Of particular importance in the context of this book is the use of a DBMS as a tool to develop applications. If we assume data to be key to an application, then their input, validation, storage, and retrieval form the basis of information provision to support decision making. Along with different ways to provide information (from formal languages, such as SQL, to display formats, such as query by example, through to natural language), Access, for example, enables the development of programs using VisualBasic, which can be used by 'interested users' as well as 'experts'.

9.5   SUMMARY

- Software engineering concerns the use of sound engineering principles, good management practice, applicable tools, and methods for software development.

- There are a number of tools that support tasks in the analysis and design process. There are also integrated toolsets that support many tasks.

- Information systems can be developed from components. These include drivers, Internet utilities, software development software, security, and database components.

- Open source components with the source code open to change are available so that adaptability for the application is facilitated.

- A database is an organized and integrated collection of data. A database management system is software that validates, stores, secures, displays, and prints the data in ways that the users require.

QUESTIONS

1 What is the difference between software engineering and information systems engineering? Is one merely a subset of the other? In that case, which is the subset?

2 What are the differences between software packages and open source components?

3 What is the difference between a database system and a knowledge management system?

9.6 FURTHER READING

Avison, D.E. and Cuthbertson, C. (2002) *A Management Approach to Database Applications*, McGraw-Hill, Maidenhead, UK.

Brown, A.W. (ed.) (1996) *Component-Based Software Engineering*, IEEE Computer Society, Los Alamitos, California.

Feller, J. and Fitzgerald, B. (2002) *Understanding Open Source Software Development*, Addison-Wesley, Harlow, UK.

Pressman, R.S. (2000) *Software Engineering: A Practitioner's Approach*, 5th edn, McGraw-Hill, London.

Raymond, E.S. (2001) *The Cathedral and the Bazaar: Musings on Linux and Open Source by an Accidental Revolutionary*, O'Reilly, Sebastobal, California.

TECHNIQUES

We have chosen to describe techniques in Part 4 separately for two reasons: first, most are common to more than one methodology and therefore to leave them to Part 6 (on methodologies) would lead to repetition there, and, second, so that the principles contained in the methodologies can be described without going into the techniques used in too much detail. Although the techniques described are used in a number of methodologies, this does not mean that they are interchangeable because, as used in any particular methodology, they could address different parts of the development process, be used for different purposes, or be applicable to different objects. More obviously, but less fundamentally, they often use different diagrammatic conventions to show the same things.

Again, we have attempted to group techniques into categories suggested by chapter headings. Some are straightforward, others less obvious, and could either be

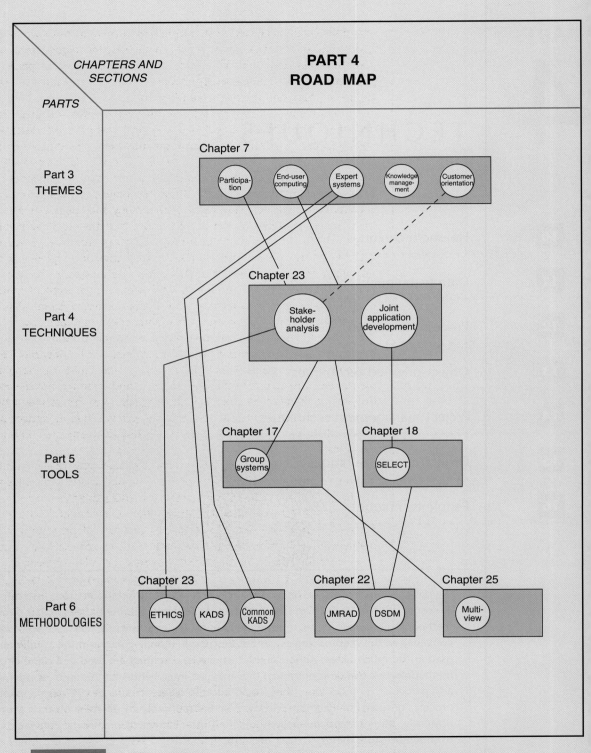

**PART 4
ROAD MAP**

Part 3
THEMES

Chapter 7

Participa-tion   End-user computing   Expert systems   Knowledge manage-ment   Customer orientation

Part 4
TECHNIQUES

Chapter 23

Stake-holder analysis   Joint application development

Part 5
TOOLS

Chapter 17

Group systems

Chapter 18

SELECT

Part 6
METHODOLOGIES

Chapter 23

ETHICS   KADS   Common KADS

Chapter 22

JMRAD   DSDM

Chapter 25

Multi-view

DIAGRAM 2   People techniques 'road map' (shows relationships between people techniques *and* themes, tools, and methodologies).

in another category or even a category of their own! As in Part 3 we show a 'road map' of the relationships between themes, techniques, tools and methodologies but this time from the perspective of a particular technique. In this example we use people techniques and show the links to themes, tools and methods (see Diagram 2).

In Chapter 10 the holistic techniques of rich pictures, root definitions, conceptual models, and cognitive mapping are described. They help to understand the problem situation being investigated by the analysts. The first three originated in Checkland's Soft Systems Methodology, but have been incorporated into other approaches, for example, Multiview. Increasingly, these techniques are being used by analysts who may be following a methodology that does not include them 'officially' as part of that approach, but nevertheless prove helpful, particularly in the early stage of a project. Rich pictures are particularly useful as a way of understanding the problem situation in general at the beginning of a project; root definitions help the analyst to identify the human activity systems they are to deal with; and conceptual models show how the various activities in the human activity system relate to each other. Cognitive mapping is used in the SODA methodology.

Entity modelling and normalization are fundamental and common to many methodologies and are described in Chapter 11. Entity modelling and normalization are techniques for analysing data. Equally fundamental, but process-oriented, are data flow diagrams, and these are introduced in Chapter 12. Many of the other techniques described in this chapter, which can be categorized as process logic, analyse processes in some respect, and these include decision trees, decision tables, structured English, and action diagrams.

Structure diagrams and matrices are used in all walks of life as well as in many information systems development methodologies and frequently at different stages in a methodology. Structure diagrams show hierarchical structures, be it a computer program, that to represent relationships between people in a department, or the structure of processing logic. Matrices show the relationship between two things, for example, entities and processes, departments and documents, or roles of people and processes. The last technique of this chapter is the entity life cycle. The technique of entity life cycle analysis is also common to a number of methodologies. The entity life cycle is not, despite its name, a technique of data analysis. We have categorized it as being a technique of process analysis, though its main aspect is that it shows how an entity changes over time. Perhaps it should have had a category of its own: time-oriented techniques!

On the other hand, object-oriented techniques (Chapter 13) can represent data and processes, indeed the same technique can represent just about everything to do with the information system. It is not surprising, therefore, that the approach has attracted so much interest over the years, even though the more traditional data and process-oriented techniques are still widely used.

We discuss three project management techniques in Chapter 14. These are linked to the project management theme and PRINCE in the methodology section. In Chapter 15 we discuss organizational techniques. These are used by management to understand the organization: its strategy, environment, and to facilitate decision making in this context. Lateral thinking includes a series of techniques aimed at problem solving. Identifying critical success factors is a commonly used technique to ensure the most important benefits of a new information system are achieved. Scenario planning, future analysis, and SWOT analysis are techniques used to identify possible outcomes in the environment. Case-based reasoning uses the experience of previous cases to inform decision making. Risk analysis techniques attempt to make known and reduce the risks associated with investments.

Finally, people techniques include stakeholder analysis to identify all the stakeholders of an information systems project and joint application workshops, where all these stakeholders or their representatives are involved in analysis and design of the information system. We use this as the basis for our road map. We can see how the themes of participation and end-use development, for example, are connected to stakeholder analysis and joint application development. There is a connection to the tool GroupSystems. This supports group decision making, so could well enhance a JAD session. ETHICS is a methodology that has been designed to emphasize people aspects.

10 HOLISTIC TECHNIQUES

10.1 RICH PICTURES

The analysis of such factors as interfaces, boundaries, subsystems, the control of resources, organizational structure, roles of personnel, organizational goals, employee needs, issues, problems, and concerns are not all contained in other techniques but are of importance in systems development. Understanding political aspects is essential for successful information systems. A high percentage of failure is due to ignoring these issues. When constructing a rich picture diagram such issues are taken into consideration.

An understanding of what the organization is 'about' need not take a diagrammatic form. It could be a mental map of some sort. We describe a possible diagrammatic form for rich pictures but we use the term rich picture rather than rich picture diagrams.

The technique stems from Checkland's Soft Systems Methodology (Section 24.1), and the description here is based on that used in Multiview (Avison and Wood-Harper, 1990). A rich picture diagram is a pictorial caricature of an organization and helps explain what the organization is 'about'. The rich picture should be self-explanatory and easy to understand.

One may start to construct a rich picture by looking for elements of structure in the problem area. This includes things like departmental boundaries, activity types, physical or geographical layout, and product types. Having looked for elements of structure, the next stage is to look for elements of process, that is, 'what is going on'. These include the fast-changing aspects of the situation: the information flow, the flow of goods, and so on.

The relationship between structure and process represents the 'climate' of the situation. Very often an organizational problem can be tracked down to a mismatch between an established structure and new processes formed in response to new events and pressures.

The rich picture should include all the important hard 'facts' of the organizational situation, and the examples given have been of this nature. However, these are not the only important facts. There are many soft or subjective 'facts' which should also be represented, and the process of creating the rich picture serves to tease out the concerns of the people in the situation. These soft facts include the sorts of thing that the people in the problem area are worried about, the social roles which the people within the situation think are important, and the sort of behaviour which is expected of people in these roles.

Representing the situation in terms of 'information systems needed' should be discouraged at this stage. These should come once the analysis has been carried out. Again, the question is not 'what systems does a manager think exist?', but rather 'what systems can be described in the situation?'. A 'system' in this sense is not about hardware and software but is a perceived grouping of people, objects, and activities which it is meaningful to talk about together.

Typically, a rich picture is constructed first by putting the name of the organization that is the concern of the analysis into a large 'bubble', perhaps at the centre of the page. Other symbols are sketched to represent the people and things that interrelate within and outside that organization. Arrows are included to show these relationships. Other important aspects of the human activity system can be incorporated. Any symbols can be used which are appropriate to the specific situation. We use crossed swords to indicate conflict and the 'think' bubbles indicate the worries of the major characters.

In some situations it is not possible to represent the organization in one rich picture. In this case, further detail can be shown on separate sheets. The perceived relative importance of people and things could be reflected by the size of the symbols on any one rich picture.

Figure 10.1 represents a rich picture for a professional association. We will use this case study in the description of rich pictures. The work concerning the case had three phases: an initial study, a full requirements analysis, and, finally, the development of some of the computer applications, including a computer system that handled some of the association's examinations.

The initial study was requested in correspondence from the secretary of the association. This was a top post in the organization. She felt that many of the systems ought to be computerized and she wished to know the type of computerization that would be appropriate for the situation, and whether the association should establish its own computer system or outsource (Section 8.3). The professional association is a professional body initiated for people working in or attempting to enter a particular profession. The current administrative system was purely manual. All the functions were under the control of the secretary. The education subsystem was administered by an education secretary.

The sorts of application included membership administration, examination administration, and tuition administration, requiring information about subjects, tutors, and fees. It was found that the workload at peak times of the year was becoming too demanding, membership was growing rapidly, and the administration and accounts occupied much of the time of the senior management, particularly that of the secretary.

Figure 10.1 represents an early draft of part of the rich picture of this human activity. If it has been well drawn; you should get a good idea of who and what is

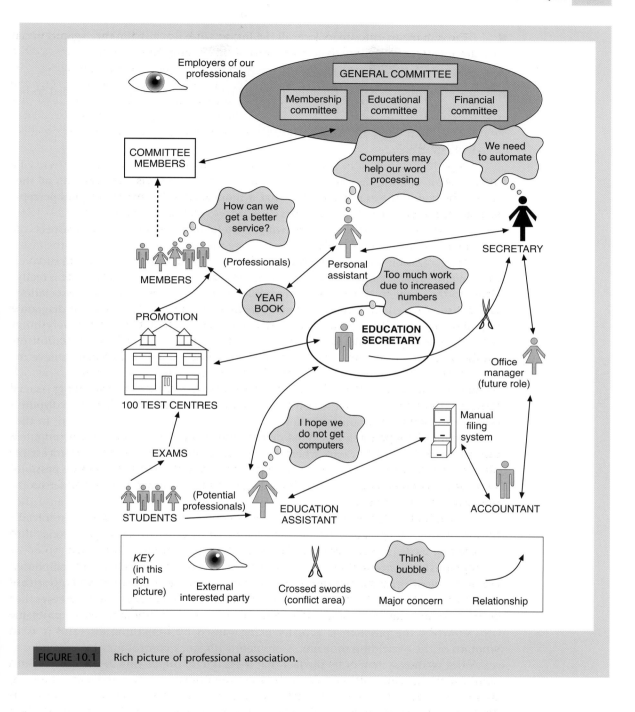

FIGURE 10.1   Rich picture of professional association.

central to the organization and what are the important relationships. Bear in mind that there is no such thing as a 'correct' rich picture. Drawing the rich picture is a subjective process.

The act of drawing a rich picture is useful in itself because:

- lack of space on the paper forces decisions on what is really important (and what are side issues or points of detail for further layers of rich pictures);
- it helps people to visualize and discuss their own role in the organization;
- it can be used to define the aspects of the organization which are intended to be covered by the information system;
- it can be used to show up the worries of individuals, potential conflicts, and political issues.

Differences of opinion can be exposed, and sometimes resolved, by pointing at the picture and trying to get it changed so that it more accurately reflects people's perceptions of the organization and their roles in it.

Once the rich picture has been drawn, it is useful in identifying two main aspects of the human activity system. The first is to identify the primary tasks. These are the tasks that the organization was created to perform, or which it must perform if it is to survive. Searching for primary tasks is a way of posing and answering the question: 'What is really central to the problem situation?' For example, it could be argued that the association aims to give an excellent service to its members (which might be implied by the diagram) or increase standards in its profession (which is not implied by the diagram). Everything else is carried out to achieve that end. Primary tasks are central to the creation of information systems, because the information system is normally set up to achieve or support that primary task.

The second way that the rich picture is of particular value is in identifying issues. These are topics or matters which are of concern. They may be the subject of dispute. They represent the (often unstated) question marks hanging over the situation. In the association, they might include: 'What do we hope to achieve by installing a computer system?' This was a major issue when the systems analysis was done. This process of identifying the issues will lead to some debate on possible changes. It might be possible for these issues to be resolved at this stage, but it is essential that they are understood. Issues are important features, as the behaviour resulting from them could cause the formal information system to fail. Unless at least some of them have been resolved, the information system will have little chance of success. In some situations, the issues can be more important than the tasks.

The analyst starts by looking at an unstructured problem situation. This emphasis on the 'problem situation' as opposed to the 'problem' is important. By looking at the problem, rather than the whole situation, it will be difficult to be able to tell whether the diagnosis of the problem is correct. All too often a client will say, 'I am having a problem with X', when the problem is actually being caused by something else and X is a symptom of the overriding problem. A problem with stock control may be caused by a weak stock records system or by the fact that there is a lot of pilfering. If the analysts are limited to the official statement of the problem, then these 'real' causes may never be uncovered. It is therefore necessary for analysts to keep eyes, ears, and minds open and avoid jumping to early conclusions about the 'problem'.

There are a number of ways in which analysts get drawn into the problem situation and a number of roles that they may be called on to play. It is important that their role and their relationship with other people in the problem situation have been well defined and well explained. Whether an external consultant, a member of the internal IT department, a representative of the supplier, or a friend giving advice, it is important to think about the roles of the client, problem owner, and problem solver.

The rich picture can help the owners of the problem sort out the fundamentals of the situation, both to clarify their own thinking and decision making and also to explain these fundamentals to all the interested parties. The rich picture becomes a summary of all that is important in the situation. An analysis of the rich picture will help in the process of moving from 'thinking about the problem situation' to 'thinking about what can be done about the problem situation'.

In the example, the problem owner in the association shown in the rich picture is the general committee of the association. The analysts found that there was conflict between the secretary and the committee for whom she acted, on how best to serve the organization in its overall goal of improving the standards of the profession. The secretary, who was the client, was expected to become the system user.

As the study was under way, the role of the education secretary became more important. He was responsible for the professional examinations, and this system became the focal point of later analysis. There was a real conflict between the secretary and the education secretary regarding how and what to automate (hence the crossed swords in the rich picture). As the education secretary became a more powerful stakeholder and the analysts homed in on the examination system, he became the client. Therefore, he is central in the rich picture shown as Figure 10.1. At the time of the first part of the investigation, it was the secretary who was central.

The building shape in the left of the picture represents the one hundred test centres. It is important to draw attention to the difficulties of handling the examinations. The role of 'students', on the bottom left of the picture, changes from wanting to be professionals to 'members' who ask 'how can we get better service' once they have passed the examination at the test centre and have entered the profession.

Other stakeholders are also included in the rich picture. Developing further the theme of computerization, some actors were less positive about the prospect. The education assistant, an important actor in the examination system, thought that computerization might reduce her status and the think bubble contains 'I hope we do not get computers'. To jump a few steps, the actual system that was implemented in this situation was not a complete success, and, in retrospect, more attention should have been paid to her views. As one of the main persons involved, her misapprehension about the 'system' should have been addressed more fully.

We have included the accounting system in our rich picture. The accountant, bottom right of the picture, was satisfied with this manual filing system at the time of the investigation, but it would be looked at in the future.

In drawing the rich picture, some things have been left out which are understood by the participants but which would not be assumed by an outsider. One of these is the social roles of the people in the association and the sort of behaviour which is expected of people in these roles. Sometimes footnotes are useful to describe or list these. A second aspect is in the level of detail. The complexity of the marking system and other regulations for admission to the association, with which the stakeholders were familiar and well understood, could not be gleaned by an outsider looking at the rich picture. A second rich picture, drawn at a greater level of detail, would help here. Rich pictures can be 'decomposed' into others of greater detail. On the other hand, alternative techniques might be more appropriate at this level of detail.

With the analysts coming in as outside consultants, it was important that these 'assumptions' are drawn out. The approach adopted here was for the analyst to ask the users for a detailed explanation of a complex situation. Where a team of analysts is available, they can be divided so that different sorts of question can be asked: those relating to management strategy, those relating to data, and those relating to people's roles. The rich picture, once drawn up, proved a very useful communication tool in this situation and was refined according to new information. No thought is given at this stage to possible solutions. One of the purposes of drawing a rich picture diagram is to avoid 'design before analysis'.

The simplicity of the final rich picture is achieved by pruning the answers so that there is as much agreement as possible and so that the final picture really does represent the important people, activities, and issues of the problem situation.

Although this technique has been used by many analysts, it is not as well used as, for example, entity-relationship diagrams or data flow diagrams. The technique may not seem as formal as others and therefore may not have the credibility with managers who may also wish to avoid their political issues being disclosed and debated. Proponents of rich pictures might argue, however, that this is not because of any weakness of the approach, but partly because of a lack of knowledge about them and partly because systems analysts are not prepared to spend enough time on analysis and rush to the design and development phases.

10.2 ROOT DEFINITIONS

The second technique originating from SSM, root definitions, can be used to define two things that are otherwise both vague and difficult. These are problems and systems. It is essential for the systems analyst to know precisely what human activity system is to be dealt with and what problem is to be tackled. The technique also originated from SSM and descriptions here are based on the Multiview approach.

The root definition is a concise verbal description of the system which captures its essential nature. Each description will derive from a particular view of reality. To ensure that each root definition is well formed, it is checked for the presence of six characteristics. Put into plain English, these are *who* is doing *what* for *whom*, and to whom are they *answerable*, what *assumptions* are being made, and in what *environment* is this happening? If these questions are answered carefully, they should tell us all we need to know.

There are technical terms for each of the six parts, the first letter of each forming the mnemonic **CATWOE**. We will change the order in which they appeared in our explanation to fit this mnemonic:

- *client* is the 'whom' (the beneficiary, or victim, affected by the activities);
- *actor* is the 'who' (the agent of change, who carries out the transformation process);
- *transformation* is the 'what' (the change taking place, the 'core of the root definition');
- *Weltanschauung* (or world view) is the 'assumptions' (the outlook which makes the root definition meaningful);

- *owner* is the 'answerable' (the sponsor or controller);

- *environment* remains the 'environment' (the wider system of which the problem situation is a part).

The word *Weltanschauung* may be new to many readers. It is a German word that has no real English equivalent. It refers to 'all the things that you take for granted' and is related to our values.

The first stage of creating the definition is to write down headings for each of the six CATWOE categories and try to fill them in. This is not always easy because we often get caught up in activities without thinking about who is really supposed to benefit or who is actually 'calling the tune'. We may question our assumptions and look around the environment even more rarely.

Even so, the difficulty for the individual in creating a root definition is less than the difficulty in getting all the individuals involved to agree on a usable root definition. Only experience of such an exercise can reveal how different are the views of individuals about the situation in which they are working together.

In trying to create the root definition for the professional association's examination system as part of the case study, the following process was followed. Initially, what were thought of as the issues and primary tasks were identified. These represented the things that the users were concerned about:

- efficient administration and management of the examinations system;

- choosing a solution which would not mitigate against the association's other systems, such as membership records management and accounting;

- building up a good reputation for the association.

Within this were identified three major components which are called the relevant systems. In the case study, the issues and primary tasks could largely be resolved by the following relevant systems:

- administration and management system;

- communication and motivation system;

- information provision system.

These relevant systems are subsystems to support a higher system which is to maintain and improve the reputation of the profession by ensuring high standards of entry into the profession.

The working root definition created was:

> A system owned and operated by the professional association to administer the examinations by registering, supervising, recording, and notifying students.

In the case when it was necessary to write the root definition, there was particular difficulty about the client. At first the obvious client was the secretary, but on further analysis the view was that the real client was the education secretary. Yet, as a computer solution became very likely, the person exercising power proved to be the treasurer, a member of the financial committee who would only give his consent to purchase a computer system if it was a particular brand. This happened to be that which he was experienced at using and one which the analysts felt later was inappropriate to the examinations system. There was little that the analysts could do about this political infighting, but at least they were aware of the problem.

It is sometimes difficult to produce a rigorous root definition because of these political or other problems. Sometimes it is impossible to resolve differences. However, unless they are resolved, they may be a source of difficulties later.

The CATWOE criteria were used to check and revise the above root definition as follows:

- *customers* – members of the association, the secretary, education secretary, and treasurer;

- *actors* – the association, its members, students attempting to join, and its full-time staff;

- *transformation* – to provide examinations which will ensure entry at the right level to the profession;

- *Weltanschauung* – the view that computer systems would be efficient and effective if they were used in this domain;

- *owners* – the general committee of the association (representing members of the association);

- *environment* – the particular profession.

Thus the first use for the root definition is to clarify the situation. People involved in an enterprise have very different views about that enterprise. These views are frequently at cross purposes. Not everyone, for example, thought that computer systems would be efficient and effective. This holds true even when the same words are used to describe things. This is because the differences are usually in the unstated assumptions or different perceptions of the environment. More significantly, there are sharp differences of opinion about whose problem the analysts are trying to solve, that is, who is the owner and who is the customer. It may not be possible to resolve differences of opinion and one root definition – a preferred root definition – might be chosen from the alternatives and used as a basis to develop the information system further.

Root definitions are particularly useful in exposing different views. We will look at an information system for a hospital to illustrate this. The different people involved in a hospital will look at the system from contrasting positions. Furthermore, these viewpoints in this problem situation are very emotive as they have moral and political overtones. In some situations this can lead to deliberate fudging of issues so as to avoid controversy. This is likely to cause problems in the future. Even if the differences cannot be resolved, it is useful to expose them.

Here are three different root definitions of a hospital system. They all represent extreme positions. In practice, anyone trying to start such a definition would make some attempt to encompass one or more of the other viewpoints, but any one of these could be used as the starting point for the analysis of the requirements of an information system in a hospital.

We will first look at the problem situation from the point of view of the patient, presenting a possible CATWOE and root definition (Figure 10.2).

THE PATIENT

CLIENT	Me
ACTOR	The doctor
TRANSFORMATION	Treatment
WELTANSCHAUUNG	I've paid my taxes so I'm entitled to it
OWNER	'The system' or maybe 'the taxpayer'
ENVIRONMENT	The hospital

A hospital is a place that I go to in order to get treated by a doctor. I'm entitled to this because I am a taxpayer, and the system is there to make sure that taxpayers get the treatment they need.

The perception of the doctors will be different:

THE DOCTOR

CLIENT	Patients
ACTOR	Me
TRANSFORMATION	Treatment (probably by specialized equipment, services, or nursing care)
WELTANSCHAUUNG	It is important to treat as many people as possible within a working week.
OWNER	Hospital administrators
ENVIRONMENT	National Health Service (NHS) vs Private practice. My work vs My private life

A hospital is a system designed to enable me to treat as many patients as possible with the aid of specialized equipment, nursing care, etc. Organizational decisions are made by the hospital administrators (who ought to try treating patients without the proper facilities) against a background of NHS politics and my visions of a lucrative private practice and regular weekends off with my family.

The views of the hospital administrators are likely to be different still:

THE HOSPITAL ADMINISTRATOR

CLIENT	Doctors
ACTOR	Me
TRANSFORMATION	To enable doctors to reduce waiting lists
WELTANSCHAUUNG	Create a bigger hospital within cash limits
OWNER	The government department of health
ENVIRONMENT	Politics

A hospital is an institution in which doctors (and other less expensive staff) are enabled by administrators to provide a service which balances the need to avoid long waiting lists with that to avoid excessive government spending. Ultimate responsibility rests with the government and the environment is very political.

FIGURE 10.2   Examples of CATWOE and root definitions from various perspectives.

We could therefore develop three sets of very different information systems depending on the view taken. The patient would have the system centred around patients' health records, the doctor would have the system designed around clinic sessions, and the administrator around the accounts.

These definitions have been deliberately controversial, but they attempt to show the private views of the participants as well as their publicly stated positions. There is no reason why definitions need to be formal and cold. Wilson (1990) carries out a similar exercise concerning the prison system. Dependent on the view taken, among other possibilities, the prison system could be seen as a:

■ punishment system;

■ society protection system;

■ behavioural experiment system;

■ criminal training system;

■ mailbag production system;

■ people storage system;

■ exclusive storage system.

These contribute to the eventual primary task definition:

A system for the receipt, storage and despatch of prisoners.

The alternative root definitions (briefly expressed above) indicate the difficulty of reconciling different viewpoints, and yet, if one is not agreed, it will be even more difficult to agree on final information systems needs. However, without looking at these wider views, information systems might be developed on the basis of a single (client's) view of the problem situation. Information systems are designed to serve the needs of people, and analysts are always brought directly into contact with power struggles between individuals and between viewpoints. Analysts have to make decisions, consciously or unconsciously, about which particular view of the situation or combination of views to work from. One option is to attempt to be 'scientifically detached', but this is only one of the options and is difficult to achieve in reality. In any case, such an aim would seem to be in conflict with the 'philosophy' of root definitions. We cannot be 'objective'.

In some Scandinavian countries there are laws or public agreements which state that the views of the workers or their representatives have to be sought and clearly represented at all stages in the analysis, design, and implementation of computer-based systems. In the USA the analysts usually focus on the opinion of the people who have commissioned them or are the senior people in that situation. Many analysts argue that they are making 'objective' decisions, innocent of any prejudice, but these may be based on personal and political assumptions that are never made explicit. The process described in this section should help to avoid this pitfall.

The system of communications is likely to be easier in smaller firms. The manager of a small firm contemplating a PC system may find this process rather long-winded and unnecessary. Nevertheless, the undercurrent in a small business can be just as political.

10.3 CONCEPTUAL MODELS

Rich picture diagrams and root definitions, and the investigation and analysis preceding their construction, give an overall view of the organization. It also provides some key definitions of the purposes to be furthered by the information system. To complete the analysis of the human activity system (following SSM and Multiview), we need to build a model which shows how the various activities are related to each other, or at least how they ought logically to be arranged and connected. This is called a conceptual model. (Unfortunately, the term conceptual model is used in some other methodologies to refer to entity modelling.)

If the analysis of the human activity system is to be helpful to the organization, then it will show any discrepancies between what is happening in the real world and what ought to be happening. This may lead to changes in the organization of human activities. The purpose of the information system is to improve things, not just to 'automate or re-automate the status quo', although, as we saw in Chapter 3, many computer information systems do little more than this. So, once conceptual models are constructed, we will have a model of the required activities, which will serve as the foundation for the information model and a set of recommendations for an improved human activity system.

What do we mean by a conceptual model and what is it for? Perhaps these questions are best explained by analogy. When architects design a building they must produce two things: first, a set of artist's impressions and a scale model to show the client what is proposed and, second, a set of plans for the builder. Together these constitute the model. They will enable the builder to say how much it will cost and how long it will take and will represent all that needs to be created for the parties concerned to decide whether to go ahead with that design, modify it, or to choose an alternative.

The model serves three purposes:

- it is an essential element in the architects' design activities;
- it is a medium of communication between architects and clients to enable the right design to be selected;
- it is a set of instructions to the builders.

In computing, we also try to create models, which will serve these three purposes, but the process is not so well known, or so well tried and tested, as it is in construction. As we will see in this chapter and on looking at the various methodologies in Part 6, there are probably in use almost as many ways of describing a proposed system as there are design teams. This creates problems for users and designers as they try to understand what is being proposed.

In information systems development there is no clear-cut distinction between artist's impressions and the engineer's blueprints. There is not one version of the model for the user and another version for the computer programmer. Some may argue that this would be a valid goal, but, furthering our analogy, artist's impressions are notoriously optimistic and vague about difficulties and engineer's blueprints are very difficult to interpret by all but the trained. It is not satisfactory for the untrained to have to accept the statement: 'trust us, we're the experts'.

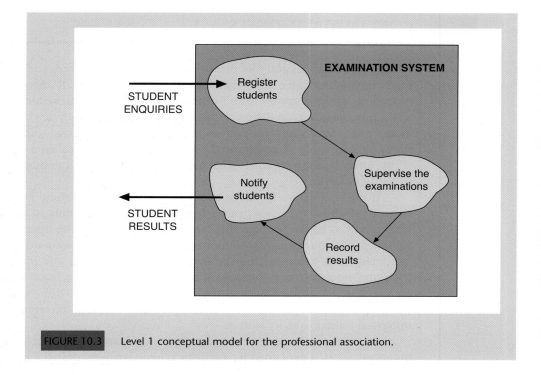

Level 1 conceptual model for the professional association.

This means that the users and the builder of the information system must both understand the conceptual model. Of course, the information represented on a model can be complex, but the real world it represents is also complex.

Returning to the case study used for illustrative purposes in the previous two sections, the main activities of the examinations system, and consequently the information to support these activities prior to computerization, is shown in Figure 10.3.

The conceptual model is formed from the chosen root definition as follows:

1. Form an impression of the system to carry out a physical or abstract transformation from the root definition.

2. Assemble a small number of verbs that describe the most fundamental activities in the defined system.

3. Develop this by deciding on what the system has to do, how it would accomplish the requirement, and how it would be monitored and controlled.

4. Structure similar activities in groups together.

5. Use arrows to join the activities which are logically connected to each other by information, energy, material, or other dependency.

6. Verify the model by comparing it against the perceived reality of the problem situation.

The conceptual model shown as Figure 10.3 was derived from the root definition which was, for the professional association:

A system owned and operated by the professional association to administer the examinations by registering, supervising, recording, and notifying students.

We start by taking significant aspects from the root definition and naming subsystems which will enable us to achieve what we require. These are the subsystems to register students, supervise the examinations, record the results, and notify the students.

So as to ensure that the most useful subsystems have been identified and understood, they are described in more detail in words and diagrammatically. In other words, there is a second layer in the conceptual model set which looks the same as the top layer, but is at a more detailed level. In other words, the technique lends itself to functional decomposition (as do many of the techniques described in this chapter).

In order to get agreement between problem solver and problem owner on these systems, it is important to ensure that there is a mutual understanding of the real-world meaning of the terms. It is necessary, for example, for the analyst to get to know what is involved in registering students (vetting enquiries and selecting potential students for registration, which is at the Level 2 conceptual model, shown as Figure 10.4) in order to understand that subsystem. As we have said above, the analyst is only concerned with 'what is conceptually necessary'. It does not matter, for example, how the enquiries are received, how the forms are sent out to be completed, or which member of staff deals with them.

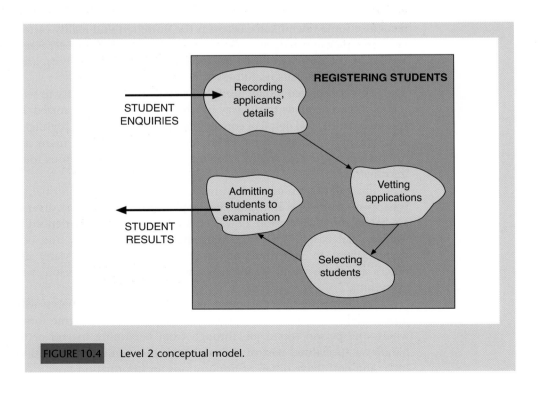

FIGURE 10.4 Level 2 conceptual model.

The conceptual model is derived from the root definition. It is a model of the human activity system. Its elements are therefore activities and these can be found by extracting from the root definition all the verbs that are implied by it. The list of active verbs should then be arranged in a logically coherent order.

We would expect the number of activities to be somewhere in the range of five to nine. Activities should be grouped to avoid a longer list, as a long list is too complicated and messy to deal with. A shorter list suggests that the root definition is too broad to be useful. Having listed the major activities, some of these may imply secondary activities. These should also be listed and arranged in logical order around their primary activities and will form Level 2 conceptual models.

Conceptual modelling is an abstract process. Following soft systems methodology (Section 24.1) the purpose of going into this abstract world of systems thinking is to develop an alternative view of the problem situation. When this alternative view has been developed, we can return to the real world and test the model. It is constructed in terms of what must go into the system, and it can therefore be set alongside the real world. We are not concerned here with how the system will be implemented. Other techniques will be used to determine this aspect.

The conceptual model illustrates what ought to be happening to achieve the objectives specified in the root definition. There is normally more than one way of doing something and so choices will have to be made about the structure of the conceptual model. Many systems analysts adopt a very positivistic approach. An inexperienced analyst may put a flowchart in front of the user and ask: 'Is this right?' Users who may have had many years of coping with 'messy' reality may well be reluctant to answer so positively. They might wish to respond: 'Yes, but ...' or 'No, but ...'. Unfortunately the politics of the situation may be such that they may be forced to say 'yes' if they recognize some resemblance between the flowchart and reality. Alternatively they may be left to 'pick at the details'. One of the problems that the user faces is the inappropriateness of the flowcharts used in conventional systems analysis, and a strength of the conceptual model is its usefulness as a communication tool.

This conceptual model needs to be compared with reality to see whether improvements should be made to the way in which activities are organized. For example, in the second or third level detail of conceptual models, they might highlight bottlenecks, such as too many small decisions waiting for the manager or too many assistants waiting to use the same price catalogue. They may also show up circuitous routes for transferring information.

In small organizations, information handling is very informal, everyone sees what is happening or works alongside the people who know. As work diversifies and more staff are taken on, information flow is based around the experienced staff who become 'walking databases'. Such an arrangement can then ossify and become increasingly dysfunctional to new functions and new personalities. Many apparently efficient offices are thrown into disarray by the loss of the one person 'who seems to know everything'.

In comparing the conceptual model with reality the analyst will ask the question: 'Does the information flow smoothly?' There are two extreme forms of organization: where one person sees a job through from beginning to end or where each person handles a specialized part of the work. Of course, most organizations have aspects of each, and both have different implications for information flow.

Many factors must be taken into account when matching functions to staff. These include the capabilities and aspirations of staff, the demands of different aspects of the business, and the need for management to keep control of what is going on. A number of these might change if a computer system were to be introduced. The conceptual model can be used as a technique for thinking about how subsystems should be organized in order to achieve the purposes set out in the root definition. Questions can be asked about which subsystems should be linked together and whether they can be handled more efficiently if they are kept separate.

The conceptual model can also be used in the design of new human activity systems, such as the setting up of a new company or department, because it shows what activities should be carried out and how they should be related to each other.

The techniques of rich pictures, root definitions, and conceptual models will be explored further in the context of SSM (Section 24.1) and Multiview (Section 25.1).

10.4 COGNITIVE MAPPING

There are techniques and methodologies designed to make sense out of situations that are variously described as complex, uncertain, confusing, wicked, and messy. For example, rich pictures are one technique used in soft systems methodology, among other approaches, to attempt to understand complexity in organizations. Cognitive mapping is a technique used in SODA, which we discuss in Section 25.2. Some of these techniques come from the management science community but are to some extent a reaction by more systemic thinkers such as Checkland, Mingers, Rosenhead, and others against the prevalent mathematical and optimizing techniques used in operations research. Our description of cognitive mapping is based on the work of Eden and Ackerman (2001).

A cognitive map is a model of the 'system of concepts' used to communicate the nature of a problem, and the concepts are related to others through an action orientation. In effect these maps show short statements (ideas, facts, circumstances, assertions, and proposals) relating to the problem situation linked by arrows showing their interrelationships; that is, how one idea might lead to or have implications for another. But it is the totality of the cognitive map that provides the most understanding. It is seen as a formal modelling technique with rules for its development. Cognitive maps can often be quite large with over 100 nodes, and they can be merged, finishing up with over 800 nodes. There is a software tool called Decision Explorer, which can be used with teams doing cognitive mapping. It draws maps, identifies clusters of nodes, and in its Group Explorer mode enables group work. Like most tools discussed in the book, it can increase productivity, but is not essential to using the technique.

The example, shown as Figure 10.5, comes from the work of Eden and Ackerman (2001), which explores the following quote about the Labour political party in the UK by Jane McLoughlin in the *Guardian* newspaper in 1986:

> The latter-day Labour party, aiming to appeal upmarket, is in a more ambivalent position. At a time when they are looking for a concordat with the unions, union opposition to profit sharing – because of the fear of collective bargaining – is hard

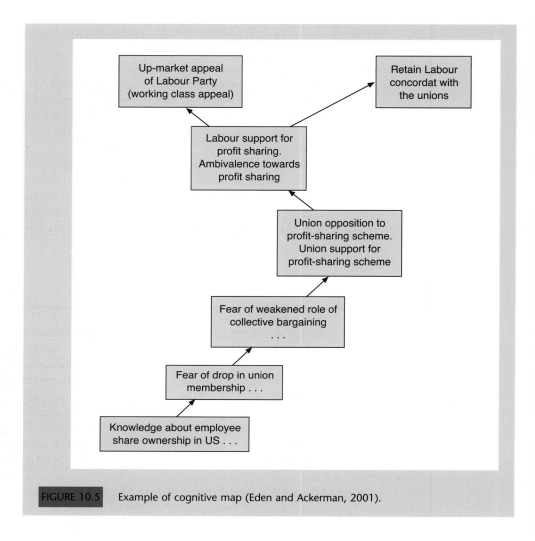

FIGURE 10.5 Example of cognitive map (Eden and Ackerman, 2001).

to avoid. American experience with employee share ownership plans since the early 1980s has led to a drop in union membership in firms with these profit sharing schemes.

The cognitive map captures important phrases which represent contrasting ideas. So, at the top of the map, upmarket appeal is contrasted with concordat with the unions. The arrows show the links between the arguments. However, the cognitive map attempts to reflect the need for action (or problem-solving) orientation, so both the words might be changed and the order of representation to reflect this, but not, of course, the meaning. Figure 10.6 shows a development of this map following a merger with another.

Each of the ideas expressed by individuals are converted to short statements in the cognitive map that are action or problem solving-oriented through a series of short interviews or discussions. The arrows connect options to desired outcomes, with the highest levels in the hierarchy expressing important goals. However, the map should

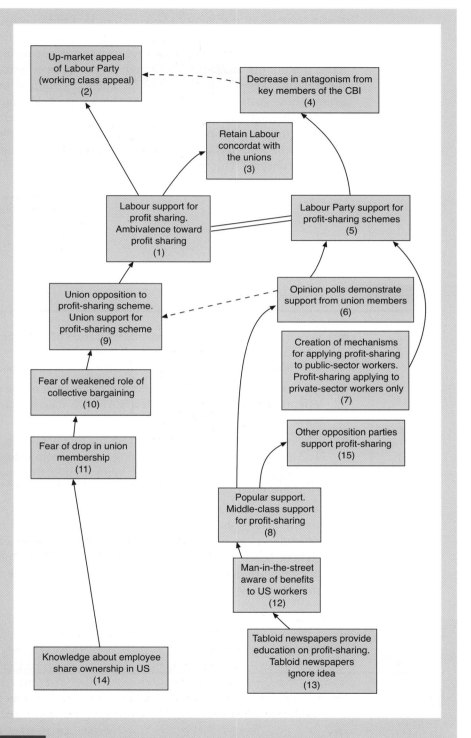

FIGURE 10.6 Development of cognitive map (Eden and Ackerman, 2001).

remain in terms of the clients' thinking, not that of the consultant. The clients should still own it and regard it as a fair representation of the situation as they see it.

The process of drawing a cognitive map therefore encourages working through the detail toward the major goals through exploration or starting with the goals and, through interviews with the client or clients, elaborate on the detail that might achieve those goals (referred to as 'laddering up' or 'laddering down', respectively).

Usually, separate cognitive maps are drawn for each client, thus reducing the possibility of 'group think', and these are merged to form that of clients as a whole and tuned so that all the team feel committed to achieving the portfolio of actions, not just their particular concerns. This will require some political astuteness and conciliation skills on behalf of the consultant.

10.5 SUMMARY

- A rich picture diagram is a pictorial caricature of an organization and helps explain what the organization is 'about'. It can represent 'soft' information representing the 'fuzziness' of many problem situations as well as 'hard' facts.

- The root definition is a concise verbal description of the system which captures its essential nature. It should reflect CATWOE (client, actor, transformation, world view, owner, and environment).

- The conceptual model is derived from the root definition. Its elements are activities and these can be found by extracting from the root definition all the verbs that are implied by it. The list of active verbs should then be arranged in a logically coherent order.

- A cognitive map is a model of the 'system of concepts' used to communicate the nature of a problem, and the concepts are related to others through an action orientation. In effect these maps show short statements (ideas, facts, circumstances, assertions, and proposals) relating to the problem situation linked by arrows showing their interrelationships. But it is the totality of the cognitive map that provides the most understanding.

QUESTIONS

1 When would you use rich pictures, root definitions, conceptual models, and cognitive maps?

2 For an organization of your choice represent appropriate information in rich pictures, root definitions, conceptual models, and cognitive maps.

10.6 FURTHER READING

Checkland, P. and Scholes, J. (1990) *Soft Systems Methodology in Action*, John Wiley & Sons, Chichester, UK.

11 DATA TECHNIQUES

11.1 ENTITY MODELLING

The theme of data modelling has been discussed in Section 5.3. Data modelling concentrates on the analysis of data in organizations and entity modelling is an important technique used to achieve this in many methodologies, including SSADM, Merise, and Information Engineering.

Just as an accountant might use a financial model, the analyst can develop an entity model. The entity model is just another view of the organization, but it is a particular perception of the organization which emphasizes data aspects. Systems analysis in general (data analysis is a branch of systems analysis) is an art or craft, not an exact science. There can be a number of ways to derive a reasonable model and there are a number of useful data models (there are, of course, an infinite number of inadequate models).

A model represents something, usually in simplified form, that highlights aspects which are of particular interest to the user, and is built so that it can be used for a specific purpose, for example, communication and testing.

An entity-relationship model views the organization as a set of data elements, known as entities, which are the things of interest to the organization, and relationships between these entities. This model helps the computer specialist to design appropriate information systems for the organization, but it also provides management with a unique tool for perceiving aspects of the business. The essence of problem solving is to be able to perceive the complex, 'messy', real world in such a manner that the solution to any problem may be easier. This model is 'simple' in that it is fairly easy to understand and to use.

Each entity can be represented diagrammatically by soft boxes (rectangles with rounded corners). Relationships between the entities are shown by lines between the soft boxes. A first approach to an entity model for an academic department of computer science is given in Figure 11.1. The entity types are student, academic staff, course, and

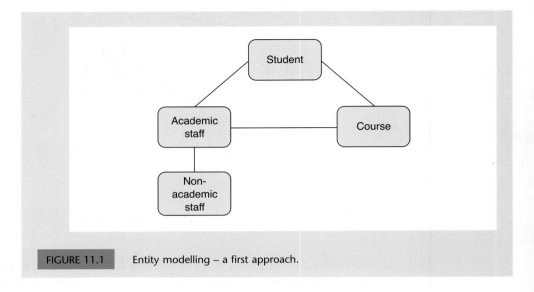

FIGURE 11.1   Entity modelling – a first approach.

non-academic staff. The entity type 'student' participates in a relationship with 'academic staff' and 'course'. The relationships are not named in Figure 11.1, but it might be that 'student' takes a 'course' and that 'student' has as tutors 'academic staff'. The reader will soon detect a number of important things of interest that have been omitted (room, examination, research, and so on). As the analysts find out more about the organization, entity types and relationships will be added to the model.

A mistake frequently made at this stage is to define the entities to reflect the processes or departments of the business, such as stock control, credit control, or sales order processing. This could be a valid model of the business but it is not an entity model and cannot be used to develop a database for the organization. Data analysis differs from conventional systems analysis in that it separates the data structures from the applications which use them. The objective of data analysis is to produce a flexible data model which can be easily adapted as the requirements of the organization change. Although the applications will need to be changed, this will not necessarily be true of the data.

The entity model is sometimes referred to as the conceptual schema or conceptual model. However, in order to avoid confusion with Checkland's conceptual models described in Section 10.3 (an entirely different model) we will use the terms 'entity model' or 'data model'.

One technique of data analysis is the entity-relationship (E-R) model, the real-world information is represented by entities and by relationships between entities. In a typical business, the entities could include jobs, customers, departments, and suppliers. The analyst identifies the entities and relationships between them before being immersed in the detail, in particular, the work of identifying the attributes which define the properties of entities.

Figure 11.2 relates to part of a hospital. The entities described are 'doctor', 'patient', and 'clinical session'. The relationships between the entities are also described. That between doctor and patient and between doctor and clinical session are one-to-many relationships (depicted by the crow's feet). In other words, one doctor can have many patients, but a patient is only assigned one doctor at a particular point in time. Further, a

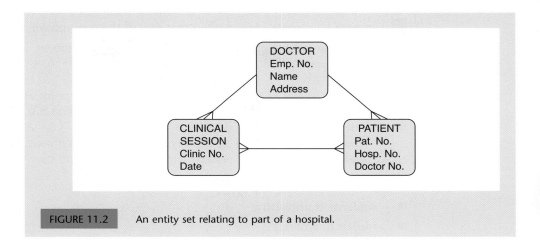

FIGURE 11.2   An entity set relating to part of a hospital.

doctor can be responsible for many clinical sessions, but a clinical session is the responsibility of only one doctor. The other relationship is many-to-many. In other words, a patient can attend a number of clinical sessions and one clinical session can be attended by a number of patients. A one-to-one relationship would be shown by a line without crow's feet.

The diagram may also shows a few attributes of the entities. The particular attribute or group of attributes that uniquely identify an entity occurrence is known as the key attribute or attribute(s). The 'employee number' (Emp. No.) is the key attribute of the entity called doctor.

The technique attempts to separate the data structure from the functions for which the data may be used. This separation is a useful distinction, although it is often difficult to make in practice. In any case, it is sometimes useful to bear in mind the functions of the data analysed. A doctor and a patient are both people, but it is their role, that is what they do, that distinguishes the entities. The distinction, formed because of a knowledge of functions, is a useful one to make. However, too much regard to functions will produce a model biased toward particular applications or users and is therefore to be avoided.

Another practical problem is that organization-wide data analysis may be so costly and time-consuming that it is often preferable to carry out entity analysis at a 'local' level, such as in the marketing or personnel areas. If a local entity analysis is carried out, the model can be mapped on to a database and applications applied to it before another local data analysis is started. This is far more likely to gain management approval because managers can see the expensive exercise paying dividends in a reasonable timescale. An important preliminary step is therefore to define the area for analysis and break this up into distinct subareas which can be implemented on a database in turn and merged later. Local data analysis should also be carried out in phases. The first phase is an overview which leads to the identification of the major things of interest in that area. At the end of the overview phase, it is possible to draw up a second interview plan and the next, longer, phase aims to fill in the detail.

Although it is relatively easy to illustrate the process of modelling in a book or at a lecture, in real life there are problems in deciding how far one should go and what level of detail is appropriate. The level of detail must serve two purposes:

1 It must be capable of explaining that part of the organization being examined.

2 It must be capable of being translated into a physical model, usually for mapping onto a computer database.

It is important to realize that there is no logical or natural point at which the level of detail stops. This is a pragmatic decision. Certainly, design teams can put too much effort into the development of the model.

Some decisions are based on the way in which the data is used. An example of this could be entity occurrences of persons who are female, where they relate to:

- patients in a hospital;
- students at university;
- readers in a library.

In the patient example, the fact that the person occurrence is female is important, so important that the patient entity may be split into two separate entities, male patients and female patients. In the student example, the fact that the person is female may not be of great significance and therefore there could be an attribute 'sex' of the person entity. In the reader example, the fact that the person is male or female may be of such insignificance that it is not even included as an attribute. There is a danger here, however, as the analyst must ensure that it will not be significant in all applications in the library. Otherwise the data model will not be as useful.

An entity is a thing of interest in the organization, in other words it is anything about which we want to hold data. It could include all the resources of the business, including the people of interest such as EMPLOYEE, and it can be extended to cover such things as SALES-ORDER, INVOICE, and PROFIT-CENTRE. Some entities are obvious physical things, like customers or stock. Others are transactions, like orders, sales, and hospital admissions. Some entities are more or less artificial. These are rather like catalogue entries in the library: the only reason to have them is to help people find books which would otherwise be difficult to locate. It covers concepts as well as objects. A SCHEDULE or a PLAN are concepts which can be defined as entities. An entity is not data itself, but something about which data should be kept. It is something that can have an independent existence, that is, can be distinctly identified.

In creating an entity model, the aim should be to define entities that enable the analyst to describe the organization. Such entities as STOCK, SALES-ORDER, and CUSTOMER are appropriate because they are quantifiable, whereas 'stock control', 'order processing', and 'credit control' are not appropriate because they are functions: what the organization does, and not things of interest which participate in functions. Entities will normally be displayed in small capitals in this book. Entities can also be quantified – it is reasonable to ask 'how many customers?' or 'how many orders per day?', but not 'how many credit controls?'. An entity occurrence is a particular instance of an entity which can be uniquely identified. It will have a value, for example, 'Jim Smith & Son' and this will be a particular occurrence of the entity CUSTOMER. There will be other occurrences, such as 'Plowmans PLC' and 'Archd Tower & Co.'.

An **attribute** is a descriptive value associated with an entity. It is a property of an entity. At a certain stage in the analysis it becomes necessary not only to define each entity but also to record the relevant attributes of each entity. A CUSTOMER entity may be defined and it will have a number of attributes associated with it, such as 'number', 'name', 'address', 'credit-limit', 'balance', and so on. Attributes will normally be displayed within single inverted commas in this book. The values of a set of attributes will distinguish one entity occurrence from another. Attributes are frequently identified during data analysis when entities are being identified, but most come later, particularly in detailed interviews with staff and in the analysis of documents. Many are discovered when checking the entity model with users.

An entity must be uniquely identified by one or more of its attributes, the **key attribute**(s). A <u>customer number</u> may identify an occurrence of the entity CUSTOMER. A <u>customer number</u> and a <u>product number</u> may together form the key atribute of entity SALES-ORDER. The key attribute functionally determines other attributes, because once we know the customer number we know the name, address, and other attributes of that customer. Key attributes will normally be underlined in this book.

There often arises the problem of distinguishing between an entity and an attribute. In many cases, things that can be defined as entities could also be defined as attributes, and vice versa. We have discussed one example relating to the sex of people. The entity should have importance in the context of the organization, otherwise it is an attribute.

In practice, the problem is not as important as it may seem. Most of these ambiguities are settled in the process of normalization (Section 11.2) and this often happens in database design. In any case, the analyst can change the model at a later stage, even when mapping the model onto a database, though the earlier the analyst gets it right the better. Entities are used by functions of the organization and the attributes are those data elements that are required to support the functions. The best rule of thumb is to ask whether the data has information about it; in other words, does it have attributes? Entities and attributes are further distinguished by their role in events (discussed below).

A **relationship** in an entity model normally represents an association between two entities. A SUPPLIER entity has a relationship with the PRODUCT entity through the relationship – supplies; that is, a SUPPLIER *supplies* PRODUCT. There may be more than one relationship between two entities; for example, PRODUCT *is assembled by* SUPPLIER. Relationships will normally be displayed in italics in this book. A relationship normally arises because of:

1. Association, for example CUSTOMER *places* order.
2. Structure, for example ORDER *consists of* order-line.

The association between entities has to be meaningful in the context of the organization. The relationship has information content, for example, CUSTOMER *places* ORDER. The action '*places*' describes the relationship between CUSTOMER and ORDER. The name given to the relationship also helps to make the model understandable. As will be seen, the relationship itself can have attributes.

The **cardinality** of the relationship could be one-to-one, one-to-many, or many-to-many. At any one time, a MEMBER-OF-PARLIAMENT can only represent one constituency, and one CONSTITUENCY can have only one MEMBER-OF-PARLIAMENT. A MEMBER-OF-PARLIAMENT *represents a* CONSTITUENCY. This is an example of a one-to-one (1:1) relationship. Figure 11.3 shows different conventions or notations of representing relationships found in methodologies. Very often, a one-to-one relationship can be better expressed

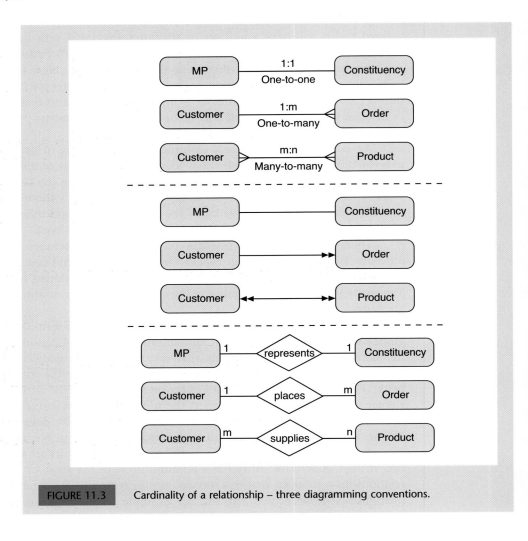

FIGURE 11.3   Cardinality of a relationship – three diagramming conventions.

as a single entity, with one of the old entities forming attributes of the more significant entity. For example, the entity above could be MEMBER-OF-PARLIAMENT, with CONSTITUENCY as one of the attributes.

The relationship between an entity CUSTOMER and another entity ORDER is usually of a degree one-to-many (1 : m). Each CUSTOMER can have a number of ORDERS, but an ORDER can refer to only one CUSTOMER: CUSTOMER *places* ORDER.

With a many-to-many (m : n) relationship, each entity can be related to one or more occurrences of the partner entity. A STUDENT can take many MODULES; and one MODULE could be taken by a number of STUDENTS (MODULE *is taken by* STUDENT; STUDENT *takes* MODULE).

In this last example (of a many-to-many relationship), entity occurrences of the STUDENT entity could be 'Smith', 'Jones', and 'Wilson', and they could take a number of modules each. For example, in Figure 11.4 Smith might take database, IS development, and expert systems; Jones might take database and IS development, and Wilson IS development and expert systems.

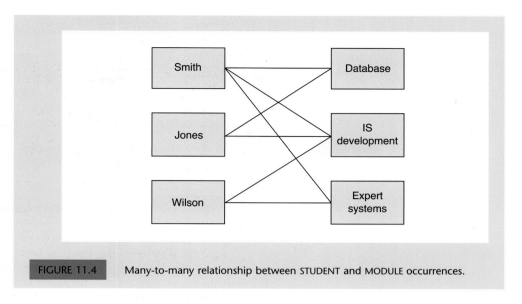

FIGURE 11.4 Many-to-many relationship between STUDENT and MODULE occurrences.

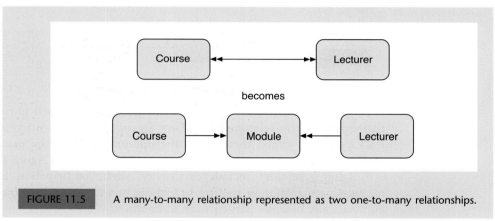

FIGURE 11.5 A many-to-many relationship represented as two one-to-many relationships.

Frequently there is useful information associated with many-to-many relationships and it is better to split these into two one-to-many relationships, with a third inter-mediate entity created to link them together. Again, this should only be done if the new entity has some meaning in itself. The relationship between COURSE and LECTURER is many-to-many, that is, one LECTURER *lectures on* many COURSES and a COURSE *is given by* many LECTURERS. But a new entity, MODULE can be described as used in the previous example which may only be given by one LECTURER and is part of only one COURSE. Therefore, a LECTURER *gives* a number of MODULES and a COURSE consists of a number of MODULES. But one MODULE *is given by* only one LECTURER and one MODULE is *offered to* only one COURSE (if these are the restrictions). This is shown in Figure 11.5.

There are other distinctions and sophistications which are often included in the model. Sometimes a 1 : m or an m : n relationship is a fixed relationship. The many-to-many relationship between the entity PARENT and the entity CHILD is 2 : m (that is, each child has two parents); but a PARENT *can beget* more than one CHILD.

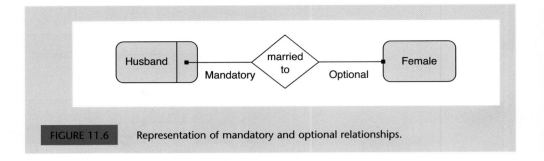

FIGURE 11.6   Representation of mandatory and optional relationships.

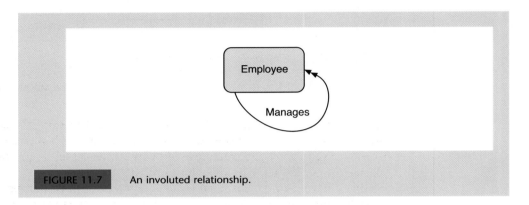

FIGURE 11.7   An involuted relationship.

While some relationships are mandatory, that is, each entity occurrence must participate in the relationship, others are optional. An entity MALE and an entity FEMALE may be joined together by the optional relationship '*married to*'. Mandatory and optional relationships may be represented as shown in Figure 11.6.

Other structures include exclusivity, where participation in one relationship excludes participation in another, or inclusivity, where participation in one relationship automatically includes participation in another.

A relationship may also be involuted where entity occurrences relate to other occurrences of the same entity. For an EMPLOYEE entity, for example, an EMPLOYEE entity occurrence who happens to be a manager *manages* other occurrences of the entity EMPLOYEE. This can be shown diagrammatically by an involuted loop, as in Figure 11.7. Some approaches suggest that these should be eliminated by creating two entities (MANAGER and EMPLOYEE in this case).

Any relationship is necessarily linked to at least one entity. We have already looked at the involuted relationship. Where a relationship is linked to two entities (as in the case of the examples in Figure 11.4), it is said to be binary. If a relationship is linked to three entities, as in Figure 11.8, it is said to be ternary. In this example, EMPLOYEE fulfils a ROLE, EMPLOYEE fulfils a CONTRACT, and ROLE fulfils a CONTRACT. Otherwise it is *n*-ary, with the value of *n* equalling the number of entities.

A good model is one that is a good representation of the organization, department, or whatever is being depicted. The process of entity modelling is an iterative process and slowly the model will improve as a representation of the perceived reality. The entity model can be looked on as a discussion document and its coincidence with the real

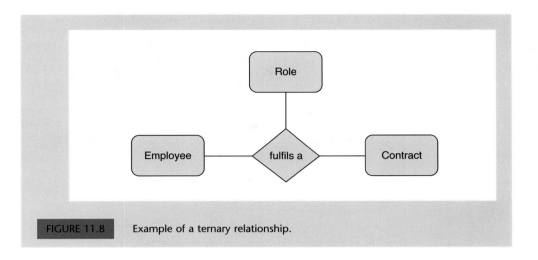

FIGURE 11.8 Example of a ternary relationship.

world is verified in discussions with the various users. However, the analyst should be aware that variances between the model and a particular user's view could be due to the narrow perception of that user. If a global entity model is built for a whole organization it is usual for entities to be grouped into important clusters.

Up to now, we have considered the data-oriented aspects of data analysis, but in practice it is useful for functional considerations to be made in order to check the model. These relate to events and operations. Entities have to support the **events** that occur in the enterprise. Entities will take part in events and in the operations that follow events. Attributes are those elements which supply data to support events.

'Tom' is an occurrence of the entity EMPLOYEE. Tom's pay rise or his leaving the company are events, and attributes of the entity EMPLOYEE will be referred to following these events. Attributes such as 'pay-to-date', 'tax-to-date', 'employment status', and 'salary' will be referred to.

Operations on attributes will be necessary following the event: an event triggers an operation or a series of operations. An operation will change the state of the data. The event 'Tom gets salary increase of 10 per cent' will require access to the entity occurrence 'Tom' (or EMPLOYEE-NUMBER '756') and augmenting the attribute 'salary' by 10 per cent. Figure 11.9 shows the entity EMPLOYEE expressed as a relation with attributes. We have to check that the relation supports all the operations that follow the event mentioned.

Some methodologies, for example, Merise (Section 20.2), also define the **synchronization** of an operation (Figure 11.10). This is a condition affecting the events which trigger the operation and will enable the triggering of that operation. This condition can relate to the value of the properties carried by the events and to the number of occurrences of the events. For example, the operation 'production of pay slips' may be triggered by the event 'date' when it equals '28th day of the month'.

Some readers may be confused by the discussion of events (sometimes called **transactions**), which are function-oriented concepts, when data analysis is supposed to be function-independent. The consideration of events and operations is of interest as a checking mechanism. They are used to ensure that the entity model will support the functions that may use the data model. This consideration of the events and operations

Employee

Emp. No.	Name	Status	Pay-to-date	Tax-to-date	Salary
756	Tom	Full	734.30	156.00	14000

Does the entity support the operations following events?
e.g. employee leaves the company
employee gets a pay rise

FIGURE 11.9   Event-driven (functional) analysis.

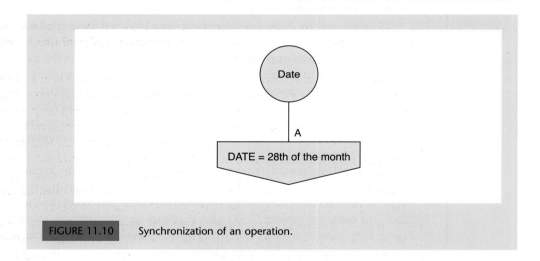

Date

A

DATE = 28th of the month

FIGURE 11.10   Synchronization of an operation.

may lead to a tuning of the model, an adjustment of the entities and the attributes. We will now look at the stages of entity analysis as a whole which are:

1   Define the area for analysis.

2   Define the entities and the relationships between them.

3   Establish the key attribute(s) for each entity.

4   Complete each entity with all the attributes.

5   Normalize all the entities.

6   Ensure all events and operations are supported by the model.

We have looked at all these elements apart from normalization which is briefly described below and discussed more fully in Section 11.2.

1 The first stage of entity analysis requires the definition of the area for analysis. This is frequently referred to as the **universe of discourse**. Sometimes this will be the organization, but this is usually too ambitious for detailed study, and as we have seen the organization will normally be divided into local areas for separate analysis.

Then we have the stages of entity-relationship modelling. It is a top-down approach in that the entities are identified first, followed by the relationships between them, and then more detail is filled in as the attributes and key attribute(s) of each entity are identified.

2 For each local area, then, the entities are defined. The obvious and major entities will be identified first. The analyst will attempt to name the fundamental things of interest to the organization. As the analyst is gathering these entities, the relationships between the entities can also be determined and named. Their cardinality can be one-to-one, one-to-many, or many-to-many. It may be possible to identify fixed relationships and those which are optional or mandatory. The analyst will be able to begin to assemble the entity-relationship diagram. The diagram will be rather sketchy, somewhat like a 'doodle' in the beginning, but it will soon be useful as a communication tool. There are computer software tools that can help draw up these diagrams and make alterations easily (see, for example, Section 17.3).

3 The key of each entity will also be determined. The key attributes will uniquely identify any entity occurrence. There may be alternative key attributes, in which case the most natural or concise is normally chosen.

4 The analyst has now constructed the model in outline and is in a position to fill in the detail. This means establishing the attributes for each entity. Each attribute will say something about the entity. The analyst has to ensure that any **synonyms** and **homonyms** are detected. A product could be called a part, product, or finished product depending on the department. These are all synonyms for 'product'. On the other hand, the term product may mean different things (homonyms), depending on the department. It could mean a final saleable item in the marketing department or a subassembly in the production department. These differences must be reconciled and recorded in the data dictionary (Section 18.1). The process of identifying attributes may itself reveal entities that have not been identified. Any data element in the organization must be defined as an entity, an attribute, or a relationship and recorded in the data dictionary. Entities and relationships will also be recorded in the entity-relationship diagram.

5 Each entity must be normalized once the entity occurrences have been added to the model. This process is described fully in Section 11.2. Briefly, the rules of normalization require that all entries in the entity must be completed (first normal form), all attributes of the entity must be dependent on all the key attributes (second normal form), and all non-key attributes must be independent of one another (third normal form). The normalization process may well lead to an increase in the number of entities in the model.

6 The final stage of entity analysis will be to look at all the events within the area and the operations that need to be performed following an event, and ensure that the model supports these events and operations. Events are frequently referred to as transactions. For this part of the methodology, the analyst will identify the events associated with the organization and examine the operations necessary on the trail of each of the events.

Events in many organizations could include 'customer makes an order', 'raw materials are purchased from supplier', and 'employee joins firm'. If, say, a customer makes an order, this event will be followed by a number of operations. The operations will be carried out so that it is possible to find out how much the order will cost, whether the product is in stock, and whether the customer's credit limit is OK. The entities such as PRODUCT (to look at the value of the attribute 'stock') and CUSTOMER (to look at the value of the attribute 'credit limit') must be examined. These attribute values will need to be adjusted following the event. You may notice that the 'product price' is not in either entity. To support the event, therefore, 'product price' should be included in the PRODUCT entity, or in another entity which is brought into the model.

Entity modelling has documentation like other methods of systems analysis. It is possible to obtain forms on which to specify all the elements of the data analysis process. The separate documents will enable the specification of entities, attributes, relationships, events, and operations. These forms can be pre-drawn using software tools and their contents automatically added to the data dictionary. We show the entity document as Figure 11.11.

As we have already stated, it may be possible to use completed documents directly as input to a data dictionary system so that the data are held in a readily accessible computer format as well as on paper forms. Entity modelling can be used as an aid to communication as well as a technique for finding out information. The forms discussed also help as an aid to memory, that is, communication with oneself. The entity-relationship diagrams, which are particularly useful in the initial analysis and as an overview of the data model, can prove a good basis for communication with managers and users. They provide a graphical description of the business in outline, showing what the business is, not what it does. Managers and users can give 'user feedback' to the analysts and this will also help to tune the model and ensure its accuracy. A user may point out that an attribute is missing from an entity, or that a relationship between entities is one-to-many and not one-to-one as implied by the entity-relationship diagram. The manager may not use this terminology, but the analyst will be able to interpret the comments made.

Data analysis is an iterative process: the final model will not be obtained until after a number of tries and this should not be seen as slowness, but care for accuracy. If the entity model is inaccurate so will be the database and the applications that use it. On the other hand, the process should not be too long or 'diminishing returns' will set in.

The entity-relationship diagram given in Figure 11.12 shows the entities for part of a firm of wholesalers. The attributes of the entities might be as shown in Figure 11.13.

The key attributes are underlined. Perhaps you would like to verify that you can understand something of the organization using this form of documentation. It is a first sketch of the business, and you may also verify the relationships, add entities and relationships to the model, or attributes to the entities, so that the model is more appropriate for a typical firm of wholesalers. For example, we have not included payments in this interim model.

ENTITY TYPE SPECIFICATION FORM

Entity name	*The standard name for the entity*
Description	*A brief description of the entity type*
Synonyms	*Other names by which the entity is known*
Identifier(s)	*Name of the key attribute(s) which uniquely identify the entity occurrences*

Date specified

Minimum occurrences *expected*   Maximum occurrences   *expected*

Average occurrences *expected*   Growth rate %   *over time*

Create authority	*The names of the users who are allowed to create the entity*
Delete authority	*The names of the users who are allowed to delete the entity*
Access authority	*The names of the users who are allowed to read the entity*

Relationships involved (cross reference)

As shown in the entity-relationship diagram

Attributes involved (cross reference)

Attributes which are found in other entities (to cross reference) different entities for access

Functions involved (cross reference)

Applications which require data contained in these and other entities

Comments

FIGURE 11.11   Entity documentation.

The entity-modelling approach to data analysis is often interview-driven, that is, most information is obtained through interviewing members of staff. It is also top-down, in that the entities are identified first and then more and more detail filled in. It has proved very useful and is included in many information systems development methodologies, as we shall see in Part 6. Methodologies usually have entity modelling preceding the process of normalization. This technique is described in the next section.

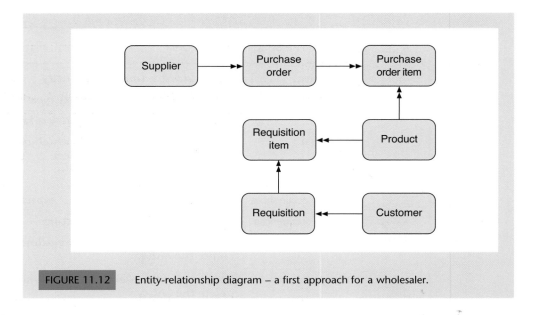

FIGURE 11.12   Entity-relationship diagram – a first approach for a wholesaler.

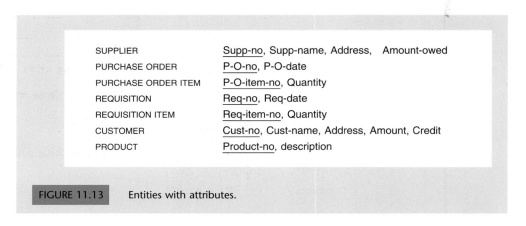

SUPPLIER	<u>Supp-no</u>, Supp-name, Address, Amount-owed
PURCHASE ORDER	<u>P-O-no</u>, P-O-date
PURCHASE ORDER ITEM	<u>P-O-item-no</u>, Quantity
REQUISITION	<u>Req-no</u>, Req-date
REQUISITION ITEM	<u>Req-item-no</u>, Quantity
CUSTOMER	<u>Cust-no</u>, Cust-name, Address, Amount, Credit
PRODUCT	<u>Product-no</u>, description

FIGURE 11.13   Entities with attributes.

11.2   NORMALIZATION

Before looking at the rules of normalization, we will briefly develop a data model to use as an example. As seen in Figure 11.14, a relation is a **table** or **flat file**. This relation is called SALES-ORDER and it could show that Lee ordered 12 of 'part number' 25, Deene and Smith ordered 18 and 9, respectively, of 'part number' 38, and Williams ordered 100 of 'part number' 87.

The entities and relationships identified in the entity-relationship model can both be represented as relations in the relational model. In Figure 11.15, there are three entities in the entity model and they are expressed as three relations: COURSE, LECTURER, and TIMETABLE.

SALES-ORDER		
CUSTOMER NAME	PART NUMBER	QUANTITY ORDERED
Lee	25	12
Deene	38	18
Smith	38	9
Williams	87	100

FIGURE 11.14 Sales-order relation.

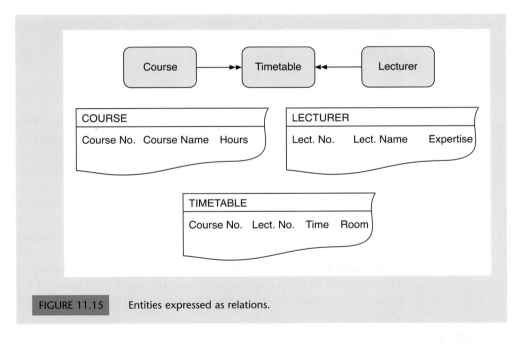

FIGURE 11.15 Entities expressed as relations.

We will now introduce some of the terminology associated with the relational model. Each row in a relation is called a **tuple**. The order of tuples is immaterial (although they will normally be shown in the text in a logical sequence so that it is easier to follow their contents). No two tuples can be identical in the model. A tuple or column will have a number of attributes, and in the SALES-ORDER relation of Figure 11.14, 'name', 'part', and 'quantity' are attributes. All items in a column come from the same **domain**, that is, the domain is the set of values from which valid attributes can be drawn. There are circumstances where the contents from two or more columns come from the same domain. The relation ELECTION-RESULT (Figure 11.16) illustrates this possibility. Two attributes come from the same domain of political parties. The number of

ELECTION-RESULT

ELECTION YEAR	FIRST PARTY	SECOND PARTY
1974	Labour	Conservative
1974	Labour	Conservative
1979	Conservative	Labour
1983	Conservative	Labour
1987	Conservative	Labour
1992	Conservative	Labour
1996	Labour	Conservative
2000	Labour	Conservative

FIGURE 11.16   Election-result relation.

attributes in a relation is called the degree of the relation. The number of tuples in a relation define its cardinality.

In the SALES-ORDER relation, the key is 'customer name'. It might be better to allocate numbers to customers in case there are duplicate names. If the customer may make orders for a number of parts, then 'part' must also be a key attribute as there will be several tuples with the same 'name'. In this case, the attributes 'customer name' and 'part number' will make up the **composite key** of the SALES-ORDER relation.

What is the key for the ELECTION-RESULT relation? On first sight, 'election year' might seem appropriate, but in 1974 there were two elections in a year, and even if all three attributes formed the composite key, there are still duplicate relations. It is necessary to add another attribute which is unique, such as an election number which is incremented by one following each election. Alternatively, it would be possible to replace 'year' by 'election date' to make each tuple unique (there will not be two of these elections on the same day). Another alternative would be the composite key of 'election year' and a new attribute 'election number in year'.

There may be more than one possible key. These are known as **candidate keys**, that is, they are candidates for the primary key. 'Customer name' and 'customer number' could be candidate keys in a CUSTOMER relation. In this circumstance one of these is chosen as the **primary key**. An attribute which is a primary key in one relation and not a primary key, but included in another relation, is called a **foreign key** in that second relation.

The structure of a relation is conventionally expressed as in the following examples:

SALES-ORDER   (<u>name</u>, part, quantity)
ELECTION-RESULT   (<u>elect-year</u>, <u>elect-number</u>, first-party, second-party)

The process of normalization is the application of a number of rules to the relational model which will simplify the relations. This set of rules proves to be useful because we are dealing with large sets of data and the relations formed by the normalization process will make the data easier to understand and manipulate. The model so formed is appropriate for the further stages in most database methodologies and the database will be shareable, a fundamental justification for the database approach.

Normalization is a technique that is used in a variety of methodologies. For example, it is used in Gane and Sarson (STRADIS), Information Engineering, SSADM, Merise and Multiview which are all discussed in Part 6. The technique of normalization is applicable irrespective of whether a relational database is envisaged or not. It is often used in its own right as an analysis technique for the structuring of data, it can be used on its own or as a means of cross-checking or validating other models, particularly an entity model. Even in structured systems methodologies which stress processes rather than data, for example, Gane and Sarson's STRADIS, it is used to consolidate all the various data stores that have been identified in a data flow diagram into a coherent data structure.

Normalization is the process of transforming data into well-formed or natural groupings such that one fact is in one place and that the correct relationships between facts exist. As well as simplifying the relations, normalization also reduces anomalies which may otherwise occur when manipulating the relations in a relational database. In this simplifying process no data are lost or added to that provided in the original set of unnormalized relations.

Normalized data are stable and a good foundation for any future growth. It is a mechanical process, indeed the technique has been automated, but the difficult part of it lies in understanding the meaning, that is, the semantics of the data, and this is only discovered by extensive and careful data analysis.

There are three levels of normalization, and the third and final stage is known as the *third normal form (TNF)*. It is this level of normalization that is often used as the basis for the design of the data model, as an end result of data analysis, and for mapping onto a database. There are a few instances, however, when even TNF needs further simplification, and these are also looked at later in this section. TNF is usually satisfactory in practice.

There are three basic stages of normalization:

1. First normal form – ensure that all the attributes are atomic (i.e. in the smallest possible components). This means that there is only one possible value for each attribute and not a set of values. This is often expressed as the fact that relations must not contain repeating groups.

2. Second normal form – ensure that all non-key attributes are functionally dependent on (give facts about) all the key. If this is not the case, split off into a separate relation those attributes that are dependent on only part of the key together with the key.

3. Third normal form – Ensure that all non-key attributes are functionally independent of each other. If this is not the case, create new relations which do not show any non-key dependence.

A rather flippant, but more memorable, definition of normalization can be given as 'the attributes in a relation must depend on the key, the whole key, and nothing but the key'.

This is an oversimplification, but it is essentially true and could be kept in mind as the normalization process is developed.

A more detailed description of normalization is now given. A key concept is **functional dependency**, which is often referred to as **determinacy**. This is defined by Cardenas (1985) as follows: Given a relation R, the attribute B is said to be functionally dependent on attribute A if at every instant of time each value of A has no more than one value of B associated with it in the relation R.

Therefore, if we know a 'customer-number', we can determine the associated 'customer-name', 'customer-address', and so on, if they are functionally dependent on 'customer-number'. Functional dependency is frequently illustrated by an arrow. The arrow will point from A to B in the functional dependency illustrated in the definition. Thus, the value of A uniquely determines the value of B.

Figure 11.17(a) is a non-normalized relation COURSE-DETAIL. Before normalizing the

---

(a) COURSE-DETAIL (Unnormalized)

COURSE	COURSE-NAME	LEVEL	MODULE	MODULE-NAME	STATUS	UNIT-POINTS
B74	Computer Science	BSc	B741	Program 1	Basic	8
			B742	Hardware 1		
			B743	Data Processing 1		
			B744	Program 2	Intermediate	11
			B745	Hardware 2		
B94	Computer Applications	MSc	B951	Information	Advanced	15
			B952	Microprocessors		
			B741	Program 1	Basic	8

(b) COURSE-DETAIL

<u>COURSE</u>	COURSE-NAME	LEVEL	<u>MODULE</u>	MODULE-NAME	STATUS	UNIT-POINTS
B74	Computer Science	BSc	B741	Program 1	Basic	8
B74	Computer Science	BSc	B742	Hardware 1	Basic	8
B74	Computer Science	BSc	B743	Data Processing 1	Basic	8
B74	Computer Science	BSc	B744	Program 2	Intermediate	11
B74	Computer Science	BSc	B745	Hardware 2	Intermediate	11
B94	Computer Applications	MSc	B951	Information	Advanced	15
B94	Computer Applications	MSc	B952	Microprocessors	Advanced	15
B94	Computer Applications	MSc	B741	Program 1	Basic	8

FIGURE 11.17   First normal form.

relation, it is necessary to analyse its meaning. Knowledge of the application area gained from entity modelling will provide this information. It is possible to make assumptions about the interrelationships between the data, but it is obviously better to base these assumptions on thorough analysis. In the relation COURSE-DETAIL, there are two occurrences of course ('COURSE'), one numbered B74 called computer science at the BSc level and the other B94 called computer applications at the MSc level. Each of these course occurrences has a number of module ('module') occurrences associated with it. Each 'module' is given a 'module-name', 'status' and 'unit-points' (which are allocated according to the status of the 'module').

1   *First Normal Form* includes the filling in of details, ensuring all attributes are in their smallest possible components. This is seen in the example in Figure 11.17(a) and is a trivial task. You may note that in Figure 11.17(a), the order of the tuples in the unnormalized relation is significant. Otherwise the content of the attributes not completed cannot be known. As we have already stated, one of the principles of the relational model is that the order of the tuples is not significant. The tuples seen in Figure 11.17(b) could be in any order in this relation. First normal form essentially converts unnormalized data or traditional file structures into fully completed relations or tables.

The key of the relation of Figure 11.17(b) is 'course' and 'module' together (a composite key) and the key attributes have been underlined. A composite key is necessary because no single attribute will uniquely identify a tuple of this relation. There were in fact a number of possible candidate keys, for example, 'module-name' and 'course-name', but we chose the primary key as above because they are numeric and unique.

Further work would have been necessary if the following was presented as the unnormalized relation:

     course, course-name, level, module-details

'Module-details' has to be defined as a set of atomic attributes, not as a group item, so it has to be broken down into its constituents of 'module-name', 'status', and 'unit-points':

     course, course-name, level, module-name, status, unit-points

2   *Second Normal Form* is achieved if the relations are in first normal form and all non-key attributes are fully functionally dependent on all the key attributes. The relation COURSE-DETAIL shown in Figure 11.17(b) is in first normal form. However, the attributes 'module-name', 'status', and 'unit-points' are functionally dependent on 'module'. In other words, they represent facts about 'module', which is not the whole key which is 'course' and 'module'. This is known as *partial dependency*. We may say that if the value of the module is known, we can determine the value of 'status', 'name', and 'unit-points'. For example, if 'module' is B743, then 'status' is basic, 'module-name' is data processing 1, and 'unit points' is 8. They are not dependent on the other part of the key, 'course'. So as to comply with the requirements of second normal form, two relations will be formed from the relation and this is shown as Figure 11.18. But this is only a partial advance to second normal form; there are elements in the first normal form relation not in this model.

The relation COURSE-MODULE is still not in second normal form because the attributes 'course-name' and 'level' are functionally dependent on 'course' only, and not on

(a) COURSE-MODULE

COURSE	MODULE	COURSE-NAME	LEVEL
B74	B741	Computer Science	BSc
B74	B742	Computer Science	BSc
B74	B743	Computer Science	BSc
B74	B744	Computer Science	BSc
B74	B745	Computer Science	BSc
B94	B951	Computer Applications	MSc
B94	B952	Computer Applications	MSc
B94	B741	Computer Applications	MSc

(b) MODULE

MODULE	NAME	STATUS	UNIT-POINTS
B741	Program 1	Basic	8
B742	Hardware 1	Basic	8
B743	Data Processing 1	Basic	8
B744	Program 2	Intermediate	11
B745	Hardware 2	Intermediate	11
B951	Information	Advanced	15
B952	Microprocessors	Advanced	15

FIGURE 11.18   First step toward second normal form.

the whole of the key. A separate COURSE relation has been created in Figure 11.19. The COURSE relation has only two tuples (there are only two courses), and all duplicates are removed. Notice that we maintain the relation COURSE-MODULE. This relation is all key, and there is nothing incorrect in this. Attributes may possibly be added later which relate specifically to the *course–module* relationship, for example, the teacher or text. The relation is required because information will be lost by not including it, that is, the modules which are included in a particular course and the courses which include specific modules. The relations are now in second normal form.

3   *Third Normal Form* (TNF) is necessary because second normal form may cause problems where non-key attributes are functionally dependent on each other (that is, a non-key attribute is dependent on another non-key attribute). In the relation MODULE, the attribute 'unit-points' is functionally dependent on the 'status' (or level) of the course, that is, given 'status', we know the value of 'unit-points'. So 'unit-points' is determined by 'status' which is not a key. We therefore create a new relation STATUS and delete 'unit-points' from the relation MODULE. We check each non-key attribute and find that there are no more such dependencies. The third normal form is given in Figure 11.20.

Sometimes the term **transitive dependency** is used in this context. The dependency of the attribute 'unit-points' is transitive (via 'status') and not wholly dependent

(a) COURSE-MODULE

COURSE	MODULE
B74	B741
B74	B742
B74	B743
B74	B744
B74	B745
B94	B951
B94	B952
B94	B741

(b) COURSE

COURSE	COURSE-NAME	LEVEL
B74	Computer Science	BSc
B94	Computer Applications	MSc

(c) MODULE

MODULE	MODULE-NAME	STATUS	UNIT-POINTS
B741	Program 1	Basic	8
B742	Hardware 1	Basic	8
B743	Data Processing 1	Basic	8
B744	Program 2	Intermediate	11
B745	Hardware 2	Intermediate	11
B951	Information	Advanced	15
B952	Microprocessors	Advanced	15

FIGURE 11.19 Second normal form.

on the key attribute 'module'. This transitive dependency should not exist in third normal form.

The attribute 'status' is the primary key of the STATUS relation. It is included as an attribute in the MODULE relation, but it is not a key. This provides an example of a **foreign key**, that is, a non-key attribute of one relation which is a primary key of another. This will be useful when processing the relations, as 'status' can be used to join the STATUS and MODULE relations to form a larger composite relation if this joint information is required by the user. The user requirements, which might include reports, are likely to contain data coming from the joining of a number of relations.

We will now consider the reasons why we normalize the relations in the first place. Unnormalized relations would have been formed by the analysts using information gained from interviews, for example, and are rough first-cut tabular representations of the data structures.

(a) COURSE-MODULE

COURSE	MODULE
B74	B741
B74	B742
B74	B743
B74	B744
B74	B745
B94	B951
B94	B952
B94	B741

(b) COURSE

COURSE	COURSE-NAME	LEVEL
B74	Computer Science	BSc
B94	Computer Applications	MSc

(c) MODULE

MODULE	MODULE-NAME	STATUS
B741	Program 1	Basic
B742	Hardware 1	Basic
B743	Data Processing 1	Basic
B744	Program 2	Intermediate
B745	Hardware 2	Intermediate
B951	Information	Advanced
B952	Microprocessors	Advanced
B741	Program 1	Basic

(d) STATUS

STATUS	UNIT-POINTS
Basic	8
Intermediate	11
Advanced	15

FIGURE 11.20   Third normal form.

Relations are normalized because unnormalized relations prove difficult to use. This can be illustrated if we try to insert, delete, and update information from the relations not in TNF. Say we have a new 'module' numbered B985 called Artificial Intelligence which has a 'status' in the intermediate category. Looking at Figure 11.17, we cannot add this information in COURSE-DETAIL because there has been no allocation of this 'module' occurrence to any 'course'. Looking at Figure 11.18(b), it could be added to the MODULE relation, if we knew that the 'status' intermediate carried 11 unit-points. This information is not necessary in the MODULE relation seen in Figure 11.20(c), the TNF version of this relation. We simply add to the MODULE relation in Figure 11.19(c), the tuple B985, artificial intelligence, intermediate. The TNF model is therefore much more convenient for adding this new information.

If we decided to introduce a new category in the 'status' attribute, called course-work, having a 'unit-points' attached of 10, we cannot add it to the unnormalized relation MODULE (Figure 11.18(b)) because we have not decided which 'module' or modules to attach it to. But we can include this information in the TNF model by adding a tuple to the STATUS relation (Figure 11.20(d)) which is coursework, 10.

Another problem occurs when updating. Let us say that we decide to change the 'unit-points' allocated to the Basic category of 'status' in the modules from 8 to 6, it becomes a simple matter in the TNF relation. The single occurrence of the tuple with the key Basic, needs to be changed from (Basic 8) to (Basic 6) in Figure 11.20(d). With the unnormalized, first normal, or second normal form relations, there will be a number of tuples to change. It means searching through every tuple of the relation COURSE-DETAIL (Figure 11.17(b)) or MODULE (Figure 11.18(b)) looking for 'status' = Basic and updating the associated 'unit-points'. All tuples have to be searched, because in the relational model the order of the tuples is of no significance. This increases the likelihood of inconsistencies and errors in the database. We have ordered them in the text only to make the normalization process easier to follow.

Another reason concerns the possible inconsistency of the data. This does not occur in the TNF relations above; but in Figure 11.17(b) the first and last tuples could have had module names 'Program 1' and 'Basic Programming', respectively, as names for the same module (B741). This would cause confusion, but the normalization process would detect the problem and the analyst will form the relation shown as Figure 11.18(b).

Deleting information will also cause problems. If it is decided to drop the B74 course, we may still wish to keep details of the modules that make up the course. Information about modules might be used at another time when designing another course. The information would be lost if we deleted the course B74 from COURSE-DETAIL (Figure 11.17(b)). The information about these modules will be retained in the module relation in TNF. The TNF relation COURSE will now consist only of one tuple relating to the 'course' B74, and the TNF relation COURSE-MODULE will consist of the three tuples relating to the COURSE B94. However, the MODULE relation (Figure 11.20(c)) will remain the same.

We have previously regarded the third normal form as the end of the normalization process and this is usually satisfactory. However, there are further levels or extensions of normalization.

Boyce-Codd Normal Form (BCNF) is one such extension. One criticism of the third normal form is that, by making reference to other normal forms, hidden dependencies may not be revealed. BCNF does not make reference to other normal forms.

In any relation there may be more than one combination of attributes which can be chosen as primary key, in other words, there are candidate keys. BCNF requires that all attribute values are fully dependent on each candidate key and not only the primary key. Put another way, it requires that each determinant (attribute or combination of attributes which determines the value of another attribute) must be a candidate key. As any

```
STUDENT-MODULE

STUDENT          MODULE          LECTURER

Bell             B741            Dr Smith
Bell             B742            Dr Jones
Martin           B741            Dr Smith
Martin           B742            Prof. Harris
```

FIGURE 11.21   Relation in TNF but not BCNF.

primary key will be a candidate key, all relations in BCNF will satisfy the rules of the third normal form, but relations in TNF may not be in BCNF.

It is best explained by an example. In fact, the third normal form relations in Figure 11.20 are also in BCNF, so we will extend the example used so far. Assume that we have an additional relation which is also in TNF giving details about the students taking modules and the lecturers teaching on those modules. Assume also that each module is taught by several lecturers, each lecturer teaches one module, each student takes several modules, and each student has only one lecturer for a given module. This complex set of rules could produce the relation shown as Figure 11.21.

Although this relation is in TNF because the 'lecturer' is dependent on all the key (both 'student' and 'module' determine the lecturer), it is not in BCNF because the attribute 'lecturer' is a determinant but is not a candidate key. There will be some update anomalies. For example, if we wish to delete the information that Martin is studying B742, it cannot be done without deleting the information that Prof. Harris teaches the module B742. As the attribute 'lecturer' is a determinant but not a candidate key, it is necessary to create a new table containing 'lecturer' and its directly dependent attribute 'module'. This results in two relations as shown in Figure 11.22. These are in BCNF. Now, deleting the information that Prof. Harris teaches Martin (the second relation will now have three tuples) will not lose the information that Prof. Harris can teach on module B742.

Fourth Normal Form can be illustrated by looking at a relation which is in the first normal form and which contains information about modules, lecturers, and textbooks. Each tuple has a module name and a repeating group of textbook names (there could be a number of texts recommended for each module). Any module can be taught by a number of lecturers, but each will recommend the same set of texts.

The relation seen as Figure 11.23 is in BCNF (and therefore TNF) and yet it contains considerable redundancy. If we wish to add the information that Prof. Harris can teach B742, three tuples need to be added to the relation. The problem comes about because all three attributes form the composite key: there are no functional determinants apart from this combination of all three attributes.

The problem would be eased by forming from this relation the two all-key relations shown as Figure 11.24. There is no loss of information, and there is not the evident redundancy found in Figure 11.23.

LECTURER	
LECTURER	MODULE
Dr Smith	B741
Dr Jones	B742
Prof. Harris	B742

STUDENT-LECTURER	
STUDENT	LECTURER
Bell	Dr Smith
Bell	Dr Jones
Martin	Dr Smith
Martin	Prof. Harris

FIGURE 11.22	BCNF.

MODULE-LECTURER		
MODULE	LECTURER	TEXT
B741	Dr Smith	Database Fundamentals
B741	Dr Smith	Further Databases
B741	Dr Jones	Database Fundamentals
B741	Dr Jones	Further Databases
B742	Dr Smith	Database Fundamentals
B742	Dr Smith	Systems Analysis
B742	Dr Smith	Information Systems

FIGURE 11.23	BCNF but not fourth normal form.

The transition to the fourth normal form has been made because of multivalued dependencies that may occur (Fagin, 1977). Although a module does not have one and only one lecturer, each module does have a pre-defined set of lecturers. Similarly, each module also has a pre-defined set of texts.

MODULE-LECTURER	
<u>MODULE</u>	<u>LECTURER</u>
B741	Dr Smith
B741	Dr Smith
B741	Dr Jones
B741	Dr Jones
B742	Dr Smith
B742	Dr Smith
B742	Dr Smith

MODULE-TEXT	
<u>MODULE</u>	<u>TEXT</u>
B741	Database Fundamentals
B741	Further Databases
B741	Database Fundamentals
B741	Further Databases
B742	Database Fundamentals
B742	Systems Analysis
B742	Information Systems

FIGURE 11.24 Fourth normal form.

Although these examples are valid, in that they do show relations which contain redundancy and yet are in TNF and BCNF, respectively, the examples are somewhat contrived. The reader will have seen that in both examples it was necessary to make a number of special assumptions. The implication is that such problems will not be found frequently by analysts when carrying out data analysis and therefore that TNF can be a reasonable stopping point for normalization.

11.3 SUMMARY

- An entity-relationship model views the organization as a set of data elements, known as entities, which are the things of interest to the organization, and the relationships between these entities.

- An entity will have attributes that describe the entity. The particular attribute or group of attributes that uniquely identifies an entity occurrence is known as the key attribute or attribute(s).

- The process of normalization is the application of a number of rules to the entities, now normally referred to as relations, which will simplify the model.

- For most situations a three-stage process of normalization to third normal form proves adequate.

QUESTIONS

1 Some argue that data is the 'lifeblood of the organization'. Do you agree? Provide reasons for your answer.

2 It is claimed that the entity-relationship model is easy for users to understand. Do you agree?

3 Complete the entity model shown as Figure 11.13.

4 For an organization of your choice, for example, a university library, suggest four or five entities and normalize them to the third normal form.

11.4 FURTHER READING

Avison, D.E. and Cuthbertson, C. (2002) *A Management Approach to Database Applications*, McGraw-Hill, Maidenhead, UK.

Connolly, T. and Begg, C. (2002) *Database Systems: A Practical Approach to Design, Implementation and Management*, Addison-Wesley, Harlow, UK.

Date, C.J. (2000) *An Introduction to Database Systems*, 6th edn, Addison-Wesley, Reading, Massachusetts.

Lejk, M. and Deeks, D. (1998) *An Introduction to Systems Analysis Techniques*, Prentice Hall, Harlow, UK.

2 PROCESS TECHNIQUES

. . . .

12.1   DATA FLOW DIAGRAMMING

The data flow diagram (DFD) is fundamental to structured systems methodologies and was developed as an integrated part of those methodologies. However, the DFD has been adopted and adapted by a number of other methodologies, not all structured systems-type, including Multiview and ISAC. In these methodologies the DFD or similar is not the major technique of the methodology but is used in conjunction with other techniques in the analysis of processes. Like entity modelling and normalization, DFDs are an important technique in a variety of systems development methodologies.

The DFD provides the key means of achieving one of the most important requirements of structured systems, that is, the notion of structure. The DFD enables a system to be partitioned (or structured) into independent units of a desirable size so that they, and thereby the system, can be more easily understood. In addition, information is graphical and concise. The graphical aspect means it can be used both as a static piece of documentation and as a communication tool, enabling communication at all levels: between analyst and user, analyst and designer, and analyst and analyst. The graphical nature of the DFD means that it can be explained easier to users and also means a more concise document, as it is argued that a picture can more quickly convey meaning than traditional methods, such as textual narrative. The DFD also provides the ability to abstract to the level of detail required. Therefore, it is possible to examine a system in overview and at a detailed level, while maintaining the links and interfaces between the different levels.

The DFD provides the analyst with the ability to specify a system at the logical level. This means that it describes what a system will do, rather than how it will be done. Considerations of a physical and implementation nature are not usually depicted using data flow diagrams, and it is possible for the logical DFD to be mapped to a variety of different physical implementations. The benefit of this is that it separates the tasks of analysis (what is required) from design (how it is to be achieved). This separation means that the users can specify their requirements without any restrictions being imposed of a design nature, for example, the technology or the type of access method. There exists a logical and physical independence, the hardware can be changed or upgraded without changing the functions of the system. Alternatively, if as often happens a functional change is required, the relevant part of the logical specification is changed and a new mapping to the physical system is designed. The change is thus effected at the logical level, which is the correct place, and the implications of the change are agreed, and only then the necessary design changes made. This improves and speeds up the maintenance process which, as we have seen, is a major time and resource-consuming activity.

The form of DFDs differs between the various proponents of structured systems analysis. The differences are relatively small and the basic concepts are the same. For example, the symbol used to represent a process differs. Gane and Sarson (1979) use a rectangle with rounded corners (a 'soft box') whereas many other authors use a circle. This means that superficially the DFDs look different but in practice the differences are relatively minor.

A logical DFD represents logical information, not the physical aspects. A data flow specifies what flows, for example, customer credit details. How it flows, for example, by carrier pigeon or via twisted copper wires, is immaterial and not represented in a logical DFD. A DFD is a graphical representation and is composed of four elements:

1   The data flow

Data flow is represented by an arrow and depicts the fact that some data is flowing or moving from one process to another. A number of analogies are commonly used to illustrate this. Gane and Sarson (1979) suggest that we think of the arrow as a pipeline down which 'parcels' of data are sent. Others think of it as like a conveyor belt in a factory which takes data from one 'worker' to another. Each 'worker' then performs some process on that data which may result in another data flow on the conveyor belt. These processes are the second element of the DFD.

2   The processes

The processes or tasks performed on the data flows are represented in this example by a soft box (see Figure 12.1). The process transforms the data flow by either changing the structure of the data (e.g. by sorting it) or by generating new information from the data (e.g. by merging the data with data obtained from another data source). A process might be 'validate order', which transforms the order data flow by adding new information to the order, that is, whether it is valid or not. It is likely that invalid orders flow out from the validation process in a different direction to valid orders. In this example the conventions used for the process symbol are as follows. The top compartment contains a reference number for the process, the middle compartment contains the description of

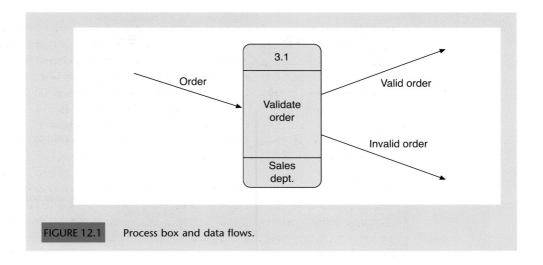

FIGURE 12.1 Process box and data flows.

the process, and the lower compartment indicates where the process occurs. Strictly speaking, this is not at the logical level and so would not always be used. A process must have at least one data flow coming into it and at least one leaving it. There is no concept of a process without data flows, a process cannot exist independently.

3   The data store

If a process cannot terminate a data flow because it must output something, then where do the data flows stop? There are two places. The first is the data store, which can be envisaged as a file, although it is not necessarily a computer file or even a manual record in a filing cabinet. It can be a very temporary repository of data, for example, a shopping list or a transaction record. A data store symbol is a pair of parallel lines with one end closed, and a compartment for a reference code and a compartment for the name of the data store. For example (see Figure 12.2), the process of validating the order may need to make reference to the parts data store to see if the parts specified on the order are valid parts with the correct current price associated with it. The data flow in this example has the arrow pointing toward the process which indicates that the data store is only referenced by the process and not updated or changed in any way. In this example we would expect to find another process somewhere on the DFD which maintained the parts data store. For example, in Figure 12.3, the new part data from process 6.2 is used to update the parts data store (the arrow points to the data store). The manner in which the access to the data store is made is usually regarded as irrelevant. However, it may be information which a designer needs, and therefore, in cases where it is not obvious, this information may be added to the DFD. In the example (Figure 12.2), it may be assumed that access to the parts file is via the part number. However, if a customer makes an order without specifying the part number, access via the part description may be required. This should then be specified (see Figure 12.4).

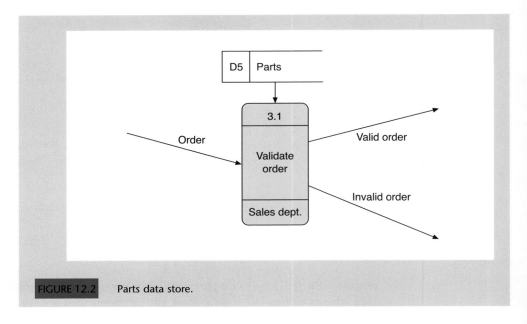

FIGURE 12.2   Parts data store.

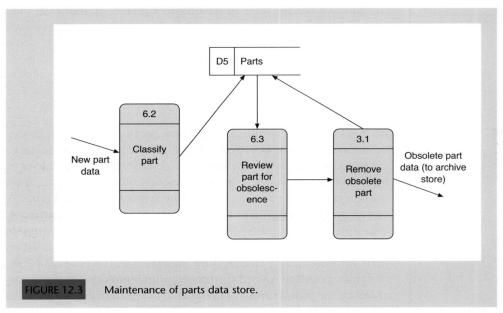

FIGURE 12.3   Maintenance of parts data store.

4   The source or sink (external entity)

The second way of terminating a data flow in a system is by directing the flow to a sink. The sink may, for example, be a customer to whom we send a delivery note. The customer is a sink, in the sense that the data flow does not necessarily continue. The

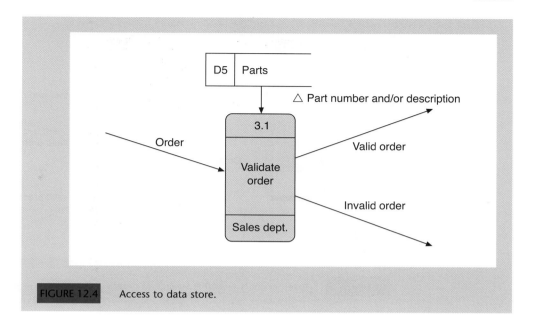

FIGURE 12.4   Access to data store.

customer is a sink down which the delivery note may fall for ever. The Department of Trade may be a sink to which a company may legally be required to provide information but never receive any in return. Sinks are usually entities that are external to the organization in question, although they need not be, another department may be a sink. It depends on where the boundaries of the system under consideration are drawn. If a DFD for the sales department is being constructed, any data flows to the production department would be represented as a sink. However, if the whole organization were being depicted, then the same data flows would go to a process within the production department. The original source of a data flow is the opposite to a sink, although it may be the same entity. For example, a customer is the source of an order and a sink for a dispatch note. Sinks and sources are represented by the same symbol which is a shadowed rectangle (see, for example, Figure 12.5). Sources and sinks are often termed 'external entities'. Figure 12.5 is an example of a data flow diagram that illustrates the combination of the four elements discussed above.

Mason and Willcocks (1994) suggest the following rules for drawing data flow diagrams assuming the analyst has described the whole logical system in narrative form:

- read the whole process a few times to get a clear picture of the system being described;
- identify the sources and sinks by circling a keyword for each of them;
- identify data stores (perhaps through the use of verbs such as 'store' or 'check' and underline them);
- draw a source entity box for the external entity which seems to start the process off and name it (entities can only link with processes);
- to its right, draw the first process box;
- from that, draw an arrow representing the primary data flow and name it;

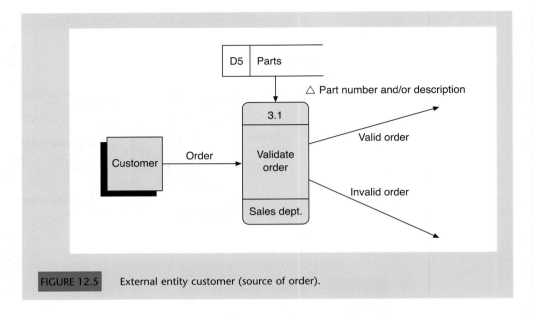

FIGURE 12.5   External entity customer (source of order).

- ■ name the process;
- ■ link it with any data stores and name these as well as the data flow entering or exiting it to and from the process (data cannot go from store to store, there must be an intervening process);
- ■ link the next process and so on until all the external entities are drawn.

We would add that all these steps will be repeated as we iterate to improve our model following discussions of it with the users.

One of the most important features of the DFD is the ability to construct a variety of different levels of DFD according to the degree of abstraction required. This means that a high-level diagram (containing the main processes) can be consulted in order to obtain a high-level (overview) understanding of the system. When a particular area of interest has been identified, then this area can be examined in more detail with a lower level DFD. The different levels of diagram must be consistent with each other in that the data flows present on the higher levels should exist on the lower levels as well. In essence it is the processes that are expanded at a greater level of detail as we move down the levels of the diagram. This 'levelling' process gives the DFD its top-down characteristic (DFD levelling is also described in the context of YSM in Section 19.2).

Usually the very top level of a DFD is known as the Context Diagram. All the processes, data stores and internal data flows are consolidated into a single process and only the external entities and the data flows between this single process are shown. Figure 12.6 is an example of a Context Diagram for an imaginary 'Sales order processing' system showing its interactions with various external entities such as Customer, Supplier, etc.

The next level down would be the Level 0 diagram showing the major processes of the 'Sales order processing' system. These major processes might be Credit Checking, Order Handling, Stock Control, Invoicing, Packaging and Delivery, etc. This level is not

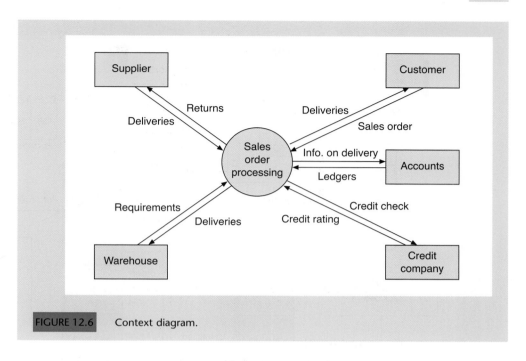

FIGURE 12.6 Context diagram.

illustrated. The next level down would be the Level 1 diagram and each major process identified in Level 0 would be decomposed into a Level 1 DFD. We have taken the 'Order Handling' major process (Reference 3.0 say) and illustrated this in Figure 12.7. So 'Order Handling' is now broken down into nine subprocesses and the figure shows the associated data flows and data stores.

Each of these nine processes can, if necessary, be expanded to still lower levels of detail. Figure 12.8 is the next level down (or an *explosion*) of the Validate Order process (Reference 3.1). This process is now expanded into five tasks with the various data flows between them. All the data flows (four in this case) in and out of Validate Order (Reference 3.1) in Figure 12.7 can be found on Figure 12.8. Any new data flows are either flows that only exist within the Validate Order process, that is they are internal to it and are now shown because we have split this down into separate parts (for example, Amended Order), or because they are concerned with errors and exceptions.

The details of errors and exceptions are usually not shown on high-level diagrams as it would confuse the picture with detail that is not required at this level. What is required at the high level is 'normal' processing and data flows. To include errors and exceptions might double the size of the diagram and remove its high-level characteristics. For example, Figure 12.8 shows new processing concerned with amending an order and a new data store which did not appear on the higher level diagram (the Parts data store). The problem is that it is sometimes difficult to decide what constitutes an error or an exception, and what is normal. Some common guidelines suggest that if an occurrence of a process or data flow is relatively rare, then it should be regarded as an exception. However, if it is financially significant, it should be taken as part of normal processing. Overall, it depends on the audience or use to be made of the DFD as to exactly what is included. At the lowest level, all the detail, including all errors and exceptions, should be shown.

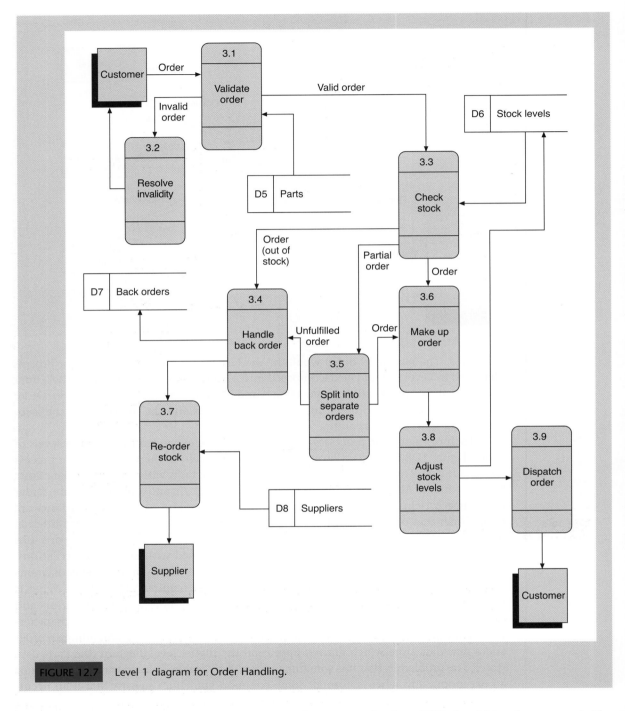

FIGURE 12.7   Level 1 diagram for Order Handling.

The question arises as to how many levels a DFD should be decomposed. The answer is that a DFD should be decomposed to the level that is meaningful for the purpose that the DFD is required. There comes a level, however, when each process is elementary and cannot be decomposed any further. No further internal data flows can be

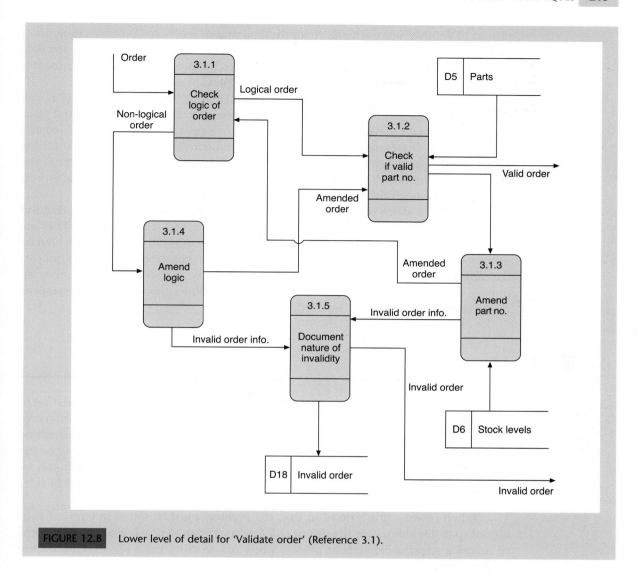

FIGURE 12.8 Lower level of detail for 'Validate order' (Reference 3.1).

identified. At this point each elementary process is described using a form of process logic. The techniques of representing process logic are described in the next four sections.

Data flow diagrams are generally logical and not physical, but they can be used to represent a physical implementation. For example, the process 'Document nature of invalidity' (Figure 12.8) might be 'type nature of invalidity on form B36 in sales office' with the B36 forms being output as part of the data flow and 'click on reason for invalidity using screen 5'. The physical DFD may then describe the present system or a proposed system.

Although it is a fundamental technique of some information systems development methodologies, e.g. Stradis, YSM and SSADM (see Part 6), DFDs have limitations even for addressing information about processes, such as how long data take to get from one process to another and the detail about the data that pass between processes in terms of peaks and troughs. Also little detail is provided about decision aspects, that is, why data flow in one way and not another. However, other techniques can be used to provide this information although none of the process techniques are as well used.

Techniques and tools closely associated with DFDs include data dictionaries as well as process logic descriptions. The data dictionary (see Section 18.1) is the central place where all the details of data flows, data stores, and processes are stored in an ordered and logical fashion. The dictionary may be manual or computerized, but the important thing is that it must be the centralized resource of the structured analysis project. It is not the same thing as the data dictionary of a database which is concerned with physical aspects of the data, although the two may very well be integrated.

The way in which process logic is described is by the use of decision trees, decision tables, structured English, and action diagrams (Sections 12.2–12.4 and 12.8). They are not complementary. A particular process is not described using all four techniques but by using whichever is the most appropriate, given the characteristics of the process concerned. So, each technique has particular strengths and weaknesses, but they all provide simple, clear, and unambiguous ways of describing the logic of what happens in the elementary processes identified in the DFD.

12.2 DECISION TREES

Decision trees and decision tables are tools which aim to facilitate the documentation of process logic, particularly where there are many decision alternatives. A decision tree illustrates the actions to be taken at each decision point. Each condition will determine the particular branch to be followed. At the end of each branch there will either be the action to be taken or further decision points. Any number of decision points can be represented, though the greater the complexity, then the more difficult the set of rules will be to follow.

When constructing a decision tree, the problem must be stated in terms of conditions (possible alternative situations) and actions (things to do). It is often convenient to follow a stepwise refinement process when constructing the tree, breaking up the largest condition to basic conditions, until the complete tree is formulated. The general format is shown in Figure 12.9. An example of a decision tree is given in Figure 12.10. At the first decision point (or node), the customer is classified into one of two types, private or trade. If the customer is trade, then a second decision point is reached. Has the customer been trading with us for less than five years, or five years or more? If the customer has been trading for five years or more, then the customer can obtain up to £5,000 credit, otherwise up to £1,000 credit can be given. If the customer was deemed private at the first decision point, then the action is to offer no credit at all.

Decision trees are constructed by first identifying the conditions, actions, and 'unless/however/but' structures of the situation being analysed gained. This can be obtained from a written statement or during interviews with users. Each sentence may form a 'mini' decision tree which combined with others could be joined together to form the version which will be verified by the users. Sometimes it is not possible to complete the decision tree because full information has not been given in the statement. For

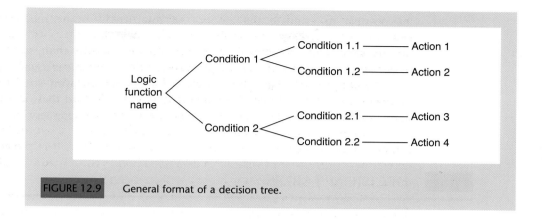

FIGURE 12.9   General format of a decision tree.

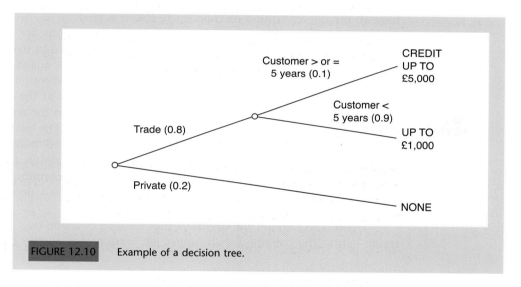

FIGURE 12.10   Example of a decision tree.

example, one branch of the decision tree may be identified, but no indication is given on the action to take on this branch. In such cases the analyst has to carry out a further investigation by interviewing staff or by using another method of systems investigation. The technique therefore helps validate the information as well as proving a useful documentation aid.

Decision trees prove to be a good method of showing the basics of a decision, that is, the possible actions that might be taken at a particular decision point and the set of values that lead to each of these actions. It is easy for the user to verify whether the analyst has understood the procedures.

Sometimes it is possible to associate probability scores for each branch once the decision tree is drawn. With this information it will be possible to compute expected values of the various outcomes and hence to evaluate alternative strategies. For example, in Figure 12.10, research may have indicated that trade customers outnumber private customers by 4:1 and that 90 per cent of trade customers are of less than five years standing. By extrapolating these figures with the total number of customers, it may be possible to evaluate the amount of total credit to be made available to all customers.

Where the number of decision nodes becomes greater than, say, 10, drawing the decision tree begins to be overly complex and a decision table is usually chosen as it can more readily represent processes with very complex decision structures. People are usually very familiar with the meaning of decision trees, and these are more graphical; therefore, decision trees are often preferred for communicating less complex logic.

12.3 DECISION TABLES

Decision tables are less graphical, when compared to decision trees, but are concise and have an inbuilt verification mechanism so that it is possible to check that all the conditions have been catered for. Again, conditions and actions are analysed from the procedural aspects of the problem situation, usually expressed in narrative form.

When constructing a decision table, the narrative is analysed to identify the various conditions and the various actions. The various actions to be executed are then listed in the bottom left-hand part of the table known as the action stub. In the top left-hand part, the conditions that can arise are listed in the condition stub. Each condition is expressed as a question to which the answer will be 'yes' or 'no'. There can be no ambiguity. All the possible combinations of yes and no responses can be recorded in the upper right-hand part of the table, known as the condition entry. Each possible combination of responses is known as a rule. In the corresponding parts of the lower right-hand quadrant, an X is placed for each action to be taken, depending on the rule associated with that column.

Figure 12.11 shows the decisions that have to be made by drivers in the UK at traffic lights. The condition stub (upper left section) has all the possible conditions

CONDITION STUB	CONDITION STUB							
Red	Y	Y	Y	Y	N	N	N	N
Amber	Y	Y	N	N	Y	Y	N	N
Green	Y	N	Y	N	Y	N	Y	N
Go with caution							X	
Stop	X	X	X	X	X	X		X
Call police	X		X		X			X
ACTION STUB	ACTION ENTRY							

FIGURE 12.11   Decision table for UK traffic lights.

(a)

Invoice > £300	Y	Y	Y	Y	N	N	N	N
Account overdue > 3 months	Y	Y	N	N	Y	Y	N	N
New customer	Y	N	Y	N	Y	N	Y	N
Put in hands of solicitor	X		X	X	X	X		X
Write first reminder letter		X	X	X		X		X
Write second reminder letter					X			
Cancel credit limit		X	X			X	X	

(b)

Invoice > £300	Y	Y	Y	N	N	N	N
Account overdue > 3 months	Y	Y	N	Y	Y	N	N
New customer	Y	N	–	Y	N	Y	N
Inform solicitor	X		X	X	X		X
Write first reminder letter		X	X		X		X
Write second reminder letter				X			
Cancel credit limit			X			X	X

FIGURE 12.12 Consolidating decision tables.

which are 'red', 'amber', and 'green'. Condition entries (upper right quadrant) are either Y for yes if the light is on (this condition is satisfied) or N for no if the light is off (this condition is not satisfied). Having three conditions in the condition stub, there will be 2 to the power of 3 ($2 \times 2 \times 2 = 8$) columns in the condition entry (and action entry). The easiest way of proceeding is to have the first row in the condition entry as YYYYNNNN, the second row as YYNNYYNN, and the final row as YNYNYNYN. If there were four conditions, we would start with eight Ys, eight Ns, and so on, giving a total of 2^4 ($2 \times 2 \times 2 \times 2 = 16$) columns.

All the possible actions are listed in a concise form in the Action Stub (bottom left). An X placed on a row/column coincidence in the Action Entry means that the action in the condition stub should be taken. A blank will mean that the action should not be taken. Therefore, if a driver is faced with Red (Y), Amber (Y), and Green (Y), the first column indicates that the driver should stop and call the police (a particular combination of conditions may lead to a number of actions to be taken). All combinations, even invalid ones, should be considered. The next column Red (Y), Amber (Y), and Green (N) informs the driver to stop. Only the Red (N), Amber (N), and Green (Y) combination permits the driver to go with caution.

Once the table is completed, rules which result in the same actions can be joined together and represented by dashes, that is, 'it does not matter'. The result of this is a consolidated decision table. Figure 12.12 illustrates an example decision table before and after the consolidation process. In the decision table represented in Figure 12.12(b),

Rules 3 and 4 of the decision table seen in Figure 12.12(a) have been merged into a consolidated Rule 2, expressing a 'doesn't matter' condition. This is because the same processing needs to be executed whether or not condition 2 is 'yes' or 'no'.

In systems analysis, there are likely to be requirements to specify actions where there are a large number of conditions. A set of decision tables is appropriate here. The first will have actions such as 'go to decision table 2' or 'go to decision table 3'. Each of these may themselves be reduced to a further level of decision tables. The technique therefore lends itself to functional decomposition.

Sometimes the values of conditions are not restricted to 'yes' or 'no', as defined in the limited entry tables described. There can be more than two possible entries, and extended entry tables are appropriate in this case. For example, the credit allowable to a customer could vary according to whether the customer had been dealing with the firm for 'up to 5 years', 'over 5 and up to 10 years', 'over 10 and up to 15 years', and so on. The rule for obtaining the right number of combinations will need to be modified. If Condition 1 has two possibilities and Condition 2 five possibilities, then the number of columns will be 2×5, that is, 10 columns.

Whereas decision trees are particularly appropriate where the number of actions is small (although it is possible to have large decision trees), decision tables are more appropriate where there is a large number of actions as they can be decomposed into sets conveniently; in other words, decision tables can better handle complexity. However, decision trees are easier to construct and give an easily assimilated graphical account of the decision structure. Decision tables have good validation procedures and, further, can be used to generate programs which carry out the actions according to the rules. Here the processing is specified by the analyst in terms of decision tables. These are transferred to computer readable format, and the programs generated automatically. Decision tables do, however, suffer from the disadvantage that no indication is given regarding the sequence that the actions are to follow (it cannot be assumed that they are to be followed in the sequence given in the decision table itself).

12.4   STRUCTURED ENGLISH

Structured English is very like a 'readable' computer program. It aims to produce unambiguous logic which is easy to understand and not open to misinterpretation. It is not a natural language like English, which is ambiguous and therefore unsuitable. Nor is it a programming language, though it can be readily converted to a computer program. It is a strict and logical form of English and the constructs reflect structured programming. Like a conventional programming language, the sequence of the commands expressed in structured English is important. It reflects the sequence in which the instructions should be followed. Although decision trees or decision tables are more suitable tools to document aspects where the system has many decision points, structured English proves to be a very useful technique to express logic in a system.

Structured English is a precise way of specifying a process, and is readily understandable by a trained systems designer as well as being readily converted to a computer program. An example is given in Figure 12.13. Structured English uses only a limited subset of English and this vocabulary is exact. This ensures less ambiguity in the use of

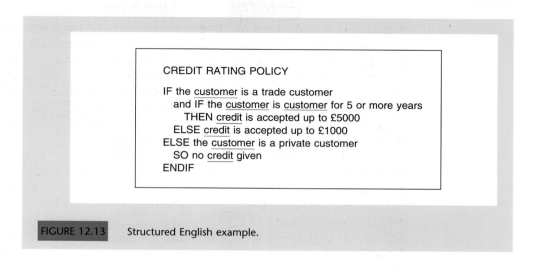

FIGURE 12.13   Structured English example.

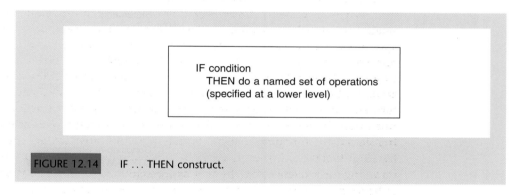

FIGURE 12.14   IF ... THEN construct.

'English' by the analyst. Further, by the use of text indentation, the structure of the process can be shown more clearly. As with all these techniques, however, although the logic can be formally expressed, there is no guarantee that the expression in syntactically correct structured English is semantically correct. That will depend on the systems investigation in the first place.

Structured English (see the example in Figure 12.13) has the following general construct:

```
IF condition 1 (is true)
   THEN action 1 (is to be carried out)
ELSE (not condition 1)
   SO action 2 (is to be carried out)
ENDIF
```

Functional decomposition can be supported in structured English by a construct using the IF ... THEN construct (Figure 12.14).

Conditions can include equal, not equal, greater than, less than, and so on. The words in capitals are keywords in structured English and have an unambiguous meaning in this context.

```
Sequencing:  Statement-1
             Statement-2
                                         Statement-2-1
                                         Statement-2-2

             Statement-3
             . . .
             . . .
             . . .
             Statement-n

Selection:   IF    Condition
             THEN  Statements
             ELSE  (not condition)
             SO    Statements

Repetition:  REPEAT
                   Statements
             UNTIL
                   Condition

Case:        CASE expression
             OF    Condition-1: Statements
                   Condition-2: Statements
                   . . .
                   . . .
                   . . .

                   . . .
                   Condition-n: Statements
                   OTHERWISE: Statements
             ENDCASE
```

FIGURE 12.15   The basic structures of structured English.

The logic of a structured English construct is expressed as a combination of sequence, selection, case, and repetition structures. Any logical specification can be written using these four basic structures (Figure 12.15):

■ *sequencing* shows the order of processing of a group of instructions, but has no repetition or branching built into it;

■ *selection* facilitates the choice of those conditions where a particular action or set of actions (or another decision and selection) are to be carried out;

■ *cases* represent a special type of decision structure (a special kind of selection), where there are several possibilities, but they never occur in combination (in other words, they are mutually exclusive);

■ *repetition* or loop instructions facilitate the same action or set of actions to be carried out a number of times, depending on a conditional statement.

The actual keywords and their number will vary according to the particular conventions used; indeed, structured English is not a 'standard', but the basic structures of sequence, selection, and repetition will be common to all.

The layout of structured English is as follows:

- the use of capital letters indicates a structured English reserved word such as IF, THEN, ELSE, and GET or the operators ADD, DIVIDE, and so on, which have particular meanings in the context of structured English;

- any data elements which are included in a data dictionary are normally underlined and these will include those items associated with the particular application, such as <u>credit</u> or <u>customer</u> in the credit rating example (Figure 12.13);

- indentation is used to indicate blocks of sequential instructions to be created together, and hierarchical structures can be built by indenting these blocks;

- blocks of instructions can be named and this name quoted in capital letters to refer to the block of instructions elsewhere in the code, and this will be particularly necessary where there are a number of places in the logic where this set of instructions needs to be performed.

When creating structured English statements, it is best to break down complex statements into a number of simple ones. Named blocks of these simple statements can be thought of as a way of effecting functional decomposition because the block can be performed in a REPEAT statement a number of times.

Structured English has many advantages, in particular its ability to describe many aspects of analysis, its conciseness, precision, and readability, and the speed with which it can be written. However, it takes time to build up skills in its use, and it is alien to many users (despite being English-like). Indeed, the terminology might be misleading to users because the structured English meanings are not exactly the same as their natural language counterparts.

There are alternative languages to structured English such as, 'pseudocode' and 'tight English'. These vary on their nearness to programming language and readability to users. For example, pseudocode has a DO-WHILE and END-DO loop structure which is similar to constructs of some conventional computer programming languages, and is obviously more programming-oriented than structured English. Tight English code seems nearer natural language than computer programming language, though it can also be interpreted by programs. When there are a number of decision points, in tight English it is usual to use a decision table or decision tree.

12.5   STRUCTURE DIAGRAMS

Like other techniques described in this chapter, structure diagrams are used by a number of methodologies. The structure diagram is a series of boxes (representing processes or parts of computer programs, usually referred to as modules) and connecting lines (representing links to subordinate processes which show the way that data and control can be passed between processes) which are arranged in a hierarchy. Each module should be small and manageable. Structure charts therefore exemplify the functional

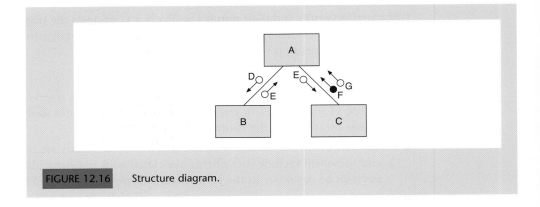

FIGURE 12.16   Structure diagram.

decomposition aspect of many of these process techniques. The basic diagram of a structure chart is shown in Figure 12.16:

■ Module A can call module B and also module C. This is shown by lines joining the boxes, which represent modules. No sequencing for these calls nor whether they actually occur is implied by the diagramming notation. When the subordinate process terminates, control goes back to the calling process.

■ When A calls B, it sends data of type D to B. When B terminates, it returns data of type E to A. Similarly, A communicates with C using data of types E and G.

■ When C terminates, it sends a flag of type F to A. A flag is used as a flow of control data. The difference in the symbol between data types and flags lie in the circle being filled in or not.

Figure 12.17 shows the structure chart for part of the processing of applications to undergraduate courses. It concerns those students that we propose to interview. CD refers to the candidate document and TR to the test result. Other charts in the set will be constructed for the processing of examination results and final assessment among others. The top-level diagram (A in Figure 12.17) will show each of these processes as a box and refer to the lower level structure charts.

The structure of a program should be designed to ensure that it minimizes the interdependence between modules (known as **coupling**), it encourages module reuse (known as **cohesion**), and eases the programming task and later maintenance. By minimizing the connections between modules and therefore their independence, coupling reduces the risk of errors or changes in one module affecting another. But cohesion, that is, the way the activities within a module are related, should be maximized as it helps ease of understanding the module and encourages reuse because the elements of the module concern similar activities which may be used in other applications. The designer should be aware of the possibilities of code reuse, both in terms of designing modules that may be reused and using modules already written.

We have so far suggested that the structure diagram relates to computer program design. But, of course, the basic technique applies to the overall design of information systems, of which the design of computer programs play a part. This sequence is not a coincidence, for many of these process techniques were used first in the structured programming movement which influenced many systems analysts. Structure diagrams

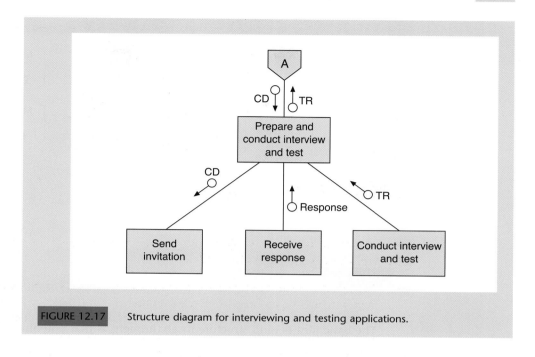

FIGURE 12.17 Structure diagram for interviewing and testing applications.

are used in SSADM, Multiview, and elsewhere, but they are described further in Section 19.3 when discussing the entity structure step, a phase in Jackson Systems Development (JSD). Jackson has been a notable contributor to both the software world (through Jackson Systems Programming) and the technical aspects of information systems.

A further variation on the same structure chart theme, but looking somewhat different, is the Warnier–Orr diagram which has been well used in the USA. As shown in Figure 12.18, the diagrams use curly brackets to show the hierarchical structure, and they are read from left to right rather than from top to bottom. Sequential processes are therefore shown within one bracket. There is a selection construct, where a choice is made between mutually exclusive possibilities, according to a condition. This is denoted by the symbol which has a plus sign within a circle. The example provided reflects a low level decision-making process, but Warnier–Orr diagrams can be used and are used to reflect the higher level processing of the structure charts of the above examples.

12.6 STRUCTURED WALKTHROUGHS

Structured walkthroughs are a series of formal reviews of a system or a program, held at various stages of the life cycle. This is an idea which has developed around structured systems analysis and design approaches, where the opportunities for such review are clearly identifiable. These are intended to be team-based reviews of a product, such as a program or design component and are not intended to be management reviews of individuals or their performance.

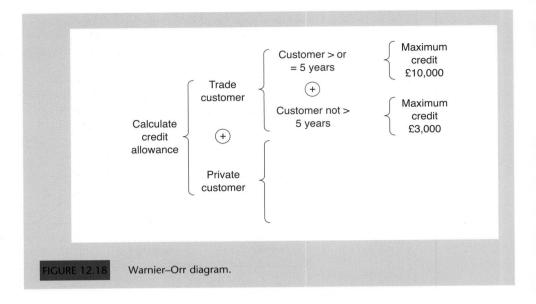

FIGURE 12.18 Warnier–Orr diagram.

The basic idea behind structured walkthroughs is that potential problems can be identified as early as possible so that their effect can be minimized. The benefits of this approach are:

- The overall quality of the systems analysis and design of the information system is improved, since more than one person is responsible for it and the analysis and design are exposed to the scrutiny of others at every appropriate opportunity.

- There is the opportunity to detect errors earlier in the development cycle than might otherwise be possible, avoiding the errors propagating throughout the rest of the systems development process.

- All team members have the opportunity to be 'educated' in the total system, resulting in a much better understanding of the total system by a greater number of organizational personnel. This means that team members can more easily take over work from each other. Other personnel, outside the development team, such as production and operational systems staff also have the opportunity to familiarize themselves with the overall system as well as particular components.

- Technical expertise is communicated through discussion that is often generated as a result of a structured walkthrough. More experienced staff will spot common sources of potential problems and discuss these with other staff, thereby transferring their own knowledge and skills. This means that the technical knowledge is dispersed more widely than would otherwise be the case.

- Inherent in structured methodologies is that technical progress can be more readily and easily assessed, and the walkthroughs provide ideal milestones and opportunities to do this.

- If carried out in the correct spirit and atmosphere, structured walkthroughs can provide an opportunity for trainee analysts and programmers to gain experience and enable them to work on complex problems more quickly, due to their participation in walkthroughs with other more experienced team members and also because of the opportunity of having walkthroughs on their work where they receive specific comments and feedback in a non-threatening environment.

Structured walkthroughs have been identified as being of considerable value in the development of information systems, and they should be held on completion of certain phases of the development as indicated. It is impractical to hold formal walkthroughs too often, as they cause unnecessary administrative overheads. The best approach is to maintain the spirit of the concept by team members discussing all decisions with others without necessarily calling formal meetings. It is intended that the approach will normally promote discussion and exchange of ideas within the team. As stated previously, formal reviews should be held on the completion of stages and certain phases within each of the stages of the life cycle, and it is suggested that walkthroughs might be held at the end of the following:

- feasibility study;
- system investigation;
- systems analysis;
- systems design;
- program specification;
- program logic design;
- implementation;
- test plan;
- implementation plan;
- operational system plan;
- user manuals;
- review and maintenance.

Formal walkthroughs should be attended by a number of team members because responsibility for the system is then placed on the whole team. All members of the team should be given the opportunity to contribute, from the most junior to the most senior. It might be appropriate to limit the number of people attending some walkthroughs to around four to six.

For maximum benefit to be derived from the walkthrough, it is important that appropriate documentation is circulated well in advance of the walkthrough and that:

- everyone attending is familiar with the subject to be reviewed;
- each attendee has studied it carefully;
- minor points of detail are discussed before the walkthrough, so that valuable time is not wasted on trivial points.

During the walkthrough it is important that:

- all errors, discrepancies, inconsistencies, omissions, and points for further action are recorded so that this can form an action list;

- one person should be allocated the responsibility of ensuring that all points from the action list are dealt with.

It should not normally be necessary to hold another walkthrough for the same activity. Walkthroughs are a very powerful technique and are most successful where they are carried out in an 'ego-less' environment, that is, one in which the individual concerned with the particular activity does not feel solely responsible for it. It is important that all team members have responsibility for the system.

Even down to the level of individual programs, it is important that all team members have access to any code produced and feel responsible for the system as a whole rather than just that program. In practice, this means that a programmer should be able to accept criticism of the program design, code, or test plan that has been produced. Equally, the programmer should not feel afraid to discuss code produced by someone else. This type of environment is encouraged by the use of structured walkthroughs because they are a formal introduction to an approach of communication. In some organizations structured walkthroughs are used extensively during coding. The idea is not to fault-find or criticize any individuals but to identify any potential problems and resolve them as early as possible in the information systems development process.

There are two specific types of walkthrough that are commonly used in programming: code reading and dry running. These are not formalized procedures but entail team members critically examining each other's work:

1 Code reading

This is performed both before testing and on completion of testing. It is normally carried out by someone other than the developer of the code being looked at. Again the idea is that work is exposed to outside scrutiny and comment as soon as possible. The aims of initial code reading are to:

- detect any coding errors in going from the program design to the code of the programming language used;
- ensure that appropriate coding standards of the organization have been adhered to;
- check that the coding is efficient in terms of the performance that the system will produce;
- cross-educate team members, as they all have the opportunity to learn from the code developed by others.

The aims of the final code reading, a task which is usually performed by the team leader, are to:

- check that the code is of good quality and adheres to organizational standards;
- confirm that testing of the code has been completed according to the appropriate test plan;
- establish that the code is consistent with the specification that it was produced from.

Code reading is a difficult and time-consuming activity but it does have a number of benefits:

■ most minor errors are discovered before testing begins, preventing more time being wasted later;

■ coding standards are maintained as programmers know that their code will be specifically checked for this and therefore they are more likely to conform in the first place;

■ technical expertise is communicated by the code reader passing on his or her knowledge to the programmer as a result of the code reading activity;

■ an ego-less environment is created where the emphasis is continually on reviewing products rather than personnel.

2   Dry running

■ This involves manually passing test data through the code. The start of the process involves the programmer listing all the variables and noting any initial values. As the test data are processed, variables are tested and updated as appropriate. This may seem a tedious task, but it has the advantage that errors and discrepancies are highlighted and it can also verify that the test data are adequate. However, if previous reviews have been performed adequately, it is only necessary to dry-run complex programs. This is because logical design errors will have been removed during the structured walkthrough of the design and clerical errors in the translation of design to code will have been found during code reading.

12.7   MATRICES

One of the most common of techniques in all walks of life is the matrix, a simple tabular expression of a relationship, usually between two things (three things would require a 3-dimensional set of matrices). We find them in many methodologies. In this section we give a few examples of their use.

A common matrix is that showing the relationship between functions and events. In Figure 12.19, which is a part-formed matrix relating to the acceptance of students on courses, the Xs at the intersections between an event row and a function column shows that an event triggers a particular function. Therefore, the event 'student enquiry' triggered the 'process enquiry' and 'selection' functions. Every event should trigger at least one function and every function should have a triggering event.

A second matrix used by many methodologies is that associating functions with entities, that is, what entities are used by each function to enable that function to be carried out? Figure 12.20 shows the entities used by functions carried out in a hospital. Frequently in methodologies, the entries reveal more than this, that is, the manner of access. Therefore, C (create), R (read), U (update), and D (delete), entries will give more information about the relationship between the two than a mere X. This is often referred

Function name / Event name	Process enquiry	Selection	Enrolment	Accounts
Student enquiry	X	X		
Student accepted		X	X	
Student registers				X

FIGURE 12.19   Function/event matrix.

Entity name / Function name	Staff member	Group session	Location	Program type	Patient
Group session attendances	R	U	R		C/U
Programs	R			R	R
Contacts traced	R				U
Assessments	R				R/U/D
Program costing	R			U	R

FIGURE 12.20   Entity/function matrix (CRUD matrix).

to as a CRUD matrix. There should be represented in the full set of matrices all the entities contained in the entity model and all the functions contained in the data flow diagrams. The CRUD matrix can also be used for the relationship between entities and events. Some cells may contain more than one entity, for example, C and R. This will show that a particular event leads to an entity occurrence either being created or simply accessed.

The systems designer may well also create a key attribute and entity matrix. This will ensure that all entities have a key. Where there are two or more Xs, this will show that an entity has a composite key. Other matrices commonly found are those associating entities and attributes and that showing the relationship between user roles and functions.

A matrix showing the document flows through the system, such as that relating the data elements in the data dictionary system with the various documents that record

Document Department	Order	Note	Invoice
Sales office	1		2
Warehouse	2/4	1/3	
Production	3	2	
Accounts	5		1
Post room			3

FIGURE 12.21 Document/department matrix.

their existence, is also commonly in use. Figure 12.21 shows the sequence by which documents are processed in various departments.

12.8 ACTION DIAGRAMS

Action diagrams are also ways of representing the details of process logic, the business rules, and are not dissimilar to structured English in that a limited subset of the natural language is used to specify a sequence of actions. They are designed to represent both the detail and the overview levels. Action diagrams are used in a number of methodologies, most notably, Information Engineering (Section 20.3). Tools can be used to check their internal consistency and also check the contents against the data dictionary as well as to make for easy construction. Tools are available which will generate program code from action diagrams.

People have sometimes commented when seeing an action diagram for the first time that, 'it doesn't look much like my idea of a diagram', and it has to be said that, compared to a data flow diagram or an entity model, it is rather lacking in diagrammatic features, such as boxes and circles. However, the basic construct of an action diagram is a bracket, which is diagrammatic. A bracket surrounds a group of actions. Actions are broadly defined, and can be parts of program code, a subroutine, a program itself, an operation, a procedure, or, at the highest level, a function.

The bracket indicates control. The actions within the bracket are performed in linear sequence like structured English or a computer program, and the brackets may be nested to indicate hierarchical structure.

Figure 12.22 represents the processing that is carried out in the function 'admit a student'.

Action diagrams support the structured programming constructs of condition, case, repetition, repeat ... until. Figure 12.23 shows selection in an action diagram

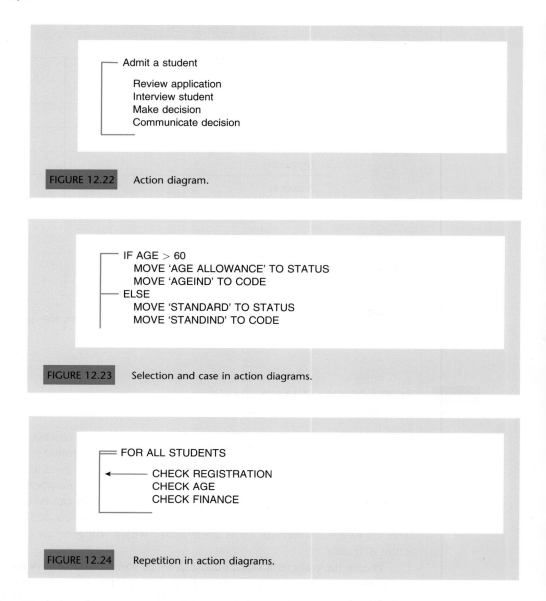

FIGURE 12.22   Action diagram.

FIGURE 12.23   Selection and case in action diagrams.

FIGURE 12.24   Repetition in action diagrams.

having an IF ... ELSE construct. If there is more than one dash in the bracket this indicates that these parts are mutually exclusive, that is, it represents the CASE structure of structured English.

The execution of a loop is indicated by a double dash at the top of the bracket and a thicker than normal line for the bracket. Figure 12.24 illustrates some repeated actions, the arrow indicates a next iteration construct, that is, skip the remaining actions and go to the next student. The arrow can also be used to indicate an escape from this bracket completely, if it points not to the bracket itself but goes through the bracket to point to an earlier bracket in a nested set.

The do ... while and do ... until construct is shown in Figure 12.25. The block of instructions to be performed is known as the process action block.

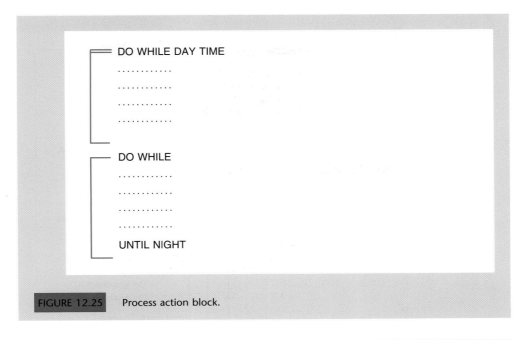

FIGURE 12.25   Process action block.

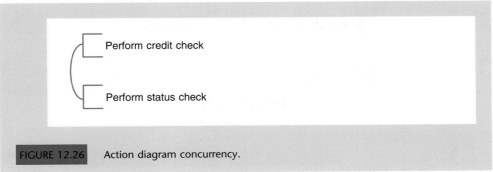

FIGURE 12.26   Action diagram concurrency.

Although brackets indicate sequences of actions, the technique can be used to show the notion of concurrency. Figure 12.26 illustrates concurrency, the link indicates that the actions in the two brackets can be performed in parallel.

Figure 12.27 extends Figure 12.24 and shows a number of the constructs of action diagramming in use.

In order to increase their applicability, action diagrams have been extended in two ways. First, so that the data required for each function or process can be identified, inputs and outputs are added to the diagrams. This requires the brackets to be extended to form a box with the required inputs for the action added to the top right-hand side and the outputs that the action produces added at the bottom right-hand side. Figure 12.28 provides a simple example.

The second extension to action diagrams is to accommodate the fact that actions often need to relate to database operations. The database operations of create, read, update, and delete are added to the action diagram conventions and the name of the

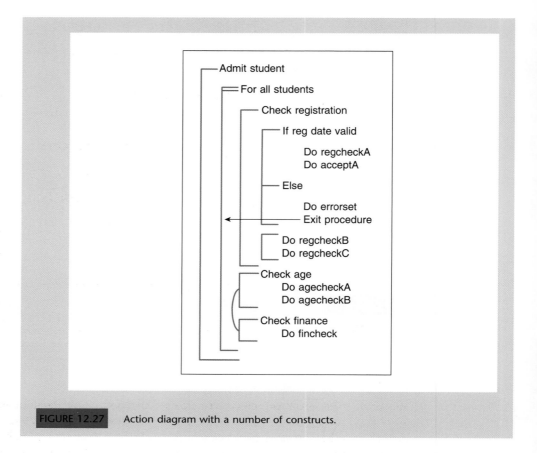

FIGURE 12.27 Action diagram with a number of constructs.

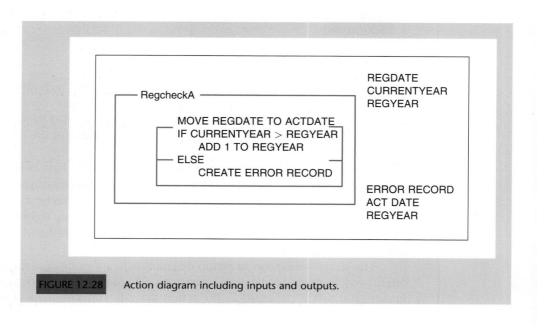

FIGURE 12.28 Action diagram including inputs and outputs.

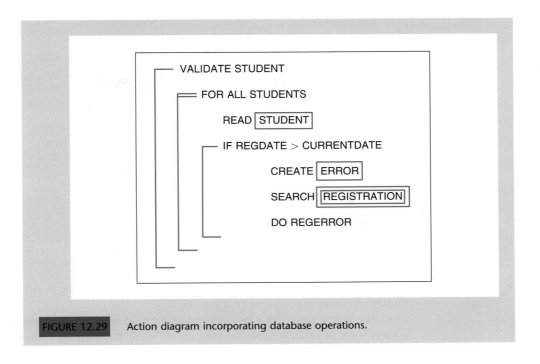

FIGURE 12.29 Action diagram incorporating database operations.

record that the operation refers to is enclosed in a box. These database operations relate to a single occurrence of the record, more complex operations relate to many occurrences and/or more than one record type, and these are represented by a double box. Searching or sorting, or, in relational environments, select and join, are examples of complex or compound database operations.

Figure 12.29 shows an example of an action diagram using the database conventions. Student records are read and processed a single occurrence at a time, 'read student' is only a single box. If we find an error, we wish to find the corresponding registration record and search the registration file. Therefore, 'registration' is in a double box.

Many argue that action diagrams are easy to construct and utilize, both by analysts and users. As well as being able to represent and communicate logic in the traditional systems development process, they are also advocated as being useful to end-users when developing their own systems using various software tools and also by information centre staff when working with users. A particular benefit of using action diagrams is that it is possible to use the same technique for representing high-level functions right through to low-level process logic.

12.9 ENTITY LIFE CYCLE

This technique also varies slightly from methodology to methodology and is called by different names, but in essence what is being achieved is substantially the same. The entity life cycle is used at a variety of stages in a number of methodologies and is one of

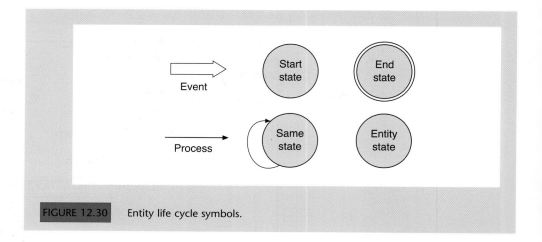

FIGURE 12.30   Entity life cycle symbols.

the few attempts to address changes that happen over **time** (most of the other techniques represent static views of a system).

The entity life cycle is not, despite its name, a technique of data analysis, but more a technique of process analysis, though we were tempted to have a chapter on time techniques with this section on its own! It does show the changes of state that an entity goes through, but the things that cause the state of the entity to change are processes and events, and it is these that are being analysed. The objective of entity life cycle analysis is to identify the various possible states that an entity can legitimately be in. The subobjectives, or by-products, of entity life cycle analysis are to identify the processes in which the entity type is involved and to discover any processes that have not been identified elsewhere. It may also identify valid (and invalid) process sequences, not identified previously, and it can form the outline design for transaction processing systems. So, as well as being a useful analysis technique in its own right, it is a useful exercise to perform as a validation of other process analysis techniques.

The documentation of the states of an entity in a diagram is one of the most powerful features of entity life cycle analysis. The diagram provides a pictorial way of communication that enables users to validate the accuracy or otherwise of the analysis easily.

The modelling conventions differ from methodology to methodology but the concepts are fairly consistent. In the following example the conventions of Information Engineering are used. Figure 12.30 shows the different symbols used, and Figure 12.31 shows a simplified example of an entity life cycle for the entity 'student' in the context of a university environment.

There is always a starting point, an event, which sets the entity into its initial state. There are three types of event. Events can be caused by external factors, such as a prospective student applies for admission into a degree programme (the starting point in the example); internal, such as a decision is made to accept the student for admission; or time-related, for example a candidate has not replied to our offer one month following our letter and is deemed to have withdrawn. There is also always (or should always be) at least one end or terminating point to finish the life cycle. In-between, there may be many different states of the entity.

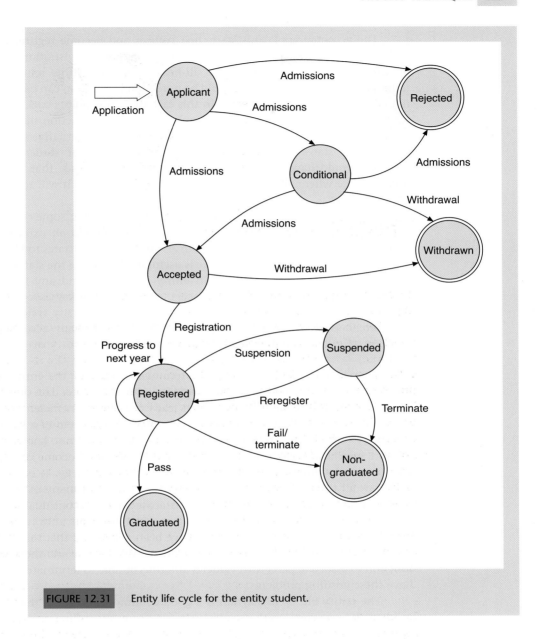

FIGURE 12.31   Entity life cycle for the entity student.

In the example, the initial state of the entity is as 'applicant'. This is triggered by an event, which is the receipt of an application for admission for one of the courses at the university. The entity changes state as a result of the admissions function, which either causes the applicant to be rejected, conditionally accepted (which means that the applicant is accepted provided certain examination grades will be achieved), or unconditionally accepted. The resultant entity states are rejected, conditional, or accepted. At any time, both conditional and accepted applicants may withdraw their applications.

The accepted applicants start their courses and become registered. They may or may not graduate. Registered students may suspend their registration for a wide variety of reasons at any time, for example, ill-health, and may either return as registered or terminate as non-graduated. It should be noted that a function can be depicted that does not change the state of the entity. In this case the arrow points back to the same entity state. 'Progress to next year' is an example of this; it is a function that does not change the state of the entity, the student is still registered. An alternative perspective, that of three entity states named first-year students, second-year students, and final-year students, would have led to a change of state. Again, we see that systems analysis is not a science where all analysts following the same approach will result in exactly the same diagram.

In this example there are a number of terminated states, some conventions suggest that there should only be one. In this case we would add an extra state, called, for example, archived, and draw arrows from all our terminated states to this archived state.

It can be seen that the technique is useful in identifying the states of an entity, the processes that cause the states of an entity to change, and any sequences that are implied. Like many other of these process techniques, the key aspects of sequence (of business rules as the applicant proceeds through the university system to graduation), selection (between alternatives, such as, accept, conditionally accept, or reject), and iteration (e.g. registered students progressing from year to year) can be expressed clearly.

It is also important to identify the terminating states of the entity. Some information systems have not always done this and found that at a later date they have no way of getting rid of entity occurrences, which leads to obvious inefficiencies. One example found by the authors concerned the vehicle spare parts system of a large organization. In this system vehicles require specific parts, but what is not known is which parts support specific vehicles. The result is that when vehicles become obsolete there is no way of withdrawing the parts that support that vehicle only. It is too dangerous to withdraw all the parts required by the obsolete vehicle, as many of these parts will be used by other vehicles. This results in a database which is continually growing as new vehicles and their parts are added. If there had been an entity life cycle analysis performed on the entity part, it would have been discovered that the entity occurrence did not terminate. The likelihood is that the organization would then have designed a function to associate parts with vehicles and thus be able to terminate the entity and not have these ensuing problems.

The entity life cycle diagram is a good communication tool that enables users to validate the accuracy of the analysis. It can form an outline design for transaction processing systems. A by-product of the analysis process is that functions in which the entity type is involved are identified. The process is therefore useful as a validation of the other process analysis techniques. These charts should be drawn for all the entities.

Some approaches develop entity life cycle diagrams further. For example, they might use separate symbols for various states of entities, such as, set-up, amended and deleted states. Others show functions on the diagram as well as entity states. The functions implied in Figure 12.31 might include 'reject student', 'conditionally accept student', and 'student withdraws'. Their explicit inclusion, by labelling arrows in more detail, might help full understanding of the overall documentation set and also might identify functions which have been omitted. Events occurring in the problem

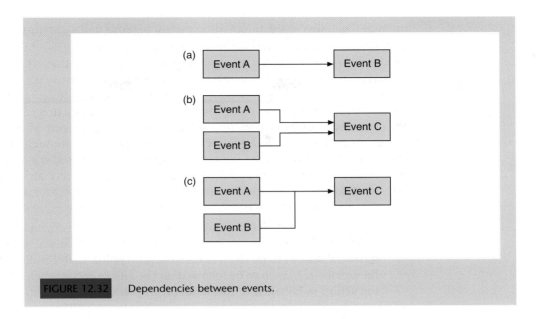

FIGURE 12.32   Dependencies between events.

situation which have not been modelled anywhere else in the documentation may also be identified.

In SSADM the entity life cycle is termed an entity life history. The diagram looks more like a hierarchical structure with the entity under consideration as the root or parent of the tree. The resulting diagrams are rather more complex than that shown in this section because they express more. These are described, with an example, in Section 20.1. The entity life history diagram is also very similar to the structure diagram of Jackson Systems Development (JSD). In JSD this is the central modelling technique used in the methodology and there are also extensions to the entity life cycle technique and these are described in JSD (Section 19.3).

In some approaches, entity life cycles are developed to provide information related to events, which are not possible to provide on standard entity life cycle diagrams. For example:

■   If incorrect information has been added to an entity at what stages can it be corrected?

■   What effect does premature termination have on the life of an entity?

■   Can events happen out of sequence and, if so, which ones are permissible?

Unless such questions are considered, the analysis work is not complete and this may lead to an information system unable to deal with all possible situations. The extra information can be captured on these **state dependency diagrams** which can be created alongside entity life cycle diagrams as they show the dependencies between events. In Figure 12.32(a) event A must take place before event B; in Figure 12.32(b) event A and event B must take place before event C; in Figure 12.32(c) event A or event B must take place before event C. Of course, the interdependencies need to be thought out first and therefore the technique encourages proper analysis. Such analysis can be a vital input to the design of the information system in terms of the application logic following events.

12.10 SUMMARY

- Data-flow diagrams provide structure to a system (or part of a system) showing independent units in a graphical and concise manner. Through functional decomposition, it is possible to examine a system in overview and at a detailed level, while maintaining the links and interfaces between the different levels. The system can be described as a logical or physical model. There are four aspects: data flows, processes, data stores, and sources/sinks.

- Decision trees and decision tables aim to facilitate the documentation of process logic, particularly where there are many decision alternatives. A decision tree illustrates the actions to be taken at each decision point. Each condition will determine the particular branch to be followed. At the end of each branch there will either be the action to be taken or further decision points.

- Decision tables are less graphical, when compared to decision trees, but are concise and have an inbuilt verification mechanism so that it is possible to check that all the conditions have been catered for. Again, conditions and actions are analysed from the procedural aspects of the problem situation expressed in narrative form. They have four elements: action stub, condition stub, condition entry, and action entry.

- Structured English is very like a 'readable' computer program. It aims to produce unambiguous logic, which is easy to understand and not open to misinterpretation. It is not a natural language like English, which is ambiguous and therefore unsuitable. Nor is it a programming language. It is a strict and logical form of English and the constructs reflect structured programming. The sequence of the commands reflects the application logic.

- The structure chart is another functional decomposition technique with a series of boxes (representing processes or parts of computer programs, usually referred to as modules) and connecting lines (representing links to subordinate processes that show the way that data and control can be passed between processes) which are arranged in a hierarchy.

- Structured walkthroughs are a series of formal reviews of a system, held at various stages of the life cycle. They are intended to be team-based reviews of a product, such as a design component.

- A matrix is a simple tabular expression of a relationship, usually between two things such as entities and database files, or data items and processes.

- An action diagram represents an alternative way of representing the details of process logic (the business rules) and is specified in the Information Engineering methodology among others.

- An entity life cycle addresses changes that happen over time. It shows the changes of state that an entity goes through from when it enters the system to when it is discarded.

QUESTIONS

In relation to a video rental chain of shops:

1 Draw a decision tree and a decision table to express the logic related to the decision whether to accept an applicant as a new customer or not.

2 Draw a data flow diagram (DFD) showing how the shop might process a registered customer wishing to rent a video.

3 Draw an entity life cycle for the entity customer.

4 Perform structured walkthroughs of your colleagues' efforts and ask them to do the same with yours.

12.11 FURTHER READING

Avison, D.E. and Shah, H.U. (1995) *The Information Systems Development Cycle: A First Course in Information Systems*, McGraw-Hill, Maidenhead, UK.

Lejk, M. and Deeks, D. (1998) *An Introduction to Systems Analysis Techniques*, Prentice Hall, Harlow, UK.

13 OBJECT-ORIENTED TECHNIQUES

13.1 OBJECT ORIENTATION

In Section 5.4 the basic concepts and a number of advantages of the object-oriented approach were identified. In this section we examine the concepts and some of the techniques further. In Chapter 21 we look at two methodologies for information systems development that utilize the object-oriented approach. Readers interested in object orientation should look at all these sections.

We begin by looking at a definition of **object-oriented programming** (Booch, 1991) and then examining the object-oriented components of that definition:

> Object Oriented Programming is a method of implementation in which programs are organised as a co-operative collection of objects, each of which represents an instance of some class, and whose classes are all members of a hierarchy of classes united via inheritance relationships.

Such definitions are not always very clear or meaningful at first sight but this definition is in fact quite comprehensive. We begin by looking at some of the components of the definition. First, we examine the concept of an object. An **object** is something to which actions are directed, it has an identity, a state, and exhibits behaviour. The identity enables it to be distinguished from other objects; the state is the current value of the dynamic properties of the object; and the behaviour is the actions that the object can itself undertake.

Formal definitions of an object or objects are not very helpful because basically an object can be anything, so we add that it should also be an abstraction of something in the problem domain, that is, it is of interest to us (in this case, as developers), given the context of our current objectives (in this case, to develop a particular system).

Yourdon and Argila (1996) informally define an object as, 'an independent, asynchronous, concurrent entity which "knows things" (i.e. stores data), "does work" (i.e.

encapsulates services), and "collaborates with other objects" (by exchanging messages), to perform the overall functions of the system being modelled.'

Strictly speaking, an object is an instance of a class of objects (i.e. a group of objects together make up a class of objects). All the objects in the class exhibit a common set of object attributes, such as structure and behaviour. Unfortunately the term 'object' is often used synonymously with class. So, strictly, the very term 'object oriented' itself should really be 'class oriented'.

A class is often illustrated by an example, which is often customer or client in many books. However, this does not really distinguish it from an entity in entity-relationship modelling for example. Therefore, a class can be a person or a place or an invoice or whatever, but it is not just the data as it would be if it was an entity. Additionally, it has actions or services that it can undertake and it can pass messages to other objects. So, it is more than just the data associated with say a customer. The customer class may include processing or code, for example, to change the status of the customer, and pass the new status to another class, such as a billing class.

Additionally, classes may be structured in a hierarchy based on inherited properties. Inheritance is a relationship among classes, such that one or more classes share the structure or behaviour of another class. The identification of classes in the design of a system is a key part. Classes are not necessarily the obvious ones we might first think of, or be the same as the entities we might identify.

Coad and Argila (1996) tell a story of a small European country that built a new social security system which kept track of pension and benefit payments, and much more besides, at great cost. They adopted an object-oriented approach and identified objects (classes) such as citizen, pension, benefit, etc. The system was not a success and was very difficult to maintain as local and European legislation changed frequently. As Yourdon and Argila say, 'nowhere was there a legislative rule object or anything similar. The secrets of legislative rules were embedded throughout the system ... and whenever one changed, it usually required that very significant system-wide changes be made.'

Therefore, objects have to be properly identified and designed. Only if this is done correctly will the benefits of object orientation be obtained. If it is not done well then there are no particular benefits to object orientation. This means that the object-oriented methodology is of key importance. However, methodologies are not dealt with until Chapter 21.

To illustrate the general benefits and concepts of object orientation we will use an example. The object we identify is customer update. Let us assume the object is an update transaction on a customer file and, further, that it is a particular transaction to update a specific record, in a specific way, made at a particular time. The object has a unique identity, for example, 16249, the number of the transaction on the transaction log, which is unique to this transaction. The object has a state, in this case the state is 'successfully completed', that is, the update has been properly made. Other possible states of the object might be 'unsuccessfully completed', 'in-process', or 'awaiting processing'. In practice, the object may have many potential states combining a variety of attributes.

The behaviour of the object is the actions (or operations) that it can undertake: it can trigger an error message, it can change the contents of a field, it can access the status of the record, it can update the log file, and so on. The behaviour of the object is completely defined by its actions.

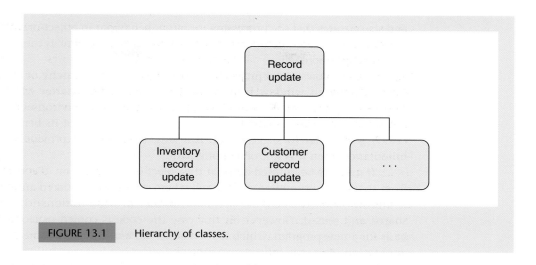

FIGURE 13.1   Hierarchy of classes.

A class is the group of objects that share a common structure and behaviour. In this example the class might be that of 'customer record update', that is, the general class of which our object 16249 is an instance (the terms 'object' and 'instance' are in fact the same and are used interchangeably). So, the class is the general form of the object.

If we compare the concepts used in the entity-relationship model, we can make an analogy in terms of the relationship between entity types and classes, and entity occurrences and objects. The entity type is the general form and an entity occurrence is a specific instance of the entity type. For those with a programming background, class is analogous to type.

Classes are often structured in a hierarchy, which shares certain properties. Our class of 'customer record update' might be a subset of a class called 'record update', which might have more than one subclass, for example, inventory record update. Thus, there is a hierarchy of classes. This is illustrated in Figure 13.1.

Hierarchy is not simply about classes and subsets or supersets of classes but also includes the object-oriented notion of **inheritance** to define the relationships in the hierarchy. Inheritance implies that the relationship is such that the hierarchy goes from classes of a general type down to classes of a more specific type, or from classes that exhibit commonality down to those with differences at the lower levels. The classes at the top are general and are then extended with more detail at the lower level in the hierarchy. In an object-oriented programming language, a lower class in the hierarchy can be produced from the higher class 'inheriting' all the higher class's structure and behaviour. The programmer can then add some more specifics and detail to the lower level class to make it perform more specifically than the higher class from which it was derived.

In our example, the class 'record update' would contain all the general features required to update a record. The class 'customer record update' would have inherited all these and then extended the class specifically to update the customer file. The benefits of inheritance include the fact that code can be reused; instead of separately writing code for 'customer record update' and 'inventory record update' we just inherit most of it from the higher class of 'record update'. This saves time and has other efficiency benefits, and also ensures that the processing (or rather behaviour in object-oriented terminology) in both 'customer record update' and 'inventory record update' is the same, that is, there is a standard approach.

MS Windows-based programs, for example, use a hierarchy of windows classes to ensure that each window behaves in the same way no matter which application is running in order to achieve a consistent windowing environment. Inheritance is central to the object-oriented concept and provides much of its benefit. Indeed Booch (1991) goes as far to suggest that 'if a language does not provide direct support for inheritance, then it is not object oriented'.

It needs to be pointed out that the object-oriented notion of code reuse is different from that in traditional programming, where code is often shared and borrowed, which is a form of reuse. There are program libraries in organizations to enable code to be shared and reused. However, in this case the code is copied or cloned and used as a basis for a new program, which is then amended and extended as necessary for the new application. This may indeed save time and effort but it is very unlikely that the original code can be returned to again because there are now two separate entities: the original program and the new program, and they develop along quite separate paths in different ways. If an error is found in the original code or a change is required to the original code, such change has to be made in both programs as the new program has changed and evolved so much it is usually impossible to go back to the original and start again.

With object orientation, and true inheritance, the higher level class could be changed and the lower level classes would inherit that new behaviour by a simple recompilation. The processing specifically required for the lower level, in this case the code to make it specific to customers, would not be affected, because the object-oriented inheritance has ensured that they are treated and organized separately. In the example, we could change the class 'record update' and then recompile the classes 'customer record update' and 'inventory record update', and this effectively means that they then inherit the changes. So, the change is made only once and is applied to all the subclasses, and in this way really effective reuse is potentially achieved.

It should be obvious that inheritance does not just happen, it needs careful design. We will examine this in more detail later, but at the very least the decision as to the classes and their hierarchical structure needs to be thought about very carefully, such that the common aspects are included in the higher level objects and the requirements of the special cases are contained in the lower levels. This is not always easy nor intuitive.

There is a further aspect relating to the definition of object-oriented programming made above that needs exploring: the organization of the program as '. . . a co-operative collection of objects'.

In the object-oriented world, objects sit around waiting to be activated, and that activation happens when the object receives a message from another object. Messages are the only way that objects communicate, and we may think of objects being fired off by messages from other objects or by an initial event. So, an object-oriented program is a series of objects organized to interrelate in particular ways to produce the functionality that is required of the program. This is sometimes referred to as co-operage. Communicating through messages makes objects independent; that is, they do not need any other object, or knowledge, to perform their job. They are triggered by a message from another object, they perform their job, which may itself involve the triggering of other objects, and when complete they usually return a message to that

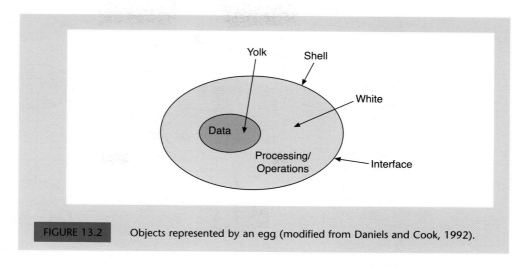

FIGURE 13.2	Objects represented by an egg (modified from Daniels and Cook, 1992).

effect to the triggering object. In traditional programming this might be thought of as a bit like a subroutine, but a subroutine is not always independent nor is it triggered by the passing of a message.

For example, we might have an object 'menu-selection' which displays a menu and obtains a selection of an option from the user. The object is fired or invoked by another object passing a message to 'menu-selection', part of the message might be the menu that should be used in 'menu-selection' itself. Let us assume that the object 'menu-selection' is the method for selection from a menu and all the associated error checking, and the message is the menu text to be used. On completion, 'menu-selection' returns the option that has been selected by the user as a message or it may invoke another object. In this way the object is independent of other objects and exists as an independent entity. The exact way that it performs its task and the data used by the object are unknown to other objects, indeed it may even be written in a different programming language. This also means that the internal workings or implementation of the object can be changed without it causing any problems or affecting the other objects.

What is important is the external interface of the object, that is, its messages. Furthermore, data and procedures are not allowed to exist externally or independently of an object, unlike in most other programming approaches. The fact that the internal processing and the details of the data are hidden (or private) is known as **encapsulation** and this is described by Booch (1991) as another of the fundamental elements of the object model.

Daniels and Cook (1992) use the analogy of an egg to illustrate the concept (see Figure 13.2). An object is an egg, the yolk is the data surrounded by the white which is the processing or operations that act on the data. The shell of the egg surrounds the whole thing and keeps it all together. It effectively hides the data and processes from the outside world, the shell is the interface and the only thing that is seen. The data and processes are said to be **encapsulated** in the object. The analogy breaks down a little because the shell of the egg, although nicely encapsulating the contents and hiding them from the outside world, does not interface very well with other eggs, nor does it

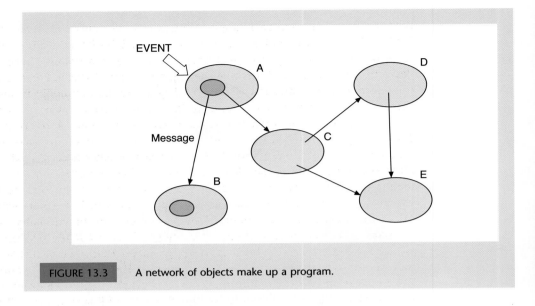

FIGURE 13.3   A network of objects make up a program.

send messages, or have an identity. In other approaches and methodologies, for example, SSADM, Merise, and Information Engineering, the data and processes exist, but are analysed, and handled separately. Encapsulation is very different.

An object-oriented program is simply a collection of interrelated objects where the connections are unidirectional paths along which messages are sent. The program begins with an initiation from outside, often an event, which triggers an object, from then on that object initiates others and so on. The activations form a network of objects that together make up the program (see Figure 13.3).

Programming an application consists of developing the objects and specifying the network or the co-operation between objects. It is one of the objectives and benefits of the object-oriented approach that in the future most of the objects needed will already exist somewhere, either within the organization or available commercially, and then development will essentially involve selecting or buying the right objects and connecting them together in an appropriate network. The path that the program takes through the network is called the thread, or the thread of control, and it can be difficult to identify once the program is invoked, because of course the objects are interacting in ways dependent on events and user responses. Also, in theory, the objects may be operating concurrently, and even on different processors.

In the discussion above the concept of an object is that of an instance or particular occurrence of a class, which means that objects are unique, and yet it is only the data, the identity, and state that are different. The general behaviour of objects in the same class is the same. Clearly it would be foolish to write the code for each object separately, so what is done in practice is that the code is written once and shared by objects of the same class. The object is really just a data structure holding the relevant data for the object, and when the object is asked to perform an operation the run-time system ensures that the data are connected with the relevant code. This means that in practice the implementation of object-oriented programs differs somewhat from the theory.

Having discussed the theory, we will now summarize the benefits that the proponents of the approach argue it generates (see also the benefits discussed in Section 5.4). As discussed above, the concept of inheritance leads to the controlled reuse of code. In theory, the organization will develop a library of object classes that deal with all the basic activities that the organization undertakes. Programming becomes the selection and connection of existing classes into relevant applications, and because those classes are well tried and tested as independent classes, when they are connected they provide immediate industrial-strength applications that run correctly the first time. Only completely new classes will need to be developed or perhaps purchased. Proponents of object orientation believe that, eventually, there will exist international libraries of object classes that developers will be able to browse to find the classes they require and buy them. The classes in these libraries will be guaranteed to perform as specified, and so new applications are easily developed. Further, existing (object-oriented) applications are modified and extended in functionality just as easily. Software development is not only quicker and cheaper but the resulting applications are robust and error-free. This attacks the problems that have bedevilled the software industry for so long, such as projects being delivered late, over budget, and full of errors. The implication is that the information systems developed using object-oriented techniques will be robust and error-free and quicker and cheaper to achieve. They should also be easier to maintain and hence address another problem that has bedevilled traditional software development.

13.2   UML (UNIFIED MODELLING LANGUAGE)

The Unified Modelling Language (UML) is a graphical language, or a notation, for modelling systems analysis and design concepts in an object-oriented fashion. It is a set of rules and semantics that can be used to specify the structure and logic of a system. Although it has the term language, this refers to UML being a graphical language rather than a programming language.

In the early days of object-oriented development each author or vendor seemed to define their own notation for their own variant of language or object-oriented approach. As a result there was a great deal of diversity and some confusion. The same concepts had a number of different notations. This was a barrier to object-oriented use. There was concern that, although the theoretical concepts of the object-oriented approach were well understood and generally well established in education, their practical use was worryingly low. So, attempts were made to standardize notations in the hope that this would remove some of the confusion and smooth the path to increased adoption of object-oriented techniques in practice.

Therefore, UML was developed, with the first standard being made available in 1997. Booch, Jacobson, and Rumbaugh set themselves seven goals as follows (Booch et al., 1997):

1   Provide users a ready-to-use, expressive, visual modelling language so they can develop and exchange meaningful models.

2   Provide extensibility and specialization mechanisms to extend the core concepts.

3 | Be independent of particular programming languages and development processes.

4 | Provide a formal basis for understanding the modelling language.

5 | Encourage the growth of the object-oriented tools market.

6 | Support higher level development concepts.

7 | Integrate best practices and methodologies.

UML is now managed and maintained by the Object Management Group (OMG), an independent and 'vendor-neutral' organization. According to Smith (2000) UML has 'broken free from its proprietary roots to become an evolving public standard.'

The first version of UML was 1.1 and at the time of writing the latest version is 1.4, but there is also a version 2.0 planned for 2002 including UML facilities for the design of web applications, enterprise application integration, real-time systems, and distributed platforms. Exactly where UML will go in the future is not clear. As new developments and technologies emerge it must evolve and this means that it will grow. The problem is that as it grows in size it becomes more complex, difficult to understand, and of less use as a standard. It may well be already. Most people only use a subset of UML and as Booch et al. (1997) says, 'you can model 80 percent of most problems by using about 20 percent of the UML.' As a response, OMG is attempting to define a UML kernel.

The UML defines 12 types of diagram, divided into three categories (OMG, 2002). The first category is static application diagrams comprising Class Diagrams, Object Diagrams, Component Diagrams, and Deployment Diagrams. The second is dynamic behaviour diagrams comprising Use Case Diagrams, Sequence Diagrams, Activity Diagrams, Collaboration Diagrams, and Statechart Diagrams. The third category represents diagrams that help to organize and manage applications, composed of Packages, Subsystems, and Models.

Like other authors, we choose only to illustrate a small subset of UML, but it is enough to understand the essence of the language and prove useful enough without being overburdensome. Six diagrams are described below (we concentrate on the dynamic). The notation with examples are described and illustrated using the Select Enterprise case tool (see Section 18.4), except for Figure 13.9, the Activity Diagram, which was developed using the Rational Rose CASE tool. Of course, although the notation of UML is standard, the way the diagrams are used is a different matter and depends on what a developer is doing or what methodology is being followed.

1 Class diagram

The class diagram is used for modelling static structure in UML, and a class is represented as a rectangle separated into three parts. The top part depicts the class name, the middle part the attributes, and the lower part the operations. Figure 13.4 shows a class diagram consisting of one class named **Student**, with attributes of RegNumber, Name and Course, and operations of ChangeCourse, Defer and TerminateReg. This tells us that a class of **Student** exists with attributes as shown and operations that the class may participate in (i.e. the common behaviour of the class). Obviously in this example things are simplified; for example, the attributes of class **Student** are likely to be rather more than three in number, and probably have more than three operations, but

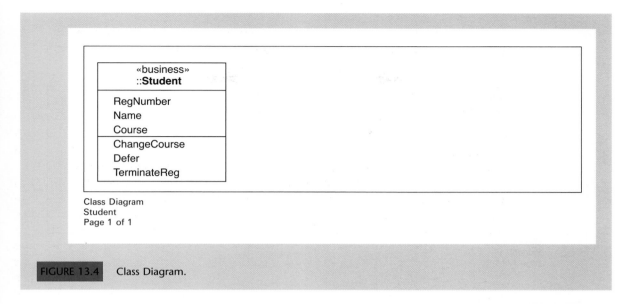

FIGURE 13.4   Class Diagram.

UML allows us to use the diagrams in the way we wish for the purpose. So, in a high-level analysis activity we would not include the detail that might appear when we are conducting a low-level design activity. In fact UML allows us to omit the attributes and/or the operations from the class diagram. So, the rectangle may only consist of the class name (for example see Figure 13.5). It is thus quite flexible. Usually the class name is in bold and additionally in italics if it is an abstract class.

An object is an instance of a class. In the example of Figure 13.4, an instance of **Student** might be Smith (i.e. an instance of class **Student**). When an object is spawned from a class it has the same structure as the class, therefore the notation is the same. But in order to differentiate an object from a class, the object name is usually underlined rather than being in bold.

Figure 13.5 shows a slightly more complex class diagram. It illustrates an association between the class of **Student** and the class of **Degree** (i.e. a student is registered for a degree). An association represents a relationship between instances of classes, similar to the relationships between entities (see Section 11.1). Unfortunately the notation in UML is different, including that to represent multiplicity, which is the term given to indicate how many objects may participate in the association. In Figure 13.5 the multiplicity is shown at either end of the association line. The * represents the range zero to infinity (0 . . . *infinity*) and the 1 indicates one and only one (*1 . . . 1*). Therefore, a student is registered for one and only one degree (at a particular time) and a degree can be taken by an infinite number of students. If there were a maximum, say 250, this would be represented as (*0 . . . 250*).

The class **Degree** is shown as having a single-inheritance hierarchy. The superclass **Degree** is composed of two subclasses, **Part-time** and **Full-time** degrees. Actually it is not really 'composed of', rather the subclasses inherit features (attributes and operations) from the superclass. However, in UML the inheritance arrow points upward. It is single inheritance because one subclass inherits from one superclass. Multiple inheritance is

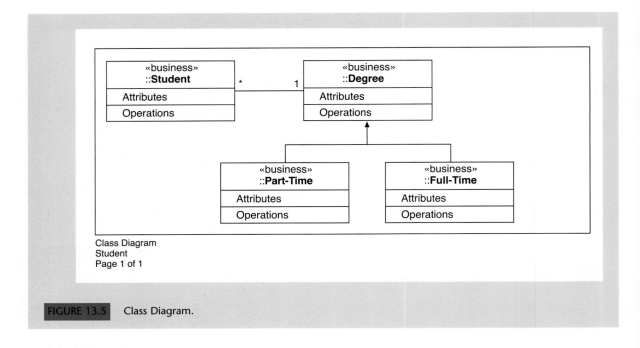

Class Diagram
Student
Page 1 of 1

FIGURE 13.5   Class Diagram.

where a subclass inherits from more than one superclass. For more details of inheritance see Section 13.1.

2   Use case diagram

Use cases describe the functionality of a system from the perspective of users or actors in the system. It is a high-level, user-oriented diagram. A use case is usually described as a high-level function of a system, and in UML the use case diagram shows the associations or interactions (as lines) between actors (stick figures) in the system and the use cases (ellipses). The diagram also shows the boundary of the system as a rectangle with the use cases within.

Figure 13.6 shows an example of a use case diagram for a student registration in a university. These are the interactions, as the users see them, which are essentially the users' requirements. The use case diagram does not depict the internal processes or workings of the system but only the flow of events as actors interact with the system. The total functionality of a system would be represented by a number of use case diagrams. The diagrams are essentially non-technical and are supposed to represent things that yield value to the actors. For this reason it is recommended that the user should participate in the construction of the diagram.

Actors although usually depicted as stick figures need not be. They can be represented as a class rectangle. Further, an actor might not be a human actor in the system. For example, it could be a non-human piece of hardware, or another system, or perhaps even a methodology. In fact it can be anything that interacts with the system.

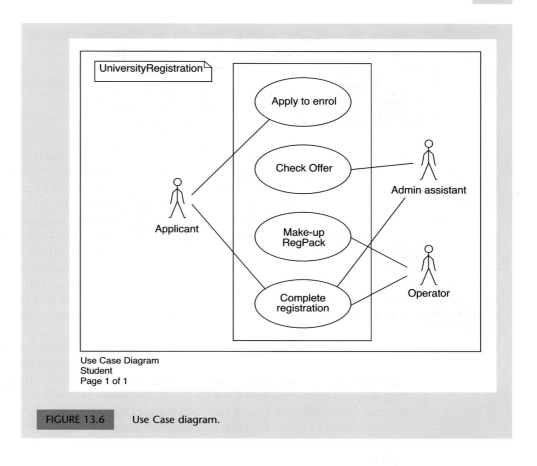

Use Case Diagram
Student
Page 1 of 1

| FIGURE 13.6 | Use Case diagram. |

Along with the use case diagram a use case textual description or specification is usually added. This is often brief, but can be a fully detailed breakdown of each interaction. Some methodologies or OO approaches recommend that the use case diagrams be the starting point for the identification of classes (e.g. Bennett et al., 1999). See also Section 21.2 on the Rational Unified Process (RUP).

3   Interaction diagrams

Unlike the previous diagrams, which were basically static, the interaction diagrams attempt to model dynamic behaviour. There are two interaction diagrams: the sequence diagram and the collaboration diagram. They both are used to describe the interaction between objects and messages in a system within a single use case. We shall only describe the sequence diagram here because the two diagrams are essentially alternative ways of modelling the same thing – interactions – and because people often seem to prefer sequence diagrams. Page-Jones (2000), for example, states that they enable him to 'clearly see who says what to whom and when … and no other diagram illuminates timing so well'. We provide examples of interaction diagrams in the following subsection.

4   The sequence diagram

The sequence diagram shows the interaction between objects and messages over time. Time is normally represented on the vertical axis with the objects (or classes) depicted from left to right on the horizontal. The order of objects in the diagram is immaterial although they are usually drawn so that the message arrows point from left to right as far as possible, just to make it more readable and less cluttered. Each object is depicted as a rectangle (i.e. by its object symbol), usually at the top of the diagram with a dotted line (though not dotted in Figure 13.7 when produced by the select CASE tool) running from the rectangle down the page, known as the object *lifeline*, which shows the object's existence during the interaction. Messages are shown by labelled arrows between the lifelines. When a message is sent from one object to another it sets off an operation of the object. A sequence diagram is often used to expand a use case to a lower level of detail. Figure 13.7 shows an example of a sequence diagram which is an expansion of part of the Check Offer use case of Figure 13.6.

We will follow what happens when the object ValidApp receives a message, CheckApp, sent by the actor StudentApplicant (not shown in this diagram, but see Figure 13.6). The object ValidApp is then invoked which means that an operation of that object is fired. This operation (or set of operations as this is still a fairly high-level diagram) confirms that a valid application exists for this person by sending a message, GenerateOffer, to Offer. The Offer object is then triggered and an offer, in the form of the

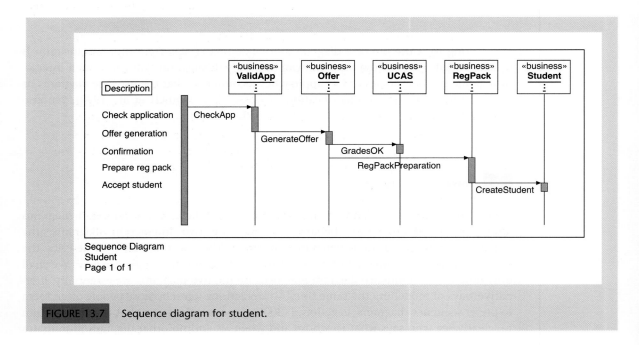

FIGURE 13.7   Sequence diagram for student.

required grades at the advanced level examination for a place on the particular course, is produced. When this has been done the Offer object sends a message, GradesOK, to the UCAS object (this is the central university admissions body in the UK) and also a message to prepare the registration pack (RegPackPreparation) is sent to the objec RegPack. This then triggers a CreateStudent message which is sent to the Student object which creates a new Student. The dotted lifeline starts lower down in the diagram because it is only at this time that the object has been created and so its lifeline starts. The other objects already exist (i.e. they have been created elsewhere), and their lifelines start at the top of the diagram. The activation period of an object is indicated by the grey rectangle on the lifeline which represents the period that the object is executing.

This is again quite a simplified example, it does not indicate what happens if errors are encountered or if the application is not valid. It should also be stated that no university functions in exactly this way, but it illustrates the principles of the sequence diagram. The strength of the sequence diagram is its simplicity and visual appeal. It is relatively easy to get a quick understanding of the flow of control and certainly much easier than looking at program code. It is also a good way of building up the specification of that flow in the first place and is relatively easy for users to understand. Other details can be included in the diagrams as necessary. For example, iteration of a message can be indicated with an asterisk.

5   Statechart diagram

A statechart diagram shows the various permitted states that an object may be in, and then transfer to, as events occur and messages are received. In concept, it is similar to the entity life cycle described in Section 12.9 except that statechart diagrams model an object rather than an entity. The general concepts will not be repeated here so readers should review Section 12.9.

In statechart diagrams (usually just called state diagrams) the state is a particular set of values of the attributes of an object at a particular time. When the value of an attribute changes, the object changes state. Obviously not all changes of attribute values are of interest. We are only interested in modelling those that are deemed to make important changes to the state of the object. For example, if a bank customer cashes a cheque the attribute 'balance', of object BankAccount, will change, but we do not usually consider the object to have changed state (unless perhaps the balance goes negative). However, if a customer tells us that their cash card has been stolen, the attribute 'suspend' will be set and this would probably be important enough for us to consider the object to have changed state.

States of an object are represented by rectangles with rounded corners (state symbols) and usually labelled with a unique name for that state. Transitions from one state to another are represented by arrows with the name of the event that triggers the change and/or the name of the attribute that changes and the condition that triggers it. Events are usually separated from attributes by a / character. A solid black dot represents the starting point for reading the diagram (i.e. the initial state). This starting point is purely notional, and an object cannot be at that point but is immediately in the first state. Similarly, the end point of the diagram is represented by a bull's eye although the object cannot leave its final state. Figure 13.8 is a statechart for object student.

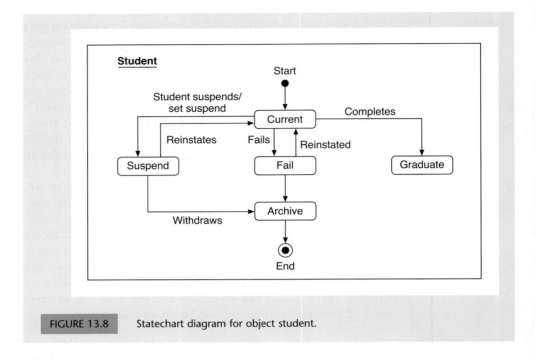

FIGURE 13.8   Statechart diagram for object student.

The diagram starts at the black dot and the object student is in state *current* (there has already been some activity for creating the object). Three possible transitions may occur. First, a student may suspend their studies and the state of the object changes to suspend. Then a student may reinstate themselves and the state returns to current or the student withdraws completely and the state changes to *archive*. Second, the student may successfully complete their studies and the state changes to *graduate*. After a specific period the state then changes to *archive*. Third, the student may fail and the state of the object changes to *fail*. If the student re-takes exams they may be reinstated, or after a specific period the state then changes to *archive*. The bull's eye indicates that *archive* is the final state of the object.

This is the basic statechart diagram. As with other diagrams there are various extensions. For example, hierarchies of states can be nested and concurrency can be represented by splitting a state symbol into two nested halves separated by a dashed line. Each half running concurrently.

6   Activity diagram

An activity diagram is described as a variation of a statechart that replaces events with activities, and focuses on internal flows and activities rather than events. Statecharts are concerned with the states of a single object, whereas an activity diagram can model the internal state of an object or a set of objects or a whole use case. An activity (or action state) is represented by a box (sometimes with curved sides).

Like statecharts they begin with a black dot (the initial state) and move directly to

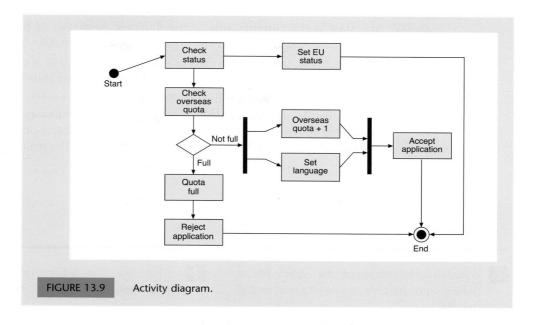

FIGURE 13.9   Activity diagram.

the first state. Figure 13.9 is an activity diagram for an operation called ProcessStudent in our student example. The first state is Check status. This is an action state because it has two possible outgoing transitions. Which one is taken depends on the 'guard condition'. In this case the applicant is either classed as EU (European Union) or Overseas. If EU the state of EU status is set. If Overseas, the quota is checked. If the quota is full, then the application is rejected. If the quota is not full, then the Overseas quota is incremental by one. The condition is in this case represented by a decision diamond after the Check Overseas quota box, with again two mutually exclusive outcomes.

Activity diagrams can indicate activities that can be performed in parallel or that must wait for another activity to complete before starting. This is represented on the diagrams by use of a synchronization bar, which is a short thick line. In Figure 13.9 the synchronization line after the condition quota 'not full' indicates that Set language and Overseas quota + 1 can be performed in parallel. The synchronization bar after these two states indicates that they must both be completed before the next activity.

Thus the UML is a standard modelling language, based on object-oriented concepts, for visualizing, specifying, constructing, and documenting the various models or artefacts required in systems development. A methodology utilizing the UML standard, known as the Rational Unified Process, is described in Section 21.2

13.4   SUMMARY

■   An object is something to which actions are directed, it has an identity, a state, and exhibits behaviour. The identity enables it to be distinguished from other objects;

the state is the current value of the dynamic properties of the object; and the behaviour is the actions that the object can itself undertake.

■ An object is an instance of a class of objects (i.e. a group of objects together make up a class of objects). Inheritance is a relationship among classes, such that one or more classes share the structure or behaviour of another class.

■ The Unified Modelling Language (UML) is a graphical language, or a notation, for modelling systems analysis and design concepts in an object-oriented fashion. It is a set of rules and semantics that can be used to specify the structure and logic of a system.

QUESTIONS

1 What is different about the object model when compared to the entity-relationship model?

2 Why have many organizations turned to the object-oriented approach? Why have many organizations not changed?

3 What are the advantages of graphical languages, like UML, over notational languages?

13.5 FURTHER READING

Fowler, M. (with Scott, K.) (2000) *UML Distilled: A Brief Guide to the Standard Object Modelling Language*, 2nd edn, Addison-Wesley, Reading, Mass., USA.

14 PROJECT MANAGEMENT TECHNIQUES

14.1 ESTIMATION TECHNIQUES

In this section we look at three estimation techniques for project management: **CoCoMo**, function point analysis (FPA), and work breakdown structure. A major problem of software development is estimating the effort required to develop programs. CoCoMo is an approximation of the effort needed based on experience of past projects. This is a formula for estimation based on the amount of program code required, that is, lines of code (measured in thousands of source instructions or KDSI). The formula, evolved from experience, is:

$$PM = 2.4(KDSI)^{1.05}$$

where PM is effort in people-months. So, if 1,000 instructions are required, then:

$$PM = 2.4(1,000)^{1.05}$$
$$= 2.692 \quad \text{(or nearly three people-months)}$$

There are further sophistications of CoCoMo taking into account other factors such as product reliability and complexity, execution time and storage requirements, experience and capability of programmers, use and experience with software tools. Such sophistications aim to increase the reliability of the formula.

Function point analysis, like CoCoMo, is an estimation technique, but somewhat more sophisticated. It tries to estimate the functionality of the system being delivered to the end-user. It does this by analysing the system in terms of information systems requirements, based on the inputs, outputs, files, updates, interfaces, reports, and enquiries, each being assigned a number of function points. An estimate of the technical complexity and such considerations as staff experience and deadline pressure can also be calibrated in the formula to make allowance for these differences. The weights for each criterion are based on measurements from previously developed systems.

This approach is used for software development estimation in methodologies such as SSADM and Merise. The criteria used are easier for analysts to estimate than lines of program code. Even so, the complexity ratios and other adjustment factors require an experienced analyst to estimate. Tables have been created which help determine the effort and elapsed time required to complete the project. At its most sophisticated, this approach will take into consideration supervision levels, documentation, quality levels required, training required, familiarization required, data conversion, reviewing required, technical support required, staff experience, and user involvement among other factors.

One of the major tasks in estimation is breaking down the project into its basic work elements. The first level decomposition will be based on the various phases and subphases, and each is broken down into its technical, management, user liaison, administrative, quality assurance, and other tasks. At the lowest level, the tasks cannot realistically be broken down further and are small enough to make estimation fairly accurate. For each task, analysts may use experience from past projects or seek advice from others for estimation. Work breakdown structure is a first phase in developing PERT charts below.

14.2 PERT CHARTS

PERT (Project Evaluation and Review Technique) is based on project network diagrams or charts with a particular feature for estimating the elapsed time of activities.

In a PERT chart the activities are represented by arrows, which join the nodes (circles). The latter represent events, that is, the completion of activities. Figure 14.1

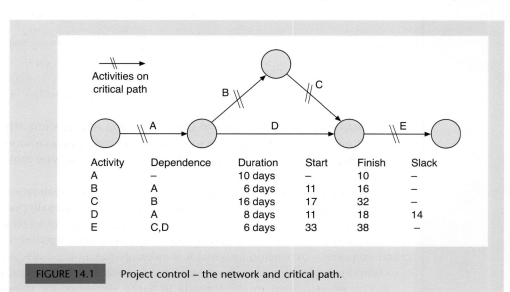

Activity	Dependence	Duration	Start	Finish	Slack
A	–	10 days	–	10	–
B	A	6 days	11	16	–
C	B	16 days	17	32	–
D	A	8 days	11	18	14
E	C,D	6 days	33	38	–

FIGURE 14.1   Project control – the network and critical path.

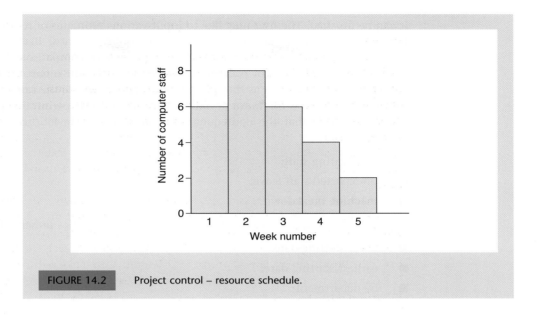

| FIGURE 14.2 | Project control – resource schedule. |

shows a network. The arrows represent the activities, though the length of the arrow does not indicate the time taken for each task. Arrows drawn from the same node indicate tasks that can be carried out simultaneously. Arrows following others indicate tasks that are dependent on the completion of these other tasks.

The manual development of networks is lengthy, and project control software makes the task much easier. Such a software tool can draw the network and highlight critical activities on which any slippage of time will cause the whole project timescale to suffer. The path of the critical activities joined together forms the critical path, and it is useful for the package to highlight these activities. In Figure 14.1, the activities A-B-C-E are on the **critical path**. Each activity on the critical path has been marked with short parallel lines. If it is possible to reduce the time of these activities, perhaps by moving resources allocated from other activities to them, then the overall project time should decrease. Activity D is not on the critical path, and there is a slack of 14 days on this activity. In other words, there can be a delay of up to 14 days on D without delaying the overall project. If feasible, it might be expedient, therefore, to move resources from activity D to an activity on the critical path. This change can be entered into the package and the results recalculated.

PERT tools such as Project 2000 (Section 17.4) can aggregate the various resources, such as the number of people working on the activity, and attempt to smooth their use throughout the project. This can be particularly useful as management reviews and when approving plans.

It is usually better to use resources as smoothly as possible in the lifetime of the project; otherwise staff will be used efficiently for only part of the project. However, unless the resources are taken out of non-critical activities, this process is likely to lead to an increase in the overall project time. Once smoothing has been done, a bar chart showing the resource allocation over time can be produced (see Figure 14.2).

Normally there is a trade-off between time and cost (assuming the same quality); in other words, the more resources allocated (and the more costly the project); the quicker it can be finished. The user may like to input various estimates of resource availability, basing them on past experience in terms of minimum, most likely, and maximum figures. This will give three different results for time/cost comparisons.

Many project control packages (see Section 17.4) will report on inconsistencies within the network, such as the same resource being used at the same time. Although the plan should allow for minor deviations, the package may permit the user to ask 'what if?' questions so that the consequences of more major deviations can be seen, for example:

- reallocating staff;
- unexpected staff leave;
- machine breakdown.

Useful reports from a package might include a list of activities presented in order of:

- latest starting date;
- earliest starting date;
- by department;
- by resource;
- by responsibility.

Packages can simulate the effects of:

- prolonging an activity;
- reducing resources applied to it;
- adding new activities.

Similarly, it can be used to show the effects of changing these parameters on project costs. The manager may be faced with two alternatives: a resource-limited schedule, where the project end date is put back to reflect resource constraints, or a time-limited schedule, where a fixed project end date leads to an increase in other resources used, such as people and equipment.

Once a project is under way progress can be monitored to:

- compare the time schedule with the actual progress made;
- compare the cost schedule with the actual costs;
- maintain the involvement of users and clients;
- detect problem areas;
- replan and reschedule as a result;
- provide a historical record, which can be used for future project planning.

14.3 GANTT CHARTS

Another way of displaying activity information is to use a Gantt chart (Figure 14.3). In this chart, the estimated duration for each activity is shown in clear boxes and the

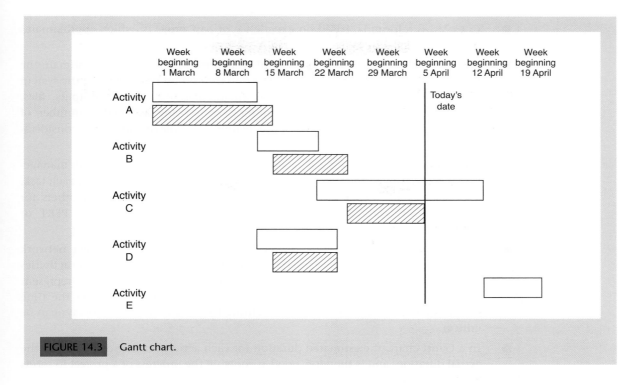

FIGURE 14.3 Gantt chart.

actual duration in patterned boxes. The Gantt chart is particularly good at showing progress.

In the example, a delay in activity A by three days is recorded, and this has set the start of activities B and C back by three days. Unlike the losses caused by delaying activity A, the gains made in reducing activity D by three days shown in the chart will not make any difference to the overall project time. In the event of delays impacting the overall duration the analyst can replan and mitigate the delay as best he or she can. Identifying and reporting delays is particularly important in organizations with many projects as the delay of one project may lead to delays in others.

A Gantt chart is often an integral part of a project management tool (Section 17.4) that may also provide guidance on how to put right any deviation from the schedule. This may be achieved by, for example, increasing the resources on some activities and rescheduling others. Goal-seeking analysis is a feature of a number of project management tools utilizing gantt charts. See Section 17.4 for examples of their use using a project management tool.

14.4 SUMMARY

■ CoCoMo, function point analysis (FPA), and work breakdown structure are estimation techniques for project management.

■ CoCoMo is a formula, based on experience of past projects, which approximates the effort needed in terms of program code required.

■ Function point analysis is a more sophisticated technique. It tries to estimate the functionality of the system being delivered to the end-user by analysing the system in terms of information systems requirements, based on inputs, outputs, files, updates, interfaces, reports, and enquiries, each being assigned a number of function points, plus an estimate of the technical complexity and other considerations.

■ Work breakdown structure is a decomposition of work into its technical, management, user liaison, administrative, quality assurance, and other tasks. For each task, analysts may use experience from past projects or seek advice from others for estimation of work. Work breakdown structure is a first phase in PERT or network analysis.

■ PERT (Project Evaluation and Review Technique) is based on project network diagrams for estimating the elapsed time of activities. In a PERT chart the activities are represented by arrows, which join the nodes (circles). The latter represent events, that is, the completion of activities. It is used for estimating the time taken to complete a project and highlighting those activities where delays can be critical.

■ In a Gantt chart, the estimated duration for each activity can be compared to the actual duration, and is therefore good at showing the progress of a project in terms of time.

QUESTIONS

1 Complete a work breakdown structure for an information systems development project following the SDLC (use the text in Chapter 3 to guide you).

2 Construct a PERT chart showing the interdependencies of the tasks and estimate the time for each activity. Use a project management tool if one is available.

14.5 FURTHER READING

Cadle, J. and Yeates, D. (2001) *Project Management for Information Systems*, Prentice Hall, Harlow, UK.

15 ORGANIZATIONAL TECHNIQUES

15.1 LATERAL THINKING

A further way to identify areas of change is to use some of the techniques used in lateral thinking. De Bono (1990) identified many techniques to try and restructure 'patterns', where patterns are people's internal models of a particular situation. The techniques range from lateral thinking 'games' to practical problem restructuring techniques. Most of these techniques, which include generating alternatives, challenging assumptions, fractionation, and brainstorming, are well known, and here we only give brief overviews. However, brainstorming is used most in systems analysis, so we will discuss this more fully.

Although we often assume that we 'naturally' search for alternatives, this is limited in practice, and the **lateral search** is aimed at looking for as many alternatives as possible. De Bono argues that the search should not be limited to obvious candidates as 'unlikely' alternatives may reveal one that will have the most impact. This is related to the second technique, that of **challenging assumptions**. But this may also be applied to asking questions about whether our basic ideas are sound. Restructuring our views and patterns may give more insight into the problem. The third technique, **fractionation**, based on functional decomposition, entails breaking things down into their constituent parts. However, in the lateral thinking context, it also involves reassembling the parts in a different way, and this may reveal a useful new view of the situation.

Brainstorming is a team activity aimed at generating a cross-stimulation of ideas. It is used in a semi-formal setting to generate ideas, where the ideas of one person serve as a stimulus to generate further ideas from other people, which in turn serve as a stimulus for further ideas, and so on. Judgement on the usefulness or validity of the ideas is 'suspended' until the brainstorming session is completed. The aim is to get a free flow of ideas.

Brainstorming is the most used of the lateral thinking techniques in systems analysis and is, perhaps, the least structured of the fact-finding techniques used in the systems development process. Different people can express their ideas together, and it therefore allows many views and opinions to be considered.

There might be problems with using lateral thinking techniques. For example, they rely on the skill, or arguably the art, of practitioners, and hence there is a lack of consistency; the techniques are not very formal or controllable; different people may be more inclined to lateral thinking than others; there is no definite stopping point in some of the techniques nor is there a definite result at the end; and there are costs involved.

Furthermore, brainstorming sessions may be difficult to arrange:

- Who does the systems analyst involve and from what business areas and should there be both management and shop-floor participation?

- How many people should be invited – the larger it is then the more ideas that can be expressed, but too large a group becomes difficult to handle?

- How can the subject matter be limited – we need a wide-ranging discussion to enable full expression of opinions, but this may lead to little being decided on the most pressing decisions?

Brainstorming sessions are therefore potentially chaotic situations, as well as potentially very enlightening, so care must be taken on their planning. But, whereas most of the methods we have discussed concern the analyst interpreting the results of interviewing or observing through the production of diagrams, for example, dataflow diagrams, entity-relationship models, and the like, brainstorming provides the opportunity for the group sharing of ideas and perceptions, which can be very helpful as well. It also provides an opportunity to gauge reactions to suggestions and proposals. It forms, therefore, part of the change management process of an information system.

Some lateral thinking techniques could be used to move out of the 'current time' constraint and help identify possible areas of future changes. They are probably better used as a tool set within more formal techniques, such as future analysis or risk analysis, though they could be used on their own as quick alternatives. They could also be used throughout the development process, for example, through stating and challenging the assumptions made at each stage.

In Figure 15.1 we show how future analysis, risk analysis, and lateral thinking might be used in the requirements analysis phase of the development of an information system in terms of change identification inputs, processing, and outputs.

15.2 CRITICAL SUCCESS FACTORS (CSFS)

Critical success factors were popularized in the information systems arena by Rockart (1979, 1982). CSFs are usually understood to be the set of factors that can be considered critical to the continued success of an organization or a business. These factors may be 'skills, tasks, or behaviours' according to Bisp et al. (1998). They can operate at a number of levels and be used for a variety of purposes. They can, for example, be used at a macro-level and used to define the critical factors for a particular industry or even for an overall economy. More usually, however, they are used at the micro-level and applied to a

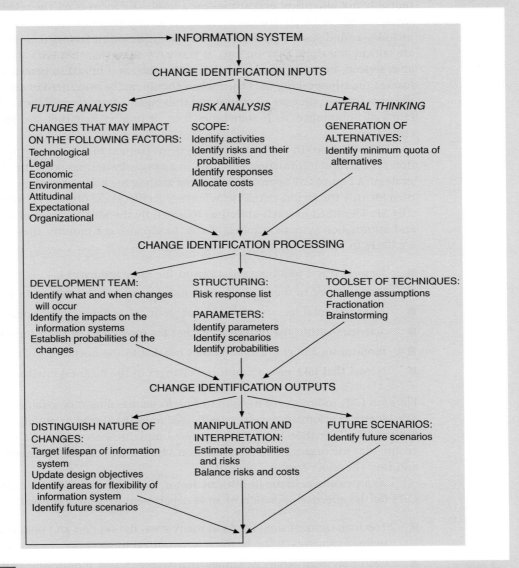

FIGURE 15.1 Techniques for improved requirements analysis – future analysis, risk analysis, and lateral thinking (from Avison et al., 1994).

business or company, or a part of a company. In the context of strategic IS planning the unit of analysis is the business unit, because, according to Ward and Griffiths (1996), this is the 'practical level to determine strategy'. Sometimes CSFs are used at the individual level, so, for example, the CSFs for a Chief Executive Officer (CEO) might be identified.

Only a limited number of factors should be identified as critical, and the limited number is an important aspect of the analysis. If too many are identified, they are probably not all critical and at too low a level. The focus is on the relatively few areas where things must go absolutely right to ensure business success. The process thus includes a fundamental assessment and prioritization of factors (i.e. those factors that are critical and those that are not). It is usually suggested that CSFs should be measurable. Indeed, not only measurable but actionable, and linked to perceived value in the market. Strictly speaking CSFs themselves should not be prioritized or ranked because, as the term implies, they are all critical and thus equally important. If they can be ranked in terms of importance, as is sometimes seen, it implies that they are probably not all critical.

CSFs are used in the information systems context to help ensure that the information systems and information provision in an organization supports the overall business strategy. A typical CSF approach might first analyse the business goals and objectives and then identify the factors critical to achieving each of those objectives, with about four to six CSFs identified for each objective, followed by the identification of the information and information systems required, if any, to support and monitor these CSFs. The CSFs are likely to include:

- factors critical to all organizations in the same industry;
- issues related to the particular organization and to its position in the industry;
- environmental factors, such as legal, political, economic, and social aspects;
- activities within the organization that are proving to be short-term problems;
- monitoring and control procedures relating to the operations of the firm;
- factors that take into account the changes in the business environment.

For each CSF, indicators or measures of performance should be established and trailed. The identified information systems will need to be developed or modified to ensure that the critical information is collected, analysed, and distributed. In other words, it helps to ensure that the organization's information systems support the agreed critical activities and thus the wider business objectives.

As an example, in the health-care sector, Arnett and Litecky (1992) identified three CSFs for the effective operation of an IS department in a small hospital. These were:

- Top management support. As in many areas the support and understanding of the senior executives in the hospital were critical to success.
- Cash-flow maintenance. Timely management and monitoring of the hospital's cash flow was critical.
- Relationship with key user managers/medical professionals. Relationships with other professionals in the hospital were vital. Key user managers provided a means to identify crucial applications as it did with the medical professionals who understood what could be done to provide better patient care. The alliance with both groups of professionals enabled the IS function to transform ideas into actions effectively.

They then went on to identify the specific skills needed by IS professionals such that the CSFs could be met and help ensure the organization's success. This is an example of cascading the CSF analysis downward to ensure that all the elements in the organization contribute to addressing the identified CSFs. In this case the critical skills required of the IS professional were identified as follows:

- ability to wear several hats (i.e. be a 'jack of all trades');
- knowledge and appreciation of the work of hospital administration (particularly regarding cash flow and accounting issues);
- knowledge and appreciation of the work of medical staff (including knowledge of medical terminology and medical software);
- negotiation skills (particularly with software vendors);
- PC and networking skills;
- a specific programming skill.

So, using the CSF technique, it is argued, helps identify those relatively few things that must be achieved to ensure success at a strategic level. Then it can be cascaded down to specific lower level activities or elements that contribute to the achieving of the overall CSFs. In this example, the skills required of the IS professional are specifically tailored to the needs of the health-care sector and the characteristics of a small hospital. It might be worth noting that the particular hospital found it very difficult to find IS staff with all the necessary skills, but at least they knew as a result of the CSF analysis what they were looking for.

15.3 SCENARIO PLANNING

One of the main concerns of the systems analyst is to ensure that the system they are designing will be suitable for the organization in the long term. We know that we cannot assume that the conditions of today will prevail in the future. Therefore we cannot assume that the system we build today for today's situation will be appropriate for the future. There are a number of techniques that can help us plan for future change. An obvious technique is forecasting, where we base our understanding of the future on present trends. However, sometimes the future cannot be planned in this way – it is much more uncertain. One technique for such circumstances is scenario planning.

Porter (1985) defines scenario planning as 'an internally consistent view of what the future might turn out to be – not a forecast, but one possible future outcome', whereas Ringland (1998) suggests that it is 'that part of strategic planning which relates to the tools and technologies for managing the uncertainties of the future', Assuming, then, that we cannot easily predict the future, how can we identify possible future outcomes? Three ways of identifying future scenarios are expert scenarios, morphological approaches, and cross-impact approaches.

In the case of **expert scenarios**, people outside the company deemed as experts in the problem area are asked for their views on possible outcomes. A consensus may emerge from the views. This might be difficult to manage, so there are skills needed from the internal people to liaise with experts. A **Delphi** approach might be used so that experts see the views of other experts and some general consensus is achieved. In the Delphi approach, people in turn give their views so that the next person can build on the previous assertions. Sometimes experts might suggest two or three possible outcomes. Some of these cannot be said to be 'expected', but they might be plausible and worth planning for. In this case the systems analyst may incorporate in the design the possibility of each of the emerging scenarios.

Morphological approaches identify a number of future states built on different assumptions. These assumptions might relate to expected states for the economy, depletions or findings of natural resources, changes in people's values or lifestyles, or changes in the political persuasion of a new government. Scenario analysis might consider different combinations of values for these key values. The spreadsheet package Excel has a scenario manager tool that can show these different scenarios side by side. For each of these different scenarios, their implications are then discussed.

Cross-impact approaches identify potential events, trends, and conditions that impact on the decision and on each other. Sometimes probabilities are assigned to each of them so the likelihood of these impact factors can be estimated.

Other techniques, such as brainstorming (as well as Delphi), may be used with these approaches to eke out possible scenarios or a consensus. Further, the approach might be used in a number of methodologies in a requirements analysis phase or, in general, to create a more robust strategy for systems design.

As Ringland (1988) shows, a number of good business choices have been based on scenario planning. A particular example is British Airways' decision following the Gulf War not to reduce capacity, a reaction of other airlines to the fall in demand. British Airways' scenario assumed that demand would go back to 'normal' levels and capacity would pick up. This proved a realistic scenario, and BA was able to provide the necessary capacity when demand did pick up and gain competitive advantage. Following 11 September 2001, however, BA has had to reduce capacity in the face of large losses. Scenarios may again suggest that demand will pick up and airlines' capacity becomes stretched, but such losses are unsustainable even in the short to medium term.

The UK National Health Service also used scenarios to plan their strategy in 1994. The future requirements of the NHS were uncertain and 30 experts provided opinions on the range of NHS services and perceptions of them. These included clinical practice, public values, the socio-political context, demography, and disease trends. Following this, 12 people participated in a weekend workshop. Such things as an ageing population, increased cost of medicines, and technology (and its greater sophistication) were predictable, but the scenarios concerned people's attitudes toward the NHS and their willingness to pay through taxes.

Having agreed possible scenarios, the organization then needs to assess the implications of present actions and alternative future decisions based on these scenarios. Scenario planning may also provide early warning and guidance so that potential problems can be detected and avoided before they occur. Further, strategy formulation can be proactively devised by considering the present implications of possible future events. Aspects of possible or desired future scenarios can also be seen and appropriately dealt with. Of course, in a methodology context, such scenario planning can ensure a greater likelihood of the information system being appropriate in the longer term despite environmental change.

15.4 FUTURE ANALYSIS

Future analysis (Land, 1982) is one of a series of techniques aimed at predicting potential change in the environment of the information system so that it can be designed to cope with that change when and if it occurs. It has two stages. The first attempts to discover the changes that may impact on the information system by classifying them into major categories. These include changes in technology, legal requirements, economic and other environmental factors, attitudes, expectations, tastes or in climates of opinion, and within the organization. Simulation, statistical forecasting, and economic modelling can all be used to help identify the changes. These changes are examined in terms of effect on the logic of the information system, on the 'traffic' of the information system, that is, changes in the volume or frequency, and on the timescale – short term or long term.

The second stage assesses the kind of future the information system under development will have to face, addressing issues such as what and when conceivable changes are likely to occur, the impact that they will have, and the probabilities of the changes. It might be necessary at this point to distinguish the nature of the changes – 'mandatory' or 'desirable'. The outcome of this stage is a target lifespan for the information system, an updated list of design objectives, identification of sections of the information system which may need extra flexibility built into them, and a number of future scenarios with which the design will have to cope.

A similar approach is Fitzgerald's (1990) flexibility analysis. Fitzgerald argues that enhancements to information systems tend to fall into three broad categories: environmental, technical, and organizational. Environmental changes might include government legislation or changes in other external agencies; organizational change may refer to changes to strategy or organizational structure; while technical change refers to technical developments or constraints. Although some changes did not fall easily into any one category, Fitzgerald suggests that 70 per cent of enhancements are attributed to organizational changes. More importantly in this context, this study suggests that 45 per cent of the changes analysed were known to the department concerned, and all but 5 per cent known by some member of the organization. But they were not allowed for in the initial designs. Flexibility analysis is about identifying these change factors.

Flexibility analysis needs to be carried out by a team that includes senior functional and strategic management and representatives of other groups in the business. This 'interdisciplinary' team is likely to have more success than a team of systems analysts alone. The latter will be able to assess how difficult and expensive it might be to incorporate the changes. Such an investigation will increase the development time of the project, but is worthwhile in the long term. The investigation and analysis phases are likely to be affected most, though such a process can work with prototyping, and some support software for flexibility analysis is available.

15.5 STRENGTHS, WEAKNESSES, OPPORTUNITIES, AND THREATS ANALYSIS (SWOT)

SWOT is an acronym for Strengths, Weaknesses, Opportunities, and Threats and is perhaps the most well-known approach to defining strategy, having influenced both practice and research for over 30 years (Zach, 1999). It is used to identify and analyse the strengths, weaknesses, opportunities, and threats that apply to a business or organization. The unit of analysis can be the overall organization, the business unit, the department, or even the individual. It can be used for a quick, 'back of the envelope' assessment or an in-depth, highly researched analysis. It is usually used as a group technique, rather than something performed by an individual, and frequently is employed initially in high-level brainstorming sessions, although it may be subsequently iterated and refined.

Business strategy has been equated with crafting and maintaining a profitable fit between a commercial venture and its environment, and SWOT analysis is the traditional means of searching for insights into ways of realizing the desired alignment. Undertaking a SWOT analysis involves describing and analysing a company's internal capabilities (i.e. its strengths and weaknesses) in relation to the competitive environment (i.e. the opportunities and threats it faces). Strategy is then formulated as a balancing act between the internal and external factors as it attempts to sustain the company's strengths, overcome its weaknesses, avert or mitigate the threats, and exploit the opportunities discovered in the SWOT analysis. SWOT is often used as a technique within some broader method or process for developing business strategy (e.g. Strategic Auditing, Balanced Scorecard, Strategic Analysis, Five Forces).

For example, as part of something called the Marketing Strategy Worksheet (MSW), SWOT is used at the organization level, first, to identify the internal strengths and weaknesses of the corporate set-up, for example, by looking at strengths and weaknesses of the marketing, finance, operations, and human resources functions. This is followed by an analysis of the external opportunities and threats at both a micro- and macro-level. At the micro-level this focuses on customers, competition, intermediaries, resources, etc. and at the macro-level on legal, technological, social, economic, and environmental opportunities and threats. This helps to steer the SWOT technique in particular directions. So, for example, it forces one to think about environmental threats and opportunities which otherwise might get forgotten. However, as in most descriptions of SWOT, these are only offered as guidelines. The outcomes of the SWOT are then documented in the worksheet and issues prioritized. MSW then goes on to use the SWOT analysis to define a Mission Statement, Objectives and Strategies, a Capsule (overview) Marketing Strategy, and finally a Budgeted Marketing Mix. As can be seen this is a marketing strategy method utilizing SWOT (Buttle, 1992).

SWOT is not specifically a technique related to information systems, but it can be, and has been, used to think through how IT could enhance the strengths and opportunities revealed by the SWOT and help counter the weaknesses and threats. For example, Zach (1999) advocates its use in the context of Knowledge Management. He argues that knowledge is an organization's most valuable resource, and that to remain competitive it must be effectively managed. However, many of the programmes to develop knowledge management do not explicitly link it or frame it within the organization's business strategy:

> In fact, most knowledge management initiatives are viewed primarily as information systems projects. While many managers intuitively believe that strategic advantage can come from knowing more than competitors, they are unable to explicitly articulate the link between knowledge and strategy.
>
> (Zach, 1999)

He argues for a framework that helps make the link between an organization's competitive position and its intellectual resources, and capabilities based on a SWOT analysis of their knowledge-based capabilities, comparing their knowledge to that of the competitor's and to the knowledge required to execute their own strategy and the information systems to support them.

SWOT, although a very popular technique in practice, has been criticized. Valentin (2001) suggests that the technique is made to look much too easy and is simply seen as answering a few questions from a checklist or filling in the quadrants of a one page worksheet. He argues that, actually, strategically significant SWOTs are not apparent at a glance and that a much more in-depth analysis is required. The examples provided, such as 'attractive customer base' or 'likely entry of potent new competitors', '... seldom reveals which factors are pivotal and which are just peripheral and they do not shed much light on the sustainability of advantages and the persistence of disadvantages'.

Hill and Westbrook (1997) have also been critical of SWOT's 'shallow' use by consultants with outcomes that are as likely to be as misleading as illuminating. Nevertheless SWOT is a well-established technique, widely used in business, and likely to remain so, partly in fact because of its simplicity but mainly because of its perceived benefits and rapid insights. In the information systems context it is typically used to help identify strategy and ensure that the business strategy is aligned with the IS strategy and IS provision.

15.6 CASE-BASED REASONING

A **case** reveals knowledge in its natural context. It represents an experience that teaches a lesson relating to the goals of the practitioner. This lesson can be useful in understanding a new situation. Therefore, we may use this learning from previous cases to solve a new problem, adapt a solution that does not quite fit, warn of possible failures, and interpret a situation. Although it is knowledge, it is specific rather than general knowledge.

Case-based reasoning is not new, even though it is relatively recent as an explicit technique in business situations, having derived from the cognitive psychology literature of the 1980s. But the principles are not new. English law is largely case-based. A lawyer will draw on previous cases that are similar to the present case that will support the client (the other lawyer will seek similar cases that will have the opposite effect). Mediators and arbitrators will also use cases represented as precedents. When doctors diagnose a patient's illness, they look for similar cases, and usually reduce the likely possibilities through the process of eliminating other possibilities. Mechanics repairing a car will often go through a similar process.

Similarly, managers making decisions might base their decision on previous experience in other cases. The manager might see particular similarities and if the case is appropriate, it should bring light to the new situation. They might be most appropriate where situations recur. But situations are rarely the same. Nevertheless, it might be feasible to adapt the old case to the new situation. Drawing on previous experiences might help the practitioner even where the situations are incomplete or fuzzy.

A reflective practitioner will learn as a consequence of reasoning on the basis of case knowledge. But such a practitioner needs to have had a number of experiences to draw on and needs to integrate these experiences in memory. The practitioner has to have the ability to understand new situations in terms of these old experiences. Further, as no two cases are alike, the ability to think about a new situation in terms of old cases is required.

The use of case-based reasoning (CBR) can therefore help solve what might be perceived as very new and difficult problems. It may speed up problem solving by reducing areas of difficulty and help in new domains. Experience gained in previous cases can help in evaluating solutions, interpreting open-ended and ill-defined aspects of the problem. Further, by drawing on less successful cases, the practitioner may prevent repeating mistakes of the past.

On the other hand, there is a danger that practitioners try to 'fit' an inappropriate case to a new situation or blindly depend on all aspects of a related case. Of course, the approach is less relevant to analysts who are less experienced and do not have the cases to draw on for support.

In information systems, CBR stemmed from artificial intelligence as expert systems software has been developed to support such reasoning. For example, expert systems (see Section 7.3) can represent the rules that formed decisions in previous cases. They can reflect the attributes of each situation for comparison purposes. Most software systems that support CBR for various types of application – Chef, Julia, Casey, Hypo, Protus, and Clavier – are therefore based on expert systems.

Such systems may use keywords relating to previous cases in new cases to use as a basis for comparison. They may ask the user questions to confirm that the cases do have significant aspects in common. Unlike humans, they do not 'forget' the experience that has been entered into the system. On the basis of all this information they look for the best match case and reveal the solution used then and possibly use experience in other cases to adapt the solution better to the new case. Those based on expert systems ought to offer the user the reasoning that lays behind the solution offered.

Watson (1997) provides a full account of numerous applications of CBR in industry and commerce. Most are used to help provide customer support for hardware and software suppliers, retailers and bankers, and for outsourcing suppliers. It can also be used to help store corporate memory supporting knowledge management systems (Section 7.4).

CBR can also be used for programmers developing new systems or maintaining old ones, as well as systems analysts designing aspects of systems used before – even identifying components used in previous systems. For example, an analyst might use CBR to identify different decision points (goods out of stock, customer exceeds credit limit) and identify other cases where these situations occur and repeat the rule (and programmers reuse the code).

15.7 RISK ANALYSIS

Risk analysis (or risk engineering) is another approach that helps to manage uncertainty and its effects. It consists of identifying areas of possible risk, estimating and allocating probabilities to the risks, identifying possible responses (which may be pre-emptive or after the fact) and allocating costs to the risks and actions. The result is a trade-off between expected risk and expected cost for different alternatives. In principle, in-depth risk analysis ought to lead to the formulation of a risk management strategy consisting of a set of response options aimed at dealing with specific sources of risks.

Various methods for risk analysis exist, for example, SCERT (Synergistic Contingency Evaluation and Review Technique). This has been used for large engineering projects but contains principles relevant to a wide variety of applications. Indeed, it is potentially invaluable in formulating corporate strategy (Cooper and Chapman, 1987). One application in the context of information systems development is in project planning. In this context, the basic risk engineering notion of alternative views and representations of any given situation applies. There are a variety of associated models, and the need to select that view which is the most appropriate to the particular circumstance is important.

SCERT consists of four stages. The first, the scope phase, identifies aspects of interest, in terms of activities, associated risks, and responses to the risks. The approach uses precedence and bar chart representations and extensive, structured, verbal documentation about the activities, risks, and responses. The second phase structures the risks and responses, identifying specific and general responses, and identifies decision rules. This leads to a risk-response list which can be represented in diagrammatic form. The parameter phase identifies parameters with which the outcomes are to be judged, and scenarios and their probability. Such parameters will include money, safety, and timescale. The final manipulation and interpretation phase estimates the probabilities along with the associated risks within an activity and attempts to strike a good balance between risks and costs. Usually an allowance is made in the budget for contingencies.

Throughout the whole process there is feedback, and this continues until the problem description, structuring, probabilities, decision rules, and their schedule implications have been agreed. More formally, the structure and parameter phases are first performed with 'primary' risks and then again for 'secondary' risks (i.e. those that are due to the responses of the primary risks). There may also be a case for looking at tertiary risks and responses as well. Generally available software supporting simulation and PERT may also be useful.

Risk analysis need not be solely concerned with identifying risk. It can also be concerned with identifying opportunities. The costs allocated to each risk need not be represented in terms of money alone and could be represented in terms of time, social, reliability, and safety metrics. The general outline of risk analysis as stated here may not be completely applicable for producing information systems or smaller systems generally, but the 'methodology' may be tailored to match the problem area. Ideally such an analysis would be undertaken at a very early stage in a project.

There are potential problems with risk analysis. For example, it will be difficult to identify all the activities and risks, and estimate (accurately) the probabilities of risks. However, there is no limit to the amount of time that could be spent attempting to analyse risk and plan reactions to it. Indeed, complexity and uncertainty may be so great that any analysis of risk must be greatly simplified. Analysis consumes resources, and this may lead to choosing the option that identifies 'general responses' to several problems rather than identify in detail every source of risk. This reduces effort in dealing with uncertainty, and general responses are a natural first line of defence in coping with 'unforeseeable' threats or opportunities.

An important result of more detailed risk analysis is that decision makers can gain an understanding of the trade-off between expected risks and costs of different alternatives, giving a firm basis on which to make and compare decisions. Risk analysis is likely to be more useful at the start of information systems development, though some of the principles can be carried through to further stages.

15.8 SUMMARY

- Lateral thinking consists of a number of techniques, from lateral thinking 'games' to practical problem restructuring techniques, including generating alternatives, challenging assumptions, fractionation, and brainstorming.

- Critical success factors are those factors – skills, tasks, or behaviours – that can be considered critical to the continued success of an organization. For a project, they will represent those elements that are crucial to its success.

- Scenario planning is an internally consistent view of what the future might turn out to be. Plans can be made on the basis of these scenarios.

- Future analysis is a technique aimed at predicting potential change in the environment of the information system so that it can be designed to cope with that change when and if it occurs.

- Strengths, Weaknesses, Opportunities, and Threats (SWOT) analysis is used to identify and analyse four crucial factors that apply to an organization. It is usually carried out by a group and used to develop a strategy with greater knowledge of the organization and its environment.

- A case reveals knowledge in its natural context. It represents an experience that teaches a lesson relating to the the goals of the practitioner. Case-based reasoning is about using these lessons in understanding a new situation. So, we may use this learning from previous cases to solve a new problem, adapt a solution that does not quite fit, warn of possible failures, and interpret a situation.

- Risk analysis (or risk engineering) consists of identifying areas of possible risk, estimating and allocating probabilities to the risks, identifying possible responses, and allocating costs to the risks and actions. The result is a trade-off between expected risk and expected cost for different alternatives, which might lead to a risk management strategy consisting of a set of response options aimed at dealing with specific sources of risks.

QUESTIONS

1 Undertake a CSF analysis of Amazon.com.

2 Use SWOT to look at a university department with which you are familiar.

3 What might be the future factors to be considered in the development of a new banking application?

4 What 'basket of techniques' might be used to estimate the risk of a student not passing the end-of-year examinations? How might this inform a strategy to make success most likely?

15.9 FURTHER READING

Boynton, A.C. (1984) An assessment of critical success factors, *Sloan Management Review*, Summer.

De Bono, E. (1992) *Serious Creativity: Using the Power of Lateral Thinking to Create New Ideas*, Advanced Practical Thinking, Harper Collins, New York.

Fitzgerald, G. (1990) Achieving flexible information systems: The case for improved analysis, *Journal of Information Technology*, Vol. 5, No. 1, 5–11.

Moynihan, T. (2002) *Coping with IS/IT Risk Management: The Recipes of Experienced Project Managers*, Springer-Verlag, London, Practitioner Series.

Porter, M.E. (1991) Toward a dynamic theory of strategy, *Strategic Management Journal*, Vol. 12, 95–117.

Ringland, G. (1998) *Scenario Planning: Managing for the Future*, John Wiley & Sons, Chichester, UK.

Watson, I.D. (1997) *Applying Case-based Reasoning: Techniques for Enterprise Systems*, Morgan Kaufmann, San Francisco.

16 PEOPLE TECHNIQUES

STAKEHOLDER ANALYSIS

Stakeholders are those people or groups of people with a stake in an information system. Traditionally in information systems, this has meant users of various kinds. But views have broadened more recently. In this section, we first look at users and then develop the concept.

In Section 1.9 we discussed the various types of user. Very often in practice, however, these all get subsumed into the one term 'user', though it is common to distinguish between user and end-user, where the end-user is a person who actually interacts with the system rather than necessarily utilizing the output or outcome of the interaction.

Each type of user may be a single individual or a group of people, or indeed diverse groups of people, internal and/or external, to the organization owning or responsible for the information system. An individual or group may undertake more than one of the roles identified in Section 1.9. In a small organization one might possibly find that a single individual might play all roles.

Therefore, there are different types of user in any system, and they need to be recognized and addressed, particularly in the design and development of a system, as they are likely to have fundamentally different requirements. Of course, there are other important ways of distinguishing users – other than by the function or role they perform in relation to the system. One distinction that is frequently made is that of skill and knowledge level. This can be an influential factor particularly in terms of the design of a system. End-users may be very knowledgeable in terms of their understanding of the application itself; that is, they are knowledgeable about banking and the current account application, or they may be knowledgeable about IT and software, or both. Equally, end-users may have little knowledge of either of these domains. The frequency with which an end-user uses a system is also important. Someone who uses the system on a regular basis, with a lot of knowledge of the system and the application, needs a very different interface to someone who uses the system irregularly and perhaps does not have as much knowledge. The occasional user will need more prompts, explanations, and guiding; for the experienced regular user this will just drive them mad. Regular professional travel agent users enter a series of short obscure codes to access and navigate their airline booking systems whereas the Internet interface for occasional users (i.e. the general public) is very different, with detailed guidance and the ability to enter destinations, dates, etc. in full or by selecting from pull-down menus, in a very laborious fashion compared to travel agents.

The term 'stakeholders' is sometimes used as a surrogate for users, but it was introduced into the information systems literature to represent a broader set of people who have involvement, influence in, or are affected by the development, use, implementation, and impact of information systems (see also Section 7.1). The term user was felt to be too narrow and limited to represent the wide range of people who are increasingly involved with information systems and their impact, especially with the ever more distributed and interorganizational nature of today's information systems. It was not just users who need to be involved, consulted, considered, and to express their opinions, but also those outside that category, such as government, society, environment, shareholder, employee, customer, supplier, patient, politician, lawyer, regulator, citizen, subject, etc. So, in IS the term 'stakeholders' was adopted to represent this broader, more diverse group.

The stakeholder concept has been used extensively and in a variety of contexts outside information systems, particularly in the strategic management area in relation to the corporation or the firm. Various stakeholder theories have been defined. Donaldson and Preston (1995) have proposed a stakeholder theory framework for 'examining the connections, if any, between the practice of stakeholder management and the achievement of various corporate performance goals'.

A stakeholder might be defined as anyone who has a stake in, or claim on, or can affect or is affected by the organization. However, Smith and Hasnas (1999) argue that it is currently understood in a narrower sense as referring only to those groups that are either 'vital to the survival and success of the corporation or whose interests are vitally affected by the corporation'. In this context they identify seven primary stakeholders:

- shareholders and investors;
- employees;
- customers;
- suppliers;
- trade associations;
- environmental groups;
- public stakeholder group, that is, the government and communities that provide infrastructures and markets (regulation and taxation agencies).

In the context of information systems, the analysis of stakeholders usually involves a rather unstructured identification of a set of relatively narrow stakeholders. It is often done in a kind of brainstorming session (Section 15.1) and then documented as a list or a set of interconnecting circles, sometimes known as a **stakeholder map**. These stakeholders are then considered as having some relevance or potential input to a system under development who then might be consulted and involved. Usually each stake-holder group is considered as having some specific requirement that needs to be considered and addressed in the system. They are seen as groups who have diverse requirements that need to be addressed by the system for it to be successful.

Kambil and van Heck (1998), for example, have used stakeholder analysis in the analysis of successes and failures in the introduction of a new IT-based trading mechanism in the Dutch flower markets. The new system and its effects on the market had the potential to lead to differential levels and allocations of costs across stakeholders. These costs and their distribution had to be considered by designers of new IT-enabled market mechanisms for it to be successful. However, the concept of stakeholder is quite limited. It appears to consist of buyers, sellers, and intermediaries, and there is no description of how the stakeholders were identified. Similarly, in relation to minimizing the risks concerned with the introduction of new IT systems, McManus (2001) suggests that: 'at the beginning of a project the manager should try to hold a risk workshop with the key stakeholder groups', but again no detail is provided as to how to do this nor how to identify the stakeholders, or any notion of a stakeholder theory.

Sometimes the stakeholders might be considered as having rights, which the system should not violate (e.g. privacy). Even more unusually, stakeholders might be identified in an attempt to minimize some detrimental effect of the system on the stakeholders. Usually the consideration of stakeholders in IS is undertaken because it is felt that it is a 'good thing' to involve a range of stakeholders. This is seen as more likely to lead to a successful information system. There is a managerial imperative underlying stakeholder analysis which sees it as 'good for business'.

However, much of the literature is not like this, but is normative and advocates that firms should address and reflect the interests of all their stakeholders, not just that of shareholders and investors, on moral or philosophical grounds. Stakeholder theory is frequently discussed in relation to business ethics and corporate social responsibility.

Introna and Pouloudi (1999) adopt this view in connection with a discussion of privacy and the possible effects of IT. They identify the following fundamental aspects of stakeholder theory (generalized):

■ Stakeholders are persons or groups with legitimate interests in procedural and/or substantive aspects of the domain of concern. Furthermore the interests of all stakeholders in the domain are of intrinsic value.

■ The ability, or influence, of the different stakeholders is unequal and the weaker should not be subsumed to the stronger.

They also argue that Stakeholder Analysis provides a way to make explicit, or give a voice to, the claims of all those stakeholders involved. Smith and Hasnas (1999) think that Stakeholder Analysis of this kind is problematic when applied to IS. It is not an easily applied 'cookbook' but requires 'substantial and non-trivial evaluation'. He identifies four problems. First, it is often unclear who constitutes the stakeholders for an IS initiative. The primary stakeholders are probably relevant, but it is difficult to determine all the others, particularly as interorganizational systems are becoming so common. 'Managers confront many new challenges in identifying all the stakeholders in such complicated webs.' Second, it is difficult to establish not only legal but also the moral rights of stakeholders in an IS context. Third, Stakeholder Theory requires managers to consider stakeholders' interests, which are often ill defined and subjective. For example, should customers be informed of potential data uses and should they be given an opportunity to 'opt out'? Fourth, the balancing of stakeholder interests is very difficult, for 'managers must contemplate a myriad of possibilities, calculate a number of cost–benefit analyses (with attention to each stakeholder's gain or loss), and balance these in some rational fashion'. This particular challenge is regarded as a significant weakness of Stakeholder Theory.

16.2 JOINT APPLICATION DEVELOPMENT (JAD)

JAD (Joint Application Development, or sometimes Joint Application Design) is a facilitated meeting designed to overcome the problems of traditional requirements gathering (see Section 3.1), in particular interviewing users. It overcomes the long time that the cycle of interviews typically takes by getting relevant stakeholders together in a meeting of a defined length, usually away from the office, which is highly focused on outcomes and making decisions.

The underlying concepts of JAD as a facilitated meeting process are not new (Andrews, 1991). According to Wood and Silver (1989) they were first developed by IBM in 1977 to help elicit requirements. However, it was not picked up by many other organizations until around the mid-1980s when it became popular. Carmel and Nunamaker (1992) estimated that there had been over 10,000 JAD-type meetings to help design and define information systems. Exactly how one knows how many such meetings there have been is difficult to imagine; nevertheless, the point is that JAD has become increasingly popular as a technique in IS development used to make development decisions and define requirements. Although used in a number of different approaches and methodologies JAD workshops are particularly associated with RAD (Rapid Application Development) (see Section 22.1).

The typical characteristics of a JAD workshop are as follows:

- *An intensive meeting of business users (managers and end-users) and information systems people.* There should be specific objectives and a structured agenda, including rules of behaviour and protocols. The information systems people are usually there to provide assistance on technical matters, for example, implications, possibilities, and constraints, rather than decision making in terms of requirements. Non-participating observers may also be present. The number of people involved in the workshops varies and this will depend on the type of system, its complexity, and its reach. Fifteen participants has been suggested as the ideal number. One of the most important people is the executive owner or executive sponsor of the system.

- *A defined length of meeting.* This is typically one or two days, but can be up to five. The location is usually away from the home base of the users, but most importantly away from interruptions. Telephones and e-mail to the outside world are usually banned. The participants are expected to attend full-time and cannot drop in and out of the meeting.

- *A structured meeting room.* The layout of the room is regarded as important in helping to achieve the meeting objectives. The round table principle is usually employed, and the walls of the room are typically covered in whiteboards and pinboards. When tools and toolsets are employed (see Section 17.1), these are usually placed at the side with the ability to display output on large screens and print when necessary.

■ *A facilitator.* This is a person who leads and manages the meeting. He or she is independent of the participants and specializes in facilitation. This person may be internal to the organization or brought in from outside and will understand the psychology of group dynamics and the tasks that the participants are undertaking. A facilitator is responsible for the process and outcomes in terms of documentation and deliverables. He or she will control the objectives, agenda, process, and discussion, using a variety of techniques to help move the meeting forward and achieve the objectives. Techniques such as brainstorming, reflection exercises, and cooling breaks will be used.

■ *A scribe.* This is a person (or persons) responsible for documenting the discussions and outcomes of the meeting (including the use of tools and toolsets).

From these characteristics it can be seen that there are a number of principles underlying JAD. First, the user design should be moved forward as quickly as possible. There may be a series of JAD meetings which either address different parts of the design area or more commonly take the design from overview to more detailed levels. Often further work is carried out between the meetings, such as the preparation of more sophisticated prototypes, but decisions are only taken at the meetings. The proponents of JAD argue that it replaces cycles of interviews and meetings on an individual basis that normally take many months. This can significantly reduce the elapsed time required to achieve the design goals. In the traditional approach, meetings usually consist of a small group or are held on a one-to-one basis. When analysts find a conflict or discrepancy between users as to requirements or interpretations, they have to reschedule all these meetings again to try and resolve things. It may be necessary to cycle round the groups more than once. Typically, this takes a great deal of time, because setting up meetings is notoriously difficult in most organizations. JAD seeks to overcome these kinds of problem with one or two major workshops.

The second key element is getting the right people together for the workshop. The right people are all those with stakes in the proposed system, including end-users, and those with the authority to make binding decisions in the area. This avoids all the time-consuming cycles that are encountered with traditional methods. RAD argues for the use of small, empowered teams giving the participants the power to make decisions that may commit other colleagues and parts of the business. This empowerment is important to successful RAD outcomes.

A third element is the commitment that the JAD meeting engenders. With traditional meetings, commitment is often dissipated over time, and decisions may be taken off the cuff in small meetings where all information is not available and implications are not fully understood. With JAD, it is all out in the open and high profile. Decisions tend not to be taken lightly, but when they are made, they are made with conviction and commitment. In particular, because JAD focuses upon the benefits of the system for the business and users, the commitment is more marked and visible.

Perhaps the most important single aspect of JAD is the facilitator. This person can make or break a workshop and is critical to determining whether the objectives are achieved. Apart from skills in handling JAD workshops, along with an understanding of group dynamics, it is the independence or neutrality of the facilitator, which is crucial. This enables facilitators to achieve more than any other stakeholder who might be regarded with suspicion by others. A facilitator is able to avoid, and smooth, many of the hierarchical and political issues that frequently cause problems and will be free from the taint of organizational history and past battles.

There have been a number of examples of JAD in action with seemingly beneficial results. For example, a 60 project study by Jones (1989) showed that projects that did not use JAD missed up to 35 per cent of required functionality which resulted in 50 per cent more code being needed in the system. Whereas when JAD was used only 10 per cent of functionality was missed with minimal impact on the code. However, Davidson (1999) in a study of JAD concluded that although the participants believed that their use resulted in favourable outcomes there was little evidence of substantive change in the ISD process (i.e. the ISD status quo was not radically changed). However, these examples were not, it seems, used in the context of the kind of cultural change required for successful RAD. There was also some evidence that JAD was sometimes used prematurely in large projects.

16.3 SUMMARY

- Stakeholders are those people or groups of people with a stake in the project. They include users of various kinds: government, society, shareholders, employees, customers, suppliers, patients, politicians, lawyers, regulators, and citizens.

- Joint Application Development (JAD) is a facilitated meeting or workshop designed to overcome the problems of traditional requirements gathering to agree a design for the information system that fully takes into account the views of users and other stakeholders.

QUESTIONS

1 Identify the stakeholders in a student administration system in a university.

2 Do you think that the views of all stakeholders should be taken into account in designing a system?

3 How can the views of such stakeholders as 'society' be ascertained?

4 In what ways does a JAD meeting overcome the problems of traditional requirements gathering approaches?

5 Why is a facilitator usually considered a necessary element of a JAD meeting?

6 What elements in the development of an information systems can JAD meetings be used for?

16.4 FURTHER READING

Vidgen, R. (1997) Stakeholders, soft systems and technology: Separation and mediation in the analysis of information system requirements, *Information Systems Journal*, Vol. 7, No. 1.

Wood, J. and Silver, D. (1995) *Joint Application Development*, John Wiley & Sons, New York.

TOOLS AND TOOLSETS

As in Part 4 we again show a 'road map' of the relationships between themes, techniques, tools, and methodologies (see Diagram 3). This time the perspective is that of a tool and a toolset. We use Project 2000 and Select in this example and show the links to themes, techniques, and methodologies.

We looked at software as a theme in Chapter 9. By tools we mean software packages that support the analysts and users in particular aspects of the application development process. Toolsets are integrated software environments. Technology has continued to develop greatly throughout the computer era, becoming much more powerful, cheaper, and more widely available. Improved graphics facilities and windowing environments have also had a major impact on tools. Indeed, some people have suggested that the latest generation of automated tools is a panacea for the problems of systems development: improving systems quality and eliminating the development and maintenance backlog. Although we do not share this belief, the quality of software has greatly improved over time so that automated tools are potentially very beneficial. In Part 5 we look at the whole range of tools that support the information systems development process.

We first look in Chapter 17 at a number of software tools: groupware (with GroupSystems as exemplar), website development (with Dreamweaver as exemplar), drawing tools (with Visio as exemplar), project management tools (with Project 2000 as exemplar), and database management systems (with Access as exemplar). In all these cases we describe briefly how the tool is used and show the screenshots generated. However, in all these cases a full description of the tool would require a book (or books), so we can only provide a flavour of their potential in this chapter.

Although the main focus of Chapter 18 is on toolsets, we start with a discussion of systems repositories as these are an essential ingredient of any toolset. Toolsets are developments on what used to be called CASE tools and are whole software

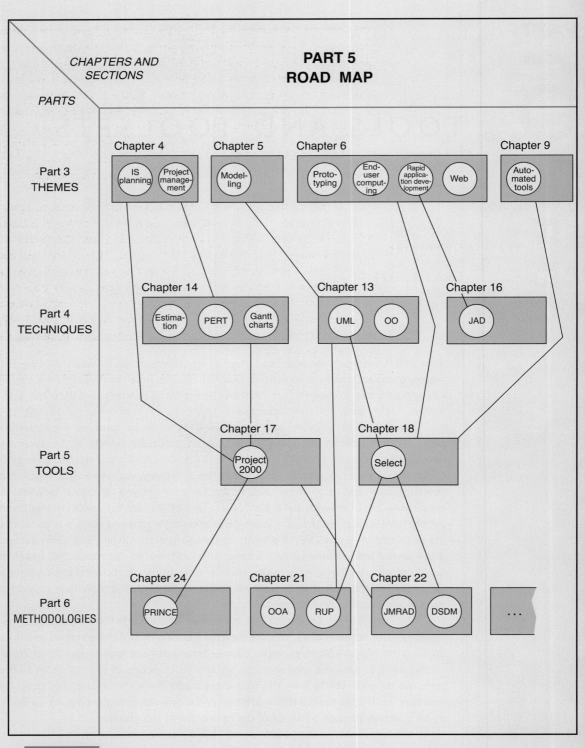

PART 5
ROAD MAP

CHAPTERS AND SECTIONS

PARTS

Part 3
THEMES

Chapter 4
IS planning | Project management

Chapter 5
Modelling

Chapter 6
Prototyping | End-user computing | Rapid application development | Web

Chapter 9
Automated tools

Part 4
TECHNIQUES

Chapter 14
Estimation | PERT | Gantt charts

Chapter 13
UML | OO

Chapter 16
JAD

Part 5
TOOLS

Chapter 17
Project 2000

Chapter 18
Select

Part 6
METHODOLOGIES

Chapter 24
PRINCE

Chapter 21
OOA | RUP

Chapter 22
JMRAD | DSDM

...

DIAGRAM 3   MS Project tool and Select toolset 'road map' (shows relationships between a tool and a toolset *and* themes, tools, and methodologies).

environments supporting the information systems development process. Some toolsets address the early stages of systems development (strategy, planning, and analysis); others address physical design, programming, and implementation stages; yet others integrate the two into a single, fully integrated development and support facility. We look at three exemplars. The first is Information Engineering Facility, a toolset supporting users of the Information Engineering methodology and one of the first of these toolsets. We then look at Oracle, at present the most widely used and one of the most powerful and inclusive toolsets. Finally we discuss Select, which is used in many universities, and we illustrate its use through screenshots.

Following this, we look in detail at the potential benefits and provide an overall evaluation of such tools and toolsets. An opportunity is taken to discuss the human, social, and organizational aspects. The likelihood of successful adoption of these tools (or, indeed, information systems in general) is as much to do with people and organizational factors as to the qualities of the software itself. We have therefore taken the opportunity in the chapter to look at a number of wider considerations in adopting software. Some of these debates are developed further in Part 7, which follows the descriptions of a number of information systems development methodologies in Part 6.

17 TOOLS

GROUPWARE: GROUPSYSTEMS

Much, indeed most, information systems development work is carried out by a project team, that is, a group of individuals working in collaboration. Software tools are now available to support group work. It takes many different forms. Some people might include e-mail in this category, for example, it can be used for information dissemination, though this has very limited groupware facilities. The most popular software of this type is Lotus Notes or Microsoft Exchange. There is also specialist software available, such as GroupSystems and others for videoconferencing. These software tools can help group work in many ways: for instance, sharing knowledge, discussing problems, co-ordinating effort, and collective decision making.

Groupware can be effective where the group is working together in a room or when the team is dispersed. For example, GroupSystems is particularly suitable for groups working together in a room and supports, for example, brainstorming, categorization, electronic whiteboards, and voting. It can be used with other software so that databases, spreadsheets, websites, and so on can inform the decision-making process. Video conferencing facilities offer people the opportunity to see as well as talk to others in another site or sites.

Lotus Notes is a well-used group support system. Whereas the emphasis in GroupSystems is on group brainstorming and decision support, Lotus places emphasis on communications between group members. It enables the documentation, sharing, storage, and access of information. It can be used to display the historical conversation over time between team members that led to a particular decision. 'Notes', for example, on viruses can be displayed on a bulletin board for all the team (or the company). The calendar can be used to co-ordinate schedules of physical and virtual meetings. In general, it helps to inform members of the project team about progress in real time as well as stimulate that progress.

The use of such systems may change the nature of group work from being largely face to face to largely online. Trust becomes a major factor as online work lacks the usual signals gained from face-to-face contact. Videoconferencing can have an obvious role here. Even web cameras used with e-mail and Internet conversations can also provide support, as can voicemail. Such systems also change roles, responsibilities, interactions, and the way work is carried out. Indeed, they may be introduced to achieve this result as well as encourage and support teamwork in general. Of course, there are also privacy and security implications as well as individuals' concerns about sharing their knowledge with others and perhaps losing their individual competitive advantage. The way such systems are introduced will therefore be a key factor in its potential for goodwill and better teamwork.

Failla (1996) provides a useful case study relating to how software is developed at IBM's international network of laboratories. Teams of work groups and managers can exist 'virtually', in many different locations. Developers write code usually in small groups while managers divide the work between group members and groups. Electronic mail, forums (shared files), conference call systems, faxes, and videoconferencing are all cited as tools supporting group work. IBM's commitment to technology supporting group work is exemplified by its purchase of Lotus for its Lotus Notes software, which it now supplies as well as uses internally.

We will look at GroupSystems software, which developed from the work of Jay Nunamaker and others at the University of Arizona (Nunamaker et al., 1991), see www.groupsystems.com for the latest version. Although it can be used for remote decision making and at different times, its most popular use is in special meeting rooms, sometimes called 'pods', where each user has a workstation with the software installed. The brainstorming feature enables each member of the team to create ideas and comment on them. These are usually expressed anonymously so that it is the ideas that have force (or not), and not who is expressing those ideas. Brainstorming should encourage unusual thinking and ideas and innovation, and the anonymity of expressing these ideas reduces the inhibiting factors. Some ideas will be rejected but others will be kept and organized into separate categories for further evaluation. At the end of the meeting there is a complete record available.

Figure 17.1 shows the basic elements of the software tool. An agenda has been agreed for the morning meeting. This starts by generating ideas on the subjects for the meeting and categorizing them. These are explored in more detail through the expression of ideas in the brainstorming part. Figure 17.2 shows how ideas are brainstormed and organized. These may then be further commented on by other members of the group with an action plan agreed.

There may be some agreements without a vote, but there is an electronic voting system that can also be used. Figure 17.3 shows how opinion can be expressed by use of a 'barometer' and Figure 17.4 how the opinions of everyone in the group can be aggregated. Such statistical information as standard deviation and mean can also be provided. Group members can vote or express their opinions in terms of rank order, true/false, yes/no, etc. Results can be displayed through a variety of charts and tables.

The system provides an electronic whiteboard; electronic handouts and information can be obtained from other sources, such as spreadsheets, databases, and web pages. We see in Figure 17.5 how an action plan can be expressed following the group discussion.

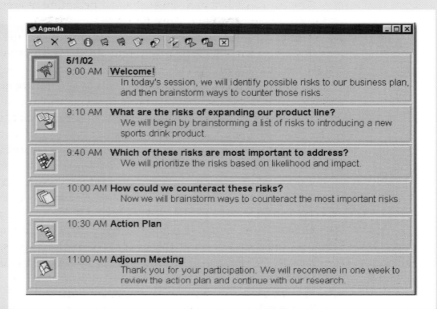

FIGURE 17.1   GroupSystems.

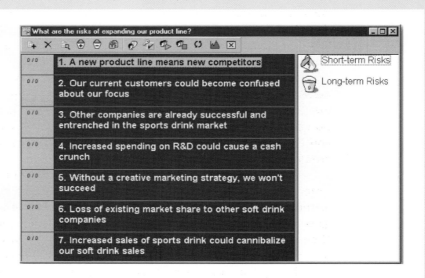

FIGURE 17.2   GroupSystems brainstorming.

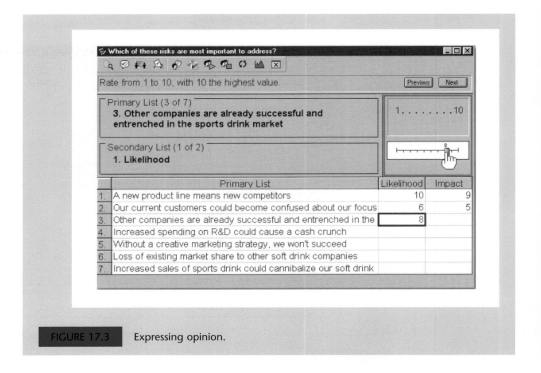

FIGURE 17.3 Expressing opinion.

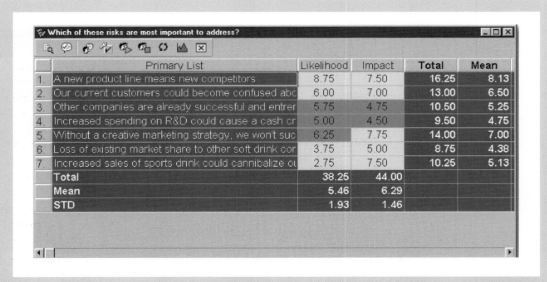

FIGURE 17.4 Aggregating opinions.

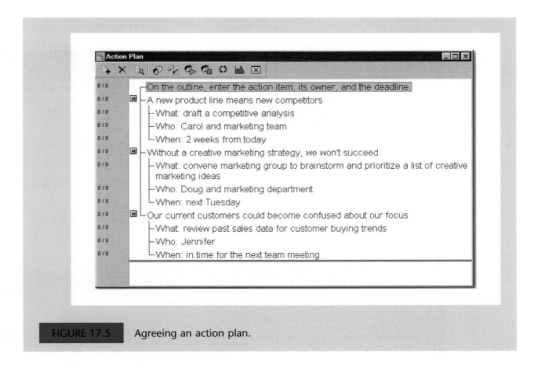

FIGURE 17.5   Agreeing an action plan.

Bikson (1996) provides a very interesting case study of GroupSystems use at the World Bank. Its use needs a facilitator who provides the technological support when needed. This may be a technical role only, or some 'project leadership' role may be included alongside the technical role, for example, to ensure that the schedule and agenda are kept.

17.2   WEBSITE DEVELOPMENT: DREAMWEAVER

Dreamweaver is one of a number of software tools that supports the production of websites. Alternatives include Microsoft's FrontPage. It is not, however, the basis for an e-commerce site. Here, a more sophisticated tool such as ColdFusion is necessary.

As Figure 17.6 shows, when opening Dreamweaver, you are confronted with a document window and several floating windows called palettes. The document window will form what will be seen in the browser window (e.g. Internet Explorer), that is, the web pages themselves.

The package comes with a tutorial, and we will use some examples from this. Figure 17.7 shows one of the web pages created alongside the HyperText Mark-up Language (HTML) code that the design reflects. HTML contains the text plus all the instructions for displaying the text (colour, bold, italic, spacing, font size, font type, pagination, etc.). These instructions reflect the mark-up code that used to be added by proofreaders for printers of newspapers and books. In this case, the mark-up code is produced by Dreamweaver itself. Users do not have to work with HTML code, but they can if that is their preference (usually computer experienced people such as

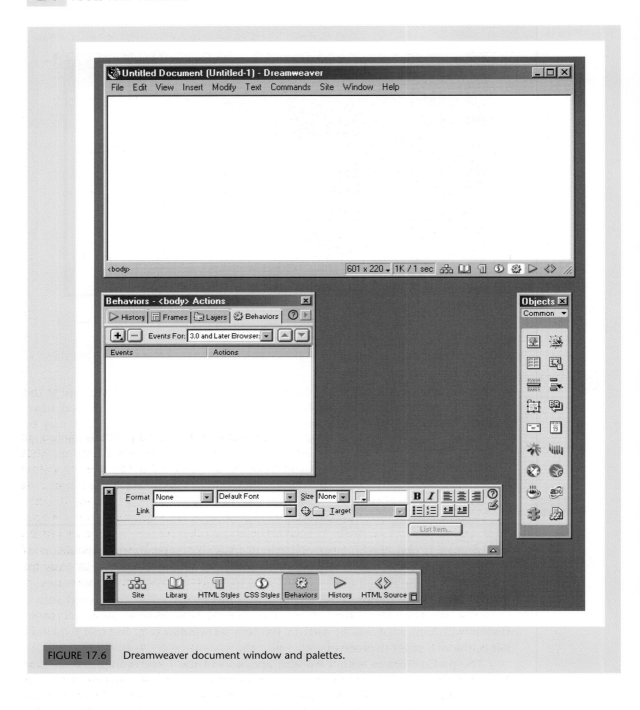

FIGURE 17.6 Dreamweaver document window and palettes.

programmers might prefer to write or edit code). The designers will specify what they want in the document window and this is translated to HTML.

Many of the commands used will be familiar to users of conventional word processors and products of the Microsoft Office suite (Ctrl + C for copy; Ctrl + V for paste;

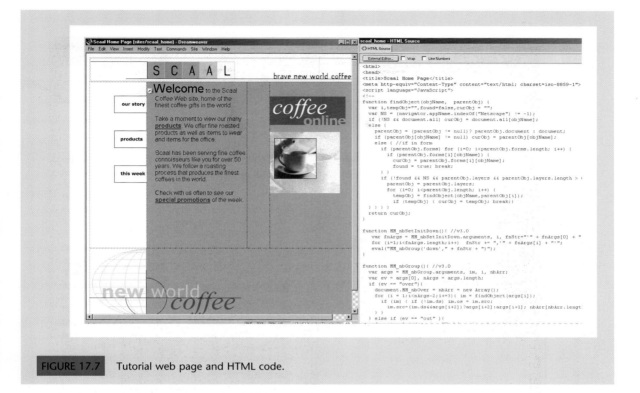

FIGURE 17.7 Tutorial web page and HTML code.

Ctrl + F for find) and there is also a spellchecker provided. Emphasis is placed on enabling the analyst to create an attractive style for the pages (some example style sheets are provided in the package), and there can be styles defined for the site so that the user sees a similar 'look and feel' for the site as a whole. Style definitions can include type (e.g. font formatting), background (e.g. colour), block (e.g. alignment and indentation), box (e.g. margin controls), and lists (e.g. numbered or bulleted). Text, images, icons, and other material can be cut and pasted from other sources into the web pages.

A particularly important page is the home page. This will normally be the users' first encounter with the website. It has therefore to be attractively designed, informative, and also enable the users to go quickly to the sections of the site that are of most or immediate interest.

The web page shows the content and also the hyperlinks to other web pages. Therefore, if the user double-clicks on products or special promotions (Figure 17.7), this will bring in these related pages. *Our story*, *products*, and *this week* are also links, but this time in the form of icons that are double-clicked rather than words. They change shade when the user moves the cursor over them, and this signals to the user that they represent links. The objects palette seen towards the bottom of Figure 17.6 can enable the use of images, tables, layers, movies, Applets, Active X controls, as well as links of various kinds.

Of course, good design is particularly important for web applications as it could be the customer who is using the application, rather than a captive user (an employee) as in most information systems. Happily, Dreamweaver, as with similar tools, provides

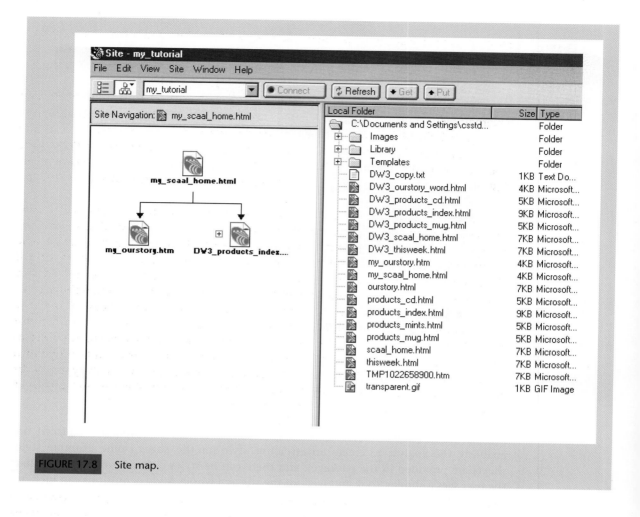

FIGURE 17.8 Site map.

analysts with a number of templates that can be used as a basis for their particular web pages. The page properties dialogue box apply to the entire page, and enables the definition of margins, and so on, while the visual properties dialogue box enables the definition of background colour, text colour, background image, etc. At first all these floating boxes can be daunting to the new user, but they separate the various requirements, and the experienced user works well in this mode.

Dreamweaver, like all modern software of this type, offers WYSIWYG (what you see is what you get), so that as analysts design the page they can preview it as it will eventually appear in a browser. Eventually the site will contain lots of pages and links between them and also links to external sites, designated universal resource locators (URLs). Figure 17.8 shows some of the linked pages for the tutorial site.

The ability to show images has, perhaps, been one of the key selling features of web pages. Dreamweaver enables images to be pasted and edited into the web page. Alternatively it can be used in conjunction with full image editors such as PaintShopPro or Photoshop. The two main image formats of the web, GIF and JPEG, among others, are supported by Dreamweaver. However, the designer has to be aware of potential downloading time problems, so images, animation, and other moving images need to be used with care. The Dreamweaver libraries can be used to store images, animation, sound files, Shockwave and Flash files, Java Applets, ActiveX controls, frames, and other components that might be used in other websites.

Another key feature of the web is the ability to link with other pages in the site and externally with only a click of the mouse. In Dreamweaver a link can be achieved by highlighting the text or image that is to be the link (for example, products in Figure 17.7), and in the link text box (bottom left in Figure 17.6) typing the location of the document to which it is linked. Other links might be to e-mail addresses. Navigation bars (list of related links) can be created, and this is another way to help guide users through the site.

Many pages on the web consist of several frames, containing text, graphics, tables, images, navigation bars, and other distinct displays. It might be useful to display the navigation bar on the page whatever scrolling the user is doing. This is made possible because each frame is independent of the others on the same page as it is an individual HTML document. Nevertheless, from the designer's point of view, it is possible to drag and drop objects from one page to another in the process of creating the web pages.

Forms used for surveys, for example, are a common feature in websites, but they can be notoriously slow and difficult to create. However, their creation is also facilitated using Dreamweaver. Again, in the object palette (see Figure 17.6), forms can be chosen as one of the options. Forms can be created using tick boxes, radio buttons, lists, drop-down menus, jump menus, and text fields. A password field enables the user's typing to be replaced by asterisks when displayed. Another option is a multi-line feedback box to be used for the user's general unstructured comments.

17.3   DRAWING: VISIO

Drawing tools help developers to create and maintain the various diagrams required in systems development. Most are designed to support the drawing of one or more of the common diagramming techniques and do not usually support any particular methodology. However, sometimes they offer the same technique drawn under the conventions of different methodologies. For example, they may give the options of drawing data flow diagrams following the Gane and Sarson (STRADIS), Yourdon, or other conventions.

Drawing tools help drawing many of the diagramming techniques described in Chapter 4, such as data flow diagrams, entity models, process logic techniques, entity life cycles, and so on. They are sometimes described as documentation support tools, being designed to take the drudgery out of drawing and revising documents, and thus making the implementation of changes easier.

Additionally, they contribute to the accuracy and consistency of diagrams. For example, in a data flow diagram, a drawing tool can check that levels of the diagram are consistent with each other. This will include ensuring that all data flows on a higher level diagram appear on the lower level ones and that the descriptions are consistent across a set of diagrams. Drawing tools can also be used to ensure that certain documentation standards and conventions are adhered to. For example, processes must have inputs and outputs, and data stores must be specified in terms of contents and flows.

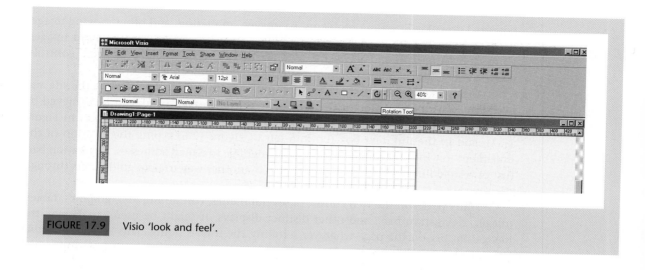

FIGURE 17.9 Visio 'look and feel'.

Most drawing tools will prevent users from doing things that are not permitted in that diagrammatic convention. With an online reference manual and context-sensitive 'help' facilities available in some tools, users can be guided through the technique.

Probably the greatest benefit of their use is that analysts and designers are not reluctant to change diagrams, because the change process is simple. Frequent manual redrawing is not satisfactory, because of the effort involved and the potential of introducing errors when redrawing. Without such drawing tools many a small change required by a user would not be incorporated into the documentation of the system.

Such drawing tools usually support only a single technique or a few basic techniques (most commonly, data flow diagrams and entity-relationship diagrams). Although useful, these are somewhat limited in the sense that, for example, much of the information required for a data flow diagram is also required, in a slightly different form, for other process logic representations and elsewhere. It makes more sense to have a central repository of all the information required for the development project. This will ensure consistency between techniques as well as within a diagramming technique. This provides the potential for integrated, co-ordinated, and consistent support throughout all aspects of the life cycle, ensuring a smooth transition from one phase to the next. With these ambitions the simple drawing tools began to evolve into more sophisticated products originally known as CASE tools but more commonly now seen as application support toolsets (see Chapter 18).

Visio is a well-used drawing tool for PCs and workstations. As can be seen from Figure 17.9, it has the same 'look and feel' as other Microsoft products. There are a number of templates available, depending on the type of diagram to be drawn. Figure 17.10 shows some database drawing types including diagrams based on Chen's entity-relationship models (ERMs) or James Martin's approach; Figure 17.11 shows some of the flowcharts which include mind mapping diagrams (see lateral thinking, Section 15.1) and total quality management; Figure 17.12 shows website diagrams; and Figure 17.13 shows data modelling diagrams, including object diagrams, data flow diagrams, UML diagrams, Jackson diagrams, Coad and Yourdon, and SSADM, all discussed in this book. Figure 17.14 shows the stencil set of all the symbols for SSADM diagrams; Figure 17.15

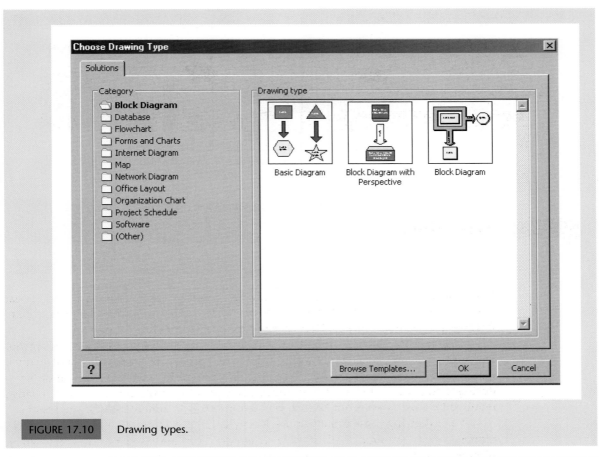

FIGURE 17.10   Drawing types.

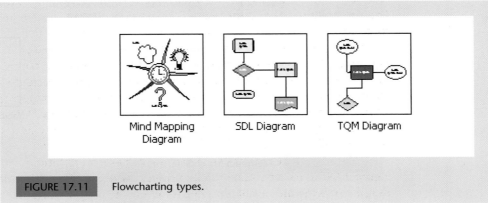

FIGURE 17.11   Flowcharting types.

shows the four basic shapes of data flow diagrams; and Figure 17.16 shows a data flow diagram being constructed using these shapes.

Although not a sophisticated integrated toolset such as the systems described in Chapter 18, Visio enables the easy creation and update of most basic diagrams used in many of the techniques and methodologies discussed in this book.

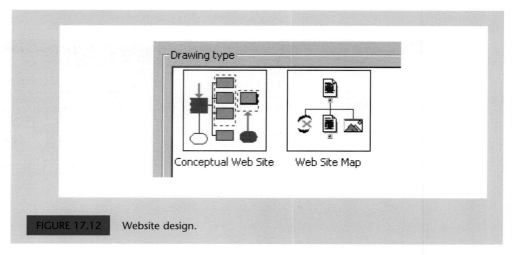

FIGURE 17.12 Website design.

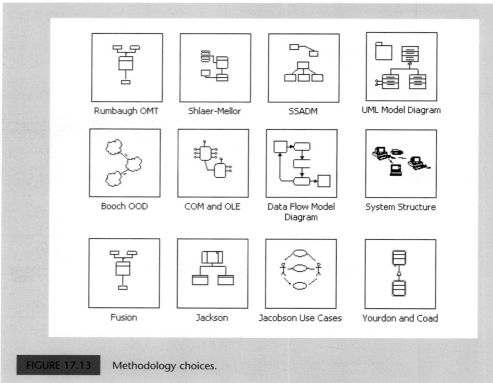

FIGURE 17.13 Methodology choices.

17.4 PROJECT MANAGEMENT: PROJECT 2000

We looked at a number of project management and control techniques in Chapter 14, and we look at a methodology, PRINCE, in Section 24.4, which is specifically designed for the project control aspects of developing projects. Here we look at the output of

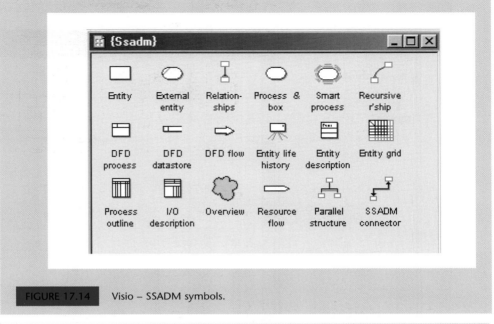

FIGURE 17.14   Visio – SSADM symbols.

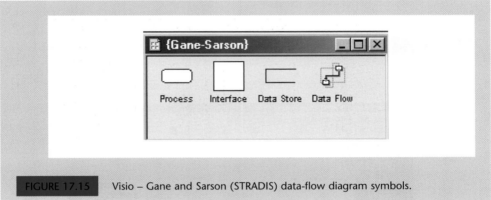

FIGURE 17.15   Visio – Gane and Sarson (STRADIS) data-flow diagram symbols.

software tools, which provide speed and accuracy to the project planning process and help to achieve the matching of project plans with their execution. In particular, we look at Microsoft's planning tool Project 2000. It features techniques we looked at such as work breakdown structure, critical path analysis, and Gantt charts in Chapter 14, plus some others like calendar management. Although essentially a package for workstations and PCs, Project 2000 will manage thousands of tasks and resources for each project, create all sorts of diagrams, ways to present information, track progress, and anticipate problems. On the other hand, no software package can eliminate the work of planning, estimating, and entering data. We will start by entering the data as shown here in Figure 17.17.

In Figure 17.18 we have added some subtasks and also shown their interdependencies as well as those between the main tasks. Note that most activities are completed sequentially, but task D, for instance, can be done in parallel with other tasks.

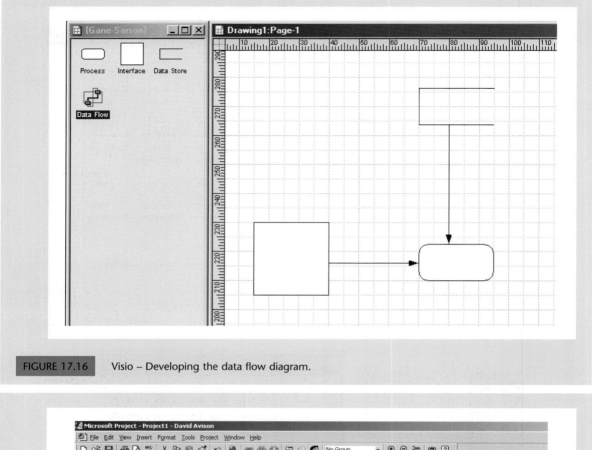

FIGURE 17.16   Visio – Developing the data flow diagram.

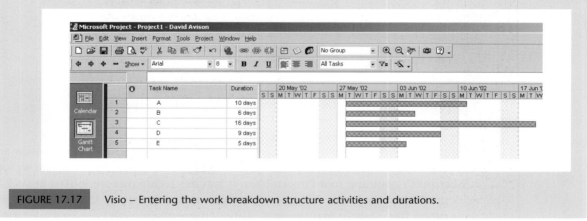

FIGURE 17.17   Visio – Entering the work breakdown structure activities and durations.

Figure 17.19 shows how these interdependencies can be displayed, along with the start and end dates.

In Figure 17.20 we show the calendar display and in Figure 17.21 part of the PERT network itself.

So far, we have not input resource usage. Figure 17.22 shows the beginnings of the resource allocation task, and this relates to material as well as human resources (Figure 17.23).

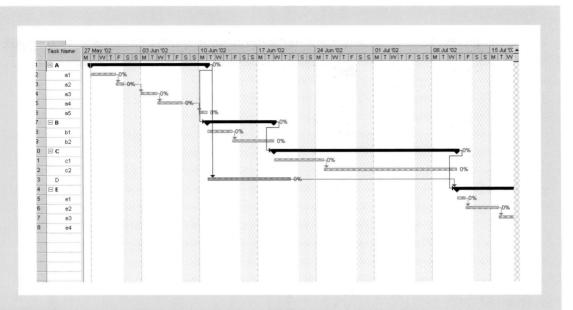

FIGURE 17.18   Visio – Interdependence of tasks.

	$\bigcirc$	Task Name	Duration	Start	Finish	Predecessors
1		⊟ **A**	**10 days**	**Tue 28/05/02**	**Mon 10/06/02**	
2		a1	3 days	Tue 28/05/02	Thu 30/05/02	
3		a2	1 day	Fri 31/05/02	Fri 31/05/02	2
4		a3	2 days	Mon 03/06/02	Tue 04/06/02	3
5		a4	3 days	Wed 05/06/02	Fri 07/06/02	4
6		a5	1 day	Mon 10/06/02	Mon 10/06/02	5
7		⊟ **B**	**6 days**	**Tue 11/06/02**	**Tue 18/06/02**	**1**
8		b1	3 days	Tue 11/06/02	Thu 13/06/02	
9		b2	3 days	Fri 14/06/02	Tue 18/06/02	8
10		⊟ **C**	**16 days**	**Wed 19/06/02**	**Wed 10/07/02**	**7**
11		c1	4 days	Wed 19/06/02	Mon 24/06/02	
12		c2	12 days	Tue 25/06/02	Wed 10/07/02	11
13		D	8 days	Tue 11/06/02	Thu 20/06/02	1
14		⊟ **E**	**6 days**	**Thu 11/07/02**	**Thu 18/07/02**	**10,13**
15		e1	1 day	Thu 11/07/02	Thu 11/07/02	
16		e2	2 days	Fri 12/07/02	Mon 15/07/02	15
17		e3	2 days	Tue 16/07/02	Wed 17/07/02	16
18		e4	1 day	Thu 18/07/02	Thu 18/07/02	17

(Sidebar icons: Calendar, Gantt Chart, Network Diagram, Task Usage, Tracking Gantt)

FIGURE 17.19   Visio – Start and end dates.

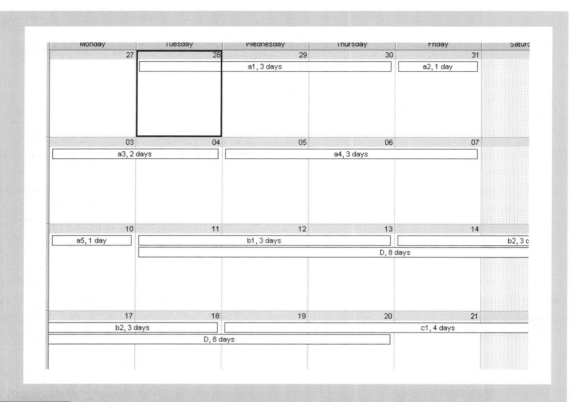

FIGURE 17.20   Visio – Calendar display.

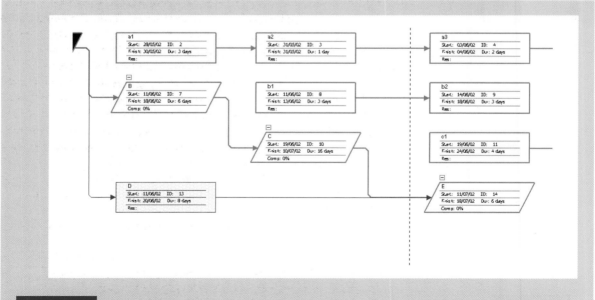

FIGURE 17.21   Visio – PERT chart.

Task Name	Work	Details		27 May '02						03 Jun '02
			S	M	T	W	T	F	S	S	M
A	**136 hrs**	Work			24h	24h	24h	8h			16h
a1	72 hrs	Work			24h	24h	24h				
Joe	*24 hrs*	Work			8h	8h	8h				
Bill	*24 hrs*	Work			8h	8h	8h				
Ted	*24 hrs*	Work			8h	8h	8h				
a2	8 hrs	Work						8h			
Joe	*8 hrs*	Work						8h			
a3	32 hrs	Work									16h
Bill(50%)	*16 hrs*	Work									8h
Ted(50%)	*16 hrs*	Work									8h
a4	24 hrs	Work									
David	*24 hrs*	Work									

FIGURE 17.22 Visio – Adding resource names.

Resource Name	Type	Material Label	Initials	Group	Max. Units	Std. Rate	Ovt. Rate	Cost/Use	Accrue At	Base Calen
Joe	Work		J		100%	£25.00/hr	£0.00/hr	£0.00	Prorated	Standard
Bill	Work		B		100%	£25.00/hr	£0.00/hr	£0.00	Prorated	Standard
Ted	Work		T		100%	£15.00/hr	£0.00/hr	£0.00	Prorated	Standard
Bill(50%)	Work		B		100%	£15.00/hr	£0.00/hr	£0.00	Prorated	Standard
Ted(50%)	Work		T		100%	£20.00/hr	£0.00/hr	£0.00	Prorated	Standard
David	Work		D		100%	£20.00/hr	£0.00/hr	£0.00	Prorated	Standard
Postage	Material		P			£0.22		£0.00	Prorated	

FIGURE 17.23 Visio – Resource details.

Assuming that the planning has been done, the project can get under way, and in Figure 17.24 we can see that all the tasks in A have been completed (denoted by ticks in the left column and a black line through their respective bars on the Gantt chart). Note that both tasks b1 and D (done in parallel) have only partially been completed.

There are many ways the data can be reported. In Figure 17.25 we display the main types (many graphical); Figure 17.26 shows the various current activity reports; Figure 17.27 shows one of these reports; Figure 17.28 shows a resource allocation report; and Figure 17.29 shows a project summary.

As for all the tools outlined in Part 5, we hope that we have given the reader some idea of the application package, though, in truth, we have only scratched the surface of the possibilities provided by Project 2000.

17.5 DATABASE MANAGEMENT: ACCESS

In this section we look at databases on personal computers (PCs). In particular, we look at Access, the database software that is part of the Microsoft Office suite of programs. The history of databases on PCs has been one of very rapid development. In the early days they were just the computer equivalent of a single user card index, for example, the patient records of a dentist. They were very restrictive in terms of the number of records

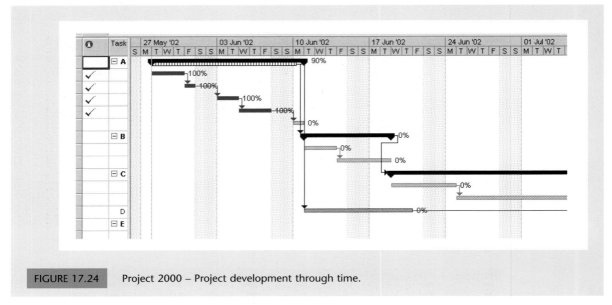

Project 2000 – Project development through time.

FIGURE 17.25 Project 2000 – Ways in which data can be displayed.

that could be held, and they could also be restrictive in terms of their update, retrieval, and sorting abilities. Nowadays they can match the most sophisticated DBMS used on large computers of a few years ago. This is due as much as anything to progress in hardware development, such as processing speeds, disk capacities, computer memory capacities, and the like.

Of course, with distributed computing and client–server systems, the largest and most sophisticated database can also be accessed using PCs. It would be foolish to put numbers to speeds, maximum number of users, size of databases, and so on as the technology changes so rapidly. All we can say for sure is that PC databases are likely

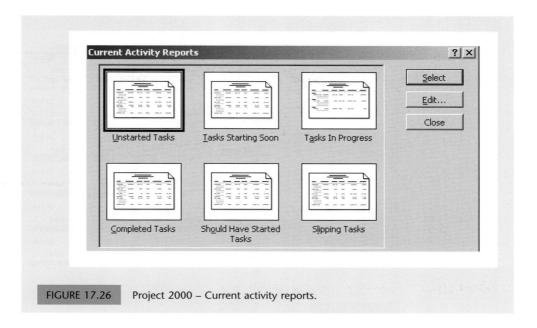

FIGURE 17.26   Project 2000 – Current activity reports.

to be smaller, with fewer users, using fewer tools, compared to corporate databases at any one time.

At the time of writing, there are three versions of Access in common use, Access97, Access2000, and Access2002. We will discuss Access2000, being the most well-used version. Like all the tools discussed in this chapter, a full discussion of Access requires a series of books, so we will look only at aspects which give a flavour of the package.

On opening Access, we see the screen as shown in Figure 17.30. It shows seven basic object types. 'Tables' are the relations, then there are options 'queries', 'forms', and 'reports' to help query the data in the database, enter data conveniently, or provide reports from the data, respectively. The option 'pages', new to the 2000 version, enables the creation of web pages. A 'macro' performs a set of commands in sequence and a 'module' is a larger program written by the user in Visual Basic. These are used for more complex or non-standard applications of the database. The database will consist of a series of related tables and associated queries, reports, forms, and so on.

Completed Tasks as of Tue 28/05/02
Project1

	ID	Task Name	Duration	Start	Finish	% Comp.	Cost	Work
May 2002								
	2	a1	3 days	Tue 28/05/02	Thu 30/05/02	100%	£1,560.00	72 hrs
	3	a2	1 day	Fri 31/05/02	Fri 31/05/02	100%	£200.00	8 hrs
June 2002								
	4	a3	2 days	Mon 03/06/02	Tue 04/06/02	100%	£560.00	32 hrs
	5	a4	3 days	Wed 05/06/02	Fri 07/06/02	100%	£480.00	24 hrs

FIGURE 17.27   Project 2000 – Completed tasks.

ID	⊙	Resource Name				Work	
1		Joe				32 hrs	
	ID	Task Name	Units	Work	Delay	Start	Finish
	2	a1	100%	24 hrs	0 days	Tue 28/05/02	Thu 30/05/02
	3	a2	100%	8 hrs	0 days	Fri 31/05/02	Fri 31/05/02
2		Bill				24 hrs	
	ID	Task Name	Units	Work	Delay	Start	Finish
	2	a1	100%	24 hrs	0 days	Tue 28/05/02	Thu 30/05/02
3		Ted				24 hrs	
	ID	Task Name	Units	Work	Delay	Start	Finish
	2	a1	100%	24 hrs	0 days	Tue 28/05/02	Thu 30/05/02
4		Bill(50%)				16 hrs	
	ID	Task Name	Units	Work	Delay	Start	Finish
	4	a3	100%	16 hrs	0 days	Mon 03/06/02	Tue 04/06/02
5		Ted(50%)				16 hrs	
	ID	Task Name	Units	Work	Delay	Start	Finish
	4	a3	100%	16 hrs	0 days	Mon 03/06/02	Tue 04/06/02
6		David				24 hrs	
	ID	Task Name	Units	Work	Delay	Start	Finish
	5	a4	100%	24 hrs	0 days	Wed 05/06/02	Fri 07/06/02

FIGURE 17.28   Project 2000 – Resource allocation report.

Project1
EBBEC Business School

as of Tue 28/05/02

Dates

Start	Tue 28/05/02	Finish:	Thu 18/07/02
Baseline Start	NA	Baseline Finish:	NA
Actual Start:	Tue 28/05/02	Actual Finish:	NA
Start Variance:	0 days	Finish Variance:	0 days

Duration

Scheduled:	38 days	Remaining:	30.57 days
Baseline:	0 days?	Actual:	7.43 days
Variance:	38 days	Percent Complete:	20%

Work

Scheduled:	136 hrs	Remaining:	0 hrs
Baseline:	0 hrs	Actual:	136 hrs
Variance:	136 hrs	Percent Complete:	100%

Costs

Scheduled:	£2,800.00	Remaining:	£0.00
Baseline:	£0.00	Actual:	£2,800.00
Variance:	£2,800.00		

Task Status

Tasks not yet started:	13
Tasks in progress:	1
Tasks completed:	4
Total Tasks:	18

Resource Status

Work Resources:	6
Overallocated Work Resources:	0
Material Resources:	1
Total Resources:	7

FIGURE 17.29   Project 2000 – Project summary.

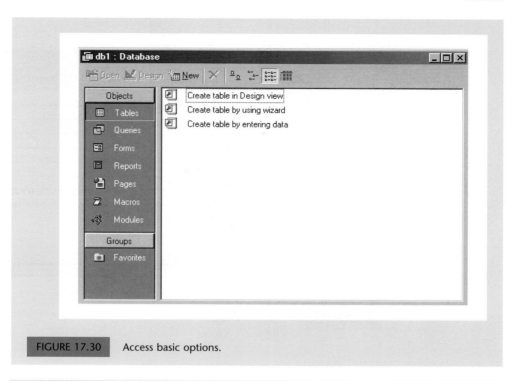

FIGURE 17.30   Access basic options.

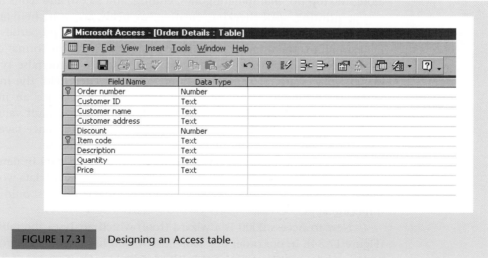

FIGURE 17.31   Designing an Access table.

In Figure 17.31, we show the design form for designing a table. This table has a composite key (see the key icon to the left) of order number and item code. We have specified most fields as text and two fields as numeric. There are many other options, such as date/time, currency, automatically generated number (often used as a primary key), a yes/no alternative, and hyperlink to a web address. You will notice that the Access interface has a 'look and feel' similar to other Microsoft products with a series of menus

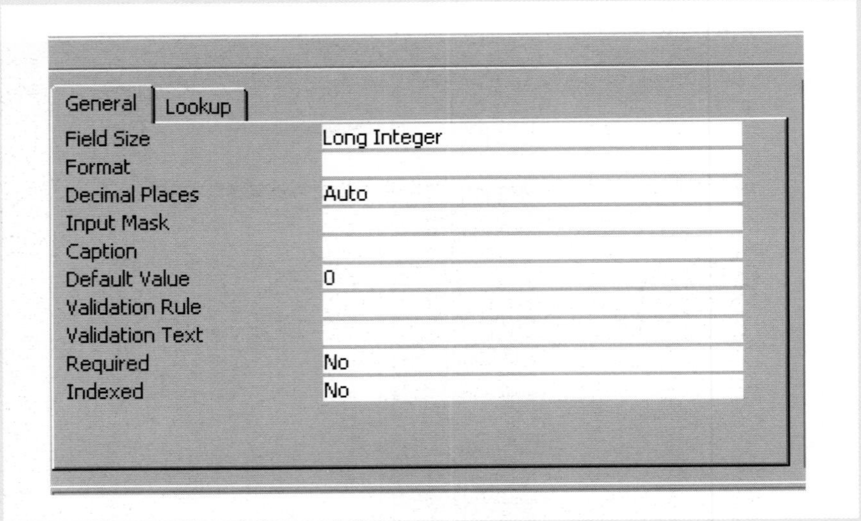

General | Lookup

Field Size	Long Integer
Format	
Decimal Places	Auto
Input Mask	
Caption	
Default Value	0
Validation Rule	
Validation Text	
Required	No
Indexed	No

FIGURE 17.32   Field properties.

along the top (for manipulating files, editing, and so on) and icons held in toolbars (for saving, printing, spell checking, creating key fields, accessing help facilities, and so on).

For each field in the table we can define a number of properties (Figure 17.32). The field size limits the number of characters for a text field, the format controls the display of the field in datasheet view (for example, currency, true/false type, or percentage), decimal places are relevant for a numeric or currency field, the input mask is useful when, for example, including a plus sign and hyphens for an international phone number, a caption provides a label for the field, and a default value is useful when a field will normally have one value more than others and hence save some keying in. A validation rule stops invalid data from entering the database.

As we see in Figure 17.33, once we begin to enter data in datasheet view, Access rightly prevents us from completing the data because rows of data would be formed with duplicate keys. According to the relational model, there should not be rows with duplicate keys.

New to Access 2000 is a wizard (tool) which analyses the tables on the database (Figure 17.34). In our order line table, the wizard has identified (through duplicate item codes and descriptions) data not in third normal form (Section 11.2). The program will help us to create a new table of item code and description, linked to the order line table using the item code. Figure 17.35 shows the initial attempt at doing this with the relationship between the two tables being mapped.

In Figure 17.36 we begin to create a query, again using an Access wizard, which is formed from data held in two tables: order details and order line. However, as the warning message informs us, we have not yet linked these tables together by a relationship. In Figure 17.37 we show how the relationship is formed using the field order number to join the tables as it is in both relations, as our linking field. As shown in

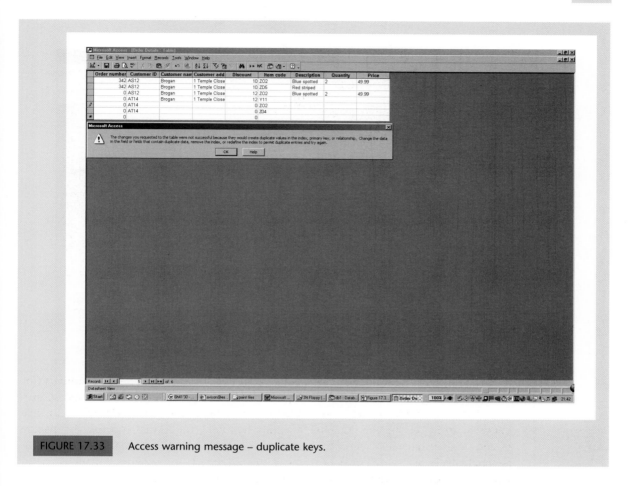

FIGURE 17.33   Access warning message – duplicate keys.

Figure 17.38, Access shows the relationship as one-to-many, with an infinity sign on the many side.

We notice in Figure 17.37 the possibility of enforcing referential integrity rules. The first of these states that you cannot enter data in the field that is used for the join in the related table, if the join field in the primary table does not have matching contents. The second rule prevents you deleting records from the primary table if there are matching records in the related table. Finally you cannot edit primary key values in the primary table if related records exist. Like the rules for normalization, these referential integrity rules help ensure that the database is well formed and easy to use.

In Figure 17.38 we show the design for the query, including the opportunity to sort the query (sorting and searching are likely to be more efficient if the fields are indexed) and only show certain records in the criteria list. For example, we could have chosen to query only those customers who ordered a certain range of products. We did not choose to limit the number of records in any way and Figure 17.39 shows the full list. We can use SQL language statements with Access as well as the query-by-example (QBE) method shown. Indeed, the equivalent SQL statement can be generated by Access, as shown in Figure 17.40. But constructing a query using QBE is more natural to the non-technical user and much easier than coding the equivalent SQL statement.

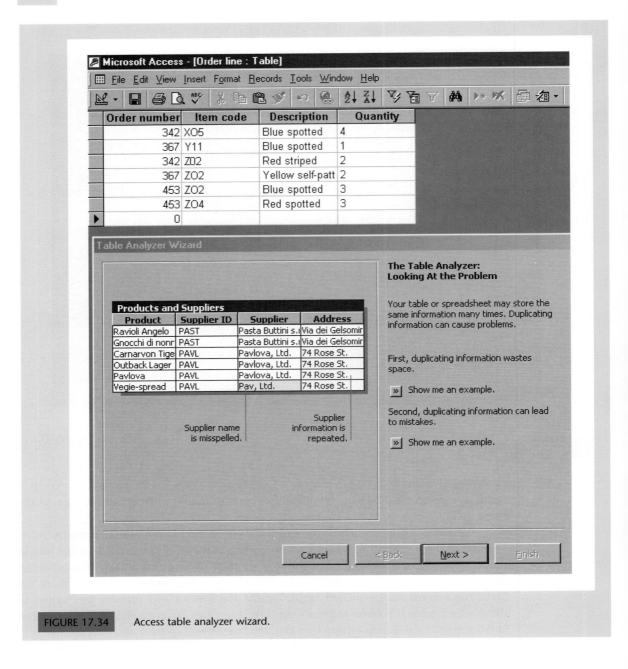

FIGURE 17.34   Access table analyzer wizard.

Forms for entering data can easily be created by using the form wizard. Figure 17.41 shows one stage in the process and Figure 17.42 shows the form created using one of the default styles. There are similar wizards for creating reports in all manner of styles and levels of detail.

Access has a documentation tool as part of the analyzer, and Figure 17.43 shows part of the automated documentation for the item table and Figure 17.44 that for the relationship between the item table and the order line table.

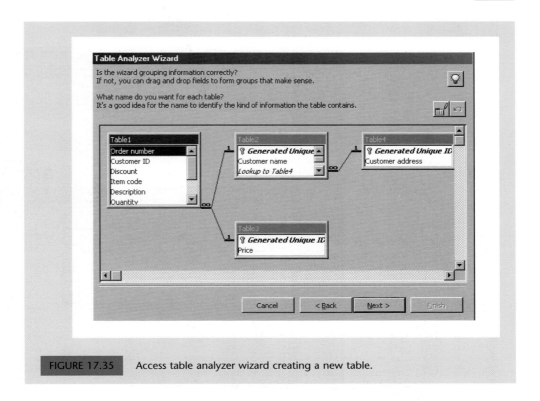

FIGURE 17.35 Access table analyzer wizard creating a new table.

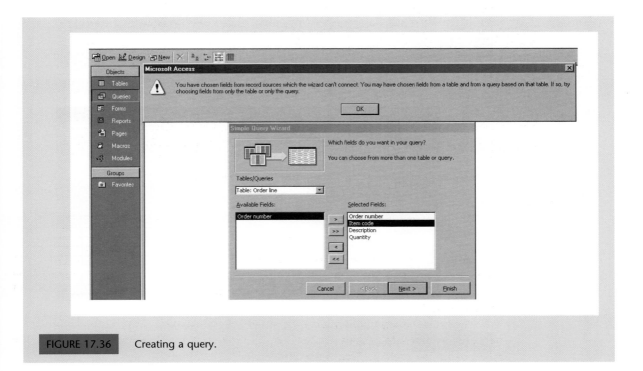

FIGURE 17.36 Creating a query.

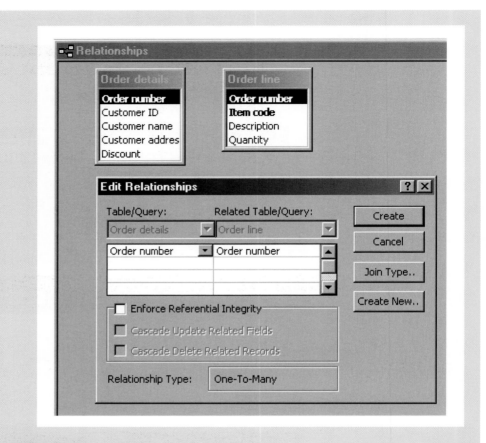

FIGURE 17.37 Establishing the relationship for the query.

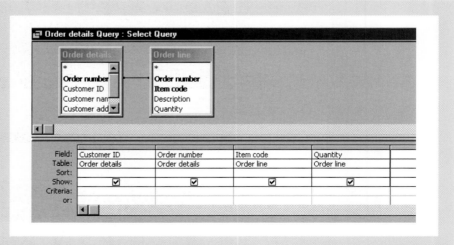

FIGURE 17.38 Access query.

Order details Query : Select Query

Customer ID	Order number	Item code	Quantity
AS12	342	ZO2	2
AS12	342	XO5	4
AS12	367	ZO2	2
AS12	367	Y11	1
AS14	453	ZO2	3
AS14	453	ZO4	3

FIGURE 17.39   Displaying the query results.

Order details Query : Select Query

```
SELECT [Order details].[Customer ID], [Order details].[Order number], [Order line].[Item code], [Order line].[Quantity]
FROM [Order details] INNER JOIN [Order line] ON [Order details].[Order number] =[Order line].[Order number];
```

FIGURE 17.40   The SQL statements for the query.

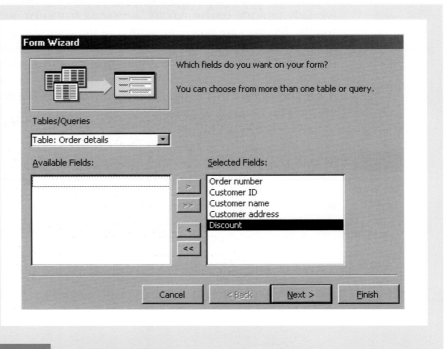

Form Wizard

Which fields do you want on your form?

You can choose from more than one table or query.

Tables/Queries

Table: Order details ▾

Available Fields:

Selected Fields:

Order number
Customer ID
Customer name
Customer address
Discount

Cancel   < Back   Next >   Finish

FIGURE 17.41   The form wizard.

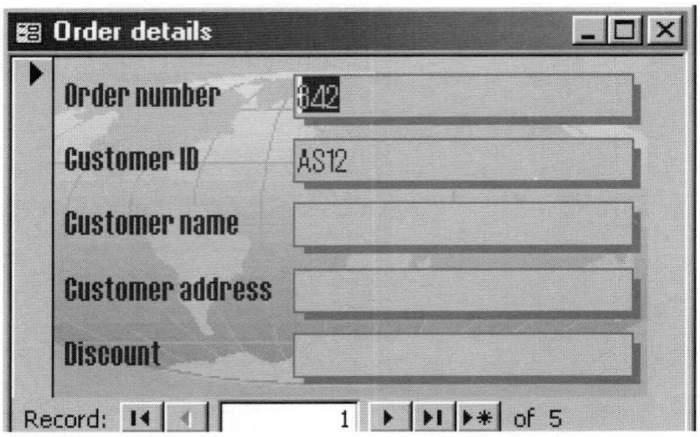

FIGURE 17.42   A wizard-generated form for order details.

Access has a number of security features. A database can be opened read-only or exclusively (via a password). Access even enables encryption and decryption of the data.

As well as enquiries and reports, you can display data using charts, such as pie charts, line graphs, bar charts, column charts, area charts, and so on. Figure 17.45 is a pie chart showing the different proportions of products ordered.

Macros are used to perform repeated actions such as opening tables and forms, regularly printing certain reports, answering particular queries, and finding particular records. Modules are programs written in the computer programming language Visual Basic for Applications. Compared to many computer programming languages, VBA is not that difficult to use. It gives flexibility in using the database. When we add the much greater sophistications and individualized applications enabled by macros and modules, it is readily evident that Access is a very powerful database management system and yet is available on personal computers.

17.6   SUMMARY

- In this chapter we illustrate the use of various tools that are commonly used to develop information systems. These include groupware to help decision support, website development software, a drawing package to support the use of graphical techniques, software for management of time and other resources used in a project, and a database management system. All the application packages described are PC-based.

Table: Order details

Properties

Date Created:	28/05/2002 22:36:32	GUID:	Long binary data
Last Updated:	28/05/2002 22:37:59	NameMap:	Long binary data
OrderByOn:	False	Orientation:	0
RecordCount:	5	Updatable:	True

Columns

Name	Type	Size
Order number	Text	50

AllowZeroLength:	False
Attributes:	Variable Length
Collating Order:	General
ColumnHidden:	False
ColumnOrder:	Default
ColumnWidth:	Default
Data Updatable:	False
DisplayControl:	Text Box
GUID:	Long binary data
Ordinal Position:	1
Required:	False
Source Field:	Order number
Source Table:	Order details
UnicodeCompression:	True

Name	Type	Size
Customer ID	Text	50

AllowZeroLength:	False
Attributes:	Variable Length
Collating Order:	General
ColumnHidden:	False
ColumnOrder:	Default
ColumnWidth:	Default
Data Updatable:	False
DisplayControl:	Text Box
GUID:	Long binary data
Ordinal Position:	2
Required:	False
Source Field:	Customer ID
Source Table:	Order details
UnicodeCompression:	True

FIGURE 17.43   Access documentation tool – tables.

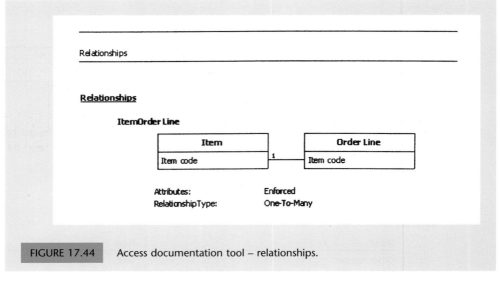

FIGURE 17.44   Access documentation tool – relationships.

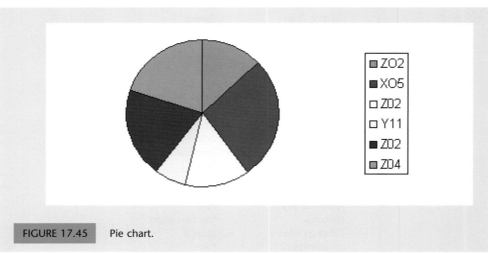

FIGURE 17.45   Pie chart.

QUESTIONS

1 Use the various packages described in this chapter, or any equivalents available to you, to draw diagrams as follows:

–   the various diagrams used in Part 4 (on techniques), using Visio;
–   plan an information systems development project, using Project;

–   set up your own personal website, using Dreamweaver;
–   develop a database application to organize and report on your CD collection, using Access.

17.7 FURTHER READING

Bucki, L.A. (2000) *Managing with Microsoft Project 2000*, Prima, Rocklin, California.

Failla, A. (1996) Technologies for co-ordination in a software factory, in C.U. Ciborra (ed.) *Groupware and Teamwork: Invisible Aid or Technical Hindrance?*, John Wiley & Sons, Chichester, UK, pp. 61–88.

Microsoft (2001) *Developing Microsoft Vision Solutions (Pro-Documentation)*, Microsoft Press.

Oliver, P.R.M. and Kantaris, N. (2001) *Microsoft Access 2002 Explained*, Babani, London.

Towers, J.T. (2001) *Dreamweaver 4 for Windows and Macintosh: Visual QuickStart Guide*, Peachpit.

18 TOOLSETS

INTRODUCTION

Over several years, software support tools have been available that help the information systems development process as a whole, not just in the drawing of some individual diagrams. These *were* generally known as **CASE** (Computer Aided Systems (or Software) Engineering) tools but we use the term information systems development toolset or, more simply, *toolset* for:

> Any integrated computer software system that is specifically designed to support a significant part of the information systems development process of an information system and the management of these tasks and processes.

Whereas the tools discussed in Chapter 17 in the main support one type of activity in the information systems development process, for example, project management, group systems work, or drawing diagrams, toolsets support several tasks; indeed, they provide a full set of tools for the analyst.

Originally CASE tools were divided into Upper and Lower CASE tools. The purpose of this distinction was to indicate which stages of the life cycle they addressed. Upper CASE includes tools that helped the strategy/planning, analysis, or logical design stages, whereas Lower CASE tools were concerned with aspects of physical design, programming, and implementation, including automatic code generation. Most toolsets integrate these elements into a single, fully integrated development and support facility.

Integration in these toolsets is particularly important. They are integrated both horizontally and vertically. Horizontal integration is the integration of different tools at a particular stage of the development cycle. At the analysis stage, for instance, there are a number of different techniques which are supported by the toolset, for example, data flow diagrams, entity models, function decompositions, and so on. These are regarded as horizontally integrated if information is shared between the tools and if changes made in

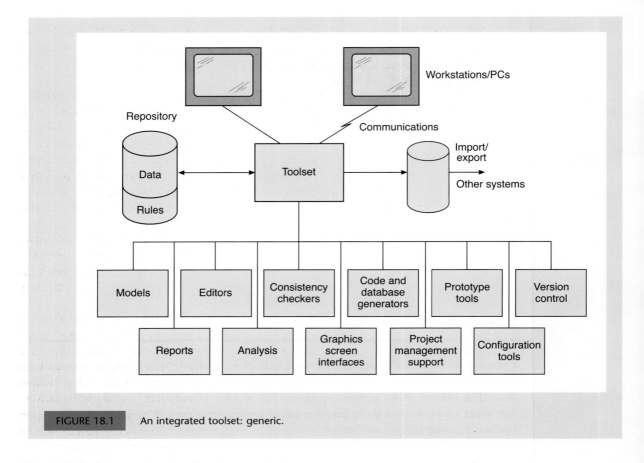

FIGURE 18.1   An integrated toolset: generic.

one diagram (using the diagram support tool) are reflected in the other diagrams, where appropriate.

Vertical integration, on the other hand, is the integration of tools between different stages of the life cycle, and this means that the results from one stage should be available in an automated form to the other stages. The results should be capable of being passed forward to subsequent stages of the life cycle (known as forward integration). Further, for highly integrated tools, the results or changes made at later stages of development should be capable of being passed backward, and be reflected in, earlier stages. This is known as reverse integration.

Another important aspect of integration is interpersonal integration. System development, in organizations of any size, is a matter of co-ordinating the work of many people and perhaps many development teams, frequently in different locations. Additionally, the work may be performed in parallel, at least within development stages, and possibly in parallel across stages. Toolsets should ensure that the work is co-ordinated and consistent. An important aspect of this is **version control**; that is, the organizing and handling of the large numbers of different versions of systems that exist.

Figure 18.1 presents a generic integrated toolset. In this chapter we look at Information Engineering Facility, Oracle and Select Enterprise. Following this, we provide an evaluation of toolsets. Before doing so, however, we discuss one of the key features of toolsets separately. This is the **repository**, seen to the middle left in Figure 18.1. This is so important because it enables the integration of all the models, definitions, and mapping of stages.

The precursors of systems repositories were **data dictionary systems** (DDSs), software tools for managing the data resource. They enabled the recording and processing of 'data about the data' (metadata) that an organization uses. They were originally designed as documentation tools, ensuring standard terminology and providing a cross-reference capability about data (and later processes) at the modelling and implementation levels. They have subsequently developed into systems repositories, which provide a central catalogue for all aspects of an information systems development project, containing all the information necessary to integrate the different stages of information systems development.

The repositories will normally contain information about the physical and operational elements of data and processes, for example, physical data items, processes, modules, code, and test data, and information about logical and functional levels as well, for example, data and process models and diagrams. But they do much more than that.

Active repositories contain information that enables the rules of a technique or an information systems development methodology to be applied. These may permit analysis, validation, and consistency and completeness checking. There may be a separate element of the repository (sometimes known as the repository manager), in which knowledge or rules are embedded. In some repositories these 'rules' (which could be the rules of the methodology) are locked (or hard-coded) into the repository. In other repositories they are more flexible and easily changed or defined in an expert systems language. In theory at least, therefore, a repository contains everything needed to support the creation and maintenance of information systems in organizations.

Repositories do not store diagrams as such, but a series of definitions about the objects in diagrams. This means that objects that appear in more than one diagram are only stored once and that diagrams are generated from the current information in the repository, as and when they are needed. When changes are made to one diagram, the effects of that change are automatically reflected when other diagrams in which the object appears are generated. This enables the basic repository information to be displayed in a number of ways according to needs. For example, an object may feature in an entity model, a data flow diagram, and an action diagram (see Chapter 12).

The repository can contain information beyond that which is needed to create software systems and include models of the organization and environment, that is, the framework of the systems. This is a view of the organization in terms of business areas, functions, hierarchies, departments, locations, strategic relationships, critical success factors, objectives, plans, and so on. Figure 18.2 shows another view of the repository reflecting the enterprise information and its mapping to data and processes in the information system, showing the mappings between them.

Many repositories are themselves relational databases, which reflects the dominant technology when they were developed. This is now somewhat inadequate, and one based on an object-oriented database management system is likely to deal better with the wide variety of data types such as image, voice, and graphics of multimedia systems.

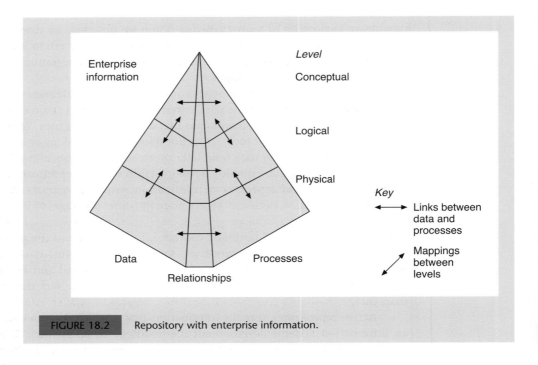

Enterprise
information

Level

Conceptual

Logical

Physical

Key

Data

Relationships

Processes

Links between
data and
processes

Mappings
between
levels

FIGURE 18.2 Repository with enterprise information.

18.2 INFORMATION ENGINEERING FACILITY

Information Engineering Facility (IEF) is an integrated toolset originally developed by Texas Instruments to support the Information Engineering (IE) methodology (Section 20.3, which might be read in conjunction with this section) and classified then as a CASE tool. It has seen much development since, and it is now called Advantage Gen and marketed by Computer Associates. In this section we are not drawing attention to the specific details of the product, but to the concepts embedded in such an integrated toolset. It supports planning, analysis, design, construction, and implementation.

These three elements are integrated via the encyclopaedia (the IEF term for the repository). The main encyclopaedia was originally designed to be held on a centralized mainframe but now runs in a client–server environment. IEF is described as being 'integrated', and this means that across the toolset there is a common look and feel, the use of an encyclopaedia to enable consistency, and the automatic generation of objects and code from higher level objects. We will consider each of the five aspects.

1 Planning

The planning software is designed to support a strategic approach to systems development following the identification of high-level business requirements. It helps in the production of three architectures: the information architecture, the business system architecture, and the technical architecture. First, planners build a subject area diagram, which is a high-level entity model of the subject areas of interest to the business. The data modelling tool enables the users (usually described as planners) to build the subject model and view the whole model or individual subject areas, which can then be 'exploded' to reveal the component entity types of the subject area. The tool ensures consistency across the diagrams and shows any relationship aggregation lines. A relationship aggregation line represents a relationship between entities in different subject areas.

Planners also construct high-level function hierarchy diagrams using the activity hierarchy diagramming tool, which enables the functions and their position in the hierarchy to be captured and displayed in various ways. The activity dependency diagramming tool is then used to document the sequence in which the functions must be performed, with arrows indicating the direction of the dependency showing what function must occur before another. There is also an organizational hierarchy diagramming tool which enables the construction and manipulation of an organization chart. Finally the matrix processor enables various interactions to be identified and depicted.

The matrix processor can be used to show the interactions between any two sets of things, but particular support is provided for 40 standard matrices, which include objectives, strategies, goals, critical success factors, entities, subjects, and functions. The tool is basically a 2-dimensional matrix (Section 12.7) with, for example, functions as rows and objectives as columns, and an entry is made in the relevant cell when a particular function supports a particular objective. The matrix may reveal that some objectives are not supported by any functions, and therefore that objectives have been lost, or that only one or two functions support the majority of the objectives and therefore these are the key functions. Planners use such matrices in a variety of ways, and the software makes the comparison and analysis that much easier. One important use of the matrix processor is to plot the interactions between functions and entities, that is, which functions affect which entities. This may be create, read, update, or delete (CRUD) (see Section 12.7). The matrix processor is also able to cluster, and this might lead to the automatic production of a new matrix where all entities affected by a particular function are clustered together.

The diagramming software for planning is integrated. Once, for example, the entities are entered using the data modelling software, they will appear automatically in the matrices concerned with entities. This means that elements are only entered once, and when they appear in a matrix none will be 'forgotten'.

2 Analysis

Analysis refines a particular area of the business identified in the planning stage, and any information captured in the planning software is automatically available to the analysis software using the encyclopaedia. In this stage (business area analysis in IE), analysts enter further details, often using the same software as in the planning stage. For example, the subject area diagram is expanded into an entity-relationship diagram using the data modelling software. Relationships between entities are now defined, including their cardinality and optionality. This is done by the use of dialogue boxes within the tool, as is the definition of the entity attributes and properties. The user can specify entity subtypes, and the diagram can be viewed with these expanded or contracted. Functions are further refined into a series of lower level processes using the activity hierarchy diagramming tool. For each process, the software, enables details to be entered. These details will include name, description, type, and any entities that the process uses. Similarly, the function dependency diagrams from the planning stage are expanded, where necessary, into a series of process dependency diagrams using the activity dependency diagramming software, and details of events that trigger processes and relationships with external objects are added. Some further matrices are also produced using the matrix processor.

The elementary processes are then defined as action diagrams (Section 12.8) using the process action diagramming tool. The action diagram defines the steps required for each elementary process and the way that they interact with the entities. The software automatically begins constructing the action diagram using information derived from other diagrams, such as the entity model, the process hierarchy, and dependency diagrams, and the analyst can insert extra actions and manipulate the action diagram as required. The process action diagramming software applies action diagramming rules and only allows entries that are semantically and syntactically correct. The information for checking semantic correctness is derived from the earlier diagrams represented in the encyclopaedia. In addition, the tool allows processes to be 'synthesized'. This may be achieved by the software asking certain relevant questions to clear up areas that have not been completed or, in certain circumstances, by automatically generating process logic based on the entity model and information from the matrices. For example, if an entity REGISTRATION has a compulsory one-to-one relationship to entity STUDENT, then a certain action logic is implied by this that can be generated by the software. All this provides the detail of the process logic upon which any subsequent code generation will be based. In certain situations, IEF can be used in analysis without the preceding planning stage having been undertaken, in which case all information is entered from scratch in the analysis software.

3 Design

In IE terms, this includes support for both business systems design and technical design, and the design software enables the designer to take the results of analysis and transform them into designs. The first stage is for each process to be transformed into a set of procedures by the dialogue design software. Dialogue flow diagrams are produced, and the software allows the designers to specify control and sequences of screens. Next, the screens themselves are designed using the screen design tool. This will automatically produce an initial attempt at the screen design, based on the information in the encyclopaedia, which can then be modified. The software also attempts to provide previously defined screen elements to the designer and so encourage consistency in design. Indeed, designers can create templates that enforce standards across applications. The screens are then prototyped, showing the layout and flow of screens, and input validation can also be performed using the tool.

The process action diagrams from analysis can also be converted into procedure action diagrams using the action diagramming software. Designers can specify the detailed logic statements and associate processes with commands from the keyboard, specify run-time error routines, and so on. Again, as in the process action diagrams, the software identifies potential errors and prevents them occurring.

Up to this stage, the design has been at the logical level and not dependent on any target hardware or software environment. Technical design now requires the business systems design to be taken to the next stage, which is physical design where the target environment is specified. Using the software, the designers can specify the target environment and the constraints that this implies. Common specifications are already stored in the encyclopaedia. Physical design is then initiated, and the data model is transformed into a physical database design of records, fields, linkages, entry points, and so on, depending on the actual database specified in the physical environment. These would be tables, rows, columns, and foreign keys in a relational database environment. The physical design can be modified and tuned by the designers as necessary, usually for performance reasons. Such changes do not modify the conceptual designs and only changes as business requirements change the logical models.

4   Construction

The next stage is construction, and the automatic production of complete application systems by the generation of code. The software supports the generation of code in a number of languages and embedded SQL calls to the database. The tool also produces screen definitions, graphical user interfaces, database definitions, referential integrity triggers (to control database deletions), and a transaction control program. The code generated is based on the logic specified in the action diagrams and the entity models.

Developers can test and modify the code without tampering with the source code. Changes are made to the code by changing the action diagrams (or further back in the analysis stage) and regenerating the code. The software 'remembers' any changes made for tuning purposes and then reapplies them to the regenerated code. Further, for small changes, not all the code needs to be regenerated and, using various dialogues, the developers can specify which components require regeneration.

5   Implementation

Finally, the implementation software (which resides on the target hardware) enables the installation of code and database on the computer. This includes the compilation, linking and binding of the application, and the allocation and building of the database, plus a facility that enables the running and testing of the application on the target computer.

6   The encyclopaedia

The encyclopaedia is the key to IEF and enables the storing of models, the concurrent use of these models, the progression from one stage to the next, and the transformation of the models ultimately into complete developed applications. The main encyclopaedia resides on the server, and subsets of the models can be downloaded to workstation clients to enable individual work and to enable teams to work on developments concurrently. Any changes to models are then uploaded back to the main encyclopaedia in a controlled way from the local encyclopaedias to ensure consistency. The encyclopaedia also provides version control, which means that multiple copies of models for different purposes can be stored and used without confusion.

The encyclopaedia stores definitions of models rather than graphical representations of the model, and therefore the software uses these definitions to produce the diagrams that are required. Many of the diagrams are based on common information, and this enables a high degree of consistency between diagrams as they are constructed as and when necessary from the stored definitions. This also enables any changes or updates made by developers to one diagram to be reflected in other diagrams automatically. For example, in an entity diagram, a change to a relationship between two entities from optional to mandatory will automatically be reflected in all other diagrams that use this information when they are next displayed, because they will access the one definition of that relationship in the encyclopaedia. The storing of definitions in the encyclopaedia rather than the storing of graphical representations not only enables models to share information but allows the information to be passed forward to subsequent stages easily.

The encyclopaedia also enables consistency checking. This can be initiated at any stage and on the whole development or subsets, such as an entity model, functions, processes, action diagrams, and so on. Some checks are enforced when information and definitions are entered. For example, an attempt to use the same name for two functions or entities would be highlighted as they were entered. Other checks will only be made upon request or before proceeding to a subsequent stage. An entity model, for example, would be checked for completeness, in that it has attributes and relationships, and that these are consistent with the functions and activities defined, before proceeding from analysis to design.

18.3 ORACLE

The core of Oracle is its well-established database software. Originally Oracle consisted entirely of a relational database system, designed to be used by a professional programmer. Now it comes with a full toolset. It is the most successful product of this type, though it is really a product range, and it is possible to purchase some tools that make up Oracle but not others. Indeed there are a number of 'toolsets', each with its suite of tools. These include the Oracle database suite, Designer/2000, Developer/2000, and Discoverer/2000. Other tools provided are outside the scope of this chapter. Many Oracle applications are developed in a PC–Windows environment, but Oracle has been designed to run on many hardware/software platforms.

Designer/2000 was formally known as Oracle CASE and is helpful in data and process modelling. Developer/2000 is used to build an application, once it has been designed using Oracle Designer/2000. Discoverer/2000 consists of a suite of user-friendly query tools designed for *ad hoc* reporting. The Oracle Database Management

System is central to these tools, though many end-users are hardly aware of its presence. In this section, we will first look briefly at the Oracle Database Management System and then look at Designer/2000 and Developer/2000.

1 Oracle Database Management System

Being a relational database system, we see data expressed in rows and columns. The main method of communicating directly with the Oracle database is by using the SQL language. Although this stands for Structured Query Language, it enables the experienced user to do more than just handle queries. It is certainly easier to use than conventional computer programming languages, but it is nevertheless not trivial. There are extensions to the basic SQL language provided in Oracle and together they form PL/SQL. The SQL optimizer attempts to make each SQL statement as efficient as possible when executed. SQL procedures can be triggered by certain events, for example, after updating or deleting a record (row).

The security features are now very sophisticated: you need system privileges to access the database and object-level privileges at different levels to query, insert, update, and delete any object stored in the database. Security also implies the ability to rollback to the previous database state should there be a problem with a particular transaction. Data are validated through data constraints, that is, only allowing permitted values of data to be entered into the database.

2 Designer/2000

The aim of these tools is to construct applications based on the Oracle Database Management System as quickly as possible; indeed its use is often referred to as rapid application development. Most of its tools are either data modelling or application generating tools. The latter are mainly used for form and report generation, but they can also be used to generate other programs in Visual Basic and for reverse engineering. They build up and require a central encyclopaedia of information about business processes and functions as well as the data resource.

The modelling tools provided include those supporting entity-relationship, function hierarchies, data flow, and process flow diagrams. There is also help to define matrices, for example, to cross functions with entities and functions with attributes, and write reports. To give only one example of the power of the tools, the repository reporting tool has more than 100 standard reports, and there are also various utilities provided to help the database administrator set up, maintain, and use the repository.

There is a generator to define the subsequent database, along with its relations, constraints, and so on. There is help provided to support normalization and resolving m : m relationships and other potential database design problems. Application module definitions are also supported that can specify screens, reports, and PL/SQL subprograms. 'Wizards', similar to those provided in the Microsoft Office suite of programs, can be used to guide the designer to generate the database and applications. Again, diagrammer tools support designing the structure of each module and many other tasks. Relevant documentation can be generated at the same time, including user and training manuals. Along with supporting a 'brand name' methodology such as Information Engineering, these tools can be used for rapid application development and other approaches. The process modeller is designed to support business process re-engineering and reverse engineering of existing systems by representing the essential aspects of each process.

The forms generator comes with a number of standard form templates that can be customized for each form. Constraints can be added to ensure data entry using the forms is validated, such as a range of numeric values or one of a list of possibilities provided in a combo box. Similarly there is a reports generator which wherever possible has a similar look and feel to the forms generator. It is possible to see the SQL statements generated and modify this generated program directly. Oracle Designer/2000 can also be used to generate programs in Visual Basic and web applications using the webserver generator and charts using the graphics generator.

Of course, such tools and diagrammers can only support information systems development, they do not do away with the necessity of having a good strategy for applications development, good planning to carry out the strategy, good fact-finding procedures and communications, and good analysis and design.

3 Developer/2000

The main features of this development suite are Developer/2000 Forms, Reports, and Graphics that run with the Oracle DBMS and the application server. This latter tool carries out the processing to produce the reports, etc. and is integrated with the web server, for web-based applications, as well as the Oracle DBMS. It should be remembered that the toolset comprising Oracle Developer/2000 consists of very powerful, complex, and sophisticated elements and is not really designed for the end-user, who is much better suited to the Discoverer/2000 toolset, with its data browser and data query tools. Further, to operate these applications efficiently requires a well-designed, modelled, and normalized database. The Oracle toolset supports the production of such databases, but human skills are still crucial.

Oracle Developer/2000 Forms can be used to create data entry screens and menus, but it can also be used to start programs and other Developer tools and create database applications. PL/SQL libraries (of reusable SQL code) and object libraries can be used so that Forms becomes a very powerful applications generator. Oracle Developer/2000 Reports enables report generation. Some reports can be used interactively. The efficient use of Reports requires a good knowledge of SQL. Oracle Developer/2000 Graphics is used to add visual 'splendour' to a report or form. Again, though the results may be user-friendly, their creation requires technical expertise, though there are over 50 predefined chart templates provided.

18.4 SELECT ENTERPRISE

Select Software Tools was a software company that developed an early CASE tool that evolved over the years as a professional toolset. It has also been widely used for teaching purposes in UK universities. Select is now owned by Aonix, based in San Diego. Aonix is itself owned by the Gores Technology Group known for its Software through Pictures (StP) product. The product line includes Select Component Factory which was made up of four tools: Select Enterprise, the modelling tool; Select Component Manager, a portal for managing components and putting them into a repository; the Process Director tool that included what is known as Select Perspective, a development methodology; and synchronization tools for Java, C++, and Visual Basic.

However, we will provide an overview of Select Enterprise, which is essentially the original but much expanded CASE tool, designed for object modelling and supporting UML. It can be used on its own and is a powerful design and development toolset itself. It enables the design of business applications quickly, leveraging best practice modelling techniques. Among other features, Select Enterprise has the following (see www.aonix. com):

- business process modelling;
- UML profile;
- graphical simulations of UML designs;
- database modelling and code generation;
- design patterns and optional component-based techniques;
- Scalable Enterprise Repository;
- intelligent document generation;
- traceability and impact analysis;
- Java, Visual Basic, C++ code synchronization;
- integration with a range of other tools.

As well as Select Enterprise there are a number of related products. For example, there exist a *Reviewer for Select Enterprise* which locates errors in syntax and UML, and *Select SSADM* and *Select Yourdon* which support users of these information systems development methodologies (see Sections 19.3 and 20.1 respectively).

The tools of the Select Enterprise product (Version 6.1) are illustrated in Figure 18.3. As can be seen, the repository is the centre of the system, which contains the various data stores and usually resides on the server. The repository management tool is the Repository Administrator, which manages the data stores. The Models Neighborhood is for managing the various models on the client workstation. The Select Enterprise tool itself enables UML modelling and more. Integrated with Select Enterprise are a number of other tools, for example, the Document Generator for creating presentations from models and the Model Copy tool which copies diagrams and other items between models.

The Select Enterprise user interface (Figure 18.3) has four separate areas or windows:

- The Explorer window (left-hand side) contains folders. There are four sets of folders available in this window accessed by various tabs (see bottom of window):
    - diagram types within the model (this tab displayed) (i.e. Process Hierarchy Diagrams, Process Thread Diagrams, Use Case Diagrams, etc.);

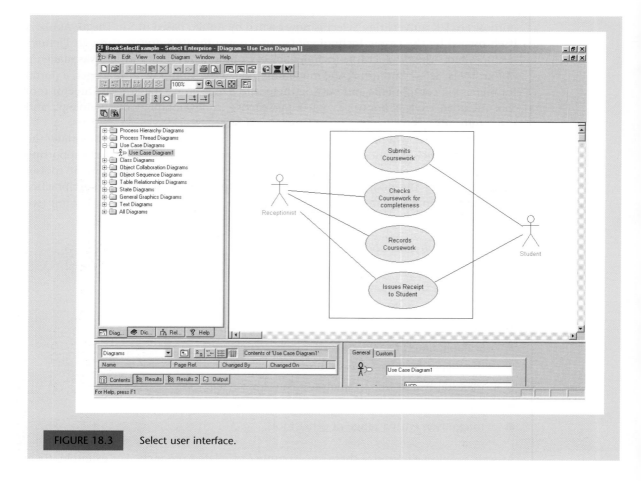

FIGURE 18.3   Select user interface.

○ dictionary items within the model (a folder for each item);
○ relationships which show associations between dictionary items and their hierarchies;
○ help contents.

■ The Output window (lower left) which has the following tabs:

○ contents displays details of the currently selected diagram or item in the Explorer window, this tab can be used to navigate through the models;
○ results displays the model objects according to the previous action performed;
○ output displays textual information (e.g. results of a consistency check).

■ The Diagram window (main) displays the selected diagram (a use case in this example) and is used to create, edit, and generally manage the diagrams.

■ The Property page (lower right) displays properties for the currently selected diagram, the tabs available depend on the actual diagram selected.

Figure 18.4 shows the Tools menu, which gives an indication of the various tools

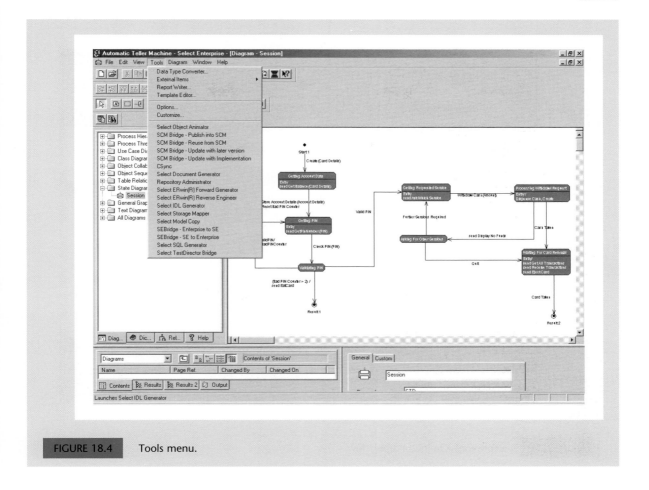

FIGURE 18.4   Tools menu.

and features available in Select. The Bridge tools interface with other products (e.g. Platinum's ERwin and Mercury's TestDirector).

The Repository Administrator window is illustrated in Figure 18.5. It is accessed from within Select via the Tools menu (Figure 18.4) and is used to create, start, and stop datastores (a datastore has to be started before it can be used) and backing up and recovering datastores.

Figure 18.6 shows a Class Diagram displayed together with some menus accessed with a right click on the mouse button showing the various options for Association, Aggregation, etc. The functions available depend on the item selected.

Figure 18.7 displays an example Sequence Diagram (see Section 13.2 for a discussion of these UML diagrams). Figure 18.8 illustrates the Object Animator, one of the facilities of Select. The function is accessed via the Tools menu (Figure 18.4) and it animates the object interactions that are defined in a Sequence Diagram. Graphically representing objects and their interactions helps users and others to understand the sequences defined in a Sequence Diagram. Obviously the dynamic interaction cannot be shown in a static screenshot, but in Figure 18.8 the line made up of little squares has

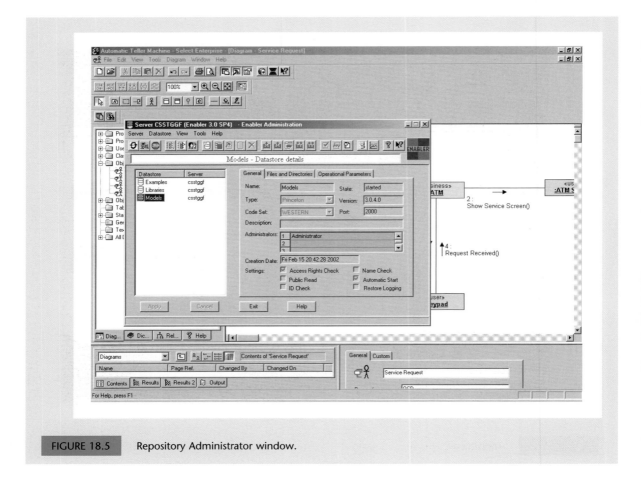

FIGURE 18.5   Repository Administrator window.

to be imagined moving from object to object, indicating the sequence of activities that occur.

As a further illustration of Select, the UML diagrams of Section 13.2 have been generated using Select Enterprise (except the Activity Diagram, Figure 13.9, which was developed using Rational Rose).

18.5   DISCUSSION

We will now look at some of the potential benefits and problems that might accrue from using integrated toolsets. We begin with the potential benefits.

1   Improvements in management and control

Applications development, particularly for large projects, is inherently difficult to manage and control. The process must therefore be tightly managed, and the IT pro-

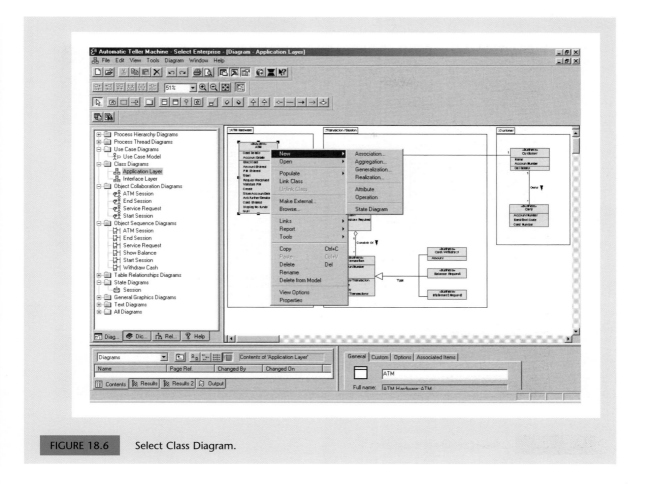

FIGURE 18.6   Select Class Diagram.

fession has not historically been very good at this, particularly in the areas of estimation and keeping to budgets and schedules. Toolsets can help in this process by providing a central repository of information concerning the project, including rules and standards to be followed, and experience from other projects, such as the length of time certain activities actually take in the organization. They can also help with estimation, risk analysis, project planning, and the monitoring of project progress. Particular support for techniques may be included, such as function point analysis, CoCoMo, PERT, and critical path analysis. These were discussed in Chapter 14. Toolsets can also structure the work of developers; for example, by handling the devolvement of tasks to developers so that work can be completed in parallel and the subsequent recombination of the work put into a coherent whole. They can also support the change control process and ensure that new versions and releases are well organized and managed.

2   **Improvements in system quality**

The problems associated with specifications have already been discussed. It is argued that tools can help overcome these problems by providing better and more complete

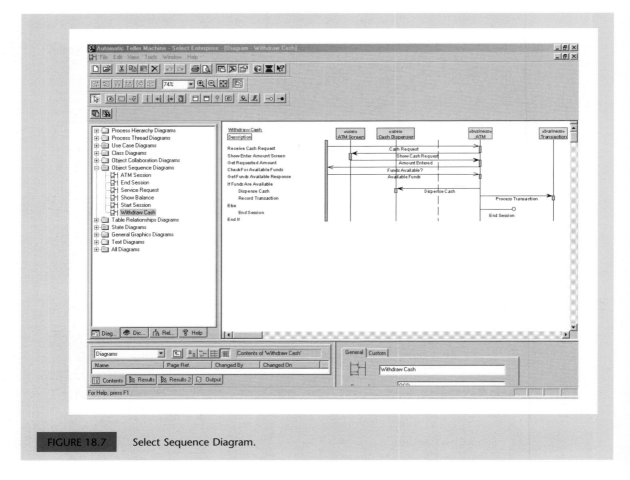

FIGURE 18.7   Select Sequence Diagram.

specifications through the use of diagrammatic representations that are easily modifiable by developers and users. These should also represent the real requirements better, partly because there is less resistance to changing diagrams because the tools make it easy.

3   Improved designs, better reflecting the specifications

Another problem of systems development is that the designs produced do not always accurately reflect the requirements specification. This can be the result of incomplete or conflicting information, and designers often make guesses or opt for whatever is the easy solution. Tools can help by providing the necessary information from the specification, having it available to designers from the repository, and by automating some of the process. This also helps to produce consistent designs, including that across applications.

4   Automated checking for consistency according to the rule base

Tools can automatically check the consistency of information input at the analysis and design stages, including information input using models and diagrams. They can highlight information that has been missed, areas that have been missed, interfaces

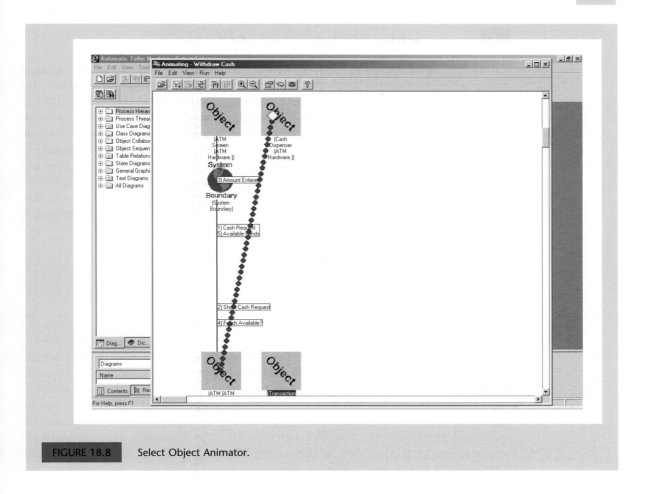

FIGURE 18.8   Select Object Animator.

that do not match, as well as incomplete information. This kind of automated consistency checking can be based on a set of rules concerning the methodology as a whole or those of the various diagramming techniques themselves. These rules would be included in the systems repository. Such checking should improve the consistency and quality of deliverables and thus the final information system, leading to less reworking and change at later stages.

5   Greater focus on analysis rather than implementation

It is often argued that the use of toolsets enables and encourages the focus of development to be changed from the later stages of the life cycle, such as design, coding, and implementation, to the earlier stages of analysis and requirements determination. Such a change of emphasis is likely to lead to better quality systems, as problems are detected and corrected at an earlier stage than with purely manual methods. The earlier in the development process that problems or errors are detected, the cheaper they are to correct.

6   Enforcement of standards and consistency

The use of tools can also help with the definition and enforcement of various standards in development. The tool itself often embodies certain conventions and standards that can help to ensure consistency in the development of individual projects and across different projects in an organization. The tool may enforce discipline by not allowing developers the freedom to ignore or contravene certain rules, procedures, and standards. It can also ensure consistency in the use of techniques, definitions, and terminology in the organization. As well as enforcing standards, they may ensure that the rules and objectives of a particular information systems development methodology are followed. Again, this may be achieved by the tool not allowing the developers the freedom to diverge from the requirements of the methodology and by the tool itself adhering to the methodology in what it does.

7   Improvements in productivity

Perhaps the most cited benefit of using tools is that of improved productivity due to a number of factors. First, it is argued that information systems are developed more quickly than with conventional methods. This is obviously a very attractive benefit, given the enduring problems of systems development in this respect. Faster systems development is achieved by improved management and control, the ability to create and change diagrams and specifications, and the automation and elimination of various manual stages, including the automatic generation of some aspects of design and the automatic generation of code. This latter benefit can potentially make a significant improvement to productivity, as the writing of code has always been a very labour-intensive part of the development process.

The second element is the ability to develop systems with fewer people. The automated support for much of the process and the automation of some tasks, it is argued, means that fewer developers are required. With fewer people, there is the added benefit that the number of interfaces and the communication required between developers is also reduced, which is also likely to enhance the speed and quality of development. The law of diminishing returns applies to systems development. This suggests that after a certain figure is reached, the more developers that are added to a project, the longer it will take to finish. This indicates that a kind of inverted economy of scale may apply to systems development, because the more interfaces there are between people, the slower things happen.

The third element contributing to improved productivity is the reduced costs of development. This is essentially an effect of the first two factors, that is, faster development and fewer people.

A fourth element of improved productivity is the ability to reuse existing development objects. The information captured by a toolset over a number of projects may eventually provide a repository of models or objects of various kinds that can be used again. These may include analysis and design models of all types and libraries of common code that can be utilized in future developments. Depending on circumstances, these models may be used in their entirety or are amended according to the requirement of the new project. This can save a significant amount of development effort and help achieve consistency between applications as well, as the standards in the original models will be incorporated into the new developments.

Reductions in maintenance

It is argued that the use of tools helps reduce the large degree of effort required for both maintenance and enhancement of existing systems. First, they can produce good and consistent documentation, which can lead to easier maintenance. Second, the better quality specification and analysis means there will be less change and thus less maintenance. Third, the improved design and implementation, including some automation, results in fewer errors at the programming, testing, and implementation stages, thus leading to less maintenance.

Accurate and effective testing is also an important element in reducing the maintenance load. Traditionally, this has been carried out by a separate group of people because the developers themselves were not trusted to test a system that they had developed effectively. Programmers were thought to be the worst people to test their own systems, as they assumed the system would work because they had written it. The consequence of having a different set of people performing the testing is that they have no knowledge of how the system was developed. Further, they could not take advantage of any verification and validation potential that the development methodology might have to offer. Toolsets can provide this enhanced testing by helping to administer and control the activity and by generating test data, applying (or even simulating) it, and analysing and comparing the results. The type of test data generated can be derived from, and reflect, the requirements of the analysis and design stages. For example, if there is a requirement that when a particular process is invoked then a subsequent process must also be performed, then this can be captured as knowledge in the repository and a particular set of tests and relevant data automatically produced. An example may be that a debit from one account must be accompanied by a credit to some other account. Such testing is more likely to test the requirement effectively than random testing, and the benefits apply both to the initial systems development and any subsequent maintenance or enhancement to the system.

Further, the traditional form of maintenance is made obsolete because changes are not made by directly reworking the code in response to errors and changing requirements, but by going right back to the analysis and design stages and amending the original diagrams and specifications and regenerating the code automatically. This helps eliminate the frequently encountered problem of introducing new errors as a result of correcting existing ones.

9

Re-engineering (or reverse engineering) of existing systems

The problem in many organizations is not so much that of developing new systems, but the maintenance and enhancement of their old systems, some of which are based on 1960s' designs, third generation languages, and dated file and access methods.

Re-engineering is the application of tools, techniques, and methods to extend the useful life of application systems cost-effectively. Re-engineering changes the underlying technology of a system without affecting the functioning of that system. Therefore, for example, the hardware platform and environment, including the programming language of the applications to reduce maintenance costs, may be changed. The rapid developments in technology have rendered many existing systems, even some that are relatively recent, obsolete, not in the functional sense, but in the programming language used and the hardware on which the system runs. Such systems can carry a high maintenance workload and be difficult to enhance. Further, many manufacturers refuse to maintain old hardware, and it is difficult to integrate legacy systems with more recently developed systems. For many organizations, the cost and resource implications of scrapping these old systems and redeveloping them from scratch on new hardware platforms is prohibitive. The normal use of tools provides support for 'forward development', that is, the top-down, linear approach to the development of new systems. Some tools are designed to support reverse engineering as well, providing the ability to capture the primary elements from current systems, such as their process logic and the data they use, including entities, attributes, names, locations, sources, edit criteria, and relationships. From this captured information, the tool can help to clean up the data definitions, produce entity models, restructure the process logic and build process hierarchies, and construct the repository for the old system. The tool can then be used in the normal forward development mode to produce new systems.

10   Strategic contribution

The potential for information systems to contribute to the achievement of the strategic objectives of the organization has been discussed in Section 4.2, and the use of these tools can help by improving the quality of systems and the speed at which those systems are developed and enhanced. Additionally, the planning elements of an integrated toolset may help to identify and prioritize those systems which are most likely to contribute to the business strategy.

11   Improved responsiveness

This is really a function of improved maintenance and enhancement of systems that have already been discussed, but the particular element emphasized here is that systems developed using a tool are likely to be more easily and quickly enhanced leading to improved responsiveness to changing and evolving business needs.

12   Portability

Many toolsets make it easier to move systems from one hardware platform or environment to another. This is really a function of the ability of some tools to generate code for a variety of different languages on different hardware platforms. For a particular application, the code can be regenerated for a different environment without affecting the functionality of the application. While this makes it easier, it does not in practice mean that there is no manual intervention required.

13   Keeping up with the state of the art

Some people argue that tools enhance the credibility of the information systems group. It indicates to the rest of the organization, and perhaps the world at large, that they are at the cutting edge of the latest technological developments. This is perhaps not a totally justifiable benefit, as it seems to be an argument for technology for technology's sake. A better justification is that it helps to attract and retain good information systems staff and increases satisfaction among developers.

Having identified the potential benefits of integrated toolsets, we will discuss the other side of the equation. The most obvious cost is that for the software and hardware which can be considerable, but probably the more important costs are those associated with the adoption of these tools:

- *Staff education and training costs*. These are costs that apply not only for the professional developers, but for users and user management as well. These costs are not just one-off, as is sometimes assumed, but are a long-term requirement, because of staff turnover and new versions of the tool.

- *Consultancy and training costs*. In some cases, the training may only be available from the vendor, and vendors may make most of their profits from consultancy and training. An associated problem relates to staff turnover, which tends to increase as experienced tool users and developers are currently much sought after.

- *Development of appropriate conditions*. The setting of standards, working practices, and the resolution of conflicts all need to be sorted out, and an appropriate environment and culture for the use of the toolset developed. Again this takes time and effort and is an initial cost of adopting a tool.

- *Integration of the new tool*. The toolset needs to be integrated into the existing development environment so as not to cause conflict. It is very unlikely that any organization will be able to change to such a development environment except in well-thought out and managed stages. All this may require organizational change and will certainly take management time and effort.

- *Customization of the tool*. There can be quite a major effort required to tailor the tool for use in the particular organization. This will take time and other resources, and systems support and consultancy from the tool vendor, which may be expensive.

- *People's time*. Often the time of people using toolsets is not properly costed, as time is often assumed to be free and to have no opportunity cost. For example, if someone goes on a course, the cost of the course is usually included but not the time lost by that person. The time put in by users is also frequently ignored.

- *The cost of recruiting experienced staff*. Probably an organization will not train everyone from scratch but will seek some developers from outside who are experienced in using and managing the toolset. Recruiting costs can be particularly expensive as these staff are in demand.

- *Other hardware costs.* It is frequently the case that the hardware needs upgrading and more workstations are required as more projects are developed. Again, these costs may not have been included in the initial estimates.

Far too many organizations have ignored the softer costs in their cost/benefit analyses and concentrated solely on the direct hardware and software costs associated with integrated toolsets. The former can easily amount to two to five times the amount spent on the tools themselves.

The evaluation of costs vs potential benefits is difficult, and the whole area of toolset use is surrounded, as are many IT developments, by a degree of 'hype', much of it emanating from vendors trying to market their products, but also, perhaps, from overenthusiastic developers seeking quick solutions. The IT community is characterized by the greeting of new approaches and products with great enthusiasm and a belief that, contrary to previous experience, this latest innovation is going to solve all known problems. Inevitably, there is then a backlash against this overly optimistic view, and a certain pessimism sets in whereby people begin to condemn the innovation as either worse than useless or nothing new and simply 'old wine in new bottles'.

Organizations that jump on the bandwagon, expecting a panacea, experience difficulties and problems. They then turn against that particular innovation and vehemently condemn it before rushing on to the next one. The truth with any innovation is usually somewhere in the middle of the two extremes. We have already seen evidence of a backlash. This is perhaps not altogether surprising considering some of the hype; for example, one vendor suggests that productivity of 25 times that of traditional development can be achieved with their product.

There are further concerns related to the particular context of this book. The first is that the technology of such toolsets might distract people from the real issues of information systems development, that is, a concentration on the tool rather than the development approach that lies behind the tool, and as a result the tool being used indiscriminately and inappropriately. Second, the tool may force people to use some methods that are not relevant or well enough defined. It has been suggested that tools are sometimes purchased and used without enough thought being given to the processes that they enforce. In other words, the tool enforces a particular approach to systems development, and it is this approach that needs to be carefully considered rather than the look and feel of the software. Some companies have found themselves implementing a particular development methodology without quite realizing it, due to their use of a particular tool. A further issue is the degree to which the methodology is supported and the way the support is implemented.

The evaluation of any toolset is not a simple process, and the statement that a toolset supports a particular methodology is only the beginning of the story. The way in which the rules are enforced is also critical. A further problem is that the vendor may interpret the rules of the methodology somewhat differently to the author of the methodology or the organization adopting the tool.

Whatever the degree of improved productivity claimed, there appear to be a growing number of indications that achieving them is more difficult, and takes longer, than might be thought. The learning period for most toolsets is long. Both developers and users need time to learn, assimilate, and become effective in using the tools. In terms of productivity, it has been suggested that the learning curve (productivity benefits plotted against time) may fall in the early stages. The length of this early stage, before improved performance is reached, has been estimated to be between six months and two years. It perhaps makes more sense to measure the length of the learning curve, not in time, but in terms of numbers of projects, in which case it has been suggested that it is not until the third or fourth project when productivity benefits begin to accrue. Clearly toolset use is not an instant panacea and some organizations may not be prepared for the kind of long-term investment that is required. The introduction of a toolset must be handled with care and people's expectations relating to benefits, problems, and timescales need to be realistically managed.

It might be that the adoption of toolsets is most successful when it is seen as part of a process of changing the culture of an IT department, that is, when it is seen as a process of organizational development. It may also be seen in the context of changing the organization as a whole, perhaps empowering users or centralizing power. It may be analysed in terms of its effect on the hierarchical structure of an organization or as an element of organization learning. The tools are not implemented in an organizational vacuum, and there are many indications that success or otherwise is heavily influenced by a range of organizational and human factors. In essence, these are characteristics of the organizational fit of the tool, or, as it is sometimes termed, the compatibility of the innovation with its context:

- the management approach;
- power structures in the organization;
- the degree of organizational creativity;
- the organizational culture;
- work patterns;
- teamwork;
- the incentive and reward systems;
- perceptions of job security;
- satisfaction levels;
- the role of champions and sponsors;
- change agents;
- the history of innovation and experimentation in the organization.

Another important aspect of the organizational dimension of analysis is the maturity of the IT department and the software development process in the organization. As we saw in Section 4.5, there are a number of models of the 'stages of growth' of IT in organizations, and there are indications that certain stages of maturity need to have been reached to allow the effective introduction of toolsets. Further, the type of tool, and its objectives and justification, might be different depending on the stage of growth at which it is introduced.

A further organizational dimension concerns the way that innovations are adopted and diffused in organizations. One strategy might be *laissez-faire* in which the tool is adopted without any deliberate organizational encouragement. A second is 'cautious', which is a slow but deliberate approach. The third is 'active', which is fast and requires a high degree of organizational and managerial push.

They also identify three types of innovation in terms of the degree and nature of the change that occurs. The first is 'compatible' innovation if the tool fits in with and does not change current working practices, such as the methodology. The second type is 'incremental', where the tool involves only small changes to current working practices, and the third is 'radical', if it requires major change and differs significantly from current experiences.

A further dimension beyond that of the project is that of the individual affected by the tool. These individuals, or stakeholders, are, first, the developers (or the primary tool users), and their perceptions and feelings are important aspects in determining success. These perceptions can be analysed in relation to the degree of change to work practices, job satisfaction, reward, communication, teamwork, and so on. It has been argued that tools sometimes require the primary users to unlearn old practices and learn new ones, and that this may result in a perceived loss of status. Further, there are indications that such changes may be more difficult for older, more experienced developers to make. However, it is not always made clear whether these difficulties are the result of the introduction of a toolset or whether it is due to the introduction of an associated methodology. We suggest that the introduction of a tool together with a new methodology into an organization is a more difficult innovation than the introduction of a tool to support an existing and well-established methodology, simply because of the greater degree of learning (and unlearning) involved.

The reaction of individual developers is not always negative, as some perceive the use of toolsets as enriching their work. Others perceive it as deskilling, reducing their creativity, and increasing the ability of management to exert control, in much the same way that supermarket checkout systems monitor and control their operators. The reaction of individuals appears to be difficult to predict, but it is likely to be a key element in the ultimate success or failure of the introduction of tools in an organization. The planning and management needs to focus on addressing these personal perception and motivation issues.

A second set of individuals, who are potentially as important as the primary users, are the secondary users, that is, the people who use (or manage) the systems that are developed with the tool. They may be involved in the development process as well as being the users of the information system produced. Their perceptions of the tool, its impact, and effects are also important, although frequently forgotten. If the secondary users perceive that the tool results in better quality systems, or faster production of systems, or improved identification of their requirements, or enabling their greater participation, or whatever advantage, then this is likely to result in the organization as a whole regarding such tools in a favourable light. Of course, the reverse is also true. Unfortunately when tools are introduced there seems relatively little emphasis on involving the secondary users or recognizing them as an important component of success.

18.6 SUMMARY

- A toolset is any integrated computer software system that is specifically designed to support a significant part of the information systems development process of an information system and the management of these tasks and processes.

- A repository contains information about the physical and operational elements of data and processes. It will also hold the rules of a technique or an information systems development methodology thus permitting analysis, validation, consistency, and completeness checking.

- In this chapter we looked at three commercial toolsets and discussed some of the potential benefits and problems that might accrue from using integrated toolsets.

QUESTIONS

1 If you have access to one of the toolsets discussed in this chapter (or an alternative), use it to draw some individual diagrams, for example those of Question 1 in Chapter 17.

2 Use the toolset to develop a small part of a system. Identify how the models integrate and how changes in one model are reflected in others.

3 Does the toolset follow the 'rules' of a particular methodology?

4 Can the toolset be customized to adapt to alternative:
- methodologies;
- models;
- notations?

5 What are the benefits of using this particular toolset as compared to the theoretical benefits identified in the chapter?

18.7   FURTHER READING

Allen, P. and Frost, S. (1998) *Component-based Development for Enterprise Systems: Applying the Select Perspective* (Managing Object Technology Series No. 12), Cambridge University Press, Cambridge.

http://www3.ca.com/ (see articles and white papers for Advantage gen)

Stone, J. (1993) *Inside ADW and IEF: The Promise and Reality of Case*, McGraw-Hill, New York.

Stowe, M.W. (1999) *Oracle Developer/2000 Handbook*, Prentice Hall, New Jersey.

PART

6

METHODOLOGIES

We begin, as in Part 5, with a 'road map' of the relationships between themes, techniques, tools, and methodologies. We adopt the perspective of methodology in this 'road map' (see Diagram 4) and use SSM and WISDM to show the links to themes, tools, and techniques.

In Part 6, we look at a number of information systems development methodologies that are well used, respected, or which typify the themes described in Part 3. Again we had a problem devising categories wherein each methodology fits like a glove. We surely have not succeeded!

We first look at process-oriented methodologies in Chapter 19. The first methodology described reflects the process modelling theme and was proposed by Gane and Sarson (1979). The main techniques used are the process-oriented ones of functional decomposition, data flow diagrams, decision trees, decision tables, and structured

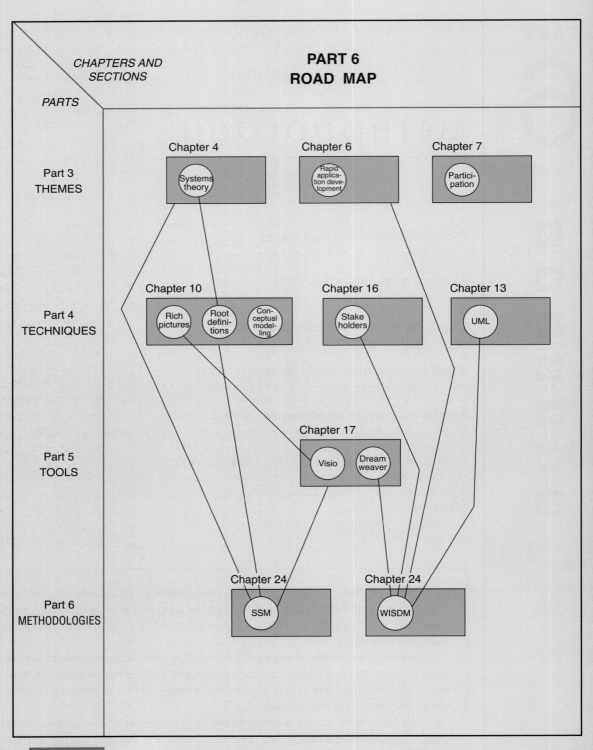

DIAGRAM 4 SSM and WISDM methodologies 'road map' (shows relationships between methodologies (SSM and WISDM) *and* themes, techniques, and tools).

English. Functional decomposition gives structure to the processes reflected in particular by the most important technique of data flow diagrams. This emphasis on structure gives the name of the methodology: Structured Analysis and Design of Information Systems (STRADIS). Yourdon Systems Method (YSM) was originally very similar to STRADIS; indeed, Gane and Sarson were at one time colleagues of Yourdon. However, more recent versions of YSM suggest that a 'middle-up' approach to analysing processes called event partitioning might be more appropriate than the top-down approach (functional decomposition). Although emphasis is placed on the analysis of processes, when compared to STRADIS, there is greater emphasis on the analysis of data as well.

Jackson's program design methodology, Jackson Structured Programming (JSP), has had a profound effect on the teaching and practice of commercial computer programming. Jackson Systems Development (JSD) is a development from JSP into systems development as a whole. An information system is seen, in effect, as a very large program. The approach is somewhat different from the methodologies described before as it concentrates on the design of efficient and well-tested software, which reflects the specifications. It is particularly relevant to applications where efficiency is paramount, for example, in process control.

In Chapter 20 we look at methodologies which exemplify blended approaches. Structured Systems Analysis and Design Method (SSADM). This has been the standard in most UK government applications and can be said to be the more modern version of the traditional information systems development life cycle approach discussed in Chapter 3. It includes the techniques of data flow diagramming and entity life histories, and recommends the use of toolsets.

Merise is a widely used methodology for developing information systems in France. Unlike other methods described above which emphasize either process or data aspects of information systems analysis and design, Merise has been designed so that both are considered equally important, and these aspects are analysed and designed in parallel. It now incorporates an alternative object-oriented approach.

Whereas STRADIS and YSM emphasize processes, Information Engineering (IE), has more emphasis on data. Similarly, whereas the fundamental techniques of the process-oriented approaches are functional decomposition and data flow diagrams, the basic approach in IE is the data-oriented entity-relationship approach. However, like the development of methodologies described in Chapter 20, IE has process-oriented aspects embedded and has been extended to include a planning phase, which is the first phase of the methodology, reflecting some of the discussion in Section 4.4.

Finally, in this chapter, we look at the methodology proposed by Welti (1999) for implementing enterprise resource planning systems, which can be regarded as a blend of applications rather than techniques and methods.

Chapter 21 looks at the object-oriented approaches, object-oriented analysis, and RUP. Coad and Yourdon's (1991) Object-oriented Analysis is significantly different from the approaches that have been discussed so far in Part 6. It is an approach that reflects the view that in defining objects (both data and processes encapsulated together) we capture the essential building blocks of information systems. It is also a unifying approach, as analysis and design can be undertaken following this approach, and applications developed using object programming languages and toolsets. The object-oriented theme leads to consistency throughout the development process.

The need to develop information systems more quickly has been driven by rapidly changing business requirements. Rapid Application Development (RAD) is a response to this need. It is based on the evolutionary and prototyping approaches discussed in Sections 6.2 and 6.3 (see also Section 6.3), and is usually enabled by toolsets. User requirements in RAD are often determined through joint applications development (JAD), which was introduced in Section 16.2. So Chapter 22 looks at methodologies aimed at rapid development of applications, James Martin's RAD, DSDM and extreme programming, along with WISDM, an approach designed to develop web applications quickly.

People-oriented methodologies are looked at in Chapter 23. Effective Technical and Human Implementation of Computer-based Systems (ETHICS) is a methodology proposed by Mumford (1995). It is a people-oriented approach (based on participation, Section 7.1) and, as the name implies, attempts to embody a sound ethical position. It encompasses the socio-technical view that, in order to be effective, the technology must fit closely with the social and organizational factors in the application domain. KADS is an approach to develop expert systems applications, whereas CommonKADS is broader and used to develop knowledge-based systems. They are people-oriented in the sense that they attempt to capture the expertise and knowledge of people in the organization.

Chapter 24 introduces what we have categorized as organizational methodologies. Soft Systems Methodology (SSM), a methodology proposed by Checkland and Scholes (1990), is influenced by systems theory (Section 4.1). Whereas many of the earlier approaches stress scientific analysis, breaking up a complex system into its constituent parts to enable analysis, systems thinking might suggest that properties of the whole are not entirely explicable in terms of the properties of the constituent elements. This is normally expressed as 'the whole is greater than the sum of the parts'. SSM addresses the 'fuzzy', ill-structured or soft problem situations, which are the true domain of information systems development methodologies, not simple, technological problems.

Information Systems Work and Analysis of Change (ISAC), a methodology developed in Scandinavia by Lundeberg et al. (1982), seeks to identify the fundamental causes of users' problems, and suggests ways in which the problems may be overcome (not necessarily through the use of computer information systems) by the analysis of activities and the initiation of change processes. It is therefore a people-oriented approach with emphasis on the analysis of change and the change process in organizations.

Davenport's (1993) Process Innovation does most to tie business process re-engineering (Section 4.3) with information technology and information systems, IT being seen as the primary enabler of process innovation as it gives an opportunity to change processes completely. We also look at PRINCE, a methodology designed for project management (Chapter 14), and Renaissance, an approach designed to ensure legacy systems (Section 6.1) are not neglected.

Chapter 25 looks at frameworks. These are approaches that describe themselves as frameworks rather than traditional methodologies. Multiview, for example, is a hybrid methodology, which brings in aspects of other methodologies and adopts techniques and tools as appropriate. In other words Multiview is a contingency approach: techniques and tools being used as the problem situation demands. It has been influenced particularly by aspects of SSM and ETHICS, but also by the proponents of process modelling and data modelling approaches. However, readers will see aspects of a number of approaches described earlier in Part 6.

SODA, described next, is an approach designed to provide consultants with a set of skills, tools, and techniques to help clients deal with messy work situations. Then we look at CMM (the Capability Maturity Model). This is a framework for evaluating processes used to develop software projects, it defines various levels of maturity and provides guidance relating to what organizations have to do in order to move from one level to another.

The last section discusses Euromethod, which results from a European initiative. It is also a framework but this time for the planning, procurement, and management of services for the investigation, development, or amendment of information systems. Other methodologies, such as SSADM, Merise, and Information Engineering, have influenced its design. This framework and associated standards will, it is hoped, help overcome the problems posed by the current diversity of approaches, methods, and techniques in information systems and help users and service providers to come to common understandings concerning requirements and solutions in information systems projects.

We have not described similar methodologies, even if both are well used, but reference this similarity where appropriate. The methodologies are described largely uncritically so that readers can follow their principles and practice, although we have commented on aspects of the methodologies where they reveal important features. However, the descriptions of the methodologies represent interpretations of the methodologies by the authors of this text, and these views may not correspond to those of the methodology suppliers! We return to the issue of interpretation in Part 7.

19 PROCESS-ORIENTED METHODOLOGIES

19.1 STRUCTURED ANALYSIS, DESIGN, AND IMPLEMENTATION OF INFORMATION SYSTEMS (STRADIS)

The major statement of Gane and Sarson's methodology of systems development called STRADIS comes in their book entitled *Structured Systems Analysis* (Gane and Sarson, 1979). The development of this structured systems approach to analysis came as a result of the earlier development of a structured approach to design. The structured design concepts were first propounded in 1974 by Stevens et al. (1974), and these ideas were later developed and refined by Yourdon and Constantine (1978), and Myers (1975 and 1978). The work of Jackson (1975) was also influential.

Structured design is concerned with the selection and organization of program modules and interfaces that would solve a predefined problem. However, it makes no contribution to the defining of that problem. This proves to be a practical limitation as the development of an information system requires both analysis and design aspects to be addressed, and, while structured design was acknowledged to provide significant benefits, these benefits were wasted if the definition of the original problem was not well stated or inaccurate.

A number of people have therefore attempted to take the concepts of structured design and apply them to systems analysis, in order to develop a method of specifying requirements and to provide an interface to structured design. In this way the techniques of structured analysis were developed. Apart from Gane and Sarson's work, DeMarco (1979), Weinberg (1978), and Yourdon (1989) are all texts on structured analysis covering some of the same ground and utilizing very similar techniques within each approach.

Gane and Sarson only relatively briefly outline a methodology of systems develop-ment in their book. The majority of the book is devoted to descriptions of the techniques which the methodology utilizes. This is in direct contrast to some other methodologies.

SSADM (Section 20.1) and ISAC (Section 24.2), for example, lay out the steps of the methodology in great detail. Therefore the most important aspect of the STRADIS methodology is the bringing together of many of the techniques which were described separately in Part 4 of this book. Nevertheless, we will continue to use the term 'methodology' in the context of STRADIS. These techniques are utilized, in some form or another, by many different methodologies, and therefore STRADIS is not unique but, along with the Yourdon Systems Method (Section 19.2), may be regarded as epitomizing those methodologies based on functional decomposition (Section 12.5) and the use of the data flow diagram (DFD), described in Section 12.1.

STRADIS is conceived as being applicable to the development of any information system, irrespective of size and whether or not it is going to be automated. In practice, however, it has mainly been used and refined in environments where at least part of the information system is automated. The methodology is envisaged to be relevant to a situation in which there is a backlog of systems waiting to be developed and insufficient resources to devote to all the potential new systems.

1   Initial study

The starting point of the methodology is an attempt to ensure that the systems chosen to be developed are those that most warrant development in a competing environment. The most important criterion in this selection process is argued to be the monetary costs and benefits of each proposal. Systems are viewed as contributing toward increasing revenues, avoiding costs or improving services. The initial study to discover this information is conducted by systems analysts gathering data from managers and users in the relevant areas. The analyst is to review existing documentation and assess the proposal in the light of any strategic plans relating to systems development that may exist within the organization. The initial study usually involves the construction of an overview data flow diagram of the existing system and its interfaces, and an estimate of the times and costs of proceeding to a detailed investigation. In addition, some broad range of final system development costs might be estimated. The initial study normally takes between two days and four weeks, depending on the size and importance of the application.

On completing the initial study, a report is reviewed by the relevant management, and they decide on whether to proceed to a more detailed study or not. If they approve of the proposal, they are committing themselves to the costs of the detailed study but not necessarily to implementing the proposed system.

The initial study might be thought to be quite close to the traditional notion of a feasibility study outlined in Chapter 3. However, there are some important differences. STRADIS does not include a review of alternative approaches to the proposal, and it is not, perhaps, as major or as resource-intensive a task as a traditional feasibility study. Furthermore, a traditional feasibility study, if approved by management, is usually in practice a commitment to the implementation of the complete proposal. Gane and Sarson do address all these aspects, but at later stages within their methodology.

2 Detailed study

This takes the work of the initial study further. In particular, the existing system is examined in detail. As part of this investigation, the potential users of the system are identified. These users will exist at three levels:

1. The senior managers with profit responsibilities, whom Gane and Sarson call the 'commissioners', whose areas will be affected. They initially commissioned the system proposal.
2. The middle managers of the departments affected.
3. The end-users; that is, the people who will actually work directly with the system.

Having identified these three sets of user, the analysts ascertain their interests and requirements by interviewing them. Next, the analyst prepares a draft logical DFD of the current system. This will usually involve constructing a DFD that extends well beyond the current system under consideration, in order to be clear exactly what and where the boundaries are in relation to other systems and to identify the interfaces between various systems.

Figure 19.1 depicts a data flow of part of a university admissions procedure. The system under consideration is that enclosed by the dotted line, but, in order to appreciate the context, a larger system is depicted which enables the interfaces to be clearly identified. Any data flow that crosses the dotted line must be addressed by both the external system and the system under consideration. In this case the diagram has highlighted the fact that those applications where the qualifications are not known require a decision to be made (see the data flow marked with the asterisk). This is a non-obvious interface which might otherwise have been neglected.

The **boundary** may be drawn in any place and could be moved. It may, for example, be more logical to include other processes within the boundary in order to minimize the number of interfaces to the external system. This is particularly important when the automation boundary is being chosen.

STRADIS describes in detail the drafting of DFDs at various levels, showing how each level is exploded into lower levels through to the level where the logic of each process box in the low-level DFD should be specified using the appropriate process logic representation, for example, decision trees, decision tables, or structured English (Sections 12.2–12.4). They suggest that DFDs and other outputs should be reviewed or 'walked through' with a number of users, so as to check their validity, and alterations made where necessary.

The detail of the DFDs and the process logic is entered into the data dictionary. The data dictionary can be either manual or computerized. On the DFD, data flows and data stores are defined using a single name which is meaningful. All the details that the name represents must be collected and stored in the data dictionary (Section 18.1).

The extent of detail that the analyst goes to at this stage in the methodology is not made clear, but it appears that not all low-level processes are specified in process logic and that not all data flows and data stores are specified in the data dictionary. It is usual to specify in detail only the most significant at this stage.

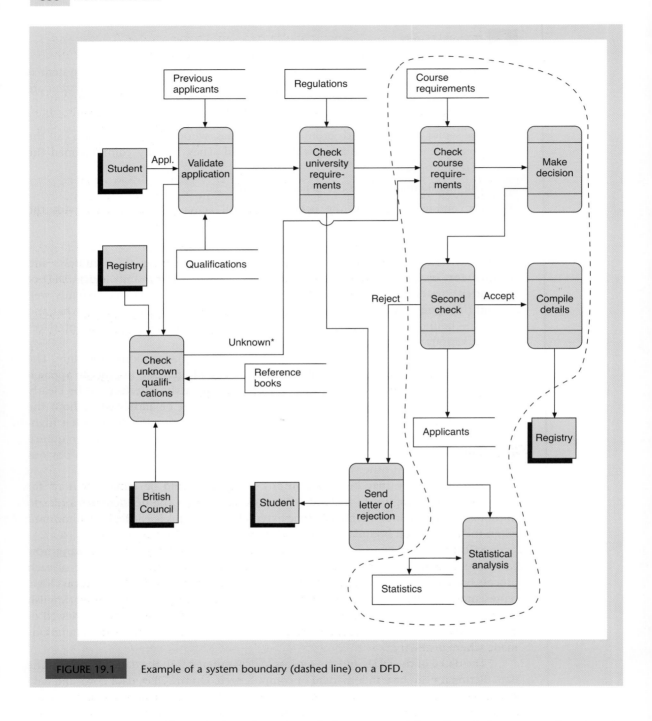

FIGURE 19.1 Example of a system boundary (dashed line) on a DFD.

The initial study estimated the costs and benefits of the proposed system in outline. These estimates are further refined within the detailed study. The analysts need to investigate the assumptions on which the estimates were based, and ensure that all aspects have been considered. They also need to consider the effects and costs of the proposed system from the point of view of organizational impact. In other words, they need to have a better estimate on which a final decision can legitimately be made.

In summary, the detailed study contains:

- a definition of the user community for a new system, that is, the names and responsibilities of senior executives, the functions of affected departments, the relationships among affected departments, the descriptions of clerical jobs that will be affected, and the number of people in each clerical job, hiring rates, and natural attrition rates;

- a logical model of the current system, that is, an overall data flow diagram, the interfacing systems (if relevant), a detailed data flow diagram for each important process, the logic specification for each basic process at an appropriate level of detail, and the data definitions at an appropriate level of detail;

- a statement of increased revenue/avoidable cost/improved service that could be provided by an improved system, including the assumptions, the present and projected volumes of transactions and quantities of stored data, and the financial estimates of benefits where possible;

- an account of competitive/statutory pressures (if any) including the system cost and a firm cost/time budget for the next phase (defining a menu of possible alternatives).

The results of the detailed study are presented to management, and a decision will be made either to stop at this stage or proceed to the next phase.

3   Defining and designing alternative solutions

The next phase defines alternative solutions to the problems of the existing system. First, the organizational objectives, as defined in the initial study, are converted into a set of system objectives. An organizational objective is a relatively high-level objective having an effect on the organization. This could include increased revenue, lower cost, or improved service. A system objective is at a lower level and relates to what the system should do to help management achieve the organizational objectives.

The system objectives should be strongly stated. This means that they should be specific and measurable, rather than general. For example, 'improving the timeliness of information' would be a weakly stated objective, and it would be preferable to state this objective more strongly, for example, 'to produce the monthly sales analysis report by the fourth working day of the following month'.

The analyst uses these objectives to produce a logical DFD of the new or desired system. The existing system DFD would normally be used as the basis for this, and the desired system may involve the introduction of new or changed data flows, data stores, and processes. The new DFD should be constructed to a level of detail which shows that the most important system objectives are being met.

The methodology then enters a design phase. At this time, analysts and designers work together to produce various alternative implementation designs which meet a variable selection of the identified system objectives. The alternatives should cover three different categories of design. First, a low-budget, fairly quick implementation which may not initially meet all the objectives; second, a mid-budget, medium-term version, which achieves a majority of the objectives; and third, a higher budget, more ambitious version achieving all the objectives. Each alternative should have rough estimates of costs and benefits, timescales, hardware, and software.

The report of this phase of the project should be presented to the relevant decision makers, and a commitment made to one of the alternatives. The report should contain the following:

- a DFD of the current system;
- the limitations of the current system, including the cost and benefit estimates;
- the logical DFD of the new system.

For each of the identified alternatives, the design will include statements covering:

- the parts of the DFD that would be implemented;
- the user interface (terminals, reports, query facilities, and so on);
- the estimated costs and benefits;
- the outline implementation schedule;
- the risks involved.

4   Physical design

The design team then refines the chosen alternative into a specific physical design which involves a number of parallel activities:

1. All the detail of the DFD must be produced, including all the error and exception handling, which has not been specified earlier, and all the process logic. The content of the data dictionary is completed and report and screen formats designed. This detail should be validated and agreed with the users.

2. The physical files or database will be designed. They will be based on the datastore contents previously specified at the logical level. Datastores are defined in the DFD as the temporary storage of data needed for the process under consideration. This has the effect of introducing many datastores scattered all over the DFD. Many of them will be very similar in content and have a significant degree of overlap.

3. The datastores need rationalizing, and the technique of normalization (described in Section 11.2) is utilized to consolidate and simplify the datastores into logical groupings. The actual process of mapping and the design of the physical files (or database) are not defined.

4. Derive a modular hierarchy of functions from the DFD. The designer seeks to identify either of two structures that any commercial data processing system is thought to exhibit. The first structure is the simplest. Here all transactions follow very similar processing paths (Figure 19.2). Such a system is termed a '**transform-centred**' system. The second structure is one in which the transactions require

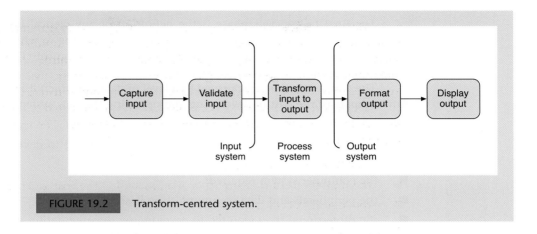

FIGURE 19.2   Transform-centred system.

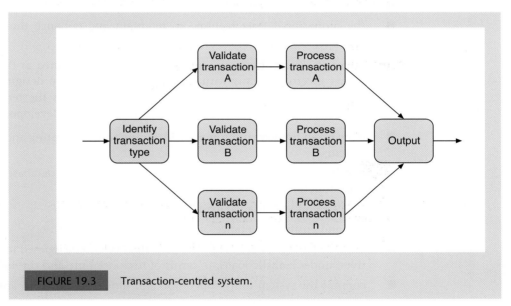

FIGURE 19.3   Transaction-centred system.

very different processing. This is termed a '**transaction-centred**' system and is illustrated in Figure 19.3.

The first step therefore is to identify which type of system is being described. It is recommended that the raw input data flow is traced through the DFD until a point is reached at which it can no longer be said to be input, but has been transformed into some other data flow. The output is traced backward in a similar fashion until it can no longer be considered to be output. Anything in-between is termed the '**transform**'. The transform is then analysed to see if it is a single transform or a number of different transforms on different transaction types. Once one or other of these high-level functional hierarchy types have been identified from the DFD, the detail of the modules in the hierarchy and the communication between them is constructed.

The final task in this phase is the definition of any clerical tasks that the new system will require. The clerical tasks are identified according to where the automated system boundary is on the DFD and according to what physical choice of input and output media has been made.

The above activities are pursued to a level of detail at which it is possible to give a firm estimate of the cost of developing and operating the new system. The major components of these costs are identified as:

- the professional time and computer test time required to develop the identified modules;

- the computer system required;

- the peripherals and data communication costs;

- the professional time required to develop user documentation and train users;

- the time of the users who interact with the system;

- the professional time required to maintain and enhance the system during its lifetime.

Subsequent phases of the methodology are not clearly defined as the methodology is effectively concerned mainly with analysis, to a lesser extent design, and hardly at all with implementation. However, the following list indicates the remaining tasks that Gane and Sarson envisage as being needed to complete the development of the system:

- draw up an implementation plan, including plans for testing and acceptance of the system;

- develop concurrently the application programs and the database/data communications functions (where relevant);

- convert and load the database(s);

- test and ensure acceptance of each part of the system;

- ensure that the system meets the performance criteria defined in the system objectives, under realistic loads, in terms of response time and throughput;

- commit the system to live operation and tune it to deal with any bottlenecks;

- compare the overall system facilities and performance to original objectives, and amend to resolve any differences, where possible;

- analyse any requests for enhancement, prioritizing these enhancements, and placing the system in 'maintenance' state.

19.2 YOURDON SYSTEMS METHOD (YSM)

YSM was originally very similar to STRADIS. Functional decomposition or top-down design, in which a problem is successively decomposed into manageable units, was the basis of the approach. However, although based on the structured approach it uses an approach known as event partitioning. This approach is neither pure top-down nor bottom-up, but is described as 'middle-out'. The analyst begins by drawing a top-level

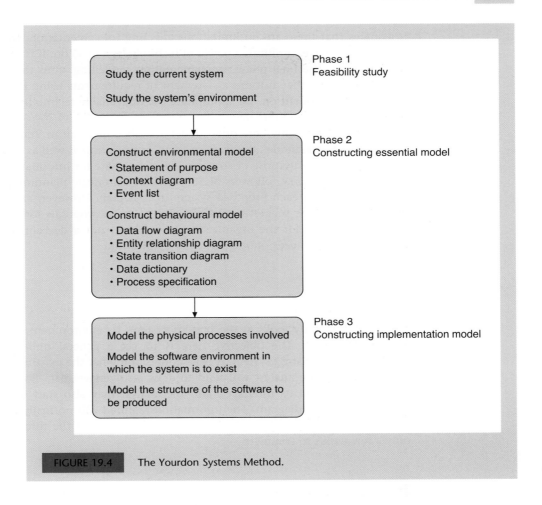

Study the current system	Phase 1
Study the system's environment	Feasibility study

FIGURE 19.4   The Yourdon Systems Method.

context diagram which indicates the system boundaries and thus the sources and sinks. Then, following interviews with the users, a textual list of the events in the environment to which the system must respond is constructed. Following this, some of the techniques described in Chapter 12 are used to document the system further.

YSM covers both the activities of the organization (although this could be at department level as well as at the level of the organization as a whole) and the system itself. Enterprise requirements need to be modelled as well as system requirements. For example, analysts may create an entity-relationship diagram and other information about data for the department, but only some of this will be appropriate for the system. Modelling at a department rather than system level will ensure consistency as well as avoiding the duplication of time and effort. Emphasis is therefore placed on modelling both the organization and the system. Many of these modelling methods are appropriate to the use of support tools, particularly toolsets (Chapter 18).

There are three major phases in the YSM approach, as shown in Figure 19.4. The feasibility study looks at the present system and its environment. Phase 2, essential modelling, aims to describe the essence of a software system in terms of how the required system must behave and what data must be stored to enable this to happen.

It assumes that there are no limitations affecting implementation, that is, it assumes unlimited resources, unlimited power of technology, and so on. It is the major phase of the approach. The final phase, implementation modelling, aims to incorporate those features found in the customer's statement of requirements using the essential model and will be dependent on the appropriate use of available technology. We will look at these three phases in more detail.

Although the only enterprise model described in detail in Yourdon (1993) is the enterprise essential model, the creation of an organization as well as system level model might suggest an enterprise or strategic planning phase for information systems development. Indeed, some followers of YSM include a strategic planning phase before the feasibility study of each proposed system in that plan. However, an enterprise implementation model is suggested and this will point to proposals for the hardware and software decisions for the organization as a whole, not a decision which should be dominated by the needs of one particular application.

1 Feasibility study

The feasibility study looks at the present system, its environment, and the problems associated with it. The objective here is to get a general understanding and an overview of the existing system. It is to understand what the existing system does (not how it works). The analyst will tend to draw an overview data flow diagram for the current system and its interfaces, and the analyst may also start to put together an entity-relationship diagram. The information required will normally be obtained from interviewing the users. This phase is much the shortest of the three, normally taking only a few weeks to complete.

2 Essential modelling

This stage gains the most emphasis in YSM. There is both an enterprise and a system essential model. We will emphasize the latter in our description as it is essentially the sum total of the systems models. The same considerations and models are reflected at the organizational level where, unusually, the 'organization' to be considered and the 'system' are the same. Having an overview of the present system, it is possible then to construct an essential model. The system essential model is a model of what the system must do in order to satisfy the users' requirements. It does not say anything about how this system is to be implemented. Therefore, it is the new logical model. In the 1993 version of YSM, essential modelling itself also has two major components:

- environmental model building;
- behavioural model building.

In some descriptions, the creation of the entity-relationship diagram is seen as part of a third parallel component, referred to as the information model. In the following description, these aspects form part of the environmental model and behavioural model building phases. The activities are the same in either case. The key difference is, perhaps, more subtle. It represents the change in the approach from one which empha-sizes processes to one which emphasizes both process and data aspects. It also enables stress to be made on the importance of comparing the data and process aspects to ensure consistency of models and therefore the integrity of the overall specification. This also separates YSM from STRADIS.

The **environmental model** defines the boundary between the system and the environment in which the system exists. The data coming from and to the environment are identified. The model consists of a statement of purpose, context diagram, and an event list.

The statement of purpose is a brief, concise, textual statement about the purpose of the system. It is provided for top management, user management, and others who are not directly involved in the development of the system. It is only about a paragraph long.

The context diagram or Level 0 data flow diagram (Figure 12.6 in Section 12.1) represents the system in a circle in the middle of the page, along with the main sources and sinks of the data entering to and from it. It identifies the people, organizations, and systems with which the system communicates. The data coming into the system that are processed in some way and then output in a different form are also identified along with any intermediary datastores. It also shows the boundary between the system and its environment.

The event list names the 'stimuli' that occur in the environment of the system to which the system must respond. An event may be flow-oriented, temporal, or a control event. A flow-oriented event is one associated with a data flow. A temporal event is triggered by reaching a particular point in time. Control events occur at an unpredictable point in time and are therefore a special case of a temporal event.

A first-cut data dictionary which describes the composition of each data element and a first-cut entity-relationship diagram highlighting the relationship between stores (the entities) may also be constructed at this time, but both are very early versions.

The **behavioural model** is a model of what the internal behaviour of the system must be in order to deal with the environment successfully. It includes a first-cut data flow diagram, entity-relationship diagram and state transition diagram and adds infor-mation to the data dictionary. A state transition diagram shows how the properties of an entity change over time and is therefore similar to an entity life cycle (Section 12.9). Note that behaviour refers to the behaviour of the system and does not imply any emphasis on people-oriented aspects. The processing behaviour of the system, that is, how the system uses its inputs to produce the required output, is shown using data flow diagrams. The structure and use of the data in the system is shown using a data dictionary and a set of entity-relationship diagrams. The dynamic behaviour of the system, describing how events in time affect behaviour, is modelled by extending the data flow diagrams (which represent control) and state transition diagrams (which represent control behaviour).

From the event list obtained in the environmental model, a data flow diagram is constructed with one process representing the system's response to each event in the event list. Stores are then drawn as needed to enable the processes to access the required data, and the input and output flows are connected to and from the processes. The data flow diagram or diagrams are then checked against the context diagram for consistency. In parallel, the control transformations are specified and the data relationships are

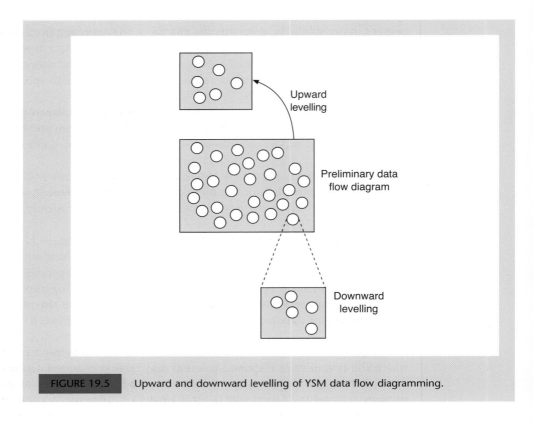

FIGURE 19.5   Upward and downward levelling of YSM data flow diagramming.

modelled. By the end of this stage, the data flow diagrams are completed by a process of levelling out, and the data dictionary, process specifications, entity-relationship diagram, and state transition diagram are also completed.

The process of levelling data flow diagrams involves restructuring so that there is a set of data flow diagrams, some the result of levelling upward and some the result of levelling downward. This is the key to the claim that YSM is middle-out rather than top-down. If the first-cut data flow diagram is too complicated with many processes, then related processes are grouped together into meaningful aggregates, each of which will represent a process in the higher level data flow diagram. A rule of thumb is suggested that each data flow diagram will have around seven processes and stores in total. Downward levelling may be necessary where it is found that a process at the middle level is not a primitive process but needs to be expressed in more detail at a lower level data flow diagram. This means that the initial process, which was a response to an event, is too complex for that middle level. The levelling process is seen in Figure 19.5.

Note that, as shown in Figure 19.6, processes are illustrated by circles in the YSM standard. Other shapes are also used to represent sources and sinks (a simple rectangle with no shadowing) and datastores (two parallel lines). Further, Yourdon (1989) recognizes two types of data flow. Discrete data flows arrive at their destination at discrete points of time (arrow) whereas continuous data flows are always available at their destination (arrow with two heads). This indicates that, although many of the techniques are

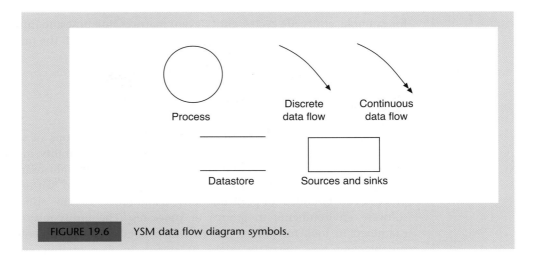

FIGURE 19.6   YSM data flow diagram symbols.

common to a number of methodologies, there are often variances in the way they are used, drawn, and so on.

Process specifications are then drawn up for every 'functional primitive', that is, every process in the bottom level data flow diagram. These are referred to as minispecs, which are detailed specifications of each data process. Essentially, they state the rules that convert the inputs to the outputs. The process specification may take the form of structured English (Section 12.4), decision tables (Section 12.3), or any other method appropriate for the process which can be verified and communicated easily to the users. These will be cross-checked with the data dictionary and entity-relationship diagram, and it might be necessary to modify the data flow diagrams as a result of this further detail.

The entity-relationship diagram also needs to be completed. YSM advocates iteration, and this diagram will also be refined from its first-cut form in stages. The knowledge gained when refining the data flow diagram will be used to help refine the entity-relationship diagram.

If the system being modelled has any real-time characteristics, then a state transition diagram is developed in addition to the entity-relationship diagram and data flow diagram. A state transition diagram specifies how a control process is to take account of its input control flows and how it is to output control flows. The effect which input control flows have depends on the 'state' of the system, and they may change the state of the system and cause control flows to be output. Moreover, the output control flows have an effect on the data flow model of system behaviour.

Like other structured approaches, 'methods' are emphasized in YSM rather than a 'methodology', and many techniques are described in detail, including entity–event matrices and function–entity matrices (Section 12.7), the specification of entities, relationships, attributes, events, and operations (Section 11.1) and normalization (Section 11.2).

The models together should describe 'what will the system do?' (e.g. the data flow diagram), 'what happens when?' (e.g. the event list), and 'what data is used by the system?' (e.g. the entity-relationship diagram). Some models link these dimensions, for example, entity life cycles; entity-event matrices link time and information, and data flow diagrams link data and processes. Together, it is argued, the models provide a full description of the system.

3   Implementation modelling

This phase starts the systems design process. The limitations of such factors as the technology available, performance requirements, and feasibility modify the essential model. Data flow diagrams and state transition diagrams are examined so that, for example, boundaries of computerization are marked, and within them groups of processes are bounded for particular devices and processes. This also includes allocating software environments to groups of processes. The entity-relationship diagram is examined to look for pointers as to which database management system might be suitable and how the data might be stored. Implementation modelling, in short, bridges the gap between specification and systems design.

19.3   JACKSON SYSTEMS DEVELOPMENT (JSD)

Michael Jackson's program design methodology, Jackson Structured Programming (JSP), which is described in Jackson (1975), has had a profound effect on the teaching and practice of commercial computer programming. Jackson (1983), on Jackson Systems Development (JSD), argues that system design is an extension of the program design task and that the same techniques can be usefully applied to both. Aspects of JSP are diffused throughout JSD, so that the JSD methodology is a significant development on its precursor, and therefore should not be seen as a 'front end' to JSP but an extension of it, where JSP is the core. 'In principle', says Jackson, 'we may think of a system as a large program.' However, the primary purpose of JSD is to produce maintainable software, and its emphasis is on developing software systems. This leads to a potential criticism of JSD in that, in the context of this text, it is oriented toward software and not to organizational need.

Given this comment, therefore, it is not surprising that JSD does not address the topics of project selection, cost justification, requirements analysis, project management, user interface, procedure design, or user participation. Further, JSD does not deal in detail with database design or file design. At least as described in his book, Jackson's methodology is not comprehensive in the sense that it does not cover all aspects of the life cycle. However, the commercial version of JSD, because of practical necessity, was extended to include some of these aspects.

The emphasis in the methodology is solving what Jackson terms the hidden path problem, that is, the path between the presentation of a specification to the design/ programming group and the completed implemented system, which could be described as a 'bundle' of documentation, listings, and executable programs. Jackson asks, 'What reasons do we have to support the claim that we have delivered what is required in the specification?' The traditional response is that the answer is found in the processes of testing and checking. But there are two problems here. We cannot be sure that the tests are complete, and, in any case, when testing is possible, the system is already complete and it is usually rather too late and too costly to repair the damage.

JSD uses transformation through process scheduling as the answer to the hidden path problem, and a major contribution of JSD lies in the areas of process scheduling and real-world modelling. Further, JSD deals with the problem of time in systems modelling and systems design in a way that most other information systems design methodologies do not, as the latter tend to model static elements in the system.

There are three major phases in JSD: the modelling phase, the network phase, and the implementation phase. In the *modelling phase*, events and entities are identified and entity structures and entity life cycles formed. In other words, analysts ask what is happening in the real world and how might this be connected to the computer world. In the *network phase*, the inputs and outputs are added to the model so far derived so that the input and output subsystems can be analysed. In other words, the analysts ask what outputs are needed from the system and what processes and operations must be added to produce these outputs. The *implementation phase* is concerned with detailed design and coding, that is, how can the specification (model plus function) be transformed to run on the hardware:

Modelling phase

1 Entity action step.
2 Entity structure step.

Network phase

3 Initial model step.
4 Function step.
5 System timing step.

Implementation phase

6 Physical system specification step.

In the entity action step the systems developer defines the real-world area of interest by listing the entities and actions with which the system will be concerned. In the entity structure step the actions performed or suffered by each entity are ordered by time. In the initial model step communications between entities are depicted in a process model linked to the real world. In the function step functions are specified to produce the outputs of the system, and this may give rise to new processes. In the system timing step some aspects of process scheduling are considered which might affect the correctness or timeliness of the system's functional outputs. In the physical system specification step the system developer applies techniques of transformation and scheduling that take account of the hardware and software available for running the system. JSD is applied iteratively, and, as increasing detail is revealed, data and functions will also be revealed. Each of these stages will be looked at in turn.

1 Entity action step

JSD aims to model the real world. In the entity action step, real-world entities are defined. These might include SUPPLIER, CUSTOMER, or PART, but, unlike the data analysis approaches, JSD is more concerned with the behaviour of the entity than its attributes or its relationships with other entities. Conventional entity modelling presents a static view of the real world, whereas JSD is concerned with modelling system dynamics.

To be defined as an entity in JSD, an object must meet the following criteria:

1. It must perform or suffer actions in a significant time ordering.
2. It must exist in the real world outside the system that models the real world.
3. It must be capable of individual instantiation with a unique name.

Entities may also be collective (e.g. BOARD OF DIRECTORS) if the instantiation has objective reality without considering its component objects. Entities may be generic (e.g. SPARE-PART) thus supporting the abstraction of classification, or specific (e.g. INNER-FAN-SHAFT). Entities that exist in the world may be ignored if it is impossible or unnecessary to model their behaviour. Therefore, only a relevant subset of the real world is modelled.

An action describes what an entity does within a system. Since the distinctive feature of JSD entities is that they perform or suffer actions, it is necessary to specify the criteria for something to be an action. These are as follows:

1. An action must be regarded as taking place at a point in time, rather than extending over a period of time.
2. An action must take place in the real world outside the system and not be an action of the system itself.
3. An action is regarded as atomic and cannot be decomposed into subactions.

Since the original version of JSD, more emphasis has been placed on the process of eliciting attributes, both action attributes and entity attributes. Whereas action attributes come from outside the system and trigger the action, entity attributes add information about the entity and will be updated by its entity actions. The actions and changes to the entity attributes form the entity life history. It is important to analyse when these changes occur so that the entity life history will have the correct time ordering. But we are now discussing the beginnings of the next step, the entity structure step.

The end result of the entity action step is a list of entities and their attributes and a list of actions and their attributes. The list of entities is liable to be much shorter than that produced by an equivalent data analysis process, particularly if the latter normalizes the entities, because the functional components of the system are excluded at this stage.

2 Entity structure step

The actions of an entity are ordered in time and are expressed diagrammatically in JSD. This is similar to the technique of entity life cycles (Section 12.9), although there are differences. They show the structure of a process in terms of sequence, selection, and iteration. The diagram shown as Figure 19.7 is read from top to bottom as a hierarchical

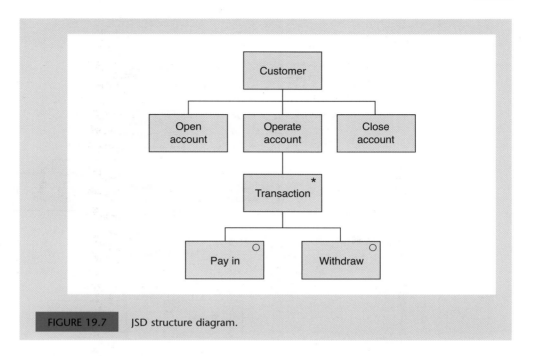

FIGURE 19.7 JSD structure diagram.

decomposition. Actions are shown as the leaves, whereas components higher up represent aggregations of actions. Each **structure diagram** is intended to span the whole lifetime of an entity, including therefore an action that causes the entity to come into existence and one that causes it to cease to exist. The model must illustrate time ordering of these elements. The lifetime of an entity may span many years in the real world.

JSD structure diagrams do not support concurrency. For example, the entity CUSTOMER in a banking system, an example discussed fully in Jackson (1983), might have been specified as a sequence (as in Figure 19.7) of OPEN-ACCOUNT, OPERATE-ACCOUNT, and CLOSE-ACCOUNT. OPERATE-ACCOUNT is an iteration of TRANSACTIONs (hence the asterisk which illustrates iteration), each of which is a selection of either PAY-IN or WITHDRAW (hence the small circle which indicates selection). Such a structure would constrain a customer to having only one account. To relax this constraint, the systems developer may be tempted to redraw the structure diagram as in Figure 19.8. It now appears that the customer may have many accounts each being operated as in Figure 19.7. The diagram now specifies that the customer can have more than one account, but not more than one at the same time. A customer may only open a new account after an existing account has been closed. The JSD structure diagram cannot show the simultaneous operation of many accounts. The answer to this problem is to specify a new entity ACCOUNT whose life history proceeds in parallel to the life history of the CUSTOMER entity. CUSTOMER now appears as in Figure 19.9(a) and ACCOUNT as in Figure 19.9(b).

In JSD, discrimination between entity roles is necessary if an entity can play more than one role simultaneously. Jackson provides an example using the entity SOLDIER. A soldier enlists in the army and may be promoted to a higher rank at various points in his career. Soldiers are also given training and may attend training courses, which they may

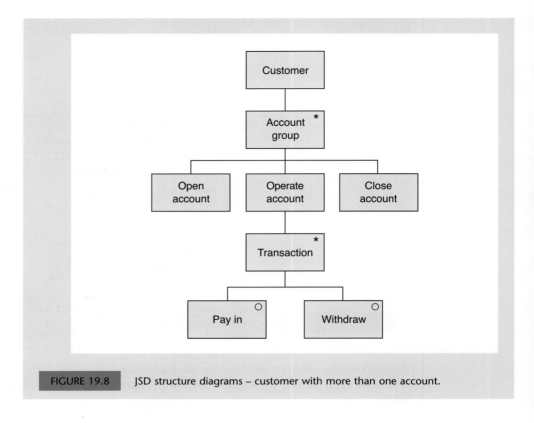

FIGURE 19.8 JSD structure diagrams – customer with more than one account.

or may not complete successfully. If successful completion of a course always leads to promotion, then these facts can be accommodated in one structure diagram. If there is no necessary connection between training and a career, then two structure diagrams are required, one for the soldier's promotion career and one for his training career. The soldier in this example is playing two roles, one as a person being trained and one as a person being promoted to a higher rank. Multiple roles may be synthesized into another structure diagram showing a selection of the possible activities in the possible roles that can be played.

Entity structure diagrams represent a sequence of activities ordered in time, without concurrency, from the 'birth' of an entity to its 'death'. One final problem addressed by the methodology in this step is that of the premature termination of the life cycle. In the real world, events may occur that prevent an entity making an orderly progression through its life cycle. For example, a soldier may be killed in battle without proceeding to retirement. It may not be feasible to draw a structure diagram for every possible variation on a prematurely terminated life cycle. JSD allows for a general specification of premature termination. This recognition of such a circumstance is an example of 'backtracking' in JSP.

The end result of the entity structure step in JSD is a set of structure diagrams. New entities and multiple roles for the same entity may have been generated during this phase.

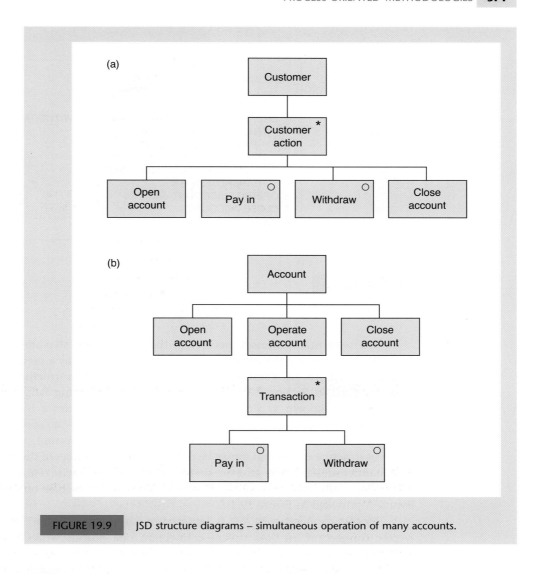

FIGURE 19.9   JSD structure diagrams – simultaneous operation of many accounts.

3   Initial model step

In this third step the systems developer creates a model that is a simulation of the real world. For each entity defined in the preceding two phases a sequential process is defined in the model that simulates the activities of the entity in such a way that it could be implemented on a computer. This is not to say that the implementation necessarily has to be computerized, merely that it could be if this were required.

In the model there will be a sequential process for each instance of an entity type, not one process for all instances. Therefore, if there are a hundred instances of entity type CUSTOMER, there will be one hundred sequential processes in the model. Moreover, the processes notionally execute at exactly the same speed as the real-world processes. So, if a customer has a bank account for 50 years, the matching processes will also execute for 50 years.

```
ACCOUNT-1 seq
   read data-stream
   OPEN-ACCOUNT; read data-stream
   OPERATE ACCOUNT itr while (PAY-IN or WITHDRAW)
      TRANSACTION sel (PAY-IN)
       PAY-IN; read data-stream
      TRANSACTION att (WITHDRAW)
       WITHDRAW; read data-stream
      TRANSACTION end
   OPERATE ACCOUNT end
   CLOSE-ACCOUNT;
ACCOUNT-1 end
```

FIGURE 19.10   JSD structure text.

The sequential processes specified in the initial model step are documented both by a diagram showing the interconnection of processes and by a pseudocode definition of each model process. **Pseudocode** is a language similar to structured English, which was described in Section 12.4, but nearer to a programming language in type. The pseudocode is known as structure text in JSD and resembles a high-level Algol-like programming language. Structure text exactly matches a corresponding entity structure diagram, and major constructs are sequence, selection, and iteration. The value of structure text is that it may be elaborated in later phases of the JSD methodology in a manner similar to the program design technique of stepwise refinement used in JSP. This process should be straightforward. An example of structure text for the ACCOUNT entity is provided in Figure 19.10.

Process connection in JSD is achieved by either data stream connection or state vector connection. In data stream connection one process writes a sequential data stream, consisting of an ordered set of messages, and the other process reads this stream. This is similar to process connection in a data flow diagram.

The JSD **system specification diagram** (SSD) models the system as a network of interconnected processes showing how they communicate with each other. In the diagram (Figure 19.11) processes are shown in boxes, with the data streams that connect processes shown as a circle with its identification given (in the example, the identification is 'C'). Arrows show the direction of data stream movement.

In Figure 19.11, CUSTOMER-0 is intended to represent a real-world instance of a customer, sending messages about his or her actions to a process that simulates this behaviour (CUSTOMER-1). A circle in an SSD indicates data stream connection. CUSTOMER-1 is sending a stream of messages to ACCOUNT-1. Since a customer can have many accounts, a double bar is used on the diagram to represent this multiplicity. Data stream connection is appropriate in the banking example, as it is not practical to telephone the customer every ten minutes to find out if he or she has paid in or withdrawn money.

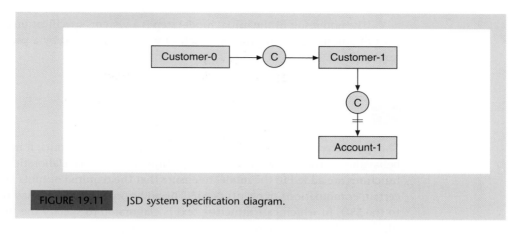

FIGURE 19.11   JSD system specification diagram.

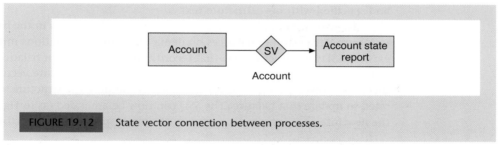

FIGURE 19.12   State vector connection between processes.

Jackson (1983) also gives the example of a lift system that finds out whether a button has been pressed in a lift by linking the button via a **state vector** to a process that models the button's behaviour. The alternative state vector connection is appropriate here because the button is essentially a switch, denoting an on or off state.

In the state vector connection, one process inspects the state vector of another process. A state vector is the internal local variable which describes and is owned by a particular process. State vector connection has no equivalent in data flow diagramming because the data flow technique permits process connection via logical files. There are no logical files in a JSD system specification diagram. State vectors are shown as a diamond on the SSD. In Figure 19.12, the data relating to the account is used to produce a report. Normally a data stream is used where a long-term view of events is required and a state vector used where a short-term snapshot is required.

Data stream connection is considered to be buffered (a data stream will be read on a first in, first out basis), so writing processes are never blocked; reading processes may lag behind writing processes. State vector connection is also unbuffered, and again no blocking occurs. State vector inspection therefore depends on the relative speeds of the processes involved. This is not true of data stream connection. If there is more than one input to a process, rules must be specified for determining which input is to be taken next. The determination may be made by fixed rules (fixed merge), or specified as part of the message stream (data merge), or determined simply by the relative availability of messages (rough merge). Such careful attention to synchronization details is absent from most other methodologies. JSD also allows for time grain markers (TGM) to indicate the arrival of particular points in real-world time (see Step 5).

The end result of the initial model step is a systems specification diagram depicting a set of communication processes each of which is specified by a pseudocode structure text.

4 Function step

The model created in the first three phases of JSD has no outputs; it models the dynamic behaviour of the real world. In the function step, further elaboration takes place, and functions are added to the model to ensure that the required outputs are produced when certain combinations of events occur. The addition of functions may require no change to the SSD, in which case structure text is elaborated to specify the functions required. Alternatively, it may be necessary to create new processes, which are added to the SSD and specified with new structure text.

To give an example, we may wish to provide the facility in the banking application to interrogate customer balances on demand. Therefore functions must be added to the existing SSD and structure text that record and display account balances. The elaboration of the ACCOUNT text is shown in Figure 19.13. Clearly, the state vector of ACCOUNT now includes knowledge of the customer's balance, because the structure text has been elaborated to update that balance. The SSD can now be amended (as in Figure 19.14) to show the new interrogation process. INTERROGATE can inspect the state vector of any ACCOUNT-1

```
ACCOUNT-1 seq
  read amount-deposited
  OPEN-ACCOUNT seq
    balance:- amount deposited
  OPEN-ACCOUNT end
  read transaction;
  OPERATE ACCOUNT itr while (PAY-IN or WITHDRAW)
    TRANSACTION sel (PAY-IN)
      PAY-IN seq
        balance:- balance + amount;
      PAY-IN end
      read transaction;
    TRANSACTION att (WITHDRAW)
      WITHDRAW seq
        balance:- balance – amount;
      WITHDRAW end
      read transaction;
    TRANSACTION end
  OPERATE ACCOUNT end
  CLOSE-ACCOUNT;
ACCOUNT-1 end
```

FIGURE 19.13 Addition of functions to structure text of Figure 19.10.

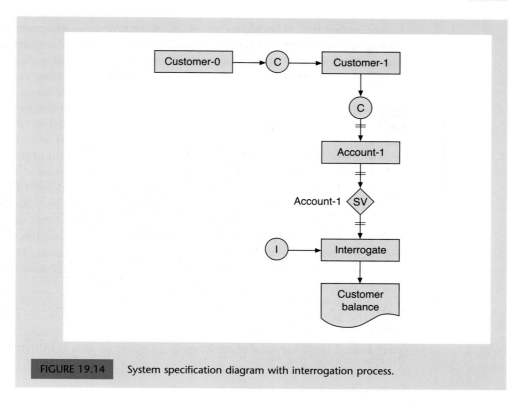

FIGURE 19.14 System specification diagram with interrogation process.

process (as indicated by a diamond symbol). It will do so when it receives a message specifying an account enquiry, and it will produce an output showing the balance of the customer's account. Therefore, the addition of functions to an initial model may cause the elaboration of existing structure texts and/or lead to the specification of new processes with their own structure texts.

Whereas the model of processes and their input and output data streams correspond to the basic system and are fairly stable, the functions represent ancillary processes and are likely to be less stable. They relate to reports, queries, and the user interface, which might change much more frequently, but the partitioning of parts of the system that change frequently into separate functions is relatively easy to carry out.

While the earlier versions of JSD did not provide many guidelines regarding data analysis, later versions do require the identification of attributes relating to entities, and these are referred to as fields of the state vector record. Update procedures and integrity constraints are also defined. However, data analysis is not as complete as in other methodologies in that, for example, it does not suggest normalization.

The end result of the function step is an amended system specification diagram with associated structure texts.

5 System timing step

The JSD modelling process so far described has not yet explicitly raised the question of speed of execution of processes and their timing. Implicitly, the model must lag to some extent behind the real world because input must take some time to arrive. In the system timing step (sometimes included within the function step) explicit consideration is given to permissible delays between receipt of inputs and production of outputs. Different parts of the system may be subject to different time lags. Timing is both important within a process and between processes. JSD uses messages known as time grain markers which act like data streams but which contain timing information. They are rough-merged with other data streams to control the arrival of messages and the timing of the execution of processes. They are used to trigger actions within processes, start and stop processes, and generally aid the synchronization of processes.

Time constraints will derive either from user requirements (e.g. for a monthly report or for an immediate response to an enquiry) or from technical considerations. Examples of the latter are state vector retrievals that must be sufficiently frequent to capture changes of state (as in a process control application) but not so frequent that they capture too many instances of the same state. The system timing step will gather information usable in the next phase when decisions are made. These decisions may concern questions relating to online, real-time, or batch implementation of aspects of the model system.

The end result of the system timing step is a specification of timing constraints using the TGMs associated with processes. The step does allow for the addition to the SSD of synchronization processes whose sole function is to ensure that certain actions have been completed satisfactorily before a further process is initiated.

6 Implementation step

Jackson's (1983) account of systems implementation is not a comprehensive treatment of all implementation considerations. Moreover 'implementation' in JSD includes activities that would be regarded in other methodologies as 'systems design', for example, file and database design, although JSD does not describe these processes in any depth.

The JSD implementation step concentrates on one major issue, the sharing of processors among processes. A system specification diagram can be directly implemented by providing one processor for each sequential process. Since there is one sequential process for each instance of an entity type (e.g. one for each customer of a bank) this might imply many thousands of processors. If this is an unacceptable implementation of the model, then the implementation step provides techniques for sharing processors among processes.

The direct opposite of providing one processor for each process is to provide one processor for all processes, which could be provided by a centralized mainframe computer. In this case, JSD provides for a transformation of the model into a set of subroutines. JSD is not recommending computer users to write their own operating systems and teleprocessing monitors, however. If these items of software are available on a machine and match the process scheduling requirements of a system, then Jackson would recommend using them. In fact, most computer-based systems are scheduled by a mixture of administrative, clerical, and software action. The structure diagram for a scheduler can be drawn alternatively to represent an online system, a batch system, or

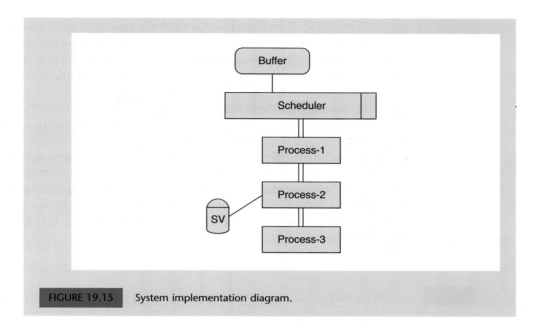

FIGURE 19.15   System implementation diagram.

a mixture of these, together with actions that may, in fact, be performed by human beings.

The JSD systems implementation diagram (or SID) is, in a way, an abstraction of all these real-world scheduling possibilities. Figure 19.15 shows the sequence of processes hierarchically: the scheduler is next to the top (drawn as a vertical bar in a box); the processes (contained in the SSD) are also shown in boxes; inversion sequences (i.e. the hierarchy of processes in terms of a main program calling subprograms) are shown as parallel lines representing the data stream as a pipe and use data contained in a state vector file (soft box) and data streams as buffers. Therefore, if we return to the banking example, the buffer could represent a data stream of credit amounts, with the processes arranged hierarchically as deposit, interest being added, and deposit account. The state vector file in this example provides data about the rate of interest. The scheduler handles the overall sequencing, and this can be represented as a process structure diagram and as structure text.

The system may be implemented by one or more real processors, thus giving rise to possible implementations that range from completely centralized to completely distributed. In general, multiple instances of common processes would share process texts (i.e. programs) as well as processors. To make process text sharing possible, it is necessary to separate the state vectors of processes from the shared process text. A concatenation of state vectors is then transformed into a file or a database. Therefore, the implementation step in JSD can give rise to perfectly conventional data processing solutions, and the information provided in the above steps gives the programmer all that is necessary to code the system using JSP procedures.

JSD's strength as a methodology lies in its determined and detailed attempt to model the dynamic aspects of real-world systems. Its treatment of concurrency, timing, and process scheduling is far more comprehensive than any other methodology discussed in this book. The model is, as far as possible, kept up to date so that it is always a fair reflection of the real world that this abstract model represents. In this way, it is possible to see what is happening in the real world and address it in the decision-making process. Entity modelling, it is argued, only represents a static view of the real world, whereas this process-oriented approach is dynamic.

It is, however, self-consciously incomplete as a methodology. Jackson wishes to say nothing about areas that are satisfactorily treated by other methodologies, only those that are not. Jackson is critical of methodologies that rely on structured decomposition, on the grounds that they confuse a method of documenting a design with the design process itself. JSD is not top-down design. Jackson is similarly critical of data modelling approaches: 'It is not much more sensible to set about designing a database before specifying the system processes than it would be to declare all the local variables of a program before specifying the executable text: the two are inextricably intertwined' (Jackson, 1983).

19.4 SUMMARY

- In this chapter we have described three methodologies that we have identified as being process-oriented. These are also called structured systems analysis approaches.

QUESTIONS

1 Identify the key elements of each of the methodologies in this chapter.

2 Construct a table that highlights their differences and common aspects.

3 Pick one of the methodologies and identify important elements of systems development that might be missing.

19.5 FURTHER READING

Gane, C. and Sarson, T. (1979) *Structured Systems Analysis: Tools and Techniques*, Prentice Hall, Englewood Cliffs, New Jersey.

Jackson, M. (1983) *Systems Development*, Prentice Hall, Hemel Hempstead, UK.

Yourdon Inc. (1993) *Yourdon Systems Method: Model-Driven Systems Development*, Yourdon Press, Englewood Cliffs, New Jersey.

20 BLENDED METHODOLOGIES

20.1 STRUCTURED SYSTEMS ANALYSIS AND DESIGN METHOD (SSADM)

SSADM is a methodology developed originally by UK consultants Learmonth and Burchett Management Systems (LBMS) and the Central Computing and Telecommunications Agency (CCTA), which is responsible for computer training and some procurement for the UK Civil Service. (CCTA is now part of the Office of Government Commerce.) SSADM has been used in a number of government applications since 1981, and its use was mandatory in many Civil Service applications. This description is based on SSADM, Version 4+ (Weaver et al., 1998).

The methodology provides project development staff with very detailed rules and guidelines to work to. It is highly structured. Another reason for its success has been in the standards provided (often exercised by completing pre-printed documents or through supporting software tools). Documentation pervades all aspects of the information systems project.

SSADM has seven stages (numbered 0 to 6 in Figure 20.1) within a five 'module' framework (the bullet points) with its own set of plans, timescales, controls, and monitoring procedures. The activities of each stage are precisely defined as are their associated end products (or deliverables), and this facilitates the use of project management techniques (the project management method PRINCE is recommended, see Section 24.4).

These modules cover the life cycle from feasibility study to design, but not implementation and maintenance. It is assumed that planning has been completed, and the stages following design are presumably seen as installation-specific, and therefore not covered by the methodology. We will now look in outline at each of the seven stages of SSADM.

- **Feasibility study**
  - 0 *Feasibility*
    - – Prepare for the feasibility study
    - – Define the problem
    - – Select feasibility options
    - – Create feasibility report

- **Requirements analysis**
  - 1 *Investigation of current environment*
    - – Establish analysis framework
    - – Investigate and define requirements
    - – Investigate current processing
    - – Investigate current data
    - – Derive logical view of current services
    - – Assemble investigation results

  - 2 *Business system options*
    - – Define business system options
    - – Select business system options
    - – Define requirements

- **Requirements specification**
  - 3 *Definition of requirements*
    - – Define required system processing
    - – Develop required data model
    - – Derive system functions
    - – Enhance required data model
    - – Develop specification prototypes
    - – Develop processing specification
    - – Confirm system objectives
    - – Assemble requirements specification

- **Logical system specification**
  - 4 *Technical system options*
    - – Define technical system options
    - – Select technical system options
    - – Define physical design module

  - 5 *Logical design*
    - – Define user dialogues
    - – Define update processes
    - – Define enquiry process
    - – Assemble logical design

- **Physical design**
  - 6 *Physical design*
    - – Prepare for physical design
    - – Create physical data design
    - – Create function component implementation map
    - – Optimize physical data design
    - – Complete function specification
    - – Consolidate process data interface
    - – Assemble physical design

FIGURE 20.1 SSADM stages.

0   Feasibility

This stage is concerned with ensuring that the project which has been suggested in the planning phase is feasible; that is, it is technically possible and the benefits of the information system will outweigh the costs. PRINCE may be used at this stage (and following stages) to help plan the project.

This phase has four steps: prepare for the study, which assesses the scope of the project; define the problem, which compares the requirements with the current position; select feasibility option, which considers alternatives and selects one; and assemble feasibility report.

Systems investigation techniques, such as interviewing, questionnaires, and so on, discussed in Chapter 3 in the context of the SDLC, are used in this stage as are the techniques of data flow diagramming (referred to as data flow models). The latter have different symbols (see Figure 20.2), but essentially the technique is the same as described in Section 12.1. Entity models (referred to as logical data structures) similar to that described in Section 11.1 are drawn. As one would expect at the feasibility stage, these are all done in outline and in not too great a detail. This detail will come in later stages.

The requirements of the new system, in terms of what the system will do and constraints on the system, are partly defined by considering the weaknesses of the present system.

Once the problem has been defined in this way, it is possible to consider the various alternatives (there might be up to five business options and a similar number of technical solutions) and recommend the best option from both the business and technical points of view. All this information is then published in the feasibility report.

1   Investigation of current environment

The second module, requirements analysis, has two stages: investigation of current requirements and business system options. This module sets the scene for the later stages, because it enables a full understanding of the requirements of the new system to be gained and establishes the direction of the rest of the project.

The first of these stages repeats much of the work carried out at the feasibility study stage but in more detail. For example, at the feasibility stage, the data flow diagrams may not have included much of the processing which is not related to the major tasks nor

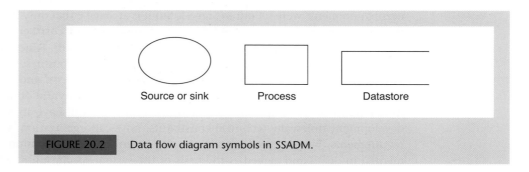

Source or sink   Process   Datastore

FIGURE 20.2   Data flow diagram symbols in SSADM.

decomposed to more than two levels of detail (Level 3 diagrams would be the norm at this stage). Further, the conflicts and ambiguities of the entity model need to be resolved. Indeed, in some projects the feasibility stage is carried out very much in outline and the investigation of current environment may have much less of a basis for the tasks of this stage.

The results of the feasibility study are examined, and the scope of the project reassessed and the overall plan agreed with management. The requirements of the new system are examined along with investigating the current processing methods and data of the current system, again in more detail than that carried out at the feasibility stage. The present physical data flow model is mapped onto a logical data flow model, and this helps to assess the present functionality required in the new system. Matrices (Section 12.7) might be constructed which, for example, show the relationship between processes and entities (i.e. which processes access the information in the various entities). Catalogues will be created, such as the user catalogue, which lists the activities carried out in each job, and the requirements catalogue, which lists the functional and non-functional requirements. Again, there is a complete description of the results of this stage assembled and reviewed as the deliverable.

SSADM suggests that decisions be made at this stage regarding customization of steps and techniques used for the particular problem situation. Users of the methodology are encouraged to think about the appropriateness of each of the steps. For example, some may be dropped or reduced in scope if a key objective is for rapid application development. Customization factors include:

- risk assessment;
- application type;
- situational factors;
- project objectives;
- available technology;
- control procedures;
- organizational constraints.

2   Business systems options

It is at this stage that the functionality of the new system is determined and agreed. The user requirements were set out in Stage 1, but it is at Stage 2 that only those requirements that are cost-justified are carried forward (using standard cost/benefit analysis techniques), and these requirements are specified in greater detail. Function point analysis (Section 14.1) is recommended for estimation. A number of business system options are outlined, all satisfying this minimum set of user requirements, and a few of these are presented to management so that one can be chosen (or a hybrid option chosen, taken from a number of the options presented). Each of these will have an outline of its cost, development timescale, technical constraints, physical organization, volumes, training requirements, benefits, and impacts on the organization. The option chosen is documented in detail and agreed as the basis of the system specification, which is the next stage of SSADM. Data flow diagrams and entity models are developed, but this stage is largely a specification in narrative.

3   Definition of requirements

This stage leads to the full requirements specification and provides clear guidance to the design stages, which follow. It is at the centre of SSADM where investigation and analysis are replaced by specification and design. For example, stress is placed on the required system design rather than the functionality of the current system. The requirements catalogue will be consulted and updated, and the logical entity model extended followed by normalization (Section 11.2) of the relations (to third normal form). The data flow model is also extended and used as a communication tool with users. User roles are defined for the new system. But it is the entity model that is emphasized at this stage and is the essential basis of the logical design of the new system. Documentation forms for all the entities and attributes (see Section 11.1) are completed.

Although the data model is emphasized at this stage, the components of each function (in terms of inputs, outputs, and events or enquiry triggers) are defined. Each function is documented in detail, and a form is used which includes space for function name, description, error handling, data flow diagram processes, events, and input and output descriptions. Jackson structure diagrams (Section 19.3) are used to show the input and output structures. Further documentation shows other details, such as the relationship between user roles and functions (via a user role/function matrix).

This stage in SSADM also has an optional prototyping phase. The methodology suggests demonstrating prototypes of critical dialogues and menu structures to users, and this will verify the analysts' understanding of the users' requirements and their preferences for interface design. As well as verifying the specification, this phase can have other benefits such as increased user commitment (Section 6.3). But these prototypes are not used as part of incremental development: they are used to form a clearer understanding of user requirements.

Entity life histories (called entity life cycles in Section 12.9) are also constructed during this phase. These document all the events that can affect an entity type and model the applicable business rules. Events affecting each entity may have been identified previously by constructing an event/entity matrix (similar to the CRUD matrix, Figure 12.20 in Section 12.7). Again, this is useful for verification purposes, as an entity should normally have at least one creation and one deletion event, and every event should lead to the update of at least one entity. Finally, at this stage, the system objectives are verified, the functions checked for completeness of definition, and the full requirements specification documented.

The diagramming conventions used in drawing entity life cycles (in SSADM called entity life histories) are very similar to the entity structure step conventions of Jackson System Development (JSD) (Section 19.3), and the technique is described in more detail there because it is of such crucial importance in JSD. In SSADM the diagrams look like hierarchies, but they are meant to be read from left to right, and, in so doing, progressively suggest the different states of the entity. Using an example from the academic world, Figure 20.3(a) shows how the entity 'student' changes over time, as an applicant,

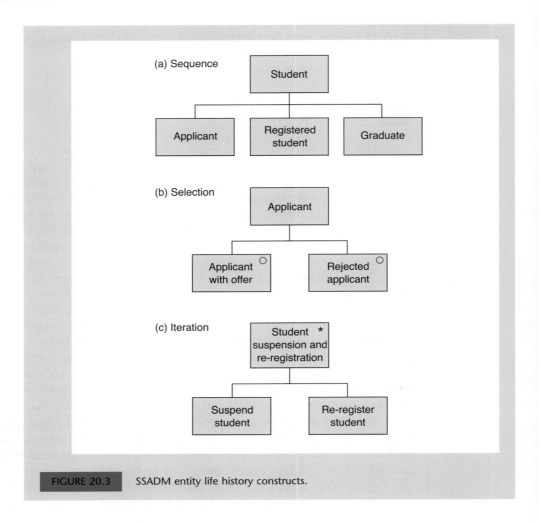

FIGURE 20.3   SSADM entity life history constructs.

registered student, and graduate (there will be other intermediary states). Figure 20.3(b) shows the use of the selection construct, whereby the small circle in the 'applicant with offer' and 'rejected applicant' boxes denote alternative conditions (these are mutually exclusive). Figure 20.3(c) shows the iteration construct, marked with an asterisk, which shows an event that may repeat (in this example, the possible repeated suspension and re-registration of a student who might regularly pay fees late).

Figure 20.4 presents an SSADM entity life history. The first level contains the events that cause an entity to be initiated into the system and those events that terminate the entity from the system. There is an iteration construct relating to whether the student is accepted conditionally or not and to reflect suspended or registered states. There are four states for the end condition: withdrawn, graduated, non-graduated, or rejected. These are all mutually exclusive (the selection construct). Notice that in this model it is not possible to show that 'graduated' can only happen from 'registered' and that 'suspended' can only terminate with 'non-graduated'. So, some information is lost when compared to the earlier entity life cycle representation described in Section 12.9.

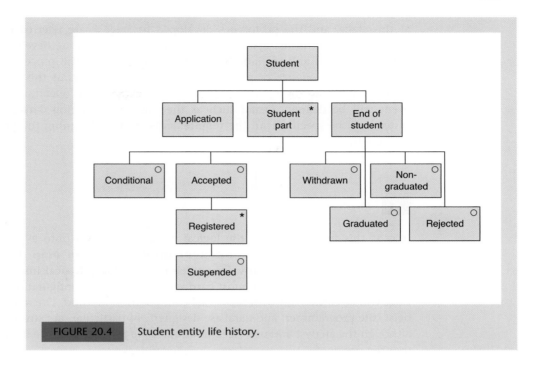

FIGURE 20.4   Student entity life history.

4 Technical system options

This stage and the following logical design stage are carried out in parallel. In the technical system options stage, the environment in which the system will operate, in terms of the hardware and software configuration, development strategy, organizational impact and system functionality, is determined.

The definition of technical options will be implementation-specific, because there are so many alternative hardware, software, and implementation strategies. The analysts need to identify constraints; for example, the hardware platform may be 'given' along with time and cost maxima and minima. System constraints might include performance, security, and service level requirements that must be met, and these will limit choice. Technical system options need to meet all these constraints, and a chosen option has to be agreed with management.

The analysts may perform an impact analysis of the various technical system options, focusing on organizational, personnel and operating changes, training requirements, systems documentation, savings, and testing requirements.

5 Logical design

This is a statement of what the system is required to do rather than a statement about the procedures or program specifications to do it. The latter is the realm of the final stage (Stage 6), the physical design. In Stage 5 the dialogue structures, menu structures, and designs are defined for particular users or user roles. User involvement is recommended at this stage, and the prototypes developed in Stage 3 are referred to. Furthermore, following the entity life cycles designed in Stage 3 (which are developed further), the update processes and operations are defined along with the processing of enquiries, including the sequence of processing. In other words, it is at this stage that further detail about how the system will apply and control the operations following each event will be defined. Detail such as the rules of validating data entered into the system will be specified. All the requirements to start designing the physical solution are now in place.

6 Physical design

It is at this final stage that the logical design is mapped onto a particular physical environment. A **function component implementation map** (FCIM) documents this mapping. The phase provides guidelines regarding physical implementation, and these should be applicable to most hardware and software configurations. However, this stage will be carried out with the actual configuration in mind. The roles of the technologist, the programmer, and database designers, in particular, are stressed in this phase, although the analyst and user need to be available to verify that the final design satisfies user requirements.

The logical data model will be converted into a design appropriate for the database management system available. The database mapping will be a key aspect of final implementation and include not only the way data and data relationships are held on the database, but also key handling and access methods. Much will depend on performance measurement so that database access is efficient, and again this will depend on the actual hardware and software configuration (including database management system).

The function component implementation map lists the components of each logical function and their mapping onto the physical components of the operational system. The principles of the FCIM are well specified in SSADM, although the form of the FCIM is somewhat ambiguously expressed. Presumably, this is seen as dependent on the standards of the particular organization. Designs are optimized according to storage and timing objectives. From this stage it should be possible to design and develop the programs necessary to provide the required functionality. It is at that point the SSADM stops and detailed software design and testing starts.

The well-defined structure of SSADM makes it teachable, and many UK university courses in information systems have used this methodology for in-depth treatment and discuss other methodologies in overview only for comparative purposes. Its three basic techniques, entity models, data flow diagrams, and entity life histories, are common to a number of methodologies and they ensure that there has been a detailed analysis of the target system. Along with the well-defined tasks, and guidance with the techniques, the methodology defines the outputs expected from the stage, and gives time and resource management guidelines.

SSADM is expected to be used with a toolset (see Part 5). The proponents of the methodology also recommend '**Quality Assurance Reviews**' based on structured walkthroughs (see Section 12.6). They are meetings held to review identifiable end products of the various phases of the methodology, such as entity models, data flow diagrams, entity life histories, and process details. Post-implementation feedback is also encouraged, and there is an audit at this time.

The successful implementation of the methodology relies on the skills of key personnel being available, though the techniques and tools are widely known, and the project team method of working, along with systems walkthroughs, encourages good training procedures and participation.

SSADM has evolved to allow a more 'pick and mix' approach, and so a rapid application development (RAD) model or a reuse approach, or an SSM front end, may be integrated as appropriate. Nevertheless, SSADM is traditionally associated with well-defined, large-scale systems development projects requiring heavy documentation, for use particularly in large, bureaucratic organizations.

20.2   MERISE

Merise is the most widely used methodology for developing information systems in France. It is used in both the public and private sectors. Its influence has spread outside France to Spain, Switzerland, and Canada. Like SSADM, Merise has become influential in the European approach, Euromethod (Section 25.4).

The essentials of the approach lie in its three cycles: the decision cycle, the life cycle, and the abstraction cycle, which cover data and process elements with equal emphasis. Although it is prescriptive to some extent, Merise permits the participation of end-users and senior management as well as data processing professionals in its decision cycle. Again, like SSADM, there are a number of software tools for use with Merise.

The project which led to Merise was launched by the French Ministry of Industry, and included research groups, consultancy and engineering firms, and academics, the inspiration coming from Hubert Tardieu. Merise has since developed into a very thorough and comprehensive methodology.

The core of the Merise approach lies in its three cycles: the decision cycle, which relates to the various decision mechanisms; the life cycle, which reflects the chronological process of a Merise project from start to finish; and the abstraction cycle, the key to Merise, which describes the various models for processes and data in each of three stages. Each of these three cycles will be considered in turn, with the major emphasis being placed on the abstraction cycle.

1   Decision cycle

The decision cycle, sometimes referred to as the approval cycle, consists of all the decision mechanisms, including those for choosing options, during the development of the information system. Decision making is a joint process concerning senior management, users, and systems developers. Decisions will include:

- technical choices regarding hardware and software;
- processing choices, such as real-time or batch;

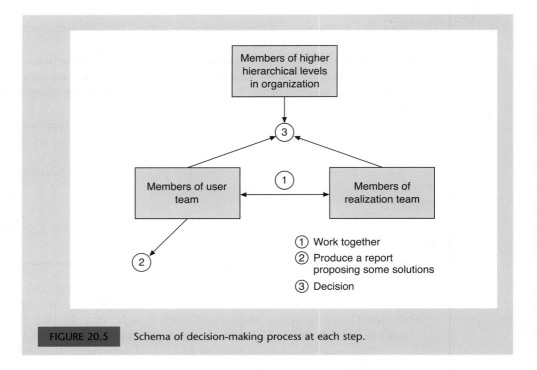

Schema of decision-making process at each step.

- user-oriented choices relating to the user interface;
- identification decisions regarding the major actors of the information system and the organization;
- financial decisions relating to costs and benefits;
- management decisions concerning the functionality of the information systems.

Each decision point during the development of an information system is identified by Merise. It is essential to know who takes the decisions, particularly those relating to the validation of the various models used by the method, and when to complete one stage to start the next. The Merise authors suggest that the decision-making process will follow the scheme as shown in Figure 20.5. The groups of users and systems developers will together discuss various options (1), and it is the responsibility of the user team to produce a report reflecting these deliberations (2). This is then discussed at a joint meeting (3) of senior management, users, and application developers, and the decision made at this point.

It is necessary to specify how a compromise should be reached in the case of conflicting views. This will depend on the norms of the specific organization, but there is a strong user element suggested in the decision-making process and this will influence the acceptance of the final system, from the point of view of operational and technical criteria and usability.

Therefore, in Merise, there are opportunities for user influence and participation, but this is not spelt out in detail as it will depend largely on the norms of the organization.

2 Life cycle

The life cycle shows the chronological progress of the information system from its creation, through its development, until its final review and obsolescence. Each of these stages is well defined in Merise. The main phases of the life cycle are:

1. *Strategic planning (at the corporate level)* – which maps the goals of the organization to its information needs, and partitions the organization into 'domains' for further analysis (such as purchasing, manufacture, finance, and personnel). For each of these a schedule of applications is devised to include a policy for human resources, software and hardware products, and system development methodology implementation. Within the frame of the strategic plan, the analysis that has just been carried out for one domain should be done for all the others, and then it will be possible to understand better and more coherently the connection between them.

2. *Preliminary study (for the domain of interest)* – which describes the proposed information systems, discusses their likely impact, and details the associated costs and benefits, which should be consistent with the strategic plans.

3. *Detailed study (for a particular project)* – of only those aspects which will be automated, including detailed specifications for the functional design (the requirements specification) and the technical design (the technical architecture of programs and files).

4. *Schedules and other documentation* – for development, implementation, and maintenance (all three at the application level).

Sometimes the last stage is defined as consisting of three separate stages: development, implementation, and maintenance.

The whole of this second cycle is similar to the conventional life cycle as found, for example, in SSADM and other methodologies, and for this reason will not be discussed further. It should be pointed out, however, that, unlike many alternative approaches, Merise includes a strategic planning phase, and in this respect Merise is similar to Information Engineering. The objective of this stage is to link the goals of the business with the information systems needs.

Nevertheless, like SSADM, the emphasis is on the analysis and design of the database and corresponding transactions. The reference to SSADM made earlier is apposite, for the nearest UK equivalent to Merise is SSADM, being the most used methodology in the UK and widely adopted by the UK Civil Service and other public and private sector organizations.

3 Abstraction cycle

The abstraction cycle is the key to Merise. Unlike many alternative approaches, the separate treatment of data and processes is equally thorough and both are taken into account from the start. The data view is modelled in three stages: the conceptual, the logical, through to the physical. Similarly, the process-oriented view is modelled through

LEVEL	CONCERN	DATA	PROCESSING
CONCEPTUAL	What do you want to do?	Conceptual data model	Conceptual processing model
LOGICAL OR ORGANIZATIONAL	Who does what, when, where, how?	Logical data model	Logical or organizational data model?
PHYSICAL OR OPERATIONAL	By what means?	Physical data model	Operational processing model

FIGURE 20.6 Merise by levels of data and processing.

the equivalent three stages of conceptual, organizational, and operational. Each of these six abstraction levels in the abstraction cycle is a representation – albeit a partial one – of the information system, and they should be consistent.

The abstraction cycle is a gradually descending approach which goes from the knowledge of the problem area (conceptual), to making decisions relating to resources and tasks, through to the technical means on which to implement it. The conceptual stage looks at the organization as a whole; the logical stage addresses questions, such as, who must do what, where, when, and how; whereas the physical stage looks at resources and technical constraints surrounding what will be the operational system. Merise is therefore independent of the technology until the later phases.

The modelling logic of Merise, outlined above, is shown in Figure 20.6. At the conceptual level the group of entities dealt with by the information system will be represented in a totally independent way from the organization and from the existing or future technical means for developing the project. At this level it is necessary to find out what the business does and the essence of the problem situation. At the logical level it is necessary to make choices (using methods developed at the conceptual level) in terms of the organization for the processing and with regard to the database models for the data, which will be part of the automated system. The physical level is the level at which constraints related to the operating system, database management system, and programming languages are going to be introduced.

An initial overall view of the system is given in the Merise flow diagram, and the construction of this precedes the conceptual models (both data and processing). The Merise flow diagram is not to be confused with the more conventional data flow diagrams. The Merise flow diagrams bring to light the information flows between the various actors in the domain studied, together with the environment. They serve as a base for developing the conceptual data model and the conceptual processing model. The actors are described in the ellipses, and arrows represent the information flows between them. So, the flow diagram showing the accounts, suppliers, and customers might be as shown in Figure 20.7, where the actors who are hatched are external to the information system. From it, we can see directions for the conceptual data model

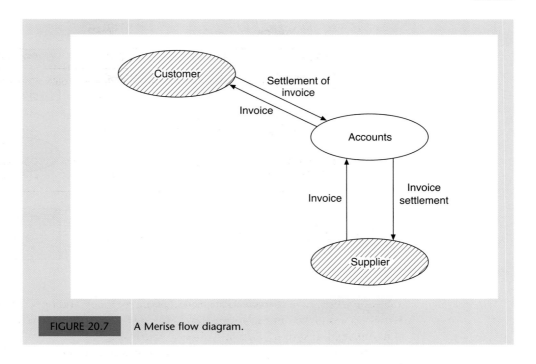

FIGURE 20.7 A Merise flow diagram.

(concerning customers, accounts, and suppliers) and for the conceptual processing model (concerning the settlement of invoices) in this example.

At the conceptual level, the information system is represented independently of its organization and of the physical and computing means that it could use. The objective of the conceptual level is to answer the question 'what?' and to understand the essence of the problem. The rules evidenced at the conceptual level are the 'management rules' of the domain under analysis.

The graphical representation of the conceptual data model (Figure 20.8) is the entity–attribute relationship model similar to that described in Section 11.1. An entity is represented by a box in Merise; a relationship is represented by an ellipse. Merise has a number of rules, which enable the verification of the model.

The conceptual processing model describes the activities of the organization. The concern of the conceptual processing model is with events, operations, and their synchronization.

Many other approaches which include the concepts of operations and events do not include that of the **synchronization** of an operation. This is the condition or conditions (events) which must have occurred to trigger the operation and a rule or set of rules regarding the necessary condition for the operation to be triggered. For example, payslips should be produced if it is the 28th of the month. The conceptual processing model related to the production of payslips might include a synchronization (28th of the month when payslips are produced) following the event that a new day has dawned (see Figure 20.9). This will trigger the process to produce payslips and routines which are dependent on whether the payslips are valid or invalid. In the figure, we also see an issuing rule, related to whether the payslips are OK or not OK, and, depending on this state, the processes that follow are different. Cheques are signed, however, whether

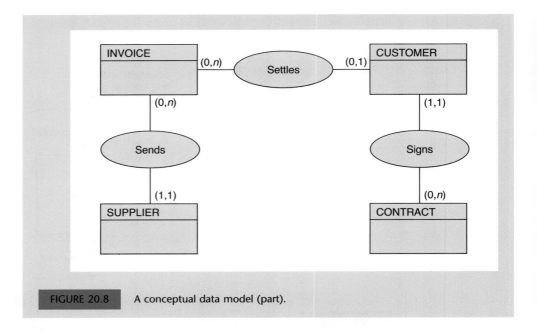

A conceptual data model (part).

the event is A or B, that is, a validated payslip is received or a corrected invalid payslip is received. These diagrams are types of **Petri nets**. Merise also provides a series of rules to enable the verification of the conceptual processing model.

Having established what to do at the conceptual level, at the logical level all the organizational alternatives are identified in order to discover who will do what, where, and when, and how the processing will be carried out. The information system is represented by taking into account the constraints imposed by these alternatives. The rules brought to light at the logical/organizational level are the 'organizational rules' of the domain under analysis. The organizational processing model is used again to clarify all the concepts described in the conceptual processing model. It is therefore a question of describing how the processing methods are executed within the organization, which could be manual (where the procedure is carried out without computing resources), conversational automatic (where the procedures are carried out by computer but with the intervention of people), or automatic (where the procedures will, once started, run without human intervention). The organizational processing model is used to define who carried out the processing, and when and how it is achieved. The organizational processing model will be based on the conceptual processing model with some changes, such as the names of departments where the processing will take place. Figure 20.9 might be amended so that processing is allocated to the personnel department (signing cheques), computing department (producing payslips), and accounts (records).

The logical data model is situated between the conceptual data model and the physical data model. It represents the world of data, described in the conceptual data model, but which takes into account the type of database management system chosen. In other words, the logical data model transforms the conceptual data model into a form that is suitable for computerization. Merise also offers a full description of the normalization process (Section 11.2).

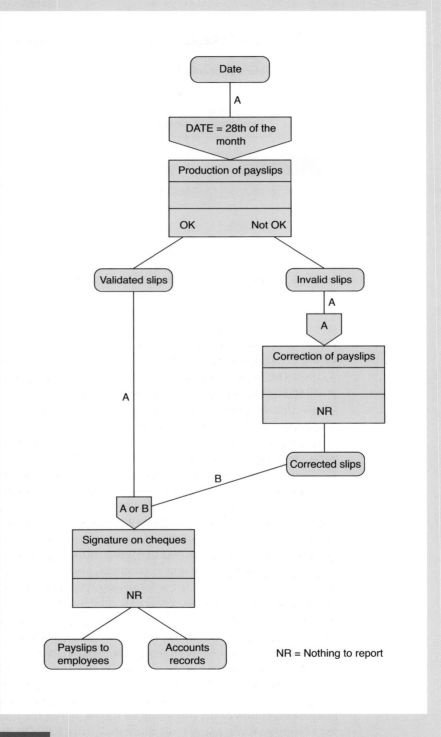

FIGURE 20.9 Conceptual processing model of the process 'production of payslips'.

CONCEPTUAL DATA MODEL		LOGICAL DATA MODEL IN BCNF
Identifier of entity	becomes a	Key
Property of identifier	becomes an	Attribute
Entity	becomes a	Relation
Relationship not of cardinality (1,1)	becomes a	Relation
Relationship of cardinality (1,1)	disappears	

FIGURE 20.10 Rules for mapping the conceptual data model to the normalized relational model.

One of the most important aspects of Merise is the detailed rules for converting from one model to the next (as well as specifying rules for creating each model), for example, there are 10 verification rules for the conceptual processing model. Therefore, the rules for mapping the conceptual data model to the logical model in relational Boyce–Codd Normal Form (BCNF) are shown in Figure 20.10, and the rules for special cases, such as those of binary and n-ary relationships, are described in detail. Rules for mapping to other data models and optimizing the relational and other data models, taking into account volume and activity, are also provided.

At the physical level, all the technical alternatives are identified which make it possible to define the computing needs, and this definition represents the last stage before the development of the software. The objective of the physical level is to answer the question 'with what means?'. The rules brought to light at the physical level are the 'technical rules'. It therefore takes into account the physical resources (database management system, hardware, support tools, and so on). Typically, the physical data model might be represented as a series of SQL definitions and the operational processing model as structured English, along with equivalent SQL queries to the database. The diagrammatic representation of the database processes and queries might be in the form of data flow diagrams and mapped onto structure diagrams. Again rules of mapping are provided.

Another important aspect of Merise is that the methodology has been designed to reflect the world where change is common, and new needs and directions can be incorporated into the design as the information systems develop. For example, guidelines are given to show how the conceptual data model and the conceptual processing model can be modified to take account of new management rules for data and processing. Further, unlike a conventional database methodology which is directed toward the static, data-oriented aspects of information systems, Merise, as we have seen, includes a thorough analysis of events, operations, and synchronization, all dynamic aspects of an information system.

Each of the six models of the abstraction cycle has a graphic formalism, with the possible exception of the physical data model, hence the methodology lends itself to the use of support tools. Many tools support all three levels of the abstraction cycle, both for data and processes, and thus ease the task of drawing the models. Some will validate, or partially validate, each of the models, help generate the required documentation at each stage, and may incorporate an applications generator, query language, and data dictionary interface, which again will lighten the task of developing information systems.

Significantly, there are a number of support tools which help the user of Merise. These tools are varied: some are design tools (e.g. to develop the various conceptual and logical models and diagrams), others are modelling and prototyping tools (to give alternative views of the final system), and yet others are execution and code generation tools (to generate the future application).

One of the important reasons for adopting an information systems development methodology is that of common standards, and, as well as the graphical support tools for each of the six models which are part of the abstraction cycle, there are standards and tools supporting strategic planning, project planning, requirements specification and the file of options, and the documentation of each entity, relationship, attribute, event, and operation defined. The strategic plan, for example, is likely to contain a diagnosis of the present situation, perspectives on the evolution of the organization, a description of the conceptual solution (what we want to do), and plans for development regarding organizational and technical solutions. It will also include, for the adopted solution, a description and information about its impact (including advantages, risks, and means), as well as reasons for rejecting other solutions.

For the processing, the overall specification is likely to include the organizational processing model, a detailed description of processes, and the operational processing model, with a list of applications, transactions, and batch chains and their arrangement into computer programs. For the data, it will include the conceptual, logical, and physical data models. It will also include a study of constraints (security and control policy), details about interfacing with existing applications and responsibilities. Appendices are likely to include definitions of relations (depending on the eventual database approach chosen), a list of states and screens for each process and their sequence, and a physical description of records or relations.

The above description can be regarded as 'classic Merise'. However, Merise has several versions in use. One significant adaptation has been the adoption of a third area to model, that of **state transitions**, to be modelled alongside data and processes. Essentially, these are entity life histories. Therefore, Figure 20.6 might be amended to include another column, that of state transition. This version is sometimes known as Merise/2. Another version separates the logical and organizational level (Figure 20.6) into two levels, forming a four-level schema. Here, organizational questions include who?, when? and where?, with the separate logical question being how? It is only at this logical stage (and the subsequent physical stage) that decisions about potential IT solutions are raised. Yet another version includes the incorporation of object modelling as an alternative to relational modelling.

20.3 INFORMATION ENGINEERING (IE)

The origins of Information Engineering (IE) differ according to which source is referenced. It appears that Clive Finkelstein first used the term to describe a data modelling methodology that he developed in Australia in the late 1970s. In early 1981 he renamed his consultancy company IE and wrote a series of articles on the methodology. In the same year he collaborated with James Martin on a two-volume book entitled *Information Engineering* (Martin and Finkelstein, 1981) and then Martin produced a later version (Martin, 1989).

Since these early days there has evolved, rather confusingly, a number of versions of IE which, while very similar in concept, have tended to develop along somewhat different lines. The reason for this is that James Martin, who is generally credited with evolving and popularizing the methodology, set up a number of independent companies based on the methodology of IE. One such initiative was an association with Texas Instruments (TI) to develop the IEF (Information Engineering Facility), a toolset to support the methodology. Martin believes that IE 'should not be regarded as one rigid methodology but, rather, like software engineering, as a generic class of methodologies' (Martin, 1991).

The version of IE described here is based upon a number of sources and is sometimes termed 'classical' IE. There also exist a number of variants of IE for different development environments. These include a package-based approach, a Rapid Application Development (RAD) approach (see Section 22.1) and an object-oriented-based version (Martin and Odell, 1992).

IE is claimed to be a comprehensive methodology covering all aspects of the life cycle. It is viewed as a framework within which a variety of techniques are used to develop good quality information systems in an efficient way. The framework is argued to be relatively static and includes the fundamental things which must be done in order to develop good information systems. The techniques currently used in IE are not part of those fundamentals, but are regarded as the best currently available to achieve the fundamentals. Therefore, the techniques can and do change as new and improved techniques emerge. The framework is also a project management mechanism, which reflects IE's philosophy of 'practicality and applicability'. It is not just a set of ideas, but is argued to be a proven and practical approach. It is also said to be applicable in a wide range of industries and environments.

There are a number of philosophical beliefs underpinning IE. One of the original was the belief that data are at the heart of an information system and that the data, or rather the types of data, are considerably more stable than the processes or procedures that act upon the data. Therefore, a methodology that successfully identifies the underlying nature and structure of the organization's data has a stable basis from which to build information systems. Methodologies which are based only upon processes are likely to fail due to the constantly shifting nature of this base as requirements change. This is the classic argument of the data modelling school of thought (Section 5.3). However, IE also clearly recognizes that processes have to be considered in detail in the development of an information system and balances the modelling of data and processes as appropriate.

A further aspect of the philosophy of IE is the belief that the most appropriate way of communication within the methodology is through the use of diagrams. Diagrams are very appealing to end-users and end-user management and, it is argued, enable them to understand, participate, and even construct for themselves the relevant IE diagrams. This helps to ensure that their requirements are truly understood and achieved. The diagrams are regarded as being rigorous enough on their own to ensure that all necessary information is captured and represented.

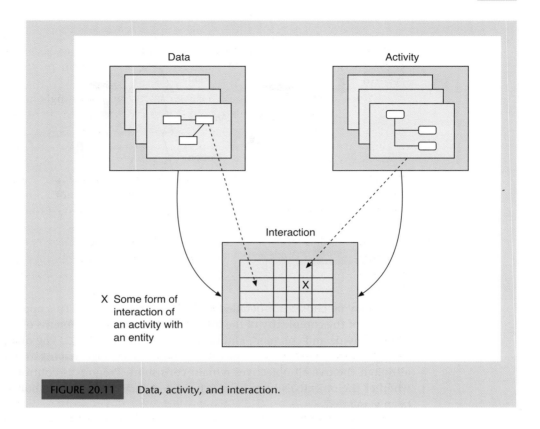

FIGURE 20.11   Data, activity, and interaction.

Each IE technique is oriented toward diagramming, and a diagram is a deliverable of each major stage in the methodology. One of the key elements in IE is the use of standard diagrams which initially are defined at high levels of abstraction and, as the methodology proceeds, they are gradually evolved, becoming more and more concrete and detailed until they ultimately form potentially executable applications. Standard symbols are used throughout, for example, boxes with square corners represent data and boxes with round corners represent activities.

The primary IE model consists of three components: data, activity, and the interaction of the data and activities (as shown in Figure 20.11). The interaction may be a matrix indicating at a high level which subject areas are used in which functions. At a lower level it may show which entity types are used by which processes. At an even lower level still, the interaction may be expressed as an action diagram (Section 12.8) and finally as actual program code.

Automated support, that is, the use of an appropriate toolset, is identified as a basic imperative for the IE methodology. A description of IEF is given in Section 18.2.

The methodology is top-down and begins with a top management overview of the enterprise as a whole. In this way separate systems are potentially related and co-ordinated and not just treated as individual projects which enables an overall strategic approach to be adopted. As the steps of the methodology are carried out, more and more detail is derived and decisions concerning which areas to concentrate upon are made. Based on the overall plan, the business areas to be analysed first are selected and then a

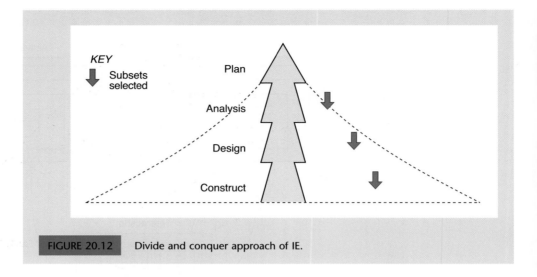

FIGURE 20.12   Divide and conquer approach of IE.

subset may be chosen for detailed design and construction. This approach to the management of the complexity of the information system requirements of an organization is termed 'divide and conquer', and is illustrated in Figure 20.12. The objectives and focus change as the methodology progresses with each stage having different objectives, although the overall objectives remain consistent. Progress is controlled by measuring whether the objectives have been achieved at each stage, not by how much detail has been generated.

The methodology is divided into four levels or layers. These levels are represented in Figure 20.13. The four levels are:

- *Information strategy planning.* The objective here is to construct an information architecture and a strategy which supports the overall objectives and needs of the organization. This is conducted at the enterprise level. One part of this planning is the identification of relevant business areas.

- *Business area analysis.* The objective here is to understand the individual business areas and determine their system requirements.

- *System planning and design.* The objective here is to establish the behaviour of the systems in a way that the user wants and that is achievable using technology.

- *Construction and cutover.* The objective here is to build and implement the systems as required by the three previous levels.

The first two levels are technology independent, whereas levels three and four are dependent on the proposed technical environment.

1   Information strategy planning (ISP)

Much of this level is really concerned with the overall corporate objectives. It may not always be part of the IE methodology, as it would normally be performed by corporate

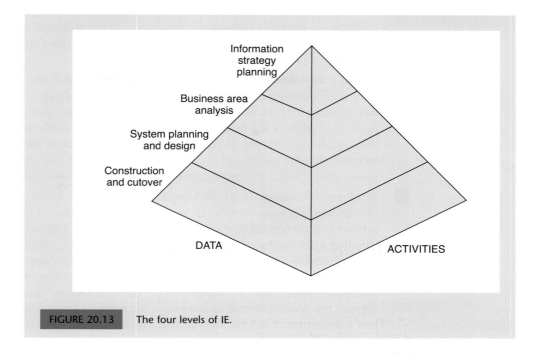

FIGURE 20.13 The four levels of IE.

management and planners. However, it is recognized as a fundamental starting point for the methodology. It implies that the organization's information system should be designed to help meet the requirements of the corporate plan and that information systems are of strategic importance to the organization. The corporate or business plan should indicate the business goals and strategies, outline the major business functions and their objectives, and identify the organizational structure. Such analysis includes any necessary re-engineering of the business processes (Section 4.3). The plan should ideally be in quantitative terms with priorities between objectives established.

ISP involves an overview analysis of the business objectives of the organization and its major business functions and information needs. The result of this analysis is what is termed 'information architectures' which form the basis for subsequent developments and ensure consistency and coherence between different systems in the organization. The resulting information strategy plan documents the business requirements and allocates priorities, which are the rationale for the development of the information systems. The plan enables these high-level requirements to be kept in view throughout the development of the project. In many other methodologies, it is argued, these needs get lost, if they are ever identified at all. It also provides a means of controlling changes to assumptions, priorities, and objectives, should it become necessary. Apart from such changes, the information strategy plan should remain relatively static. Information strategy planning is a joint activity of senior general management, user management, and information systems staff. It involves the performance of four tasks as follows:

1   *Current situation analysis.* This is an overview of the organization and its current position, including a view of the strengths and weaknesses of the current systems. This overview will include an analysis of the business strategy, an analysis of the

information systems organization, an analysis of the technical environment, and a definition of the preliminary information architecture (data subject areas, such as customer or product, and major business functions).

2   *Executive requirements analysis.* Here, managers are provided with an opportunity to state their objectives, needs, and perceptions. These factors will include information needs, priorities, responsibilities, and problems. This also involves the identification of goals of the business and how technology can be used to help achieve these goals and the way in which technology might affect them. Critical success factors (CSFs) for the overall organization are identified, and these are also decomposed into CSFs for the individual parts of the organization (see Section 15.2).

3   *Architecture definition.* This is an overview of the area in terms of information (the identification of global entity types and the decomposition of functions within the subject areas described in the preliminary information architecture in the current situation analysis above), an analysis of distribution (the geographic requirements for the functions and the data), a definition of business systems architecture (a statement of the ideal systems required in the organization), a definition of technical architecture (a statement of the technology direction required to support the systems including hardware, software, and communications facilities), and a definition of information system organization (a proposal for the organization of the information systems function to support the strategy).

4   *Information strategy plan.* This includes the determination of business areas (the division of the architectures into logical business groupings, each of which could form an analysis project in its own right), the preparation of business evaluations (strategies for achieving the architectures, including migration plans for moving from the current situation to the desired objective), and the preparation of the information strategy plan itself (a chosen strategy including priorities for development and work programs for high-priority projects).

2   Business area analysis

The business areas identified in the information strategy plan are now treated individually, and a detailed data and function analysis is performed. Maximum involvement of end-users is recommended at this stage. The tasks of business area analysis are as follows:

■   *Entity and function analysis.* This is the major task of the stage. It involves the analysis of entity types and relationships, the analysis of processes and dependencies, the construction of diagrammatic representations of the above, such as entity models (Section 11.1), function hierarchy diagrams, similar to that shown as Figure 5.1, and process dependency diagrams (a kind of data flow diagram (Section 12.1) but without datastores), and the definition of attributes and information views.

■   *Interaction analysis.* This examines the relationship and interactions between the data and the functions, that is, the business dynamics. Figure 20.14 is an example of a function/entity-type interaction matrix. In this example, the order processing function of a business is shown in the form of an entity-relationship model, a

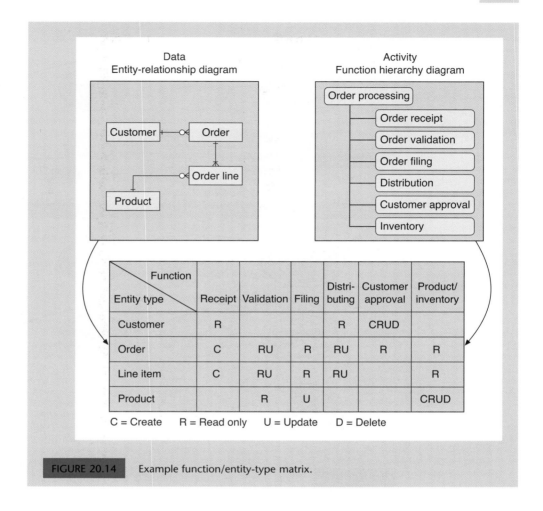

Example function/entity-type matrix.

function/process hierarchy diagram, and the matrix of interactions between the two. In this example, the matrix maps the interactions in terms of whether the function creates, reads, updates, and/or deletes the entities (CRUD matrix). The example is somewhat simplified, but it readily shows that orders and order lines are never deleted. This may be an error, or it may indicate that an order archiving function is required. Interaction analysis also involves an analysis of entity life cycles (Section 12.9), an analysis of process logic (Sections 12.2–12.4), and the preparation of process action diagrams (Section 12.8).

- *Current systems analysis.* This models the existing systems in the same way as for the entity and function analysis task in order that the models can be compared in the confirmation task (below), so that a smooth transition from one to the other can be achieved. The phase includes the construction of procedure data flow diagrams (Section 12.1) and the preparation of a data model by **canonical synthesis**. Because this is a technique not described previously, an example of its use will be provided. Canonical synthesis is a technique for pulling together all the data identified in separate parts of the organization, whether they be reports, screens,

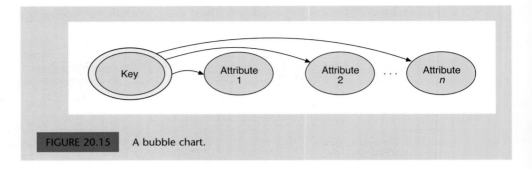

FIGURE 20.15   A bubble chart.

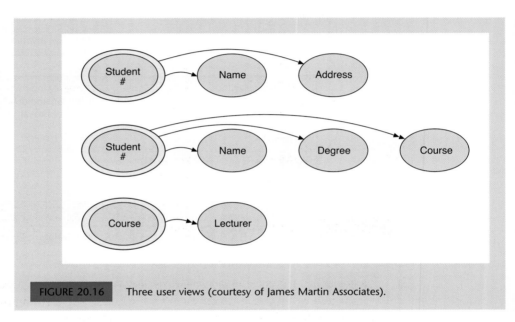

FIGURE 20.16   Three user views (courtesy of James Martin Associates).

forms, diagrams and so on, in fact all sources, into a coherent structure, which is the entity model. The technique involves the drawing of bubble charts (user view analyses) and synthesizing all the data into an entity model. A bubble chart is a graph of directed links between data item-types (Figure 20.15). A double ellipse represents a key, an arrow represents a one-to-one dependency, and a double arrow represents a one-to-many dependency. In this case, the key completely determines (or identifies) the attributes, therefore the data are normalized. A separate bubble chart is constructed for each separate user view of the data. Figure 20.16 shows an example of three user views in a university environment. View 1 might be a secretary's view, View 2 a registrar's view, and View 3, a course manager's view. The process of canonical synthesis combines the separate views into one data model. Each view is normalized (Section 11.2) and combined with another, and any duplications in the graph are eliminated. Figure 20.17 is the result of the combination of Views 1 and 2, and Figure 20.18 is the synthesis of all three views.

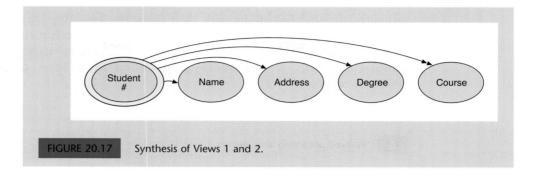

| FIGURE 20.17 | Synthesis of Views 1 and 2. |

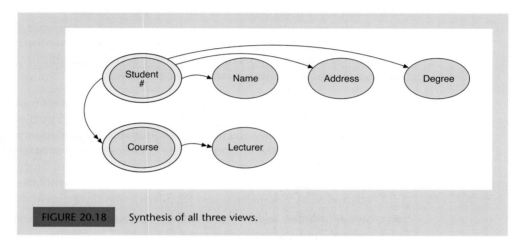

| FIGURE 20.18 | Synthesis of all three views. |

- *Confirmation*. This is the cross-checking of the results of the above, in terms of completeness, correctness, and stability. Hypotheses concerning business changes are also examined to see what effects these might have.

- *Planning for design*. This step includes the definition of design areas (which identify those parts of the model to be developed), the evaluation of implementation/ transition sequences, and the planning of design objects. This includes the identification of areas where existing reusable objects (models and code) or components could be utilized. This may involve the reuse of objects generated internally or the purchase of objects externally. This is now an important area for IE, with the objective of speeding up the development process. In addition, areas where objects being designed for this particular area might be required themselves in the future for reuse should be designed with this in mind. Design for reuse involves additional requirements such as flexibility and ease of use (Section 4.6). The effective identification of objects for reuse requires an appropriate repository (Section 18.1).

The output from business area analysis is the business area description, which contains the business functions, and each function is broken down into its lower level processes and the process dependencies. On the data side, the entity types, relationships, and attributes are described, along with their properties and usage patterns. The level of detail here is much greater than that arrived at during the construction of the architectures performed during the information strategy planning stage. This information provides the basis for the broad identification of business processes requiring computer support.

3   System planning and design

This level is divided into business system design and technical design. In some versions of IE, these are termed external design and internal design.

In the area of business systems design, for each design area identified, the facts gathered are used to design a system to fulfil the identified business requirements. The design is taken up to the point at which technical factors become involved, therefore it is the logical design. The steps involved are as follows:

■ *Preliminary data structure design.* In order to ensure integration and compatibility for all systems in the business area, this step is performed at the level of the whole business and not just the design area. It involves a first attempt at converting the entity model to the structure of the chosen database management system. This includes a summary of data model usage (basically an analysis of the way the data are used by the functions to produce a quantifiable view, sometimes referred to as volumetrics) and the preparation of the preliminary data structure.

■ *System structure design.* This involves the mapping of business processes to procedures, and the interactions are highlighted by the use of data flow diagrams. This phase involves the definition of procedures and the preparation of data flow diagrams.

■ *Procedure design.* This stage involves the development of data navigation diagrams (access path analysis, which examines the types and volumes of access required to particular entity types), the preparation of dialogue flows (i.e. the various hierarchies of control of user interaction), and the drawing of action diagrams (Section 12.8). Hierarchically structured dialogues and menus can be represented in action diagrams, but non-hierarchical menus require an alternative diagrammatic representation. For this purpose, IE uses dialogue flow diagrams (sometimes called dialogue structure diagrams), a simple example being illustrated in Figure 20.19. In overview, the horizontal lines represent screens and the vertical lines potential jumps or transfers between screens. This will depend on the choices made by the user. A horizontal line with bars at both ends represents a procedure, which could be a screen or a menu. Horizontal lines without bars represent a procedure step, that is, a part of a procedure. A vertical line between procedures indicates that control is transferred from the procedure at the tail of the arrow to the procedure or step pointed to by the arrow. If the tail of the arrow has a loop, this represents a link transfer which means that control may return to the originating procedure with the context retained. The example shown in Figure 20.19 is the structure of a menu system for handling customer orders. The first procedure is the main order menu, and the user can select three options: check order, create order,

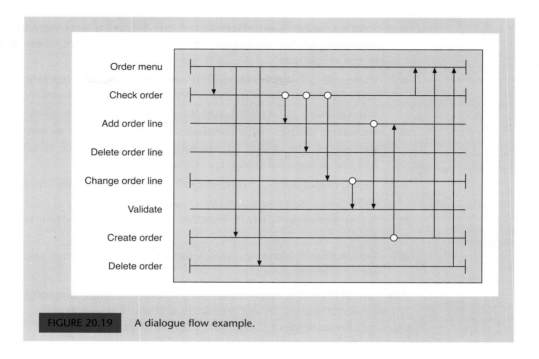

Order menu
Check order
Add order line
Delete order line
Change order line
Validate
Create order
Delete order

FIGURE 20.19   A dialogue flow example.

or delete order. In check order, the customer order number is entered, and the options of adding an order line, deleting an order line, or changing an order line can be made. These are link transfers as the context, that is, the order details for the selected customer, is retained on return. Note that add order line and change order line have a link transfer to validate, which is a procedure step of some other procedure.

■ *Confirmation.* Again, as part of business systems design there is a stage to confirm completeness, correctness, and usability. Matrices are used to analyse completeness. For correctness, the question 'does it follow the IE rules?' is asked. For usability, verification is normally achieved by the users commenting on a prototype.

■ *Planning for technical design.* The final phase of this stage involves the definition of implementation areas and the preparation of technical design plans.

At the end of this stage a business systems specification is produced which details, for each business process, the information flows and user procedures, and for each computer procedure, the consolidated and confirmed results of business area analysis, plus the dialogue design, screens, reports, and other user interfaces. The scope of the proposed computer systems is defined along with the work programmes and resource estimates for the next stage.

The computerized aspects of the business systems identified above are designed at a technical level such that the final construction and operation of the systems can be planned and costed. The tasks of this technical design phase are as follows:

■ *Data design* – which includes preparation of data load matrices, refinement of the database structure, design of data storage, and the design of other files.

- *Software design* – which includes the definition of programs, modules, reuse templates, integration groups, the design of programs/modules, and the definition of test conditions.

- *Cutover design* – which includes the design of software and procedures for bridging and conversion, the planning of system fan-out (the phases in which it should be implemented by location), and the definition of user training.

- *Operations design* – which includes the design of the security and contingency procedures, the design of operating and performance monitoring procedures, and the design of software for operations.

- *Verification of design* – which includes benchmark testing and performance assessment.

- *System test design* – which includes the definition of system tests and acceptance tests.

- *Implementation planning* – which includes a review of costs and the preparation of the implementation plan.

The output from this stage is the technical specification, including the hardware and software environment, its use, standards, and conventions. It also includes the plan and resources for subsequent construction and cutover.

4   Construction and cutover

This level includes the stages of construction, cutover, and production. Construction is the creation of each defined implementation unit and includes the following tasks:

- *System generation* – which includes the construction of the computing environment, preparation of development procedures, construction of database and files, generation of modules, generation of module test data, performance of integration tests, and generation of documentation.

- *System verification* – which includes the generation of system test data, performance of system tests, generation of acceptance test data, performance of acceptance tests, and obtaining approval. The use of test support tools is recommended.

Construction is completed once the acceptance criteria are satisfied.

Cutover is the controlled changeover from the existing systems and procedures to the new system. The tasks are:

- *Preparation* – which includes the preparation of the cutover schedule, training of users, and the installation of hardware.

- *Installation of new software* – which includes the conversion to the new software and execution of trial runs.

- *Final acceptance* – which includes agreement of the terms for acceptance and transferring fully to the new system.

- *Fan-out* – which means the installation at all locations.

- *System variant development* – which is to identify requirements, revise analysis and design, and perform construction and cutover where a particular location requires a variance from the norm.

Cutover is regarded as complete when the system operates for a period at defined tolerances and standards, and passes its post-implementation review.

Following cutover, production is the continued successful operation of the system over the period of its life. The tasks are to ensure that service is maintained and that changes in the business requirements are addressed:

■ *Evaluate system* – which includes performance measurement, comparing benefits and costs, user acceptability, and making a comparison with the design objectives.

■ *Tune* – which includes monitoring performance, tuning software, and reorganizing databases.

■ *Maintenance* – which includes correcting bugs and modifying the system as required.

The levels, stages, and tasks of IE outlined above are described in a sequence that would suggest that a top-down classic waterfall model is in operation. This is not necessarily the case, and much of the development after the information strategy planning level, and particularly after the business area analysis level, can be performed in parallel. To support parallel development a co-ordinating model is constructed. This is essentially a high-level model of data and processes, which identifies and highlights dependencies and necessary interfaces between systems and subsystems. This enables complex activities to be broken down into manageable components that can be developed independently. IE is also claimed to be able to support a variety of paths through the development layers. For example, reverse engineering starts at the bottom of the framework, that is, with an existing implementation, and deduces business rules from that system. This might be useful when existing legacy systems are to be included in an IE framework. It can support re-engineering which is a combination of forward and reverse paths through the framework. Developers may reverse engineer an existing application back to an appropriate point and when the design rules have been identified, combine these with some new requirements, and then forward engineer it to implementation. As mentioned above, IE is dependent on a suitable toolset with a sophisticated repository to provide the capability to reverse and re-engineer.

20.4 WELTI ERP DEVELOPMENT

In this section we consider Norbert Welti's approach to developing ERP projects, as described in Welti (1999). The description is based on his experience implementing SAP R/3 projects, which is the most common ERP solution base, but the approach can be used for other ERP projects. He has used the approach for ERP projects involving many countries as well as many sites; indeed, most ERP projects are large and complex. SAP have developed their own methodology called Accelerated SAP, and we look at this briefly at the end of this section.

The ERP system, along with the organizations in which it is implemented, is large and complex. The components of SAP R/3, for example, include separate modules for

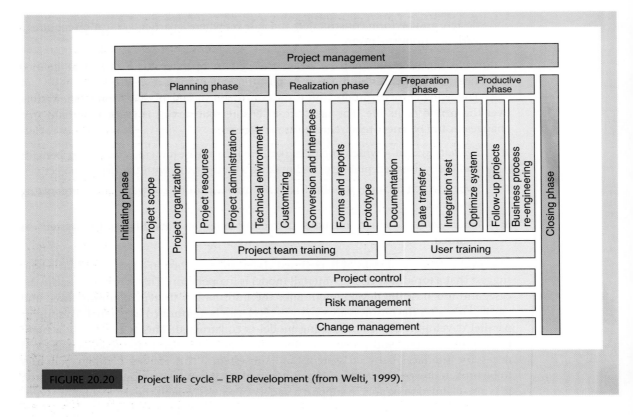

FIGURE 20.20   Project life cycle – ERP development (from Welti, 1999).

financial accounting, controlling, fixed assets management, project systems, workflow, industry solutions, human resources, plant maintenance, quality management, production planning, materials management, and sales and distribution. Of course, not all these need to be implemented in one time slot for any organization: they can be implemented in an evolutionary fashion or only few modules chosen. Even so, the ERP project is likely to be the largest and perhaps most expensive IT project for most organizations that choose this option. Welti argues, therefore, that such projects require a different approach than that for most other IT projects in organizations.

Figure 20.20 describes the project life cycle tailored for this approach. In the following, we highlight only those aspects that take on special importance in an ERP project. The four major phases are:

1   *Planning.* This involves defining the scope of the project (including locations and departments involved), allocating resources (e.g. human, both internal and consultancy, hardware and software), suggesting objectives and targets (e.g. response times, reliability targets, and other savings), planning the detailed activities, and setting up the technical environment. Obviously a major aspect of this phase relates to determining which modules of the ERP system will be adopted for which sites, whether these modules are likely to necessitate much adaptation, and whether much (expensive) ERP consultancy time might be necessary. Further, because of the size, scope, and risk of an ERP project, there needs to be decisions related to adaptation by the organization: 'The company must be made

aware of the fact that adopting the philosophy of the standard software means adapting its own organization, processes and procedures to the software standard, and not vice versa' and later 'company strategy must follow the processes described in the standard software, and not the other way round' (Welti, 1999). The approach suggests that an external consultant needs to be on the project team to advise on customization scheduling and project control, and another on the steering committee to advise on project management issues in particular. Other external consultants may be hired, but this is expensive and experience suggests that little know-how is transferred from them to the company employees. Even worse, because ERP consultants are in such high demand, there is a risk of taking on poorly qualified people. They should be evaluated very carefully for a high level of experience, skills, and competence. New hardware, including networks, is likely to be required and this takes time to acquire and implement.

2   *Realization.* This involves developing a prototype, customizing the system, and creating reports and forms. The prototype needs to reflect the organization's processes and procedures in the ERP system's structures, with customization where necessary. Skilled consultants can be invaluable in this phase, as customization can be particularly difficult, although there are now tools to help in this work. Data needs to be converted to the standards of the appropriate ERP modules. Further, the ERP modules need to interface with the legacy systems in the organization, unless they will also be implemented as ERP modules. The conversion and interface aspects are likely to be particularly time consuming and critical, and often very problematical. Regarding reports and forms, the ERP system is likely to produce standard ones, which might need customization. Other issues to be decided in this stage are the authorization of access to sensitive data. The system will produce the information, and it is necessary for the organization to decide on access rights.

3   *Preparation.* There is likely to be some parallel operation of the realization and preparation stages. The preparation phase involves developing the final system, final customizing, integrating the modules, performing quality tests, documenting the system, migrating the data, and final preparations for changeover. This changeover may be immediate for all modules and/or sites or a step-by-step approach, involving one site and/or module at a time over a period of some years. On the other hand, it often involves some compromise between the two. Apart from the large and complex nature of ERP projects, the various aspects of this phase are likely to be similar to many other projects and methodologies.

4   *Productive.* This involves management acceptance of the system and fine-tuning. The latter will include optimization to ensure that all the modules are running together efficiently. It is particularly interesting that Welti emphasizes business process re-engineering at this time. It is not surprising, however, in view of the approaches insistence that the organization needs to change to fit in with the ERP system (improving and adapting its organization, processes, and procedures to the software). This is not ideal: in our view the organization might have to change, but for other reasons than fitting in with IT constraints. However, the implication is that the implementation of ERP systems is too complex for it to happen any other way. Even so, the approach strongly suggests that BPR should happen *after* the ERP

system is implemented, since political and other problems of BPR would make implementation of the ERP unmanageable at the same time, and it is only after implementation that the functionality and the potential of the ERP system will be apparent.

Running throughout all four phases are the activities of training, project control, risk management and change management. These are similar to other development projects in nature, but are likely to take on greater significance due to the complexity, cost, risk, and political implications of such a large change impacting on all departments, sites, and people.

SAP itself has developed a methodology called Accelerated SAP or ASAP, which is designed for smaller and more straightforward ERP projects. The methodology has six phases:

1. *Project preparation.* This phase sets up the project team and planning for the project.
2. *Design business blueprint.* This is an outline of the expected SAP system to be implemented.
3. *Simulation.* In this phase the design and configuration of the ERP system are completed in detail and agreed.
4. *Validation.* In this phase the planned system is implemented and tested fully.
5. *Final preparation.* In this phase the interfaces between the ERP modules are written and the system becomes operational.
6. *Support.* This refers to the ongoing maintenance and upgrading, where necessary, of the ERP system.

ASAP is appropriate only for straightforward applications where the ERP modules 'fit' in well with the organization (or the organization's processes can be adapted easily to the ERP). In addition it would only be appropriate for the central ERP modules of finance, sales, distribution, and control. In these cases, however, it is expected that the ERP system can be implemented well within a one-year period.

20.5   SUMMARY

■   In this chapter we have described four methodologies which we classify as being blended, that is, being formed from parts of, or perhaps, the 'best of', other methodologies, techniques, and tools (and applications in the case of ERP).

QUESTIONS

1 In what ways are the first two methodologies (SSADM and Merise) discussed similar and different?

2 Why do you think that both these methodologies became recommended standards for use in government departments in the UK and France, respectively?

3 Do you think the first three methodologies conform fully to the method engineering theme that was discussed in Section 6.5?

4 Is the Welti ERP methodology distinct because it applies to a particular type of information system?

20.6   FURTHER READING

Eva, M. (1994) *SSADM Version 4: A User's Guide*, second edition, McGraw-Hill, Maidenhead, UK.

Martin, J. (1989) *Information Engineering*, Prentice Hall, Englewood Cliffs, New Jersey.

Quang, P.T. and Chartier-Kastler, C. (1991) *Merise in Practice*, Macmillan, Basingstoke, UK (translated by D.E. and M.A. Avison from the French: *Merise Appliquée*, Eyrolles, Paris, 1989).

Weaver, P.L., Lambrou, N., and Walkley, N. (1998) *Practical SSADM+*, Pitman, London.

Welti, N. (1999) *Successful SAP R/3 Implementation*, Addison-Wesley, Harlow, UK.

21
OBJECT-ORIENTED
METHODOLOGIES
....

OBJECT-ORIENTED ANALYSIS (OOA)

There have been many different approaches to the analysis and design of object-oriented systems. Books have proliferated, and it appears they continue to do so. For example, Booch (1991, 1994), Coad and Yourdon (1991), Coad and Argila (1996), Jacobson et al. (1999), Kruchten (2000), Martin and Odell (1992), Mathiassen et al. (2000), and Rumbaugh et al. (1991).

Of these competing methodologies, particularly those focusing on analysis, possibly the most well known is the Coad and Yourdon Object-oriented Analysis (OOA) methodology. This approach was published before the advent of UML and was first described in 1990. It has been updated and enhanced since (e.g. Yourdon and Argila, 1996). As is sometimes the case with methodologies it is difficult to identify which is the definitive version of OOA, indeed there does not seem to be one and perhaps marketing considerations have had some influence here. For example, the version of OOA that Yourdon has written with Argila includes additional elements from other authors, such as Jacobson. It also includes some elements from the older structured analysis methods, which is interesting, for Yourdon was closely associated with structured methodologies (see Section 19.2) before deciding that object-oriented methods were the answer. So rather than describe these more hybrid versions we stick with the more pure 1991 description of Coad and Yourdon which for our purposes includes all the basics that are needed. Yourdon now uses the UML notation (Section 13.2) in his approach but this description sticks with the original notation.

OOA consists of five major activities:

■ finding class-&-objects;
■ identifying structures;
■ identifying subjects;

- defining attributes;
- defining services.

Coad and Yourdon emphasize that these are activities that need to be performed. They should not necessarily be seen as stages or sequential steps. They point out that many analysts prefer to iterate around the various activities in a variety of sequences. Nevertheless, we shall describe them in this order which progresses from a high level to increasingly lower levels of abstraction.

1 Finding class-&-objects

This activity is about increasing the analyst's understanding of the problem domain and, as a result, identifying relevant and stable classes and objects that will form the core of the application. Coad and Yourdon describe this as the 'system's responsibilities'. The problem domain is the general area under consideration, and the system's responsibilities are an abstraction of those elements that are required for the system that is conceived. It is the system's responsibilities which are modelled. The analysis of the problem domain is not particularly original nor examined in great detail by Coad and Yourdon. The approach recommended is first-hand observation, talking (or rather listening) to 'domain experts', reading (or 'read, read, read' as they suggest), gathering experience from previous, and related, systems, and finally prototyping. Later versions of the approach from Yourdon and Argila also recommend the use of entity models, data flow diagrams, and linguistic analysis techniques to help in this activity. See Section 5.4 for an example of why finding the correct class-&-objects is so important.

The relevant classes and their associated objects are filtered out from the problem domain. The specific term class-&-objects (represented by a particular symbol as shown in Figure 21.1) includes a class (the bold inner box) and the objects in that class (the outer box). In the symbol, the class is divided into three parts. The top part is for the name of the class-&-object, the middle part for the attribute names, and the lower part for the services. An object in OOA is an abstraction from the problem domain, about which we wish to keep information (attributes of the object) and with which we can interact (the services). A class is a description of one or more objects with a common set of information and interactions.

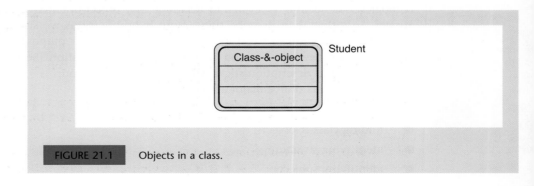

FIGURE 21.1   Objects in a class.

An example in the domain of university student administration might be the classes of registration, student, course, registration-clerk, and so on. For the class registration, attributes might include date, number, and fee. Services might include create, renew, terminate, suspend, approve, and check-qualifications. An object might be an instance of the class Student, for example, the attributes and processing for student Smith. An object embodies the notion of encapsulation (see Section 5.4).

Coad and Yourdon offer a set of helpful hints in order to find relevant class-&-objects:

1   Most importantly, look for structures which is the second activity of OOA as is discussed later.

2   Look at other systems with which the system under consideration interacts as a way of prompting potential class-&-objects.

3   Ask what physical devices the system interacts with. In our student administration system it is difficult to think of any example, although perhaps the photo booth might qualify. In a manufacturing system it is more obvious, for example, a weighing platform or a bottling machine. (It should be noted that these devices are not the technology with which the system might be implemented.)

4   Examine the events that must be remembered and recorded, for example, the date of registration, then the roles that people play, for example, the owner, manager, and client.

5   Examine the physical or geographical locations of relevance and also the organizational units, for example, divisions and teams.

An examination of all these factors will help to reveal relevant class-&-objects. This is by way of a checklist, and may or may not lead to the identification of all the relevant ones, but it is argued that it is a useful starting point. However, even with object orientation, the traditional problems of systems analysis remain, including users and stakeholders not really knowing what they require. Yourdon suggests that a common problem in OOA is the identification of too many objects, and so a criterion for evaluating objects is provided. This Coad and Yourdon term 'what to consider and challenge' is somewhat similar to the criteria that are applied when building entity models:

■   *Needed remembrance*. Is there anything, that is, any data, that must be kept by the system for this object? If there are no data, it probably means it is not an object.

■   *Needed behaviour*. Is there any behaviour, that is, processing or functionality, that must be kept by the system for this object? If there is no behaviour, it probably means it is not an object, and it will certainly not be an object if there is no needed remembrance and no behaviour.

■   *More than one attribute*. An object is likely to have more than a single attribute, and it should be reviewed if it has only one.

■   *More than one object in a class*. If there is only one object in a class, then it should be seriously challenged, indeed Coad and Yourdon suggest that this is a 'suspect' object.

■   *Always applicable attributes*. Are the attributes common, that is, applicable to each object in the class? If not, it is probable that the model should contain a class hierarchy. If the object is 'student' and the attribute 'employer', but this does not apply to full-time students, then it is likely that we have two subtypes of student, full-time and part-time. (This is examined in a subsequent activity.)

- *Always applicable behaviour.* Similarly, we apply the same test to the behaviour, or in Coad and Yourdon terminology, services. If certain services do not apply to all instances of the object, then we should consider subtypes or breaking down the structure.

- *Domain-based requirements.* Ensure that all the objects are derived from the domain and not from implementation considerations. For example, 'student' is clearly derived from the domain, whereas 'registration-card' or 'application-form' are about a particular design of implementation. It is recommended that the model is kept at the highest possible level of abstraction, because the concept of a registration-card may not exist in some possible implementations, that is, it is a design consideration. Application-form is a similar case. It might preclude a design which enables a direct application via the telephone. In this case, no application form is completed, and therefore the object should be less specific and focus on the logical requirement or event rather than the document or the implementation. In the examples we might prefer to consider a registration-complete object or an application-event object rather than the registration-card or application-form, respectively.

- *Not merely derived results.* Derived results, that is, things that can be derived or calculated or implied from other attributes, should be avoided. For example, holding a student's examination grade (A, B, or C) as well as the percentage mark, is not relevant, as the grade can always be derived from the mark. Such consideration avoids duplication and helps to simplify things.

The end result of the class-&-objects activity is a set of relevant classes and, for each class, the associated objects modelled using the appropriate conventions. These classes and objects should have been challenged and accepted or modified according to the guidelines outlined above. These class-&-objects will form the basic structure of the system under consideration.

2   Identifying structures

The next activity is to organize the basic **classes-&-objects** into hierarchies that will enable the benefits of inheritance to be realized (see Section 5.4). This involves the identification of those aspects or objects that are common or generalized, and separating them from those that are specific. (Yourdon points out that some analysis of structure will probably already have occurred in the class-&-objects activity.)

Coad and Yourdon use the terms 'generalization' and 'specialization' (which they shorten to 'gen-spec') for what is otherwise known as the identification of superclasses and subclasses. First, each class-&-object is examined to identify the gen-spec structure for each class. In other words, the generalized form of the class is examined and any specific subclasses are identified. There may be many ways of breaking down the

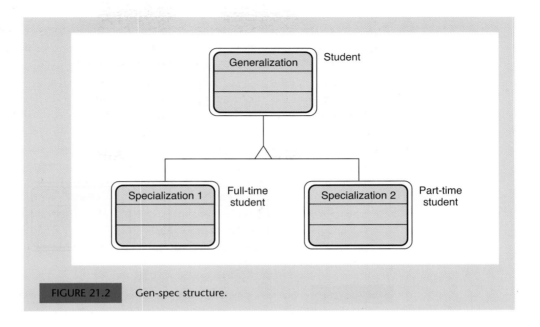

FIGURE 21.2 Gen-spec structure.

generalized elements into specific elements but what should ideally be identified are those that will lead to the greatest degree of inheritance.

(1) Gen-spec structure
The gen-spec structure is graphically modelled as in Figure 21.2 and usually reflects a hierarchy of classes. Therefore, for example, we may break our student-class into full-time-student and part-time-student, keeping as much as possible that is common to both the lower level classes in the higher level class. This will enable all the common aspects (data and behaviour) to be inherited from the higher level to the lower levels. The benefits of this were seen in Section 5.4. Any specific factors or requirements (known as specializations) for the lower levels can then be added to the general ones inherited from the higher level. Therefore, for example, all those aspects common to all types of student will be included in the high-level class of student, such as registration and qualifications. Those attributes and services specific to part-time-student, possibly employer details (full-time students would not have employers) and processing of student progress reports to employers, would be added at the lower level. This would mean that in implementation, the code for part-time-student could mostly be inherited from student and only a small addition need specifically be added for part-timers.

As a way of testing the gen-spec structures, Coad and Yourdon suggest asking the following questions of each specialization, that is, the lower level classes:

■   *Is it in the problem domain?* Does it make sense in terms of the business or organization? In the example, do we really have a distinction between part-time and full-time students that is of relevance in this context? Objects should not be broken down just for the sake of it. Some students are male and some are female, but we must ask whether this is of importance and relevance in the problem domain. In most cases it probably is not and we would distinguish between male and female

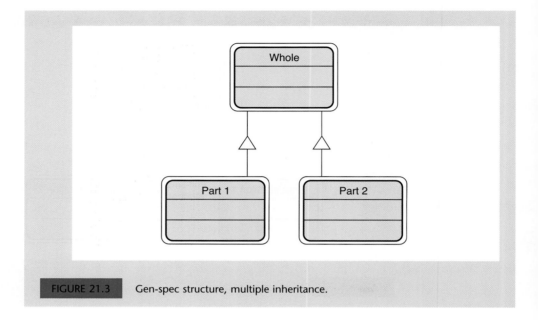

FIGURE 21.3 Gen-spec structure, multiple inheritance.

simply by an attribute of gender at the generalization level rather than identifying separate classes of male-student and female-student.

- *Is it within the system's responsibilities?* Again, if the system does not need to make a distinction then it should not be broken down.

- *Will there be inheritance?* Are there some attributes and/or services that are common (shared) and some that are specific? If there are not, then there is not much point in breaking it down.

- *Will the specializations meet the 'what to consider and challenge' criteria?* This will be detected from the class-&-objects activity above.

At this stage, the diagrams are drawn to indicate the class hierarchies. They are usually hierarchies, although multiple inheritance is allowed. This is where a specialization (lower level) inherits elements from more than one generalization (higher level). An example might be a specialization course-exam which inherits some aspects from the exam, such as common examination standards and procedures which apply to all courses in the university, and some aspects from the course, such as examination weightings and course-specific data and procedures, for example, that it is laboratory-based or has practical sessions. If there is multiple inheritance, then the gen-spec structure becomes a lattice rather than a hierarchy (see Figure 21.3). It should be noted that at this stage the model simply indicates that there are some attributes and behaviour that are general and some that are specific, they do not specify the detail.

(2) Whole-part structure

OOA also identifies what are termed whole-part structures. These are hierarchies of objects which indicate that one object is composed or made up of a series of subobjects. The notation is illustrated in Figure 21.4. The distinction between the gen-spec structure

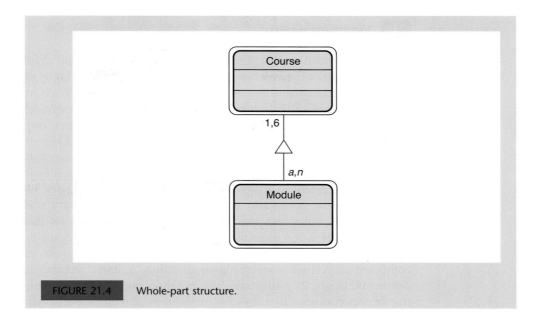

FIGURE 21.4   Whole-part structure.

and the whole-part structures is indicated by the triangle. The cardinality of the relation-ship may also be indicated on the model, for example, that a course may be composed of a minimum of one module and a maximum of six modules. A module, on the other hand, may not necessarily be part of any course (Figure 21.4). Coad and Yourdon suggest that there are three types of whole-part structures that might be considered:

1   The 'assembly and its constituent parts'-type, for example, an organization is composed of various departments.

2   The 'container and its contents'-type, for example, a lecture hall and its seats.

3   The 'collection and its members'-type, for example, the football club and its players and helpers.

A set of criteria for considering and challenging the identification of whole-part struc-tures are similar to those used for gen-spec structures as outlined above, with the exception of the inheritance test.

Whole-part structures often present people with difficulties, and this is usually to do with their purpose in relation to an object-oriented approach. It seems that they have been introduced to capture elements that have been found to be needed but not captured in the traditional object-oriented methods, for example, in gen-spec structures. Whole-part structures do not imply any notion of inheritance by the parts from the whole, they simply indicate that an object is composed of various other objects or parts. Coad and Yourdon suggest that whole-part structures are particularly useful for identifying class-&-objects at the edges of the problem domain, and these objects are dealt with by other systems.

Diagrams may be constructed that include both gen-spec structure and whole-part structure together.

3   Identifying subjects

The third activity of the OOA methodology is the identification of subjects. The purpose of this is to reduce the complexity of the model produced so far by dividing or grouping it into more manageable and understandable subject areas. This is somewhat analogous to the levelling of a DFD in other approaches, and is about presenting relevant chunks of the model to users or designers that are understandable on their own but are also set in context as part of a larger whole. Obviously in a small system there may be no need for this, but in larger systems with more than about 20–30 classes it becomes important. Guidelines are provided for the grouping of related classes together and it is a bottom-up process which produces a top-down view. The groupings may be based on any criteria that are relevant to the area of concern, and might involve a traditional, functional decomposition but could also be based on problems or issues that emerge from the problem domain. For example, in a university problem domain, the subject layer might be admissions, courses, exams, appeals, and so on, where admissions might be composed of classes concerning applications, criteria, acceptance, references, and payments. Figure 21.5 illustrates the notation used and shows the structure layer for the subject courses. The subject identification provides a particular view or picture of the system and there may be a number of relevant, and overlapping views. At any particular point, the most useful view is used depending on the objectives, which might be explanation to senior management, or verification by a user, or the creation of a work-package for an analyst or designer.

4   Defining attributes

In this activity, the attributes of the class-&-objects are defined. This is very similar to the identification of attributes for entity models (Section 5.3). It is the data elements of the object that are defined. The only difference is that attributes that define the state of the object are perhaps given more prominence; for example, things that might be defined using an entity life history diagram are emphasized (Section 12.9). Examples of attributes for an object student might be student-number, name, address, date-of-birth, suspended, or current. Attributes are normally listed by name in the middle part of the class-&-objects box (Figure 21.6). Attributes that 'point' to other objects are included. In relational database terms this means that foreign keys are included. For example, the attribute course above is in effect a pointer from the student object to another object called 'course'. In the model these objects would be connected with a line to indicate a relationship, and the degree and cardinality of the relationship expressed. This part of the identification of attributes is termed 'instance connection' by Coad and Yourdon and indicates that the connection is between instances of the individual objects rather than between classes. This is the same for entity models, where the relationships connect occurrences of the entity type rather than the entities themselves.

For each named attribute that has been identified, a short description is specified along with various constraints that apply to the attribute. These may include domain information, the allowable range, any default value, the various states that may apply,

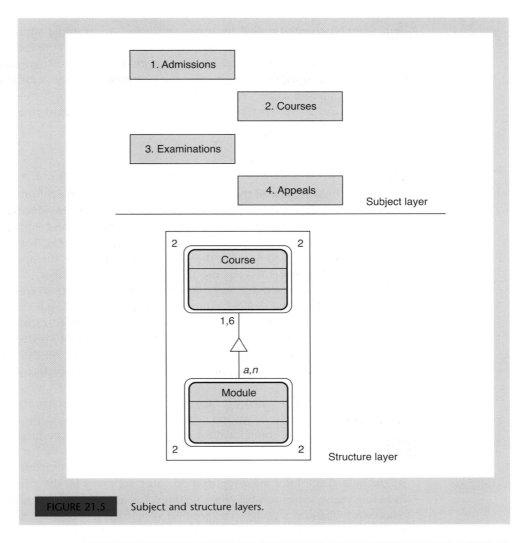

FIGURE 21.5 Subject and structure layers.

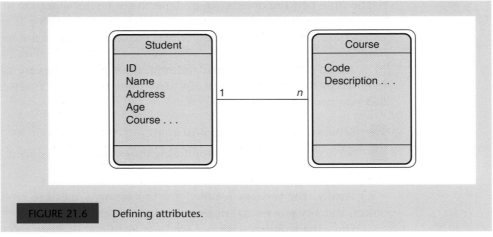

FIGURE 21.6 Defining attributes.

and any constraints implied by other attributes. An example would be: 'if in object student the attribute registration-suspended is set, then attribute fee must be zero'.

All implementation considerations associated with attributes are deferred to design. Therefore, the attributes should not be normalized nor performance considered, and specific identification keys are not defined.

5 | Defining services

In this, the final activity of the OOA methodology, the services of the class-&-objects are defined. In the object-oriented approach, as we have seen, the objects are composed of data and processing. The previous activity defined the data, and this activity defines the processing, or in Coad and Yourdon's terminology, the services. The terms 'method' or 'behaviour' are also used to mean the same thing. A service is the operation or processes performed by the object in response to the receipt of a message.

In the previous activity, attributes that defined the state of an object were identified. In this activity, the services required to change or modify states are identified. In the student object, we might have identified a state of suspended-registration. This would imply that we need to define the services to suspend a student's registration and perhaps to unsuspend, or reinstate, the registration of that student. All the services needed to achieve the changes of state identified in the entity life history diagrams should be fully defined.

Next, what are termed the 'algorithmically simple' services are defined. Yourdon later changes the terminology and calls these 'implicit' services. These are the ones that are likely to appear in some form for each class-&-object in the model; they are create, release (i.e. delete), connect, and access. The services required for create, delete, and access are fairly obvious. For example, what is required to create an object student might be a check for a valid registration form, followed by the allocation of the next available registration number, the creation of a new object, and then the return of a 'successful creation' message. The connect is perhaps less obvious, but means a service that creates or terminates a mapping between objects, that is, the establishment of a relationship between objects. An example might be the allocation of a new student to a personal tutor as this would require the creation of a mapping from object student to object tutor. These algorithmically simple services are usually not included on the OOA diagrams.

As can be imagined, if the algorithmically simple services are identified, this will be followed by the identification of any algorithmically complex services. These are classified into two types:

1. Services concerned with calculations.
2. Services concerned with monitoring the external environment; that is, the services required to detect and respond to events.

Finally, the services required for processing a message received from another object, and any processing triggered by the message, are defined.

Once the required services have been identified they are specified in detail using

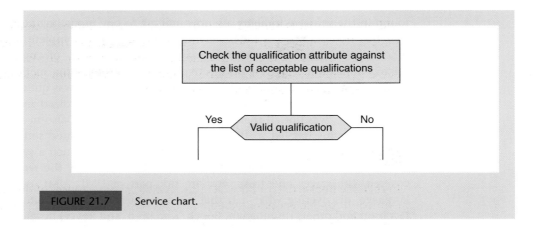

FIGURE 21.7   Service chart.

either a form of structured English notation (Section 12.4) or via a service chart, which is a kind of program flowchart. Figure 21.7 provides an example of a service chart.

It should be emphasized again that the description of the methodology as a linear series of activities is not necessarily how it would actually be approached. Some analysts might identify a few key class-&-objects, then drive down through the activities, and then iterate the process with other objects. It does not really matter as long as the outcome is a complete set of OOA models and diagrams. A further aspect that needs highlighting is the importance of the activities of identifying reusable objects, classes, and services, and therefore, ultimately, reusable code.

The methodology of OOA, as its name implies, does not include design and implementation phases, although the authors address design in some detail in other sources. In this book we will not extend the description into detailed design because that is not our focus. However, an important aspect of the transition from analysis to design in object-oriented methods is that it is not a question of changing, or introducing, new concepts. The transition is simply a matter of extending the detail of the object-oriented models and specifications, and adding components concerning human interactions (such as dialogue design), task management (such as real-time tasks, communication, and hardware considerations) and data management (e.g. designing the database). The detailed design stage slowly becomes program language-dependent, that is, we need to know what the target program language is, and the actual implementation will normally take place in an object-oriented programming language in order to utilize most easily the object-oriented concepts. Coad and Yourdon point out that the results of the OOA can be implemented in a non-object-oriented language, although it would be much more difficult.

21.2   RATIONAL UNIFIED PROCESS (RUP)

In 1998 Jacobson stated that the methods war was over (Jacobson, 2000). He believed that a standard had been achieved, and that standard was the Unified Modelling Language (UML) (Sections 13.1 and 13.2). He states, 'that all the different methods found in the software industry are now moving to one modelling language: UML', and that this new standard is far better described and more complete than any previous modelling language. This may or may not be true, and, of course, Jacobson was talking from quite a narrow perspective concerning modelling methods; nevertheless, for object-oriented approaches the standardization of UML was quite an advance.

However, Jacobson recognized that having a standardized modelling language, such as UML, was not all that was needed. As he says, 'You also need to know how to use it', and this has led to the development of the associated software development process or, in our terms, a methodology. The process by which a system is developed, for example, the type of things that have to be done, how the requirements are discovered, the stages and tasks, etc. are not part of UML. UML is only a modelling language, discovering what it is that needs to be modelled is quite different. For this Jacobson and others (Rumbaugh, Booch, Kruchten, and Royce) developed and evolved a process that has become known as the Unified Process and which utilizes UML for modelling.

Jacobson's early work was in the telecommunications industry with Ericsson where some of the ideas behind the Unified Process were developed, but he left Ericsson in 1987 to establish a company called Objectory, based in Stockholm. Objectory is a concatenation and abbreviation of the term 'Object factory', and the product of the company was a process for developing systems. In 1995 the Rational Software Corporation acquired Objectory. Rational had also been developing a number of software development practices, particularly in relation to software architecture and iterative development, and these concepts were combined with those of Objectory to form what was first called the Rational Objectory Process (first released in 1997) but became the Rational Unified Process (RUP) in 1998. Jacobson et al. (1999) describe RUP as a 'full-fledged process able to support the entire software development life-cycle'.

Jacobson does not like the term 'method' (or methodology) used to describe the Unified Process. He says, 'a method is usually a set of interesting ideas and general step by step descriptions. However, it typically does not guide developers in how to use it in commercial product development.' For Jacobson methods are embodied in textbooks and are primarily used for educational purposes, but they do not guide developers as to how to use them to develop commercial software. To achieve this the method has to be 'processified' into a real software engineering process. Therefore, the Unified Process as described in textbooks is essentially the fundamental and conceptual ideas of its methodology whereas the Process (e.g. RUP) is the processified software engineering process, typically converted and delivered as a product. Jacobson says that he would never recommend his book (Jacobson, 1992) to be used for commercial development, but it would be useful for acquiring and learning the basic ideas before developing a process on the basis of his method. Jacobson (2000) goes on to identify a number of shortcomings of methods:

- they are paper products, typically frozen in a book;
- they are rarely tried or tested in real projects (before publication);
- they are simple introductions (they are insufficient for use in real, commercial development projects);

■ they focus on developing new systems and have little to say concerning evolving development or maintenance;

■ they are rich in notations but lack semantics.

RUP, as a product, is available from Rational Software as a CD or via the Internet. It is essentially a hyperlinked website description of the process in HTML, and has been described as 'an electronic coach or e-coach' which is an interesting view of methodology. The latest version (at the time of writing) is v2002 and contains what are known as 'variants' of RUP. These are pre-packaged development cases for different types of software development organization. For example, there is a standard RUP and also a variant for e-business. The description provided here is of the standard RUP.

The Unified Process is described as 'use-case driven, architecture centric, iterative and incremental' (Jacobson et al., 1999), and this perspective is argued to make the process unique. Use-cases have been described in Section 13.2 as part of UML. In the Unified Process they are used to capture the user requirements. A use-case describes an element of the functionality of a system that gives a user 'a result of value'. They thus focus on things of specific value to a particular user (or group of users) and in this way overcome the growth of 'wish lists' or vague general functionality that might be nice to have but is not essential to the system. The sum of these use-cases (called the use-case model) depicts the total functionality of the system. But they are argued to be more than this because they are used to drive the development process, through design, implementation, and testing. Therefore, the system is designed based on the use-cases, it is implemented to support the use-cases, and is tested based upon the content of the use-cases.

RUP is an 'architecture-centric' process. Software architecture is compared to the architecture of a building, in that it is a blueprint of the building design that allows people to 'see' the building before it is actually built. The architecture of a system is similar but provides different views of the system. It contains details of the hardware, the operating system, the database, the network, etc. (i.e. the platform for the system), plus the non-functional requirements (non-functional requirements might concern reliability, performance, conformance, user interface standards, etc.). The architecture is defined in outline at the beginning but evolves and develops in tandem with the needs of the software system as it develops. Many other methodologies ignore the development of the architecture and just concentrate on the development of the software part of the project.

RUP is also described as iterative and incremental because its authors believe that user requirements cannot be fully and accurately defined initially at one go. Requirements evolve with improved understanding and change over time. Therefore, the project is not seen as one large activity with a 'big bang' outcome at the end but as a series of controlled incremental iterations which helps to minimize risk and reduce the chance of the system not meeting its goals at the conclusion. It is suggested that this means it is not a waterfall or life cycle approach (although as seen in Chapter 3 the life cycle is also supposed to be iterative). It is in fact much more like the spiral model (see Section 6.2).

These three key concepts of RUP (use-cases, architecture, and iteration) are described as being like a three-legged stool, without one of the legs the stool falls over (Jacobson et al., 1999). Other authors identify six (or more) core elements of RUP. For example, Kruchten (2000) also identifies tool support and use of components as critical to RUP.

The RUP has a number of 'cycles' which together make up the development of a project and run throughout its life. Each cycle consists of four phases: Inception, Elaboration, Construction, and Transition. Figure 21.9 indicates the phases and the workflows of RUP. The shapes in the figure indicate the relative emphasis of each phase in that particular workflow. Therefore, the major emphasis in construction is on implementation, as would be imagined but there are elements of other workflows as well. Each phase is composed of a number of iterations involving all the core workflows (see the blue box which depicts the second iteration of the elaboration phase). The number will be determined by the circumstances. So a development is not one pass through the workflows but a series of iterations round them for each of the four phases.

A workflow is a sequence of activities that 'produces a result of observable value' (Kruchten, 2000), and there are nine core process workflows in RUP. The workflows are shown in Figure 21.9, with the first six being termed engineering workflows and the bottom three support workflows (i.e. Configuration and change management, Project management, and Environment).

An interesting aspect of RUP is the concept of a worker (i.e. someone who performs a role in the development process). It is not actually an individual but someone performing that role, or as Kruchten (2000) looks at it, it is someone wearing a particular 'hat' at a particular time. RUP actually defines a list of all workers (of which there are around 30) potentially involved in the process, ranging from architect, systems analyst, and designer, through to stakeholder, project manager, and change control manager. A worker is associated with a set of 'cohesive' activities, meaning activities best performed by one person, in relation to the manipulation (e.g. creation, update) of an artefact. An artefact might be a use-case, a model, a piece of code, etc. It is part of the philosophy that the artefacts are created and maintained in a CASE toolset. In RUP design artefacts might be stored in Rational Rose or Select (see Section 18.4) while the project plan might be in Project 2000 (see Section 17.4). The major artefacts of RUP are specified in Figure 21.8. RUP also has a set of guidelines which relate to artefacts, activities, or steps. They might specify, for example, what is good practice, what makes for a quality artefact, or a heuristic. So they might give advice on how to conduct a review, how to model a use-case, how to check something, good user interface design, etc.

The workflows themselves will now be examined, starting with the engineering ones followed by the support workflows. Different descriptions of RUP vary in the number of workflows that are identified. We look at the nine workflows described by Kruchten (2000), but in some descriptions the first and last of the engineering workflows are not included (i.e. business modelling and deployment).

1 The business modelling workflow

This starts with the development of the Business Model. This is essentially establishing the context for the system being developed and the shape of the organization in which the system is to be deployed. It might include the identification of current problems and

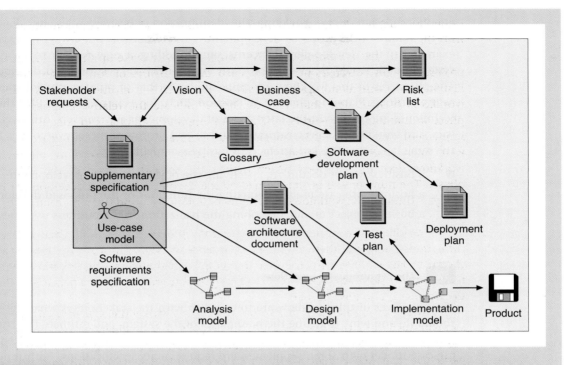

FIGURE 21.8 Major artefacts of the Rational Unified Process (RUP).

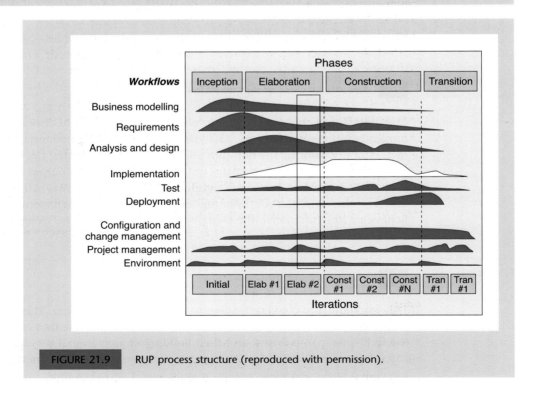

FIGURE 21.9 RUP process structure (reproduced with permission).

areas for redesign or re-engineering, the identification of business rules, etc., depending on the nature of the proposed development. This workflow is not always necessary, for example, if the development concerns simply adding a new feature to an existing system, but it would be essential for any major new business-oriented development. The objectives of this workflow are quite similar to that of other methodologies, such as the Business Planning phase of IE (Section 20.3), for example, but in RUP the same techniques are used as in the later stages of development (i.e. workers, artefacts, activities, and workflows), thus ensuring an end to end process and that everyone is talking the same language. The key artefacts of business modelling are:

- a business vision document, specifying the objectives of the development;
- a business use-case model, depicting the functions of the proposed development;
- a business object model, describing the realization of the business use-cases.

2 The requirements workflow

The objectives of this workflow are to establish with the stakeholders what the system should do and why, to define the boundaries of the system, and estimate the costs and timescales involved. A 'vision' of the system is developed which is then translated into a use-case model with some supplementary requirements specifications. Both functional and non-functional (e.g. minimum response times) requirements are collected and analysed. The key stakeholder and user needs and the high-level features are defined, and then these have to be converted into specific software requirements. Again the use-case model is used to express this.

3 The analysis and design workflow

The objective of this workflow is to convert the requirements from (2) above into an implementation specification. Analysis ensures that the functional requirements are met, typically ignoring the non-functional requirements and the run-time environment. So, analysis is a logical view of the system. Design takes the output of the analysis and adapts it to the constraints of the architecture and the non-functional requirements. This involves the activities of Defining and Refining the Architecture, Analysing the Behaviour (the functions), the Design of components and the Design of the Database.

4 The implementation workflow

This workflow is to convert the designs into an implementation. This involves planning the process, converting the classes and objects from (3) above into components, testing the individual components, and then building an operational version of the system in parts, known as 'the builds'. The separate software components are then incrementally integrated into a complete system, usually over a period of time.

5   The test workflow

This workflow tests and verifies the interaction of components, that all requirements have been implemented, and that a quality product has been developed in terms of the absence of defects and fitness for purpose. The system is tested for reliability, functionality, and performance. Testing is not a single phase in the project, it occurs throughout the life cycle and at all stages. Clearly it differs in the early stages to the later stages. The type of testing may include Benchmark tests, Configuration tests, Functionality, Installation, Integrity (resistance to failure), Load tests, Performance, Stress tests, etc. These might involve the creation of test cases, procedures, scripts, etc. to help to test comprehensively.

6   The deployment workflow

This workflow deploys the finished software to the users and involves:

- testing the software in its operational setting (beta-testing);
- training the end-users;
- migrating from existing software (including database conversion);
- packaging the software (if it is a shrink-wrap software package);
- installing the software.

The exact nature of the deployment workflow will depend on whether the system is a traditional custom-made, in-house developed piece of software or a package, and whether, for example, it is to be delivered via an Internet download. The deployment workflow is important in RUP, and it is suggested that deployment activities are often ignored by other methodologies and approaches.

7   The configuration and change management workflow

This workflow tracks and maintains the integrity of the project. The artefacts developed in the project represent a significant investment and their use should be maximized. Artefacts must be identified and stored, and the various history and versions controlled. The workflow involves monitoring and managing change requests, change costs, and keeping control of the various versions of products and artefacts. It also involves the management of the configuration of hardware and software. Tool support is advised for what is described as the 'tedious aspects' of the workflow.

8   The project management workflow

This workflow provides a framework for managing software projects and managing risk. It also provides guidelines for planning, staffing, monitoring, and generally performing project management. Again the use of tools such as Project 2000 and techniques such as

Gantt charts and PERT are emphasized (see Sections 14.4 and 14.5). RUP recognizes that project management has been a particularly difficult aspect of software development and so devotes a workflow to helping ensure that a project is successful in this respect and in particular addresses risks.

In planning there are two levels of plans, a 'coarse-grained' plan (the phase plan) and a set of 'fine-grained' plans (the iteration plans). The phase plan relates to the major milestones of the project, from project approval through to product release, while the iteration plans relate to the detail of the current iteration and possibly the next iteration. Part of this workflow examines potential risks to the project, for example, requirement creep or difficulties in recruiting key specialisms. These risks are assessed as to their probability and their potential impact on the project. If a risk is assessed as serious then attempts are made actively to mitigate the risk together with the development of contingency plans to be enacted if the risk actually occurs. As part of project management RUP recommends that detailed project metrics (quantitative measures) be established and kept. These might relate to progress, productivity, levels of reuse achieved, customer satisfaction, etc. and are important not only for effectively managing the current project but for learning and improving the management of future projects.

9   The environment workflow

This workflow is about supporting the project with relevant processes, methods, and tools in an organization. As we have seen the use of tools is a key element of RUP so the activities concern the selection, procurement, implementation, and management of appropriate tools and support processes.

RUP, according to Rational, is based on experience and best practices and is suitable for a wide range of projects and organizations. It is use-case-driven and focuses on developing software iteratively, and provides phases, workflows, guidelines, and frameworks for software development. It is designed for and utilizes UML for its modelling elements and is based upon the integral use of tools to support its processes.

21.3   SUMMARY

■   In this chapter we have described two methodologies that are object-oriented: object-oriented analysis and the rational unified process.

QUESTIONS

1 What do you see as the common features and differences between object-oriented analysis (OOA) and rational unified process (RUP)?

2 In what ways is RUP different to other, non-object-oriented methodologies, for example, Information Engineering (IE), discussed in Chapter 20?

3 Why do the RUP authors not like to call it a methodology? Do you agree with them and why?

4 Do both these approaches (OOA and RUP) conform fully to the object modelling theme in Section 5.4, and do they use all the object techniques discussed in Chapter 13?

21.4 FURTHER READING

Coad, P. and Yourdon, E. (1991) *Object Oriented Analysis*, 2nd edn, Prentice Hall, Englewood Cliffs, New Jersey.

Jacobson, I., Booch, G., and Rumbaugh, J. (1999) *The Unified Software Development Process*, Addison-Wesley, Boston.

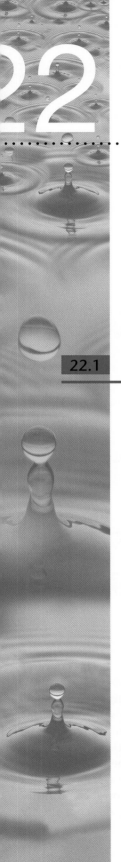

22 RAPID DEVELOPMENT METHODOLOGIES

· ·

22.1   JAMES MARTIN'S RAD (JMRAD)

The goal of rapid development of applications has been around for some time and with good reason, as the objective of speeding up the development process is something that has been on the agenda of both general management and information systems management for a long time. The need to develop information systems more quickly has been driven by rapidly changing business needs. The general environment of business is seen as increasingly competitive, more customer-focused, and operating in a more international context. Such a business environment is characterized by continuous change, and the information systems in an organization need to be created and amended speedily to support this change. Unfortunately, information systems development in most organizations is unable to react quickly enough, and the business and systems development cycles are substantially out of step. In such a situation, the notion of rapid application development (RAD) is obviously attractive.

RAD (Rapid Application Development) has been discussed in general terms in Section 6.4, and this should be reviewed along with this description of James Martin's RAD methodology, which we term JMRAD in order to distinguish it from the general form of RAD and other specific RAD methodologies, for example, Dynamic Systems Development Method (DSDM), described in Section 22.2.

Martin is, of course, also known for the development of the Information Engineering (IE) methodology (Section 20.3), and it comes as no surprise to find that his version of RAD is set firmly in the context of IE, as illustrated in Figure 22.1.

JMRAD is actually a combination of techniques and tools that are, for the most part, already well known and dealt with elsewhere in this book. We identify the following as the most important JMRAD characteristics:

■   it is not based upon the traditional life cycle (Chapter 3), but adopts an evolutionary/prototyping approach (Sections 6.2 and 6.3);

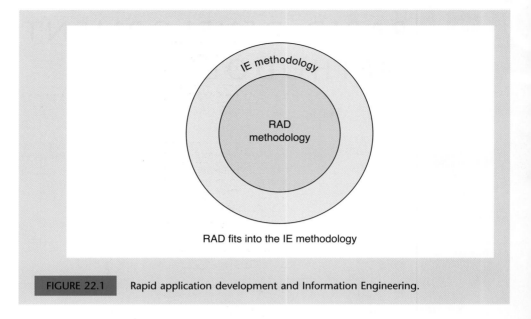

RAD fits into the IE methodology

FIGURE 22.1   Rapid application development and Information Engineering.

- it focuses upon identifying the important users and involving them via workshops at early stages of development;
- it focuses on obtaining commitment from the business users;
- it requires a toolset with a sophisticated repository (Chapter 18).

JMRAD has four phases which we shall describe in turn (Figure 22.2):

1. Requirements planning.
2. User design.
3. Construction.
4. Cutover.

1   Requirements planning

JMRAD devotes a lot of effort to the early stages of systems development. This concerns the definition of requirements. There are two techniques used in this phase, both of which are really workshops or structured meetings. The first is joint requirements planning (JRP), and the second is joint application design (JAD). In some other RAD methods, these are not separated; indeed, Martin points out that they may in practice be combined with some of the functions of JRP being subsumed into JAD.

The role of JRP Workshop is to identify the high-level management requirements of the system at a strategic level. The participants in JRP are senior managers who have a vision and understanding of the overall objectives of the system and how it can contribute to the goals and strategy of the organization. If this understanding does not already

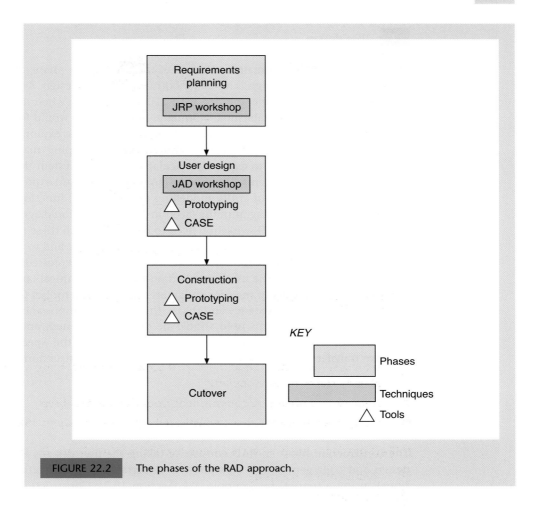

FIGURE 22.2 The phases of the RAD approach.

exist, the workshop may be used to help determine such an understanding or vision. The JRP is a creative workshop that helps to identify and create commitment to the goals of the system, to identify priorities, to eliminate unnecessary functions, and so on. Martin separates JRP from JAD because there are different people involved. In JRP, the participants need to have a combination of overall business knowledge and specific knowledge about the area that the proposed system is addressing along with its requirements. They also need to have the necessary authority and seniority to be able to make decisions and commitments. Applications often cross traditional functional boundaries, and ensuring the right people are involved is difficult but absolutely critical. Martin suggests that if the right people are not available the workshop should not take place. The participation of substitute personnel, without the authority to make decisions, who have frequently to refer back to their superiors, could negate one of the main workshop objectives which is to get the requirements identified and agreed in the shortest possible time.

The detail of the workshops will be discussed in the next section as they are the same as JAD workshops.

2   User design

JAD (Section 16.2) is the main technique of the user design phase; indeed, it contains little else. In fact, user design is in reality both analysis and design. As mentioned above, the JRP workshop may be combined with JAD in situations where the overall requirements are already well established. Normally, however, JAD would follow on from JRP. Prototyping (Section 6.3) is advocated to enable the quick exploration of processes, interfaces, reports, screens, dialogues, and so on. Prototyping may be used for the overall system or be used to explore particular parts of the system that are contentious or present particular problems. The user design is developed and expressed using the four diagramming techniques of entity modelling (Section 11.1), functional decomposition (Section 12.5), data flow diagramming (Section 12.1), and action diagrams (Section 12.8). The participants in the JAD workshop need to be familiar with these techniques, but the emphasis is on getting the requirements as correct as possible and to reflect the business needs. Therefore, the language used in the workshop and expressed in the diagrams is that of the business and the users, rather than the more technical language of information systems. The results of the user design are captured in a toolset (Chapter 18) which checks both internal consistency and that with other applications and corporate models. Where necessary, the terms used should be discussed, defined, and entered into the repository of the toolset. The use of a toolset enables the speedy, accurate, and effective transfer of the results into the next phase, the construction phase.

3   Construction phase

The construction phase in RAD consists of taking the user designs through to detailed design and code generation. This phase is undertaken by information systems professionals using a toolset, for example, IEF (Section 18.2). Construction in Martin's RAD methodology is highly dependent on the presence of an IE-based toolset and is performed by creating a series of prototypes which are then reviewed by the key users. In this way the screens and designs of each transaction are prototyped, and the users then approve them. If they do not approve them, they will request changes, and the process goes on through a series of iterations. By prototyping and the use of the toolset, these iterations are achieved quickly, and testing is enabled. Some of these key users will already have been involved in the earlier phase of user design. Construction is performed by small teams of three or four experts in the use of the toolset. These experts are known as **SWAT teams**. SWAT stands for 'skilled with advanced tools', and the approach requires them to work quickly, making maximum possible use of reusable designs and code that already exist. Teams are kept small so as to reduce the number of interfaces and interactions between people in the teams. One of the problems of traditional development is low productivity which, it is argued, results from the large teams of developers involved, the consequent large communications network, and the number of communications. Normally there is a SWAT team member allocated to developing each transaction in a system. In practice, there is often only one developer for a particular part of the system, and this reduces the number of potential interactions with other developers for the area to zero. Using this approach, it is argued that the core of a system can be built relatively quickly, typically in four to six weeks, and then it is progressively refined and integrated with other aspects developed by other team members.

Once the detailed designs have been agreed, the code can be generated using the toolset and the system tested and approved. Because of the way that the construction has occurred, there should not be any surprises to the users when they see the finished version. All associated documentation is then produced and database optimization is performed.

4　Cutover

The final phase is cutover, and this involves further comprehensive testing using realistic data in operational situations. The users are trained on the system, organizational changes (implied by the system) are implemented, and finally the cutover is effected by running the old and the new systems in parallel, until the new system has proved itself and the old system is phased out.

JMRAD adopts an evolutionary or timebox approach to development and implementation (see Section 6.4). Typically, it recommends implementation of systems in a 90-day life cycle. The objective is to have the easiest and most important 80 per cent of system functionality produced in the first 90-day timebox and the rest in subsequent timeboxes. This forces users and developers to focus on only those aspects of the system that are necessary and probably most well defined for development in the first timebox. Everything else is left until later. The knock-on benefit of this is that with experience and use of the basic system, developed in the first timebox, users often find that their requirements evolve in different directions from those originally envisaged. In other words, the benefits of an evolutionary approach accrue. The other advantage of the timebox is that it creates a focus on achieving an implementation in the specified period. In order to achieve this, the functionality must be trimmed accordingly. The timebox approach contrasts with the traditional approach where every conceivable requirement is implemented together, and the resulting complexity often causes long delays in implementation.

22.2　DYNAMIC SYSTEMS DEVELOPMENT METHOD (DSDM)

As with JMRAD above DSDM attempts to address the ongoing problem of the length of time it takes to develop information systems. In 1994 a group of systems developers from interested companies came together to form an independent or 'not for profit' Consortium to discuss and attempt to define a standard RAD (Rapid Application Development) method (see Section 6.4). There was some concern that RAD was becoming tainted with a 'quick but dirty' image whereas the Consortium believed that RAD could and should not only be rapid but also practical and professional. The method they defined became known as DSDM (Dynamic Systems Development Method). Although their debt to Martin has been acknowledged (Stapleton, 1997) it appears that Martin's RAD was felt not to encompass certain principles nor to provide a total RAD solution, but probably equally important was its close association with proprietary elements, such as IE and IEF (Sections 18.2 and 20.3). The Consortium originally contained 17 members representing a mix of organizations, in terms of size, vendors, and user organizations. The Consortium rapidly grew to over 200 member organizations by 1996, including ICL, IBM, the British Ministry of Defence, British Telecom and British Airways, and according to Stapleton now has over 1,000 members. The Consortium does inevitably have various product and service vendors in its membership, but has striven not to let particular proprietary products influence or define the method and they describe the method as 'vendor-independent'. The Consortium operates with a Management Committee, a Directorate, and has various Technical Committees and Working Groups, one of which is a Training and Accreditation Group to help disseminate the approach and accredit practitioners in the use of the method. Certification is undertaken in association with the BCS (British Computer Society).

Rapid Application Development (RAD) is defined by the Consortium as 'an approach to building and maintaining computer-based systems, which combines effective use of tools and techniques, prototyping and tight project delivery timescales' (www.dsdm.org, 2001), and the first detailed definition of DSDM was published in 1995. After a period of monitoring and reviewing experience in practice a second version was published later the same year, and DSDM has since become well known and influential, especially in the UK but also increasingly in Europe as a whole and to a lesser extent the rest of the world. DSDM Version 3 was produced in 1997 and as well as being a general update includes additional material relating to the management of business process change in organizations. At the time of writing Version 4 has just been published but is not generally available outside the DSDM membership. Recently eDSDM has been produced which is a version of DSDM tailored to organizations and projects undertaking e(lectronic)-business initiatives including organizational and architectural change issues.

DSDM, despite its name, is more of a framework than a method, which sometimes disappoints people looking for a tightly defined methodology, and much of the detail of how things should actually be done and what the various products will contain is left to the organization or individual to decide (Stapleton, 1998). To try and define every possible detail and possibility would be contrary to the RAD ideals, and as Stapleton (1997) states, '... it would be disastrous for a RAD method to become known as bureaucratic or overcomplex'. DSDM is defined at a higher level than just a set of techniques and tools. It is argued that an organization needing a RAD approach requires a more fundamental change to their development process. Therefore, DSDM provides 'a framework of controls for building and maintaining systems which meet tight time constraints and provide a recipe for repeatable RAD success. The method not only addresses the developer's view of RAD but also that of all the other parties who are interested in effective system development, including the users, project managers and quality assurance personnel' (www.dsdm.org, 2001).

While some of the detail may be missing, DSDM clearly identifies its underlying principles. These principles are critical to DSDM project success, and if even one is ignored or not applied then the whole project is endangered and the general advice is to reconsider the use of DSDM if they cannot be guaranteed. There are nine principles, as follows:

1   Active user involvement is imperative.

2   Teams must be empowered to make decisions. The four key variables of empowerment are: authority, resources, information, and accountability.

3   Frequent delivery of products is essential.

4   Fitness for business purpose is the essential criterion for acceptance of deliverables.

5   Iterative and incremental development is necessary to converge on an accurate business solution.

6   All changes during development are reversible (i.e. you do not proceed further down a particular path if problems are encountered, you backtrack to the last safe or agreed point, and then start down a new path).

7   Requirements are baselined at a high level (i.e. the high-level business requirements, once agreed, are frozen). This is essentially the scope of the project.

8   Testing is integrated throughout the life cycle (i.e. 'test as you go' rather than testing just at the end where it frequently gets squeezed).

9   A collaborative and co-operative approach between all stakeholders is essential.

Although speed of delivery is not specifically mentioned in these principles, only alluded to, it is clearly a key principle of DSDM. Historically, of course, there have been problems in this area, and DSDM recognizes that the business often needs solutions faster than they can be delivered and that deadlines are frequently set with no reference to the work involved (i.e. the deadline is outside the control of those tasked with the delivery of the project). In situations of tight deadlines it is tempting to introduce extra resources and people to a project, but as has often been observed (e.g. Brooks, 1974) this frequently makes things worse as there is a considerable learning curve for new people joining a project and existing people are diverted to help bring the new people up to speed. Therefore, a late-running project cannot alter the deadline nor can it add resources, so the only thing left is to reduce the functionality. This is the RAD solution and the one that DSDM adopts.

1   DSDM process

This section should be read in conjunction with the more general description of RAD in Section 6.4, for DSDM embraces the general concepts of timeboxing, Moscow Rules, JAD workshops, prototyping (Section 6.3), etc. The DSDM framework defines a set of phases that any new or enhancement development project should undertake. This includes the initial identification of a problem or opportunity to be addressed through the development of the system to keeping the system operating successfully.

Figure 22.3, known in DSDM as the 'three pizzas and a cheese diagram' depicts the phases and the main products that need to be produced in each phase together with the various pathways through the process. As can be seen the feasibility and business studies are performed sequentially and before the rest of the phases because they define the scope and justification for the subsequent development activities. The arrows indicate the normal forward path through the phases including iteration within each phase while the dashed arrows indicate the possible routes back for evolving and iterating the phases.

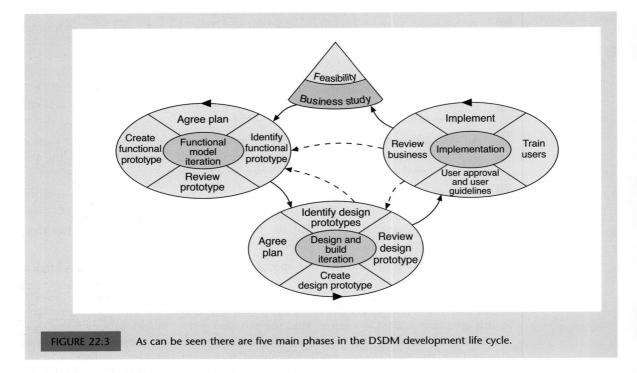

FIGURE 22.3 As can be seen there are five main phases in the DSDM development life cycle.

In fact the sequence in which the last three phases are undertaken or how they are overlapped is not defined but left to the needs of the project and the developers.

The five main phases in the DSDM development life cycle are:

1 *Feasibility study.* This includes the usual feasibility elements, for example, the cost/benefit case for undertaking a particular project, but also, and particularly important, it is concerned with determining whether DSDM is the correct approach for this project. DSDM recognizes that not all projects are suitable for RAD and DSDM. Some guidelines are provided but it is not simply that projects of type *X* are suitable and that projects of type *Y* are unsuitable. It is more concerned with the maturity and experience of the organization with DSDM concepts. Having said that, there is a feeling that one should be very careful in going ahead with engineering, scientific, or particularly computationally complex applications. Howard (1997) says that DSDM is not recommended for real-time applications. Projects where all the requirements must be delivered at once may also not be suitable for DSDM (i.e. where there are no 'should haves' or 'could haves', in Moscow Rules terms see Section 6.4). In general, business applications, especially where the details of the requirements are not clear but time is critical, are particularly suitable for DSDM. The feasibility study is 'a short, sharp exercise' taking no more than a few weeks, in dramatic contrast to some traditional feasibility studies that take years. Therefore, it is not particularly detailed but highly focused on the risks and how to manage them. A key outcome is the agreement that the project is suitable and should proceed.

2 *Business study.* This is also supposed to be quick and is at a relatively high level. It is

about gaining understanding of the business processes involved, their rationales, and their information needs. It also identifies the stakeholders and those that need to be involved. Traditional requirements gathering techniques, such as interviewing, take too long, so facilitated JAD-type workshops (see Section 16.2) are recommended. The high-level major functions are identified and prioritized as is the overall systems architecture definition and outline work plans. These plans include the Outline Prototyping Plan; this defines all the prototypes to be included in the subsequent phases (i.e. the prototyping strategy and the configuration management plan). These plans get refined at each phase as more information becomes available. The other major output is the Business Area Definition, usually containing an overview DFD and Entity Model or business Object Model, if the environment is object-oriented. DSDM is applicable to both structured or object-oriented development approaches, or indeed to any other. DSDM advocates using 'what you know' and is not prescriptive concerning analysis and design techniques.

3   *Functional model iteration*. Here the high-level functions and information requirements from the Business Study are refined. Standard analysis models are produced followed by the development of prototypes and then the software. This is described as a symbiotic process with feedback from prototypes serving to refine the models and then the prototypes moving toward first-cut software, which is then tested as much as is possible given its evolving nature.

4   *System design and build iteration*. This is where the system is built ready for delivery to the users. At the least the 'minimum usable subset' of requirements will be delivered; that is, the 'must haves' and hopefully some of the 'should haves' will also be delivered but this depends on how the project has evolved during its development. As indicated above testing is not a major activity of this stage because of the ongoing testing principle. However, some degree of testing will probably be needed as in some cases this will be the first time the whole system has been available together.

5   *Implementation*. This is the cutover from the existing system or environment to the new and includes training, development, or rather completion, of the user manuals and documentation. Completion because, like testing, these should have been ongoing activities throughout the process. Ideally user documentation is produced by the users rather than the specialist developers. Finally a Project Review Document is produced which assesses whether all the requirements have been met or whether further iterations or timeboxes are required.

As mentioned above DSDM adopts an incremental approach and uses the RAD concept of timeboxing. The normal concept of a timebox is the overall period from the start of the project to the scheduled end, when something tangible and usable is delivered to the users. This may be followed by a second timebox when something additional is delivered. However, rather confusingly DSDM although using the term in this way also applies it to describe a subphase within a project (a nested timebox). So in DSDM there are investigation timeboxes, analysis timeboxes, prototype timeboxes, development timeboxes, etc. Therefore, they apply timebox principles to any subphase or stage of the project, rather than just to the overall project. The principles relate to the

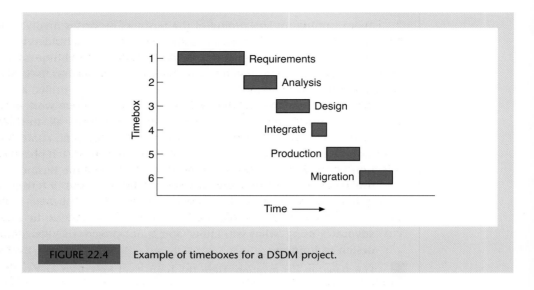

FIGURE 22.4   Example of timeboxes for a DSDM project.

fact that these are not activity-based but a series of fixed deadline timeboxes in which as much is undertaken as is needed to make something or produce a particular output in the shortest possible time. Figure 22.4 illustrates an example from a DSDM project that is broken down into six timeboxes. Each such timebox is recommended to be between two and six weeks long although as is the case with many of the recommendations in DSDM it depends on the nature of the particular situation. Every effort is made to stick to the timescales of these internal timeboxes but they are not completely unchangeable and may have to be modified as the project evolves or as more information becomes available. DSDM addresses the management of these timeboxes in some detail but devotes relatively little attention to how to manage the overall timebox except to indicate that Moscow Rules should be applied and that not everything can, or should be, delivered in a single increment. Indeed Stapleton (1997) says that the reason for this is that 'incremental delivery has no distinct DSDM flavour'.

DSDM emphasizes the key role of people in the process and is described as a 'user centred' approach. Overall there is a Project Manager, requiring all the skills of traditional project managers, only more so as the focus is on speed! The Project Manager is responsible for project planning, monitoring, prioritization, human resources, budgets, timeboxes, scoping, etc. The use of software project management and control tools are recommended; for example, PRINCE2 (see Section 24.4).

On the user side there are two key roles, the first is that of Ambassador User; this is someone (or more than one) from the user community who understands and represents the needs of that community. The second is the Visionary User; this is the person who had the original idea or vision as to how the project might help in the business or organization. As well as defining the original vision they have a responsibility to make sure that the vision stays in focus and does not become diluted. In other contexts this might be described as the project champion. On the IT side, although they are crucial, there are in general no particular specialist roles; that is, no distinction is made between different IT roles, such as analysts, designers, programmers, etc. Everyone has to have flexible skills and be capable of turning their hand to whatever is required at any particular time. Of course, in practice particular skills may have to be imported at times but the key IT team members are generalists and do not change. One exception to this is the specific role of Technical Co-ordinator, responsible for the technical architecture, technical quality, and configuration management. A particular requirement for all is good communication skills.

DSDM recommends small development teams composed of users and IT developers. A large project may have a number of teams working in parallel but the minimum team size is two, as at least one person has to be from the IT side and one from the business or user side. The recommended maximum is six as it has been found that above this number the RAD process can prove difficult to sustain.

DSDM does not recommend any specific software tools but does recommend that appropriate tools are identified and used appropriately in the process. Indeed the use of some, such as prototyping tools, are implicit in the method, others are recommended but optional. We have already seen that project management tools might be appropriate but analysis, design, construction, and documentation tools, or integrated toolsets, are all potentially appropriate. The key factor is whether they will speed up the process and increase quality, but what they must not do is get in the way of the DSDM principles, i.e. speed. So, it is not so much what tools you use but more how you use and apply them.

DSDM has some similarities with Extreme Programming (see next section), and it is argued that their use can be combined, with DSDM being used as the overall methodology and extreme programming being used for the code development.

22.3 EXTREME PROGRAMMING (XP)

Extreme Programming also attempts to support quicker development of software, particularly for small and medium-sized applications and organizations (it is said to work best where the whole project requires 3 to 10 programmers). It is more a series of principles for developing software rapidly than a step-by-step methodology. Jeffries (2001) defines Extreme Programming as 'a discipline of software development with values of simplicity, communication, feedback and courage'.

On communication, the approach stresses the role of teamwork – 'open and honest communication' – and the importance of communications with customers, in particular through continuous testing, referred to as 'concrete and rapid feedback'. This should ensure quality. Courage is necessary to develop the programs at top speed and to throw code away and start again if necessary. Programmers should look for simple solutions, not complex ones and develop through a series of simple steps. The focus is therefore on incremental development, with each release being put into operation quickly.

A number of organizations are utilizing XP in their software development to reap its potential efficiency gains. This is a less structured or lightweight methodology, which places emphasis on teamwork. This team consists of customer, management, and developers. Extreme Programming is a process that convenes these people and assists them in succeeding together.

The customer must define their requirements in **User Stories**; these are the things that the system needs to do for its users. A crucial component of defining a User Story is the definition of test scenarios, so that testing is always upfront in XP. An

Architectural Spike is an aid to figure out answers to tough technical or design problems. This is usually a very simple program to explore the potential solutions; it builds a system that only addresses the problem under examination and ignores all other concerns. A spike is not a high-quality piece of code, therefore; it is expected that it will be thrown away. The purpose behind the use of a spike is to reduce the risk of a technical problem or increase the reliability of a user story's estimate.

Paired programming – two programmers per workstation – is particularly put to good use and reduces the potential risk when a technical difficulty threatens to hold up the system's development. While one programmer is keying in the best way to perform a task, the other is 'thinking more strategically' about whether the whole approach will work, tests that may not work yet, and ways of simplifying. The roles should reverse frequently.

A release planning meeting is where a release plan is created. The release plan is then used to create iteration plans for each iteration. Each iteration is one to three weeks of the project. In iteration planning, acceptance tests are created from User Stories and scheduled. The customer specifies scenarios to test when a User Story has been correctly implemented. A story can have one or many acceptance tests, whatever it takes to ensure the functionality works. Indeed, tests are said to drive development in XP.

Although we have described XP as a 'lightweight methodology', we see phases as follows:

1. *Planning* the scope of the project, the priority of the functions, the members of the team, the contents of each increment, and estimating costs and arriving at a schedule for release of the increments. Story writing by users and clients can help by suggesting scope, content, costings, and timings. (The planning phase may be preceded by an *exploration* phase where the customer suggests change through story boards and is assured that the technical people understand the requirements in outline.)

2. *Designing* on the principle of simplicity, feedback, and courage, and enabling incremental change – an increment may typically take one to three weeks. There will normally be a daily meeting of all the participants at this phase onwards. (This phase may be engulfed by the urge to develop and be subsumed in that next phase.)

3. *Developing* the code using paired programming, testing using programmer and user data, gaining rapid feedback, developing that extra code which ensures that the test works fully, and continuously integrating with already implemented code. Each release of the developing project may be rolled out to users every two to five iterations.

4. *Productionalizing* may also be seen as part of developing, but the tests at this time ensure fitness for production of the 'whole system', perhaps parallel running, ensuring good performances for running the software, so that this phase naturally runs into *maintenance*.

Unlike many methodologies, documentation is not a prime concern – delivering software is seen as the primary goal. This is seen as part of XP being a 'light' methodology.

22.4 WEB IS DEVELOPMENT METHODOLOGY (WISDM)

There are a number of approaches that have been proposed for developing web applications. They are available in books and on the web. However, none have been taken up widely. It appears that many web developers simply develop their sites and associated applications by trial and error or by using software such as Dreamweaver to guide development (Section 17.2). Others use a more conventional approach and modify it as appropriate for web development. Indeed, it could be that web applications are like any other, but with different emphases, such as those on interface design and security, and also the usual necessity for rapid development, hence its inclusion in this chapter.

Here we offer an approach known as WISDM, which is a modification of Multiview (Section 25.1) for web development (see Vidgen et al., 2002):

> Many of the approaches to Web development have focused on the user interface and in particular the look and feel of a Web site, but have failed to address the wider aspects of Web-based information systems. At the same time, traditional IS methodologies – from the waterfall lifecycle to rapid application development (RAD) – have struggled to accommodate web-specific aspects into their methods and work practices. Although Web sites are characterized historically as graphically intense hypermedia systems, they have now evolved from cyber-brochures into database-driven information systems that must integrate with existing systems, such as back office applications. Web-based IS therefore require a mix of Web-site development techniques together with traditional IS development competencies in database and program design.

Essentially, the authors argue that Multiview can be drawn upon in a specific situation by particular people to create WISDM a modification of Multiview used locally and uniquely for web development in practice. The book contains a complete case study related to a theatre booking system. As seen in Figure 22.5, emphasis is placed on design, and human–computer interaction and the user interface, in particular.

We will concentrate here on differences in emphasis when compared to the Multiview framework expressed in Section 25.1. Unlike conventional methodologies, there is no a priori ordering of the five aspects of the methods matrix, each one being emphasized alone (or with others) as appropriate during the lifetime of the project.

Organizational analysis represents *value creation* and stresses strategy as relationship building and maintaining with a broad range of stakeholders that includes customers, employees, government, suppliers, labour organizations, and so on. As the users of websites can be broader and different than conventional applications, a broad view of stakeholders is essential (Section 16.1). In an age where dotcom failure is noticeable, the right strategy may also be emphasized more than normal. For some organizations, the website is the most prominent aspect of the company and its main source of income, so it is essential to get it right.

Information analysis represents the *requirements specification*. This is a formalized specification of the information and process requirements of the organization. The specification might be in the form of a document with graphical notations, but it might also be in the form of a software prototype (an executable specification). The indicative approach in WISDM is to use UML (Section 13.2). It is used to create structural

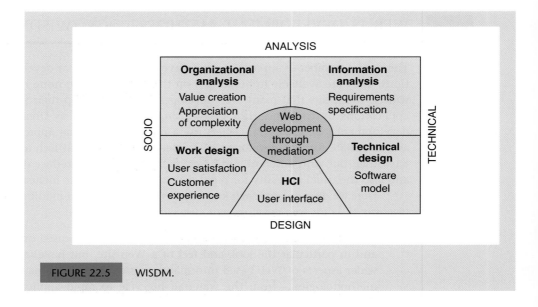

FIGURE 22.5   WISDM.

(class model), behavioural (use-case and interaction diagrams), and process-oriented (activity diagrams) models of the problem situation. In general, web content analysis and management is a major concern including such factors as consistency, navigability, and tracking, again concerns that will have more prominence in web applications development.

Work design represents *user satisfaction*. The traditional concern of the socio-technical approach to IS development has been with job satisfaction and genuine user participation in the development process (see ETHICS, Section 23.1). WISDM extends this view to incorporate the interests of external users, such as customers, who may be using the information system as part of their social activities. Customer satisfaction with a web IS is assessed using the method, and the Internet enables the designers to reach outside the organization to find potential external users during the development process as well as when the site is operational. WISDM uses an instrument known as WebQual to assess e-commerce offerings against a range of qualities using a 7-point Likert scale. As seen in Figure 22.6, there are 23 questions related to usability, information, interaction, and convergence (the overall view of the website).

Technical design represents the *software model*. A formalized model of the software in terms of data structures and program design is needed to support software construction. There are some technical restraints in developing web applications; for example, a variant of HTML will be used for the pages and an Internet server will host the pages. JavaScript is likely to be needed for some processing. The extensible mark-up language (XML) might be used to provide a notation for defining the content and presentation of data. The data are likely to use a relational database management system, such as Access or Oracle (Sections 17.5 and 18.3, respectively). ColdFusion might be used to convert files to HTML format, effectively automating much of the functionality of the implementation. Vidgen et al. (2002) recommends that in some instances functions may be supplied by a third party, for example, the handling of credit card payments.

Usability

1. I find the site easy to learn to operate
2. My interaction with the site is clear and understandable
3. I find the site easy to navigate
4. I find the site easy to use
5. The site has an attractive appearance
6. The design is appropriate to the type of site
7. The site conveys a sense of competency
8. The site creates a positive experience for me

Information

9. Provides accurate information
10. Provides believable information
11. Provides timely information
12. Provides relevant information
13. Provides easy to understand information
14. Provides information at the right level of detail
15. Presents the information in an appropriate format

Interaction

16. Has a good reputation
17. It feels safe to complete transactions
18. My personal information feels secure
19. Creates a sense of personalization
20. Conveys a sense of community
21. Makes it easy to communicate with the organization
22. I feel confident that goods/services will be delivered as promised

Convergence

23. What is your overall view of this website.

| FIGURE 22.6 | WebQual questions. |

Human–Computer Interface (HCI) represents the *user interface* and is located as an overlapping space in technical design and work design. The shape of this space reflects its role in pointing toward analysis but its foundations are solidly in design. The interface design draws on website design principles for page layout, navigation schemes, and usability in the context of work design. Templates and style sheets, such as those provided by Dreamweaver (Section 17.2), may be used for pages so that there is a common 'look and feel' to the site. Because the reach of websites can be very different when compared to conventional applications, this phase might include promotion plans and the monitoring of the use of the site. Emphasis is also placed on security issues, such as authentication.

22.5 SUMMARY

■ In this chapter we have described four methodologies that are oriented toward speed of development. RAD and DSDM concentrate on developing information systems rapidly, with XP mainly concerned with programming software quickly, and WISDM on web development.

QUESTIONS

1 What do you see as the common features and differences between the four approaches discussed in this chapter?

2 In what ways, if any, do they potentially sacrifice quality for speed of development?

3 Why is cultural change important in DSDM?

4 Do you think the key feature of their success is use of toolsets?

22.6 FURTHER READING

Beck, K. (2000) *Extreme Programming Explained*, Addison-Wesley, Boston.

DSDM Manual Version 3 (1998) DSDM Consortium, Tesseract Publishing, Surrey, UK.

Jeffries, R. (2001) *Extreme Programming Installed*, Pearson Education, London.

Martin, J. (1991) *Rapid Application Development*, Prentice Hall, Englewood Cliffs, New Jersey.

Stapleton, J. (1997) *DSDM Dynamic Systems Development Method, The Method in Practice*, Addison-Wesley, Harlow, UK.

Vidgen, R., Avison, D.E., Wood, R., and Wood-Harper, A.T. (2002) *Developing Internet Applications*, Butterworth-Heinemann, Oxford.

23 PEOPLE-ORIENTED METHODOLOGIES

23.1   EFFECTIVE TECHNICAL AND HUMAN IMPLEMENTATION OF COMPUTER-BASED SYSTEMS (ETHICS)

ETHICS is an acronym, but the name of this approach is meant to imply that it is a methodology that embodies an ethical position. ETHICS, devised by Enid Mumford (Mumford, 1995), is a methodology based on the participative approach to information systems development (discussed in Section 7.1). In addition, it encompasses the socio-technical view that for a system to be effective the technology must fit closely with the social and organizational factors.

     The philosophy of ETHICS is thus different from most information system development methodologies and is also explicitly stated, which is also not common in most methodologies. The philosophy is one which has evolved from organizational behaviour and perceives the development of computer systems not as a technical issue but as an organizational issue which is fundamentally concerned with the process of change. It is based on the socio-technical approach of the social sciences as developed by a number of authors, one of the most influential being Davis (1972). Mumford (1983a) defines the **socio-technical approach** as:

> one which recognizes the interaction of technology and people and produces work systems which are both technically efficient and have social characteristics which lead to high job satisfaction.

Elsewhere, in Mumford and Weir (1979), **job satisfaction** is defined as:

> the attainment of a good 'fit' between what the employee is seeking from his work – his job needs, expectations and aspirations – and what he is required to do in his job – the organizational job requirements which mould his experience.

In order to ascertain how good this fit is, a theory for measuring job satisfaction has been developed based on the various views of what is important in job satisfaction and these have been integrated into a framework derived from Parsons and Shils (1951). Five areas of measurement are identified as follows:

1. *The knowledge fit* – a good fit exists when the employees believe that their skills are being adequately used and that their knowledge is being developed to make them increasingly competent. It is recognized that different people have widely different expectations in this area, some wanting their skills developed, others wanting to remain static and opt for an 'easy life'.

2. *The psychological fit* – a job must fit the employee's status, advancement, and work interest (some of the Herzberg, 1966, motivators). These needs are recognized to vary according to age, background, education, and class.

3. *The efficiency fit* – this comprises three areas. First, the effort–reward bargain, which is the amount an employer is prepared to pay (as against the view of the employee about how much he is worth). Although this is probably the prime area of importance to management, it is in practice sometimes way down the list of employee needs. Second, work controls, which may be tight or loose but need to fit the employee's expectations. Third, supervisory controls, such as the necessary back-up facilities, for example, information, materials, specialist knowledge, and supervisory help.

4. *The task-structure fit* – this measures the degree to which the employee's tasks are regarded as being demanding and fulfilling. Particularly important are the number of skills required, the number and nature of targets, plus the feedback mechanism, the identity, distinctiveness, and importance of tasks, and the degree of autonomy and control over the tasks that the employee has. This measure is seen to be strongly related to technology and its method of employment. Technology can affect the task-structure fit substantially and, it is argued, has reduced the fit by simplification and repetitiveness. However, it is also seen as a variable which can be improved dramatically by designing the technical system to meet the requirements of the task-structure fit.

5. *The ethical fit* – this is also described as the social value fit and measures whether the values of the employee match those of the employer organization. In some organizations, performance is everything, while others value other factors, for example, service. Some firms are paternal or welfare-oriented, others aim to achieve the characteristics of 'success', and so on. The better the match of an organization's values with those of the employee, the higher the level of job satisfaction.

A second philosophical strand of the ETHICS methodology is participation. This is the involvement of those affected by a system being part of the decision-making process concerning the design and operation of that system. Those affected by a system include the direct users and also the indirect users, such as management, customers, suppliers, and so on. Of course, there are limits to this. For example, competitors will be affected, but it is unlikely that they will be asked to participate. Participation is important in many methodologies, but has been described as vital in ETHICS (Hirschheim, 1985). In some other methodologies no more than lip service is paid to participation, sometimes being regarded simply as 'allowing the users to choose the colour of the workstations that they use'. In ETHICS, users are involved in the decisions concerning the work process and how the use of technology might improve their job satisfaction.

In ETHICS the development of computer-based systems is seen as a change process and therefore it is likely to involve conflicts of interest between all the participants or actors in that process. These conflicts are not simply between management and worker but often between worker and worker and manager and manager. The successful implementation of new systems is therefore a process of negotiation between the affected and interested parties. Obviously major affected and interested parties include the users themselves, and if these people are left out of the decision-making process, the process of change is unlikely to be a success. This is not just because of resulting disaffection among the user group but, more positively, because they have so much to contribute in making the implementation a success. They are probably the most knowledgeable about the current workplace situation and the future requirements. Mumford (1983a) summarizes:

> All change involves some conflicts of interest. To be resolved, these conflicts need to be recognized, brought out into the open, negotiated and a solution arrived at which largely meets the interests of all the parties in the situation ... successful change strategies require institutional mechanisms which enable all these interests to be represented, and participation provides these.

It is recognized in practice that participation means different things to different people and that the parties involved may have quite different reasons for wanting participation and quite different expectations concerning the benefits. Management may see it as a way of achieving changes that would otherwise be rejected. This is perhaps not the ideal view for management to take but if the resulting participation is real then so be it, although the end result may not exactly turn out as they expect. The point being that it is not a prerequisite for everybody to hold the view that participation is a moral or ideological necessity, enlightened self-interest will do just as well.

The philosophical commitment to participation outlined above begs the question of exactly how it is to be achieved. There appears to be quite a degree of freedom involved, and, although there exist 'ideal' types of participation, in practice a variety of forms are acceptable for it still to be 'ETHICS'. In fact, it can be used by an expert group to design a system for another, non-participating group. However, this is not recommended. Nevertheless, it shows that ETHICS is a methodology which has quite a level of flexibility. It is better, Mumford argues, to use it in some form, rather than not at all. The implication being that its use, even stripped of some of its most important participatory trappings, is better than other more traditional methods which concentrate purely on technical and economic objectives.

Mumford distinguishes between structure, content, and process. Structure is the mechanism of participation which, as discussed in Section 7.1, can be consultative, representative, or consensus. Consultative participation involves the participants giving evidence to the decision makers which, possibly, will influence the decision makers but does not bind them in any way. This is the weakest form of participation and not recommended for detailed design. Representative participation is a structure where selected or, preferably, elected representatives of the various interests are involved in the decision-making process. This is most appropriate for the tactical or middle management-type of decision making. In computing terms, this might be at the system definition stage where the system outline and boundaries are discussed and a fairly wide spectrum of interests are involved. The third form of participation is consensus, where all the constituents are involved in the decision making. This is most suitable at the detailed design stage where the decisions probably affect the day-to-day work practices of the people involved. Clearly it is difficult to involve everybody in everything, and what usually happens is that design groups are formed to do the work and present alternatives to the whole constituency, which takes the final decisions.

The content of participation concerns the issues and the boundaries of activities that are within the remit of participation. Generally, prior to any participation, management will want to keep certain things as their own prerogative. One objective of the process of participation is the gaining of relevant knowledge and information by the participants. In general, the users involved in participation will not have previously had the necessary knowledge, information, and, perhaps, confidence to discuss issues and make decisions. Without this, participation is only of a very limited kind. The users must have as much information and knowledge as is necessary to make informed decisions, or at least as much as anyone else. Without the acquisition of this information and knowledge they will be at a disadvantage and subject to undue influence from more powerful groups. True participation means equal knowledge and thus, it might be argued, equal power for all groups. Training and education of users is therefore a very important aspect of ETHICS.

Participation usually involves the setting up of a steering committee and a design group or groups. The steering committee sets the guidelines for the design group and consists of senior managers from the affected areas of the organization, senior managers from management services and personnel, and trade union officials (if the organization is unionized). It is recommended that the steering committee and the design group meet once a month during the course of the project. The design group designs the new system including:

- choice of hardware and software;
- human–computer interaction;
- workplace reorganization;
- allocation of responsibilities.

All major interests should be represented, including each section and function, grade, age group, and so on. The design group includes systems analysts, although their role is not the normal one of analyst and designer, but one of educator and adviser. This often involves the analysts in a learning process themselves. If the area of the design is large, involving many departments or sections, then a design group may first design in outline and then hand over to detailed design groups. A participative design requires the appointment of a facilitator to help the design group manage the project and educate the group in the use of ETHICS. The role is multifaceted and concerns motivation and confidence-building of the design group; it is not one of decision making or persuading. For this reason, the facilitator must be neutral and preferably external, if not to the organization, then to the department. The role is very important. In one situation that Mumford quotes, the facilitator withdrew, and the confidence of the design group declined and the importance of the group in the eyes of the management also declined. ETHICS has 15 steps (Mumford, 1986) as follows (unless stated otherwise, the work in the steps that follow are performed by the design group).

1 Why change?

The first meeting of the design group considers this rather fundamental question and addresses the current problems and opportunities. The result should be a convincing statement of the need for change. Presumably, if no convincing statement for change is arrived at, the process stops there, although this is not made explicit.

2 System boundaries

The design group identifies the boundaries of the system it is designing and where it interfaces with other systems. Four areas are considered: business activities affected (e.g. sales, finance, and personnel); existing technology affected; parts of the organization affected (e.g. departments and sections); and parts of the organization's environment affected (e.g. suppliers and customers).

3 Description of existing system

This is to educate the design group as to how the existing system works. In practice, it is found that people will know the detail of their own jobs and those that they interact with directly, but will probably have little knowledge of the whole system. In this step, two activities are undertaken. First, a horizontal input/output analysis is described with inputs on the left, activities in the middle, and outputs on the right. Second, a vertical analysis of the design area activities is made at five different levels. The lowest level is of the operating activities, that is, the necessary activities of a day-to-day nature. These should have appeared in the horizontal analysis. The problem prevention/solution activities are also identified. These are the key problems or variances that occur and how they are corrected. Third, the co-ordination activities are identified. These are activities that have to be performed together or in a particular sequence or at a particular time. These are both interdepartmental and intradepartmental co-ordinations. Fourth, the development activities are recorded. These are the things or areas that need improving. Fifth, the control activities are identified, indicating how the system is controlled, how it is judged to be meeting targets or objectives, and how it is monitored.

4, 5 and 6 Definition of key objectives and tasks

Three questions are asked in order to help define the key objectives. First, why do particular areas exist, what is their role, and what is their purpose? Second, given this, what should be their responsibilities and functions? Third, how far do their present activities match what they should be doing? From this, the key objectives can be listed and these form the design objectives of the new system. In addition, the key tasks that need to be performed to achieve the key objectives are defined in outline, along with their key information needs.

7   Diagnosis of efficiency needs

Weak links in the existing system are identified and documented. Mumford talks about them as variances, which is a 'tendency for a system or subsystem to deviate from some desired or expected norm or standard' (Mumford, 1983a). Mumford identifies two types of variance. First, systemic or key types, which are inherent in the system and cannot be completely overcome. They can only be eased. An example is provided by the variances connected with the *financial desire* to keep stocks small and the *service desire* to be able to supply customers with what they want. The second type of variance is operational. These are variances due to poor design or lack of attention to changing circumstances and can usually be completely eliminated in the new system. Examples could include bottlenecks, insufficient information, and inadequate equipment.

8   Diagnosis of job satisfaction needs

This step measures the job satisfaction needs. This is achieved by use of a standard questionnaire provided in the ETHICS methodology. The design group may alter the questionnaire to fit their organization and requirements. The results are discussed democratically and the underlying reasons established for any areas where there are poor job satisfaction fits. In addition, formulations for improving the situation in the new design are made, and everybody is encouraged to play a major part in this design work. Where there have been knowledge or task-structure problems of fit, these are susceptible to improvement by a redesign of the system. Other areas of poor fit, such as effort–reward or ethical, may be improved somewhat in this way, but will probably require changes in personnel policies, or more radically, organizational ethos.

9   Future analysis

The new system design needs to be both a better version of the existing system and able to cope with future changes that may occur in the environment, technology, organization, or fashion. Therefore, an attempt is made to try and identify these changes and to build a certain amount of flexibility into the new system. This may involve the design group in interactions with people outside the organization in order to identify and assess some of the potential changes.

10   Specifying and weighting efficiency and job satisfaction needs and objectives

Mumford identifies this as the key step in the whole methodology. Objectives are set according to the diagnosis activities of the three previous steps. The achievement of an agreed and ranked set of objectives can be a very difficult task and must involve everyone, not just the design group itself. Often objectives conflict and the priorities of the various constituencies may be very different. These differences may not all be resolved, but one of the stated benefits of ETHICS is that at least these differences are aired. Ultimately, a list of priority and secondary objectives is produced. The criterion for the systems design is that all priority objectives must be met along with as many of the secondary ones as possible. At this stage a certain amount of iteration is recommended, to review the key objectives and tasks from Steps 4 and 5.

11   The organizational design of the new system

If possible, this should be performed in parallel with the technical design of Step 12, because they inevitably intertwine. The organizational changes which are needed to meet the efficiency and job satisfaction objectives are specified. There are likely to be a variety of ways of achieving the objectives, and between three and six organizational options should be elaborated. The design group specifies in more detail the key tasks of Step 5 and addresses the following questions, the answers forming the basic data for the organizational design process:

- What are the operating activities that are required?
- What are the problem prevention/solution activities that are required?
- What are the co-ordination activities that are required?
- What are the development activities that are required?
- What are the control activities that are required?
- What special skills are required, if any, of the staff?
- Are there any key roles or relationships that exist that must be addressed in the new design?

Each organizational option is rated for its ability to meet the primary and secondary objectives of Step 10, and should identify the sections, subsections, work groups, individuals, their responsibilities, and tasks. In order to meet the job satisfaction objectives, it is almost inevitable that the design group will have to consider the socio-technical principles of organizational design and be provided with information and experience in relation to design. The socio-technical approach is the antithesis of Taylorism (Taylor, 1947) which is to break each job down into its elemental parts and rearrange it into an efficient combination. The traditional car assembly line which requires its operators to perform small, routine, repetitive jobs, is regarded as the ultimate example of Taylorism in action. The requirements of the machine are given priority over the requirements of the human being. This has, it is argued, inevitably led to a bored, disaffected, and ultimately inefficient workforce.

    Although ETHICS uses aspects of socio-technical design, the socio-technical school assumes a given technology, whereas, in ETHICS, the technology is part of the design. Further, they assume shop-floor situations, rather than the office and high-level organizational situations which concern ETHICS.

    Mumford recommends the consideration of three types of work organization pattern. The first is task variety, and involves giving an individual more variety in work by providing more than one task to be performed or by rotating people around a number of different tasks. This is the more traditional approach, but is limited especially where the expectations of job satisfaction are more sophisticated. In this case, the principles of job enrichment might be appropriate. This is where the work is organized in such a way that a number of different skills, including judgemental ones, are introduced. In particular, it involves the handling of problems and the organization of the work by the individual without supervision. This may require an increased skill level on behalf of the individual, but leads to enhanced job satisfaction. A further stage in job enrichment is the incorporation of development aspects into a job. This means that the individual has the freedom to change the way the job is performed. This leads to constant review and the implementation of new ideas and methods. Obviously this cannot be introduced into every job, but there are probably more opportunities than at first imagined.

As important as individual jobs is the concept of what Mumford calls self-managing groups. Here, groups are formed that have responsibility for a relatively wide spectrum of the tasks to be performed. These groups are preferably multi-skilled, so that each member is competent to carry out all the tasks required of the group. They are encouraged to organize themselves, their work, and their own control and monitoring, which may include their own target setting. This can provide a very stimulating and satisfying work environment for the group members. Again, self-managing groups are not always possible and require a good deal of management goodwill at first, but nevertheless can prove very effective.

12   Technical options

The various technical options that might be appropriate, including hardware, software, and the design of the human–computer interface, are specified. Each option is evaluated in the same way as the organizational options, that is, against efficiency, job satisfaction, and future change objectives. As mentioned in Step 11, the organizational and technical options should be considered simultaneously, as often one option implies certain necessary factors in the other. It is advised that one option should exist which specifies no change in technology, so as to be able to see how much could be achieved simply with organizational changes.

The organizational and technical options are now merged to ensure compatibility and are evaluated against the primary objectives and the one that best meets the objectives is selected. This selection is performed by the design group with input from the steering committee and other interested constituencies.

13   The preparation of a detailed work design

The selected system is now designed in detail. The data flows, tasks, groups, individuals, responsibilities, and relationships are defined. There is also a review to ensure that the detail of the design still meets the specified objectives. Obviously, the design detail includes the organizational aspects as well as the technical.

14 **Implementation**

The design group now applies itself to ensuring the successful implementation of the design. This involves planning the implementation process in detail. This will include the strategy, the education and training, the co-ordination of parts, and everything needed to ensure a smooth changeover.

15 **Evaluation**

The implemented system is checked to ensure that it is meeting its objectives, particularly in relation to efficiency and job satisfaction, using the techniques of variance analysis and measures of job satisfaction. If it is not meeting the objectives, then corrective action is taken. Indeed, as time progresses, changes will become necessary and design becomes a cyclical process.

Quite a common reaction to ETHICS is for people to say that it is impractical. First, it is argued that unskilled users cannot do the design properly, and, second, that management would never accept it, or that it removes the right to manage from managers. In answer to the first problem Mumford argues that users can, and do, design properly. They need some training and help along the way, but this can be relatively easily provided. More importantly, they have the skills of knowing about their own work and system, and have a stake in the design. This is much more than many traditional analysts and designers. To answer the second point, managers have often welcomed participation and can be convinced of its benefits. There are many success stories. It is not always the management that needs to be convinced, sometimes it is the users who are sceptical about participation, seeing it as some sort of management trick. The job of a manager is to meet the corporate objectives, not simply oversee people and make every last decision. This is often counterproductive to achieving those objectives, often resulting in very high staff turnover rates, which is not productive.

Mumford admits that it is not easy, quite the reverse, but the benefits are, she claims, worth it. Mumford shows how users can design their own systems and how they come to terms with their design roles, illustrated by experiences. For example, a group of secretaries at Imperial Chemical Industries (ICI) in the UK designed new work systems for themselves in the wake of the introduction of word processing systems, and a group of purchase invoice clerks helped design a major online finance system. One of the most interesting aspects, and most telling concerning the power of ETHICS, is the fact that the clerks designed three different ways of working with the computer system to do essentially the same thing. The one used depends on the clerk. Few professional systems design teams would design a number of alternative ways to achieve the same task.

ETHICS has also been used by a number of large companies to assist the building of very large systems. One of the first major uses of ETHICS in the development of a large system was Digital Equipment Corporation's XSEL, an expert system for their sales offices which helped to configure DEC hardware systems for particular customers.

In some situations it has become a method of requirements analysis in particular, and a version has been defined which is referred to as **QUICKETHICS** (QUality

Information from Considered Knowledge). In order to create and maintain managers' interest, it can be organized as a drama having four 'acts':

- self-reflection;
- self-identification;
- group discussion;
- group decision.

In this approach, each manager describes his or her work role and relationships, along with information needs ranked as 'essential', 'desirable', and 'useful' on an individual basis. This provides an opportunity for self-reflection. Meeting then as a group, each manager gives a short description of his or her mission, key tasks, critical success factors, and major problems. This provides an opportunity for self-identification and encourages questions and discussion. Then managers may write the essential information needs on cards placed on a magnetic board explaining the reasons for their importance. This provokes group discussion because it soon becomes apparent that managers have many overlapping needs. These common needs can be agreed as forming a 'core' module of the proposed information system, delivering essential information needs in the group decision process. Once this is implemented, 'desirable' needs can guide future development. The requirements analysis phase may only involve two days of management's time. ETHICS has changed over time, as for all information systems development methodologies, but the importance of user involvement and participation in systems design has endured the process of change.

23.2 KADS

In this section we examine a formalized approach to expert systems development known as KADS (Wielinga et al., 1993; De Greef and Breuker, 1992) which had its origins as a European Union ESPRIT research project, with partners from commercial companies and universities. There is also a development of KADS known as CommonKADS. We will first look at KADS and then CommonKADS.

KADS adopts the view that developing an expert system is a modelling activity and that it is not the case that the system has to be filled only with knowledge extracted from a human expert. It is rather a computational model of desired behaviour, which may also reflect aspects of the behaviour of an expert. It is not the functional and behavioural equivalent of an expert; the system may actually do things in different ways and utilize different approaches to human experts.

Figure 23.1 illustrates the various models that are constructed in KADS. It also shows the relationships between the models in the sense that information in a higher level model is used in the construction of the lower level model. The model does not necessarily imply that the sequence has to be followed in the linear top-down fashion that the diagram suggests; in fact, KADS advocates a spiral approach rather than a waterfall life cycle. The spiral model (Section 6.2) has been adapted for KADS and is illustrated in Figure 23.2. It begins in the centre with the process circling around with each pass adding a degree of functionality or progress, and only when a number of circles

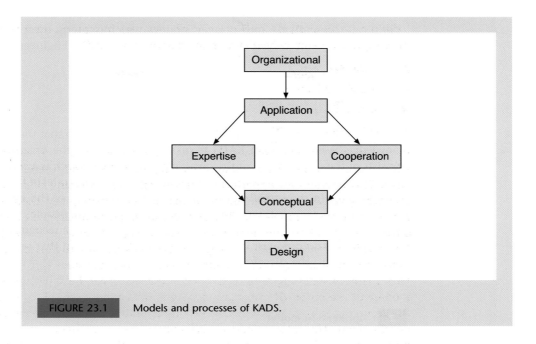

FIGURE 23.1   Models and processes of KADS.

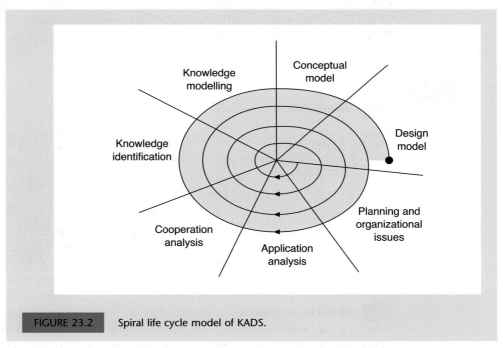

FIGURE 23.2   Spiral life cycle model of KADS.

have been made is the process complete. The breakdown or decomposition of the process into the development of these different models is the way that KADS attempts to address the complexity of expert systems. A model is an abstraction that eliminates certain detail but concentrates on certain key features of the area being modelled. Wielinga et al.

(1993) call this a 'divide and conquer' strategy which is a term used by James Martin in describing the same concept in the context of Information Engineering (Section 20.3).

1   Organizational model

The first step of KADS is concerned with defining the problem that the expert systems (or knowledge-based system in KADS terms) is addressing in the organization. This step consists of the construction of the organizational model, which is a socio-organizational analysis of the environment. This is essentially a high-level model of the functions, tasks, and problems in the organization, including an assessment of the effects of the introduction of the expert system on the organization and the people. Unfortunately, the form that this model takes is not specified in detail, but it is a recognition by KADS that expert systems do not exist in an organizational vacuum and that organizational issues are important to the success of expert systems.

2   Application model

Next an application model is constructed which narrows the focus from the organization to the area of application and defines what problem the system is going to solve, and the overall function and purpose of the system. Again, we are not told the detail of this stage nor the exact form of the model.

3   Task model

The next stage is to develop the task model which decomposes the overall function of the system described in the application model into a series of tasks and subtasks that the system will perform. Each task is defined by the information input to the task and the goal that is achieved by the task. These are known as input/output specifications. The tasks are then assigned to agents which might be the expert system, the user, or some other system. This will depend on what or who could best perform each task. Finally, any constraints or specific requirements for the tasks are defined; for example, that the output of the task must be in the terminology of a particular type of user.

4   Model of co-operation

The next step is to define the model of expertise and the model of co-operation. The model of co-operation is the definition of how the system and the user will work together at the task level and interact when using the system in various modes, for example, in solving a problem, seeking advice, or requesting an explanation. This is an important stage because in practice the execution of an expert system usually requires a complex set of interfaces and interactions between users or groups of users and the system. This is typically more complex than that for a traditional information system.

5 Model of expertise

Next the model of expertise is developed. This is the key task in the methodology, and the model of expertise is effectively the functional specification of the problem-solving part of the expert system. Unlike many expert systems approaches, this model is a specification of the desired behaviour and the types of knowledge involved, rather than the specification of detailed rules.

In KADS, a process of knowledge identification is undertaken as a preparation phase before construction of the model of expertise. This is a kind of systems investigation of the area of concern prior to the building of the model. Data is collected and tasks identified using a variety of techniques, for example, structured interviews, rational task analysis, workflow analysis, and repertory grid analysis. A glossary and lexicon of terms are also developed to help understand and document the area of concern prior to any formal conceptualization of knowledge. After this, a knowledge-modelling phase is undertaken, which involves the identification and definition of four types or layers of knowledge. Some typical techniques and representations that might be used in this process are tree diagrams, decision trees, laddering, data modelling diagrams, think-aloud protocols, and scenario simulation. KADS suggests that a prototype of the problem-solving aspect of the system can be implemented as a way of validating the requirements and the knowledge models.

The first type of knowledge identified is the **domain knowledge** which involves the identification of concepts, properties, relationships between concepts, and relationships between properties and structures. Concepts are things or objects in the knowledge domain. For example, in the domain of credit rating for loans in a banking application, a concept might be customer, account, or application. In practice, these concepts should be as low level or elementary as possible. A property is an attribute of a concept; for example, a customer might be active or passive, or an application significant or not. Relationships between concepts are identified. For example, an applicant is a customer. Causal relationships between property expressions are also identified; for example, a customer with a transaction in the last year causes customer to be active or a value over a certain amount causes the application to be significant. Structures are also identified, and this is a way of breaking complex objects down into more manageable components. In practice, an account might be broken down into current or deposit, and deposit into short-term and long-term, open or closed, and so on. The examples used are illustrative and would in practice be at more elementary levels.

The second type of knowledge defined is **inference knowledge**. Inference knowledge is that which uses the domain knowledge to infer or produce additional information. KADS advocates the separation of domain knowledge from inference knowledge as a matter of philosophy, on the basis that it allows multiple use of the same domain knowledge. Inference knowledge is identified in the form of 'knowledge sources'. These are the processes that generate elementary pieces of information using domain information. For example, within a specific domain, the process by which a particular piece of information is compared to another piece of information, in order to see if they are similar, might be a knowledge source, or, in terms of our earlier example, the action or reasoning in the rejection of a loan application might be an inference knowledge source. Knowledge sources use domain knowledge, but the process is defined as independently as possible of the information in the knowledge domain and in principle could be applied to a variety of different situations. An extension of this idea is the generation of 'interpretation models' of typical inference knowledge for a particular task, which might be reused in a different domain. For example, a credit assessment interpretation model might form a template in the alternative domain of assessment for tenancy agreements. Such interpretation models would guide the knowledge engineer by providing a template for knowledge acquisition in the new domain and perhaps also save significant development time.

The third type of knowledge is **task knowledge** which is information about how the elementary knowledge sources can be combined to achieve a particular higher level objective. These higher level processes are called tasks; for example, the combination of various knowledge elements might be the definition of the task of verification of a hypothesis. The tasks are decomposed into a number of subtasks which may be inference tasks, problem-solving tasks, or transfer tasks. A transfer task is one that requires interaction with an external agent. The structure of the subtasks and the control dependencies are described using structured English (Section 12.4). Due to the independence of the knowledge sources from the domain knowledge, the task knowledge is also independent and may be thought of as representing fixed strategies for achieving problem-solving goals.

The fourth category of knowledge is **strategic knowledge** which identifies the strategies, goals, high-level rules, and tasks that are relevant to the solution of a particular problem. Although the need for strategic knowledge is identified in KADS, little work has been done on the definition of such knowledge, and Wielinga et al. (1993) concede that most systems developed with KADS have identified little or no knowledge of this type.

The description of the categories of knowledge relevant to KADS is described in what information systems people might feel is a bottom-up way and that it might be better if a top-down view were adopted. Figure 23.3 provides this architecture, showing the four levels and their interactions.

1   Conceptual model

The conceptual model is the combination of the model of co-operation and the model of expertise, and together this provides an application-independent specification of the system to be built.

2   Design model

The design model introduces the computational and representational techniques into the conceptual model. For example, the constraints of the hardware, software, and the

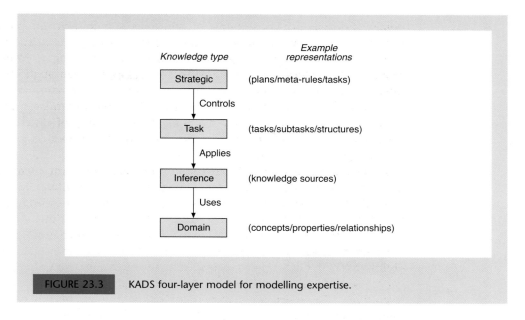

Knowledge type

Example representations

Strategic — (plans/meta-rules/tasks)

Controls

Task — (tasks/subtasks/structures)

Applies

Inference — (knowledge sources)

Uses

Domain — (concepts/properties/relationships)

FIGURE 23.3   KADS four-layer model for modelling expertise.

external world are now defined for the purposes of implementation. This is similar to the separation of the logical and physical models familiar in much information systems development but has not usually been present in approaches to expert systems development. However, the transformation from the conceptual model to the design model is by no means automatic or indeed well defined. In principle, the designer in KADS is free to proceed in whatever way is thought best providing the conceptual specification is achieved. A completely independent approach can cause problems because it is then difficult to provide explanations of the systems reasoning in domain and conceptual language terms, unless there exist some clear linkages. KADS makes a few recommendations, but the process is essentially still in development and the subject of research. For inference knowledge, a computational technique that can realize the inferences needs to be selected. This requires elements that support (a) algorithms, (b) input–output data structures, and (c) a representation of domain knowledge (usually via production rules, as described in Section 7.3). For domain knowledge, a database is required that supports all the domain knowledge elements, for example, concepts, properties, and relationships. Most conventional databases are not adequate in this respect. For task knowledge, a control technique for executing tasks is required, which might be a blackboard (Section 7.3) or even a simple procedure hierarchy. For strategic knowledge, a production system that handles meta-rules is suggested.

As can be seen KADS is a little different to other methodologies as it focuses on principles and models rather than the processes, phases, steps, and tasks that need to be followed and undertaken.

23.3   COMMONKADS

KADS (above) relates essentially to the development of expert systems whereas CommonKADS relates to the wider domain of knowledge management. As we saw in

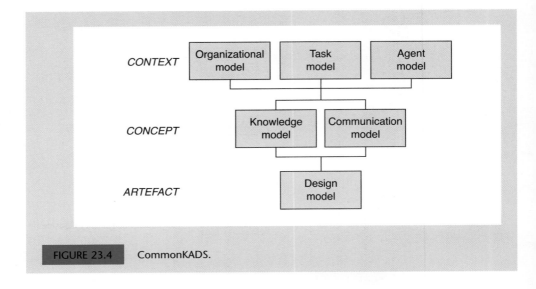

FIGURE 23.4 CommonKADS.

Section 7.4 knowledge management is about levering knowledge as an important organizational resource. We have referred to information systems development greatly in this book, yet knowledge, that is, the ability to use information in action for a particular purpose, is even more important than information, which is much more commonplace. In this description of CommonKADS, we use the text of Schreiber et al. (2000) and the website http:/www.commonkads.uva.nl as our major source. Along with KADS itself, its design has been influenced by soft systems methodology (Section 24.1) and the organizational learning literature, for example, Argyris (1993).

In this description, we will discuss in particular areas of divergence with KADS (Section 23.2). Figure 23.4 shows the general approach of CommonKADS from context, through concept, to artefact. Within this structure, there are six models:

1 Context

- *Organization model.* This concerns a review of potential knowledge-based solutions and comes from organizational analysis, which discovers problems, opportunities, and potential solutions for knowledge systems, establishes their feasibility, and assesses the organizational impacts.

- *Task model.* A task forms part of a business process. The task model analyses the global task layout, its inputs and outputs, needed resources (including agents) and competences, goals, preconditions, and performance criteria.

- *Agent model.* Agents carry out a task, be they human, information systems, knowledge, or culture/power related, or a combination of these. The agent model describes the characteristics of agents – competences, authority to act, and constraints.

2 Concept

■ *Knowledge model.* The knowledge model details the types, roles, and structures of the knowledge used in a task, and the reasoning requirements of the prospective system.

■ *Communication model.* This model defines the various needs and desires of the agents and the dialogue exchanges with other agents involved. The key aspect concerns the knowledge transfer between agents.

3 Artefact

■ *Design model.* The above models together constitute the requirements specification for the knowledge system, and these are translated into a technical system solution. Therefore, a specification for the information system, including the software components (software architecture, algorithm design, data structure design, and hardware), is made here based on the knowledge and communication models.

Knowledge is modelled using a variant of the UML class diagram (Section 13.2). Modifications are necessary, as UML is not designed to model inferences and tasks, a requirement in CommonKADS. Modelling in this approach has also been influenced by Yourdon, from the structured analysis school, as well as object modelling. The authors argue that they 'take a middle line between data and process modeling'.

There are three stages in the process of knowledge-model construction: knowledge identification, knowledge specification, and knowledge refinement:

1 *Knowledge identification.* At this stage, information sources that are useful for knowledge modelling are identified. Existing model components such as task templates and domain schemas are identified, and reusable components are also identified. Knowledge identification may start with a description of knowledge items in the organization model and the characterization of the application task in the task.

2 *Knowledge specification.* At this stage the specification of the knowledge model is carried out. A task template is chosen and an initial domain model is constructed to which further detail is added. The inference knowledge, domain knowledge, and task knowledge are identified.

3 *Knowledge refinement.* In the final stage, the knowledge model is validated and the knowledge bases completed. A technique used at this stage is the simulation of the scenarios gathered during knowledge identification. This should ensure that the knowledge model can generate the problem-solving behaviour required.

As for the CommonKADS approach as a whole, Schreiber et al. (2000) provide a detailed explanation of this aspect of the methodology. For example, for each of these stages, it lists a number of activities to be carried out at the stage and guidelines to help carry out these activities. Support is also provided on how to ascertain the knowledge of the experts in knowledge elicitation. These techniques include interviewing, protocol analysis (analysing how the expert solves problems), and repertory grids.

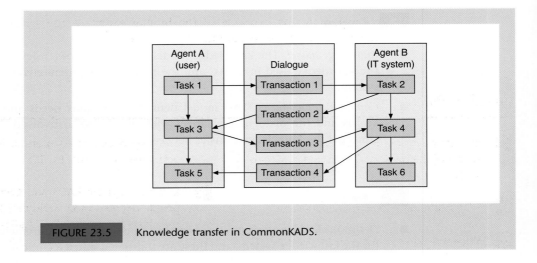

FIGURE 23.5 Knowledge transfer in CommonKADS.

We have stated that the key aspect of the communication concerns the knowledge transfer between agents. This is illustrated in the dialogue diagram shown as Figure 23.5, which shows the overall information flow.

The design modelling stage includes design of the system architecture, choice of implementation (hardware and software) platform, specification of the architectural components, and the applications. In effect, it converts the requirements into the design of an information system. Quality criteria for the design are seen as code reuse, maintainability, adaptability, explanation, and support for knowledge elicitation. The last two are stressed in knowledge systems (and expert systems – see KADS in the previous section): the ability of the system to explain the rationale behind a reasoning process and support for obtaining knowledge from the knowledge workers. The approach authors see object orientation as the prevailing modelling approach and particularly suitable to these applications. Prototyping is suggested to form the basis for the reasoning system as well as develop the user interface aspects.

These are perhaps early days in the establishment of an accepted methodology for the development of knowledge management systems. However, CommonKADS, being based on KADS and the related knowledge-based expert systems applications, offers potential in supporting knowledge management systems development. The influence of its expert systems/knowledge engineering inheritance is, however, marked.

An alternative approach, perhaps more managerial in philosophy which puts knowledge management more in its organizational and environmental perspective, is given by Tiwana (2000).

23.4 SUMMARY

- In this chapter we have described three methodologies that we have classified as people-oriented. ETHICS uses the tenets of participation and the socio-technical approach for information systems development. KADS and CommonKADS attempt to incorporate the expertise of the human expert in the system and manage knowledge for the organization.

QUESTIONS

1 In what ways does ETHICS correspond to the tenets of the participative approach (Section 7.1)?

2 Why is the name of ETHICS significant?

3 What is meant by a socio-technical approach, and why does it not feature in most methodologies other than ETHICS?

4 In what ways are KADS and CommonKADS people-oriented methodologies? How might they have been otherwise classified?

23.5 FURTHER READING

Mumford, E. (1995) *Effective Requirements Analysis and Systems Design: The ETHICS Method*, Macmillan, Basingstoke, UK.

Schreiber, G., Akkermans, H., Anjewierden, A., de Hoog, R., Shadbolt, N., Van de Velde, W., and Wielinga, B.J. (2000) *Knowledge Engineering and Management: The CommonKADS Methodology*, MIT Press, Cambridge, Massachusetts.

Wielinga, B.J., Sterner, Th. A., and Breuker, J.A. (1993) KADS: A modelling approach to knowledge engineering, in B.G. Buchanan and D.C. Wilkins (eds) *Readings in Knowledge Acquisition and Learning, Automating the Construction and Improvement of Expert Systems*, Morgan Kaufmann, San Mateo, California.

24 ORGANIZATIONAL-ORIENTED METHODOLOGIES

SOFT SYSTEMS METHODOLOGY (SSM)

As discussed in Section 4.1, general systems theory attempts to understand the nature of systems. Scientific analysis breaks up a complex situation into its constituent parts for analysis. Although this works in the physical sciences, it is less successful in the social sciences and in management science. One tenet of systems thinking is that the whole is greater than the sum of the parts: properties of the whole are not explicable entirely in terms of the properties of its constituent elements. Human activity systems are complex and the human components, in particular, may react differently when examined singly as when they play a role in the whole system. Something is lost when the whole is broken up in the 'reductionist' approach of scientific analysis.

The systems principle also implies that we must try to develop application systems for the organization as a whole rather than for functions in isolation. It may take only a few hours by Concorde to cross the Atlantic, but this progress is partly lost if it takes as many hours to get from home to Heathrow Airport and from JFK Airport to the hotel in New York along with the requirement to be at the airport two hours before the flight. It is the transport system we should be looking at, not the airline system in isolation. Further, organizations are '**open systems**' and therefore the relationship between the organization and its environment is important. We should always be looking at 'the system' in terms of the wider system of which it is part.

Systems theory would also suggest that a multidisciplinary team of analysts is much more likely to understand the organization and suggest better solutions to problems. After all, specialisms are a result of artificial and arbitrary divisions. In the information systems context, a systems approach should prevent an automatic assumption that computer solutions are always appropriate. It will also help in problem situations which have been studied from only one narrow point of view. Such an approach is not appropriate in the study of large and complex problem situations.

Checkland (1981) has attempted to adapt systems theory into a practical methodology. By methodology he means the study of methods to achieve certain purposes. 'For any particular problem situation, the study will lead to a subset of principles which can be applied for that particular situation.' He argues that systems analysts apply their craft to problems which are not well defined. These 'fuzzy', ill-structured or soft problem situations, usually also complex, are common in organizations. The description of one category of systems, **human activity systems**, also acknowledges the importance of people in organizations. It is relatively easy, it is argued, to model data and processes (the emphasis placed in many of the preceding methodologies discussed), but to understand the real world it is essential to include people in the model, people who may have different and conflicting objectives, perceptions, and attitudes. This is difficult because of the unpredictable nature of human activity systems. There is no such thing as a repeatable experiment in this context. The claims for the soft systems approach are that a true understanding of complex problem situations is more likely using this approach than if the more simplistic structured or data-oriented approaches are used, which address mainly the formal or 'hard' aspects of systems.

Wilson (1990) gives an analogy. He considers two examples of problems. The first is a flat tyre. The solution is clear. The second is 'What should the UK government do about Northern Ireland?' (a more recent example might be 'What should the United Nations do about the Middle East?'). The solution to these problems are not clear, and it would be difficult to find any solutions that satisfied all the interested parties. Wilson suggests that hard methodologies, that may be suitable for solving 'burst tyre-type problems', are inappropriate for organizational problem situations. It is not only a question of techniques and tools, but also culture, concepts and language.

Another difference between hard and soft systems thinking is that in hard systems thinking a goal is assumed. The purpose of the methods used by the analyst (or engineer) is to modify the system in some way so that this goal is achieved in the most efficient manner. Hard systems thinking is concerned with the 'how' of the problem. In soft systems thinking, the objectives of the system are assumed to be more complex than a simple goal that can be achieved and measured. Systems are argued to have purposes or missions rather than goals. Understanding is achieved in soft systems methods through debate with the actors in the system. Emphasis is placed on the 'what' as well as the 'how' of the system. The term 'problem' in this context is also inappropriate. There will be lots of problems, hence the term **'problem situation'** – 'a situation in which there are perceived to be problems' (Wilson, 1990).

The methodology of Checkland has been developed at Lancaster University. It was developed through **'action research'** whereby the systems ideas are tested out in client organizations. The analysts neither dictate the way the action develops nor step outside as observers: they are participants in the action and results are unpredictable. The practical work provides experience which can be used to draw conclusions and to modify these ideas. This proves to be a successful approach, because, as we have said, it is not possible to develop a good 'laboratory model' of human activity systems and set up repeatable experiments.

Each action research project therefore furthers knowledge which can be used in future soft systems work, and provides some benefits in a particular problem situation. Change is therefore achieved through the learning process as theory and practice meet and affect each other. Checkland's book is aptly titled *Systems Thinking, Systems Practice*!

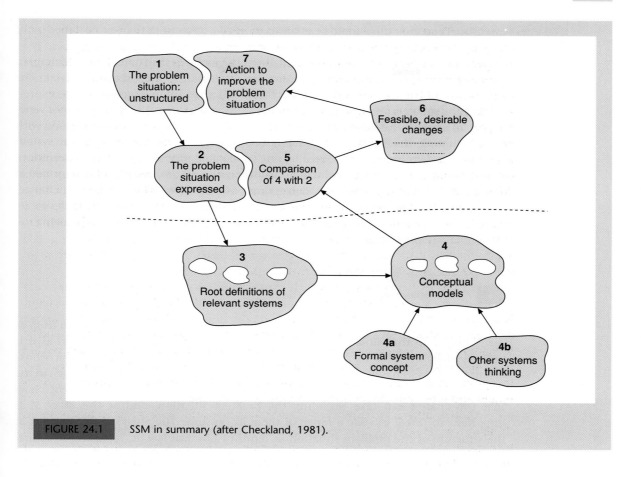

FIGURE 24.1   SSM in summary (after Checkland, 1981).

Checkland has carried out extensive studies, both theoretical and practical, on the analysis of organizations in his action research projects. The central focus of the methodology is the search for a particular view (or views). This *Weltanschauung* (assumptions or world view) will form the basis for describing the systems requirements and will be carried forward to further stages in the methodology. The world view is extracted from the problem situation through debate on the main purpose of the organization concerned – its *raison d'être*, its attitudes, its 'personality', and so on. Examples of world view might be: 'This is a business aimed at maximizing long-term profits' or 'This is a hospital dedicated to maintaining the highest standards of patient care'.

The original version of soft systems methodology is given in Checkland (1981). We will outline this version (Mode 1) below. This will be followed by a brief outline of the changes made to the approach (Mode 2) as found in Checkland and Scholes (1990).

Figure 24.1 shows the seven stages of SSM. Stages above the dotted line are 'real-world' activities involving people in the problem situation, whereas stages below the dotted line are activities concerned with thinking about the problem situation. Checkland argues that this is a logical sequence for description purposes, but that it is possible to start a project at a place other than at Point 1. Further, the analyst is likely to be working on a number of stages simultaneously, and backtracking and iteration are essential. Therefore, this should be taken as more of a framework than as a detailed set of prescriptions which must be followed.

Stages 1 and 2 are about finding out about the problem situation. This unstructured view gives some basic information from the views of the individuals involved. The application of the CATWOE criteria (Section 10.2) gives some structure to the expressions of the problem situations, and in Stage 3 the analyst selects from these those views which he or she considers gives insight to the problem situation. Stage 4 is to do with model building, that is, what the systems analyst might *do* (as against what the system *is* – the root definition). There must be one conceptual model for each root definition. Stage 5 compares the conceptual models from Stage 4 and the root definitions formed at Stage 2. This comparison process leads to a set of recommendations regarding change, and Stage 6 analyses these recommendations in terms of what is feasible and desirable. Stage 7, the final phase, suggests actions to improve the problem situation, following the recommendations of Stage 5.

1   The problem situation: unstructured

The first two stages are concerned with finding out about the problem situation from as many people in that situation as possible. There will be many different views as it is unlikely that the views of the problem owner, that is, the person or group on whose behalf the analysis has been commissioned, the other people taking part as 'actors' in the problem situation and other stakeholders, will coincide. There will be different views that the analyst can take regarding the problem situation, and at this stage it is important to reveal as wide a range of them as possible. The analyst will also look at the structure of the problem situation in terms of physical layout, reporting structure, and formal and informal communication patterns. These activities carried out in the problem situation are also studied along with how these activities are controlled. The 'climate' of the situation, that is, the relationship between structure and process can also be very revealing.

2   The problem situation: expressed

Given the informal picture of the problem situation gathered in Stage 1, it is feasible to attempt to express it in some more formal way. Checkland does not prescribe a method of doing this, but he and many users of the approach tend to draw rich picture diagrams of the situation (Section 10.1).

The rich picture is used as an aid in discussion between the problem solver and the problem owner, or may simply help the problem solver better understand the problem situation. This stage is concerned with finding out about the problem situation.

The rich picture can be used as a communication technique between the analysts and the users of the system, and therefore uses the terminology of the environment. It will usually show the people involved, problem areas, controlling bodies, and sources of conflict. From the rich picture, the problem solver extracts problem themes – things noticed in the picture that are, or may be, causing problems. The picture may show

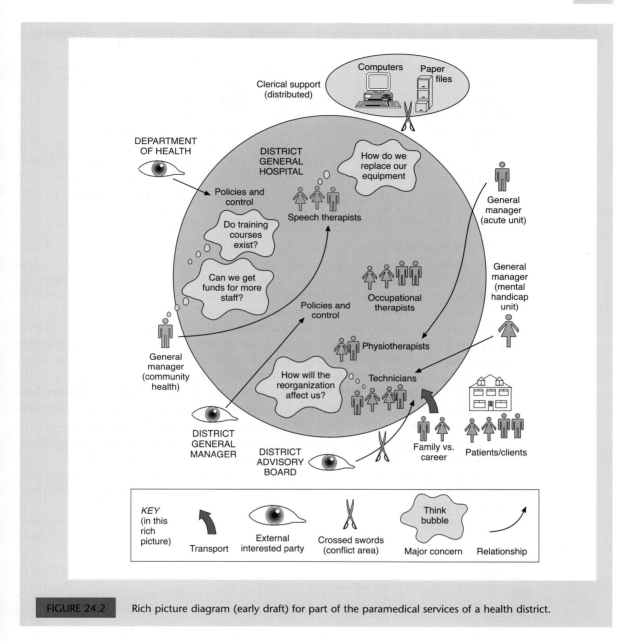

FIGURE 24.2   Rich picture diagram (early draft) for part of the paramedical services of a health district.

conflicts between departments, absences of communication lines, shortages of supply, and so on. Rich pictures are intended to help in problem identification, not in the process of recommending solutions. In general, SSM concentrates on understanding problem situations, rather than developing solutions.

Rich pictures prove to be a very useful way of getting the user to talk about the problem situation. They may stimulate the drawing out of some of the parts of the 'iceberg' which normally lie hidden when using traditional 'methods of investigation. Figure 24.2, an example rich picture chart (from Avison and Catchpole, 1987), highlights areas of conflict and concerns in the problem situation, a branch of a community health service in the UK.

3 Root definitions of relevant systems

Taking these problem themes, the next stage of the methodology involves the problem solver imagining and naming relevant systems. By relevant is meant a way of looking at the problem which provides a useful insight, for example:

Problem = Conflicts between two departments

Relevant systems = System for redefining departmental boundaries

Several different relevant systems should be explored to see which is the most useful, but, in any case, this may be changed afterwards. It is at this stage that debate is most important. The problem solver and the problem owner decide which view to focus on, that is, how to describe their relevant system. For example, will the conflict resolution in our health example be 'a system to impose rigid rules of behaviour and decision making in order to integrate decisions and minimize conflict' or will it be 'a system to integrate decisions of actors through increased communication and understanding between departments' or even 'an arbitration system to minimize conflict between departments by focusing disagreements through a central body'?

After constructing a rich picture, a root definition (Section 10.2) is developed for the relevant system. A root definition is a kind of hypothesis about the relevant system and improvements to it that might help the problem situation:

The root definition is a concise, tightly constructed description of a human activity system which states what the system is (Checkland, 1981).

Using the CATWOE checklist technique, the root definition is created. A root definition for a hospital administration system could be: 'to provide a service which gives the best possible care to the patients and which balances the need to avoid long waiting lists with that to avoid excessive government spending'. But alternative root definitions could have been 'a system for employing medical and administrative staff', 'a system to generate long waiting lists to illustrate the high status of consultants', or 'a system to encourage the use of private health facilities'.

4 Building conceptual models

When the problem owners and the problem solvers are satisfied that the root definition is well formed, a conceptual model (Section 10.3) can be developed using this root definition (Figure 24.3). In this context, the conceptual model is a diagram of the activities showing what the system, described by the root definition, will do. (The term 'conceptual model' is used in some other methodologies to refer to entity modelling.) This stage in the methodology is about model building, but the model is meant to describe something relevant to the problem situation; it is not meant to be a

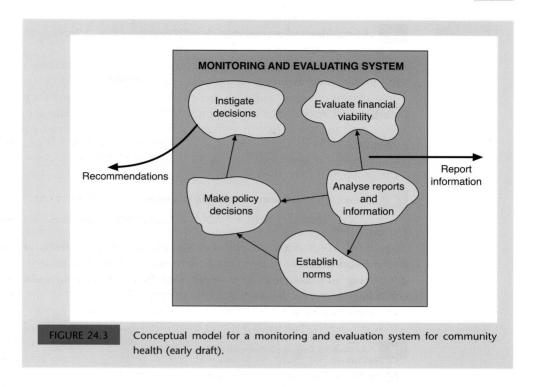

FIGURE 24.3 Conceptual model for a monitoring and evaluation system for community health (early draft).

model of the situation itself (otherwise it stifles radical thought about the problem situation).

This interpretation is different to that implied in a mathematical model, or an architect's model. The conceptual model such as that shown in Figure 24.3, can again be used as a debating point so that the actors can relate the model to the real-world situation. Analysts need also to check the conceptual model against a general model of any human activity system (the 'formal system' model, Stage 4a in Figure 24.1). Checkland includes among these prerequisites a purpose, measure of performance, a decision-taking process, connectivity, and an environment. Checkland also suggests evaluating the conceptual model through looking at the work of other systems thinkers, such as Beer, Churchman, and Vickers, and thereby improve the model (Figure 24.1, Stage 4b).

Usually there is a conceptual model drawn for each root definition, and the drawing up of several root definitions and conceptual models becomes an iterative process of debate and modification toward an agreed root definition and conceptual model. An agreed statement is never easy to achieve as the process described is meant to draw out the different ideologies and conflicts, so that the final version represents an understanding of the problem situation. Similar processes were described in the ETHICS methodology. There is a danger that these final versions represent a conservative compromise. This is not what is intended. In SSM, if the ideological conflict is central to the problem situation, it has to be represented. The approach is meant to represent a holistic view to consider a complex problem, not a simplistic view representing a 'political' compromise.

5   Comparing conceptual models with reality

The next stage concerns the comparison of the problem situation analysed in Stage 2 through rich pictures alongside the conceptual models created in Stage 4. It is also about a comparison of views, and since these views are those of human activity systems, made by people, we may not be comparing similar things. The debate about possible changes should lead to a set of recommendations regarding change in order to help the problem situation.

6   Assessing feasible and desirable changes

On assimilating these views, Stage 6 concerns an analysis of proposed changes from Stage 5 so as to draw up proposals for those changes which are considered both feasible and desirable. Checkland's methodology does not limit itself to changing or developing new information systems, though this would be valid in the context of this book.

7   Action to improve the problem situation

This final stage is about recommending action to help the problem situation. Note that the methodology does not describe methods for implementing solutions. The methodology helps in understanding problem situations rather than provide a scheme for solving a particular problem.

Although we have discussed rich pictures, root definitions, and conceptual models, the methodology relies much less on techniques and tools than most other methodologies, particularly 'hard' methodologies. These provide tools for use in particular situations at particular times in the development of the information systems project. SSM provides all actors, including the analysts, opportunities to understand and to deal with the problem situation, that is, the human activity system. The analysts are perceived as actors involved in the problem situation, as much as those of the client and problem owner – they are not perceived as outside onlookers providing objectivity.

The process is iterative and the analysts learn about the system and are not expected to follow a laid-down set of procedures. This does present problems: it is difficult to teach and to train others, and it is difficult to know when a stage in the project has been satisfactorily completed. However, these features are also its strengths, because it does not have any preconceived notions of a 'solution' and use of the methodology gives a better understanding of the problem situation.

One possible way that SSM can be fitted in the information systems development process is by using it as a 'front end' before proceeding to the 'hard' aspects of systems development. This would seem to be appropriate because SSM concerns analysis whereas the harder methodologies tend to emphasize design, development, and implementation. The Multiview methodology (Section 25.1) also draws on SSM in the early parts of the systems definition process.

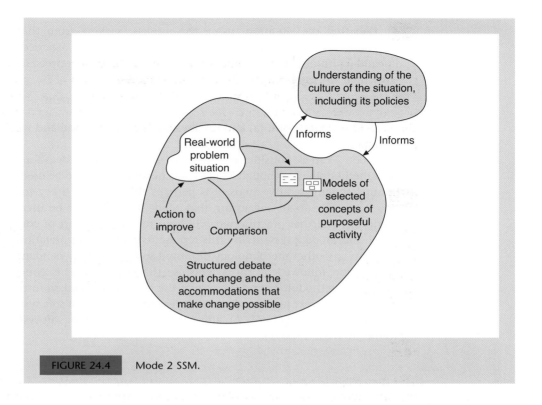

FIGURE 24.4   Mode 2 SSM.

SSM Mode 1, described in Checkland (1981), is still the version most commonly referred to and possibly the most useful in an information systems context. However, there is an alternative version proposed in Checkland and Scholes (1990) based on lessons learnt from action research practice. This sees the 7-stage methodology given above as just one option in a more general approach.

In Mode 2, the problem situation is seen as a product of history and can be looked at in many different ways. People using SSM will follow two strands of enquiry, which together should lead to changes being implemented which improve the problem situation. These two strands are described as a 'logic-driven stream of enquiry' and a 'cultural stream'.

The logic-driven stream considers models of human activity systems, and a comparison of these models is made with an examination of our views of the real world and the ensuing debate concerns change. The cultural stream examines three aspects of the problem situation: the intervention itself, the situation as a social system, and the situation as a political system. The two streams are seen to interact and the process viewed as a continual one.

A useful diagrammatic representation of Mode 2 SSM is shown as Figure 24.4. The four activities are:

1 Finding out about a problem situation, including culturally/politically.
2 Formulating some relevant purposeful activity models.

3 Debating the situation, using the models, seeking from that debate both (a) changes which would improve the situation and are regarded as both desirable and (culturally) feasible, and (b) the accommodations between conflicting interests which will enable action-to-improve to be taken.

4 Taking action in the situation to bring about improvement.

As Checkland points out, (a) and (b) are intimately connected and will gradually create each other.

Mode 2 can be considered as more of a framework of ideas for exploration rather than a methodology, although Mode 1 was never proposed to be used prescriptively nor without frequent iterative steps. It is perhaps this which is a key to interpreting SSM: Mode 2 is really about suggesting that Mode 1 should not be used as a step-by-step prescription and that practitioners will tend to use some sort of compromise between Mode 1 and Mode 2. Essentially this represents a loose interpretation of Mode 1. SSM, more than any other methodology discussed so far, is very dependent on the particular interpretation followed by those who use the approach. This concept of framework rather than methodology and the role of the interpreter is taken further in an information systems context in Multiview. A 30-year retrospective of soft systems methodology is found in Checkland (1999). An alternative interpretation of soft systems methodology is found in Wilson (2001).

24.2 INFORMATION SYSTEMS WORK AND ANALYSIS OF CHANGES (ISAC)

The ISAC methodology was developed by a research group at the Swedish Royal Institute of Technology and at the University of Stockholm. The methodology has been developed by use and experience in a number of commercial organizations and Swedish government agencies. Most users of the methodology are Scandinavian, although a number of users are claimed in other parts of Europe and North America. The methodology is closely associated with Mats Lundeberg (described in Lundeberg et al., 1982). It is interesting in that it was an early approach used which emphasized organizational issues rather than technological ones, but unlike SSM (Section 24.1), covers most phases of the life cycle.

Although the methodology covers information systems development as a whole, some users only apply the analysis and design parts of it, which are probably its best known aspects. ISAC is a problem-oriented methodology and seeks to identify the fundamental causes of users' problems. The methodology begins at an earlier stage than most methodologies and does not assume that the development of an information system is necessarily the solution to the problem. If a need for an information system is not identified, then the role of the methodology terminates. Need is established only if it is seen that an information system benefits people in their work, so that pure financial benefit to the organization, or some other benefit, is not thought to be enough of an indication of need for an information system. An information system is thought to have no value in its own right and without benefiting people should not be developed.

ISAC is a people-oriented approach and they are seen as the important factors in organizations. The term 'people' includes all people in an organization: users, managers, workers, as well as people usually thought of as outside the organization, such as customers and funders (i.e. stakeholders, see Section 16.1). People in an organization may have problems concerning the activities that they perform. These problems may be overcome, or the situation improved, by analysis of these activities and the initiation of various changes. The ISAC authors believe that the people best equipped to do this analysis, in terms of their knowledge, interest, and motivation, are the users themselves. The methodology attempts to facilitate this by providing a series of work or method steps and a series of rules and techniques which, it is claimed, can be performed by these users. An important part of this process is the education of the users to understand the organization better and to improve communication between people in the organization.

If the need for an information system is established, then the methodology emphasizes the development of a number of specific information subsystems rather than one 'total' system. The subsystems are local systems tailored to groups of individual needs, and these subsystems may well overlap in content and function. However, it is argued that the benefit that accrues is the specific relationship to the local needs. The assumption is therefore that solutions to subproblems will give solutions to the organization's problems as a whole (which perhaps conflicts with the holistic, systems view described in Section 4.1).

In ISAC terms, an information system is an organized co-operation between human beings in order to process and convey information to each other, it does not necessarily involve any form of computerization.

The major phases of ISAC are:

1. Change analysis.
2. Activity studies.
3. Information analysis.
4. Data system design.
5. Equipment adaptation.

The first three phases are classified as problem-oriented work and focus on users and their problems, whereas the latter two phases focus on information systems-oriented work. Within each phase a number of work steps are identified and within these work steps various techniques are employed.

1 Change analysis

Change analysis seeks to specify the changes that need to be made in order to overcome the identified problems. Change analysis begins with the analysis of problems, the current situation, and needs. The following method steps are used:

- *Problem listing*. This is a relatively unstructured, first-attempt look at current problems and any anticipated future problems.
- *Analysis of interest groups*. ISAC acknowledges that problems are not necessarily

objective. They are relative to the viewpoint of the participants in the organization. At this stage, the different interest groups are identified. These interest groups may be end-users, public users, departmental managers, and so on.

■ *Problem grouping*. Here, the identified problems are grouped into related sets or categories.

■ *Description of current activities*. The activities that the identified problems relate to, plus the activities undertaken by the concerned interest groups, are now modelled. This activity model is a functional view and shows processes performed on inputs to produce outputs. These aspects are not just concerned with information, but include physical activities, inputs, and outputs, such as the loading of a lorry. The activity model is documented in the form of an A-graph (an activity-graph).

An A-graph depicts three things:

1. Sets which can be real or physical sets, concerning, for example, people or services or stock, or they can be message sets, containing only information or they can be a combination of both.
2. Activities.
3. Flows, which can be shown in detail or in overview.

Activities are transformations of sets into new sets. Flows represent the movement of sets to and from activities. They are very similar to data flow diagrams (Section 12.1), except that they also represent physical objects as well as data flows. Figure 24.5 shows an example of an overview A-graph concerned with the dispatch of goods. The message set 'orders' flows into the activity 'produce shipping list' which results in a message set 'shipping list'. This itself flows to an activity called 'load lorries' which has input flows of real sets 'empty lorries' and 'goods'. A-graphs exhibit a hierarchical structure capable of showing an overview picture which can then be broken down to show the detail at lower levels. The A-graph is supplemented by narrative or descriptive text and property tables. The property tables show quantitative information such as volumes:

■ *Description of objectives*. The previously identified interest groups are perceived to have a variety of different general objectives and desires. Here, firmer and more specific objectives are defined and these are unified into a single set of objectives, via a process of negotiation and compromise. An attempt is made to reach a situation where the achievement of a set of agreed objectives solves the problems that have been identified.

■ *Evaluation of current situation and analysis of needs for changes*. This is where all the previous work comes together and enables the methodology to progress. What is wanted (the objectives) is compared to what is available. What is available is described by the activity model, but this is tempered by the problems that have been identified. The differences between what is wanted and what is available are defined as the needs for changes. These needs are then evaluated and prioritized according to the values of the different interest groups involved. This evaluation of the importance of the various needs for changes leads directly into the next stage which is the generation and study of different change alternatives.

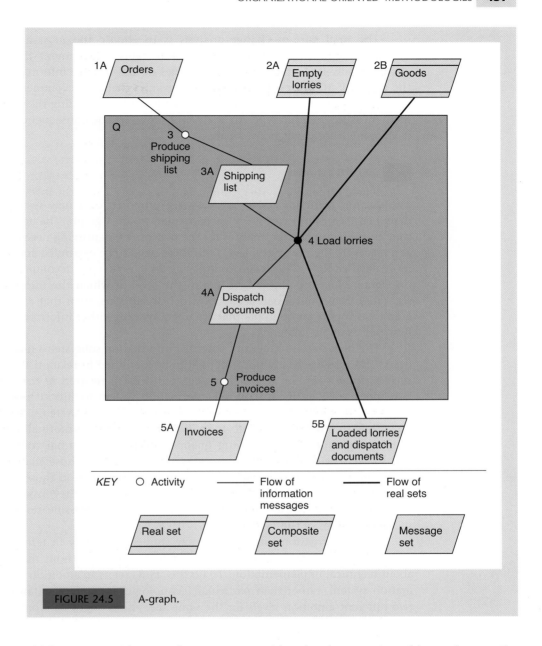

FIGURE 24.5   A-graph.

ISAC gives no guidance on how to generate ideas for changes, since this requires creativity in the context of the situation rather than the use of techniques, except to say that an analysis of flows and activities might be helpful. ISAC does not presuppose that the solution to the problems lies in automation or indeed in the construction of any form of information system. The type of solution is not constrained and may involve purely organizational and physical changes that do not result in the generation or modification of information systems. Once possible changes have been generated they are described through a new A-graph. The changes and the models are then analysed and evaluated from human, social, and economic feasibility viewpoints.

The final part of change analysis is to choose the most appropriate change approach based on the previous evaluations, and to document the reasons for the choices made. If the recommended changes do not involve information systems then the role of ISAC ceases. More likely, however, is that the recommendations involve a combination of types of change, and a plan is made concerning the necessary development measures for each type. An analysis of the effect and consequences of these parallel development measures is also made.

2 Activity studies

The starting point for activity studies is a proposal for a new system modelled and described in a number of ways, in particular, as an A-graph. The activity models that were produced in change analysis for the purpose of identifying needs for changes were at a relatively high overview level, and these need to be expanded and investigated at a more detailed level. This is shown as Figure 24.6, which is a decomposition of Process 4 on Figure 24.5. The object is to get to the level at which the information system is separated from the human activities which it supports, such that each process on the graph has inputs and outputs that are unequivocally either information or some other flow (for example, materials).

The next step is to identify potential information subsystems relating to groups of users. The subsystems are not supposed to be identified in relation to artificial criteria, such as some common technical aspect, but only in relation to commonality in use. ISAC does not identify any overall information system totality. It is more relevant to identify a number of subsystems. These information subsystems are then classified according to whether they are formalizable or not. An unformalizable information system might be one concerning qualified decisions, informal contacts, know-how, and so on. The formalizable subsystems are divided into those that seem sensible to automate, in terms of cost, social desirability, and so on, and those that are not. The automated ones are further classified according to whether they involve calculations or simply involve storing and retrieving information. These classifications are the basis for subsequent steps of the methodology.

Each information subsystem is now studied separately in terms of its costs and benefits. ISAC attempts to do this cost/benefit analysis without making assumptions about technical implementation. To do this, ISAC refers to ambition levels for an information system, rather than particular technologies for implementation. For example, two different ambition levels for the same subsystem might be a one-second response time compared with a three-hour one. Each ambition level will have a different cost/benefit associated with it.

The steps in this phase are as follows:

- *Analysis of contributions.* This is a study of the benefits (not quantified) expected to accrue from the change. It is a refinement of the earlier work done in change analysis and the results are documented in a property table. It is emphasized that this analysis must be performed in the context of the environment and the way in which the environment uses the information. This may require a more detailed analysis of the environment than has been done up to this point.

- *Generation of alternative levels of ambition.* A number of alternatives are generated for

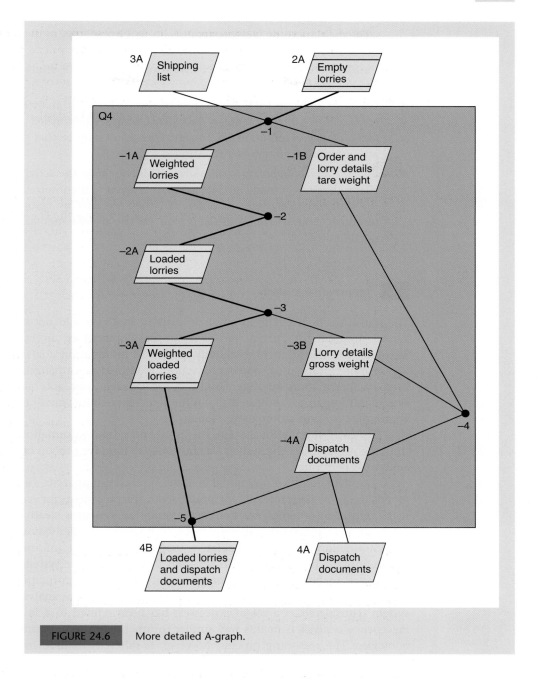

FIGURE 24.6 More detailed A-graph.

each subsystem and documented. The alternatives must be realistic. There is no point in generating ambition levels that do not fulfil minimum requirements in terms of, for example, frequencies or volumes or cost.

■ *Test of ambition levels*. Here the ambition levels are tested to see if they are practical. ISAC envisages a number of ways that they might be tested; for example, if similar information systems exist elsewhere, then it is likely that such a system can be created. Prototyping is also suggested, but not a prototype of the technology, rather one of the provision of information to the user.

■ *Cost/benefit analysis.* This is a conventional cost/benefit study of each identified level of ambition.

■ *Choice of ambition level.* The results of the cost/benefit analyses are evaluated in conjunction with the human and social analyses performed at an earlier stage, and a choice of ambition level made. One result may be that the development of an information system is discontinued.

■ *Co-ordination of information subsystems.* This concludes the activity studies and is, in effect, the project plan. Special emphasis is given to the interrelationships between the different subsystems in order that they are sensibly co-ordinated. Priorities, resources, and schedules are allocated for the developments, and the plans are documented.

3 Information analysis

The transition from change analysis to activity studies would not be made unless the agreed proposal for change included the development of an information system. Similarly, the transition from activity studies to information analysis is made only if one or more information systems have been identified as formalizable. The techniques used in information analysis assume a formalizable and automatable information system, although it is indicated that a limited degree of information analysis might be appropriate for non-automatable systems.

For each information system, the input and output information sets are extracted from the A-graphs for the system. At this time, an iterative process of function and data analysis is performed.

The ISAC term for functional analysis is precedent analysis, because ISAC recommends that it be performed by reasoning about the precedents for each information set. If the output information set from an information system is clearly derivable from its input set, then precedence analysis stops. If, however, the derivation is not clear, then the information set that immediately precedes the output information set must be deduced. If the derivation of this set from the inputs to the system is not clear, then precedence analysis continues. The precedents from each information set are analysed until the input sets are reached. At each stage of precedence analysis the information system (considered as a set of processes) has been refined to a lower level of detail. Precedence analysis is in this way similar to functional decomposition in other methodologies. The reasoning process, however, is different in that, instead of enquiring about the logical structure of a process, ISAC concentrates on the transformation that must have been necessary to produce the output information set currently being studied. If this transformation is not clear, then a simpler problem must be solved. The question is asked: 'What was the nature of the information set that immediately preceded the transformation of the current output set?' In this way the definition of processes is implicit. At any stage a process is always a black box (or using ISAC notation a black dot).

The result of precedence analysis is a set of information precedence graphs (I-graphs). I-graphs describe information sets and precedence relations between in-

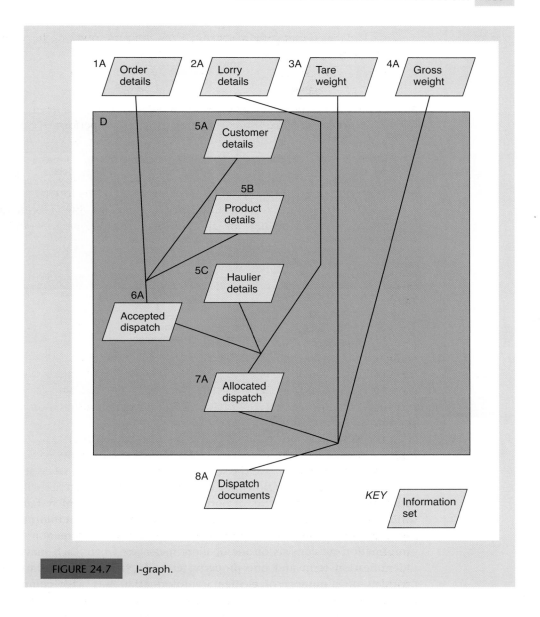

| FIGURE 24.7 | I-graph. |

formation sets. They are more precise than A-graphs in that they not only show input and output sets but also show relationships between sets. Figure 24.7 shows an example of an I-graph derived from the A-graph of Figure 24.6. It shows the input and output information sets and the precedence relations. For example, it shows that, in order to derive the 'accepted dispatch' information set, we first need the 'order details', 'customer details', and 'product details' information sets.

Reasoning about the transformations that need to be performed on information sets requires knowledge of the structure of information, and that is why component analysis is performed at the same time as precedence analysis.

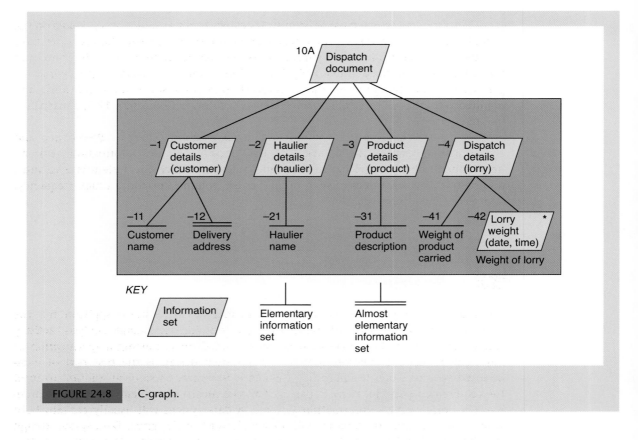

FIGURE 24.8   C-graph.

In component analysis the structure of the information sets is studied. An information set is either a data flow or a datastore. An information set will either have been specified as a basic input to, or output from, the information system being studied; or will have been from a preceding process or a set of permanent information. An information set may be compound, that is, it may itself contain information sets. An elementary information set consists of one or more messages, where each message consists of an identification term and one property term. An 'almost elementary' information set consists of a number of elementary information sets with common identification terms. Therefore, an almost elementary information set corresponds to a logical record with a key (identification term) and a number of data-item types (property terms).

ISAC documents information sets by means of a C-graph (component graph). This graph is a hierarchy showing the decomposition of an information set into subsets. Figure 24.8 is an example of a C-graph for the 'dispatch document' information set. The lowest level on the graph shows either elementary or almost elementary sets.

A further step in information analysis concerns process logic analysis. This has been ignored by ISAC during precedence analysis in order not to complicate things, but must now be addressed. Process analysis means the detailed description of the information processes in the information system. An information process is the transformation of one or more information sets into some other information set or sets. These transformations are at the logical level and do not depict implementation aspects.

The processes which have previously appeared simply as nodes or black dots on the I-graphs are now identified and named. The relationships between the processes have already been described in the C-graphs, so that all that needs doing is for the content of the process to be specified individually. This is done using a process table that defines the prerequisites for the process, the conditions, permitted states for conditions, and required actions. A process table is effectively a decision table (Section 12.3) constrained by prerequisites.

The final stage of information analysis is property analysis. Precedence and component analysis are structural descriptions of an information system. Requirements that are specific to the environment in which the system is used must also be specified. Examples of such properties are volumes, response times, frequency, and security requirements.

4   Data system design

Transition to data system design implies a fundamental change in the application of the ISAC methodology. Up to this point the ISAC activities of change analysis, activity studies, and information analysis have concentrated on producing a specification of requirements for information systems. Data system design is the first part of data-oriented systems work, the purpose of which is to design a technical solution to meet the requirements specification. A data system is a means of implementing the requirements of one or more information systems. A data system will usually contain both manual and computerized parts, both of which must be designed. Data system design is followed in ISAC by an activity known as equipment adaptation. Data system design, therefore, assumes types of equipment but not specific equipment.

The design activity starts with a study of processing philosophy. Processes that are to be performed on a computer are differentiated from those that are not. A decision is made on the mix of batch and online processing and centralized vs distributed processing. The results of activity studies are particularly relevant to determination of processing philosophy, and the identification of processes performed in information analysis enables preliminary 'process collections' to be made grouped by some common requirement (e.g. response time).

The next stage of data system design is data structure design and program delimitation and design. Information analysis has typically decomposed data and functions below the level of files and programs, and appropriate groupings are now made.

The design of a permanent data set is performed, first, by consolidating or aggregating more primitive objects (e.g. elementary information sets) into higher level groupings, on the basis of functional dependency, and, second, by considering access requirements and search paths for efficient retrieval and storage.

Program delimitation consists of putting a boundary around a group of processes defined on an I-graph. The number of processes so grouped will clearly partially determine the size and complexity of the program, and these two factors are a constraint on the delimitation. The other important constraint is the nature of the decisions that have been made about file and database design.

Once programs have been delimited and files or a database have been designed, the overall structure of the system can be recorded in a D-graph (a form of program run-chart). The next step is to specify each program, which is completed in some detail in the ISAC approach, and Jackson systems programming is recommended (see Section 19.3).

The final stage in data system design is the design of manual routines. Some information processing activities are naturally manual, and all computer-based systems will have associated manual routines. ISAC recommends that users design their own work routines.

<h2>5   Equipment adaptation</h2>

The preceding phase of data system design has produced an 'equipment-independent' solution. This is now adapted to fit particular equipment. Equipment adaptation consists of equipment study, adaptation of computer-based routines, and the creation of side-routines.

The equipment study involves collecting and evaluating technical specifications and cost and performance characteristics, and formulating an equipment strategy. Possible options might be, for example, the use of existing computer facilities, the purchase or rent of new equipment, or the use of bureau facilities. Accurate sizing of the configuration required is performed at this stage. The final choice of equipment is documented in an E-graph, which is a mapping of the D-graph onto a particular hardware configuration.

Adaptation of computer-based routines consists of two tasks. First, physical data structures must be designed, and, second, the program specifications must be adapted. Files and databases are mapped to specific storage devices, and retrieval and linkage mechanisms are specified. Outputs are mapped to specific output peripherals, such as workstations or printers. Input formats are mapped to specific methods of data capture. Any of these mappings may alter the data structures of computer programs, and thus the structure of the programs must be adapted. Finally, side-routines are specified. These are work-routines that are a necessary consequence of the choice of a particular set of equipment. For example, side-routines might be specified for data preparation or output handling.

The emphasis on the methodology is placed on analysis and design aspects of information systems development where appropriate. The methodology seeks to identify the fundamental causes of users' problems in the present system. These problems may be overcome or the situation improved by analysis of these activities and the initiation of various changes. The authors of this methodology believe that the people best equipped to do this analysis, in terms of their knowledge, interest, and motivation, are the users themselves. The methodology attempts to facilitate this by providing a series of work or method steps and a series of rules and techniques which, it is claimed, can be performed by these users. It is accepted that this might lead to a series of self-contained application systems which might be regarded as 'inefficient' from some points of view.

The methodology does not assume that the development of a computer information system is necessarily the solution to the problem. Need is established only if it is seen that an information system benefits people in their work. It has been traditional in Scandinavian countries, sometimes backed up by legislation, that technology is only implemented with the approval of the workers in that workplace. This people-oriented methodology has a wide view of the stakeholders of an information system, including users, managers, workers, and also those usually thought of as outside the organization, such as customers and funders. Development of ISAC has related to broadening the view toward business process analysis and BPR (Sections 4.3 and 24.3).

24.3   PROCESS INNOVATION (PI)

Business process re-engineering was discussed as a theme in Section 4.3, and an approach to implementing classic BPR called Process Innovation (PI) has been devised by Tom Davenport (Davenport and Short, 1990; Davenport, 1993) which suggests five stages as follows:

- develop the business vision and process objectives;
- identify the processes to be redesigned;
- understand and measure the existing process;
- identify the IT levers;
- design and build a prototype of the new process.

1   Develop the business vision and process objectives

Davenport and Short argue that it is not enough to attempt to eliminate obvious bottle-necks and inefficiencies from processes; it is necessary to redesign the entire process according to a business vision. In this phase, the organizational strengths and weaknesses need to be identified, along with an analysis of the market and the opportunities it provides. A knowledge of the innovative activities of competitors will also be useful. But a business vision will only come as a result of the creative thinking of executives and others.

There needs to be an effective linkage between business strategy and business processes. Where strategy implies radical business change, this suggests radical changes to business processes and process innovation rather than the more usual incremental change. Examples given of such a vision include developing systems with a customer perspective, improving product quality, and taking best practice from the industry. Process innovation may lead to more complex processes. Davenport argues that process simplification or rationalization only leads to marginal change and therefore implies a lack of vision. A more radical vision, it is argued, will imply objectives which might include cost reduction, time reduction, increasing the quality of products, and empowering staff. Key activities in developing process visions include:

- assess existing strategy with respect to processes;
- consult with process customers for performance objectives;
- set up performance objectives and functionality targets.

2   **Identify the processes to be re-engineered**

At this stage the major processes are identified, along with their boundaries. The critical processes of the organization are considered for IT-enabled re-engineering. Processes which are of high impact, of great strategic relevance, or presently conflict with the business vision in some way are selected for consideration and a priority attached to them. It is unlikely that they can all be re-engineered in parallel. There may be somewhere between 10 and 20 processes identified for innovation. For businesses, these might include:

- customer contact;
- inventory management;
- product design;
- personnel support;
- product marketing;
- production;
- supplier management;
- customer feedback;
- human resource management;
- financial management.

The processes are classified according to beginning and end points, interfaces, owners, functions, users, and departments involved. It is important that the process owner, usually a senior manager, is motivated toward making the change. If there are difficulties in identifying these processes, senior manager workshops may help, as will interviewing senior managers. An alternative approach is to consider re-engineering all processes, but this may neither be feasible nor efficient. For example, there may be constraints preventing re-engineering of some processes due to the necessity of supporting some legacy systems. Some of these may need to be kept because of the degree to which they are embedded in the organization. It is rare that a 'clean slate' may be assumed.

3   **Understand and measure the existing process**

Processes cannot be redesigned before they are understood. The present processes need to be documented. This will help communications within the group studying the process. It will also help to understand the magnitude of the change and the associated tasks. Understanding existing problems should help to ensure that they are not repeated. It also provides measures which can be used as a base for future improvements. For example, measuring the time and cost consumed by process areas that are to be re-designed can suggest initial areas for redesign in a process. However, although designers should be informed by past process problems and errors, they should work as if in virgin territory, otherwise processes will be tampered with rather than redesigned. Key activities in this stage are:

■   document the current process flow;

■   measure the process in terms of new process objectives;

■   measure the process in terms of new process attributes;

■   identify problems and weaknesses of the existing process;

■   identify short-term improvements in the process.

4   Identify the IT levers

The accepted view in information systems is that business requirements should be determined first before considering IT solutions. However, the benefits of simply auto-mating existing processes are likely to be minimal. IT can be used to change processes completely. Davenport and Short argue that an awareness of IT capabilities can influence process redesign and should be considered in the early stages.

IT capabilities can enable better information access and co-ordination of processes. IT can make new process design options feasible, rather than simply to support them. One distinguishing aspect of this approach, compared to most well-used information systems development methodologies, is that the latter concentrate on the development and implementation of information systems, whereas business innovation sees IT as the most powerful design tool providing opportunities for process re-engineering which is fundamental and broader.

A list of eight IT capabilities, along with organizational impacts, are suggested:

■   *Transactional*. IT can transform unstructured processes into routine transactions.

■   *Geographical*. IT can transfer information rapidly and across long distances.

■   *Automating*. IT can reduce the need for human intervention in processes.

■   *Analytical*. IT can enable complex analytical methods to be incorporated into processes.

■   *Integrating*. IT can support the co-ordination of tasks and processes.

■   *Informational*. IT can bring in vast amounts of information to be included into a process.

■   *Sequential*. IT can reorder the operation of tasks and allow them to be processed in parallel where appropriate.

■   *Knowledge orientating*. IT can be used to capture and disseminate knowledge to improve the process.

- *Tracking.* IT enables monitoring the status, inputs, and outputs of tasks.
- *Simplifying.* IT can be used to simplify communication so that, for example, intermediary stages are not required.

5   Design and build a prototype of the new process

In this final stage, the process is designed and the prototype built through successive iterations. Design comes from a review of the information collected in the first four stages. It is suggested that the design team consist of key process stakeholders as well as those from the IT side who debate possible design alternatives.

Key activities at this stage are:

- 'brainstorm' design alternatives;
- assess feasibility, risk, and benefit of design alternatives and select the preferred process design;
- prototype the new process design;
- develop a strategy for changing to the new process;
- implement the new organizational structures and systems.

Davenport suggests process design at three levels: a process level, subprocess level, and activity level. At the process level, the inputs, outputs, interfaces, flow, and measures are specified. At the subprocess level, the objective, performance metrics, the performers, IT enablers, information needs, and activities in the process are defined. At the activity level, the information needed, decision points, the performers, and value-added are defined.

Process models may be rapidly generated and even automatically coded via the use of a toolset (Chapter 18). Such a design needs to satisfy general design criteria, such as satisfying the objectives set, simplicity, control mechanisms, and the generalization of tasks which can be executed by more than one person. It is suggested that prototypes are more likely to lead to systems which are accepted by the users as well as being produced faster than the conventional approach.

Davenport discusses the potential role of IT in process innovation. As well as in the design and build stage where the impact of IT is most obvious both in the design and the prototyping stages, all the phases can be supported by information systems and information technology. Executive information systems should provide managers with information about current business performance and market factors. Computer-supported conferencing may help in the brainstorming activities. When identifying the processes to be redesigned, information about the performance of present processes can be provided and simulation packages may help to identify alternative approaches which are potentially more successful.

Although the above concentrates on the role of IT in process innovation it is not to the exclusion of other factors such as the need for empowerment and participation in decision making and process planning, and the need for teamwork.

24.4 PROJECTS IN CONTROLLED ENVIRONMENTS (PRINCE)

PRINCE is a structured and standard approach for project management, and like SSADM (Section 20.1) it was first developed for UK government applications although it is now used elsewhere. It was developed through the CCTA (the Central Computer and Telecommunications Agency), now part of the Office of Government Commerce, and the latest version is called PRINCE2.

A project is seen as having a defined and unique set of products (we have tended to use the term deliverables) at the end and during the project's development, a set of activities and their sequence to construct the products, appropriate resources to undertake the activities, a finite lifespan, and an organizational structure with defined responsibilities. The project aims are to deliver the end products at a specified quality within budget and on time.

The management structure of a PRINCE project consists of a project board, with a senior executive as a member along with a senior user, but a project manager fulfils the day-to-day management with team leaders reporting to the project manager. However, some flexibility in this structure is permitted. The management champion the project having agreed the business case, outlining the justification, commitment, and rationale for the project. All the stakeholders should be involved during the project as appropriate.

The formation of detailed plans is a cornerstone of the approach. The highest level of plan is the project plan, that is, an overall plan for the project, and this is broken down into stages. A detailed plan gives a further breakdown of activities within each stage. Although the project plan is important in showing the overall scope of the project, major deliverables, and resources required, it is the stage plans that are used for day-to-day control. The technical aspects include the product breakdown structure as well as PERT charts (Section 14.2), which link the activities, showing their interdependencies, to create the end date. Resource plans identify the resource type, amount, and cost of each resource at each stage. Gantt charts (Section 14.3) are used to help resource allocation and smoothing.

Meeting quality expectations, like time and cost, are also seen as important aspects of the approach. There are quality controls, which are defined in the technical and management procedures, and the descriptions of the deliverables in terms of fitness for purpose also represent a statement about quality.

PRINCE produces a set of reports which help control, in particular the monitoring of actual progress against plan and against the business case. Some of these reports are expected to form the basis of discussions at meetings. These meetings are normally held at the initiation at the end of each stage in the project (and sometimes at mid-stage as well). The reports highlight such things as progress, exceptions, and requests for change.

However, the first document produced is the project initiation report, which outlines the business case, defines a high-level plan, formally initiates the project, lists overall objectives for the project, and defines personnel responsibilities. It may be more detailed, for example, identifying job descriptions for each person, providing a detailed cost/benefit analysis for the business case (similar to that in a feasibility report), examining the risks associated with a project, and dividing the project into well-defined stages.

End stage assessment is a control point, which, if successful, signifies acceptance of the deliverables promised for that stage and provides authority to go on to the next stage. Mid-stage assessment may occur if the stage is of long duration, problems have been identified such as deviation from the plan, or there have been requests for change.

At the end of the project there is a project closure report, which lists the project's achievements in terms of deliverables achieved, performance in terms of comparisons of actual against forecast duration, cost and resource usage, and quality in terms of errors or exceptions. It also provides information to help organizational learning, for example, experience with the use of tools and development methodologies. The report also includes formal acceptance letters from senior technical staff, users, and operations staff. There will also be a post-implementation review.

24.5 RENAISSANCE

Renaissance is another European ESPRIT initiative involving a collaboration of company and university partners. The project addresses system evolution and maintenance, rather than new development, so it has particular links with the theme of legacy systems (Section 6.1). Its focus is generally on software engineering aspects rather than wider information systems development. As we will see, it also has links to object orientation (Section 5.4), toolsets, and other themes.

It provides an approach to ensure that legacy systems can be adapted to reflect changes in the environment. The main objectives of Renaissance are to propose 'a more methodological approach to evolution and re-engineering which is consistent with current development and maintenance practices used in industry' (www.comp.lancs. ac.uk/projects/renaissance/). Both this website and Warren (1999), which includes two interesting legacy system case studies, are good sources of material on this approach.

Renaissance first presents a framework for the evolution of legacy systems. The use of the term 'framework' suggests that it is expected to be adapted according to the particular organization. It has three viewpoints:

1. *Technical.* This includes an understanding of the technologies used, along with documentation and maintenance processes.

2. *Economic.* This includes an understanding of the business value of the system and cost and risk estimates for different evolution strategies.

3. *Managerial.* Decisions based on the previous two views.

The framework also identifies three role categories:

1. *Strategic.* This role is concerned with defining market strategies and identifying future needs, aiming at cost reduction and quality improvement. There will be a focus on managerial and economic views.

2. *Operational.* This role is concerned with providing control over the evolution of legacy systems and negotiations with customers.

3   *Service*. This role is concerned with ensuring that the level of service required is achieved in the technical view.

A process model is defined which suggests various activities:

1   *Trade-off analysis*. This is a thorough investigation of open technical issues, technical market trends, and business goals. This view of the legacy system as a business asset along with an understanding of present-day technologies will prove a good basis for further work.

2   *Issue assessment*. This looks at the scope and direction of the project and in particular ensuring that the legacy system is a good basis for evolution from a technical and business point of view.

3   *Decision analysis*. This involves choosing the best evolutionary strategy from a number of possibilities from the point of view of costs, benefits, and risks, and developing a project plan to carry out this strategy. One strategy will be to do little apart from required maintenance, but many will involve much greater change.

4   *Solution implementation*. This involves the design of a solution that satisfies the requirements set out at the earlier phases, having understood the extent and effects of the required change. It also includes creating a programme for validating the evolved system.

5   *Solution deployment*. This concerns the validation and acceptance of the evolved system ready for running it operationally. There may be a period of parallel running before the organization is fully dependent on the evolved system.

6   *Kaizen improvement*. This phase is based on the Japanese approach to business improvement and suggests continuous evaluation, incremental change, and improvement through tuning. Therefore, the legacy system is continually being refined.

Renaissance suggests six possible evolution strategies:

1   *Continued maintenance*. This relates to the fixing of small problems that would be expected in any system maintenance.

2   *Revamp*. This might involve modernizing the user interface, such as changing from a command to a graphics user interface, but not involving change to the basic hardware and software. Software products are available that will enable the user interface to be changed without changing the application software otherwise.

3   *Restructure*. This will involve more fundamental change to the software, but not the hardware. It might concern changing old-fashioned 'spaghetti code' into more structured code resulting from good software engineering practice.

4   *Rearchitecture*. This involves change to both the hardware and software. Migration of the application to the Internet may involve this more radical rearchitecture, though it might also be a much lesser revamp. The hardware platform may be changed from a mainframe environment to a client–server approach, and this would be classified as rearchitecture. Relational or object DBMS might replace conventional files (or hierarchical or network DBMS). This is perhaps a more

risky and costly approach; for example, data migration may present a problem. However, the new design should be more flexible as well as more efficient.

5 *Redesign with reuse.* This involves more new software modules and is the most radical change, but it will reuse some parts of the present system.

6 *Replacement.* This involves replacing the legacy system with a new system.

The four strategies 2 to 5 are appropriate to the Renaissance approach, although legacy systems may undergo most of these during their lifetime (and sometimes a combination strategy at one time). Strategy 1 falls under standard maintenance of systems, while Strategy 6 requires developing a new system to replace the legacy system. Each approach requires planning, development, delivery, acceptance, and deployment, but in the spirit of evolutionary change this will be a continual process.

24.6 SUMMARY

■ In this chapter we have looked at five methodologies that we have classified as organizational oriented.

QUESTIONS

1 What do you think links these five methodologies? What are the differences between them? Can you suggest an alternative, better classification?

2 SSM has been very influential in terms of systems development ideas. Why do you think this is?

3 What makes ISAC different to other methodologies, for example, SSADM, described in Chapter 20?

4 How does PI relate to the 'classic' and 'new' forms of business process reengineering (BPR) described in Section 4.3?

24.7 FURTHER READING

Bentley, C. (2002) *PRINCE2: A Practical Handbook*, Butterworth-Heinemann, Oxford.

Checkland, P. (1981) *Systems Theory Systems Practice*, John Wiley & Sons, Chichester, UK.

Davenport, T. (1993) *Process Innovation*, Harvard Business School Press, Cambridge, Massachusetts.

Lundeberg, M., Goldkuhl, G., and Nilsson, A. (1982) *Information Systems Development – A Systematic Approach*, Prentice Hall, Englewood Cliffs, New Jersey (for ISAC).

Warren, I. (1999) *The Renaissance of Legacy Systems: Method Support for Software-System Evaluation*, Springer-Verlag, London.

25 FRAMEWORKS

MULTIVIEW

Multiview 1

Multiview perceives information systems development as a hybrid process involving computer specialists who will build the system, and users for whom the system is being built. The methodology therefore looks at both the human and technical aspects of information systems development. In this aspect and others, it has been greatly influenced by the work of Checkland and Mumford, but has fused these ideas with those found in 'hard' methodologies, such as STRADIS and IE.

Multiview is a **contingent** methodology rather than highly prescriptive, because the skills of different analysts and the situations in which they are constrained to work always has to be taken into account in any project. Avison and Wood-Harper (1986) describe Multiview as an **exploration** in information systems development. It therefore sets out to be flexible: a particular technique or aspect of the methodology will work in certain situations but is not advised for others.

The methodology will be seen by readers of this text as truly 'multi-view', because it includes many of the techniques used by the other methodologies and its stages parallel those of other methodologies. The authors of Multiview claim, however, that it is not simply a hotchpotch of available techniques and tools, but a methodology which has been tested and works in practice. It is also 'multi-view' in the sense that it takes account of the fact that as an information systems project develops, it takes on different perspectives or views: organizational, technical, human-oriented, economic, and so on.

The five stages of Multiview are as follows:

- analysis of human activity;
- analysis of information (sometimes called information modelling);

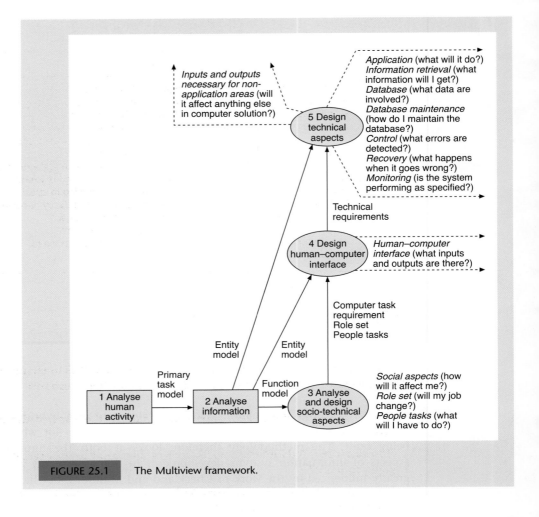

FIGURE 25.1   The Multiview framework.

- analysis and design of socio-technical aspects;
- design of the human–computer interface;
- design of technical aspects.

They incorporate five different views which are appropriate to the progressive development of an analysis and design project, covering all aspects required to answer the vital questions of users. These five views are necessary to form a system which is complete in both technical and human terms. The five stages move from the general to the specific, from the conceptual to hard fact, and from issue to task. Outputs of each stage either become inputs to following stages or are major outputs of the methodology. The Multiview methodology is shown in outline in Figure 25.1. The two analysis-oriented stages are shown in boxes and the three design-oriented stages in circles. The arrows represent information passing between stages, and the dotted arrows represent outputs of the methodology. The outputs of the methodology, shown as dotted arrows in Figure 25.1, are listed in Figure 25.2, together with the information that they provide and the questions that they answer.

OUTPUTS	INFORMATION
Social aspects	How will it affect me?
Role-set	Will my job change? In what way?
People tasks	What will I have to do?
Human–computer interface	How will I work with the computer?
	What inputs and outputs are there?
Database	What data are involved?
Database maintenance	How will I maintain the integrity of data?
Recovery	What happens when it goes wrong?
Monitoring	Is the system performing to specification?
Control	How are security and privacy handled?
Information retrieval	What information will I get?
Application	What will the system do?
Inputs and outputs for non-application areas	Will it affect anything else on the computer system?

FIGURE 25.2	Multiview methodology outputs.

The authors argue that to be complete in human as well as in technical terms, the methodology must provide help in answering the following questions:

1. How is the computer system supposed to further the aims of the organization installing it?

2. How can it be fitted into the working lives of the people in the organization that are going to use it?

3. How can the individuals concerned best relate to the machine in terms of operating it and using the output from it?

4. What information system processing function is the system to perform?

5. What is the technical specification of a system that will come close enough to doing the things that have been written down in the answers to the other four questions?

Too often, the authors argue, methodologies and role players have only addressed themselves to a limited subset of these questions: for example, computer scientists to Question 5, systems analysts to Question 4, users to Question 3, trade unions to Question 2, and top management to Question 1. Multiview attempts to address all these questions and to involve all the role players or stakeholders in answering all these questions. The emphasis in information systems, it is argued, must move away from 'technical systems which have behavioural and social problems' to 'social systems which rely to an increasing extent on information technology'.

Because it *is* a multi-view approach, it covers computer-related questions and also matters relating to people and business functions. It is part issue-related and part task-related. An issue-related question is: 'What do we hope to achieve for the company as a

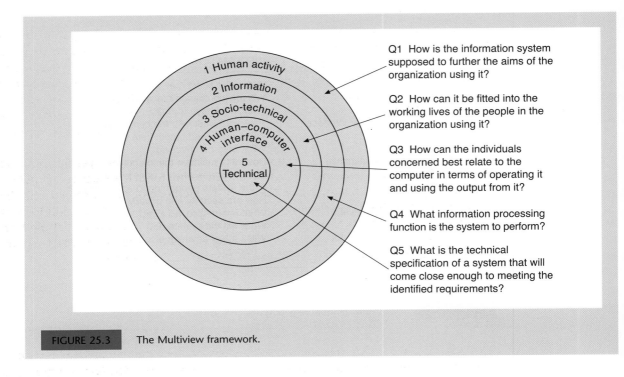

Q1 How is the information system supposed to further the aims of the organization using it?

Q2 How can it be fitted into the working lives of the people in the organization using it?

Q3 How can the individuals concerned best relate to the computer in terms of operating it and using the output from it?

Q4 What information processing function is the system to perform?

Q5 What is the technical specification of a system that will come close enough to meeting the identified requirements?

| FIGURE 25.3 | The Multiview framework. |

result of installing a computer?' A task-related question is: 'What job is the computer going to have to do?'

The distinction between issue and task is important because it is too easy to concentrate on tasks when computerizing and to overlook important issues which need to be resolved. Too often, issues are ignored in the rush to 'computerize'. But you cannot solve a problem until you know what the problem is! Issue-related aspects, in particular those occurring at Stage 1 of Multiview, are concerned with debate on the definition of system requirements in the broadest sense, that is, 'what real-world problems is the system to solve?' On the other hand, task-related aspects, in particular Stages 2–5, work toward forming the system that has been defined with appropriate emphasis on complete technical and human views. The system, once created, is not just a computer system, it is also composed of people performing jobs.

Another representation of the methodology, rather more simplistic, but useful in providing an overview for discussion, is shown in Figure 25.3. Working from the middle outward we see a widening of focus and an increase in understanding the problem situation and its related technical and human characteristics and needs. Working from the outside in we see an increasing concentration of focus, an increase in structure, and the progressive development of an information system. This diagram also shows how the five questions outlined above have been incorporated into the five stages of Multiview.

The first stage looks at the organization – its main purpose, problem themes, and the creation of a statement about what the information system will be and what it will do. The second stage is to analyse the entities and functions of the problem situation described in Stage 1. This is carried out independently of how the system will be developed.

The philosophy behind the third stage is that people have a basic right to control their own destinies and that, if they are allowed to participate in the analysis and design of the systems that they will be using, then implementation, acceptance, and operation of the system will be enhanced. This stage emphasizes the choice between alternative systems, according to important social and technical considerations. The fourth stage is concerned with the technical requirements of the user interface. The design of specific conversations will depend on the background and experience of the people who are going to use the system, as well as their information needs.

Finally, the design of the technical subsystem concerns the specific technical requirements of the system to be designed, and therefore to such aspects as computers, databases, control, and maintenance. Although the methodology is concerned with the computer only in the latter stages, it is assumed that a computer system will form at least part of the information system. However, the authors do not argue that the final system will necessarily run on a large mainframe computer. This is just one solution, many cases show applications being implemented on a microcomputer.

1   Analysis of human activity

This stage is based on SSM (Mode 1). The very general term 'human activity' is used to cover any sort of organization. This could be, for example, an individual, a company, a department within a larger organization, a club, or a voluntary body. They may all consider using a computer for some of their information systems. The central focus of this stage of the analysis is to search for a particular view (or views). This *Weltanschauung* will form the basis for describing the systems requirements and will be carried forward to further stages in the methodology. This world view is extracted from the problem situation through debate on the main purpose of the organization concerned.

First, the problem solver, perhaps with extensive help from the problem owner, forms a rich picture of the problem situation. The problem solver is normally the analyst or the project team. The problem owner is the person or group on whose behalf the analysis has been commissioned. This picture can be used to help the problem solver better understand the problem situation. The rich picture diagram is also very useful to stimulate debate, and it can be used as an aid to discussion between the problem solver and the problem owner. There are usually a number of iterations made during this process until the 'final' form of the rich picture is decided. The process here consists of gathering, sifting, and interpreting data which is sometimes called 'appreciating the situation'. Drawing the rich picture diagram, examples of which are given in Figures 10.1 and 24.2, is a subjective process. There is no such thing as a 'correct' rich picture. The main purpose of the diagram is to capture a holistic summary of the situation.

From the rich picture the problem solver extracts problem themes, that is, things noticed in the picture that are, or may be, causing problems and/or it is felt worth looking at in more detail. The picture may show conflicts between two departments, absences of communication lines, shortages of supply, and so on. Taking these problem themes, the problem solver imagines and names relevant systems that may help to relieve the problem theme. Several different relevant systems should be explored to see which is the most useful. Once a particular view or root definition (Section 10.2) has been decided upon, it can be developed and refined. Thus, by using the CATWOE checklist, the root definition can be analysed by checking that all necessary elements have been included. For example, have we identified the owner of the system, all the actors involved, the victims/beneficiaries of the system, and so on?

When the problem owner and the problem solver are satisfied that the root definition is well formed, a conceptual model (or activity model) of the system is constructed by listing the 'minimum list of verbs covering the activities which are necessary in a system defined in the root definition ...'. Examples of conceptual models are seen in Figures 10.3, 10.4, and 23.3. At this stage, therefore, we have a description in words of what the system will be (the root definition) and an inference diagram of the activities of what the system will do (the conceptual model).

The completed conceptual model is then compared to the representation of the 'real world' in the rich picture. Differences between the actual world and the model are noted and discussed with the problem owner. Possible changes are debated, agendas are drawn up, and changes are implemented to improve the problem situation.

In some cases the output of this stage is an improved human activity system, and the problem owner and the problem solver may feel that the further stages in the Multiview methodology are unnecessary. In many cases, however, this is not enough. In order to go on to a more formal systems design exercise, the output of this stage should be a well-formulated and refined root definition to map out the universe of discourse, that is, the area of interest or concern. It could be a conceptual model which can be carried on to Stage 2, the analysis of entities, functions, and events.

2   Analysis of information

The purpose of this stage is to analyse the entities and functions of the application. Its input will be the root definition/conceptual model of the proposed system which was established in Stage 1 of the process. Two phases are involved: (a) the development of the functional model and (b) the development of an entity model.

a   *Development of a functional model.* The first step in developing the functional model is to identify the *main* function. This is always clear in a well-formed root definition. This main function is then broken down progressively into subfunctions (functional decomposition), until a sufficiently comprehensive level is achieved. This occurs when the analyst feels that the functions cannot be usefully broken down further. This is normally achieved after about four or five subfunction levels, depending on the complexity of the situation. A series of data flow diagrams, each showing the sequence of events, is developed from this hierarchical model. This stage is therefore greatly influenced by the process modelling theme (Section 5.2). The hierarchical model and data flow diagrams are the major inputs into Stage 3 of the methodology, the next stage, which is the analysis and design of the socio-technical system.

b   *Development of an entity model.* In developing an entity model, the problem solver extracts and names entities from the area of concern. Relationships between entities are also established. Again, this stage is greatly influenced by the data modelling them (Section 5.3). The preceding stage in the methodology, the analysis of the human activity systems, should have already given this necessary understanding and have laid a good foundation for this second stage. The entity model can then be constructed. The entity model, following further refinement, becomes a useful input into Stages 4 and 5 of the Multiview methodology.

3   **Analysis and design of the socio-technical aspects**

The philosophy behind this stage (influenced by ETHICS, Section 23.1) is that people have a basic right to control their own destinies and that, if they are allowed to participate in the analysis and design of the systems that they will be using, then the implementation, acceptance, and operation of the system will be enhanced. It takes the view therefore that human considerations, such as job satisfaction, task definition, morale, and so on, are just as important as technical considerations. The task for the problem solver is to produce a 'good fit' design, taking into account people and their needs and the working environment on the one hand, and the organizational structure, computer systems, and the necessary work tasks on the other.

An outline of this stage is shown in Figure 25.4. The central concern at this stage is the identification of alternatives: alternative social arrangements to meet social objectives and alternative technical arrangements to meet technical objectives. All the social and technical alternatives are brought together to produce socio-technical alternatives. These are ranked, first, in terms of their fulfilment of the above objectives and, second, in terms of costs, resources, and constraints – again both social and technical – associated with each objective. In this way, the 'best' socio-technical solution can be selected and the corresponding computer tasks, role-sets, and people tasks can be defined.

The emphasis of this stage is therefore *not* on development, but on a statement of alternative systems and choice between the alternatives, according to important social and technical considerations.

It is also clear that, in order to be successful in defining alternatives, the groundwork in the earlier stages of the methodology is necessary and, in order to develop and implement the chosen system, we must continue to the subsequent stages. An important technique applicable to this stage is future analysis (Section 15.4). This aids the analyst and user to predict the future environment so that they are better able to define and rank their socio-technical alternatives.

The outputs of this stage are the computer task requirements, the role-set, the people tasks, and the social aspects. The computer task requirements, the role-set, and the people tasks become inputs to the next stage of the methodology, that is, the design of the human–computer interface. The role-set, the people tasks, and the social aspects are also major outputs of the methodology.

4   **Design of the human–computer interface**

Up to now, we have been concerned with what the system will do. Stage 4 relates to how, in general terms, we might achieve an implementation which matches these requirements. The inputs to this stage are the entity model derived in Stage 2 of the

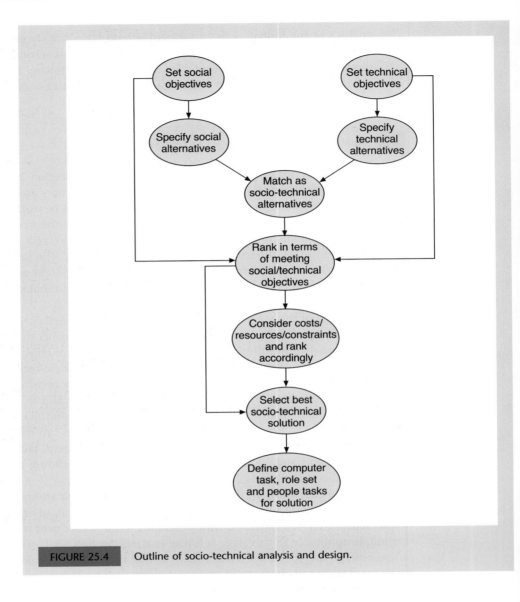

FIGURE 25.4   Outline of socio-technical analysis and design.

methodology and the computer tasks, role-set, and people tasks derived in Stage 3. This fourth stage is concerned with the technical design of the human–computer interface and makes specific decisions on the technical system alternatives. The ways in which users will interact with the computer will have an important influence on whether the user accepts the system.

A broad decision will relate to whether to adopt batch or online facilities. In online systems, the user communicates directly with the computer through a terminal or workstation. In a batch system, transactions are collected, input to the computer, and processed together when the output is produced. This is then passed to the appropriate user. Considerable time may elapse between original input and response.

Decisions must then be taken on the specific conversations and interactions that particular types of user will have with the computer system and on the necessary inputs and outputs and related issues, such as error checking and minimizing the number of keystrokes. There are different ways to display the information and to generate user responses. The decisions are taken according to the information gained during Stages 1 and 2 of Multiview.

Once human–computer interfaces have been defined, the technical requirements to fulfil them can also be designed. These technical requirements become the output of this stage and the input to Stage 5, the design of technical subsystems. The human–computer interface definition becomes a major output of the methodology.

5 Design of the technical aspects

The inputs to this stage are the entity model from Stage 2 and the technical requirements from Stage 4. The former describes the entities and relationships for the whole area of concern, whereas the latter describes the specific technical requirements of the system to be designed.

After working through the first stages of Multiview, the technical requirements have been formulated with both social and technical objectives in mind and also after consideration of an appropriate human–computer interface. Therefore, necessary human considerations are already both integrated and interfaced with the forthcoming technical subsystems.

At this stage, therefore, a largely technical view can be taken so that the analyst can concentrate on efficient design and the production of a full systems specification. Many technical criteria are analysed and technical decisions made which will take into account all the previous analysis and design stages. The final major outputs of the methodology might include:

■ *the application subsystem* which is concerned with performing the functions which have been computerized from the function chart;

■ *the information retrieval subsystem* which is for responding to enquiries about data stored in the system;

■ *the database* in which all the data are organized;

■ *the database maintenance subsystem* which permits updates to the data and provides the information necessary to check for data errors;

■ *the control subsystem* which checks for user, program, operator, and machine errors and alerts the system to their presence;

■ *the recovery subsystem* which allows the system to be repaired after an error has been detected;

■ *the monitoring subsystem* which keeps track of all system activities for management purposes.

Figure 25.5 shows a schematic of these requirements for the technical specification. These subsystems cover all the things that have to be done by the computer system and the people operating it. These parts, or subsystems, may be implemented in different ways and in different combinations. For example, the information retrieval

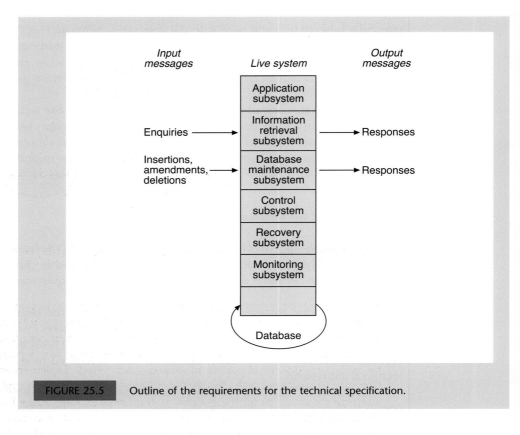

Input messages   Live system   Output messages

- Application subsystem
- Information retrieval subsystem
- Database maintenance subsystem
- Control subsystem
- Recovery subsystem
- Monitoring subsystem

Enquiries → ... → Responses

Insertions, amendments, deletions → ... → Responses

Database

FIGURE 25.5   Outline of the requirements for the technical specification.

subsystem may be just another aspect of the database management system, and this may also include many of the necessary functions for control and recovery. The Multiview authors have separated them out because it is necessary to be sure that each one of them is catered for in the system.

Following full testing of all aspects of the system, there is a recognition that there will still be changes required, and this should be regarded as 'the norm'. Information systems will develop, and this requires an ongoing relationship between users, analysts, system creators, or owners. The authors recommend that the Multiview framework be applied for these changes (at least with a 'token run') so as to ensure that the system is still meeting its real objectives.

Multiview2

A new version of Multiview was published as Multiview2 (Avison et al. 1998). The original conception of Multiview posited a three-way relationship between the analyst, the methodology, and the situation. Avison and Wood-Harper (1990) suggested that parts of this relationship were missing in many descriptions of IS development (ISD), and that methodologies often contained unstated and unquestioning assumptions about the unitary nature of both the problem situation and the analysts involved in investigating it. Despite this criticism of other methodologies, Multiview1 itself offered no further

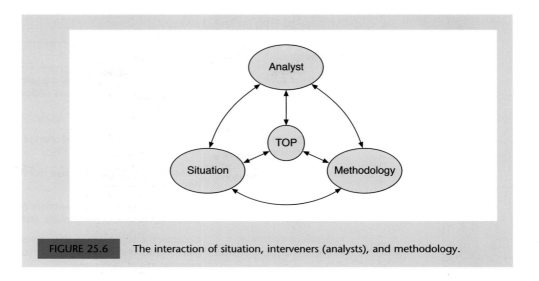

FIGURE 25.6   The interaction of situation, interveners (analysts), and methodology.

guidance on how any given instantiation of the triad (analyst–methodology–situation) might come about in actual practice. Mitroff and Linstone (1993) is used to inform the particular occurrence of Multiview2 under any given set of circumstances (Figure 25.6).

Multiview2 offers a rich implementation of the multiple perspective approach as far as ISD is concerned. As we have seen Multiview1 implemented such an approach through a five-stage methodology. These five stages were then typically presented as a waterfall structure. In Multiview2 the outcomes of ISD are posited as consisting of three elements: organizational behaviours, work systems, and technical artefacts, which are reflected in the parts: organizational analysis, socio-technical analysis and design, and technical design and construction, respectively (Vidgen, 1996). The fourth part of Multiview2, information modelling, acts as a bridge between the other three, communicating and enacting the outcomes in terms of each other (Figure 25.7). The proposed

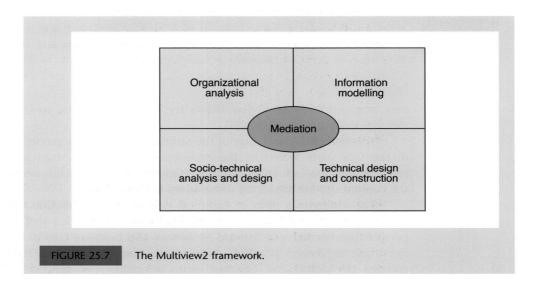

FIGURE 25.7   The Multiview2 framework.

Part	Change	Rationale
Organizational analysis	Inclusion of strategic assumption surfacing and testing (SAST, Mason and Mitroff, 1989)	To strengthen the conceptual analysis of SSM with real-world stakeholder analysis (Vidgen, 1994)
	Radical change and business process redesign	IT as business enabler, rapid change in business environments (Wood et al., 1995)
	Introduction of ethical analysis	Stakeholders can have different moral ideals (Wood-Harper et al., 1996)
	Consideration of non-human stakeholders	To support a symmetrical treatment of social and technological factors (Vidgen and McMaster, 1996)
	Inclusion of technology foresight and future analysis	Consider the impact of the intervention on stakeholders (Avison et al., 1994, 1995) and the potential role of technology
Information modelling	Migration to Object-Oriented Analysis (from structured methods)	The principles of OO are more compatible with systems thinking than are the process/data separation and data flow metaphor of structured methods (e.g. the notion of systemic transformation and state change)
Socio-technical analysis and design	Ethnographic approaches to supplement ETHICS	Ethnographic approaches to socio-technical design (Randall et al., 1994; Avison and Myers, 1995) aid the analyst in understanding how work is accomplished (Sachs, 1995)
Technical design and construction	Construction of technical artefacts is incorporated within the scope of the methodology (Multiview1 stopped at technical design)	Prototyping, evolutionary, and rapid development approaches to system development require that analysis, design, and construction be more tightly integrated (Budde et al., 1992)

FIGURE 25.8   Changes in the content from Multiview1 to version Multiview2 (Avison et al. 1998).

new framework for Multiview shows the four parts of the methodology mediated through the actual process of ISD.

Together with the change in the Multiview2 framework go changes to the content of the four parts, reflecting the experiences of applying Multiview through action research and developments in IS theory and practice. The major amendments made in the content of Multiview2 are summarized in Figure 25.8.

The Multiview2 parts of technical design and construction (T), socio-technical analysis and design (P), and organizational analysis (O) align well with the multiple perspective approach put forward by Mitroff and Linstone (1993). However, there are important differences of emphasis and definition. For example, the T perspective is equated by Mitroff and Linstone with rationality and functionalism, whereas in

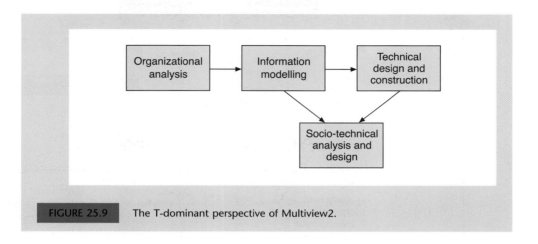

FIGURE 25.9   The T-dominant perspective of Multiview2.

Multiview2 the technical design stage is concerned with the detail of computer system design and construction. In unbounded systems thinking, therefore, it would be perfectly feasible to have a T perspective of the analysis of human activity. The authors consider it more insightful to apply the TOP Multiple Perspective as a basis for informing the *approach* taken to ISD.

The T perspective reflects a rational, engineering-based approach to systems development in which the aim is to produce technical artefacts that will support purposeful human and organizational activity. The O perspective is typified by the development of a shared understanding and organizational learning, within the process of ISD. It can be visualized as a learning cycle including discovery, invention, production, and generalization, as well as double-loop learning to bring about the surfacing and challenging of deep-rooted assumptions which were previously unknown or undiscussable (Argyris and Schön, 1978). The P perspective represents the fears and hopes of individuals within the organization and deals with situations of power, influence, and prestige (Knights and Murray, 1994).

The TOP multiple perspective approach described by Mitroff and Linstone can be used to inform the different views that can be taken of the three sets of outcomes – organizational behaviours, work, and technical artefacts – within any given problem context. As an example of adopting a singular perspective of the system development process, Figure 25.9 offers a predominantly T perspective of Multiview2. This can be seen to be very much in line with what is often taken to be conventional wisdom as far as ISD is concerned, but here is taken to be the embodiment of the logical, rational view. It incorporates the agreement–analysis modes of thinking described by Churchman (1971) and Mitroff and Linstone (1993), and describes the technical interest of prediction and control identified by Habermas earlier. We also point out that alternate life-cycle models, such as iterative and evolutionary development, although generally more sympathetic to the O and P perspectives, may still be reduced in practice to a T-dominant view of ISD in which it is believed that the 'real' requirements are 'captured' more effectively than with a waterfall life-cycle model.

Multiview2 offers a systematic guide to any ISD intervention, together with a reflexive, learning methodological process, which brings together the analyst, the situation, and the methodology.

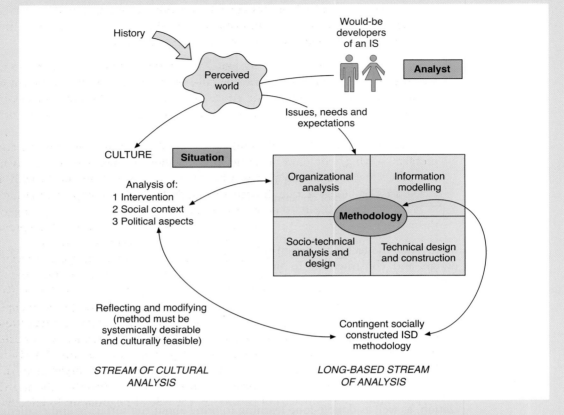

Constructing the information systems development methodology (from Avison et al., 1995).

However, although the authors recommend a contingent approach to ISD, Multiview2 should not be used to justify random or uncontrolled development. An IS methodology, such as Multiview2, provides a basis for constructing a situation-specific method (Figure 25.10), which arises from a genuine engagement of the analyst with the problem situation (Wastell, 1996).

Although Multiview has been in a continual state of development since 1985, the reflections on Multiview in action have suggested this radical redefinition of Multiview into Multiview2 which takes these experiences into account, along with the more recent literature and recognizing the new 'era' of the domain of information systems (see Chapter 26).

25.2 STRATEGIC OPTIONS DEVELOPMENT AND ANALYSIS (SODA)

We look briefly at SODA as an alternative framework approach. According to Eden and Ackerman (2001), SODA is:

an approach which is designed to provide consultants with a set of skills, a framework for designing problem solving situations and a set of techniques and tools to help their clients work with messy problems.

The **consultant** needs to have the skills to facilitate the processes that lead to efficient and effective problem solving, and the skills to construct a model of the content of the problem situation. Therefore, the consultant works with the problem-solving groups, should be flexible, and needs to be aware of the important role of individuals in the process.

Therefore, like SSM and Multiview, it is not seen as a prescriptive approach to problem solving, but more a framework to guide the problem solver to investigate complex situations. Similarly, it is a cyclic and contingent approach, with all uses of SODA seen as being unique. Indeed this guide through a complex situation has been developed more recently to an approach known as **Journey Making**, suggesting that the journey is as important as the outcome. This stresses the impact of the process as well as the outcome on personalities, roles, politics, and power dimensions.

The SODA framework is seen in Figure 25.11. It has four perspectives relating to the individual, nature of organizations, consulting practice, and technology and technique. The focus on the individual stresses his or her attempt to understand or 'make sense' of the organization in order to 'manage and control' that world. Cognitive mapping is seen as a very important technique (Section 10.4) to help this process of understanding. The perspective on the nature of organizations also focuses on the individuals within them as it stresses the political and power aspects as important explanations of decision making. Participants are seen as continuously negotiating their roles in organizations.

The third perspective of consulting practice brings together the individual and organizational perspectives, but centres on the role of negotiation in effective problem solving, the consultant facilitating this negotiation, and managing consensus and commitment. These three building blocks come together through appropriate technology and technique, the main technique being cognitive mapping.

Cognitive maps are usually created individually with clients, and these are then merged to represent the views of all clients. The merged map helps to set the agenda for the workshop that follows. A workshop of the client team as a whole can help to ensure full client commitment to all the emerging issues (not just their own part of the map), understanding all the detail, yet moving to the specified actions. This requires negotiation, the merged map is not a *fait accompli*, and the workshop will probably include a number of cycles before agreement and commitment. Typically, it will last one or two days. A full case study concerning the use of SODA in the UK National Audit Office is provided in Ackerman and Eden (2001).

25.3 CAPABILITY MATURITY MODEL (CMM)

The Capability Maturity Model is strictly speaking not a methodology for systems development; it is a framework for evaluating processes used to develop software projects. The CMM classifies the maturity of these processes in an organization into five levels, with Level 5 being the most mature. The CMM framework specifies the characteristics that the

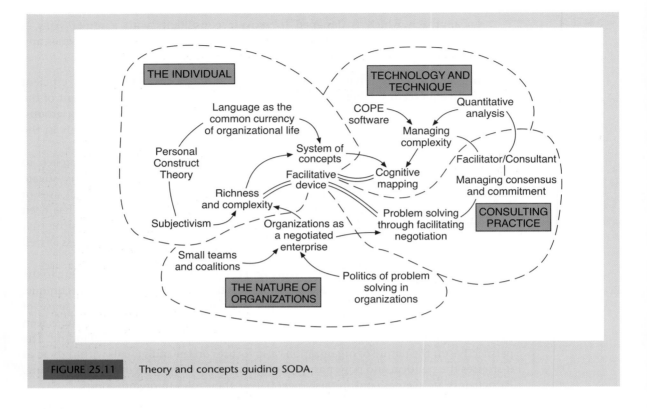

FIGURE 25.11   Theory and concepts guiding SODA.

various levels should have rather than prescribing any particular processes. It also provides advice and guidance relating to the improvements necessary to move from a lower maturity level upward. However, the CMM although being a maturity framework and not prescriptive does embody a certain philosophy concerning the way information systems and software should be developed.

CMM was created by the Software Engineering Institute (SEI) at Carnegie Mellon University for the US Department of Defense (DoD) to help assess the software engineering capability of their vendors and subcontractors (McGrew et al., 1999). The SEI was founded in 1984 and is a federally funded research and development centre sponsored by the DoD. Its original goal was to 'advance software engineering practice' in the light of the increasing dependence of the military on software and the increasing recognition that software was problematic in terms of its delivery, escalating costs, and customer dissatisfaction. A not unfamiliar story, and one that has also been found in the commercial sector. Today the long-range goal of the SEI is to 'make the acquisition, development, and sustainment of software-intensive systems *predictably better, faster, and cheaper* for the DoD' (SEIa, 2001).

In 1987 the first version of a maturity framework was defined (Humphrey, 1989), and this evolved, with experience of use, into what is now known as the CMM for Software (Paulk et al., 1993, 1995; Weber, 1991). According to Paulk et al. (1993) CMM 'provides software organizations with guidance on how to gain control of their processes for developing and maintaining software and how to evolve towards a culture of software engineering and management excellence. The CMM was designed to guide software organizations in selecting process improvement strategies by determining current process maturity and identifying the few issues most critical to software quality and process improvement.' CMM Version 1.0 was published in 1991, and reviewed by the software community resulting in Version 1.1 (Paulk et al., 1993a) which was released in 1993. Since this time SEI has been working on CMM Version 2 which was under review by members of the SEI software community. However, Version 2 has not yet been released.

SEI has also defined a number of other capability maturity models (CMMs), based on the success of the original CMM for Software. These relate to wider areas and other issues than just software engineering; for example, they have defined a People model (P-CMM), a Software Acquisition model (SA-CMM) and a Systems Engineering model (SE-CMM) among others. They have also defined a model for integrating these individual models in an organization, known as CMMI (Capability Maturity Model Integrated Discipline). It appears that the development of CMMI has now become the main focus of the work of SEI and that Version 2 of SW-CMM has been incorporated into CMMI Version 1.02 and that organizations new to CMM should use this version but that existing users should continue using SW-CMM Version 1.1.

This is all quite confusing, and we will only describe, from here on, the CMM for Software Version 1.1. As indicated this is commonly known just as CMM, but because of the various other SEI CMMs it should really be called by its full name which is SW-CMM, Version 1.1. Indeed there are other maturity and quality process models that are not produced by SEI which also cause confusion, so strictly speaking we should call it the SEI SW-CMM, Version 1.1. These other models or framework for software processes include ISO 9000-3, Trillium, SPICE, BOOTSTRAP, and TickIT.

The CMM is designed to help organizations improve their software processes by providing a path for them to move from *ad hoc* development through to more disciplined software processes in a staged approach. The CMM framework provides a context in which policies, procedures, and practices are defined and established that enable good practices to be repeated, transferred across groups, and standardized. CMM has five maturity levels shown in Figure 25.12 and characterized as follows.

1 Initial level

Development is characterized as *ad hoc* or possibly chaotic. Processes are generally not defined, and success or failure depends on the capabilities of the individuals involved. Success can sometimes be achieved because individuals perform 'heroically', but this is generally not sustainable over time as there are few repeatable processes and often those heroic individuals move on. Typically development is *ad hoc* and lurches from crisis to crisis, software is typically delivered late and over budget, and there is little effective management and control. This has been the norm in the past for software development and is still frequently seen in organizations. This is the initial stage from which organizations are trying to escape and move to a more mature process where development is not so dependent on the individuals but more on the characteristics of the management process. Fine (2001) says that this level might be better called the Heroic Level as any success is so dependent on a few star performers. He also reveals that CMM implementers

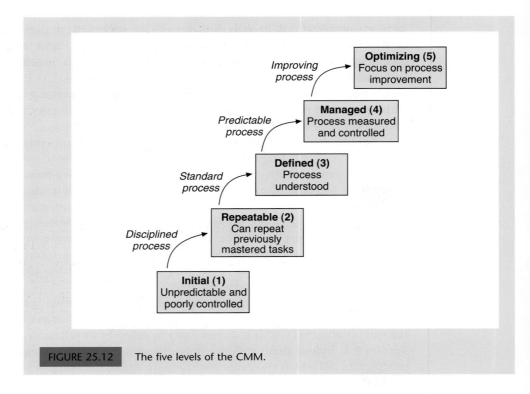

The five levels of the CMM.

often joke that many companies would be at Level 0 rather than 1 if such a level existed (i.e. the situation is quite poor out there).

2   Repeatable level

At Level 2 policies for managing software development are identified and established based on experience. Basic software development processes are in place, SEI characterizes an effective process as one which is 'practiced, documented, enforced, trained, measured and able to improve' (Paulk et al., 1993a). Management process and controls are also established for planning, estimating, and tracking costs, schedules, functionality, etc. Project standards are defined and followed. Specific processes are not defined and may differ between projects. For an organization to be in Level 2, software projects and processes are essentially managed and under control with realistic plans based on performance of previous projects (i.e. previously mastered tasks are repeatable).

3   Defined level

At Level 3 the standard software engineering and management processes are documented and form a coherent, integrated, and standard approach to software development for the organization as a whole. The process is well defined, relatively stable, and recognized as the organization's approach to software development. Paulk et al. (1993a)

characterizes well defined as 'including readiness criteria, inputs, standards and procedures for performing the work, verification mechanisms (such as peer reviews), outputs,
and completion criteria'. There should exist a group responsible for maintaining and
improving these standard processes and an organization-wide training programme for
communicating and imparting knowledge and skills concerning the process. Individual
projects may tailor the standard process for the needs of the particular project but it
should remain a well-defined, coherent, and integrated process. Overall, management
should understand and be in control of quality and technical progress on each project.

4   Managed level

At Level 4 quantitative quality and productivity measures are established for key software
development activities across all projects and goals set that will help ensure consistency,
understanding, and improvement of the processes. A software process database should
be used to collect and help analyse the data resulting in processes that are now predictable and operate within specified limits with any exceptions able to be quickly
identified and remedied, ensuring high-quality software and predictable processes. The
level is characterized as measured and predictable.

5   Optimizing level

At Level 5 the whole organization is focused on continuous process improvement on a
proactive basis. The ability to identify strengths and weaknesses, to assess new technologies and process innovations, and take action to improve things on this basis is in
place. The level is one of continuous process improvement on a planned and managed
basis as a standard activity.

The levels provide a set of stages and criteria which organizations can measure themselves against and attempt to move up the levels as a way of achieving a more mature
software process.

     Having identified Maturity Levels, CMM defines a number of further elements to
its structure. These are represented in Figure 25.13. Each Maturity Level (except Level 1)
contains a number of Key Process Areas that need to be focused upon in order to achieve
a particular Maturity Level. They are shown in Figure 25.14.

     The goals specify the scope, boundaries, and intent of each of these Key Process
Areas and help determine if they have been satisfied for the level. According to Paulk
et al. (1993b) an example of a goal from the Software Project Planning key process area
might be 'Software estimates are documented for use in planning and tracking the
software project.'

     Further, each Key Process Area has a number of attributes or Common Features that
are used to test whether the implementation and institutionalization of a Key Process
Area is effective, repeatable, and lasting. These Common Features are Commitment to
Perform, Ability to Perform, Activities Performed, Measurement and Analysis, and
Verifying Implementation. Activities Performed relates to implementation activities

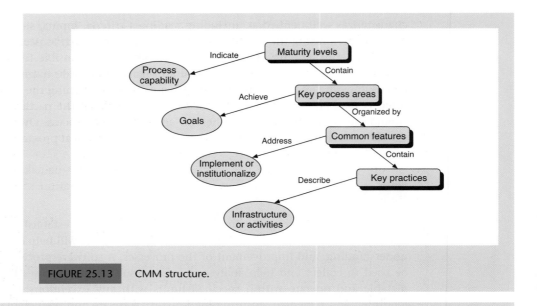

FIGURE 25.13 CMM structure.

Levels \ Process categories	Management **Software project planning, management, etc.**	Organizational **Senior management review, etc.**	Engineering **Requirements analysis, design, code, test, etc.**
5 Optimizing		Technology change management Process change management	Defect prevention
4 Managed	Quantitative process management		Software quality management
3 Defined	Integrated software management Intergroup co-ordination	Organizational process definition Training programme	Software product engineering Peer reviews
2 Repeatable	Requirements management Software project planning Software project tracking and oversight Software subcontract management Software quality assurance Software configuration management		
1 Initial	*Ad hoc* processes		

FIGURE 25.14 Key Process Areas grouped according to level and process category.

whereas the rest relate to the institutionalization factors (i.e. the elements that ingrain the process into the culture of the organization). So, for example, Ability to Perform describes the conditions which must be present, such as adequate resources, necessary training, etc. Commitment to Perform specifies the organizational policies and senior management sponsorship which must be present to ensure that the process is created and that it endures over time. Finally the Key Practices describe the infrastructure and activities that ensure the effective Implementation and Institutionalization of the Key Process Area. An example of a Key Practice might be 'that adequate resources and funding are provided for planning the software project'; this might then be broken down into detail which specifies that developers with experience and skills are available and that relevant tools, such as spreadsheets, estimation software, project scheduling, etc. are also available.

It can be seen that the specification of all these Key Process Areas, Goals, Common Features, and Key Practices and their interrelationships is an enormous task on its own. The Report documenting the Key Practices is itself nearly 400 pages which has to be got to grips with before the processes can be implemented and institutionalized. Thus, CMM provides a very detailed set of elements and definitions for each level which defines what is necessary, and must be in place, for organizations to be considered as having reached a particular level and what they have to achieve in order to move to the next level. For example, according to McGrew et al. (1999), there are at least 121 Key Practices that must be implemented in order to move from Level 1 to Level 2 and that on average it takes 23 months (Johnson and Broadman, 1996). Organizations must move from level to level in sequence; that is, levels cannot be skipped, otherwise some of the essential foundations or building blocks of effective software processes will be missed.

By specifying the key practices in detail CMM emphasizes that it is not requiring or espousing 'a specific model of the software life cycle, a specific organizational structure, a specific separation of responsibilities, or a specific management and technical approach to development. The intention, rather, is to provide a description of the essential elements of an effective software process. The key practices are intended to communicate principles that apply to a wide variety of projects and organizations, that are valid across a range of typical software applications, and that will remain valid over time. Therefore, the approach is to describe the principles and leave their implementation up to each organization, according to its culture and the experiences of its managers and technical staff' (Paulk et al., 1993b).

Although originally developed for the military, CMM has over the years become increasingly popular in commercial business (Diaz and Sligo, 1997; Jalote, 2000) as a basis for improving software processes and has become very influential in relation to software quality. For example, the processes of the two largest producers of software, IBM and Microsoft, have been compared against the standards of the CMM, with the basic assumption that the CMM is 'still the best way to produce quality software' (Phan, 2001).

It is difficult to know exactly how many organizations have formally adopted the CMM but certainly some of the major producers of software have done so. However, Gray (1996) reports that most organizations 'seem to still be at Level 1' with *ad hoc*, even chaotic processes, but according to McGuire (2000) the implementation of CMM leads to impressive improvements and he states that there are 'compelling statistics on reduced cycle time, increased productivity, fewer defects, and decreased risk throughout the software life cycle'. More specifically Lawlis et al. (1995), in a study of 52 defence projects, found lower costs and better scheduling with higher levels of CMM. Broadman and Johnson (1996) also found improvements in productivity, schedules, and quality, as did Herbsleb et al. (1994) suggesting that companies implementing CMM achieved averages of 35 per cent improvements in software productivity and 39 per cent reductions in post-delivery defects. Improvements are also reported in individual companies, for example, Hughes Aircraft (Willis et al., 1998), who were the first organization to achieve 'SEI-assisted' Level 3, Boeing (Fowler, 1997), Motorola (Diaz and Sligo, 1997), and Infosys (Jalote, 2000).

CMM is essentially about introducing discipline into software development by formalizing, standardizing, and institutionalizing a set of processes. These processes relate to a particular view of technical software development and embody the assumption that an engineering approach is the best way to develop such systems. It is based on a manufacturing and product-building view of systems development. This is not accepted by all, and they have argued that software development has conceptual differences, for example, it is not usually designed and built and then mass-produced, and it changes and evolves over time incrementally. These differences, it is sometimes argued, means that software is not like a traditional product mass manufacturing process but is perhaps more like a creative art than a science, and needs to be treated as such. Also it is pointed out that CMM is really only concerned with the narrower software development process rather than the wider process of information systems development and thus misses many of the real, complex issues of systems development. Further, CMM, although including some processes relating to requirements identification, adopts the view that requirements are inherently definable and that it is just a question of working hard enough, and having the right processes in place, to identify the requirements successfully. Clearly this is just one view of the world and it contrasts sharply with other views (e.g. SSM, see Section 24.1), where requirements are more problematic, are more perceptual than absolute, and are not 'discoverable' in this way.

These criticisms relate to some fundamental differences in philosophies and assumptions relating to systems development; nevertheless it is clear that the CMM view is widely accepted in some quarters and is an important 'approach' to systems development practice, if not a methodology in its own right. Some have suggested that although there are these broad differences in approaches, of which CMM is one end of the spectrum, it does not necessarily mean that one is always right and the other wrong. For example, Fitzgerald and Fitzgerald (1999) have argued that in certain circumstances CMM may be an appropriate approach to systems development. Such circumstances being where requirements are narrowly scoped and definable, where the circumstances are akin to manufacturing, where the environment is relatively stable, where the processes are predictable, and where the human element in the problem domain is not the primary issue. Fitzgerald and Fitzgerald (1999) use the example of the software elements of a telecommunication system, that is, the software controlling large switching and communications infrastructure systems, and indeed these have been successfully developed in a company having achieved a high CMM maturity level.

25.4 EUROMETHOD

With the introduction of the single European market and the removal of various barriers to trade, it was predictable that at some point the European Commission would turn its attention to service and procurement standards in the information systems arena. The lack of standards in the area and the fragmentation of the information systems services and tools marketplace is perceived as a barrier to open competition and the principles of the single or open market. In 1989, the European Commission (EC), through its IT standardization policy unit, established Euromethod as an initiative to facilitate cross-border trading within the European Union (EU) in the acquisition of information systems. Clearly it was also intended to enhance and promote the overall competitiveness of the European information systems industry in a global context and thereby European industry in general. The description below is based on CCTA (1990, 1994a, b), Jenkins (1994), Stewart (1994), and Turner and Jenkins (1996).

The objective of Euromethod is to provide a public domain framework for the planning, procurement, and management of services for the investigation, development, or amendment of information systems. This framework and associated standards would, it was hoped, help overcome the problems posed by the current diversity of approaches, methods, and techniques in information systems used in Europe and help users and service providers to come to common understandings concerning requirements and solutions in information systems projects.

The focus of Euromethod is on the marketplace, and it seeks to smooth the path for those requiring and procuring information systems services and those potentially providing such services. It seeks to enable all suppliers to compete on an equal footing, no matter which European country they are from, by providing a common terminology that can bridge the different cultures and methods employed across the EU member states. Euromethod only addresses those arrangements where there is likely to be a contractual relationship between a customer and supplier. It does not address the situation where information systems services are provided to users by an in-house IT facility or department.

Euromethod was based on experiences with existing methods as follows:

- SSADM from the UK;
- Merise from France;
- DAFNE (DAta and Function NEtworking) from Italy;
- SDM (System Development Methodology) from the Netherlands;
- MEIN (MEtodológica INformática) from Spain;
- Vorgehensmodell from Germany;
- IE (Information Engineering) from the UK/US.

Some of these methodologies are described in Chapter 20 (i.e. SSADM, Merise, and IE).

The scope of Euromethod is supposed to cover all stages of procurement through to completion of an information systems adaptation and the associated planning and management elements. In practice some elements, such as the requirements

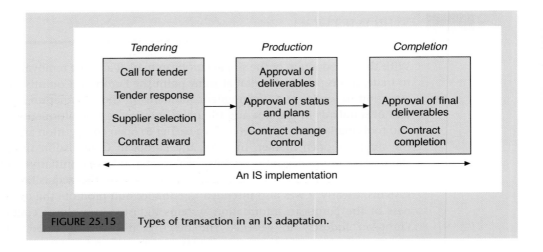

FIGURE 25.15 Types of transaction in an IS adaptation.

specification stage, are addressed in more detail than others, and some things are missing altogether, such as technical architecture.

An information systems adaptation, to which Euromethod might apply, consists of any development or modification of an information system, including organizational, human, and technical elements, providing that the initial (or current) state and the required final state can be defined. For example, an information system adaptation might be a feasibility study, a system design, an enhancement, or a reverse engineering project. So, Euromethod can be applied at any stage of a project and applied many times in a development.

Euromethod focuses on the understanding, planning, and management of the contractual relationships between customers and suppliers of information systems adaptations. The key transactions required between customers and suppliers are identified. Figure 25.15, for example, summarizes the high-level transactions required in the process of tendering, production, and completion of an information systems adaptation. This focus results in Euromethod identifying and defining the deliverables required between customers and suppliers. Each transaction implies one or more decision points, each of which needs supporting by a deliverable. Euromethod identifies a hierarchy of deliverables as in Figure 25.16. The target domain is the part of the organization affected by the information systems adaptation, and the information systems descriptions are the documentation designs and specifications, whereas the operational items are deliverables that can be installed as part of the information system itself. This could be a screen or a prototype. The project domain is the temporary organization established to adapt an information system and manage the process. The deliverables on this side are divided into plans for the production process and reports to manage the process. The delivery plan is the key definition of the process of defining the customer/supplier transactions in the overall context of the information systems adaptation, that is, the problem situation. Figure 25.17 represents the planning process to produce the delivery plan.

Euromethod recognizes that different types of information systems adaptation require different approaches depending on the situation. Differences may be due to the complexity or uncertainty of the environment. Euromethod provides guidelines and support for a variety of different situations. Guidelines exist for the identification

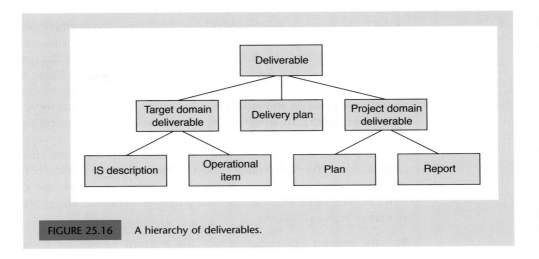

FIGURE 25.16 A hierarchy of deliverables.

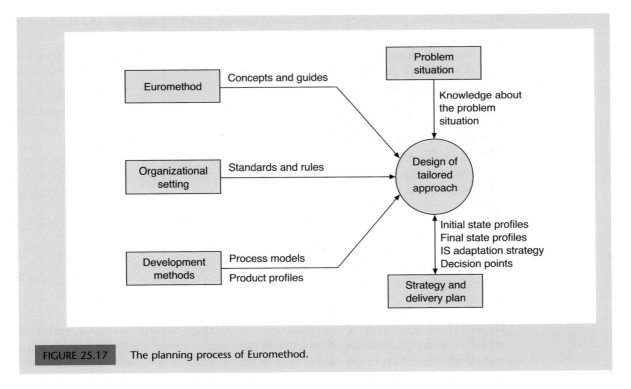

FIGURE 25.17 The planning process of Euromethod.

of important situational factors, the assessment of complexity, uncertainty and risks, and the definition of a strategy for the IS adaptation. The delivery planning process of Figure 25.17 illustrates the context of this situation-driven approach.

Euromethod is not another information systems development methodology but is a framework. It seeks to provide guidance as to how to map or bridge a particular method into the basic Euromethod framework. In this sense a method might include a European systems development methodology (e.g. SSADM), a project management approach (e.g.

PRINCE), or a procurement standard (e.g. TAP, Total Acquisition Process). (TAP is the UK public sector preferred procurement method for IS/IT services.) Guidelines are provided that help bridge between Euromethod concepts and those of the specific method.

These principles result in three Euromethod models. These are the transaction model, the deliverable model, and the strategy model. The transaction model helps understand, manage, and facilitate customer/supplier interactions across organizational boundaries during an information systems adaptation. It identifies a set of generic customer/supplier transactions in information systems adaptations, including, for each, the goals, the key roles, and responsibilities in both the customer and supplier organizations. The deliverable model defines the target domain for an information systems adaptation, what an information system is, the scope of the information systems adaptation, and the essential properties. The essential properties are expressed as a set of views as follows:

- *the business information view* – the relevant knowledge about the information resource;

- *the business process view* – the relevant knowledge about processes and their use of the information resource;

- *the work practice view* – the relevant knowledge about individual actors and their use of the information resource.

These views are further developed, and the computer systems required to support these essential properties are identified. The business information view is developed to identify the computer systems' data view, the business process view to the computer systems' function view, and the work practice view to the computer systems' architecture view.

The strategy model reflects the situation-driven principle above and helps define the approach required which reduces, or contains, the risks of a particular problem situation. The strategy options relate to systems installation, systems construction, systems description (or modelling), and project control.

In practice, the development of a Euromethod delivery plan involves the following tasks:

- assessment of the problem situation;
- definition of a strategy;
- definition of decision points.

The first stage, assessment of the problem situation, helps to clarify the requirements of the information systems adaptation for both customer and supplier. First, the initial state of the adaptation, that is, the current state of the existing information system, is defined. A good definition of the initial state is crucial to enable the supplier to understand the starting point of the adaptation. Second, the desired final state of the adaptation is defined. This includes the elements of the initial state that are to be changed, the additional items to be produced, the documentation, the data, the interfaces, and so on. The initial and final states are defined in terms of Euromethod essential properties and the views that they represent (see above). As various existing methods and methodologies will have already been defined in these terms, this should enable each final state deliverable to be assessed as to which approach might be most appropriate for its production.

This first stage also involves the determination of the situational factors and an assessment of their complexity and uncertainty. Such factors might include the complexity of the business processes, the heterogeneity of the users, the attitude and ability of the actors involved, the stability of the environment, and the requirements and the quality of the specifications.

These factors are now used for the next task, to define an appropriate strategy for the production of the final state deliverables based upon the strategy model. For example, the strategy option chosen for system construction might be evolutionary and participatory in situations where the complexity of requirements is judged to be high and the understanding of the business processes is low. In practice, the analysis is more sophisticated than this, as Euromethod provides heuristics for the suitability of the approach and examples of how to reduce risk.

Finally, once the strategy has been defined, the decision points are identified. These are a by-product of the deliverables exchanged between customers and suppliers and their identification is based on the transaction model. Euromethod identifies three categories of decision: investment, design, and systems acceptance. For each decision point, the decision to be made is identified plus the roles of those involved, the transactions they represent, and the deliverables that are exchanged. The full documentation of each deliverable is made according to Euromethod product profiles. Both project and target domain deliverables are identified. The profile for target domain deliverables consists of:

- the deliverable type;
- the information system view; that is, the essential properties of the transaction model as described above;
- the computer system view;
- the IS properties within each view;
- non-functional properties;
- scope (of the deliverable);
- state (of the deliverable);
- degree of formality (of the deliverable).

Some of this information is similar in type to that required for initial and final states, and this reflects Euromethod's approach to standard terms and definitions. These concepts are again used in the method's bridging process and enable relevant external methods for the decision points and deliverables to be identified and used.

The sequence and schedules of the decision points are also identified, and the total documentation provides the basis of the contractual agreement for the information systems adaptation between customer and supplier.

However, the high ideals of Euromethod are difficult to achieve in reality. There are different versions of Merise and other country standard approaches that are used in practice, so agreeing one for the whole of Europe is not easy. In practice, this means that Euromethod has influenced SSADM, Merise, and so on by providing agreed standards, rather than led to an imposition of one approach throughout Europe. However, it is often seen as adding yet another layer to already bureaucratic methodologies, such as SSADM and Merise.

Euromethod is a Europe-wide initiative that the EC have decided is important and in which they have invested. The concept of method bridging is clearly attractive, and it supports a common understanding about IS development across Europe. Whatever its originators set out to do, it has proved to be more of a contingency framework (like Multiview), to be adapted and to adapt local methodologies, such as SSADM, rather than a 'super-methodology'.

25.5   SUMMARY

- In this chapter we have described four approaches that we classify as frameworks rather than methodologies, mainly because they provide guidance to the developer in choosing methods, techniques, and tools rather than a prescriptive step-by-step approach.

QUESTIONS

1 Do you agree with the distinction made between frameworks and methodologies?

2 Multiview might also be described as a 'blended' methodology (see Chapter 20). Why is this? What elements have been blended? Where have they come from?

3 What are the five levels of CMM? How does an organization move from one level to another?

4 Why does Euromethod include elements relating to 'procurement' rather than development of information systems?

25.6   FURTHER READING

Ackerman, F. and Eden, C. (2001) SODA – journey making and mapping in practice, in Rosenhead, J. and Mingers, J. (2001) *Rational Analysis for a Problematic World Revisited – Problem Structuring Methods for Complexity, Uncertainty and Conflict*, 2nd edn, John Wiley & Sons, Chichester, UK.

Avison, D.E. and Wood-Harper, A.T. (1990) *Multiview: An Exploration in Information Systems Development*, McGraw-Hill, Maidenhead, UK.

Paulk, M.C., Weber, C.V., Curtis, B., and Chrissis, M.B. (1995) *The Capability Maturity Model, Guidelines for Improving the Software Process*, Addison-Wesley, Reading, Massachusetts.

Turner, P. and Jenkins, T. (1996) *Euromethod and Beyond*, Thomson, London.

PART
7
ISSUES AND FRAMEWORKS

In the first edition of this book, published in 1988, the area of information systems development methodologies was described as a jungle, and we concluded that this was unlikely to change much in the future due to the continuing developments in information technology, information systems, and organizations as a whole. In the second edition published in 1995 we thought that not much had changed in this respect, and that it was still 'a methodology jungle'. Six years later we feel we can say that perhaps there is not quite the diversity of methodological approaches that there were.

Although some newer methodologies have been adopted, most notably the OO methods based on UML, many have disappeared, and perhaps the picture has become a little clearer. In the previous edition we made reference to an estimate that there were over 1,000 brand name methodologies worldwide (Jayaratna, 1994), but we suggested that this figure should not be taken too literally because we felt that many of them were probably very similar and differentiated only for marketing purposes. Today we feel the figure would be considerably smaller, possibly less than a hundred – with the number of fundamentally different methodologies even smaller. Therefore, we conclude that there is some improvement in the situation and that the area is less of a 'jungle' than it was. Nevertheless it is still quite confusing, especially for newcomers to the field.

Chapter 26 attempts to review developments and discuss the various issues as a way of providing some help in understanding the 'jungle'. The treatment is both theoretical and philosophical, as well as practical. The nature of such discussions is that there are few hard and fast facts, and much of the chapter involves our interpretations and opinions. We hope that they are based on sound judgement and experience, but they also recognize that there will be those who make different interpretations. Nevertheless we hope that this chapter contributes to informed debate concerning methodologies.

In Chapter 27 we provide a checklist and framework for comparing methodologies, and we use the framework to compare methodologies discussed in the book. The framework consists of philosophy, model, techniques and tools, scope, output, practice, and product. Again, we do not suggest an objective comparison, indeed our discussion is sometimes philosophical in nature, our purpose is more to raise issues and engender debate.

26 ISSUES

WHAT IS A METHODOLOGY?

In Chapter 2 we provided a working definition of the term 'methodology', and, although this has been adequate for our purposes, we will now look in more depth at the question 'what is a methodology?'. The term is not well defined either in the literature or by practitioners. There is very little agreement as to what it means other than at a very general level. The term is used very loosely but also very extensively.

This loose use of the term does not, of course, mean that there are no definitions, simply that there are no universally-agreed definitions. At the general level, a methodology is regarded as a recommended series of steps and procedures to be followed in the course of developing an information system. In a brief *ad hoc* survey, this proves to be about the maximum that people will agree to, and, of course, such a definition raises many more questions than it answers. For example:

- What is the difference between a methodology and a method?
- Does a methodology include a specification of the techniques and tools which are to be used?
- Does a collection of techniques and tools constitute a methodology?
- Should the use of a methodology produce the same results each time?

The questions that arise are fundamental as well as numerous. Unfortunately the problem will not be solved here; the most that can be achieved is that the issues will be aired. The information systems community has regularly debated the meaning of the term methodology in an information systems context, and as yet it has not come up with any universal definition.

One of the most useful definitions for the authors is that provided by the British Computer Society (BCS) Information Systems Analysis and Design Working Group as long ago as 1983. They defined an information systems methodology as:

a recommended collection of philosophies, phases, procedures, rules, techniques, tools, documentation, management, and training for developers of information systems.

(Maddison, 1983)

Utilizing this definition, we suggest that a methodology has a number of components which specify:

- how a project is to be broken down into stages;
- what tasks are to be carried out at each stage;
- what outputs are to be produced;
- when, and under what circumstances, they are to be carried out;
- what constraints are to be applied;
- which people should be involved;
- how the project should be managed and controlled;
- what support tools may be utilized.

In addition, a methodology should specify the training needs of the users of the methodology. On the other hand, the frameworks discussed in Chapter 25 are far less prescriptive.

Apart from the above, we believe that a methodology should also specifically address the critical issue of 'philosophy'. We mean by this the underlying theories and assumptions that the authors of the methodology believe in and that have shaped the development of the methodology. This identifies those sometimes unwritten aspects and beliefs that make a methodology an effective approach to the development of information systems in the eyes of their authors. We believe that the definition of a methodology should include specific reference to its philosophy as this has a critical bearing on the understanding of a particular methodology. An information systems development methodology is therefore much more than just a series of techniques along with the use of software tools.

Utilizing these ideas and beliefs we extend the BCS definition of a **methodology** as follows:

A systems development methodology is a recommended means to achieve the development, or part of the development, of information systems based on a set of rationales and an underlying philosophy that supports, justifies and makes coherent such a recommendation for a particular context. The recommended means usually includes the identification of phases, procedures, tasks, rules, techniques, guidelines, documentation and tools. They might also include recommendations concerning the management and organization of the approach and the identification and training of the participants.

Some methodologies are, of course, more comprehensive than others, which is why we include the statement about 'development or part development' and, as mentioned above, the 'rationales and underlying philosophy' are not always made clear but we believe that they always exist and are the key to understanding a particular methodology. For example, they will shed light on the ethical stance that a methodology incorporates. We include 'a particular context' in the definition because it is clear that methodologies are not universal in their applicability, despite some methodology authors seemingly thinking they are. For us there are always limitations to the applicability, and thus we believe that those contexts and limits should be addressed. Together the philosophy and the context help illuminate the assumptions that the authors of the methodology are making, which is why we do not specifically include a reference to 'assumptions' in our definition. In practice, many methodologies, particularly commercial ones, are products that are 'packaged' and might include:

- manuals;
- education and training (including videos);
- consultancy support;
- tools and toolsets;
- *pro forma* documents;
- model-building templates, and so on.

Some have argued (e.g. Flynn, 1992) that the term 'methodology' is not apt in the context of systems development and that the term 'method' is perfectly adequate to cover everything that we mean by a methodology. Indeed Flynn states that 'the term methodology was popular for a time in the 1980s' implying that it is no longer much used. This is contrary to our experience, although it is true that the term 'method' is also used. For us, this might be argued to substitute one ill-defined word for, another, but more importantly we believe that the term 'methodology' has certain characteristics that are not implied by 'method', for example, the inclusion of 'philosophy' which we have already suggested is key. Methodology is thus a wider concept than method.

Checkland (1981) has distinguished between the two terms and says that a methodology:

> ... is a set of principles of method, which in any particular situation has to be reduced to a method uniquely suited to that particular situation.

In Checkland (1985), he argues that information systems development must be seen as a form of enquiry in the context of the general model of organized enquiry, which consists of three components: an intellectual framework, a methodology, and an application area. This suggests a hierarchy of elements to enquiry.

The first element is the **intellectual framework**, which comprises the ideas that we use to make sense of the world. This is described as the philosophy that guides and constrains the enquiry. It consists of ontological assumptions, that is, beliefs about the fundamental nature of the physical and social world and the way it operates, and epistemological assumptions, that is, the theory of the method or grounds of knowledge. These terms are discussed in Section 27.2. It also consists of ethical values, which should be articulated, that may serve to guide or constrain the enquiry.

The second element is the methodology. This is the operationalization of the intellectual framework of ideas into a set of prescriptions or guidelines for investigation which require, or recognize as valid, particular methods and techniques.

The third element is the application area; that is, some part of the real world that is deemed to be problematical and worthy of investigation.

This is a useful framework for discussions of research and enquiry, but we need to know how well it relates to the world of information systems development methodologies. Working backward, it would seem that the application area is that of information systems development in general. The methodology element is equivalent to the collection of phases, procedures, rules, methods, and techniques that are usually considered to be a methodology in the information systems world. The intellectual framework is the element that is often missing from methodologies, or rather it is not missing, for it exists, but is not explicitly articulated. In our definition, much of this intellectual framework element is included in what we term the underlying philosophy, which we include in the definition of methodology itself.

26.2 THE RATIONALE FOR A METHODOLOGY

It is important to discover why people adopt a particular methodology. Obviously this varies substantially between organizations and individuals, but we can identify three main categories of rationale: a better end product, a better development process, and a standardized process.

1 A better end product

People may want a methodology to improve the end product of the development process, that is, they want better information systems. This should not be confused with the quality of the development process, addressed below. It is difficult to assess the quality of information systems produced as a result of using a particular methodology. For example, we cannot know that the use of the methodology produced the particular results. The same results might have occurred if the system had been developed using another methodology or without using any methodology at all.

Even if we had some way of comparing the results of using different methodologies, the elements that are perceived to constitute measures of quality differ considerably from person to person, and there is little agreement within the information systems community on this issue. The following represents our attempt to address some of the components of quality of an information system:

- *Acceptability* – whether the people who are using the system find the system satisfactory and whether it fulfils their information needs. This includes business users and managers and their requirements.

- *Availability* – whether it is accessible; when and where required.

- *Cohesiveness* – whether there is interaction between components (subsystems) so that there is overall integration of both information systems and associated manual and business systems.

- *Compatibility* – whether the system fits with other systems and other parts of the organization.

- *Documentation* – whether there is good documentation to help communications between operators, users, developers, and managers.

- *Ease of learning* – whether the learning curve for new users is short and intuitive.

- *Economy* – whether the system is cost-effective and within resources and constraints.

- *Effectiveness* – whether the system performs and operates in the best possible manner to meet its overall business or organizational objectives.

- *Efficiency* – whether the system utilizes resources to their best advantage.

- *Fast development rate* – whether the time needed to develop the project is quick, relative to its size and complexity.

- *Flexibility* – whether the system is easy to modify and whether it is easy to add or delete components.

- *Functionality* – whether the system caters for the requirements.

- *Implementability* – whether the changeover from the old to the new system is feasible, in technical, social, economic, and organizational senses.

- *Low coupling* – whether the interaction between subsystems is such that they can be modified without affecting the rest of the system.

- *Maintainability* – whether it needs a lot of effort to keep the system running satisfactorily and continuing to meet changing requirements over its lifetime.

- *Portability* – whether the information system can run on other equipment or in other sites.

- *Reliability* – whether the error rate is minimized and outputs are consistent and correct.

- *Robustness* – whether the system is fail-safe and fault-tolerant.

- *Security* – whether the information system is robust against misuse.

- *Simplicity* – whether ambiguities and complexities are minimized.

- *Testability* – whether the system can be tested thoroughly to minimize operational failure and user dissatisfaction.

- *Timeliness* – whether the information system operates successfully under normal, peak, and every condition, giving information when required.

- *Visibility* – whether it is possible for users to trace why certain actions occurred.

Maximization of all these criteria is, of course, not attainable; indeed, some actually work against each other. Ideally, the most appropriate information systems methodology can be chosen and then 'tuned' so that emphasis can be given to those criteria which are particularly important in the problem situation. Such tuning, or even any consideration of tuning, is rare in methodologies.

2   A better development process

Under this heading comes the benefits that accrue from tightly controlling the development process and identifying the outputs (or deliverables) at each stage. This results in improved management and project control. It is usually argued that productivity is enhanced with the use of a methodology; that is, we can either build systems faster, given specific resources, or use fewer resources to achieve the same results. It is sometimes also argued that the use of a methodology reduces the level of skills required of the analysts, which improves the development process by reducing its cost.

For some, the problems of developing information systems can be improved by adopting the quality standards that have proved popular in manufacturing and industrial processes. These standards are designed to ensure the quality of processes rather than that of the end product, and this sometimes leads to emphasis on conformity to the standard irrespective of whether this helps the quality of the system.

Another problem argued in Avison et al. (1994) is that the traditional manufacturing process is quite different from the process of developing software products. For example, the product of software is a 'one-off' rather than a mass replication of a design. There are schemes which recognize these difficulties and attempt to interpret the standards in methods applicable to software development. Although such standards have not yet made a large impact, either in terms of coverage or improved quality, they are helping to raise the issues and level of debate concerning quality in the development of information systems.

3   A standardized process

The needs associated with this category relate to the benefits of having a common approach throughout an organization. This means that more integrated systems can result, that staff can easily change from project to project without retraining being necessary, and that a base of common experience and knowledge can be achieved. In short, all the normal benefits of standardization can be achieved, including the specific benefit of easier maintenance of systems.

All the reasons contained in the above categories have been specified, in some form or other, by the authors or vendors of methodologies as being benefits of adopting their particular approach. In contrast purchasers might well be more interested in:

1. Improved systems specifications.
2. Easier maintenance and enhancement.

Methodologies rarely directly address improvement of the maintenance task (but see Section 24.5), although vendors often claim it as an indirect benefit as the information system developed will require less maintenance through use of the methodology. Further, some approaches – particularly those discussed in Chapter 25 – suggest flexibility within a framework, rather than 'a standardized process'.

26.3   ADOPTING A METHODOLOGY IN PRACTICE

An organization thinking of adopting or purchasing a methodology has a number of concerns. These relate to what they get and whether they are guaranteed successful information systems as a result.

What do they get? To address the first question, they get what the vendor or methodology author gives them, and this differs greatly:

- a methodology can range from being a fully fledged product detailing every stage and task to be undertaken to being a vague outline of the basic principles in a short pamphlet;
- a methodology can cover widely differing areas of the development process, from high-level strategic and organizational problem solving to the detail of implementing a small computer system;
- a methodology can cover conceptual issues or physical design procedures or the whole range of intermediate stages;
- a methodology can range from being designed to be applicable to specific types of problem in certain types of environment or industry to an all-encompassing general-purpose methodology;
- a methodology may be potentially usable by anybody or only by highly trained specialists or be designed for users to develop their own applications;
- a methodology may require an army of people to perform all the specified tasks or it may not even have any specified tasks;
- a methodology may or may not include tools and toolsets.

The variations on this theme are numerous. It is clear that methodology adopters should be aware of what their needs are and choose their methodology accordingly. This does not always seem to be the case. One organization that adopted a particular methodology found that they had to write detailed manuals themselves to specify what was required of their development staff. What they purchased was a management overview without any detail.

Some methodologies are purchased as a product, others are available by purchasing a licence, others are obtained through a contract for consultancy work, some come as part of the purchase of a tool, and some by a combination of the above. As can be imagined from this, the cost of methodologies varies considerably. Some are effectively free, and this is the case for Merise. Often the initial purchase of the methodology product is the least of the investment, and it is the training, additional hardware and software, and ongoing consultancy costs that mount up and eventually dwarf the initial purchase price. What is also clear is that the potential organizational costs of adopting a methodology, particularly if it is adopted as a company standard, are enormous. These organizational costs are not the purchase price, but the costs of embedding the methodology in the culture of the organization, the opportunity costs of not doing something else, the costs of training and educating users and managers to participate in the use of the methodology, and so on. There may also be large costs associated with changing methodologies, as once a particular methodology becomes embedded in an organization it is not easy to change the development culture.

These costs are usually seriously underestimated in the evaluation of the cost of a methodology. It also indicates that the IT or systems development department should not necessarily be the ones to make decisions concerning the adoption of a particular methodology. It appears that in the majority of cases the decision to adopt a standard methodology and the choice of the particular methodology is made by the IT/IS department. This is often because this department assumes it as its role and prerogative. Indeed, it has been suggested that this assumption of technical expertise is the structural basis of IS professionals' power in organizations (Markus and Bjørn-Andersen, 1987). It can legitimately be argued that the users, and business managers in general, should be making such decisions, as they are the ones who have to make the actual investment, not just in terms of money, but in time and effort, and ultimately business success, as a result of methodology decisions. However, the assumption that it is an IT decision is frequently accepted and encouraged by the rest of the organization. Information systems development is often seen as a technical issue that the technicians should decide upon. After all that is what they are paid for! We have not taken this view in this book.

However, we know of instances where IT departments have attempted to involve users and business managers in decisions concerning methodologies without success. The users and managers preferred to leave it to the IT department despite the potential significant implications on the degree of user involvement in development that the different methodologies under consideration embodied, and ultimately on the overall future success of the business. Equally, there are some cases where users and managers have not been consulted in the choice of methodology at all, and they have refused to co-operate in developments as a result.

Markus and Bjørn-Andersen (1987) argue that the choice of methodology is in practice made by corporate IS rather than by involving individual analysts who have to work with the methodology following the decision. Therefore, the power structure is argued to be conspiring against the users and the business managers, as discussed above, and against the information systems worker as well.

The answer to the second question posed above, '*are they guaranteed successful information systems as a result of using the methodology?*', is clearly 'no'. However, this does raise the question of what a methodology is supposed to produce. If two teams of developers are using the same methodology on a similar project, in the same type of environment, can the same results be expected, and if not, why not?

Clearly the developers may interpret the demands of the methodology differently and thus end up with different results. The methodology may give a lot of leeway to the developers in terms of how they perform the specified tasks, and so the results will be different. The developers may have varying skill levels, which will also produce differing results. However, it is sometimes argued that, given these variations, multiple uses of the same methodology in the same circumstances should yield roughly the same results. The tighter, more specific the methodology, the more reproducible the results, particularly where the methodology specifies the exact techniques and tools to be employed under each circumstance.

This is a highly contentious area, but the implication is that if the results are to some degree reproducible, then we must be sure that the methodology specifies 'a best' way of producing information systems. We cannot say *the* best way, because there may be trade-offs between quality, quantity, skill levels, reliability, generality, and so on. But we want a methodology that will produce good results. This implies that a methodology is not just a helpful set of guidelines that enables the developer to organize the development process more effectively and efficiently, but that it embodies a good way of developing systems. If it is reproducible then it leads to the development of particular solutions, and thus if we adopt a methodology, then this methodology must be, to our minds, a good way of doing things. If it is not, it will lead to problems, because the nature of the methodology will exclude other ways of doing things. For example, the adoption of a data flow diagram-based methodology will, if it is rigidly followed, exclude the kind of analysis that the SSM methodology recommends. There will, for example, be no analysis of conflict between various actors in the existing system.

The question of repeatability or reproducibility is obviously not one that can be easily tested in practice. It is impossible to create exactly the same environment in an organization for two sets of developers to develop systems which we can then compare. Checkland (1987) highlights the problem by challenging developers of systems perceived to be successful to prove that another methodology would not have been better. And, of course, they cannot. He asks the developers of systems, where there have been problems, to *prove* it was not their incompetence that led to the problems rather than the methodology. Once again they cannot. It has been suggested that two development teams could work independently on developing a system to the same requirements in the same environment enabling a legitimate comparison of the systems at the end. However, the very fact that there are two sets of developers will undoubtedly influence the results. For example, the fact that one set will have talked to a user first will influence the results when the second set of developers talks to that same user. Even if flawed, the results of such experimentation would be interesting, but it seems the practical problems are insurmountable as the authors have no knowledge of any such attempt, let alone a systematic study.

This lack of repeatability, or rather the ability to demonstrate repeatability, is often used to suggest that information systems is not really an engineering discipline. However, engineering is also a creative profession. Will two engineers design the same bridge or two electronic engineers design the same circuit for a particular function? Probably not, but the degrees of freedom in designing a bridge are greater than that of designing a particular circuit; that is, the two designs of the circuit will probably be more similar than the two designs of the bridge. With information systems, the degrees of freedom are typically even greater than for the bridge. The adoption of an information systems methodology can thus be argued to be an attempt to reduce the degrees of freedom.

If this is the case, then the implication still holds that the methodology should embody a best way of developing systems. This is not always appreciated when methodologies are being selected and may result in the development of inappropriate systems. The question whether the methodology embodies a best way of developing systems is rarely asked. The more usual questions are:

- whether it fits in with the organization's way of working;
- whether it specifies what deliverables (or outputs) are required at the end of each stage;
- whether it enables better control and improved productivity;
- whether it supports a particular set of tools.

As has been observed earlier, there exist a large number of different methodologies. This implies that there are large numbers of 'best' ways of developing information systems. Many of them are probably quite similar when closely examined, but many of them do differ substantially on fundamentals. It is the identification of these fundamentals that are of importance in our opinion, and Section 27.2 will discuss the comparison of methodologies. But, first, we categorize a number of eras of methodology evolution.

26.4 EVOLUTION AND DEVELOPMENT OF METHODOLOGIES

In considering the evolution and development of methodologies we have identified a number of methodology 'eras' as follows.

1 Pre-methodology era

The first era is known as the pre-methodology era and information systems, say until the early 1970s, were developed and implemented without the use of an explicit or formalized development methodology. In these early days, the emphasis of computer applications development was on programming and solving various technical problems. Indeed most of the problems were perceived to be in the technical arena, particularly those resulting from the rather limited hardware of the time. Developers were technically trained but rarely fully understood the business or the organizational context in which the systems were being implemented, and they were typically not very good at communicating with non-technical people. The needs of the users were rarely well established with the consequence that the system designs were often inappropriate to the real requirements of the application and the business. The approach to development was usually individualistic, depending on the experience and skills of the programmer, and based on some simple rules-of-thumb. This approach often resulted in poor control and management of projects. Emphasis was also placed on maintaining operational systems to get them working properly rather than on developing new systems and responding to the needs of users.

However, despite these problems, the demand for computer-based business systems was steadily increasing and management was demanding more appropriate systems for their expensive outlay. This led to a number of changes. First, there was a growing appreciation that analysis and design required different people with different skills to that of programmers. This led to the systems analyst as the key role in systems development. Second, there was a growing appreciation of the desirability for standards and a more disciplined approach to the development of information systems in organizations. Therefore, the first information systems development methodologies were established.

2 Early-methodology era

The early-methodology era of the 1970s and early 1980s was characterized by an approach to building computer-based applications that focused on the identification of phases and stages that it was thought would help control and enable the better management of systems development and bring a discipline to bear. This approach has come to be known as the Systems Development Life Cycle (SDLC) or the 'waterfall model'. It consisted of a number of stages of development that had to be followed sequentially (it has been discussed extensively in Chapter 3). There were a number of variants of the SDLC but usually the major stages were: feasibility study, systems investigation, analysis, design, development, implementation, and maintenance. One phase had to be completed before the next one began (hence the term waterfall), and each phase had a set of defined outputs or deliverables that had to be produced before the phase could be deemed complete. Therefore, it was also a mechanism for project control. In systems development it also became associated with a set of techniques, such as flowcharting, that were applied to particular phases. There was also the notion of iteration around the phases, as things changed and problems were encountered, although this was often ignored in practice.

The SDLC has a number of features to commend it (Chapter 3). It is tried and tested and, for some, it is well 'proven'. The use of documentation standards helps to ensure that proposals are complete and that they are communicated to both users and developers. There are controls and these, along with the division of the project into phases of manageable tasks with deliverables, help to avoid missed cutover dates and disappointments regarding what is delivered. Unexpected cost overruns and unrealized benefits are also less likely. The approach also ensures that developers are trained and follow a well-formed, standard process and that users are also trained to enable them to use the systems effectively.

However, as we have seen in Section 3.6 there are a number of serious weaknesses or limitations to the approach, as well as limitations in the way it is used.

3   Methodology era

As a response to one or more of the limitations or criticisms of the SDLC a number of different approaches to systems development began to emerge in the mid to late 1980s, running through till the mid to late 1990s, and what we term 'the methodology era' began. In this era the term methodology was probably used for the first time to describe these different approaches, and methodologies proliferated.

Broadly speaking these methodologies emerged from one of two sources:

- those developed from practice;
- those developed from theory.

The methodologies in the first category have typically evolved from usage in an organization and then been developed into a commercial product. The second category of methodologies have typically been developed in universities or research institutions. These are usually written up in books and journals, although occasionally may have evolved into commercial products.

The commercial methodologies evolving from practice are the most widely known and some claim large numbers of users. They each have a different history, but it was often typically the case that system developers in an organization found that particular techniques they were using, or had helped to develop, were more useful than others, and they then concentrated on improving the use and effectiveness of these techniques. Typically, the people concerned would find that the organization for which they were working was not interested in investing in the development of the technique. Sometimes this resulted in the developers leaving the organization, and either setting up their own company or joining an existing consultancy company, where the opportunity to develop the techniques and methods was greater, using the clients as guinea pigs. At this stage, it was not the methodology itself, but the consultancy work developing information systems that was sold to clients.

Most of the early methodologies relied on one technique, or on a series of closely related techniques, as the foundation stone of the methodology. Commonly, these techniques were either entity modelling or data flow diagramming, but usually not both. It was only later that methodology authors began to include other techniques and to widen the scope and include prescriptions and phases or stages for development. Slowly these informal and somewhat *ad hoc* procedures or 'cookbooks' evolved into the early methodologies. From time to time the development of the methodologies would go through periods of introspection, where various aspects would be added and others dropped, and then the revised methodology would be put to the test, again by usage.

Sometimes consultants using the same methodology in a consultancy company would discover that they were doing things quite differently from their colleagues. They had their own styles and favourite elements, and yet they were supposed to be applying the same methodology. It was at this stage that some of these consultancy companies realized that it was no longer possible to rely on an ill-defined, inadequately researched, often conflicting set of procedures and techniques. Rather than selling consultancy, the realization began to dawn that the methodology itself had to be the product. In one organization, this happened when it was discovered that no one person had responsibility for the methodology and its content. People in the organization could add things to it as they thought fit, and they did. The main reason for this state of affairs was the nature of consultancy business. Consultants were charged out on the basis of the amount of time they spent on a client's project, and there was no mechanism for accounting for time spent developing a methodology. Therefore, nobody was responsible for the methodology because at that stage it was not something that was sold.

Eventually most organizations with a potential methodology product grasped the nettle and invested resources (people and time) into developing the methodology as a product. This involved ensuring that the methodology was:

- written up;
- made consistent;
- made comprehensive;
- made marketable;
- updated as needed;
- maintained;
- researched and developed;
- evolved into training packages;
- provided with supporting software.

The consultancy houses had finally invested in their methodologies. As a result of this investment, a number of things have happened.

Filling the gaps

It was realized that most of the methodologies had some gaps in them or, if not complete gaps, they had areas that were treated much less thoroughly than others. This was usually as a direct result of their background of development that had typically involved a concentration on a single, or small set, of development techniques. These gaps needed to be filled because their clients assumed that the methodologies covered the whole spectrum of activities necessary. It was often quite a surprise for users to find that this was not the case. For example, a methodology based on entity modelling techniques might have been very powerful for data analysis and database design, but not so comprehensive when it came to specifying functions and designing the applications, and might not provide any support for dialogue design. Almost all information systems methodologies went through a process of filling the gaps to make the methodology more comprehensive.

Expanding the scope

Another process was that of expanding the scope of methodologies. This occurred because the methodologies did not address the whole of the life cycle of systems development. Frequently, the implementation phase was not included, some did not include design, others did not address analysis. So, decisions were taken to expand the scope of the methodologies.

One of the most important aspects of this expansion of scope was for methodologies to expand into the areas of strategy and planning. The traditional life cycle of systems development usually started with a stage termed 'project selection' or 'problem identification', which was characterized by the identification of some problem to be solved, some area of the business where computerization was a possible option, or some application that needed building. The development process was viewed as a one-off, *ad hoc* solution to the identified problem, and, while this may have been a reasonable approach in the early days of systems development, it was now no longer valid. Organizations had had many such 'identified problems' solved in this one-off manner and found that, although the individual problem may have been solved to some extent, the existence of a variety of different one-off systems in a business did not lead to harmony nor any general improvement to business processes.

Further, it was realized that these individual problems were not so 'individual', and that almost all areas of the business needed to interact and integrate in some way. In particular, the requirements of tactical and strategic levels of management needed integration across traditional boundaries. A series of systems, developed as individual solutions, at different times, and without reference to each other, is unlikely to be the ideal starting point for such integration. Yet, for many organizations, this is just what existed, and methodologies were forced to address themselves to this situation if they were to provide more than improved implementations of one-off systems.

Therefore, in order to achieve this integration, and because the market was demanding it, some methodologies turned themselves to the topic of information systems strategy. This involved the recognition that:

1   Information systems were becoming a fundamental part of the organization, and that they could contribute significantly to the success, or otherwise, of the enterprise.

Information was increasingly being regarded by organizations as an important, and previously neglected, resource, in the same way as the more traditional resources of land, labour, and capital.

It was realized that such a resource was not free, as had been previously assumed, but needed to be controlled, co-ordinated, and planned. Further, the controlling and planning had to take place at the highest level in an organization in order for these resources to contribute effectively to fulfilling the organization's objectives. So, the starting point for effective information system development methodologies was now seen as a strategic plan for the organization, including a specification of the way in which information systems would contribute to the achievement of that plan.

In practice, it was found that, although most organisations, but by no means all, had some kind of strategic or corporate plan, this plan did not usually address the role of the information systems. For this reason, some methodologies incorporated the development of the required strategy plan into their scope. This not only helped to ensure that the information systems met the high-level needs of the organization, but effectively pushed the information system function up the hierarchy of importance in the organization.

Gaining competitive advantage

Another reason for addressing information systems strategy at a high level in an organization was the developing management belief that not only could the information system make the running of the business easier and more efficient, but that information systems and information technology could change the position of the organization in relation to its business competitors. The idea that information systems could enable business change and advantage was prevalent, and this meant that most commercial methodologies introduced strategic and planning phases. This, it was argued, not only ensured that the business and information systems strategy was in alignment, but it also often led to the influencing and determination of business strategy by the identification of new opportunities that information systems could provide.

The process of expanding their scope and 'filling the gaps' has continued for most commercial methodologies. After the introduction of strategic and business planning phases and tasks, the next development was to integrate new and evolving techniques and approaches, such as object-oriented techniques and the introduction of support tools into the methodology package.

As existing methodology vendors sought to fill the gaps and expand the scopes of their products, a number of other organizations entered the marketplace with new methodology products. These were only new in the sense that they sought to blend together what were seen as strong features of a variety of existing methodologies, in particular, the combination of entity modelling techniques with data flow diagramming techniques (see Chapter 20 on Blended Methodologies and SSADM in particular).

There were also other pressures that led to the development of more formalized methodologies, for example, the requirements of certain large organizations or standards bodies. Fitzgerald (1996), for example, suggests that the ISO (International Standards Organization) and the SEI (Software Engineering Institute) were influential in this respect, as was the perceived wisdom in some quarters that 'better methods will solve the problems of IS development'.

This process of expanding the scope and filling the gaps has sometimes resulted in methodologies becoming extremely large and often cumbersome. They seek to be comprehensive and provide all things to all people, but in doing so they have perhaps lost their original specialist focus and sown the seeds for some of a growing discontent with methodologies that we shall examine later. This expansion and filling of gaps also tended to result in some methodologies adopting a process that looks not unlike the conventional SDLC. This is relatively easy to understand as the SDLC, as its name implies, addresses the whole process and even with the advent of new techniques there was still seen to be a need for a life cycle type of process in some cases.

The second basic category of methodology has evolved from an academic or theoretical background. These are generally less well known than the commercial methodologies and may have relatively few users, although their influence is often substantially greater than their user base. Academic methodologies were usually developed by individuals who evolved and popularized the methodologies by means of action research and consultancy.

Typically these methodologies started life as research projects in universities or research institutions. Here the researchers took a more theoretical viewpoint and were less concerned by commercial considerations, although they often wanted access to real situations in order to test and experiment. The income from consultancy was also no deterrent. What intrigued the academic researcher, in particular, was that there did not seem to be any standard techniques or approaches based upon sound theoretical concepts. This was clearly a challenge which was taken up by a number of people from a variety of different background disciplines. It was sometimes felt that methods were already available and successfully being used in other disciplines and that these only needed a small amount of adaptation to be useful in the area of information systems development. Mathematicians, psychologists, linguists, social scientists, engineers, sociologists, and others turned their attention to the challenge. This did not, of course, happen all at the same time but some of the approaches have proved interesting and useful.

In areas other than information systems, the development of techniques and methods by academics has been very influential on practice, particularly in the areas of database design and software engineering. But in the case of information systems development methodologies, the impact was relatively low. Some argued that the research-based methods were not good enough, nor practical enough, or that they were no better than the new methods that the practitioners were already developing themselves. Slowly academics persuaded organizations to try their methods under their guiding hands on a consultancy basis. Others adopted a practice known as action research, which includes the experimentation with and testing of the methodology in a practical situation with the academic playing dual roles of participant and researcher.

As this process evolved, the methods became more practical, and the academic methodologies played an increasingly important role. The adoption of some elements from academic methodologies into commercial methodologies sometimes happened, while others attempted to combine the data and process techniques of entity modelling and data flow diagramming from commercial methodologies with academic methodologies, such as SSM and Multiview.

We characterize the above as the methodology era because of the apparent proliferation of methodologies during this period. This does not mean that every organization was using a methodology, particularly a named methodology purchased from a vendor, and the claims of methodology vendors at the time certainly need to be viewed with some suspicion. Nevertheless, many organizations were using a methodology of some kind, albeit frequently an in-house-developed methodology, which might or might not be based on a named commercial methodology.

A survey conducted in the UK by Fitzgerald et al. (1999) found that 57 per cent of the sample were claiming to be using a methodology for systems development, but, of these, only 11 per cent were using a commercial development methodology unmodified, whereas 30 per cent were using a commercial methodology adapted for in-house use, and 59 per cent a methodology which they claimed to be unique to their organization (i.e. one that was internally developed but not solely based on a commercial methodology). So, the picture seems to emerge that the majority of organizations were using some kind of methodology, but that most of these were developed or adapted to fit the needs of the developers and the organization. Therefore, although large-scale use of commercial methodologies is not the case, we justify the term methodology era on the number of organizations using a methodology of some kind, albeit often home-grown or adapted. Additionally, we argue that the influence of commercial methodologies is considerably larger than their use.

4   Era of methodology reassessment

The most recent era, from the mid to late 1990s onward, is characterized by a serious reappraisal of the concepts and practicalities of the methodologies of the methodology era. As a result some organizations have turned to yet different methodologies and approaches while others have abandoned their use of methodologies completely.

Methodologies were often seen as a panacea to the problems of traditional development approaches, and, as we have also seen, they were often chosen and adopted for the wrong reasons. Some organizations simply wanted a better project control mechanism, others a better way of involving users, still others wanted to inject some rigour or discipline into the process. For many of these organizations, the adoption of a methodology has not always worked or been the total success its advocates expected. Indeed, it was very unlikely that methodologies would ever achieve the more overblown claims made by some vendors and consultants. Some organizations have found their chosen methodology has not been successful or appropriate for them and have adopted a different one. For some this second option has been more useful, but others have found the new one not to be successful either, and some organizations appear to cycle through methodologies on a regular basis. This has led some developers and organizations to reject methodologies in more general terms and attack the concepts upon which they are based. This has been termed a 'backlash against methodologies', which we now discuss. The criticisms of methodologies are deliberately couched in generic terms and are not related to specific methodologies:

■   *Productivity*. The first general criticism of methodologies is that they fail to deliver the suggested productivity benefits. It is said that they do not reduce the time taken to develop a project, rather their use increases systems development lead-times when compared with not using a methodology. This is usually because the methodology specifies many more activities and tasks that have to be undertaken. It specifies the construction of many more diagrams and models, and in general the production of considerably more documentation at all stages. Much of this may be felt by users to be unnecessary. As well as being slow, they are resource-intensive. This is true, first, in terms of the number of people required, from both the development and user side, and, second, from the point of view of the costs of adopting the methodology, for example, the purchase costs, training, tools, organizational costs, and so on.

■ *Complexity*. Methodologies have been criticized for being over-complex. They are designed to be applied to the largest and most comprehensive development project and therefore specify in great detail every possible task that might conceivably be thought to be relevant, all of which is expected to be undertaken for every development project.

■ *'Gilding the lily'*. Methodologies develop any requirements to the ultimate degree, often over and above what is legitimately required. Every requirement is treated as being of equal weight and importance which results in relatively unimportant aspects being developed to the same degree as those that are essential. It is sometimes said that they encourage the creation of 'wish lists' by users.

■ *Skills*. Methodologies require significant skills in their use and processes. These skills are often difficult for methodology users and end-users to learn and acquire. It is sometimes also argued that the use of the methodology does not improve system development skills or organizational learning.

■ *Tools*. The tools that the methodology advocates are difficult to use and do not generate enough benefits. They increase the focus on the production of documentation rather than leading to better analysis and design.

■ *Not contingent*. The methodology is not contingent upon the type of project or its size. Therefore the standard becomes the application of the whole methodology, irrespective of its relevance.

■ *One-dimensional approach*. The methodology usually adopts only one approach to the development of projects and while this may be a strength it does not always address the underlying issues or problems. In some cases the approach needs a more political, organizational, or other dimension.

■ *Inflexible*. The methodology might be inflexible and does not allow changes to requirements during development. This is problematic as requirements, particularly business requirements, frequently change during the long development process.

■ *Invalid or impractical assumptions*. Most methodologies make a number of simplifying yet invalid assumptions, such as a stable external and competitive environment. Many methodologies that address the alignment of business and information systems strategy assume the existence of a coherent and well-documented business strategy as a starting point for the methodology. This may not exist in practice.

■ *Goal displacement*. It has frequently been found that the existence of a methodology standard in an organization leads to its unthinking implementation and to a focus on following the procedures of the methodology to the exclusion of the real needs of the project being developed. In other words, the methodology obscures the important issues. De Grace and Stahl (1993) have termed this 'goal displacement' and talk about the severe problem of 'slavish adherence to the methodology'. Wastell (1996) talks about the 'fetish of technique' which inhibits creative thinking. He takes this further and suggests that the application of a methodology in this way is the functioning of methodology as a social defence which he describes 'as a highly sophisticated social device for containing the acute and potentially overwhelming pressures of systems development'. He is suggesting that systems development is such a difficult and stressful process that developers often take refuge in the intense application of the methodology in all its detail as a way of dealing with these difficulties. Developers can be seen to be working hard and diligently, but this is in reality goal displacement activity because they are avoiding the real problems of effectively developing the required system.

- *Problems of building understanding into methods.* Introna and Whitley (1997) argue that some methodologies assume that understanding can be built into the method process. They call this 'method-ism' and believe it is misplaced. Method-ism assumes that the developers need to understand little or nothing about the problem situation, and that the method will somehow 'bring to light' all the characteristics that need to be discovered. Therefore, all that needs to be understood is the method itself. This, it is argued, is far too constraining and prevents real understanding of the problem situation emerging and being acted upon. It also inhibits the contingent use of methodologies. Introna and Whitley are not against methods as such, just this underlying assumption and its implications.

- *Insufficient focus on social and contextual issues.* The growth of scientifically-based, highly functional methodologies has led some commentators to suggest that we are now suffering from an overemphasis on the narrow, technical development issues, and that not enough emphasis is given to the social and organizational aspects of systems development. Hirschheim et al. (1996), for example, argue that changes associated with systems development are emergent, historically contingent, socially situated, and politically loaded and that as a result sophisticated social theories are required to understand and make sense of IS development. They observe that these are sadly lacking in most methodologies.

- *Difficulties in adopting a methodology.* Some organizations have found it hard to adopt methodologies in practice. They have found resistance from developers who are experienced and familiar with more informal approaches to systems development and see the introduction of a methodology as restricting their freedom and a slight on their skills. One organization experienced these problems to the extent that they had to introduce the methodology by setting up a new development team from scratch, recruited from new graduates not tainted with the old ways of doing things. In other cases it has been the users who have objected to a methodology, because it did not embody the way they wished to work and included techniques for specifying requirements that they were not familiar with and did not see a good reason to adopt.

- *No improvements.* Finally in this list, and perhaps the acid test, is the conclusion of some that the methodology has not resulted in better systems, for whatever reasons. This is obviously difficult to prove, but nevertheless the perception of some is that 'we have tried it and it didn't help and it may have actively hindered'.

We thus find that for some the great hopes in the 1980s that methodologies would solve most of the problems of information systems development have not come to pass.

Strictly speaking, a distinction should be made in the above criticisms of methodologies between an inadequate methodology itself and the poor application and use of a methodology. Sometimes a methodology vendor will argue that the methodology is not being correctly or sympathetically implemented by an organization. While this may be true to some extent, it is not an argument that seems to hold much sway with methodology users. They argue that the important point is that they have experienced disappointments in their use of methodologies.

So, for the reasons above, some organizations have rejected the use of a methodology altogether and are returning to a less formal, more off the cuff, perhaps more flexible approach. While for others, it is not the concept of a methodology that is the problem, it is simply the inadequacy of the current methodologies, and they continue to seek a different and better methodology. Still others seek, not a better methodology, but an alternative to traditional in-house systems development. The directions we see these organizations moving in this era of methodology reappraisal are as follows:

1. *Ad hoc development.* This might be described as a return to the approach of the pre-methodology days in which no formalized methodology is followed. The approach that is adopted is whatever the developers understand and feel will work. It is driven by, and relies heavily on, the skills and experiences of the developers. This is perhaps the most extreme reaction to the backlash against methodologies, and in general terms it runs the risk of repeating the problems encountered prior to the advent of methodologies. One area where, in the authors' experience, methodologies are not being used is in the development of web-based applications. Many of these applications are currently being developed in a very *ad hoc*, trial-and-error manner relying on the skills and experience of a few key personnel in organizations. Not unlike the development approach of the pre-methodological era! We have chosen to illustrate WISDM (Section 22.4), but it is true that no methodology has become a standard for web development. Another group of organizations are pinning their faith on the evolution of toolsets to guide and automate the development process.

2. *Further developments in the methodology arena.* For some there is the continuing search for the methodology holy grail. Methodologies will continue to be developed and existing ones evolve. For example, object-oriented techniques and methodologies have been gaining ground over process and entity modelling approaches for some time, although whether this is a fundamental advance is debatable. It may be that component-based development, which envisages development from the combination and recombination of existing components, will make a long-term impact. But this may simply be the current fashion to be overtaken by the next panacea at some point in the future. It may be that the RAD approaches will prevail, or perhaps the need for flexibility will favour prototyping approaches. The current emphasis on knowledge, rather than information, may make approaches like CommonKADS popular. With the importance of web

applications, focusing on customers as stakeholder might make Customer Relationship Management (CRM). But these are conjectures made at the time of writing and it is difficult to predict the future. What we do know, based on past experience, is that proposed new solutions will come and go, some will be easily forgotten while others will probably stand the test of time and make genuine contributions. However, we believe it unlikely that any single approach will provide the solution to all the problems of information systems development.

3   *Contingency*. Most methodologies are designed for situations which follow a stated or unstated 'ideal type'. The methodology provides a step-by-step prescription for addressing this ideal type. However, situations are all different and there is no such thing as an 'ideal type' in reality. We therefore see a contingency approach to information systems development where a structure is presented but tools and techniques are expected to be used or not (or used and adapted), depending on the situation as being a third movement of this present era. Situations might differ depending on, for example, the type of project and its objectives, the organization and its environment, the users and developers, and their respective skills. The type of project might also differ in its purpose, complexity, structuredness, and degree of importance, the projected life of the project, or its potential impact. The organization might be large or small, mature or immature in its use of IT. Different environments might exhibit different rates of change: the number of users affected by the system, their skills, and those of the analysts. All these characteristics could affect the choice of development approach that is required. A contingent methodology allows for different approaches depending on situations. This is a reaction to the 'one methodology for all developments' approach that some companies adopted, and is a recognition that different characteristics require different approaches. There are, however, potential problems of the contingent approach as well. First, some of the benefits of standardization might be lost. Second, there is a wide range of different skills that are required to handle many approaches. Third, the selection of approach requires experience and skills to make the best judgements. Finally, it has been suggested that certain combinations of approaches are untenable because each has different philosophies that are contradictory. Multiview aims to provide a framework which helps people make such contingent decisions (Section 25.1).

4   *External development*. We also see a movement toward external development in a variety of ways (Chapter 8). In particular we discuss the use of packages and outsourcing. Some organizations are attempting to satisfy their systems needs by buying packages from the marketplace. Clearly the purchasing of packages has been commonplace for some time, but the present era is characterized by some organizations deciding not to embark on any more in-house system development activities but to buy in all their requirements in the form of package systems. This is regarded by many as a quicker and cost-effective way of implementing systems for organizations that have fairly standard requirements. Only systems that are strategic or for which a suitable package is not available would be considered for development in-house. The package market is becoming increasingly sophisticated, and more and more highly tailorable packages are becoming available. Integrated packages which address a wide range of standard business functions, purchasable in modular form, known as Enterprise Resource Packages (ERPs) have

emerged in the last few years and have become particularly popular with large corporations. The key for these organizations is ensuring that the correct trade-off is made between a standard package, which might mean changing some elements of the way the business currently operates, and a package that can be modified to reflect the way they wish to operate. There are dangers of becoming locked in to a particular supplier and of not being in control of the features that are incorporated in the package, but many companies have taken this risk. For others, the continuing problems of systems development and the perceived failure of methodologies to deliver, has resulted in them outsourcing systems development to a third party. The client organization is no longer so concerned with how a system is developed and what development approach or methodology is used, but with the end results and the effectiveness of the system that is delivered. This is different to buying in packages or solutions, because normally the management and responsibility for the provision and development of appropriate systems is given to a vendor. The client company has to develop skills in selecting the correct vendor, specifying requirements in detail, and writing and negotiating contracts rather than thinking about system development methodologies.

The above features of the present era of methodology reappraisal as we see it are not mutually exclusive, and some organizations are moving to a variety of these approaches. Some aspects are being absorbed or incorporated into some existing methodologies (i.e. the 'filling the gaps' and 'blending' process is still continuing). This present era is not one where all methodologies have been abandoned. It is an era where there is diversity and perhaps a more realistic view of the limitations of methodologies. For some, however, it is about the abandonment of methodologies altogether. For others, it is seeking improved methodologies, but moving away from the highly bureaucratic types of the methodology era. For still others it is about moving out of in-house systems development altogether. But it should also not be forgotten that even in the post-methodology-era some are still using methodology era methodologies effectively and successfully.

Our identification and characterization of these methodology eras has been done to provide a more categorized view of the history and evolution of methodologies and to make such a history more understandable. However, it has been criticized by some because they do not recognize the concept of the methodology era itself. They argue there was never a period when methodologies proliferated, particularly in terms of their use; we disagree but as with any historical categorization it is open to debate and interpretation. Our hope is that we have engendered, and contributed to, such a debate.

26.5   SUMMARY

- In this chapter we have further refined the definition of the term 'methodology' to include the critical issue of 'philosophy', or underlying theory behind a methodology. The philosophy is key to understanding the methodology.

- We also looked at the rationale for adopting a methodology under the headings: a better end product, a better development process, and a standardized process.

■ The issue of what you get when you buy or adopt a methodology in practice is addressed. This varies considerably from a fully comprehensive product, including manuals and software, covering the range of the life cycle, to a short paper or a book.

■ Next an historical examination of the evolution of methodologies is undertaken which identifies four methodology eras: a pre-methodology era, an early-methodology era, a methodology era, and the current era which is described as an era of methodology reassessment. This means that we are now in an era which is perhaps more critical and demanding of methodologies and that does not see them as a panacea to the problems of systems development. In this era a range of approaches exist, including the use of a methodology through to *ad hoc* development without a methodology or outsourcing of development.

QUESTIONS

1 How would you define a methodology and why?

2 In the context of a company with which you are familiar, choose a methodology, and identify a convincing rationale for adopting it that might persuade the Chief Executive.

3 What would you expect to find in the box if you purchased a methodology from a well-known source?

4 Why is the current methodology era described as one of reassessment?

26.6   FURTHER READING

Fitzgerald, B., Russo, N.L., and Stolterman, E. (2002) *Information Systems Development: Methods in Action*, McGraw-Hill, Maidenhead, UK.

Introna, L.D. and Whitley, E.A. (1997) Against method-ism: Exploring the limits of method, *Information Technology and People*, Vol. 10, No. 1, 31–45 (MCB University Press).

27 METHODOLOGY COMPARISONS

COMPARISON ISSUES

There are two main reasons for comparing methodologies:

- *an academic reason* – to better understand the nature of methodologies better (their features, objectives, philosophies, and so on) in order to perform classifications and to improve future information systems development.

- *a practical reason* – to choose a methodology, part of one, or a number of methodologies for a particular application, a group of applications, or for an organization as a whole.

The two reasons are not totally separate, and it is hoped that the academic studies will help in the practical choices and that the practical reasons will influence the criteria applied in the academic studies. In this section we look at a number of different approaches to the comparison of methodologies which have been attempted, and discuss some of the issues that arise from such comparisons.

We provide the following list of 'ideal-type' criteria that might be considered in assessing methodologies:

- *Rules*. Methodologies should provide formal guidelines to cover phases, tasks, and deliverables, and their ordering, techniques and tools, documentation and development aids, and guidelines for estimating time and resource requirements.

- *Total coverage*. A methodology should cover the entire systems development process from strategy to cutover and maintenance.

- *Understanding the information resource*. A methodology should ensure effective utilization of the corporate information resource, in terms of the data available and the processes which need to make use of the data.

- *Documentation standards*. There should be agreed standards, and all output, using the methodology, should be easily understandable by both users and analysts.

- *Separation of logical and physical designs*. There should be a separation of logical descriptions and requirements (e.g. what an application does, what the interactions are, and what data are involved).

- *Validity of design*. There should be a means of checking for inconsistencies, inaccuracies, and incompleteness.

- *Early change*. Any changes to a system design should be identifiable as early as possible in the development process.

- *Inter-stage communication*. The full extent of work carried out must be communicable to other stages, with each stage being consistent, complete, and usable.

- *Effective problem analysis*. The methodology should provide a suitable means for expressing and documenting the problems and objectives of an organization.

- *Planning and control*. Careful monitoring of an information system is required, and a methodology must support development in a planned and controlled manner to contain costs and timescales.

- *Performance evaluation*. The methodology should support a means of evaluating the performance of operational applications developed using it.

- *Increased productivity*. The use of a methodology should lead to increases in productivity.

- *Improved quality*. A methodology should improve the quality of analysis, design, and programming products and hence the overall quality of the information system.

- *Visibility of the product*. A methodology should maintain the visibility of the emerging and evolving information system as it develops.

- *Teachable*. Users as well as technologists should understand the various techniques in a methodology in order that they can verify analysis and design work and train others to use them.

- *Information systems boundary*. A methodology should allow definition of the areas of the organization to be covered by the information system. These may not all be areas for computerization.

- *Designing for change*. The logical and physical designs should be easily modified.

- *Effective communication*. The methodology should provide an effective communication medium between analysts and users.

- *Simplicity*. The methodology should be simple to use.

- *Ongoing relevance*. A methodology should be capable of being extended so that new techniques and tools can be incorporated as they are developed, but still maintain overall consistency and framework.

- *Automated development aids*. Where possible software tools should be used since they can enhance productivity.

- *Consideration of user goals and objectives*. The goals and objectives of potential users of a system should be noted, so that when an information system is designed it can be made to satisfy these users and assist them in meeting goals and objectives.

■ *Participation*. The methodology should encourage participation through simplicity and the ability to facilitate good communications.

■ *Relevance to practitioner*. The methodology has to be appropriate to the practitioner using it, in terms of level of technical knowledge, experience with computers, and social and communications skills.

■ *Relevance to application*. The methodology must be appropriate to the type of system being developed, which might be real-time, distributed, web-based, etc.

■ *The integration of the technical and the non-technical systems*. The methodology should not only address the technical and non-technical aspects of a system but should make provision for their integration.

■ *Scan for opportunity*. The methodology should enable the system to be thought about in new ways. Rather than being viewed as simply a solution to existing problems it should be seen as an opportunity to address new areas and challenges.

■ *Separation of analysis and design*. This separation ensures that the analysis of the existing system and the user requirements are not influenced by design considerations.

Of course, the above 'ideal-type' requirements will not be found in any one methodology. However, the above criteria form a useful checklist but clearly need to be tailored for the particular purpose. Other commentators have taken these debates further and suggested a much broader range of issues that they feel are relevant in the comparison of methodologies. Bjørn-Andersen (1984), for example, identifies a checklist that includes criteria relating to values and society:

1 What research paradigms/perspective form the foundation for the methodology?

2 What are the underlying value systems?

3 What is the context where a methodology is useful?

4 To what extent is modification enhanced or even possible?

5 Does communication and documentation operate in the users' dialect, either expert or not?

6 Does transferability exist?

7 Is the societal environment dealt with, including the possible conflicts?

8 Is user participation 'really' encouraged or supported?

This checklist is useful as it focuses attention on some wider issues that are often ignored. It is, of course, a subjective list and makes a number of assumptions, for example, that user participation is a desirable feature.

Another comparison framework is NIMSAD (Normative Information Model-based Systems Analysis and Design) (Jayaratna, 1994). This is based on the models and epistemology of systems thinking and to a large degree evaluates and measures a methodology against these criteria. The evaluation has three elements:

■ the 'problem situation' (the methodology context);

- the intended problem solver (the methodology user);
- the problem-solving process (the methodology).

The evaluation of the elements is wide-ranging and expressed in terms of the kinds of question that require answers. The questions concerning the first element (the problem situation) deal with the way in which the methodology helps the understanding and identification of the following:

- the clients and their understandings, experiences, and commitments;
- the problem owners, their concerns, and problems;
- the situation that the methodology users are facing, its diagnosis as structured or unstructured;
- the ways in which the methodology might help the situation;
- the culture and politics of the situation, including the risks associated with using the methodology in various circumstances;
- the views of the stakeholders concerning 'reality', for example, is there an objective real-world problem out there, and what is the relationship of this to the methodology's philosophical assumptions about reality?;
- the dominant perceptions in the problem situation; for example, are they technical, political, social, and so on?

The questions concerning the second element (the intended problem solver) ask about:

- the methodology users' beliefs, values, and ethical positions;
- the relationship of the above to that assumed or demanded by the methodology;
- the way in which mismatches in the above two may be handled or reconciled; for example, can the methodology processes be changed, and does the methodology help to achieve this?;
- the methodology users' philosophical views, for example, science or systems-based;
- the methodology users' experience, skills, and motives, in relation to those required by the methodology.

The questions concerning the third element (the methodology itself) ask about the way in which the methodology provides specific assistance for:

- understanding the situation of concern and the setting of boundaries;
- performing the diagnosis; for example, the models, tools, techniques, and the levels at which they operate, how they interact, what information they capture, what is not captured, what happens when people disagree, and so on;
- defining the prognosis outline, for example, the desired states, what constitutes legitimate states, and the handling of conflict;
- defining problems;
- deriving notional systems; for example, are they derived at all, and if so how, and in what ways are they recorded?;
- performing conceptual/logical and physical design, including who is involved and

what are the implications; for example, does it lead to systems improvements or systems innovation?;

■ implementing the design; for example, how does it handle alternatives and how does it ensure success?

One feature of this framework is that it recommends that the evaluation be conducted at three stages. First, before intervention (i.e. before a methodology is adopted), second, during intervention (i.e. during its use), and finally, after intervention (i.e. after an assessment of the success or otherwise of the methodology). These stages are an important feature of the framework and introduce the important element of organizational learning.

A number of other commentators have suggested alternative approaches to an overall feature analysis when selecting methodologies. They adopt a more pragmatic approach and suggest that there is no benefit to be gained from attempting to find, in isolation, a 'best' methodology, because the approaches are not necessarily mutually exclusive. One or more approaches may be suitable, depending on the circumstances. Therefore, there should be a search for an appropriate methodology in the context of the problems being addressed, the applications, and the organization and its culture.

Davis (1982) advocates the contingency approach, that is, the selection of an appropriate approach as part of the framework or methodology itself. Davis offers guidelines for the selection of an appropriate approach to the determination of requirements, rather than to the selection of a methodology itself (although the same principles may well apply). Davis suggests measuring the level of uncertainty in a system. This will help ascertain the appropriate methodology. There are four measures:

1. System complexity or ill structuredness.
2. The state of flux of the system.
3. The user component of the system, for example, the number of people affected and their skill level.
4. The level of skill and experience of the analysts.

Once the level of uncertainty has been ascertained, the appropriate approach to determining the requirements can be made. For low uncertainty, the traditional method of interviewing users would be appropriate. For high levels of uncertainty, a prototype or an evolutionary approach would be better. For intermediate levels of uncertainty, a process of synthesizing from the characteristics of the existing system might be appropriate.

Avison and Taylor (1996) identify five different classes of situation and appropriate approaches as follows:

1. Well-structured problem situations with a well-defined problem and clear requirements. A traditional SDLC approach might be regarded as appropriate in this class of situation.
2. As above but with unclear requirements. A data, process modelling, or a prototyping approach are suggested as appropriate here.
3. Unstructured problem situation with unclear objectives. A soft systems approach would be appropriate in this situation.

4   High user–interaction systems. A people-focused approach, for example, ETHICS, would be appropriate here.

5   Very unclear situations, where a contingency approach, such as Multiview, is suggested.

In addition to some of the conceptual problems of comparing methodologies discussed above, we also discovered a number of practical problems in attempting to compare methodologies themselves. First, methodologies are not stable, but are in fact moving targets that are continuing to develop and evolve. Therefore, there exists a version problem, and it is often difficult to know which version of a methodology is being applied in a particular situation or which is the latest version. Second, for commercial reasons, the documentation is not always published or readily available to people or organizations not purchasing the methodology. Third, the practice of a methodology is sometimes significantly different from that prescribed by the documentation or the authors of the methodology. This is sometimes talked about in terms of the espoused version of the methodology and the way that it is actually used in practice. Fourth, consultants or developers using the methodology often interpret aspects of the methodology in quite different ways.

A further problem in undertaking comparisons concerns terminology, in particular, the use of different terms for the same phenomena and similar terms for different phenomena. Information systems continues to exhibit rather more than its fair share of these. It is unhealthy, as it not only leads to confusion and poor communication, but to a restriction of development, due to the inability to enhance and expand upon earlier research work. Progress in most successful disciplines is usually a process of evolutionary development because 'out of the blue' quantum leaps are rare. Any restriction in evolution is therefore very serious. One problem is that sometimes 'new' approaches only express a new terminology and make no substantial contribution to the state of the art.

A common approach to methodology comparison attempts to identify a set of idealized 'features', followed by a check to see whether different methodologies possess these features or not. The implication being that those that do possess them or at least score highly on a features rating are 'good', and that those that do not are 'less good'. The set of features must be chosen by somebody and are thus subjective, although often purported to be objective. The most obvious indication of this is the kind of comparison conducted by particular methodology vendors in which their methodology scores highly and the competition poorly. The comparison has been designed to give this result. We are more familiar with this kind of comparison in relation to cars or soap powders.

We identify our own set of comparison criteria below, in the full knowledge that they are subjective and can be criticized in exactly the same way as all the other attempts discussed above:

1   What aspects of the development process does the methodology cover?

2   What overall framework or model does it utilize? For example, is it systems development life cycle-based, linear, or spiral?

3   What representation, abstractions, and models are employed?

4 What tools and techniques are used?

5 Is the content of the methodology well defined and described, such that a developer can understand and follow it? This applies not only to the stages and tasks but also to the philosophy and objectives of the methodology.

6 What is the focus of the methodology? Is it, for example, people-, data-, process-, and/or problem-oriented? Does it address organizational and strategic issues?

7 How are the results at each stage expressed?

8 What situations and types of application is it suited to?

9 Does it aim to be scientific, behavioural, systemic, or whatever?

10 Is a computer solution assumed? What other assumptions are made?

11 Who plays what roles? Does it assume professional developers, require a methodology facilitator, involve users and managers, and, if so, how and to what degree?

12 What particular skills are required of the participants?

13 How are conflicting views and findings handled?

14 What control features does it provide and how is success evaluated?

15 What claims does it make as to benefits? How are these claims substantiated?

16 What are the underlying philosophical assumptions of the methodology? What makes it a legitimate approach?

Perhaps the most important aspects of this list in terms of comparing methodologies has been found to be the final one. The features of a methodology are highly dependent upon the philosophy, and without this understanding the methodology is difficult to explain. Some methodologies, especially the more commercial ones, do not always explicitly state their underlying philosophy: it has to be searched for and interpreted, and this makes analysis difficult. Others are more explicit, some of the object-oriented methodologies make great play of explaining the reasoning behind the concept of objects. However, relatively few explain their philosophy or in Checkland's terms the 'intellectual framework of enquiry'.

Despite all the difficulties identified, which may imply failure from the outset, comparisons continue to be made, because it is becoming increasingly important in a world where large numbers of widely differing methodologies claim the same promises of universal applicability and overall usefulness.

27.2 FRAMEWORK FOR COMPARING METHODOLOGIES

The reader should now be aware that comparing methodologies is a very difficult task, and the results of any such work are likely to be criticized on many counts. There are as many views as there are writers on methodologies. The views of analysts do not necessarily coincide with users, and these views are often at variance with those of the methodology authors. Therefore, the following is simply another set of views and is unlikely to satisfy all the players in the methodologies' game.

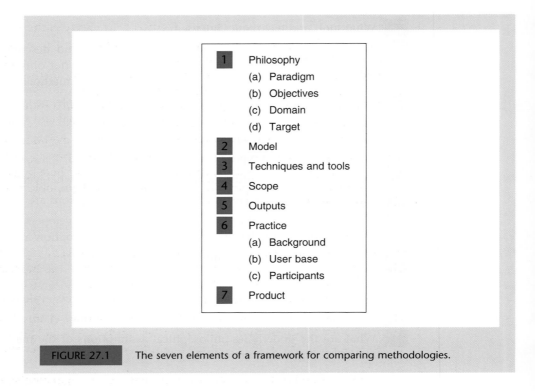

FIGURE 27.1 The seven elements of a framework for comparing methodologies.

There are seven basic elements to our framework as follows, some elements are broken down into a number of subelements (see Figure 27.1).

The framework is not supposed to be fully comprehensive, and one could envisage a number of additional features that might usefully be compared for particular purposes, for example:

- the speed at which systems can be developed;
- the quantity of the specifications and documentation produced;
- the potential for modification by users to suit their own environment.

However, we believe that this gives a set of features that proves to be a reasonable guide when examining an individual methodology and when used as a basis for comparing methodologies. The headings are not mutually exclusive and there are obviously inter-relationships between them. For example, aspects of philosophy are reflected in some senses in all the other elements.

Each of the above-listed elements in the framework will be described, and then a sample application of the framework is made to some of the methodologies of Part 6. The reader is also invited to apply the framework to methodologies of his or her own choice.

1　Philosophy

The question of philosophy is an important aspect of a methodology because it underscores all other aspects. As discussed in Section 26.1, it distinguishes, more than any other criterion, a 'methodology' from a 'method'. The choice of the areas covered by the methodology, the systems, data or people orientation, the bias or otherwise toward a purely IT solution, and other aspects are made on the basis of the philosophy of the methodology. This philosophy may be explicit but in most methodologies the philosophy is implicit. Indeed, many feature analyses have neglected this aspect completely, partly because methodology authors seldom stress their philosophy.

In this context we regard 'philosophy' as a principle, or set of principles, that underlie the methodology. It is sometimes argued that all methodologies are based on a common philosophy to improve the world of information systems development. While this is true to some extent, this is not what is meant here by philosophy.

As a guide to philosophy the four factors of paradigm, objectives, domains, and applications are highlighted.

(a) Paradigm

We identify two paradigms of relevance. The first is the science paradigm, which has characterized most of the hard scientific developments of recent times, and the second is the systems paradigm, which is characterized by a holistic approach.

The term paradigm is defined here, in the sense that Kuhn (1962) uses it, as a specific way of thinking about problems, encompassing a set of achievements which are acknowledged as the foundation of further practice. A paradigm is usually regarded as subject-free, in that it may apply to a number of problems regardless of their specific content.

As Checkland (1981) summarizes it, the science paradigm consists of reductionism, repeatability, and refutation:

> We may reduce the complexity of the variety of the real world in experiments whose results are validated by their repeatability, and we may build knowledge by the refutation of hypotheses.

The science paradigm has a long and successful history and is responsible for much of our current world. The systems paradigm has a much shorter and less successful history, but was evolved as a reaction to the reductionism of science and its perceived inability to cope with living systems and those categorized as human activity systems.

Science copes with complexity through reductionism, breaking things down into smaller and smaller parts for examination and explanation. This implies that the breakdown does not disrupt the system of which it is a part. Checkland argues that human activity systems are systems which do not display such characteristics, they have **emergent properties** (i.e. the whole is greater than the sum of the parts) and perform differently as a whole or as part of a system than when broken down to their individual components. This led directly to the development of the systems paradigm which is characterized by its concern for the whole picture, the emergent properties, and the interrelationships between parts of the whole. The science and systems paradigms are closely related to concepts of hard and soft thinking discussed in Section 4.1.

In a series of papers, Iivari et al. (2000/2001) extend the debate, distinguishing between ontology and epistemology. Ontology is concerned with the essence of things and the nature of the world, and two extreme positions of realism and nominalism are identified. Realism, according to Hirschheim (1985), 'postulates that the universe comprises objectively given, immutable objects and structures. These exist as empirical entities, on their own, independent of the observer's appreciation of them.' On the other hand, according to Hirschheim and Klein (1989), nominalism is where:

> reality is not a given immutable 'out there', but is socially constructed. It is the product of the human mind. Social relativism is the paradigm adopted for understanding social phenomena and is primarily involved in explaining the social world from the viewpoint of the organizational agents who directly take part in the social process of reality construction.

Epistemology is the grounds of knowledge. The term relates to the way in which the world may be legitimately investigated and what may be considered as knowledge and progress. It includes elements concerned with sources of knowledge, structure of knowledge, and the limits of what can be known. Again, two extreme positions are frequently identified: positivism and interpretivism. Positivism implies the existence of causal relationships which can be investigated using scientific methods whereas interpretivism implies that there is no single truth that can be 'proven' by such investigation. Different views and interpretations are potentially legitimate and the way to progress is not to try and discover the one 'correct' view but to accept the differences and seek to gain insight by a deep understanding of such complexity.

Lewis (1994) brings these elements together in a framework, shown in Figure 27.2, that identifies objectivist and subjectivist approaches as positions between the ontology of realism and nominalism and the epistemology of positivism and interpretivism. We find this a helpful framework for thinking about and identifying the underlying philosophies of methodologies. For example, if we believe in an ontology of nominalism we should not adopt a methodology based on an assumption of realism. A subjectivist approach might help us think about data collected in the analysis of a system not as 'facts' but more as perceptions from a particular point of view. Sales targets are not necessarily a set of facts, but perhaps part of a political process which is negotiated between sales personnel, management, and directors. This negotiation may have

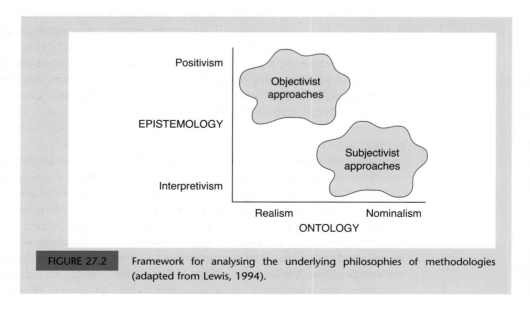

FIGURE 27.2   Framework for analysing the underlying philosophies of methodologies (adapted from Lewis, 1994).

far-reaching implications, relating to people's lives, remuneration, job satisfaction, self-esteem, and so on. Furthermore, we need ways of handling these different perceptions. This may mean, for example, that we need a methodology that focuses on the high-lighting of different opinions and interpretations or one that allows a series of different designs in order to accommodate different perceptions.

It is sometimes argued that not only do methodologies adopt particular philosophical assumptions that we should be aware of but that individual techniques and tools also embody and reflect these concepts. Entity, process, and object modelling are usually all seen as objectivist techniques, but Lewis (1994) argues that 'this does not rule out the possibility that they could be employed as part of an alternative (subjectivist) paradigm'. He suggests that some analysts use the technique in this way in practice. They do not think of particular entities and relationships as representations of reality, but as representations of interpretations of reality. They use it as a way of negotiating a shared understanding or interpretation of the problem domain rather than as a way of correcting the user's ambiguities and misunderstandings.

This raises some interesting issues, for if a generally perceived objectivist technique can be used in a subjectivist manner, then this implies that the techniques themselves are not such an important feature in determining the characteristics of a methodology as usually thought. However, we could argue that entity models are not generally used in a subjectivist way but, even if they can be, the technique is still objectivist because it pushes the user of the technique in that general direction. It is a sophisticated developer that does not seek to resolve differing views to one version of reality. It can be argued, however, that it is not so much whether a technique assumes an independent existence of reality or a consensus interpretation of reality but whether it is able to handle differing perceptions of reality that cannot be resolved by consensus.

Another issue is that the content and expression of a technique can 'frame' and limit the user's perception of the problem situation and potential solution to that allowed by the technique. This framing effect can also apply to tools and even methodologies themselves.

This is a complex area, but the purpose of the discussion has been to indicate the importance of a methodology's underlying philosophies and assumptions and that developers need to be aware that they should match their beliefs to that of the authors of the methodology. As may be appreciated, this discussion of ontology and epistemology is an oversimplification of a long history of philosophical debate, and the reader is referred to Burrell and Morgan (1979), Searle (1995), Walsham (1993), and Klein et al. (2000, 2001) for more detailed treatments.

(b) Objectives

One fairly obvious clue to the methodology philosophy is the stated objective or objectives. Some methodologies state that the objective is to develop a computerized information system. Others, for example, ISAC, have as an objective to discover if there really is a need for an information system. So, there exists a difference in that some methodologies are interested only in aspects that are 'computerizable' while others take a wider view and direct their attention to achieving solutions or improvements no matter what this implies. Such improvements might involve manual, procedural, managerial, organizational, educational, or political change. This is an important difference, because it determines the boundaries of the area of concern. The problem with concentrating only on aspects to be computerized is that this is an artificial boundary in terms of the logic of the business. There is no reason why the solution to a particular problem should reside only in the area that can be automated. More likely the problem needs to be examined in a wider context.

It has often been found that 'computerization' *per se* is not the answer. What is required is a thorough analysis and redesign of the whole problem area. It may be viewed as 'putting the cart before the horse' to decide that an IT system is the solution to a particular problem. Clearly a methodology that concerns itself solely with providing an IT solution is quite a different methodology from one that does not. In choosing and understanding a methodology, it is important to ask the question: 'could the use of this methodology lead to the implementation of a purely organizational or non-IT solution?' If the answer is 'no' then the methodology is not addressing the same problems as one to which the answer is 'yes'. It is interesting to note that many of the most widely used commercial methodologies would seem to answer 'no' to this question, whereas most of the academic methodologies would probably answer 'yes'. An exception would be the 'new' BPR methodologies, whose focus is not primarily on IT but on generalized improvements to business processes.

(c) Domain

The third factor relating to philosophy is the domain of situations that methodologies address. Early methodologies, such as the conventional life cycle approach discussed in Chapter 3, saw their task as overcoming a particular and sometimes narrow problem. Obviously the solving of the problem, often through the introduction of a computer system of some kind, might be beneficial to the organization. However, the solution of a number of these kinds of problem on an *ad hoc* basis at a variety of different points in time can lead to a mishmash of different physical systems being in operation at the same time.

Even if the developments of solutions to the different problems have been well co-ordinated, and the later systems have been designed with the earlier systems in mind, it is often found that the systems and problems interrelate and the solution to a number of interrelated problems is different to the sum of the solutions to the individual problems viewed in isolation. This has led to a number of methodologies adopting a different development philosophy. They take a much wider view of their starting point and are not looking to solve, at least in the first instance, particular problems. The argument is a basis of a number of approaches, for example, the systems and strategic approaches described in Sections 4.1 and 4.2. In other words, it is argued that in order to solve individual problems, it is necessary to analyse the organization as a whole, devise an overall information systems strategy, sort out the data and resources of the organization, and identify the overlapping areas and the areas that need to be integrated. In essence, it is necessary to perform a top-down analysis of the organization, sort out the strategic requirements of the business, and in this way ensure that the information systems are designed to support these fundamental requirements.

(d) Target

The last aspect of philosophy is the applicability of the methodology. Some methodologies are specifically targeted at particular types of problem, environment, or type or size of organization, while others are said to be general purpose.

2   Model

The second element of the framework concerns an analysis of the model that the methodology adheres to. The model is the basis of the methodology's view of the world, it is an abstraction and a representation of the important factors of the information system or the organization.

The model works at a number of levels: first, it is a means of communication; second, it is a way of capturing the essence of a problem or a design, such that it can be translated or mapped to another form (e.g. implementation) without loss of detail; and, third, the model is a representation which provides insight into the problem or area of concern.

Models have been categorized into four distinct types:

1. Verbal.
2. Analytic or mathematical.
3. Iconic, pictorial, or schematic.
4. Simulation.

The models of concern in the field of information systems methodologies are almost exclusively of the third type. The reason for the current dominance of iconic, pictorial, or schematic models is the perceived importance of using the models as a means of communication, particularly between users and analysts. Further important aspects of the models in information systems development are to ensure that the information necessary is captured, at the appropriate stage, and that this information is that required to be able to develop a working system.

3   Techniques and tools

A key element of the framework is the identification of the techniques and tools used in a methodology, but as these have been extensively discussed in Parts 4 and 5 they will not be further elaborated here.

4   Scope

The scope of a methodology is the next element in the framework. Scope is an indication of the stages of the life cycle of systems development which the methodology covers (Chapter 3). Further, an analysis of the level of detail at which each stage is addressed is useful. The problem with using the stages of the life cycle as a basis for the examination of scope is that there are methodologies that do not follow a life cycle, they may adopt a more iterative, evolutionary, or spiral model (Section 6.2). Nevertheless we think an examination of the scope of a methodology in relation to the life cycle is still useful.

5 Outputs

The next element in the framework concerns the outputs from the methodology. It is important to know what the methodology is producing in terms of deliverables at each stage and, in particular, the nature of the final deliverable. This can vary from being an analysis specification to a working implementation of a system and all its related procedures.

6 Practice

The next element of the framework is termed the practice and is measured according to: (a) the methodology background (discussed in Section 26.4 in terms of commercial or academic); (b) the user base (including numbers and types of user); (c) the participants in the methodology (e.g. can it be undertaken by users themselves or must professional analysts be involved); and what skill levels are required. The practice should also include an assessment of difficulties and problems encountered, and perceptions of success and failure. This should be undertaken by investigating the experiences of prior users of the methodology. This will inevitably be subjective, depending on who is consulted, but it can be a revealing exercise. In examining the practice, the degree to which the methodology can be, and is, altered or interpreted by the users according to the requirements of the particular situation should be assessed. It is also important to assess any differences there appear to be between the practice and the theory of the methodology.

7 Product

The last element of the framework is the product of the methodology, that is, what purchasers actually get for their money. This may consist of software, written documentation, an agreed number of hours training, a telephone help service, consultancy, and so on.

27.3 COMPARISON

In this section we offer a discussion of some of the methodologies we have described in this text in the context of the comparison framework identified in Section 27.2 above. This discussion is illustrative, rather than comprehensive, so we do not include all methodologies from Part 6. For example, we exclude a number of methodologies because of their restricted application domain such as KADS (expert systems development), Welti ERP, and Renaissance (legacy systems). We also exclude those that are frameworks, such as Euromethod, SODA, Multiview, and CMM. We hope readers will regard our comparison as a basis for stimulating debate rather than a statement of 'facts' about methodologies. It represents only our subjective view.

1   Philosophy

Element 1 of the framework concerns the identification of the philosophy of the methodology. There are a number of subelements to philosophy which we will examine in turn.

The first subelement is paradigm, and it provides ample illustration of the difficulties in attempting to compare methodologies. In the discussion of the framework, we identified the science paradigm and the systems paradigm to be of critical importance. We suggest that SSM and ETHICS belong to the systems paradigm and that STRADIS, YSM, IE, SSADM, Merise, JSD, OOA, RUP, DSDM, and ISAC belong to the science paradigm.

(a) Paradigm

It is clear that SSM adopts the systems paradigm, indeed it is explicitly stated to do so by the methodology author. This is one of the few cases where the issue is addressed as part of the methodology itself. But even if we were not so told, it is clear that the methodology uses many systems concepts and avoids a reductionist approach.

In ETHICS it is the belief in the interaction of the social and the technical subsystems (the socio-technical approach) that leads to an advocacy of the participative design philosophy. The work system is analysed for variances or weaknesses which prevent the systems objectives being realized. These variances are often discovered at subsystems boundaries, particularly where the social and technical subsystems meet. The ideas of job enrichment and participative design are particular solutions to the more common variances which are encountered. In addition, ETHICS makes no attempt to break down the system into its constituent parts for the purpose of understanding the problems. Therefore, the underlying paradigm for ETHICS is, we believe, the systems paradigm.

In the analysis of paradigm, ISAC generates the most discussion. ISAC is probably one of the less well-known and used methodologies we describe, but it is important in relation to its philosophical contribution. While it is clear that ISAC is firmly in the participative tradition, we believe that this does not mean it automatically incorporates the systems paradigm. The ETHICS methodology is also highly participative, but it is more the socio-technical aspects which lead us to classify that as being of the systems paradigm. ISAC adopts a more reductionist approach to the understanding of systems. Its authors state (Lundeberg et al., 1982) that:

> The only way to solve complex problems is to divide them into sub-problems until they become manageable. A requirement for this to work is that the solution to the sub-problems gives the solution for the problem as a whole, that is, that the division in sub-problems is coherent.

This would appear to be a categorical endorsement of the science paradigm, and despite its socio-technical spirit we classify ISAC to be in the science paradigm, although if we accept the notion of a continuum it would not be at the extreme end. We also, on the basis of their clear reductionist approaches and their acceptance of the ontological position of realism, identify STRADIS, YSM, IE, SSADM, Merise, JSD, RUP, DSDM, and OOA to belong to the science paradigm.

IE, for example, adopts what is termed the 'divide and conquer' approach which is clearly reductionist, and JSD describes its approach to modelling as attempting to reflect the real-world situation; for example, in the entity action step, 'real-world entities are defined' without any discussions of the real world being socially constructed or any problems that might be encountered concerning differing perceptions of the real world.

One of the interesting aspects of applying the comparison framework is not so much whether the classification is right, but the discussion and debate that it generates. The debate proves insightful and causes many significant questions to be asked of the methodologies, some of which prove difficult to answer.

(b) Objectives

The second subelement of philosophy concerns the objectives of the methodology. There are many objectives that could be discussed, but for the purposes of this framework it is of prime importance whether the objective is to build a computerized information system or whether wider improvements and more general problem solving are involved. Some of our methodologies indicate their position more clearly than others. ISAC, for example, decides on information systems development as the suitable development measure only if the change analysis indicates that there are problems and needs in the information systems area. In other situations, other development measures are chosen, for example: (i) development of the direct business activities, such as production development, product development, or a development of distribution systems; (ii) organizational development; or (iii) development of personal relations (communication training). We therefore see that ISAC is very much more than the development of IT systems, as are SSM and ETHICS.

PI also has objectives that are much wider than the development of computerized systems. Its objectives focus on improving and redesigning business processes for an organization as a whole, and, although IT is usually regarded as an important enabler of process innovation, many of the specified improvements and redesigned processes are achieved without the construction of computer systems. DSDM, although often resulting in the design of computer systems, is sometimes used to address organizational or general problem-solving issues.

On the other hand we classify STRADIS, YSM, IE, SSADM, Merise, JSD, RUP, and OOA not as general problem-solving methodologies, but as having clear objectives to develop computerized information systems. Some methodologies claim that they are applicable whether the system is going to be automated or not, for example, STRADIS, but we can find no evidence that this is ever put into practice, and an examination of the activities of these methodologies illustrates that their main focus clearly embodies an assumption that a computerized system is to be constructed.

Apart from objectives concerning whether a computerized system is the goal or not, there are other objectives of importance in comparisons. For example, in ETHICS there are objectives relating to improving the quality of working life and enhancing the job satisfaction of users, and a clear ethical position implying that it should not be used in circumstances where an IT system might dehumanize work.

(c) Domain

The next subelement for analysis is that of domain. This is related to the above subelement of objective but focuses on what aspects or domain the methodology seeks to address. Of particular interest is the distinction between those methodologies that seek to identify business or organizational need for an information system, that is, those which address the general planning, organization, and strategy of information and systems in the organization, and those concerned with the solving of a specific, pre-identified problem, for example, the need to provide a wider range of marketing information to the salesforce.

Often the key to this distinction is the starting point of the methodology. IE, PI, and SSM are identified as being of the planning, organization, and strategy type. In PI the development of information systems is clearly driven by the identified improvements to the processes required for the benefit of the business and organization. IE has as its first stage information strategy planning. Here an overview is taken of the organization in terms of its business objectives and related information needs and an overall information systems plan is devised for the organization. This clearly implies that it is an approach adopting the philosophy that an organization needs such a plan in order to function effectively, and that success is related to the identification of information systems that will benefit the organization and help achieve its strategic objectives.

SSM is quite different to IE, and yet we also classify it as a methodology of the planning, organization, and strategy type. Such terminology might not easily be associated with SSM, but it is clearly not a specific problem-solving methodology in the sense that it does not assume that a well-defined, structured problem already exists. Much of its focus is on the understanding of these wider issues and the context in which the problem situation exists. The term 'problem situation' in SSM is not meant to imply the existence of a well-defined problem, quite the reverse. However, SSM is not usually thought of as a methodology that addresses planning, organization, and strategy, but if we remove the managerial implications from these terms, this is fundamentally what it is about. It is attempting to identify the underlying issues that help in the understanding of the problem situation, including the purpose of the organization. Later stages of the methodology assess feasible and desirable change and recommend action to improve the situation, the results of which can be the development of information systems.

STRADIS, YSM, SSADM, Merise, JSD, OOA, RUP, DSDM, ISAC, and ETHICS are classified as specific problem-solving methodologies; that is, they do not focus on identifying the systems required by the organization but begin by assuming that a specific problem is to be addressed.

(d) Target

The final subelement of philosophy in the framework is concerned with the target system to be developed, that is, whether the methodology is aimed at particular types of application, types of problem, size of system, environment, and so on. This is also a difficult area, because most methodologies appear to claim to be general purpose. Such a claim is clearly made within certain assumptions. In the majority of cases, a large organization with an in-house data processing department is assumed. Further, it is often assumed that bespoke (tailor-made) systems are going to be developed, rather than, for example, the use of application packages. An exception is IE, where alternative approaches are envisaged. OOA and RUP are considered to be general purpose, although it is suggested that they are not very helpful for simple, limited systems or systems with only a few class-&-objects. STRADIS is also stated to be general purpose and applicable to any size of system, yet the main technique is data flow diagramming, which is not particularly suitable for all types of application, for example, the development of management information systems or web-based systems. Therefore, the claims of the methodology authors have to be tempered by an examination of the methodology itself. JSD, for example, has been described as most suitable for real-time processing applications. SSM has been developed to be applicable in human activity situations where very complex (wicked) problem situations exist.

The size of organizations that the methodologies address is also an important aspect of target. Whereas STRADIS, YSM, IE, SSADM, Merise, OOA, and RUP have all been designed primarily for use in large organizations, Multiview has been designed to be applicable in relatively small organizations. There is, however, a version of SSADM, called MicroSSADM, which is intended to help develop information systems in smaller environments or where the target system is PC-based.

2   Model

The second element of the framework deals with the model or models that the methodology uses. This can be investigated in terms of the type of model, the levels of abstraction of the model, and the orientation or focus of the model.

In this subsection, we will concentrate on examining the various models of process that methodologies use. The primary process model used is the data flow diagram. In STRADIS it is the primary model of the methodology. It also appears in YSM, SSADM and ISAC as an important model, although not the only one. It is also used in Wilson's (1990) description of SSM (but not in Checkland's version), referred to as 'a "Gane and Sarson" type diagram'. It also features in IE, though in a slightly different form, termed a 'process dependency diagram', but it plays a less significant role than, for example, in STRADIS. The data flow diagram is predominantly a process model, and data are only modelled as a by-product of the processes.

The models in JSD, ETHICS, SSM (Checkland), and PI are also, in their various ways, process-oriented, but they do not use data flow diagrams. The structure diagram is used in JSD to model aspects of process, and we see that this depicts the structure of processes rather than the flow of data between processes, which dramatically changes the focus of what is important in JSD and helps to explain why it is regarded as more suitable for real-time process applications than data flow diagram-based methodologies. In SSM, the rich picture, which is a model of the problem situation, is also, in part, a model of processes, structures, and their relationships. ETHICS uses a socio-technical model which involves the interaction of technology and people and the processes performed. It is interesting to note that of the identified model types, this is not a pictorial model-type but a 'verbal' or narrative model. In OOA and RUP the basic models are an integration of both process and data orientation, often in the same diagram, which as we have seen is a key element of the object-oriented approach.

3   Techniques and tools

The third element of the framework is that of the techniques and tools that a methodology employs. These have been examined in Parts 4 and 5, respectively. The techniques to be used in a methodology are usually made explicit by the authors which makes it relatively easy to compare and contrast. Many of the models discussed above are closely reflected in the techniques used but there are sometimes differences in the way the models are used and their importance in the methodology. Many methodologies appear to include the techniques as part of the methodology. STRADIS is an example of a methodology which is largely described in terms of its techniques, but others, such as, YSM, SSADM, JSD, OOA, and RUP, also have specific techniques which are regarded as fundamental to the methodology. Other methodologies, for example, ISAC, do not rely on particular techniques quite so much, and it is relatively easy to envisage similar but alternative techniques being used without affecting the essence of the methodology.

Some methodologies, for example, IE, explicitly suggest that the techniques are not a fundamental part of the methodology and that the current recommended techniques can be replaced, or substituted, as better techniques become available, providing, of course, they address the same fundamentals. This is potentially an important conceptual difference between methodologies, and it is a useful exercise to strip a methodology of its techniques and see what, if anything, is left. For example, are the phases and tasks of the methodology described in terms of when and how to use the techniques? Obviously those methodologies that allow new techniques to be incorporated are somewhat more flexible, but achieving this in practice is not so easy. For example, in a methodology which advocates the clear separation of the modelling of data and processes, such as, SSADM, Merise, or IE, it would be quite difficult to accommodate an object-oriented modelling technique, which integrates the two without amending the fundamentals of the methodology. Similarly it would be difficult to imagine OOA or RUP accommodating anything other than object-oriented techniques and models, particularly ones which did not incorporate the essential combination of data and process. Therefore, the identification of the fundamentals is an important part of any comparison. This also raises interesting issues about how methodologies can legitimately develop and evolve over time without losing the essence of the methodology.

The comparison of the tools of methodologies begins with whether any are specifically advocated. SSM, for example, does not advocate, or even mention, any tools, but most methodologies, such as YSM, IE, SSADM, Merise, JSD, OOA, and PI, recommend the use of tools to some degree. These range from simple drawing tools through to tools supporting the whole development process, including prototyping, project management, code generation, simulation, and so on. The degree of recommendation varies considerably. Some, such as IE and RUP, suggest that the process should not be contemplated without the use of tools, the process being too complicated and time consuming. Others, for example, SSADM and OOA, argue that they might be helpful but are not necessarily essential. An important element of comparison is whether the methodology, like IE, implies the use of a specific brand-name tool, or whether appropriate tools from any vendor can be used. In practice, there is often a trade-off to be made between the degree that the tool is specific to the methodology and the degree of lock-in to a particular vendor.

4 Scope

The fourth element of the framework is scope. For the purposes of this text we examine methodologies in terms of the stages of the life cycle they address. We identify nine

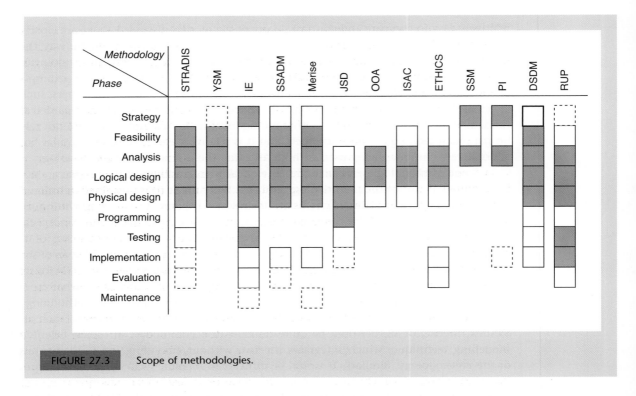

| FIGURE 27.3 | Scope of methodologies. |

stages: strategy (planning), feasibility, analysis, logical design, physical design, program-ming, testing, implementation, and maintenance. This is not the only possible approach to the analysis of scope and, depending on the methodologies being compared and the purpose of the comparison, other dimensions may be more appropriate. Any analysis of the scope of a methodology is difficult and subjective. Using the stages of the life cycle may misrepresent those methodologies that are not designed to follow such a structure, for example, prototyping methodologies, in which case a definition of scope based on the spiral model might be more appropriate. It is therefore important that scope is not viewed in isolation from the rest of the framework and that the earlier warnings con-cerning comparisons are heeded.

Figure 27.3 summarizes the results of the analysis of scope. Shaded areas indicate that the methodology covers the stage in some detail which may include the provision of specific techniques, and tools of support. An unshaded area means that the methodology addresses the area, but in less detail and depth. In this case there is less guidance from the methodology and more is left for the developers to interpret and perform for themselves. The broken lines indicate areas that are only briefly mentioned in the methodology, but no procedures, techniques, or rules are provided although the methodology recognizes that the area should be addressed. The identification that a methodology covers a par-ticular stage does not necessarily mean that there exists a defined stage of that name but that within the methodology there are elements that can be construed to be equivalent to that stage.

In our analysis of scope, *strategy* is used to indicate whether the methodology addresses any aspects which relate to an organization-wide context, and that deals with overall information systems strategy, purpose, and planning, rather than just that of the particular system or area of concern. IE and PI are identified as addressing this in some detail, as is SSM which also deals with the wider context, although in a significantly different way to the others. SSADM, Merise, DSDM, and, to a lesser extent YSM and RUP, also include aspects of a strategic nature.

The next stage is *feasibility* which is defined as the economic, social, and technical evaluation of the system under consideration. STRADIS, YSM, SSADM, DSDM, and Merise include detailed aspects for the evaluation of feasibility in their methodologies. IE, ISAC, PI, and RUP also address feasibility, but less comprehensively. However, it should be noted that the way in which they deal with feasibility differs considerably. For example, ISAC does not identify a specific feasibility phase (it is contained in some of the analysis steps) and STRADIS checks and rechecks feasibility at many stages throughout the methodology. ETHICS and SSM are identified as dealing in detail with feasibility, although in quite a different way from the others as it is not financial but social feasibility of change which is addressed. ETHICS focuses on social and technical 'fit' and SSM on feasible and desirable change. In Figure 27.3, these methodologies are depicted as open boxes rather than shaded boxes because, although their social focus is comprehensive, the other aspects of feasibility are not.

The *analysis* stage, which includes user requirements analysis, is covered in detail, although in a wide variety of different ways by all the methodologies except JSD. JSD does not specifically address user requirements analysis but begins with an assumption that they are given. The *logical design* stages are covered in detail by all the methodologies except SSM and PI which do not cover the stage or indeed most subsequent stages. *Physical design* is covered in detail by all except OOA, ISAC, and ETHICS, which are less explicit. ISAC suggests the use of JSP in the data systems design phase.

The next stage we identify is that of the physical development of the system, characterized as *programming*. Only STRADIS, IE, JSD, DSDM, and RUP cover programming, with JSD judged to address it in most detail. Some methodologies suggest or assume that other approaches are used for the physical development of the system. ISAC, for example, recommends the use of JSP, and OOA recommends an object-oriented language. In such cases we do not include this as being covered in the scope of the methodology. *Testing*, which includes the planning as well as the testing of systems, programs, and procedures, is addressed by STRADIS, IE, JSD, and RUP, but only in detail by IE and RUP.

Implementation, in which we include planning and implementation of technical, social, and organizational aspects, is covered by IE, SSADM, Merise, DSDM, and ETHICS, although not in as much detail as earlier stages, with STRADIS and PI addressing it, but in less detail. JSD is a special case, because its interpretation of implementation is simply technical, covering the sharing of processors among processes. RUP deals in detail with the technical issues of implementation but does not address the social and organizational aspects to the same extent. Nevertheless, we classify this as detailed coverage. Post-implementation *evaluation* and review concerns the measurement and evaluation of the implemented system and a comparison with the original objectives. This is addressed by IE, DSDM, RUP, and ETHICS, with ETHICS particularly focusing on the evaluation of 'fit', STRADIS and SSADM cover evaluation in less detail.

The final stage in the analysis of scope is *maintenance*, which we regard as being covered by a methodology only if it is specifically addressed in terms of tasks. The fact that maintenance may in general be improved by the use of the methodology in earlier stages is not regarded as coverage of maintenance for the purposes of this analysis. With this definition we find that only IE and Merise mention maintenance in any detail.

A glance at Figure 27.3 illustrates that the main focuses of most of these methodologies are at the analysis and design stages, but that there are wide scope variations, and that to assume all methodologies are the same in this respect, as people often do, is obviously incorrect.

5 Outputs

The fifth element of the framework is concerned with outputs. This is an investigation of what is actually produced in terms of deliverables at the end of each stage of the methodology. The outputs of methodologies differ quite substantially, not only in terms of what should be produced but also in the level of detail that the methodology specifies. This is closely related to the degree that the methodology is seen as a blueprint for action; that is, how detailed are the rules about how to proceed and how much is left to the discretion of the analyst.

A related issue concerns how, and to what extent, the analysts know that they are proceeding correctly. As an example, ISAC specifies in some detail the outputs of the change analysis stage (A-graphs), but the process of generating change alternatives is not described in any detail. This is regarded as the creative part of the methodology and not amenable to specification. The identification of such areas in a methodology is regarded as an important contribution to an understanding of that methodology.

6 Practice

The penultimate element of the framework is the practice or use of the methodology. It contains the subelements of background, user base, applications, and players. The background of the methodology broadly identifies its origins in terms of academic or commercial. STRADIS, YSM, IE, SSADM, DSDM, and OOA lie in the commercial sphere, whereas Merise, JSD, ISAC, ETHICS, SSM, RUP, and PI have academic backgrounds, at least in part, though this does not mean that they are not now commercial methodologies.

The user base, perhaps surprisingly, is often difficult to discover and is possibly less widespread than vendors would have us believe. Vendors have a habit of suggesting that any company that has expressed interest in their methodology, or has requested an evaluation version, is a user. There is a view that commercial methodologies are not in as widespread use as is claimed but finding evidence is difficult. Fitzgerald et al. (1999) found that 57 per cent of organizations were using a systems development methodology, but, of these, only 11 per cent used a commercial development methodology, 30 per cent used a commercial methodology adapted for in-house use, and 59 per cent a methodology which was claimed to be unique to the organization (i.e. internally developed and not based on a commercial methodology). A similar finding concerning the adaptation of methodologies was found in a study conducted in the Republic of Ireland, although in this case the proportion using methodologies was only 40 per cent (Fitzgerald, 1996). In the USA Russo and Wynekoop (1995) reported on a survey that identified generic types of methodology and found that, of 132 organizations using a methodology, 77 per cent were using a structured approach, with 8 per cent using a prototyping/iterative approach, and 5 per cent using a RAD approach. Therefore, it would appear that commercial methodologies are not as well used as some might believe but nevertheless they are clearly influential on the practice of systems development.

The last subelement of practice requires an analysis of the participants involved, in some contexts these are referred to as 'actors' or 'stakeholders'. This requires answers to the questions 'who is supposed to use the methodology?' and 'what roles do they perform?', 'who are the other stakeholders', etc. It also attempts to identify the skill levels required. The traditional view of information systems development is that a specialist team of professional systems analysts and designers perform the analysis and design aspects and professional programmers design the programs and write the code. The system is then implemented by the analysts. Although the exact roles have different names, in general systems development is undertaken by professional technical developers. This view is taken by STRADIS, YSM, IE, SSADM, Merise, JSD, OOA, and RUP. ETHICS takes a different view, and users have a much more proactive role. In ETHICS, the users perform the analysis and design themselves and the data processing professionals are used as consultants as and when required. In addition, ETHICS incorporates a facilitator role, whose task is to guide the users in the use of the methodology. Facilitators do not actually perform the tasks themselves, but smooth the path and ensure that the methodology is followed correctly. The facilitator should be expert and experienced in the use of the methodology. Introna and Whitley (1997) advocate what they term 'a formal apprenticeship' in the use and applicability of a range of methodologies and the context in which they might be used to overcome the problems of method-ism discussed earlier.

The levels of skill required by the players varies considerably. In almost all methodologies considerable training and experience is necessary for at least some of the players. Further, many make significant demands on the users, in which case the methodology would be expected to include training aspects. This may significantly increase the time and costs required to develop a project. ETHICS, which makes heavy demands on the users, recognizes and addresses this problem. Even where methodologies adopt the more traditional roles, professional analysts and designers can find them quite difficult to learn at first (and some complain laborious as well), with new vocabularies, techniques, and tools to work with. Other methodologies, while not going as far as ETHICS, have a much wider range of stakeholders involved, particularly from the business side as well as the professional systems developers, for example, SSM, ISAC, PI, and DSDM.

7 Product

The final element of the framework is that of product. This describes what is supplied when purchasing a methodology and at what cost. Most methodologies have a range of products and services available, which can be taken or not, although there is likely to be a minimum set. The product is also likely to be changing rapidly, mainly due to the increasing numbers of support tools available. The product can range from large and copious sets of manuals, for example, SSADM, to a set of academic papers and a book, as in the case of SSM. RUP has a range of documents, books, and specifications but also has a multimedia website, and indeed claims that the methodology product is actually delivered using this web technology, 'so it's not in books or binders but literally at the developers' fingertips'. Some methodologies require consultants, facilitators, and/or training courses to be used as part of the product. Some methodologies offer certification of competency for developers. There is, for example, a certificate of proficiency scheme for SSADM.

This discussion of methodologies using the framework is by no means comprehensive, but is intended to be illustrative of the issues that the framework raises. It is likely to be contentious. It is meant to stimulate debate, to open discussions rather than be taken as a statement of facts.

27.4   SUMMARY

- In this chapter we examine the comparison of methodologies. We identify two main reasons for wanting to compare methodologies. First, an academic reason, to understand the nature of methodologies better, and, second, a practical reason, to choose a methodology for use in an organization.

- A general framework for comparing methodologies is discussed (NIMSAD). This is a broader framework than most and has three main elements as follows: the problem situation (context); the problem solver (methodology user); and the problem-solving process (the methodology itself).

- A more specific framework for comparing methodologies is proposed. This framework has seven elements. The first element relates to the identification of the underlying philosophy behind the methodology (i.e. what gives it its particular flavour and why the authors think it is an appropriate way to develop information systems). The second element relates to the models that the methodology uses (i.e. the way that the 'real world' is modelled and abstracted). The third element is the specific techniques and tools that are recommended. The fourth element suggests comparing the scope of the methodologies, the fifth the outputs of the methodology, the sixth the practice (e.g. number and experience of existing users), and finally the sixth element is the nature of the product itself (i.e. what you actually get when you procure a methodology).

- The final section of the book takes many of the methodologies described in Part 6 and uses the framework, described above, to compare them. The value of such a comparison is not necessarily the outcome but the enhanced understanding that comes from asking questions of methodologies and discussing the issues that arise. For example, the comparison of scope reveals that quite different aspects are addressed in very different ways by different methodologies.

QUESTIONS

1 Why do you think such great importance is attached to the philosophy of a methodology?

2 What elements do you regard as most important in the comparison of methodologies?

3 What would be your criteria for comparison if you were making a choice of a methodology for potential adoption in a public service organization, such as a hospital?

4 Undertake a comparison of three methodologies with which you are familiar using just three criteria. What did you learn from the comparison?

5 Why are some methodologies essentially a set of recommended techniques while others say that in a particular stage or phase any 'appropriate' techniques may be used?

27.5 FURTHER READING

Checkland, P. (1981) *Systems Thinking, Systems Practice*, John Wiley & Sons, Chichester, UK.

Hirschheim, R., Klein, H.K., and Lyytinen, K. (1996) Exploring the intellectual structures of information systems development: A social action theoretical analysis, *Accounting Management & Information Technology*, Vol. 6, Nos 1/2, 1–64.

Jayaratna, N. (1994) *Understanding and Evaluating Methodologies, NIMSAD: A Systemic Framework*, McGraw-Hill, Maidenhead, UK.

Olle, T.W., Sol, H.G., and Verrijn-Stuart, A.A. (1982) *Information Systems Design Methodologies: A Comparative Review*, North Holland, Amsterdam.

Russo, N.L. and Stolterman, E. (2000) Exploring the assumptions underlying information systems methodologies: Their impact on past, present and future ISM research, *Information Technology & People*, Vol. 13, No. 4.

Bibliography

Ackerman, F. and Eden, C. (2001) SODA – journey making and mapping in practice, in J. Rosenhead and J. Mingers (eds) *Rational Analysis for a Problematic World Revisited – Problem Structuring Methods for Complexity, Uncertainty and Conflict*, 2nd edn, John Wiley & Sons, Chichester, UK.

Ackoff, R. L. (1971) Towards a system of system concepts, *Management Science*, Vol. 17.

Amoroso, D.L. and Cheney, P.H. (1991) Testing a causal model of end-user application effectiveness, *Journal of Management Information Systems*, Vol. 8, No. 1, 63–89.

Andrews, D.C. (1991) JAD: A crucial dimension for rapid application development, *Journal of Systems Management*, March, 23–31.

Angell, I.O. and Smithson, S. (1991) *Information Systems Management: Opportunities and Risks*, Macmillan, Basingstoke, UK. This text emphasizes the management of information systems within business organizations, suggesting that the real problems associated with information systems are human, managerial, social, and organizational, rather than technological.

Ansoff, H.I. (1965) *Corporate Strategy*, McGraw-Hill, New York.

Argyris, C. (1993) *Knowledge for Action: A Guide to Overcoming Barriers to Organization Change*, Jossey-Bass, San Francisco.

Argyris, C. and Schön, D. (1978) *Organizational Learning: A Theory of Action Perspective*, Addison-Wesley, Reading, Massachusetts.

Arnett, K.P and Litecky, C.R. (1992) Retooling systems analyst skills for small hospitals, *Journal of Systems Management*, June.

Avison, D.E. and Catchpole, C.P. (1987) Information systems for the community health services. *Medical Informatics*, Vol. 13, 2.

Avison, D.E. and Myers, M.D. (1995) Information systems and anthropology: An anthropological perspective on IT and organizational culture, *Information Technology & People*, Vol. 8, No. 3, 43–56.

Avison, D.E. and Taylor, A.V. (1996) Information systems development methodologies: A classification according to problem situations, *Journal of Information Technology*, Vol. 11.

Avison, D.E. and Truex, D. (submitted for publication) *Method Engineering: Reflections on the Past and Ways Forward*.

Avison, D.E. and Wood-Harper, A.T. (1986) Multiview – an exploration in information systems development, *Australian Computer Journal*, Vol. 18, 4.

Avison, D.E. and Wood-Harper, A.T. (1990) *Multiview: An Exploration in Information Systems Development*. McGraw-Hill, Maidenhead, UK.

Avison, D.E., Powell, P.L., and Adams, C. (1994) Identifying and incorporating change in information systems, *Systems Practice*, Vol. 7, No. 2, 143–159.

Avison, D.E., Powell, P., Keen, P., Klein, J.H., and Ward, S. (1995) Addressing the need for flexibility in information systems, *Journal of Management Systems*, Vol. 7, No. 2, 43–60.

Avison, D.E., Wood-Harper, A.T., Vidgen, R.T., and Wood, J.R.G. (1998) A further exploration into information systems development: The evolution of Multiview2, *Information Technology & People*, Vol. 11, No. 2, 124–139.

Bahrami, A. (1999) *Object-oriented Systems Development*, McGraw–Hill, Boston.

Baskerville, R., and Pries-Heje, J. (2001) Racing the e-bomb: How the Internet is redefining information system development methodology, in L. Russo, B. Fitzgerald, and J. DeGross (eds) *Realigning Research and Practice in Information System Development*, Proceedings of the IFIP TC8/WG8.2 Working Conference, 27–29 July, Boise, Idaho.

Beck, K. (2000) *Extreme Programming Explained: Embrace Change*, Addison-Wesley Longman, Boston.

Benbasat, I., Dexter, A.S., Drury, D.H., and Goldstein, R.C. (1984) A critique of the stage hypothesis: Theory and empirical evidence, *Communications of the ACM*, Vol. 27, No. 5, 476–485.

Bennett, S., McRobb, S., and Farmer, R. (1999) *Object-oriented Systems Analysis and Design Using UML*, McGraw-Hill, London.

Benyon, D. (1990) *Information and Data Modelling*, McGraw-Hill, Maidenhead, UK.

Bergeron, F. and Berube, C. (1988) The management of the end-user environment: An empirical investigation, *Information and Management*, Vol. 14, No. 2, 107–113.

Beynon-Davies, P (1995) Information systems 'failure': The case of the London Ambulance Service's Computer Aided Despatch project, *European Journal of Information Systems*, No. 4, 171–184.

Bikson, T.K. (1996) Groupware at the World Bank, in C.U. Ciborra (ed.) *Groupware and Teamwork: Invisible Aid or Technical Hindrance?*, Wiley, Chichester, UK, pp. 145–183.

Bisp, S., Sorensen, E., and Grunert, K.G. (1998) Using the key success factor concept in competitor intelligence and benchmarking, *Competitive Intelligence Review*, Vol. 9, No. 3, 55–67.

Bjørn-Andersen, N. (1984) Challenge to certainty, in T.M.A. Bemelmans (ed.) *Beyond Productivity: Information Systems Development for Organizational Effectiveness*, North Holland, Amsterdam.

Boehm, B. (1999) Making RAD work for your project, *Computer*, Vol. 32, No. 3, 113–114.

Boehm, B.W. (1988) A spiral model for software development and enhancement, *IEEE Computer*, Vol. 21, No. 5.

Booch, G. (1991) *Object-oriented Design with Applications*, Benjamin/Cummings, Redwood City, California.

Booch, G. (1994) *Object-oriented Analysis and Design with Applications*, 2nd edn, Benjamin/Cummings, California.

Booch, G. (1995) *Object Solutions: Managing the Object-oriented Project*, Addison-Wesley, Boston.

Booch, G., Jacobson, I., and Rumbaugh, J. (1997) The Unified Modeling Language, Notation Guide Version 1.1, available at http://www.rational.com/uml/index.jsp

Booch, G., Jacobson, I., and Rumbaugh, J. (1998) *Unified Modeling Language – User's Guide*, Addison-Wesley, Boston.

Booch, G., Jacobson, I., and Rumbaugh, J. (1999) *Unified Modeling Language 1.3*, White paper, Rational Software Corp., available at http://www.rational.com/uml/index.jsp

Boynton, A.C. (1984) An assessment of critical success factors, *Sloan Management Review*, Summer.

Boynton, A.C. and Zmud, R.W. (1984) An assessment of critical success factors, *Sloan Management Review*, 25 (Summer), 17–27.

Braa, K., Sorensen, C., and Dahlbom, B. (eds) *Planet Internet*, Studentliteratur, Lund.

Brancheau, J.C. and Wetherbe, J.C. (1990) The adoption of spreadsheet software: Testing innovation diffusion theory in the context of end-user computing, *Information Systems Research*, Vol. 1, No. 2.

Brinkkemper, S., Lyytinen, K., and Welke, R.J. (eds) (1996) *Method Engineering: Principles of Method Construction and Tool Support*, Chapman & Hall, London.

Broadman, J.G. and Johnson, D.I. (1996) Realities and rewards of software process improvement, *IEEE Software*, Vol. 29, No. 11, 99–101.

Brooks, F.P. (1974) *The Mythical Manmonth*, Addison-Wesley Longman, Boston.

Brown, A.W. (ed.) (1996) *Component-based Software Engineering*, IEEE Computer Society, Los Alamitos, California, p. 140.

Bubenko, J.A. Jr (1986) Information system methodologies – a research view, in T.W. Olle, H.G. Sol, and A.A. Verrijn-Stuart (eds) *Information Systems Design Methodologies: A Comparative Review*, North Holland, Amsterdam.

Bucki, L.A. (2000) *Managing with Microsoft Project 2000*, Prima, Rocklin, California.

Buckingham, R.A., Hirschheim, R.A., Land, F.F., and Tully, C.J. (eds) (1987) Information systems curriculum: A basis for course design, *Information Systems Education: Recommendations and Implementation*, Cambridge University Press, Cambridge.

Budde, R., Kautz, K., Kuhlenkamp, K., and Züllighoven, H. (1992) *Prototyping – An Approach to Evolutionary Systems Development*, Springer-Verlag, Berlin.

Burke, G. and Peppard, J. (1995) *Examining Business Process Re-engineering: Current Perspectives and Research Directions*, Kogan Page, London

Burrell, G. and Morgan, G. (1979) *Sociological Paradigms and Organisational Analysis*, Heinemann, London.

Buttle, F. (1992) The marketing strategy worksheet: A practical tool, *Cornell Hotel Restaurant Administration Quarterly*, Vol. 33, No. 3.

Cadle, J. and Yeates, D. (2001) *Project Management for Information Systems*, Prentice Hall, Harlow, UK.

Cameron, J.R. (1989) *JSP & JSD: The Jackson Approach to Software Development*, IEEE Computer Society Press, Los Angeles.

Jones, C. (1993) *Assessment and Control of Software Risks*, Prentice Hall, Englewood Cliffs, New Jersey.

Card, D. (1995) Is timing really everything? *IEEE Software*, September.

Cardenas, A.F. (1985) *Database Management Systems*, 2nd edn, Allyn and Bason, Boston.

Carmel, E. and Nunamaker, J. (1992) Supporting joint application development (JAD) with electronic meeting systems: A field study, in J.I. DeGross, J.D. Becker, and J.J. Elam (eds) *Proceedings of the Thirteenth International Conference on Information Systems (ICIS)*, ACM, Baltimore.

Carmel, E. (1995) Does RAD live up to the hype? *IEEE Software*, September, 25–26.

CCTA (1994a) *Euromethod Overview*, CCTA, Norwich, UK.

CCTA (1994b) *Using Euromethod in Practice*, CCTA, Norwich, UK.

CCTA (1990) *Euromethod Project, Phase 2, Deliverable 1, State of the Art Report*, Eurogroup, CCTA, Norwich, UK.

Checkland, P. (1981) *Systems Thinking, Systems Practice*, John Wiley & Sons, Chichester, UK.

Checkland, P. (1985) From optimising to learning: A development of systems thinking for the 1990s, *Journal of the Operational Research Society*, Vol. 36, 9.

Checkland, P. (1987) *Systems Thinking and Computer Systems Analysis: Time to Unite*, DEC Seminar Series in Information Systems, presentation given at the London School of Economics, 5 November 1987.

Checkland, P. (1999) Soft systems methodology: A 30-year retrospective, in *Systems Thinking, Systems Practice*, John Wiley & Sons, Chichester, UK.

Checkland, P. and Scholes. J. (1990) *Soft Systems Methodology in Action*. John Wiley & Sons, Chichester, UK.

Chen, J. (2001) Building web applications, *Information Systems Management*, Winter, Vol. 18, No. 1.

Churchman, C.W. (1971) *The Design of Inquiring Systems, Basic Concepts of Systems and Organization*, Basic Books, New York.

Ciborra, C.U. (1996) The platform organization: Recombining strategies, structures, and surprises, *Organization Science*, Vol. 7, No. 2, 103–118.

Coad, P. and Argila, C. *Case Studies in Object Oriented Analysis and Design*, Yourdon Press, New Jersey.

Coad, P. and Yourdon, E. (1991) *Object Oriented Analysis*, 2nd edn, Prentice Hall, Englewood Cliffs, New Jersey.

Cockburn, A. (2002) *Agile Software Development*, Pearson-Longman, Harlow, UK.

Cooper, D.F. and Chapman, C.B. (1987) *Risk Analysis for Large Projects – Models, Methods and Cases*, John Wiley & Sons, Chichester, UK.

Cooper, R.B. and Zmud, R.W. (1990) Information technology implementation research: A technology diffusion approach, *Management Science*, Vol. 36, No. 2, 123–139.

Currie, W. L. and Galliers, R. (1999) *Rethinking Management Information Systems*, Oxford University Press, Oxford.

Currie, W.L. (2001) Application outsourcing: A new business model for enabling competitive electronic commerce, *International Journal of Technology Management*, Special Issue on Enabling Organizational Competitiveness Using Electronic Commerce (forthcoming).

Daniel, R.H. (1961) Management data crisis, *Harvard Business Review*, September–October, 111–112.

Daniels, J. and Cook, S. (1992) Making objects stick, in R. Tagg and J. Mabon (eds) *Object Management*, Aldgate Publishing, Aldershot, UK.

Daniels, J. *Why RAD Is Bad*, Presentation to the BCS Specialist Group, Imperial College, 10 July.

Davenport, T.H. (1993) *Process Innovation*, Harvard Business School Press, Cambridge, Massachusetts.

Davenport, T.H. and Prusak, L (1998) *Working Knowledge: How Organizations Manage What They Know*, Harvard Business School Press, Boston.

Davenport, T.H. and Short, J. (1990) The new industrial engineering: Information technology and business process redesign, *Sloan Management Review*, Vol. 31, No. 4, 11–27.

Davenport, T.H. and Stoddard, D. (1994) Re-engineering: Business change of mythic proportions, *MIS Quarterly*, Vol. 18, 121–127.

Davidson, E.J. (1999) Joint Application Design (JAD) in practice, *Journal of Systems and Software*, Vol. 45, No. 3, 215–223.

Davis, L.E. (1972) *The Design of Jobs*, Penguin, Harmondsworth, UK.

Davis, G.B. Strategies for information requirements determination, *IBM Systems Journal*, Vol. 21, 2.

De Bono, E. (1990) *Lateral Thinking for Management*, Penguin, Harmondsworth, UK.

De Grace, P. and Stahl, L. (1993) *The Olduvai Imperative: CASE and the State of Software Engineering Practice*, Pentice Hall, Englewood Cliffs, New Jersey.

De Greef, P. and Breuker, J. A. (1989) Analysing system-user cooperation, *Knowledge Acquisition*, Vol. 4.

DeMarco, T. (1979) *Structured Analysis and System Specification*, Prentice Hall, Englewood Cliffs, New Jersey.

Diaz, M. and Sligo, J. (1997) How software process improvement helped Motorola, *IEEE Software*, Vol. 30, No. 5, 75–81.

Donaldson, T. and Preston, L.E. (1995) The stakeholder theory of the corporation: Concepts, evidence, and implications, *Academy of Management Review*, Vol. 20, No. 1, 65–91.

DSDM Manual Version 3 (1998) DSDM Consortium, Tesseract Publishing, Surrey, UK.

Dyché, J. (2002) *The CRM Handbook: A Business Guide to Customer Relationship Management*, Addison Wesley, Boston.

Earl, M. and Khan, B. (1994) How new is business process re-design?, *European Management Journal*, Vol. 12, No. 2, 20–30.

Earl, M.J. (1989) *Management Strategies for Information Technology*, Prentice Hall, Hemel Hempstead, UK.

Eden, C. and Ackerman, F. (2001) SODA – the principles, in J. Rosenhead and J. Mingers (eds) *Rational Analysis for a Problematic World Revisited – Problem Structuring Methods for Complexity, Uncertainty and Conflict*, 2nd edn, John Wiley & Sons, Chichester, UK.

Espejo, R. and Harnden, R. (eds) (1989) *The Viable System Model: Interpretations and Applications of Stafford Beer's VSM*, John Wiley & Sons, Chichester, UK.

Essex, P. and Magal, S.R. (1998) Determinants of information center success, *Journal of Management Information Systems*, Fall, Vol. 15, No. 2.

Eva, M. (1994) *SSADM Version 4: A User's Guide*, 2nd edn, McGraw-Hill, Maidenhead, UK.

Eva, M. and Guilford, S. (1996) Committed to a RADical solution, paper given at *4th BCS ISM Conference*, edited by Fitzgerald and Jayaratne, N. (eds) *Proceedings of the Fourth BCS Conference on Information Systems Methodologies*, University College, Cork.

Evan, W. and Freeman, R.E. (1988) A stakeholder theory of the modern corporation: Kantian capitalism, in T. Beauchamp and N. Bowie (eds) *Ethical Theory and Business*, 3rd edn, Prentice Hall, Englewood Cliffs, New Jersey.

Evans, J.S. (1991) Strategic flexibility for high technology manoeuvres: A conceptual framework, *Journal of Management Studies*, Vol. 28, No. 1, 69–89.

Fagin, R. (1977) Multivaried dependencies and a new normal form for relational databases, *ACM Transactions on Database Systems*, Vol. 2, 3.

Failla, A. (1996) Technologies for co-ordination in a software factory, in C.U. Ciborra (ed.) *Groupware and Teamwork: Invisible Aid or Technical Hindrance?*, John Wiley & Sons, Chichester, UK, pp. 61–88.

Feeny, D., Willcocks, L., Rands, T., and Fitzgerald, G. (1993). Strategies for IT management: When outsourcing equals rightsourcing, in S. Rock (ed.) *Directors Guide to Outsourcing*, Institute of Directors/IBM, London.

Feeny, D.F., Earl, M.J., and Edwards, B. (1996) Organisational arrangements for IS: Roles of users and specialists, in M.J. Earl (ed.) *Information Management: The Organisational Dimension*, Oxford University Press, Oxford.

Feigenbaum, E.A. (1982) *Knowledge Engineering in the 1980's*, Department of Computer Science, Stanford University, Stanford, California. [Quoted in Giarratano, J. and Riley, G. (1994) *Expert Systems, Principles and Programming*, PWS Publishing, Boston.]

Feller, J. and Fitzgerald, B. (2002) *Understanding Open Source Software Development*, Addison-Wesley, Harlow, UK.

Fine, E. (2001) Where heros go, *IIE Solutions*, Vol. 33, No. 5, 26–31.

Fitzgerald, B. (1994) The systems development dilemma: whether to adopt formalised systems development methodologies or not?, in W.R.J. Baets (ed.) *Proceedings of the Second European Conference on Information Systems*, Nijenrode University Press, Breukelen, The Netherlands.

Fitzgerald, B. (1996) Formalized systems development methodologies: A critical perspective, *Information Systems Journal*, Vol. 6, No. 1, 3–23.

Fitzgerald, B. (1999), An empirical investigation of RAD in practice, in T. Wood-Harper, N. Jayaratne, and B. Woods (eds) *Proceedings of the BCS Information Systems Methodologies Conference*, Springer-Verlag, London, pp. 77–87.

Fitzgerald, G. (1990) Achieving flexible information systems: The case for improved analysis, *Journal of Information Technology*, Vol. 5, No. 1, 5–11.

Fitzgerald, G. (1994) Strategic outsourcing of IT in the UK, Keynote address given at *Proceedings of the 5th Australasian Conference on Information Systems*, edited by G. Shanks and D. Arnott, published by Monash University, Melbourne, Australia, pp. 27–40.

Fitzgerald, G. (1998) Evaluating information systems projects: A multidimensional approach, *Journal of Information Technology*, Vol. 13, No. 1, 15–28.

Fitzgerald, G. (2000) *IT at the Heart of Business*, British Computer Society, Swindon, UK.

Fitzgerald, G. and Fitzgerald, B. (1999) Categories and contexts of ISD: Making sense of the mess, in J. Pries-Heje et al. (eds) *European Conference on Information Systems (ECIS)*, Copenhagen Business School, Copenhagen.

Fitzgerald, G. and Willcocks, L. (1994) *A Business Guide to Outsourcing Information Technology, A Study of European Best Practice in the Selection, Management and Use of External IT Services*, Business Intelligence, Wimbledon, UK, p. 372.

Fitzgerald, G., Philippides, A., and Probert, P. (1999) Information systems development, maintenance and enhancement: Findings from a UK study, *International Journal of Information Management*, Vol. 40, No. 2, 319–329.

Flynn, D.J. (1992) *Information Systems Requirements – Determination and Analysis*, McGraw-Hill, Maidenhead, UK.

Fowler, K.M. (1997) SEI CMM Level 5: A practitioner's perspective, *Crosstalk*, Vol. 10, No. 9.

Fowler, M. (with Scott, K.) (2000) *UML Distilled: A Brief Guide to the Standard Object Modelling Language*, 2nd edn, Addison-Wesley, Reading, Massachusetts.

Freeman, R.E. (1984) *Strategic Management: A Stakeholder Approach*, Harper Collins, Boston.

Galliers, R.D. and Sutherland, A.R. (1991) Information systems management and strategy formulation: the 'stages of growth model' revisited, *Journal of Information Systems*, Vol. 1, No. 2.

Gane, C. (1989) *Rapid Systems Development*, Prentice Hall, Englewood Cliffs, New Jersey.

Gane, C. and Sarson, T. (1979) *Structured Systems Analysis: Tools and Techniques*. Prentice Hall, Englewood Cliffs, New Jersey.

Gibson, C. and Nolan, R. (1974) Managing the four stages of EDP growth, *Harvard Business Review*, Vol. 52, No. 1, 76–78.

Gilb, T. (1988) *Principles of Software Engineering Management*, Addison-Wesley Longman, Harlow, UK.

Goldsmith, R.F (1994) Confidently outsourcing software development, *Journal of Systems Management*, Vol. 45, No. 4.

Gray, P. (1996) Information resource management: The capability maturity model (book), *Information Systems Management*, Vol. 13, No. 2.

Greiner, L. (2000) Tapping into the best tools, *Computer Dealer News*, Vol. 16, Issue 12, 25–27.

Grover, V. (2001) Power of Modern Information Technology is Impetus for Business Process Change, *Information Management*, Vol.. 14, No. 1/2.

Grover, V. and Malhotra, M. (1997) Business Process Re-engineering: A tutorial on the concept, evolution, method, technology and application, *Journal of Operations Management*, Vol. 15, 193–213.

Grundén, K. (1986) Some critical observations on the traditional design of administrative information systems and some proposed guidelines for human-oriented system evolution, in H-E. Nissen and G. Sandsröm (eds) *Quality of Work versus Quality of Information Systems*, Lund University, Sweden.

Guimaraes, T. (1996) Assessing the impact of information centers on end-user computing and company performance, *Information Resources Management Journal*, Vol. 9, No. 1, Winter, 6–15.

Hammer, M. (1990) Re-engineering work: don't automate, obliterate, *Harvard Business Review*, Vol. 90, No. 4, 104–112.

Hammer, M. and Champy, J. (1990) *Re-engineering the Corporation: A Manifesto for Business Revolution*, Harper Business, New York.

Hammer, M. and Champy, J. (1993) *Re-engineering the Corporation: A Manifesto for Business Revolution*, 2nd edn, Harper Business, New York.

Hardgrave, B.C. (1995) When to prototype: Decision variables used in industry, *Information and Software Technology*, Vol. 37, No. 2, 113–118.

Henderson, J.C. and Treaty, M.E. (1986) Managing end-user computing for competitive advantage, *Sloan Management Review*, Vol. 27, No. 2, Winter, 3–14.

Herbsleb, J. et al. (1994) Software process improvement: State of the payoff, *American Programmer*, September.

Herzberg, F. (1966) *Work and the Nature of Man*, Staple Press, New Hope, Minnesota.

Hill, T. and Westbrook, R. (1997) SWOT analysis: It's time for a product recall, *Long Range Planning*, Vol. 30, No. 1, 46–52.

Hirschheim, R. (1985) Information systems epistemology: An historical perspective, in E. Mumford, R.A. Hirschheim, G. Fitzgerald, and A.T. Wood-Harper (eds) *Research Methods in Information Systems*, North-Holland, Amsterdam.

Hirschheim, R. and Klein, H.K. (1989) Four paradigms of information systems development, *Communications of the ACM*, Vol. 32, No. 10.

Hirschheim, R., Earl, M., Feeny, D., and Lockett, M. (1988) An exploration into the management of the information systems function: Key issues and an evolutionary model, paper given at *Information Technology Management for Productivity and Strategic Advantage, IFIP TC-8 Open Conference, Singapore, March.*

Hirschheim, R., Klein, H.K., and Lyytinen, K. (1996) Exploring the intellectual structures of information systems development: A social action theoretical analysis, *Accounting Management & Information Technology*, Vol. 6, Nos 1/2, 1–64.

Holland, C.P. and Light, B. (2001) A stage maturity model for enterprise resource planning systems use, *Database for Advances in Information Systems*, Vol. 32, No. 2.

Hough, D. (1993) Rapid delivery: An evolutionary approach for application development,, *IBM Systems Journal*, Vol. 32, No. 3.

Howard, A. (1997) A new RAD-based approach to commercial information systems development: The dynamic systems development method, *Industrial Management & Data Systems*, Vol. 5, 175–177.

Huff, S.L., Munro, M.C., and Martin, B.H. (1988). Growth stages of end-user computing. *Communications of the ACM*, Vol. 31, No. 5, 542–550.

Hume, S., DeVane, T., and Slater, J.S. (1999) Transforming an organization through prototyping: A case study, *Information Systems Management*, Fall, Vol. 16 No. 4; *IBM Systems Journal*, Vol. 32, No. 3.

Humphrey, W.S. (1989) *Managing the Software Process*, Addison-Wesley, Reading, Massachusetts.

Iivari, J., Hirschheim, R., and Klein, H.K. (2000/2001) A dynamic framework for classifying information systems development methodologies and approaches, *Journal of Management Information Systems*, Winter.

Introna, L.D. and Pouloudi, A. (1999) Privacy in the information age: Stakeholders, interests and values, *Journal of Business Ethics*, Vol. 22, No. 1, 27–38.

Introna, L.D. and Whitley, E.A. (1997) Against method-ism: Exploring the limits of method, *Information Technology and People*, Vol. 10, No. 1, 31–45.

Jackson, M. (1983) *Systems Development*, Prentice Hall, Hemel Hempstead, UK.

Jackson, M.A. (1975) *Principles of Program Design*, Academic Press, New York.

Jacobson, I. (updated by Bylund, S.) (2000) *The Unified Software Development Process*, Cambridge University Press, Cambridge.

Jacobson, I., Booch, G., and Rumbaugh, J. (1999) *The Unified Software Development Process*, Addison-Wesley, Boston.

Jacobson, I., Christerson, M., Jonsson, P. and Øvergaard, G. (1992) *Object-oriented Software Engineering: A Use Case Driven Approach*, Addison-Wesley, Wokingham, UK, 582 pp.

Jacobson, I., Griss, M., and Jonsson, P. (1997) *Software Reuse Architecture, Process and Organization for Business Success*, AWL, Harlow, UK.

Jalote, P. (2000) *CMM in Practice: Processes for Executing Software Projects in Infosys*, Addison-Wesley, Reading, Massachusetts.

Janson, M.A. and Smith, L.D. (1985) Prototyping for systems development: A critical appraisal, *MISQ*, December.

Jayaratna, N. (1994) *Understanding and Evaluating Methodologies, NIMSAD: A Systemic Framework*, McGraw-Hill, Maidenhead, UK.

Jeffries, R. (2001) *Extreme Programming Installed*, Pearson Education, Harlow, UK.

Jenkins, T. (1994) Report back on the DMSG sponsored UK Euromethod Forum '94, *Data Management Bulletin*, Summer Issue, Vol. 11, 3.

Johnson, D.I. and Broadman, J.G. (1996) Realities and rewards of software process improvement, *IEEE Software*, Vol. 29, No. 11, 99–101.

Jones, C. (1986) *Programming Productivity*, McGraw-Hill, New York.

Kambil, A. and van Heck, E. (1998) Re-engineering the Dutch flower auctions: A framework for analyzing exchange organizations automation, *Information Systems Research*, Vol. 9, No. 1, 1–19.

Kettelhut, M.C. (1992) Supporting end-user database development, *Data Resource Management*, Vol. 3, No. 3, 29–39.

King, J.L. and Kraemer, K.L. (1984). Evolution and organizational information systems: An assessment of Nolan's stage model, *Communications of the ACM*, Vol. 27, No. 5, 466–475.

King, W.R. and Thompson, S.H.T (1997) Integration between business planning and information systems planning: Validating a stage hypothesis, *Decision Sciences*, Vol. 28, No. 2.

Klein, H., Hirschheim, R.A. and Lyytinen, K. (1995) *Information Systems Development and Data Modeling: Conceptual and Philosophical Foundations*, Cambridge Tracts in Theoretical Computer Science, Cambridge University Press, Cambridge.

Knights, D. and Murray, F. (1994) *Managers Divided: Organization Politics and Information Technology Management*, John Wiley & Sons, Chichester, UK.

Kraushaar, J.M. and Shirland, L.E. (1985) A prototyping method for applications development by end-users and information systems specialists, *MISQ*, September.

Kruchten, P. (1995) The 4+1 view model of architecture, *IEEE Software*, Vol. 12, No. 6, November, 42–50.

Kruchten, P. (2000) *The Rational Unified Process An Introduction*, 2nd edn, Addison-Wesley, Reading, Massachusetts.

Kuhn, T.S. (1962) *The Structure of Scientific Revolutions*, 2nd edn, University of Chicago Press, Chicago.

Lacity, M. and Hirschheim, R. (1993) *Information Systems Outsourcing: Myths, Metaphors and Realities*, John Wiley & Sons, Chichester, UK.

Land (1982) Adapting to changing user requirements, *Information and Management*, Vol. 5.

Lawlis, P.K., Flowe, R.M., and Thordahl, J.B. (1995) A correlation study of the CMM and software development performance, *Crosstalk*, Vol. 8, No. 9, 21–25, September.

Lederer, A.L. and Mendelow, A.L. (1989) Information systems planning: Incentives for effective action, *Data Base*, Fall.

Lewis, P.J. (1994) *Information Systems Development: Systems Thinking in the Field of IS*, Pitman, Lonoon.

Liebenau, J. and Backhouse, J. (1990) *Understanding Information: An Introduction*, Macmillan, Basingstoke, UK.

Lincoln, T.J. and Shorrock, D. (1992) Cost justifying current use of information technology, in T.J. Lincoln (ed.) *Managing Information Systems for Profit*, John Wiley & Sons, Chichester, UK.

Ljubic, T. and Stefancic, S. (1994) Problems in the introduction of RAD principles put to praxis, *Proceedings of the Fourth International Conference on Information Systems Development (ISD94), Methods & Tools, Theory & Practice*, Moderna Organizacija, Bled, Slovenia.

Lundeberg, M., Goldkuhl, G., and Nilsson, A. (1982) *Information Systems Development – A Systematic Approach*, Prentice Hall, Englewood Cliffs, New Jersey.

Maddison, R.N. (ed.) (1983) *Information System Methodologies*, Wiley Heyden, Chichester, UK.

Mansuy, J.E. (1989) Evolutionary development srategy for MIS, *Journal of Systems Management*, July.

Marchand, D.A., Davenport, T.H., and Dickson, T. (2000) *Mastering Information Management*, Prentice Hall, Harlow, UK.

Markus, M.L. and Bjørn-Andersen, N. (1987) Power over users: Its exercise by systems professionals, *Communications of the ACM*, Vol. 30, 6.

Martin, J. (1989) *Information Engineering*, Prentice Hall, Englewood Cliffs, New Jersey.

Martin, J. (1991) *Rapid Application Development*, Prentice Hall, Englewood Cliffs, New Jersey.

Martin, J. and Finkelstein, C. (1981) *Information Engineering*, Vols 1 and 2, Prentice Hall, Englewood Cliffs, New Jersey.

Martin, J. and Odell, J.J. (1992) *Object Oriented Information Engineering (OOIE) – Object Oriented Methods A Foundation*, Prentice Hall, Englewood Cliffs, New Jersey.

Mason, R. and Mitroff, I. (1981) *Challenging Strategic Planning Assumptions*, John Wiley & Sons, New York.

Mason, D. and Willcocks, L. (1994) *Systems Analysis, Systems Design*, McGraw-Hill, Maidenhead, UK.

Mathiassen, L., Munk-Madsen, A., Nielsen, P.A., and Sage, J. (2000) *Object Oriented Analysis and Design*, Marko Publishing, Aalborg, Denmark.

McCracken, D.D. and Jackson, M.A. (1982) Lifecycle concept considered harmful, ACM SIGSOFT, *Software Engineering Notes*, Vol. 17, 2.

McFarlan, F.W. (1984), Information technology changes the way you compete, *Harvard Business Review*, May–June, 98–103.

McGrew, J.F., Bilotta, J.G., and Deeney, J.M. (1999) Software team formation and decay, *Small Group Research*, April, Vol. 30, No. 2, 209–234.

McGuire, E.G. (2000) The Culture Side of CMM, Research Briefs, Cutter Consortium, www.cutter.com/consortium/research/2000/crb000613.html

McKeen, J.D. and Smith, H.A. (1996) *Management Challenges in IS*, John Wiley & Sons, Chichester, UK.

McLeod, G. and Smith, D. (1996) *Managing Information Technology Projects*, Boyd & Fraser, Danvers, Massachusetts.

McManus, J. (2001) Risk in software projects, *Management Services*, Vol. 45, No. 10.

Melao, N. and Pidd, M. (2000) A conceptual framework for understanding business processes and business process modelling, *Information Systems Journal*, Vol. 10, No. 2, 105–129.

Michell, V.A. (1994) *IT Outsourcing: The Changing Outlook*, International Data Corporation, London, pp. 13–21.

Mirani, R. and King, W.R. (1994) Impacts of end-user and information center characteristics on end-user computing support, *Journal of Management Information Systems*, Summer, Vol. 11, No. 1.

Mitroff, I. and Linstone, H. (1993) *The Unbounded Mind, Breaking the Chains of Traditional Business Thinking*, Oxford University Press, Oxford.

Moad, J. (1993) Does reengineering really work?, *Datamation*, Vol. 39, 15.

Moynihan, E. (1993) *Business Management and Systems Analysis*, McGraw-Hill, Maidenhead, UK. This text provides a hybrid approach to the subject, treating the business and computer sides with equal importance and emphasizing the necessary integration of the two in the information systems development process.

Mumford, E. (1983a) *Designing Human Systems*, Manchester Business School, Manchester.

Mumford, E. (1983b) *Designing Participatively*, Manchester Business School, Manchester.

Mumford, E. (1986) *Using Computers for Business*, Manchester Business School, Manchester.

Mumford, E. and Weir, M. (1979) *Computer Systems in Work Design – The ETHICS Method*, Associated Business Press, London.

Mumford, E. (1989) *XSEL's Progress*, John Wiley & Sons, Chichester, UK.

Mumford, E. (1995) *Effective Requirements Analysis and Systems Design: The ETHICS Method*, Macmillan, Basingstoke, UK.

Myers, G. (1975) *Reliable Software Through Composite Design*, Petrocelli/Charter, New York.

Myers, G. (1978) *Composite/Structured Design*, Van Nostrand Reinhold, New York.

National Audit Office (1999) *Government on the Web*, A Report by the Comptroller and the Auditor General, HC 87, 13 December.

National Audit Office (2002) *Government on the Web II*, A Report by the Comptroller and the Auditor General, 25 April.

Nauman, J.D. and Jenkins, A.M. (1982) The new paradigm for systems development, *MISQ*, September.

Nolan, R.L. (1973) Managing the computing resource: A stage hypothesis, *Communications of the ACM*, Vol. 16, No. 7, 399–405.

Nolan, R.L. (1979) Managing the crises in data processing, *Harvard Business Review*, Vol. 57, 2.

Norris, G., Wright, I., Hurley, J.R., Dunleavy, J., and Gibson, A. (1998) *SAP: An Executive's Comprehensive Guide*, John Wiley & Sons, New York.

Nunamaker, J., Dennis, A., Valacich, J., Vogel, D., and George, J. (1991) Electronic meeting systems to support group work, *Communications of the ACM*, July, 41–61.

Oliga, J. (1988) Methodological foundations of systems methodologies, in R.L. Flood and M.C. Jackson (eds) *Critical Systems Thinking: Directed Readings*, John Wiley & Sons, Chichester, UK.

Olle, T.W., Sol, H.G., and Verrijn-Stuart, A.A. (1986) *Information Systems Design Methodologies: A Comparative Review*, North Holland, Amsterdam.

OMG (2002) Introduction to OMG's Unified Modeling Language, http://www.omg.org/gettingstarted/what_is_uml.htm

Orman, L. (1998/9) Evolutionary development of information systems, *Journal of Management Information Systems*, Vol. 5, No. 3.

Page-Jones, M. (2000) *Fundamentals of Object-oriented Design in UML*, Addison-Wesley, Reading, Massachusetts.

Parsons, T. and Shils, E. (1951) *Towards a General Theory of Action*, Harvard University Press, Massachusetts.

Patane, J.R. and Jurison, J. (1994) Is global outsourcing diminishing the prospects for American programmers? *Journal of Systems Management*, Vol. 45, No. 6.

Paulk, M.C., Curtis, B., Chrissis, M.B., and Weber, C.V. (1993a) Capability Maturity Model, Version 1.1, *IEEE Software*, Vol. 10, No. 4, July, 18–27.

Paulk, M.C., Weber, C.V., Garcia, S.M., Chrissis, M.B., and Bush, M. (1993b) *Key Practices of the Capability Maturity Model, Version 1.1*, Software Engineering Institute, CMU/SEI-93-TR-25.

Paulk, M.C., Weber, C.V., Curtis, B., and Chrissis, M.B. (1995) *The Capability Maturity Model, Guidelines for Improving the Software Process*, Addison-Wesley, Reading, Massachusetts, 441 pp.

Peppard, J. and Preece, I. (1995) The content, context and process of business process re-engineering, in G. Burke and J. Peppard (eds) *Examining Business Process Re-engineering: Current Perspectives and Research Directions*, Kogan Page, London, pp. 157–185.

Phan, D.D. (2001) Software quality and management, *Information Systems Management*, Winter, Vol. 18, No. 1, 56–68.

Plato, J.J. (1995) Prototyping: Proceed with caution, *Information Systems Management*, Fall, Vol. 12, No. 4.

Ploskina, B. (1999) Rational adds quality to rapid application development, *ENT*, Vol. 4, Issue 21, August, 25–27

Porter, M.E. (1980) *Competitive Strategy*, Free Press, New York.

Porter, M.E. (1985) *Competitive Advantage*, Collier-Macmillan, New York.

Porter, M.E. (1991) Toward a dynamic theory of strategy, *Strategic Management Journal*, Vol. 12, 95–117

Pralahad, C.K. and Hamel, G. (1990) The core competence of the corporation, *Harvard Business Review*, May/June, 79–91.

Prahalad, C.K. and Hamel, G. (1994) Strategy as a field of study: Why search for a new paradigm? *Strategic Management Journal*, Vol. 15, 5–16.

Pressman, R.S. (2000) *Software Engineering: A Practitioner's Approach*, 5th edn, McGraw-Hill, London.

Probasco, L. (2000) *The Ten Essentials of RUP: The Essence of an Effective Development Process*, Rational White Paper.

Pyron, T. (2000) *Using Project 2000*, Que Macmillan, Indianapolis, Indiana.

Quang, P.T. and Chartier-Kastler, C. (1991) *Merise in Practice*. Macmillan, Basingstoke (translated by D.E. and M.A. Avison from the French: *Merise Appliquée*, Eyrolles, Paris, 1989).

Quinn, J. (1992) *The Intelligent Enterprise*, Free Press, New York, 1992.

Radding, A. (1999) Enterprise RAD tools: Can they do the job? *InformationWeek*, Issue 716, November, 1–5.

Randall, D., Hughes, J., and Shapiro, D. (1994) Steps towards a partnership: Ethnography and system design, in M. Jirotka and J. Goguen (eds) *Requirements Engineering: Social and Technical Issues*, Academic Press, London, pp. 241–258.

Raymond, E.S. (2001) *The Cathedral and the Bazaar: Musings on Linux and Open Source by an Accidental Revolutionary*, O'Reilly, Sebastobal, California.

Ringland, G. (1998) *Scenario Planning: Managing for the Future*, John Wiley & Sons, Chichester, UK.

Rockart, J.F. (1979) Chief executives define their own data needs, *Harvard Business Review*, Vol. 57, No. 2, 238–241.

Rockart, J.F. (1982) The changing role of the information systems executive: A critical success factors perspective, *Sloan Management Review*, Fall.

Rockart, J.F. and Flannery, L.S. (1983) The management of end-user computing, *Communications of the ACM*, Vol. 26, 10.

Rosenhead, J. (1989) *Rational Analysis for a Problematic World: Problem Structuring Methods for Complexity, Uncertainty and Conflict*, edited by J. Rosenhead, John Wiley & Sons, Chichester, UK.

Ross, J.W. and Feeny, D.F. (2000) The evolving role of the CIO, in R. Zmud (ed.) *Framing the Domain of IT Management: Glimpsing the Future through the Past*, Pinnaflex, Cincinnati, Ohio.

Rumbaugh, J., Blaha, M., Premerlani, W., Eddy, F., and Lorensen, W. (1991) *Object Oriented Modelling and Design*, Prentice Hall, Englewood Cliffs, New Jersey.

Russo, N.L. and Wynekoop, J.L. (1995) The use and adaptation of system development methodologies, *Proceedings of the 6th Information Resources Management Association International Conference*, Idea Group Publishing, Hershey, Pennsylvania.

Sachs, P. (1995) Transforming work: Collaboration, learning, and design, *Communications of the ACM*, Vol. 38, No. 9, 36–44.

Schreiber, G., Akkermans, H., Anjewierden, A., de Hoog, R., Shadbolt, N., Van de Velde, W., and Wielinga, B.J. (2000) *Knowledge Engineering and Management: The Common KADS Methodology*, MIT Press, Cambridge, Massachusetts.

Searle, J.R. (1995) *The Construction of Social Reality*, Allen Lane, Penguin Press, Harmondsworth, UK.

SEIa (2001) SEI Mission, http://www.sei.cmu.edu/about/overview/sei/mission.html

Silk, D. (1990) Managing information systems benefits for the 1990s, *Journal of Information Technology*, Vol. 5, No. 4.

Smith, A. (1997) *Human Computer Factors: A Study of Users and Information Systems*, McGraw-Hill, London.

Smith, H.J. and Hasnas, J. (1999) Ethics and information systems: The corporate domain, *MIS Quarterly*, Vol. 23, No. 1.

Smith, R. (2000) Defining the UML kernal, *Software Development*, October, Rational Software Corp., available at http://www.sdmagazine.com/articles/2000/0010/

Stapleton, J. (1997) *DSDM Dynamic Systems Development Method, The Method in Practice*, Addison-Wesley, Harlow, UK. This source also contains a number of case studies of DSDM development projects.

Stapleton, J. (1998) Giving RAD a good name, *The Computer Bulletin*, November.

Stevens, W.P., Myers, G.J., and Constantine, L.L. (1974) Structured design, *IBM System Journal*, Volume 13, 2.

Stewart, J. (1994) *IS Notice: Euromethod*, CCTA, Norwich, UK, p. 61.

Strassmann, P. (1990) *The Business Value of Computers*, The Information Economics Press, New Canaan, Connecticut.

Subramanian, G.H. and Zarnich, G.E. (1996) An examination of some software development effort and productivity determinants in ICASE tool projects, *Journal of Management Information Systems*, Vol. 12, No. 4.

Sumner, M. and Klepper, R. (1986) The impact of end user computing on information systems development, *Computer Personnel*, Vol. 10, No. 4.

Sutcliffe, A. (1988) *Jackson Systems Development*, Prentice Hall, Hemel Hempstead, UK.

Taylor, F.W. (1947) *Scientific Management*, Harper & Row, New York.

Tayntor, C.B. (1994) New challenges or the end of EUC? *Information Systems Management*, Summer, Vol. 11, No. 3. The DSDM website: http://www.dsdm.org/

Tiwana, A. (2000) *The Knowledge Management Toolkit*, Prentice Hall, Upper Saddle River, New Jersey.

Tudhope, D. (2000) Prototyping praxis: Constructing computer systems and building belief, *Human–Computer Interaction*, Vol. 15 No. 4.

Turner, P. and Jenkins, T. (1996) *Euromethod and Beyond*, Thomson, London.

Valentin, E.K. (2001) SWOT analysis from a resource-based view, *Journal of Marketing Theory and Practice*, Vol. 9, No. 2, Spring.

Van Slooten, K. (1996) Situated method engineering, *Information Resources Management Journal*, Vol. 9, No. 3.

Vidgen, R. (1994) Research in progress: Using stakeholder analysis to test primary task conceptual models in information systems development, in *Proceedings of the Second Annual Conference on Information System Methodologies*, BCS IS Methodologies Specialist Group, 31 August–2 September, Edinburgh.

Vidgen, R. (1996) A multiple perspectives approach to information system quality. Unpublished PhD thesis, June, University of Salford.

Vidgen, R. and McMaster, T. (1996) Black boxes, non-human stakeholders and the translation of IT through mediation, in W.J. Orlikowski, G. Walsham, M. Jones, and J.I. DeGross (eds) *Information Technology and Changes in Organizational Work*, Chapman & Hall, London, pp. 250–271.

Vidgen, R., Avison, D.E., Wood, R., and Wood-Harper, A.T. (2002) *Developing Web Information Systems*, Butterworth-Heinemann, London.

Walker, R. (1998) *Software Project Management, A Unified Framework*, Addison–Wesley, Boston.

Walsham, G. (1993) *Interpreting Information Systems in Organisations*, John Wiley & Sons, Chichester, UK.

Ward, J. and Griffiths, P. (1996) *Strategic Planning for Information Systems*, 2nd edn, John Wiley & Sons, Chichester, UK.

Ward, J.M. (1985) Evaluating IS projects and charges for services, *Management Accounting*, Vol. 63, No. 1.

Warren, I. (1999) *The Renaissance of Legacy Systems*, Springer-Verlag, London.

Wastell, D. (1996) The fetish of technique: Methodology as a social defence, *Information Systems Journal*, Vol. 6, 1.

Watson, I. (1997) *Applying Case Based Reasoning*, Morgan Kauffman, San Francisco, California.

Weaver, P.L. (1993) *Practical SSADM Version 4: A Complete Tutorial Guide*, Pitman, London.

Weaver, P.L., Lambrou, N., and Walkley, N. (1998) *Practical SSADM+*, Pitman, London.

Weber, C.V., Paulk, M.C., Wise, C.J., and Withey, J.V. (1991) *Key Practices of the Capability Maturity Model*, Software Engineering Institute, CMU/SEI-91-TR-25.

Weinberg, V. (1978) *Structured Analysis*, Prentice Hall, Englewood Cliffs, New Jersey.

Welti, N. (1999) *Successful SAP R/3 Implementation*, Addison-Wesley, Harlow, UK.

Wielemaker, M.W., Elfring, T., and Volberda, H.W. (2000) Strategic renewal in large European firms: Investigating viable trajectories of change, *Organization Development Journal*, Vol. 18, No. 4, 49–68.

Wielinga, B.J., Sterner, Th.A., and Breuker, J.A. (1993) KADS: A modelling approach to knowledge engineering, in B.G. Buchanan and D.C. Wilkins (eds) *Readings in Knowledge Acquisition and Learning, Automating the Construction and Improvement of Expert Systems*, Morgan Kaufmann, San Mateo, California.

Willcocks, L. and Fitzgerald, G. (1993) Market as opportunity? Case studies in outsourcing information technology and services, *Journal of Strategic Information Systems*, Vol. 2, No. 3, 223–242.

Willcocks, L., Fitzgerald, G., and Lacity, M. (1996) To Outsource IT or not?: Recent research on economics and evaluation practice, *European Journal of Information Systems*, Vol. 5, 143–160

Willis, R.R. (and eight others) (1998) *Hughes Aircraft's Widespread Deployment of a Continuously Improving Software Process*, Software Engineering Institute, CMU/SEI-98-TR-006.

Wilson, B. (1990) *Systems: Concepts, Methodologies and Applications*, 2nd edn, John Wiley & Sons, Chichester, UK.

Wilson, B. (2001) *Soft System Methodology*, John Wiley & Sons, Chichester, UK.

Wirth, N. (1971) Program development by stepwise refinement, *Communications of the ACM*, Vol. 14, 4.

Wood, J. and Silver, D. (1989) *Joint Application Design: How to Design Quality Systems in 40% Less Time*, John Wiley & Sons, New York.

Wood, J.R.G., Vidgen, R.T., Wood-Harper, A.T., and Rose, J. (1995) Business process redesign: Radical change or reactionary tinkering?, in G. Burke and J. Peppard (eds) *Examining Business Process Reengineering: Current Perspectives and Research Directions*, Kogan Page, London.

Wood-Harper, A.T., Corder, S., Wood, J., and Watson, H. (1996) How we profess: The ethical systems analyst, *Communications of the ACM*, Vol. 39, No. 3, 69–77.

Wysocki, R.K. and DeMichiell, R.L. (1997) *Managing Information Across the Enterprise*, John Wiley & Sons, New York.

Yoon, Y., Guimaraes, T., and O'Neal, Q. (1995) Exploring the factors associated with expert systems success, *MIS Quarterly*, Vol. 19, 1.

Yourdon, E. (1989) *Modern Structured Analysis*, Prentice Hall, Englewood Cliffs, New Jersey.

Yourdon and Argila (1996) *Case Studies in Object-oriented Analysis and Design*, Yourdon Press, Prentice Hall, New Jersey.

Yourdon, E. and Constantine, L.L. (1978) *Structured Design*, 2nd edn, Yourdon Press, New York.

Yourdon Inc. (1993) *Yourdon Systems Method: Model-driven Systems Development*, Yourdon Press, Englewood Cliffs, New Jersey.

Yourdon, E. (2000) *Computerworld*, 21 August, Vol. 34, Issue 34, 36.

Zach, M.H. (1999) Developing a knowledge strategy, *California Management Review*, Vol. 41, No. 3, 125–145.

Zuboff, S. (1988) *In the Age of the Smart Machine*, Basic Books, New York.

INDEX